Ann Granger has lived in cities in many parts of the world, since for many years she worked for the Foreign Office and received postings to British embassies as far apart as Munich and Lusaka. She is married, with two sons, and she and her husband, who also worked for the Foreign Office, are now permanently based near Oxford.

Also by Ann Granger

Fran Varady crime novels
Risking It All
Watching Out

Mitchell and Markby crime novels
Say It With Poison
A Season For Murder
Cold In The Earth
Murder Among Us
Where Old Bones Lie
A Fine Place For Death
Flowers For His Funeral
Candle For A Corpse
A Touch Of Mortality
A Word After Dying
Call The Dead Again
Beneath These Stones
Shades Of Murder
A Restless Evil
That Way Murder Lies

Asking for Trouble

and

Keeping Bad Company

and

Running Scared

Ann Granger

headline

ASKING FOR TROUBLE first published in Great Britain in 1997
by HEADLINE BOOK PUBLISHING

KEEPING BAD COMPANY first published in Great Britain in 1997
by HEADLINE BOOK PUBLISHING

RUNNING SCARED first published in Great Britain in 1998
by HEADLINE BOOK PUBLISHING

First published in this omnibus edition in 2005
by HEADLINE BOOK PUBLISHING

A HEADLINE paperback

10 9 8 7 6 5 4 3 2 1

ISBN 0 7553 2657 1

Printed and bound in Great Britain by
Mackays of Chatham plc, Chatham, Kent

HEADLINE BOOK PUBLISHING
A division of Hodder Headline
338 Euston Road
London NW1 3BH

www.headline.co.uk
www.hodderheadline.com

Asking for Trouble

Chapter One

The man from the council housing department came on Monday morning. He served us with summonses, one each.

'According to our procedure!' he informed us in a voice pitched nervously high. He wasn't very old, curly-haired, his round cherubic face doing its best to express authority but losing out to an expression of incipient panic.

I can't believe he was seriously scared of us. Granted we outnumbered him but we weren't strangers. He, and various of his colleagues, had been before. In the past we'd locked them out, so that they had to shout up at the windows to communicate with us. But that day we'd let him in. It was decision day. We knew it and he knew that we did. There was no longer any point in those spirited exchanges hurled between pavement and windowsill. It was a curiously muted ending to a long-running dispute.

All the same he watched us anxiously, just in case we tore up the individual summonses in a last protest. Squib took his from its envelope and turned it over as if he expected to see something written on the back. Terry pushed hers into the pocket of her knitted coat. Nev looked for a moment as if he were going to refuse to accept his, but took it eventually. I took mine and said, 'Thanks for nothing!'

The official cleared his throat. 'I shall be attending the court tomorrow, together with the council's solicitor, to apply for an order for immediate possession. We anticipate it will be granted. We're prepared to give you until Friday to enable you to find alternative accommodation. But the matter is now in the hands of the court and its bailiffs. So it's no use arguing with me! Argue it out with the court tomorrow, if you want. But it won't do any good.'

He was still defensive, though no one bothered to answer him. We'd always known we'd lose. Even so, the reality of knowing we were out induced a physical sickness in the stomach. I turned away and stared at the window until I could control my face.

It was one of those slate-coloured mornings, threatening to tip rain at any moment, though it would probably hold off until evening. Dense cloud cover kept the traffic fumes and other odours trapped at street-level. You could even smell the charred meat and burnt onions from the Wild West hamburger bar which was two streets away.

I hadn't been feeling very cheerful that morning, even before our visitor came, because I'd lost my job the previous Friday. The manager had found out that my address was 'irregular' and that was that. Irregular meant I was currently living in a squat.

Although technically our occupation was illegal, no one had prevented us moving into an empty – and to all intents ownerless – house, and now we'd been there long enough for our presence to have acquired an air of permanency. Moreover, we had a purpose. We called ourselves the

Jubilee Street Creative Artists' Commune, though none of our work would have attracted a subsidy from the Arts Council or the National Lottery. But in between conforming to the norm or plummeting to the depths, whatever our individual destinies might be, we planned stupendous careers from the anonymity of Jubilee Street. In every way we possibly could, in fact, we deceived ourselves. Dreams beat reality any day.

By the way, I have to leave Squib out of the great careers scenario. Squib lived strictly from day to day and hadn't formed even the ghost of a plan that anyone had ever heard of.

Nev had plans. They came in the form of a twenty-page synopsis for his novel, which was likely to rival *War and Peace* in length. Every day he tapped away relentlessly on an old W H Smith manual machine. I've sometimes wondered if he ever finished it.

Squib was a pavement artist. He could copy anything. Some people would say that wasn't truly creative because it wasn't original, but they hadn't seen what Squib could do with a box of chalks and a few clean slabs. Old masters, which had been reduced by familiarity and brown varnish to the status of museum pieces, emerged breathing new life from Squib's fingers. They spoke so eloquently to passers-by that several were visibly disconcerted by the vibrancy of the chalked faces at their feet. In an episode which Squib regarded as deeply embarrassing, a passing art critic became so enthusiastic that he talked of presenting Squib to the world, together – presumably – with some purpose-acquired slabs to work on. The idea of being taken up by the establishment had so terrified Squib that he'd simply melted away with his tin of chalks and taken to improving the pavements of the provinces until he thought it safe to return to London.

As for me, I still clung to my early ambition to be an actress. Life had somewhat got in the way. I'd dropped out of a college course in the Dramatic Arts. Since then, apart from some Street Theatre, the role of star of stage and screen had eluded me. I still hoped to make it some day. Short term, keeping the wolf from the door was enough to occupy me. That, and maintaining an eye on the other two.

We three had moved into the house first. Soon afterwards we'd been joined by Declan, a small wiry fellow with straggling shoulder-length hair and features like a good-natured elf. Both his arms had been heavily tattooed: a fearsome snake on one; a sacred heart on the other. He recalled having the sacred heart done, but claimed to have no recollection of the snake being tattooed. He'd woken up one morning with a monumental hangover and there it was, crawling up his arm. 'I thought I had the DTs,' he observed. Sometimes he'd stretch out his arm and study the snake thoughtfully. I think it worried him.

Declan had arrived as a rock musician without a group, owing to his former group's lead guitarist having been accidentally electrocuted whilst rehearsing in a church hall.

'The poor sod's hair stood on end,' Declan would relate with mournful wonder. 'God rest his soul, it was bloody funny to see. Until we realised he was dead, you know. That sobered us up. We all stood round trying to remember how to do resuscitation while we waited for an ambulance. Though we could see he was a goner. On top of which, the amp was just about fried and we hadn't got the dosh to buy another. Just then, would you believe it? A wee man came running in, mouthing off at us because we'd fused all the lights in the place. It pissed us off that much, him no showing any respect for the dead like it, that the drummer and I, we picked him up, kicking and yelling like a banshee, and dropped him out of the window. It wasn't a long drop. He bounced. But we got done for assault, all the same.'

Declan played bass and a bass-player needs a group.

A little later Lucy and her two children had come along. Lucy wasn't an artist of any sort. She'd run away from a violent husband and had been staying at a battered women's refuge a few streets away. I'd got talking to her one day while I was serving in Patels' corner greengrocer's shop. She was buying carrots for the children to gnaw. Raw carrots are full of vitamin C, don't contain the sort of acids which drill holes in tooth enamel, and are cheaper than most fruit.

She was trying to get herself somewhere permanent to live and a job. The refuge was full and she felt she couldn't stay there much longer. The palm of her left hand was badly scarred where her husband had forced it down on a glowing red hotplate during a row about his dinner being late. The scars were unsightly and had impaired the hand's flexibility. She was conscious of it and always told anyone who asked that she'd done it herself, by accident. She'd told me the truth one evening after she'd come to live at the house. I'd expressed amazement that she'd stayed with him so long and put up with so much abuse.

'It's not easy walking out with two kids,' she'd said.

But she had walked out when he started hitting the

children, as well as her. She said he had a drink problem. In my view he had a head problem. But it had underlined for me, if I'd been in any doubt, how precious my independence was.

As for the house, that stood all by itself at the end of a row of redbrick terraced others. It was older than the terrace, we thought early Victorian, and once it must have stood here in a big garden. All that was left of the garden was a patch of jungle at the back and a litter-strewn strip between the front of the house and the pavement. There were holes indicating posts for railings but those too had gone. The house had dirty white stucco facing, dropping off in patches, a pillared front entrance, sash windows which stuck and a water-logged basement. When it was new it must have been graceful and welcoming. Now it was like the dishevelled old baglady who lived down the street, out of tune with the world around, kept together by grime and makeshift repairs. All the same, we'd been prepared to take it on and make something of it.

Unfortunately, we weren't allowed to. Within weeks, we were informed by the council, which legally owned it, that the house was scheduled to come down as part of redevelopment plans for the area, and there was nothing we could do about it. We'd asked the council, when we'd moved in, to give us a regular tenancy, a request which they'd ignored. Now a stream of communications couched in official mandarin fluttered through the letterbox, and the council cut off the electricity, just in case we still hadn't got the message. They hadn't turned off the water but perhaps they hadn't needed to, since they were calling in the bailiffs.

Nev suggested we try to get the house listed as of

architectural interest. We wrote to English Heritage and the National Trust. They thanked us for our letter but the house wasn't interesting enough and they didn't want it.

One by one, the people moved out of the terraced houses, leaving empty, boarded-up shells. We hung on like legionnaires in a desert fort. It became a battle of wills between us and the rampaging Rif warriors as represented by a string of council officials.

The uncertainty caused a shake-out of residents. The council, hoist with its own petard, rehoused Lucy and her children, one of whom was asthmatic. Declan, too, had left, to go no one knew where, though he spoke vaguely of having heard of a group needing a bass guitarist. There'd been a couple of mean-looking blokes at the door asking for him about a week before that, so we reckoned he was in some kind of trouble. But who wasn't? We never asked people personal questions.

Terry, however, had arrived, a small damp figure with dark blond hair, parted centrally and falling to either side of her pinched little face, like spaniel's ears. Her appearance coincided with the electricity being cut off, so that for me, from the start, she symbolised the deterioration in our situation. It was uncharitable of me to think that way, but, as things turned out, dead right.

On that Monday morning, until the moment we were handed our final notices to quit, I hadn't thought things could get worse. The manager of the mail-order packing department where I'd been working had the usual idea of squatters, and he hadn't been able to get rid of me fast enough. There had been nothing wrong with my work – despite the fact that it was boring and badly paid. I'd never turned up late or skived off early. I never broke anything, or packed the wrong item by mistake, or sent off something totally inappropriate to a customer for a joke. But he claimed I hadn't been 'completely frank' about my circumstances and 'the company had a policy'.

I wouldn't have taken that job if I could have got any other. I was earning hardly more than I would have got on the dole and the conditions we'd worked in were like something out of Dickens. But it was better than no job. Now I was unemployed, technically homeless and soon to be literally so, and thoroughly fed up.

Our silence seemed to rattle the man from the council, who added, 'Look here, you've really got to get out by Friday. The bailiffs will put you out by force if necessary. The police will be on standby and it won't be any good climbing up on the rooftop or putting your feet into bags of cement or anything like that.'

We all just looked at him. A remark like that really wasn't worth answering. Even Squib wouldn't have done something like that.

Nev said, 'Anyone who got up on this roof would fall straight through it! You've got to be joking.'

I was feeling a little sorry for our visitor so I asked him if he wanted a cup of tea. We'd only just brewed up. Nev had lit a fire in the hearth with a load of kindling he'd got from chopping up an old wooden garden seat out the back and we had the kettle going, hanging from a hook screwed into the arch of the grate.

Declan fixed that up when he was living here. It was at the time the electricity had been cut off. He said his granny in Ireland had cooked for a family of thirteen all her life, just using a pot hanging from a hook. Declan was full of stories like that. You couldn't believe half of them.

But the other half, which sounded just as mad, you could believe so you never knew which were true and which weren't.

We didn't do all our cooking in the hearth. We had a stove fed by Calor gas bottles. But that cost money to run and so, whenever we could, we used the open fire.

He refused the tea but he didn't look so nervous. Instead he looked pompous and I stopped feeling sorry for him. 'We've written several times explaining what would happen. You've had several stays of execution. We've done everything we could to be reasonable. All these houses are due to come down. The others are already empty. The squatters in those saw sense and moved out. Only you lot stay on. We've explained all this till we're blue in the face. You must have had the letters.'

'I know all that,' I said, trying to sound ultra-polite and reasonable. 'We understand the council's argument, but we've got our point of view, too. We're homeless. Or we will be if you put us out of here. Will the council house us?'

'We can't,' he said wearily. 'We haven't got anywhere. Mrs Ho and her children had priority. Of the remaining four of you, Miss Varady, you're the only one who could argue you have any real link with the borough at all, and that's pretty tenuous! All we can do is put you on the list. We're not responsible for the other three. You and they will have to try the private sector.'

'No private landlord would take us on. And we couldn't afford the sort of rent he'd charge if he would! Look, we keep the place clean,' I went on. 'We don't hold wild parties or do anything you wouldn't do yourself. We don't let other people doss here. We're really very good tenants.

Or we would be if you'd let us pay rent and put us on a regular footing. That's all we ask. What's wrong with it?'

'The house is due to come down within the next six months. In the meantime, it's unsafe, not up to habitable standard. The electricity has been cut off.' He didn't look cross or unpleasant, just rather tired. 'We explained all that in our letters, too. You did read them, didn't you?'

Squib spoiled things then, by saying, 'Yeah, we used 'em to make spills to light the fire. Saved on matches.'

The housing official went red in the face and read us the riot act again, and then he drove off. Only just in time. While he'd been inside the house, talking to us, I'd been able to see, through the window, a couple of kids hanging round his shiny new Fiesta, and in another few minutes they'd have been inside it. The last he would have seen of it would have been the exhaust fumes and a squeal of skidding tyres.

We held a council of war after our visitor had left. We knew we had to go, of course. We just didn't know where. It was the end of summer and none of us fancied being out on the street just as the cold weather was about to start. Anyway, it was a lot less dangerous living in a squat, even one with an unsafe roof and dry rot in the staircase, like this one. As the man had said, we didn't qualify for any help.

Terry sat on the bare staircase, twisting a strand of hair round her finger and waiting for someone else to suggest something, so that she could criticise it. She was the world's greatest whinger, evaded housework and always jibbed at parting with her share of the house-keeping money. Looking at her I just wished she'd disappear and Declan come back. At least Declan was good at fixing things and good company as well.

It's dangerous to wish. Sometimes your wish is granted and then you're stuck with it.

She had noticed my scowls and immediately made herself look small and helpless. It was something she was very good at and which had led us to adopt her in the first place. I was the actress in our company, but that girl had missed her vocation, believe me. She peered through the curtains of hair and said pathetically, 'I haven't got anywhere else to go.'

'None of us has!' I snapped.

We all got up and trailed back into the main room. The three of them sat around looking at me, just like hopeful puppies. Each one of them was nursing a mug of tea. We each had our own mugs and no one ever drank from someone else's. It was a house rule.

Nev asked, 'What do we do, Fran?' in a trusting sort of way which made it all so much worse.

It was always down to me in the end. The trouble was, I was really out of ideas. I had to say something. They expected it. So I said, 'If we could get an old van, we could go on the road.'

'I'd rather doss in a doorway,' Squib said straight away. 'I've tried that New-Age stuff. Digging holes in mud before you can crap and having to listen to folk music all night long. Forget it.'

'He's got a point. It's all right in summer,' Nev added. 'But wintertime, it's no joke.'

'The police keep moving you on, anyway,' Terry tossed in her usual handful of objections. 'And it's really awful in a tent when it rains. They always leak. You'd do just anything to get somewhere dry, anywhere. I know, I've tried it.'

'I like it here,' said Nev wistfully. 'In this house.'

Squib took off his woolly hat and looked into it. Perhaps he thought he'd find an idea in there. He didn't, so he smoothed a hand over his shaven head and put the hat back again carefully.

'I don't,' said Terry. 'It's got rats.'

'Everywhere's got rats,' said Squib. 'Rats is all right. I've had some really nice pet rats. I had a white one. I carried it inside my coat. It never bit me, not once. I sold it to a bloke in a pub. He give me a fiver for it. Mind you, he was pissed at the time. I reckon that rat bit him, after he got it home. It bit other people. It never bit me. Animals like me.'

That was true. Terry mumbled it was because Squib smelled like barnyard and the animals just accepted he was one of them. The pouty, discontented look on her face grew worse. She had wrapped herself in an old knitted coat she always wore and was sulking. The coat was grubby and matted, but I'd seen the label in it once, and it was a very expensive one. I'd remarked on it and Terry had promptly said she'd got the coat from Oxfam. I hadn't believed her then and it set me wondering again now. She might have stolen it. She was inclined to be light-fingered although she wasn't stupid enough ever to touch anything of mine or Nev's. We probably didn't have anything she wanted. Only a complete nutter would have touched anything of Squib's. The dog would have had him in a flash. Even if the dog hadn't been there on guard, Squib's belongings wouldn't invite investigation.

As I said, we never asked people about themselves. If they were desperate enough to want to share a condemned house riddled with dry-rot, illegally and without electricity, then they needed a place to stay, not questions. Only, sooner or later, most people told you something about themselves. Not Terry. She'd never said a word. But whatever her background, there'd been money around there. You could tell. It made me wonder about the coat even more.

We talked about our problem all morning but we didn't get anywhere. It ended with an argument, not about what we should do, but about Squib's dog.

Terry said it had fleas. It was always scratching. You could say anything you liked about Squib, but not about his dog. It was a funny-looking dog with one ear turned over and one pointing up. Its legs were crooked. Squib had found it on a pile of rubbish when it was a puppy. He thought someone had chucked it out because it was the runt of a litter. Anyhow, he'd looked after it and it grew up all right except for the crooked legs. It was a nice dog. It was friendly to everyone except when guarding Squib's gear. We all liked it, except Terry. But she didn't like anything.

So when she insulted his dog, Squib told her a few home truths. They were well into a squabble when I lost my temper. I always tried to keep my temper in the house because once one person starts yelling, everyone starts. But we were already arguing and, somehow, Terry's moaning was the last straw. Her criticism of the house itself had hurt. We'd taken her in, given her a home there, and all she could do was to let us know it wasn't up to her accustomed standard.

I yelled, 'You're a real pain in the bum!' Only I didn't say 'bum'. 'Nobody asked you to move in with us. We let you stay here and I don't think there's been one day when you haven't whinged from morning till night! We've all got problems! You're no worse off than the rest of us.' Remembering the coat label, I added, 'I know your type. When you've had enough, you'll just push off back wherever you came from!'

She turned absolutely white. She pushed back the spaniel's ears and hissed, 'Shut it, Fran! You don't know anything about me! You fancy pushing us around, that's all! Do this, do that! You give the orders and we all jump, right? Well, wrong! I don't! And that's what you don't like. You always act like some kind of Mother Superior! This is a commune, we've got equal rights, OK? Equal say? Just because Nev's a nervous wreck and Squib's got no brains, they let you do the thinking and talking for them and you think you can do the same for me! You can't, you don't and you'd better remember it!'

There was a viciousness in her voice that I hadn't heard before, but it wasn't that which shook me. It was the accusation itself. I hadn't thought of myself as overbearing, pushing anyone around. I didn't like the picture much and it made me defensive.

'I don't order anyone around! I'm just trying to be helpful! If you tried, it would be something! Even Squib tries!'

Squib looked surprised at getting a compliment. It must have been a first for him. He said, 'Thanks, Fran!'

Nev said nervously, 'Look, we've got to stick together. We mustn't all fall out now.'

'You, Squib and I were together – she came along later and she can go any time!' I shouted. I was still mad at her and madder because she'd rattled me. I'm not proud of any of this. I shouldn't have turned on her like that. She was right when she said I knew nothing about her.

Looking back, I don't remember exactly how Terry got to be with us. I think Lucy introduced her. I'd once wondered if Terry had stayed originally because she fancied Declan who was still with us at that time. I think perhaps he'd fancied her just a little. But it didn't stop him leaving. He was better off without her, if you ask me. But then, I never liked her, not from the beginning. It's no use pretending. But I would never have wanted what happened. None of us would have wanted it.

All that was on Monday morning. We didn't have a lot of time to waste, so on Monday afternoon, Nev and I made a long trek up Camden way, to see a squat he'd heard about. Just to see if there'd be room for us there. Only, when we got there, it was all boarded up and empty so their council had been and cleared everyone out. Pity, it was a classier area than the one we'd been living in. We went to Camden Lock and messed about. We saw a few people we knew and asked around.

Squib had gone up West with the dog. He'd taken along his chalks and a picture postcard of El Greco's *Assumption of the Virgin* and the idea was to find a patch of pavement. He couldn't afford to waste time, not with the weather threatening to break up again.

Terry hadn't said what she was doing and we hadn't asked her. None of us expected her to be doing anything useful, like finding us another place to live.

I suppose I oughtn't to talk about the dead like that. You're not supposed to. You're supposed to say nice things about dead people or they come back and haunt you. I know that's right because Terry haunted me. It was probably because of all the sour things I'd said about her over the time she'd been with us, quite apart from what I said after – well, after it happened.

Going back to Monday. Nev and I got back from Camden quite late. Some people had invited us to stay and eat with them. They were vegetarian, like Nev, so it was all beans but it was quite nice, very spicy and hot, but I knew I'd suffer later.

When we got back, the place was very quiet. It was dark because the electricity was disconnected. We used candles. Only, apart from the emptiness and the usual dry-rot smell, there was something else. It was a sort of impression, a different, foreign one. I knew, just knew, that someone had been there who wasn't one of us. A stranger. A real stranger, someone totally outside our circle and not from the council. There was a very faint perfume as well, a type of cologne. I worked in a cut-price chemist's shop one time. I know colognes. I know good ones from cheap ones. This was a good one, the sort that sells well at Christmas.

The scent of it there in the hall made me cross. I thought perhaps Terry had been shop-lifting again and I was always telling her off about that. It was possible she'd had more money than she let on, and had gone out and bought it for herself. Those colognes, frankly, smell better on a woman than a man, just my opinion. She always kept quiet if she had any money. She'd spend it on junk or on glossy magazines, the sort which tell you how to transform your semi-detached into something you'd be happy to invite a *Hello!* camera team into. And that at a time when we were putting buckets under the leak in the roof and were living on bread and marge.

I mentioned the cologne smell to Nev but he said he couldn't make it out, not with the smell of the dry rot as well. The other thing, the impression of someone, an outsider, having been there, I kept to myself. It wasn't something easily explained. Lucy had been into the paranormal and she'd have told me I was a natural psychic. I don't believe in that sort of thing. Or I don't think I do. If I had to explain what I felt at that moment, looking back with hindsight, I think I scented danger. If I'd been a cavewoman, it'd have been a woolly mammoth outside the cave. Only this wasn't outside, it was inside, with us.

We went into the main room and got the fire going again because it was getting very chilly. Neither of us said anything, but we were both thinking that it was going to be a whole lot colder next week, when chances were we'd be sleeping rough until we found some new place to stay. After a while Squib came back with the dog and a four-pack of lager. He'd also brought a packet of sausages which he roasted over the fire using a metal shovel as a frying pan.

They smelled delicious. The fat spat up and fell in the flames so they roared up, red and yellow. It was very cosy and we felt happy. When they were done, crispy and dark brown, Squib offered them all round. Say what you like about Squib, he always shared. Nev refused the sausages because he didn't eat meat and I refused them because the beans we'd eaten earlier lay on my stomach. Besides, I knew Squib probably hadn't eaten that day.

Squib cut up half the sausages for the dog and put them up on the mantelshelf to cool off. Then he asked, 'D'you think Terry will want any when she gets in?'

I said, 'Why bother about her? She never bothers about

us.' That shows how I was feeling just then, because even if I didn't like her, she was one of us and I wouldn't normally have left her out.

But she didn't come back that night, or we thought she hadn't. We didn't see her.

The next morning she still wasn't around and Squib suggested she might have done a runner, like Declan.

'She's found somewhere else to live,' he said. 'She's ditched us and moved in with some others. After the council came, you can't blame her. There's probably no point in hanging around here.'

Knowing that he was right, that our days here were numbered, didn't make us feel any better. But it was still a relief to think we'd seen the back of Terry. She was one fewer to worry about.

Nev suggested we ought to check her room and see if her things had gone. If it was empty, fine. We could forget her.

We trooped upstairs, all three of us, and the dog. The dog was good at getting up and down the staircase even with its crooked legs.

But outside Terry's room the dog began to act strangely. Its pointy ear flattened out to match its other ear and it crouched down and began to make a weird whining in its throat.

Squib knelt down and stroked its head and asked it what was wrong. But it just lay down and looked miserable.

Nev said, 'Perhaps it's eaten something it shouldn't.'

That worried Squib who'd heard of squatters' dogs being poisoned. He was sitting on the floor outside the door, trying to get the dog to open its mouth so he could see if its tongue was stained, when Nev and I opened the door to Terry's room.

She was there, after all. She must have stayed behind indoors the previous day, when we'd gone out. She'd been there when we came back and there all night. There when Squib cooked his sausages downstairs and there when I got up in the night because of the beans.

Hanging there from the ceiling light.

I remember the scene very clearly, almost as if my mind took a snapshot of it which I can take out and mentally consult. The room, like the rest of the house, must have been beautiful once. Pale sun was shining through the tall, thin windows, one of which still had half a broken brass rod across the top of it. The sun just clipped the rod and made it gleam like gold. The corners of the high ceiling were festooned with ancient cobwebs and dead spiders. Running all around was a plaster frieze in Greek 'egg and dart' pattern. In the very middle of the ceiling a sculpted plaster round, caked with dust, displayed intertwined oakleaves and acorns. It was easy to imagine an ornate light, a chandelier perhaps, hanging from it in days gone by.

There was nothing hanging from it now but Terry. There was a length of something round her neck which turned out later to be the dog's lead. Squib hardly ever used it because the dog was very well behaved and always kept to heel. It had been lying around the house and now it was round Terry's throat.

Even given the shock of the moment, or perhaps because of it, the shutter in my mind snapped her in the same detail. She – rather, that thing which had been Terry

– wore tattered jeans. The front zip fastening was undone and they gaped open over her bare stomach. A considerable gap had opened up between the gaping waist of the jeans and the bottom of a badly shrunk and faded tee-shirt. I could see her lower rib cage protruding over the convex stomach muscles, pulled taut. Her feet were bare, mottled mauve. She had the makings of a first-class bunion on her left big-toe joint, but it wasn't ever going to trouble her now.

Like the room, she'd been pretty once, and, like it, she wasn't now. Overnight the weight of her body had elongated her neck to resemble a giraffe-necked African tribeswoman whose head is supported on a stack of metal coils. The doglead had cut into her throat horridly, causing her face to puff and turn black with congested blood. Her mouth was open and her swollen tongue protruded as if, even in death, she was dishing out one last insult to us. Her eyeballs were popping out at us, netted over with crimson veins.

Nev gasped, 'Gawd! She's topped herself!'

I had no reason, then, to suppose he wasn't right. There was a rickety old chair nearby, lying on its side, not far from Terry's dangling bare toes. I imagined her climbing on to it, fixing the noose, jumping off.

You don't die quickly that way. The old-time hangmen knew how to knot a rope to break the neck. This way, she'd simply strangled, slowly. Her flailing feet had kicked over the chair. Perhaps, in a moment's realisation of how it was going to be, she changed her mind, and sought out the chair's support again, intending to release the pressure on her neck, disentangle herself from the noose and climb down, bruised but wiser.

She wouldn't have been the first to change her mind, nor the first to discover it wasn't that easy. You didn't fool around with death. It liked to be taken seriously. So, whether, in the end, she'd intended it or not, there she was.

And there we were, with a dead body for company, and an awful lot of trouble in store.

Chapter Two

I couldn't have guessed all that lay ahead following our horrifying discovery. But I was aware that we'd receive much unwelcome attention from the authorities. The other two weren't thinking ahead, too busy coping, or not, with the sight of that hanging shape. Nev rushed out and could be heard being sick in the loo. It turned out that he'd never seen a dead body before. I had, but it didn't make it any easier looking at her.

Squib left the dog and came into the room. He'd stood his ground, but he had an even chalkier complexion than usual. He always had a pinched look about him and now must have resembled that white rat he'd once kept as a pet.

'We'd better get out of here!' he said. He was sweating. I could smell the odour, rising up from him as from a hunted animal. 'Come on, we're wasting time! Let's get our gear together and go!'

'Don't be daft,' I told him. 'The council knows all about us, our names, everything. They'll find us.'

'Why'd she do it?' he asked. 'Was she worried about us being chucked out? Here—' His eyes gleamed. 'That's what we tell that wally from the council! We tell him, he drove her to it!'

'Shut up, Squib!' I told him. I needed to think. No one else was likely to do any constructive thinking. It would be down to me, as usual. Squib in a blind panic wanting to run and Nev throwing up, that was likely to be the sum total of their contribution. Looking after Nev and Squib was sometimes like looking after a pair of infants. You had to do all the thinking for them and be worrying every five minutes where they were and what they were doing.

Nev came back, still looking ill but trying to pull himself together. 'Oughtn't we to – take her down?' His voice couldn't rise above a whisper and it cracked on the last word. 'We oughtn't to leave her hanging there. It's obscene.'

It was obscene. He was right. But we couldn't touch her. We mustn't touch anything. I explained the point forcibly to them both.

Squib looked relieved. He wasn't keen to touch her. Nev, however, reacted with a cry of dismay.

'We can't leave her hanging there!' His voice sounded like something produced by computer. The sounds were all there, making up the words, but it wasn't human.

He made a sudden lurch towards her and before I could stop him, he grabbed her legs. I don't know what he thought he was going to do. Lift her down unaided, maybe. But as almost as soon as he touched her, he staggered back with a strangled scream.

'She's stiff . . . '

The body, set in motion by his clumsy attempt, began to rotate on the doglead like a grotesque mobile hanging from the ceiling. I took a look up at the light fixture. It wasn't going to hold much longer. It was astonishing it'd held out so long. Any moment now, especially with the movement, the body was likely to come crashing down without our help. If it did, we'd be in even more trouble.

But the stiffness, if Nev was right, had set me thinking. I wasn't clear on the finer point of rigor, but had an idea it took around twelve hours to come on and then lasted around another twelve before it passed off gradually, depending on circumstances. If she was good and stiff, she'd died yesterday afternoon. We had to fetch the police at once or we'd have to explain the delay.

Nev wasn't in any state to object further and nodded listlessly.

'I say we oughta make a run for it!' Squib objected, unconvinced. He didn't like the law. It wasn't too keen on him. The dog sat up and lifted its muzzle to let out a howl as if it agreed with him.

'Hear that?' Squib pointed at the dog. 'She didn't like him, Terry didn't. She was always saying he'd got fleas. He hasn't. But he's crying for her, see? Animals are better than humans, that's what I think. Animals have got decency.'

'Decency', I told him sharply, 'means we fetch the police.'

We might have argued about it for ages, but it got settled for us. There was a shout from downstairs.

We stared at one another, all panicking. I ran downstairs and would you believe it? There was the man from the council again. This time he had a colleague with him, a sweaty, tubby charmer with a malevolent scowl.

'We came to check you're preparing to move out,' the

first one said, 'and to make sure you mean to attend today's hearing.'

I'd forgotten the hearing. It hardly seemed to matter now. They were the last people we needed there and I wondered frantically how to get rid of them. 'We can't!' I blurted. 'I mean, we'll see you there. We're getting ready to leave, so you can't come in, not just now.'

He came nearer to where I stood, halfway down the uncarpeted stair, and frowned up at me. 'It's Fran, isn't it? You're in charge here, aren't you? You always seem to speak for the others.'

That, I recalled ruefully, was what Terry had accused me of.

The reason I always spoke for the others was because, left to themselves, they always said the wrong thing. I was thinking wildly now, trying to think of the right thing to say, to find some way of explaining.

'Something's happened. One of our friends has – has had an accident. I've got to fetch help.'

'What kind of accident?' It was the fat one speaking now. He moved forward, looking nasty.

'Fran?' The younger one looked at me, worried. 'Do you need an ambulance?'

It crossed my mind that he wasn't such a bad sort. But I hadn't time for character analysis.

The other one snapped, 'Drugs, you bet! One of 'em's oh-dee'd! They would choose this bloody morning to do it! How long's he – she – been unconscious?'

'We're not druggies!' I shouted. 'None of us is!'

That was absolutely true. It was another house rule. No drugs. Terry sometimes had cannabis. But that was it.

Fatso was sniffing the air now. 'I'm not so sure!'

'The smell's the dry rot!' I snapped at him.

There was a creak on the stair behind me and I heard the dog growl. Squib's voice soothed it. Then he spoke.

'You can't go upstairs,' he said. 'One of our mates is dead.'

That put the cat amongst the pigeons. The first council official was up the stairs like a greyhound, racing past me and Squib and pushing Nev aside on the landing. The dog began to bark and wanted to jump up at him but Squib held it by its collar.

'Where?' the official was yelling. 'Are you sure?'

'She topped herself!' Squib yelled back at him. 'It was you coming yesterday to tell us we'd gotta quit that did it! She got depressed!'

The fat man was plodding heavily up the stairs. He squeezed past me giving me a dirty look. He had BO, the sort his best friend hadn't told him about. The stair creaked. I hoped the dry rot would give way under his weight but it didn't. Probably just as well. We'd have had two corpses.

Nev mumbled, 'She's in there! We didn't touch her!'

The two men had opened the door to Terry's room. There was silence and then the fat man began swearing.

We heard him say, 'The press will get hold of this!'

The thinner one told him to shut up. Then they began whispering together. Eventually the first one came out of the room and spoke to us all.

'We'll fetch the police. You lot stay here. Don't let anyone in. Don't talk to anyone!' He paused. 'My colleague, Mr Wilson, will stay with you.'

Fatty plodded across the landing, glowering. He looked

an awful lot less confident than when he'd arrived. Squib's dog, not liking the look of him, growled again.

He moved back. 'What sort of dog is that? Is it a pit bull?'

'Does it look like a pit bull?' I asked. 'It's about half the size, to start with.'

'He's got a bit of Staffordshire in him, I reckon,' said Squib with pride. 'Once he gets his teeth into something, he don't let go.'

'For Gawd's sake,' said Wilson to his council colleague, 'Hurry up and get back here with the cops!'

We waited for the police, all of us sitting in the living room, Wilson included. He sat by the door like a heavy, with his arms folded over his beer belly, in case any of us tried to rush him. When he wasn't watching us, he was watching the dog.

Squib huddled in the far corner with his arms round it, whispering into its pointy ear. It kept turning its head and looking up at him. Once or twice it licked his face. No way was anyone going to be able to claim it was dangerous. I hoped.

Nev was managing well. He sat by the hearth, only a nervous twisting of his hands betraying stress. From time to time he glanced at me for reassurance and I smiled back. It took some doing on my part. I didn't feel like smiling. My head was in a whirl and I knew I had to sort it out before the police got there.

To begin with, they'd ask us about Terry and there wasn't very much we could tell them. We could suggest they ask Lucy. That was about it. I tried hard to remember all the things she'd said, every word since she'd arrived. But I hadn't liked her and I hadn't talked to her unless I'd had to, so there you were. All opportunities missed.

She'd been very well spoken, an upper-class sort of voice. She reminded me of the girls at the private day school I attended until they politely requested my dad to take me away. Of course, she used to use all kinds of words she'd picked up out there in the streets, trying to sound like just anyone else around the area. But it hadn't worked. She still sounded different. There was that woolly jacket with the expensive label. She'd had that with her when she came. She was wearing it the night she arrived with Lucy. I know she didn't get that jacket from Oxfam. She'd brought that with her from home, wherever home was.

As for her friends, I didn't even know if she had any, or where she went during the day. The police would ask if either Nev or Squib had been her boyfriend. Neither had. Nev was generally considered to be with me, but the arrangement was a platonic one. I acted, if anything, as Nev's minder. He didn't cope well on his own. Squib had his dog for company. He didn't really need people.

Declan was the one Terry had been keen on. But we didn't know where Declan had gone and anyway, he'd had troubles of his own. I didn't want to put the police on to Declan. I'd liked him.

So, to come back to the most important question, why? Why should she kill herself? I couldn't accept it, even though I'd seen the evidence. She hadn't appeared depressed or worried, more than any of us were worried about the eviction. Despite Squib's theory, I didn't believe she'd worried enough about that to take such extreme action. Generally, she'd just been her normal, grousing self. Alarm bells were starting to ring at the back of my brain and I didn't like the sound of what they were trying to tell me.

I remembered how she'd been dressed when we found her, just in the unzipped jeans and crumpled shirt. I couldn't understand why the jeans weren't zipped up. If she'd been walking around like that before she died, the jeans would've ended up round her ankles. So, had she pulled them on in a hurry and, with suicide in mind, not bothered with the zip? Or, an idea, as grotesque as it was unwelcome popped into my head, had someone else dressed her unconscious body, panicking, fumbling with the zip and giving up? I remembered the aroma of cologne in the house when Nev and I returned from Camden and my feeling that some outsider had been there in our absence.

I put that unpleasant thought on hold and concentrated on another. The rigor. Accepting that she had died yesterday afternoon, the police would want to know where we'd all been, when was the last time we'd seen her and if she'd appeared distressed in any way. They were unlikely, in the circumstances, to accept anyone's plea of total ignorance and absence from the scene, without some confirmation. We were not the sort of people whose word they took. So what we were looking for here were alibis, not to put too fine a point on it.

Nev and I, with luck, could prove that for part of the time we were eating Mexican bean stew with his friends. As for Squib, a pavement artist must have hundreds of witnesses to his activities. But all of them would have been hurrying by, glancing at a hunched figure rubbing industriously at a square of paving with chalks. Some would have taken a closer look at the picture, but few would have troubled to look closely at the artist.

I must have shifted in my chair because I met Wilson's beady gaze fixed on me. He had tensed as I moved and probably thought I was planning to leap through a pane of glass and run off down the street like they do in movies. If so, he watched too much television.

Nev said, 'I need a glass of water,' and stood up.

Wilson ordered, 'You just stay where you are, sunshine!'

'He's been sick!' I snapped. 'You stay there, Nev. I'll go and get you the water.' I marched over to Wilson and stood over him. 'You don't have any right to prevent me!' I told him. 'And don't forget, your mate was here yesterday and our friend died right afterwards!'

'You've got a big mouth!' he said.

'And you've got a fat gut!' I told him.

'All right,' he snarled. 'You won't be so lippy when the police get here. Go and get him his glass of water. Where's the kitchen?'

'It's the next room. If I leave the door open, you'll be able to see me in there from just outside this room, OK?'

He grunted and moved out into the hall where he could see both the living-room door and the kitchen door. I went into the kitchen and turned on the tap. I had a drink of water myself while I was there, even though I could feel Wilson's eyes boring into my back. Then I took Nev's glass back with me.

He said, 'Thanks, Fran!' and sipped at it. After a moment, he whispered, 'Stick with me, won't you, Fran? I don't think I can manage to face the police alone!'

I smiled again. But he was going to have to manage somehow because they'd interview us separately for sure.

Honestly, I'd never seen so many coppers in my life, not all in one house. They brought all sorts of equipment, lights and cameras and I don't know what else. It would have been interesting to watch if we hadn't been at the centre of it all.

A Detective Sergeant Parry arrived. He had crewcut ginger hair and bright blue eyes too close together. His eyebrows were almost non-existent and possibly by way of compensation he was trying, not very successfully, to grow a moustache. It sprouted unevenly along his upper lip with varying thickness and hue as if it were infected with mange. His manner was sarcastic. Whatever he told him, he obviously didn't believe any of it.

'All right, what happened?' He'd produced a notebook and was thumbing wearily through it.

We told him we didn't know.

'Don't give me that. And don't waste everyone's time, mine, yours, the inspector's. Do you know how much an investigation like this costs the taxpayer? No, don't suppose you do. You lot don't pay any taxes. Just scroungers, live off the social. Come on, let's have the whole story.'

What can you say to someone like that? We said nothing.

'What is this?' He scowled at us. 'Someone told you you've got a right to silence? Got something to hide?'

'No,' I said patiently. 'We already told you that we just don't know what happened.'

He sighed. 'Look, it was a game, right? It went wrong.

It was a stupid bet or something. You were pissed out of your skulls at the time. Or high as kites. Which? Both? There will be a post mortem. We'll find out what you were using. It'll be much easier if you tell me now. Stand you in good stead before the court.'

'What court?'

'Coroner's court. What other? Sounds to me as if bad conscience is troubling you.'

I'd meant to keep cool but at that, I couldn't. 'I thought you were supposed to make tactful and sympathetic inquiries when this sort of thing happens – not try and invent something you can stick on us?'

'Sassy little madam, aren't you?' He pointed his Biro at me. 'But you're talking yourself into a lot of trouble, lady. Don't cheek me! I'm writing it all down here.' He tapped the pad. 'Every word.'

I told him, 'That moustache looks like something the cat brought up. Go on, write that down. You're supposed to write it all down, not just pick out the bits which suit you.'

He put his notepad and Biro away. 'All right, have it your own way. We'll go down to the station and interview you all there. It'll be recorded on tape. You can make all the smart remarks you want, darling. But when the tape's played back they won't sound so clever.'

I asked, 'Are we being arrested? What's the crime?'

He looked mock-shocked. 'Of course not, dear! The very idea!'

I knew we could refuse but, on the other hand, we were hardly flavour of the month and it might be best not to make things worse. So we went.

* * *

They took our fingerprints. I'd never been involved in a suicide enquiry, but this didn't seem justified to me. I asked why. 'For elimination. Once we don't need them any longer, they'll be destroyed,' I was told.

I asked, 'Elimination from what?' But I didn't get any answer.

They split us all up so that we couldn't confer. I don't know where Nev and Squib went. Nev looked awful as he went out, grey-faced, sweating and looking as guilty as hell. I hoped the police realised he wasn't well.

I sat for ages in a bare little room, watched by a bored copper who kept scraping his finger round inside his ear and inspecting the tip of it to see what he'd found there. I wished they'd offer me a cup of tea, but they didn't. Eventually, Parry came again and said Inspector Morgan would like to talk to me.

Before we left the house, the younger, nicer, council official had come back and I'd found out his name was Euan. So now I began to wonder if they were all Welsh and if they were, what they were all doing in this part of London. Were they all plotting some sort of revenge for the death of Llewellyn?

Inspector Morgan turned out to be a woman. I suppose they thought that was clever of them, all girls together stuff, and I'd confide in her. But I did get that cup of tea at long last.

She was quite young which surprised me. I'd always imagined inspectors would be old fellows with grey hair and bad teeth. Or, if they were women, built like brick barns. Morgan was smartly dressed though her hair was a bit dowdy. If she looked like anything, she looked like a schoolteacher. She had something of the same manner, bossy but wary at the same time.

'Miss Varady?' she asked, although she knew I was. 'I don't think I've come across that surname before.'

'It's Hungarian,' I told her. 'But before you start checking on me, I'm British by birth.'

My father came from Hungary with his parents in the fifties when they had the revolution. He was five years old at the time.

'I see,' she said. 'Well now, Francesca—'

I interrupted her to ask, 'What's your first name?'

She looked surprised so I went on, 'Because if you're going to call me by my first name, I ought to be able to call you by yours. Otherwise, I call you Inspector, and you call me Miss Varady.'

The copper by the door hid a grin.

She took that quite well. 'Fair enough,' she said. 'Just when we're on our own, then, my name's Janice. So, Francesca—' She underlined it faintly. 'Just carry on telling me about yourself, and the squat, and your friends – and Theresa Monkton.'

'We called her Terry.' There really wasn't more I could say than that. We hadn't known her very long. I had nothing but my own guesswork for the things I'd deduced about her, so I couldn't mention any of them. She hadn't talked about herself. Lucy might know something. I told Inspector Janice all this.

'What about her other friends?' she asked.

'I don't know. She didn't say. No one ever came to the house.'

'Had there been any disputes between you, any of you, at the house?'

There'd been plenty, Terry being so lazy and grumbling all the time. But I thought quickly before I answered. I didn't like the drift of the question. What did they think had happened?

I said, 'Nothing much, just the usual squabbles about whose turn it was for the washing-up. She kept herself to herself. We always tried to respect one another's privacy. Even people like us have the right to a private life, you know! It's not easy, when you're all living together. You have to be careful not to ask questions and we didn't.'

'Which of the men was her boyfriend?'

'Neither! People come and go in squats! It just happened that we were two women and two men!' For good measure, I added, 'I don't have to stay here and be grilled by you, you know.'

'You volunteered to come to the station, Francesca.'

Not that I remembered. I said so.

'We know it's been a shock,' she said soothingly. 'But we need to know the circumstances. We're grateful for your cooperation. Now, let's get through it as quickly and painlessly as possible, shall we? Tell me the last time you saw her.'

'Alive? Yesterday around lunchtime. Next time I saw her, she was dead.'

'Hanging from the ceiling?'

'Of course, hanging from the ceiling! Where else?' Morgan was waiting. 'Nev wanted to take her down because she looked so hideous, hanging there. But I told him, we mustn't touch her. We had to tell your lot. But the council men turned up first.'

'But you were going to notify the police?'

'Yes!' I said fiercely. 'Believe it or not, we were!'

'Oh, I believe you, Francesca. Why shouldn't I?'

'Because we're squatters. Don't tell me the law's impartial. Tell your sergeant. He doesn't know it.'

Janice's eyes were pale grey and now they looked like bits of steel. For a few minutes she forgot she was being nice to me and this was a cosy girls' chat. 'You've a complaint against Sergeant Parry?'

Not if I knew what was good for me, I didn't.

'Lovely feller,' I said. 'Every woman's dream.'

She was studying me. 'We'll be getting a complete post mortem report. But there are already one or two things which puzzle us. You're absolutely certain that when you left the house yesterday, you all left together?'

'I told you, yes! Nev and I went over to see if we could get a place to live up Camden way. Squib went somewhere else. Up West, probably. He was looking for a clear piece of pavement to make a picture. He's a pavement artist.'

'Yes, we're checking on that. Why do you call him Squib? I understand his name is Henry.'

'He doesn't look like a Henry. I didn't give him the name Squib. He's always had it as far as I know. No one calls him anything else.'

If she'd known Squib she could have worked out for herself that he had a low-wattage brain and someone somewhere made a joke about his being damp.

I added, 'But he's all right. He likes animals and they like him.' I leaned forward. 'I know what he looks like and I know what you're thinking, but Squib is all right! You can trust him!'

'And Nevil Porter? What about him?'

I fixed her with a look and said very quietly because I wanted her to listen and take it in: 'Don't bully Nev. It would be easy for you to do that. He couldn't resist. He'd tell you anything you wanted him to say whether it was the truth or not. He's been ill, had a breakdown. He's very intelligent but he can't cope. That's why he packed in his studies. Get a doctor to talk to him. And you can check all this. He hasn't done anything and if you got him to confess to anything, his medical history would mean you couldn't take it into court. So leave him alone.'

She gave a thin smile. 'We already know some of this. We've had a call from his family's solicitor.'

That was quick. They hadn't wasted much time. But I guessed what had happened. Once they'd got Nev on his own, he'd panicked and asked for that solicitor. 'Did Nev ask for a lawyer?'

'Yes.' Then she asked silkily, 'We appreciate that he's very nervous and it appears he has a medical history of breakdown. But all the same, why should he need a solicitor? Wouldn't a family friend do? Or one of the doctors who treated him? If he hasn't done anything, he only needs to answer a few routine questions.'

I was angry because I'd just tried to explain all that and it was as if I hadn't spoken. But I knew I mustn't lose my temper. I met her eye and said firmly, and nice and clearly, just the way they'd taught us to speak up at that school, 'Surely he's entitled to have his solicitor?'

She blinked. 'Yes.'

'So what's the problem?'

I'd hit the ball back into her court. She didn't like it, but there wasn't much she could do but give me a frozen smile. The corners of her mouth turned up, but her lips stayed clamped together. It was more like rictus than a smile and reminded me of Terry.

I thought about Nev again. He must have been really afraid he'd go to pieces when he asked for the family lawyer. He would have known that the first thing that legal eagle would do, would be pick up the telephone and inform Nev's parents he was in trouble. Next thing, they'd be down here from the wilds of darkest Cheshire before you could say knife.

Still, I was relieved to know Nev had someone looking after his interests. But it had made the police even more suspicious. Neither Squib nor I had anyone to look after our interests. But we were probably luckier than Nev. I'd met Nev's father once and he would be the last person I'd want around if I had problems. He's one of those who are always ready to tell you what you ought to do, even if any idiot can see you're in no state to do it. When Nev had his breakdown, his father just stood over him telling him to pull himself together! What use is that?

'Why, when you came home and, according to what you told Sergeant Parry and me, you cooked sausages, didn't someone go upstairs and ask Theresa if she wanted to join you? Didn't you usually eat together?'

I don't know why she had to repeat the same set of questions so many times in as many ways. Either she was slow to get the picture, or she thought that, eventually, I'd start contradicting myself.

I repeated for the *n*th time, 'I told you, Nev and I had already eaten and Nev's vegetarian. You can check everything I've said. I don't know what Terry did after we left her Monday midday. We didn't go up to her room when we got in because we thought she was out of the house and would be back later. I also told you she didn't confide in us. She just went off and did her own thing.'

'So why did you go up to her room this morning? Had something happened to make you suspicious?'

'No! We just thought she'd gone for good – and we were checking.'

But she had gone for good, poor Terry. I wished I'd phrased it differently. All the same, trust her to make trouble for everyone else, even in dying.

The image kept coming back to me, although I tried to keep it away. It was as if that hanging body was there in the room with us, the purplish-black face which hadn't looked like Terry at all, her delicate features bloated and discoloured and her swollen tongue protruding at us in a grotesque, childish gesture of defiance.

It seemed Morgan could read my mind. 'When you found her, Francesca, did you notice the bruises?'

The alarm bells were jangling ever louder. Every visible bit of Terry's skin had been mottled mauve and grey when I saw her, but since then, a doctor must have had a closer look. They couldn't have done a post mortem yet, only a preliminary check, establishing death. But someone, unless Janice was even more devious than I had already credited, had noticed bruises.

'You mean, as if she'd fallen?' I, too, could be devious.

'Uh-huh. More as if someone had hit her.'

'Someone had roughed her up recently?' This was very bad news.

'Well, we don't know, do we, Francesca.' She gave me that rictus smile. 'Or at least, I don't. There appear, on cursory examination, to be bruises on her thighs and upper arms and a serious contusion on the side of her head resulting from a blow hard enough to knock her cold. Also a graze on the right hip.'

Getting worse.

'So I'll ask again, were there ever any fights in that house?'

'I'll tell you again, no! We may have had a few spats. No punches were thrown – ever!'

'These spats? Were they ever – emotional in origin?'

I sighed. 'Whom would we have been fighting over? Nev? Squib? You've got to be joking. We had house rules and it kept the peace, more or less.'

But I was thinking of something else. Janice was, too.

'How about the way she was dressed, when you found her. Did it strike you as unusual?'

I admitted it bothered me a little.

'It bothers me, too,' she said. 'Jeans and a shirt. No underwear of any kind. Did she usually go around without any knickers on?'

'How should I know?' I snapped. 'She never wore a bra. She didn't have much to put in one. The graze on the hip. Was the skin broken?'

'Definitely and a couple of wood splinters lodged in it. Forensics will find the origin of those. Did she ever bring men back to the house?' The last question was slipped in like a knife beneath my guard. I knew what she was getting at, but I thought she was wrong.

'She didn't bring back anyone, male or female. If she was on the game, she was operating well away in another part of town. I never saw any sign of it.'

Janice abandoned that line of questioning and the tone of it, becoming conciliatory again. 'I'd like, if I may, to ask you about the dogleash. The dog belongs to the one you call Squib, is that right?'

'Yes. The leash just lies round the house. The dog's very well trained and it isn't often he put it on a leash.'

'So anyone could have got hold of the leash? Is that what you're saying? We can expect to find all your fingerprints on it?'

The question hit me with an unpleasant jolt to the solar plexus. So this was why they'd been in such a hurry to take our fingerprints, before we could object. The sick feeling below my chest intensified.

I didn't want to say anything else to make her more suspicious of me. But I'd been told by someone who reckoned he knew that there still wasn't any really reliable way of taking clear fingerprints off rough surfaces. Not clear enough to stand up in court, anyway. To be used as evidence, so the person who told me said, there had to be sixteen points of similarity between a print taken at a scene of crime and one taken off a suspect. And that's an awful lot. That dogleash was a scuffed-up bit of old leather. They'd be lucky to get sixteen points of similarity off that.

She was still giving me that steely look. I countered it with one of my own.

'I don't think I should answer any more of these questions without a lawyer.'

'My goodness,' she said. 'First Porter, now you. What's your reason for wanting a legal adviser, Francesca?'

'Simple. You indicated you only wanted to ask about the circumstances leading to our finding Terry's body. You did say there were a few things puzzling you. But this line of questioning seems to me far more than is necessary for a suicide. I'm not daft. You think you've got yourselves a case of murder.'

Chapter Three

When they realised I really wasn't going to answer any more questions, the interview came to an abrupt end – for the time being. They weren't keen to see any more of us legally represented, even by the most incompetent of lawyers, at that stage. They didn't know for sure they had a murder case. For that they'd await the final report of the post mortem. Janice thanked me icily for all my help and murmured that they might need to talk to me again. What was my address?

I pointed out they knew. She said, still smiling, she understood we were about to be evicted within the next few days. I told her it was still the only address I had, and suggested she ask the council what it meant to do about us. I was asked to wait outside.

Eventually someone came to tell me they'd been in touch with the council and understood it meant to rehouse me – though not Squib or Nev. All this was news to me. The police must have put pressure on and succeeded where all else had failed. But it made me uneasy, as it turned out, rightly so.

They also brought me a transcript of everything I'd told

them. I signed after I'd read it a dozen times because I wanted to be sure what I was putting my name to. Then I asked, 'Can I go now?'

They weren't happy about it but they let us all go. We trailed back to Jubilee Street to find a gallant specimen of the Old Bill was guarding the entrance to our house. He wouldn't let us in. We told him all our gear was in there and, as far as we were concerned, it was still our home. He told us we'd have to wait till someone told him officially he could let us inside. After some argument, he let us know that the forensic team was busy in there, and nothing had to be disturbed.

'What are they looking for?' Squib asked, as we walked away. 'They got the body. They took photos of the place.'

I didn't want to worry Nev, so I just said that the police were like that, pernickety.

Squib made what, to his mind, was a joke. 'They think we strung her up, do they?'

He cackled away happily and I didn't tell him that he'd hit the nail right on the head. That's exactly what their nasty little minds were thinking.

Shut out of the house, we were at a loose end, if that's not an inappropriate expression in the circumstances. Nev and Squib went down the pub and I went to the corner shop to talk to Ganesh.

I'd walked along the stretch of pavement going to and from the house or the shop at the corner I don't know how many times. I knew every crack. I knew all the places rain collected and where edges stuck up and could trip you. I could walk down the street in the pitch dark and not put a foot in a puddle or fall flat on my face. Quite often, I had walked down it in pitch dark because the street lighting was inreliable. The council never came around and fixed our pavement or resurfaced our road.

The reason they gave was that the area was due for redevelopment. It was as part of the redevelopment that our row of houses was scheduled to come down. I don't know what they intended putting up in their place. Smart flats, probably, for young executives.

If you kept going when you got to the end of the street, you got to the river. Looking across, you could see on the far side the luxury flats built in the docklands for Yuppies, before Yuppies became an endangered species, like snow leopards. Looking down the narrow defile between crumbling brick terraces towards those shining towers always made me feel like Judy Garland gazing at the Emerald City. Because of that, and the way the sun sparkled on all the glass of the high-rise office blocks, I called it 'the Crystal City'.

'Sounds like a football team,' Ganesh said.

'That's Crystal Palace. I'll call it what I like.'

Sometimes of a summer evening, Gan and I walked down there and sat on a crumbling wall above the mudflats, looking across and making up stories about the people who lived there. Once, we actually went across there and walked round, but we felt like little green men just dropped in from Mars. It was so clean, so prosperous. The people looked so fit and healthy, well dressed and trim. They had a purposeful air as if they were all going somewhere and knew where it was. We couldn't wait to get back again.

Now the developers were starting, at a much slower rate, on our side of the river. Our houses sprawled around the edge of the cleared building sites like a shanty town or squatter camp in the Third World, clinging to the skirts of a big city. Most of the people round here had no more chance of making it across the great divide to the affluent part of the area than they could sprout wings and fly.

It was the older ones who were bewildered. Old men who'd worked all their lives down at the docks before the work disappeared and the wharves became tourist sights. Old women who'd lived here all through the Blitz and who still scrubbed their front doorsteps. People like Ganesh's parents, who'd come here thinking that it would be upward and onward in a new country and who had worked hard to achieve success, but who had found themselves trapped now in this urban wilderness, a far cry from anything they'd ever imagined.

I think Mr Patel was hoping the development would bring quality housing nearer, as it had done across the river, because no one round here had very much money at the moment. If people started moving in who had more dosh, they might spend some of it in his shop. He had all kinds of plans, speciality Indian foods and so on. I didn't like to suggest the council might decide to bulldoze his shop as well. Everyone needs a dream.

Right opposite the shop, on the other corner of the street, was a disused chapel and burial ground. We called it 'the graveyard'. The building was locked up, the glass in its mock-Gothic windows broken, weeds growing from cracks in the masonry. It had originally been a congregational chapel. It had changed hands and religious viewpoint several times since then. The last people to use it as a place of worship had been the Church of the Beauteous Day.

The Church of the Beauteous Day had been really

something. When they turned up of a Sunday morning, whole families dressed in their best, it was like Mardi Gras. And they knew how to worship with songs and cymbals, all right. To say nothing of trombones, choirs and hand-clapping. When they weren't making music they were listening to the preacher, the Reverend Eli, and shouting joyously 'Hallelujah!' and 'Yes, Lord!' For one day a week, they brought light and life and faith to our street. But the premises weren't suitable for all their social events and they moved out, led away by the Reverend Eli, a tiny man with crinkled grey hair. Away he took all those smiling ladies in the floral hats, smart young men, little boys with bowties and little girls with snowy socks, like Moses leading the children of Abraham into the desert. I don't know whither he led them. Some said to Hackney. I was sorry. I missed them, especially the Reverend Eli, who, when he saw me, would sing out, 'You ready to repent, child?' and beam a gold-toothed smile.

Though the chapel was abandoned, the burial ground was still in use, by the living. A crazy old baglady named Mad Edna had her home there among the headstones with a tribe of feral cats for company. People taking a short cut through the graveyard were alarmed when Mad Edna sprang out from behind a tomb, like Magwitch the convict in *Great Expectations*, and began a conversation with them. She always treated them graciously, as if they'd come to call on her. She told me she'd been a débutante once, long ago, and I believed her. The council was having trouble over demolishing the chapel because of the graves alongside it, so Edna was safe for the time being.

A load of fruit and veg had been delivered to the shop during the afternoon. It was stacked on the pavement and

Ganesh was moving it, putting some on display outside the shop, and carrying the rest down the side alley to the yard at the back.

He was wearing grubby jeans and an old Fair Isle sweater, because it was a mucky job, and his long black hair was tied back with a piece of ribbon. He ties his hair back when he's working because it's more convenient and because his father insists on it. If Mr Patel had his way, Ganesh would be working round the shop wearing a suit and with his hair trimmed short back and sides, or so Ganesh reckons.

Parents have ambitions for their children, I suppose. My dad had ambitions for me. Sometimes I hope that I'll still manage to fulfil some of them, someday, and he'll know, in heaven. I'd like to please him, even at this late date. Make up for all the disappointment.

Ganesh looked up as I came along the pavement. His expression had been worried but it cleared. 'Fran! Thank God you're all right! What's going on? I've been worried sick about you! Someone said a person had died in your house!'

'Someone did,' I told him. 'Terry.'

We both looked down the street towards the house. Besides the police, quite a few sightseers had gathered. There was a van parked, just down from the police vehicles, which hadn't been there earlier. My heart sank, if possible, further. If it had been any one of the other of us, there wouldn't have been half the fuss. Nev, with his history of breakdown, would have been written off as suicide. Squib hanging from the light fitting would have been written off as one fewer problem for society. They might have said the same about me. But Terry – there was something about Terry. She was going to be trouble. The police sensed it, just as I'd always sensed it. They knew they were not going to be able to write her off, just like that. They were doing it all by the book to head off any criticism at a later date.

Ganesh didn't like the sight of all the activity down the street either. He dusted his hands and wiped them on his sweater, and by mutual accord, we set off down the alley.

The yard was full of stuff. Empty crates, full crates, packing cases, dismembered cardboard boxes baled up for the refuse people to take, and everywhere scraps of squashed fruit and withered leaves.

Ganesh picked out a couple of apples and handed me one. I was surprised to find I was hungry. We sat down side by side and between bites at the apple, I told him as much as I could. It wasn't much. Inspector Janice had given strict instructions that I wasn't to talk to anyone about anything. But Ganesh wasn't just anyone. Anyway, if he'd already heard someone had been found dead in the house, he knew nearly as much as I did.

However, I'd had some theatrical training, so I made a good story of it and finished up on a highpoint by suggesting the police thought it was murder.

Cheap theatricals didn't impress Ganesh who looked sceptical. 'Gossip around the place says she hanged herself.'

Word travelled fast. 'They think someone helped her.'

'Who?' That was Ganesh for you, always the awkward question.

'Us, probably. We didn't.' Something had occurred to me and it made things worse. 'Gan, if it's true, if someone killed her, she let him into the house.'

We had fixed up a proper lock on the front door. Or

rather, Declan had. We locked it when we went out to stop anyone else taking over our squat, quite apart from the council getting in and repossessing us. When we were at home, we locked ourselves in as a matter of principle. Apart from the council, there were plenty of people out there who might like to make trouble for us, the developers for a start. We even blocked up the letterbox after dark to prevent anyone pushing lighted rags through it. That had happened elsewhere.

If one of us was alone in the house, we took extra care. Entrance was strictly by the front door. Terry would have locked it and not opened it for anyone she didn't know and trust. The downstairs windows didn't open easily. The wooden frames had swollen with damp and warped with age. The old sash cords didn't work. Just to push the window open an inch took two people and more effort than it was worth.

'When the police realise that, it's going to make it look worse for us,' I concluded. 'Like an inside job.'

'She knew people outside,' he said, 'people she'd have let in. Let the police go and hassle them.'

'That's the point, Gan. I can't name a single one. We knew nothing at all about her, where she went, what she did when she left the house. She was always suspicious, secretive.'

Ganesh said unkindly that Terry had always struck him as a headcase.

At this point, his father came out to see why Ganesh had stopped working. Mr Patel has a sort of sixth sense which tells him where and when anyone he's employing isn't working one hundred per cent. I've worked in the shop on a Saturday and I know.

When he saw me, he looked relieved. 'Ah! There you are, Francesca! We have all been extremely worried about you, my dear. What on earth is going on?'

'She's just telling me about it, Dad!' Ganesh said patiently.

'Terry's dead, Mr Patel,' I told him.

'That other girl? This is very bad. How has she died?'

His brow furrowed into deep worry lines as I told him. Unwarily I let slip that the police thought the death might be suspicious. As that, he erupted, jabbing a forefinger at me in accusation and looking as if he was going to have a fit.

'Murder! Murder, are you saying, Francesca? In this street? So near to my shop? In this place where you are living?' He rounded on Ganesh. 'Have I not told you so?'

Ganesh snapped back at him in Gujarati and, the next thing, they were at it hammer and tongs with me unable to understand a word.

But I didn't need a translator. I could guess what it was all about. After a while Mr Patel turned and stamped off back into the shop.

Ganesh, breathing heavily, said, 'Sorry about that.'

'Never mind. I understand.'

'Look, they do like you!' He thrust out his jaw pugnaciously. 'Don't get Dad wrong. I know he flew off the handle then, but that's because murder on the doorstep isn't what he expected to hear about. It wasn't anything to do with you!'

'Leave it, Gan!' I said sharply.

The muscles around his mouth and jawline tightened and he got up and began to stack some empty crates, throwing them around with unnecessary force. After a few minutes, when he'd got the anger out of his system, he sat down again and asked in a reasonably normal voice, 'Yesterday afternoon, that's when the police think she died?'

'They haven't said, but we were all out of the house between one-thirty and around seven when Nev and I got home. Squib came in later. The body was stiff. I'd guess some time during the afternoon.'

He was looking thoughtful. 'Look, it's probably nothing, but yesterday afternoon, I noticed this guy . . . '

Irritatingly, he fell silent.

'Go on, then! Where?' I prompted in frustration.

'Hanging around in the street. By the post box on the other side about half way down. I'd never seen him before. I took a good look at him because, well, if a stranger starts hanging around casing places, you do, don't you?'

'If he was thinking of breaking in anywhere round here, he was being a bit optimistic!' I said. 'No one round here's got anything worth pinching.'

'He didn't look that type. He was a big chap, six-footer, well built, pretty fit. He'd have been aged about, oh, early thirties, and he was well dressed. Casual clothes, I mean, but nothing he'd got down the market. Quality gear. Sort of huntin', shootin' and fishin' things. Tweed jacket.'

I thought about this. 'What time was this?'

'I couldn't swear to it. Early on, around three or just before. At least, that's when I saw him. I don't know exactly what time he arrived. I was in the shop. I came out and there he was. I fooled around outside to watch him, then went inside and tried to keep an eye on him through the window. Then I was distracted and when I looked again, he'd gone.'

'Did he have a car?'

'If he did, he hadn't parked in this street. But he was definitely looking at the houses and it could have been yours.'

I thought about this for a while. That there'd been no car parked in the street didn't surprise me because no one who had a decent car and any sense would park it around here. He might have been an estate agent or a property developer or any of the people connected with the proposed redevelopment. It was more than likely that's who he was. I suggested this to Ganesh.

'I thought of that. He wasn't making any notes or taking any photos. He looked shifty, as if he didn't want to be seen.'

'Then he probably *was* a property developer!' I got up. 'Show me exactly where you saw him.'

We went back into the street and Ganesh pointed out the spot. The pillarbox is about twenty feet from our house, on the other side of the street. The stranger could well have been watching our place. I know it was a squat but I still called it 'ours'.

'I think he realised I'd spotted him,' Ganesh went on. 'Because he stooped and made out he was reading the collection times on the box. He wasn't any great actor, I can tell you! Think I ought to tell the police?'

'Perhaps you should.' I was more worried by the news than I wanted to let on.

Just then a car turned into the street and pulled up sharp by us. I recognised it as Euan's Fiesta. He got out and came over to us, glancing worriedly down the street towards the activity outside the house.

'There you are, Fran!'

'Suddenly everyone's looking for me,' I murmured.

'You forgot about the court, didn't you?' He gave a wry grimace. 'So did I – nearly! We got our order for immediate possession. But I don't suppose that now you want to stay in that house? Not now this has happened.'

'Yes, there's been a murder!' Ganesh broke in angrily before I could speak. 'And still you lot come harassing her, wanting to throw her out on to the street!'

Euan had reddened angrily but he wasn't going to argue with Ganesh who was a by-stander and not, in Euan's view, involved. He turned his back on him and went on to me, 'But cheer up, Fran. I've got some good news for you. We've got you temporary accommodation.'

So I'd been told correctly at the police station. But I still asked suspiciously, 'What sort of accommodation?'

'A flat. Only for six months, mind!'

'Oh, great!' Ganesh burst out. 'So this is what it takes for you lot to offer her somewhere decent to live? A violent death?'

'It's not marvellous,' Euan warned me, still ignoring Ganesh. 'But it's somewhere. Come over to my office and I'll give you the key.'

He drove off and I said goodbye to Ganesh. As I was walking off, however, I heard someone calling my name. I turned round, and saw Mr Patel hurrying after me.

'Francesca!' He came up panting. 'I wanted to say to you that I am truly very sorry about shouting like that and the carry-on.'

'It's OK, Mr Patel,' I told him.

'No, no!' he said excitedly. 'It is not OK! It is terrible, terrible! Such a crime! But you are all right, my dear. That is good. You are not hurt.'

'I'm not hurt,' I assured him.

He waved his hands. 'You see, it is very difficult for us, for my wife and myself. You are obviously of good family and an educated young woman. An education is a fine thing. But you should not be living like that, in that place. You see what happens in such places?'

I told him I appreciated his concern but he shouldn't worry about me. He looked at me in a lost way as if he couldn't think of anything more to say, much as he wanted to say something, a worried man with a balding head and a Biro stuck behind one ear, trying to make sense of something beyond him. Then he gave up and went back to the shop.

I knew what he wanted to say. He couldn't understand how someone like me, who was neither deranged nor a criminal, could end up living on her own or with a group of other loners in a condemned house. It puzzled him that I hadn't any family or anyone to care for me. It seemed all wrong to him and it presented a threat. Most of all, he was worried about the effect I had on Ganesh.

I could have told him that I wasn't the cause of the problems he had with Ganesh.

About six months ago Ganesh's sister, Usha, had married a chap named Jay who was in accountancy and had prospects. Ganesh had been mooching about scowling ever since. He felt he was being left behind here. 'One more year!' he'd told me privately, 'One more year and I'm out!'

But he hadn't told his people that yet. They knew though. They were putting pressure on him. He hadn't said so to me, but I guessed what their answer to the problem would be. It would be a pretty sixteen-year-old with beautiful manners and a dowry. They thought I'd be the obstacle. They were wrong.

I started wondering and worrying about Euan's promised flat.

Chapter Four

Euan was right. The best you could say about that flat was that it was somewhere. It was on the fifth floor of one of a pair of condemned tower blocks. The building was already half empty and pretty well all vandalised. The lift didn't work. The staircase was graffiti-covered. There was a hole in the corridor ceiling outside my door with funny stuff hanging out of it which looked to me like asbestos lining. So he was also right to say it wasn't marvellous.

My heart sank when I saw it, but I knew I couldn't stay in the house where Terry had died. This would have to be it for a few weeks, anyway. Euan had come with me and I told him thanks.

Naturally I offered the hospitality of my new roof to Nev and Squib. Nev accepted gratefully. Squib, a natural loner, looked uneasy. Living with others had already shown itself too likely to attract attention. We went to Jubilee Street in another attempt to collect our belongings. Either the council or the police had boarded up the house and we had to break in at the back. We put everything portable into black plastic rubbish sacks and took them over to the shop so that Ganesh could ferry them in the van to my new abode. He wasn't able to do it straight away, so while we waited for him to be free, Squib and Nev went to the pub and I went for a last walk round the neighbourhood I'd got to know so well, or what the developers had left of it. Not that I was going far, but even a block or two is moving away.

I was walking through the graveyard when Edna jumped out from behind a headstone, doing her Magwitch impersonation.

'Where are you going in such a hurry, dear?' she asked.

'Nowhere,' I told her. 'I'm not in a hurry.' Even the thought of not being waylaid by Mad Edna any more made me feel sad. I sat on a tomb. She sat down beside me and began rummaging in her grubby coat. She had an excited air about her, like a child who has learned a new trick and is going to try it out.

Eventually she produced a gold-coloured Benson and Hedges cigarette packet, very clean and not crushed. She held it tenderly in her mittened hands and touched it with a yellowed nail sticking through the chopped-off ends of the glove-fingers. She stroked it reverently a few times, then opened it with infinite care and very hospitably offered me a cigarette.

I declined but she continued to push the gold box at me, peering up into my face to make sure I'd noticed how beautiful it was, if only card. If it had been real gold, she wouldn't have been happier and she wanted me to share her pleasure in it.

I said, 'It's nice, Edna!' but still refused a cigarette.

She looked disappointed but took one herself.

She'd got matches, too. One of those little booklets you get for free in bars and restaurants. Watching her struggle to light it, I offered help, struck the paper match for her and lit her smoke.

Before handing the booklet back, I read the name on it. It came courtesy of a wine bar in Winchester. She didn't like me studying it, or even holding it, and snatched it away, tucking it and the precious gold-coloured packet away in some best-not-to-think-about place. The mittens didn't hide how rheumatism had swollen her knuckle joints. She oughtn't to have been living rough in a graveyard. But I knew anyone'd have a dreadful job moving her out. She liked it there. She smelled a bit high, though, and I moved along the tomb as far as I could.

Two of the feral cats lounged nearby in the long grass watching us through half-closed eyes. Another was curled up asleep on a grave. Wherever Edna sat, a cat or two was generally nearby. She was part of their extended tribe.

As she was puffing happily on her cigarette, I told her I was being moved into a temporary flat.

'Why don't you get yourself a little place in Chelsea?' she asked. 'Chelsea is interesting. Wonderful parties. Although some people think living there rather fast.' She gave a rasping cough. She wasn't used to this amount of fresh tobacco.

Mentally she was back in her débutante days again, whenever they'd been. I had no idea how old she was. She always appeared incredibly ancient.

I told her I depended on the council and had to stay in the borough. She mumbled at that and began ferreting among several plastic carrier bags she always had with her. Smoke curled up into her eye and made her squint. Knowing that Edna normally collected her smokes from bins and gutters, I wondered about the gold packet and asked, 'Splashing out, Edna? Buying the ciggies in a proper packet now?'

'He dropped it,' she muttered. 'He didn't see. I saw, though. He didn't see me. He walked through here.' She waved the cigarette at the path through the long grass and tipsy headstones.

'Who was he?' I wasn't really interested, just making conversation with her. She seemed reasonably sane today.

'Smart young fellow,' she said. 'Stranger. Well set-up. He'd left his car over there . . . ' This time she pointed behind us to an open patch behind the buildings in the road beyond, accessible through a gap, which the Church of the Beauteous Day had cleared so that the Reverend Eli could park his purple transit van there.

'I don't like strangers. They keep coming these days and telling me I can't live here any more. Where should I live? What about the cats? I've told them, I've got to look after the cats. So when he came through, I hid and watched him. He was up to no good.'

The hairs prickled on the back of my neck. 'How do you know, Edna?'

'He looked it. Dodging about from headstone to headstone, didn't want to be seen. So busy hiding himself away, he didn't spot me. I was over there.' She waved at a jumble of overgrown bushes.

It didn't surprise me the stranger hadn't spotted her. In her dirty coat and with her amorphous outline, she blended perfectly into her surroundings. I'd often passed by her myself, and jumped out of my skin when she'd greeted me. She had a trick, like the cats, of sitting perfectly still and watching. I'd seen her sitting on the grass, quite surrounded by them, just blinking her eyes at them as they blinked back. I'd sometimes speculated whether they were the spirits of the dead buried in this place. That Edna could communicate with them didn't surprise me in the least.

'When was this you saw the man, Edna?'

She looked vague. Days were all the same to her. 'Must've been yesterday,' she said uncertainly.

I asked her if it had been morning or afternoon but she couldn't remember. She wasn't, however, completely out of touch. Unexpectedly, she asked, 'Is that right the girlie hanged herself, dear?' She peered at me with a flicker of interest in her rheumy old eyes.

'That's right, Edna.'

She puffed on the cigarette, staring ahead. It was impossible to say what she made of it. She didn't seem surprised or frightened. Even her curiosity, now I'd confirmed the rumour, was cured.

It was hopeless. She may have seen the same fellow Ganesh saw. We'd never be able to establish it for sure.

She came to life and leaned towards me confidentially. 'Got something to show you!'

My spirits rose briefly. What else had she found? I should have known better.

She took me to a corner of the graveyard and proudly showed me some new kittens, mewing blindly but safely inside a ramshackle stone tomb. The tomb's inscription commemorated Josiah and Hepzibah Wilkins who'd died within a week of one another of the influenza in 1819, leaving seventeen children. There had been enough money to build them a decent monument so I suppose there'd been money to take care of the seventeen children. Perhaps the older ones had looked after the younger ones.

The fact remained that if anyone asked questions of Edna, they'd get nothing sensible in reply. She might or might not be a vital witness. Her only concern was for the cats and what would happen to her and to them, if the developers succeeded in levelling the surrounding monuments.

I gave Edna all the loose change in my pocket and she squirrelled it away in another hiding place in her grubby old coat.

'Call again!' she invited, as I walked away.

We were allowed to remove our furniture, such as it was, from the house. We ferried it over to the new flat in several lots, using the Patels' van. Between us we manoeuvred it up the filthy staircase and staggered with it along open windswept balconies lined with unwelcoming doors. Some flats were abandoned and boarded up. Others, though still inhabited, were nearly as well barricaded, like medieval castles. It didn't promise a spirit of neighbourliness.

The flat itself had been cleared and swept out, but still looked as if a major riot had taken place in it. The walls were pitted and scarred; parts of the skirting had been ripped out. There was something very odd about the kitchen sink unit which was at an angle. Anything placed on the draining board simply slid down into the basin.

Squib, looking more than usually perplexed, wandered around rattling loose fittings and opening cupboards. Eventually he said, sounding pleased, 'Got it!'

We waited apprehensively, expecting him to turn round, holding some furry creature he'd found lurking in the corner.

Instead, empty-handed but triumphant, he declared, 'Worked it out. It's the wrong place. The council gave you the wrong key, Fran.'

I told him I wished that could be true. Sadly, I thought it wasn't. This, despite all appearances, was home sweet home.

He shook his head. 'Can't be. Look, they condemned our house and it was better than this. They got it wrong, Fran.'

He took some persuading and, finally accepting my argument, became offended and muttered, 'Well, I'm not staying here.'

I found that hurtful, considering I'd generously offered him the shelter of my roof. For Squib, of all people, to object . . . But he said he'd been offered a place in a hostel and he'd try it out. The police had told him he had to stay there so they could find him again. But if the hostel made a fuss about the dog, he'd leave.

I suggested that if the hostel wouldn't take the dog, Mad Edna might look after it for a while. The dog would probably like being in the churchyard and Edna, in her crazy way, could be relied upon for something like that.

But Squib wouldn't even think about being parted from the dog, even temporarily. Besides, he thought the cats were quite capable of ganging up on a dog. He'd seen them do it.

I leaned over the balcony to watch him walk across the wasteland between the condemned blocks, his rucksack on his back and the dog trotting nicely by his heels.

Euan, whom I liked more and more, had promised to try and rustle up some extra furniture. He had a friend in the Salvation Army. At least the hot water was working.

It was ages since I'd lived in a place with hot water. While Nev dragged our existing furniture around trying to make the place look habitable, I spent an hour cleaning out the bathroom before I got in the tub and lay there in the steaming water, just looking up at the cracks in the ceiling and another hole in the plaster where the lavatory cistern was coming away.

As it turned out, Nev only stayed twenty-four hours before his parents descended on the place. I wasn't surprised to see them. I don't think Nev was, either. He'd had the air of a condemned man about him since walking in the door.

His father stood in the middle of the sitting room, heels together, bolt upright, hands clasped behind his back as if he were reviewing the troops. His mother looked at me just as my old headmistress did when I was being carpeted for something.

I've mentioned my school before. My mother ran off and left my dad and me when I was seven, so I was brought up by Dad and my Hungarian Grandma Varady. I think my father felt he owed it to me somehow to give me every opportunity he could because my mum had left. I always told people she was dead, because we didn't know where she was and for me, it was as if she was dead. So they scraped and saved, Dad and Grandma Varady, and paid for me to go to this school for young ladies.

I was in and out of trouble from the first day I went there and by the time I got to be fifteen they told my father it really wasn't worth keeping me on there. They meant they wanted me to go.

They wrote a final report on me. It read, 'Francesca is extremely bright but lacks application. She has consistently failed to take advantage of the opportunities offered by this school.'

I have never been so ashamed of anything in my life as I was the day I watched my father read that report. He and Grandma Varady had gone without virtually every luxury to keep me at that school and I'd let them both down completely. I was sorry, but it was too late. I loved them both and wouldn't have hurt them for the world, but I had hurt them.

If they'd been angry, shouted and stamped up and down, it would have helped, but they didn't say anything. Dad even said, 'Never mind, *édesem*,' and hugged me because he was afraid the report might have hurt *my* feelings. Grandma Varady had to be forcibly restrained from marching round to the school and socking the headmistress. She came of a long line of Austro-Hungarian hussars. We had faded sepia portraits of some of them, waxed moustaches, tight jackets with frogging, tighter pants and shiny boots. She firmly believed that the answer to every problem was a cavalry charge.

I went away and shut myself in my room and howled. Afterwards I made a resolve that never again would I ever act as plain stupid as that. But I suppose I have.

Anyhow, the upshot of the visit from the Porters was that they frogmarched poor Nev away with them, back to that luxury gaol they called home. The way they talked to him, he might just as well have been four, not twenty-four. Even worse, they told him their very good friend, some high-powered head-doctor, had a whole set of bright new ideas for treating Nev's nervous breakdown.

As he left he said, 'I'll be in touch, Fran. I've left you my books.'

I said, 'Thanks!' but I knew I'd seen the last of him. So I just added, 'Good luck!' He might just as well have left me the books in his will. It was that final.

His mother gave me a really nasty look. His father didn't look at me at all during the whole time he was there. He was pretending I wasn't there. Anything he couldn't handle, he pretended didn't exist – like poor Nev's illness.

I knew that, for better or worse, my life had changed for ever. Probably for worse.

Chapter Five

I was on my own. I hadn't lived completely on my own for quite some while. It was a strange feeling, rattling around that depressing flat. But, although I might be alone, I certainly wasn't forgotten, not by the police at any rate. Janice Morgan was presumably busy on more important matters and I was left to the tender mercies of Sergeant Parry. His expression of sceptical disbelief at whatever I said and his ginger moustache began to haunt my dreams.

'You're getting paranoid,' said Ganesh, heaving a sack of potatoes around, preparatory to slitting it open and emptying it into a bin.

'How can you say that?' I'd been having my usual moan but still felt I'd every right to sound incredulous. 'Parry's on my neck from morning till night. Always the same questions, dished up in different ways. What do the police think I know?'

'How about Nev and Squib, are they chasing them in the same way?'

'That's what I came to tell you this morning. I tried to phone Nev last night and his father told me Nev is in a private clinic. They've got him hidden away where the police can't question him. As for Squib, I went over to the hostel yesterday. It's run by some kind of religious group. They smile all the time and their skins look as if they've been sitting in the bath too long.'

'Hey!' interrupted Ganesh disapprovingly. 'They're doing their best, right!'

'All right. Anyhow, Squib wasn't there. They said he'd be back this evening and, if I wanted, I could leave a note pinned on a corkboard they've got in the entrance. So I did, though I don't suppose Squib will even look at the corkboard and I can't count on anyone telling him I was there. They call him Henry,' I added. 'Just like the police do.'

'It's his name.' Ganesh can be very irritating. 'You can't expect them to call him Squib.'

I wasn't going to argue about that. I had other things on my mind. 'Let's face it, Gan, I'm the only one the Bill can really get at, and I'm the one getting the treatment. They can't seem to get it into their thick heads that it's wasting everyone's time and getting none of us anywhere. It's certainly not going to find out exactly what happened to Terry, if we ever do that.'

Ganesh grunted and tipped out the spuds. They rolled and bounced down into the bin with a strong smell of earth.

Grumbling to Ganesh worked off some of the frustration but I couldn't pretend the continual police questioning wasn't worrying me. They were starting to wear me down, which was the name of the game as far as they were concerned, I suppose. I was beginning to get confused in my own mind. They'd managed to convince me I hadn't told them everything or that I'd forgotten something of great importance. I'd started racking my brains in the still of the night.

'Quiet today,' I offered Ganesh. The shop had been empty but as I spoke a woman came in with a grubby child in tow and started picking over the vegetables.

Ganesh glared at her. 'Who's doing any business with half the houses emptied around here? You want those beans or don't you, love?'

She moved away from the beans and stared mistrustfully at the newly decanted spuds. 'I want potatoes but those are covered in mud.'

'They grow in the ground,' Ganesh told her. 'What do you expect?'

'I expect them cleaner than that. Mud weighs, mud does. It's heavy. I'm not paying for mud.'

Ganesh sighed and pushed the top potatoes around. 'These are cleaner.'

'I'll pick 'em out, thanks!' she said crossly, shoving him aside. She began to pick out one potato at a time, peering at each for signs of mud or damage.

'I ask you,' said Ganesh to me. 'Who wants to be a greengrocer?'

'Beats being a police suspect,' I told him. 'Leave you to it, Gan. See you later.'

There was a car parked opposite the shop, outside the graveyard. Someone, a woman, was attempting to talk to Edna. Our resident baglady was huddled in a heap among her plastic bags and I could tell she was pretending to be deaf. When I appeared the woman lost interest in Edna, who scurried away among the tombs. The newcomer called out to me, 'Francesca!' It was Inspector Janice.

'Glad to see you,' she added as I joined her.

'What is it now?' I asked grumpily. I really had had enough.

'Nice to know you're pleased to see me, too,' she retorted.

'Don't take it personally,' I told her. 'But I'm not. I'm out of a job, living in a set left over from an old Hammer movie, and every time I turn round, there's a copper wanting to ask me questions.'

'No questions,' she assured me. 'I was going to suggest we take a drive.'

It was an unmarked car and she was in plainclothes. Janice liked her clothes very plain. She was wearing a sort of blazer today, with broad navy stripes. It made her look as if she'd been leaning against newly painted railings. However she dressed, and had she been riding a tricycle, no one around here would have had any doubt who or what she was.

'Give me a reason,' I suggested.

'I'm trying', she said, 'to get you off the hook. That's what you want, isn't it?'

'Go on.' I had justification in feeling suspicion. Greeks bearing gifts, and all the rest of it. The way they worked, Parry had been sent to wear me down and now I was at rock bottom, Janice was moving in for the kill.

I winced as the last word crossed my mind. But Janice was smiling, conciliatory today in voice and manner. Softening me up.

'You told us you were out of the house for the whole of Monday afternoon and early evening. You were in Camden with Porter, so you say. I'd like to believe it and we've done our best to check it out. But so far, anywhere we've asked, everyone has denied knowing either you or

Nevil or seeing anyone like you on that day.' She waited.

I sighed. 'They would. They don't want to be involved. You can't blame them.'

She hunched her shoulders. 'I thought we could drive around there. You might see someone. Look, I'm in my own time. I don't have to bother with this!'

I got in the car.

'Theresa Monkton's family has been in touch,' she said casually, as we drove off.

That startled me. 'You found them?'

'They found us.' She explained that apparently the family had been trying to find Terry for some time. She'd left home before but this time they'd feared something had happened to her. They'd kept a sharp watch on the news reports concerning any unidentified young women. The best they were hoping for was an amnesia victim. The worst – the worst of their fears had come true. I felt sorry for them.

We drew a blank around Camden High Street. We called at the house where we'd had the Mexican bean stew, but the people Nev knew had left, or so the others there said. I thought they were lying. They just didn't want to get involved, just like all the others Janice had already asked. I wasn't surprised but, what with one thing and another, my life at the moment was akin to trying to paddle a canoe with a tennis racket.

It was a nicer day weather-wise than it'd been for a while. Pale sunshine inspired shops to put out racks of clothes on the pavements. But Camden was having one of its grotty days, nonetheless, its gutters choked with litter. There were a couple of stalls with fruit and veg in side alleys, adding to the debris with dropped leaves and squashed fruit. They made me think of Ganesh and I wished I hadn't bothered him with my troubles. He had enough of his own. There were plenty of people about but no one and nothing of any help to me.

'We're wasting our time,' I said, exasperated. 'I can't prove we were here. But it's the truth.'

We carried on looking without much joy. Then, just as we were giving up, I did see a couple I recognised, a man and a girl. The man was called Lew, I knew that, but I couldn't remember the girl's name. I leapt out of Janice's car and raced after them, yelling, 'Lew!'

They very nearly took off, but I managed to grab his arm. His girlfriend misinterpreted my enthusiasm at seeing him and took a swing at me. It took a fraught few minutes trying to explain. She was quite a bit taller than me and several pounds heavier, and neither Lew nor anyone else seemed inclined to intervene, although a few gathered to watch and cheer us on. Eventually, I managed to make them both understand that I wanted some help from them, not to break up their one-to-one relationship. As our fight broke up, the onlookers drifted away. One or two left small coins on the pavement, perhaps under the impression we'd been taking part in some Street Theatre.

During all the time I was in active danger of getting seriously done over by an enraged Amazon in fishnet tights and combat boots, Janice had been hanging about in the background, not making any effort to come to my rescue, much as all the other gawpers. When she saw things had calmed down, she joined us. Grudgingly they told her they'd seen me and Nev on the Monday afternoon at Camden Lock and we'd had a coffee together. I could see neither of them liked being asked to give me an alibi. But at least they didn't issue flat denials and perhaps their reluctance made Janice more inclined to believe them.

I told them thanks and that I was sorry I'd had to ask them. They weren't very gracious about it, but at least supplied names and an address before the Amazon hauled her man away like a hunting trophy. It wasn't my fault but I knew they didn't see it that way, and if I knew what was good for me, I'd stay away from that part of town. I'd had my last free meal of beans.

'Well, it helps, Francesca,' Janice said encouragingly.

'Not much,' I told her.

'No, not much,' she agreed. She was honest, at least. But I still didn't trust her.

Since she was feeling generous towards me, I asked her about the post mortem. 'Is this or isn't this a murder inquiry? If not, why do I need an alibi? If it is murder, I should be told so, outright. I don't have to cooperate if I don't know what's going on.'

She didn't answer at once. She pulled over behind a stall selling curtain material, and twisted in her seat to face me.

'It's not that easy to answer your question, Fran. It wouldn't be the first case where foul play has been suspected and then, after exhaustive and costly inquiries, it's been decided the injuries were accidental or self-inflicted. People do harm themselves in a multitude of ways. I wouldn't like to guess how often an investigation's taken time, money and manpower, everyone's got frustrated and tired, and still we've ended up closing the file. No one likes that. On the other hand, murder has been made to look like suicide before. The killer's found it easier to try and fake a suicide than to fake an accident. In this case, we've an apparent suicide, but with so many inconsistencies about it that we have to be suspicious. Sergeant Parry, who was one of the first officers to see the body—'

I interrupted bitterly, 'I know what Parry thinks! He thinks we had something to do with it!'

'No,' she contradicted me. 'You don't know what Sergeant Parry thinks. Despite anything he may have said to you, he's not leaping to any conclusions about this, nor am I. Parry is a very experienced officer. I, for one, respect his opinion. So, if we haven't a suicide, what do we have?'

Janice glowered through the windscreen at the billowing net curtaining strung along the trader's stall ahead. 'The worst is trying to explain all this to the family. Suicide appals most relatives. They want to believe it's an accident. Even murder is more acceptable to them. They can't be responsible for the accident or the murder – but the suicide leaves them with a personal burden of guilt. If I went to Theresa's family today and said, sorry, folks, the murder theory was a mare's nest. It was suicide, after all. You know, they'd be more upset than if I went to them and named a killer?'

'But yourself,' I persisted. 'You think that, out there somewhere, is a killer?'

'Personally and off the record, yes, I think so. But hunches, mine or Parry's, aren't enough, even when there's circumstantial evidence to back them up. Eventually it has to be proved to the satisfaction of a jury. That's not easy. Juries nowadays mistrust forensic evidence. They shouldn't but they do. A couple of cases of verdicts declared unsafe which get wide media coverage, and there you are! Unsupported confessions are no longer acceptable. The boundaries of reasonable doubt get hazier every day. I think someone attacked her, that she was either naked or was stripped partially naked in the process, there was some struggle which took place on the floor and the splinters of wood entered her skin. She then received a blow to the head which rendered her either unconscious or semi-conscious. The attacker finished the job, making it look like a suicide. There's evidence to support all that. But as yet, *I* don't know why and *I* don't know who.'

'I don't know who, either!' I hadn't missed the stressed pronoun.

'You see why I keep asking about a fight,' Janice said. 'If the bruises were come by in an earlier incident, some significant physical evidence drops out of things.'

'No fight,' I said.

She smiled. 'I'm glad you didn't invent one. It wouldn't have helped – either of us. I think someone killed her, Francesca. But I need to be sure. I can't afford a mistake.'

I must have looked surprised because she flushed. 'You have to understand, there are – certain tensions among police officers as amongst people working together in any job. I have – there are certain people who resented my promotion. They'd like to see me fall flat on my face. Clash of personalities, call it. An office of any kind is a claustrophobic place. You get that.'

She'd said more than she'd intended and looked away, embarrassed.

I was thinking of the blow to Terry's head. She would have to have been disabled in some way or she'd have put up a fight. Perhaps she did put up a fight and that's when he hit her. I must have sat there thinking for long enough to make Janice curious.

'Remembering something, Francesca?'

'Nothing that matters.'

'Why don't you let me decide that?'

I was in no mood to be patronised and said so.

'Sorry,' she said. 'I didn't mean it to come out like that. But if there's anything, tell me. You want the killer found, don't you?'

'Of course I do,' I said. 'He chose to string her up from the light fitting and leave her there to strangle to death.'

'People get sexual kicks all ways. Maybe he sat there and watched because that's the sort of thing he likes. There are a lot of very sick people around, Francesca, and a lot of them act and look normal – most of the time.'

'You don't have to tell me! Do you think I haven't come across enough weirdos?' I couldn't help sounding exasperated. 'This wasn't a sex game gone wrong. This was someone who wanted her dead. Someone who hated her enough to do what he did, quite deliberately and for no other reason than to kill.'

'So,' she was watching me carefully with her pale grey gaze. 'Any ideas who? If you're so sure, you must have some theory.'

'I don't have a theory,' I told her. 'But I do know there was someone else in the house that afternoon while we were away. The place reeked of one of those male colognes when Nev and I got home. Ganesh saw a stranger earlier, acting odd. He told one of your boys in blue about it.'

'He told Sergeant Parry. We haven't been able to find anyone else who saw the man he described. He's a friend of yours, Mr Patel, isn't he?'

'Yes. Sometimes I lend a hand in the shop on a Saturday. But he didn't make up seeing someone just to help me out.'

'I didn't say that. Why should he have felt it necessary to do that?'

They like doing that, the police. They like asking you the sort of questions which, however you answer them, you sound guilty. They have suspicious minds. Even when they try to be fair, as I suppose Janice was, it comes out sounding like a caution. They can't help it. It's the mentality they have or the way they train them at police college. I could have told her that Edna had also seen a stranger, well dressed, and too intent on sneaking through the churchyard to notice her or that he'd dropped his cigarettes. But what use was Edna as a witness? Even if I could get her to talk to Janice? From what I'd seen earlier, Janice herself hadn't been having much luck with Edna. I wondered suddenly why she'd been trying.

'For about the hundredth time,' I said, 'I didn't have anything to do with her death and I don't know who killed her or why.'

'Neither do I, Francesca,' she said cheerfully. 'But by the time I've finished, I shall!'

'Bully for you!' I muttered.

The stallholder, squat, grubby little fellow, had had enough of us sitting there chatting. He came storming up and mouthed through Janice's window.

'Listen, darling, this undercover obbo or what? I'm selling a few yards of nylon net, not bleedin' heroin!'

'Got a stallholder's licence?' Janice asked.

'Do me a favour, doll!' he pleaded. 'Haven't you coppers got anything else to do but harass honest businessmen?'

'Get a licence!' Janice told him.

I could see something was bothering her as we drove off.

After a moment she asked, sounding bemused, 'Francesca, tell me honestly, do I look like a policewoman?'

'To some people, perhaps,' I told her diplomatically.

She seemed puzzled.

When I got back to the flat, Ganesh was waiting for me, sitting on the landing. A net of oranges lay on the top stair by him.

He greeted me with, 'I came to see how you were getting along in this place.'

His voice and manner were more sympathetic than when we'd last spoken at his shop, and put me vaguely in mind of someone visiting a friend in hospital. Dealing with a person who is ill and one who's having trouble must be similar. The oranges, presumably, equated with taking flowers to the patient. I've always thought that it was nicer to take fruit to the sick than flowers. Fruit doesn't make you think of funerals.

'Don't ask!' I said as I opened the flat door to let us in. 'I've been trawling Camden with Inspector Janice, trying to find an alibi.'

'And did you?' Ganesh dropped the string of fruit on the table and gave me a sharp look.

I told him what had happened. 'It's something,' I finished.

He shrugged and looked disapprovingly round the flat. 'I'll make us a cup of tea,' he said and went out into the kitchen whence I could hear him rattling crockery.

Whilst it's always nice to have a lover, sex can get in the way and sometimes what's needed is just a friend. That's what Ganesh is, a friend.

A friend is someone you can tell your troubles to, argue

with, not see for weeks and then meet again and take up where you left off, all without getting tied up and wrung out emotionally. Problems, I think, are what constitute the basis of the friendship between Gan and me. He has his problems and I have mine. I don't entirely understand his, nor he mine, but it doesn't matter. I listen to him and he listens to me. It doesn't solve anything but it certainly helps.

Of course, I'd be fooling myself if I told you the familiar man/woman chemistry played no part at all. Sometimes I see Ganesh looking at me with half a question in his eyes, and I dare say he catches me looking at him in the same way from time to time. But that's as far as it's ever got. Things between us work well as they are and you know what they say, if a thing's not broke, don't fix it. Sometimes I think it's a pity, though.

Right now I felt absolutely whacked. I really didn't want to talk to anyone, even Ganesh, but I needed all the support I could get.

As we sat in the kitchen drinking the tea he said, 'I've tried asking around too, Fran, customers, mostly. But it's hard to get anyone to talk about it now. It was a nine-day wonder. Now all they do is moan about our prices. If they ever knew anything they've forgotten it.'

'My impression exactly,' I said gloomily. 'But thanks for trying, anyway.'

'Dad says, he still needs someone in the shop on a Friday and Saturday, if you want to earn some extra money.'

I told him I didn't think his father really wanted me around the place. I was a bird of ill-omen, filling Gan's head with ideas of independence and a free lifestyle, consorting with suspicious types, at odds with the police.

'They like you,' Ganesh said obstinately. 'You personally. The other – it's a clash of cultures. They don't understand but they still like you.'

'They think I'll lead you astray,' I said unwisely.

He got angry then. 'For God's sake, Fran! Do you think I want to spend my entire life flogging spuds and bananas to old women with string bags? Listen!'

He leaned across the table. 'I've been thinking. We both need to get out of where we are. There is a way. If I've learnt something from the shop it's the basics of running a business. You and I together, we could run any kind of business we liked! We can go to the bank, get them to put together a small business package for us! Get one of those Start-Up grants! I've been keeping my eye open, looking for a suitable place. And if we needed help with the accounts, to start off, Jay would do that for us, no charge, family.'

It was the most hare-brained idea I'd heard in a long time and coming from Ganesh, whom I saw as sensible, it was unbelievable. He didn't honestly think it would work, did he? Even if I had the aptitude for business, which I don't. I supposed his family had been giving him hassle and that's what had brought all this about, but he'd betrayed himself with the idea of Jay helping with the accounts. With one breath he was talking of branching out on his own. With the next, he was still relying on the family network.

Rather unkindly I retorted, 'Forget it. It's a barmy idea. It'd drive me round the bend. I certainly couldn't stick your brother-in-law coming round once a week to audit the books!'

'You might,' he said touchily, 'think about it.'

'I've got the police on my back right now. How'm I supposed to think about anything else? I can't even think straight about what happened at the house any longer!'

He mumbled a bit and I could see he was annoyed with me. But I couldn't imagine myself, even when the present crisis was over, sitting over the books every evening with or without Jay at my shoulder, trying to make them balance. Worrying about staff and business rates, profit and loss? I think I'd pitch myself out of the window. But it illustrated, if nothing else did, the reason why Ganesh and I couldn't ever progress beyond friendship. When it came down to lifestyles, he was a traditionalist at heart. Me, I was just me, a gypsy if anything, an urban nomad. No fixed abode, no fixed employment, no fixed anything. Another word for that is freedom.

But none of that helped right now. I didn't want to hurt his feelings and tried politely to explain to him how I saw it. He said it didn't matter and took himself off, still looking huffy. Alone, I sat eating the oranges, one after the other. It's called comfort-bingeing.

I did need the extra money so, in the end, I went over to the shop and helped out. I thought the customers would recognise me and ask me questions, but Ganesh had been right. All they were worried about was making sure I didn't sell them any bruised fruit and making me pick all the yellow leaves off the greens.

Going back to the flat in the evenings was something I began to dread.

For the first time in my life I was actually afraid, although I didn't tell Ganesh. I hadn't been frightened in the squat or in any other place I'd lived in and I'd lived in some crummy ones. But that tower block was unbelievable. The winds whistled round it and right through it and when I woke up in the middle of the night I had a dreadful feeling of being lost in some kind of nightmarish desert. I felt that when dawn came I'd find everyone had gone and left me entirely alone in that place. I can't describe it. I wouldn't wish it on my worst enemy.

I took to switching on the light if I awoke and reading till morning. I was getting through Nev's books at the rate of about one a night and getting bags under my eyes as well. I told myself I was at least making up for my missed education. Nev's book choice was on the heavy side.

One afternoon Inspector Janice turned up on my doorstep. With luck I'd at least seen the last of Parry. It was the first time Janice had tackled me in the surroundings of my own home.

I made her coffee and let her have the armchair Euan had got from the Sally Army for me. When she sat in it, the springs collapsed under her. Her knees shot up to chin level and she grabbed the balding plush arms and glared at me.

'I was being polite!' I told her. 'Not playing a practical joke on you. You can sit on this one, if you prefer.' I indicated the tubular aluminium and plastic effort I was sitting on.

She struggled to the edge of the armchair and perched there. Her mug of coffee was on the floor by her feet. 'This is a dreadful place for you to be living in!' she blurted. 'How did you get into all this mess, Fran? You're young, fit and you've got all your marbles!'

For the first time she wasn't wearing her police hat to

ask questions. She really wanted to know, for herself. Perhaps for that reason I didn't resent her words.

'It's a place,' I told her. 'You don't want to know the story of my life. I became homeless. It's easier than you think.'

'Tell me!' she persisted.

'The person I was living with became ill. She had to go into hospital long-term. She was the tenant, not me, and the landlord wanted me out.'

I was telling her the truth but still not telling her how it really was. After Dad died, Grandma Varady and I had stayed on together. But after a while she became confused. I think it was Dad dying. She couldn't really cope with it. She began to talk as if he was still alive and even worse, she began to call me Eva, which was my mother's name. It was as if she couldn't remember that my mother had left.

'Bondi's late this evening, Eva,' she'd say. Bondi was the name she'd had for my father whose name had been Stephen.

She also started getting up in the middle of the night believing it was morning and wandering out of the house and down the street in her nightgown. Her doctor found her a place in a home. I'd always sworn I'd never let Grandma Varady go into such a place but things never turn out the way you expect. I couldn't look after her. She no longer knew who I was. She lived about six months in the home and died there in her sleep. By then I was already living at the first of many 'irregular' addresses.

I said to Janice, 'Look, I've had jobs, dozens of them. But when employers find out you don't have a regular address, they can't get rid of you fast enough. Or else they take advantage of the situation to offer you slave wages. You drop out of the system. You have to fight to get your foot back in the door.'

'So tell me about systems!' she invited. 'All systems exclude you if you don't kick your way in. Try making it as a woman officer in the CID.'

She had a point but I didn't want her to think I was whingeing and I told her so. 'I'll get out of here one day, one way or another, on my own two little flat feet! Getting this murder business behind me would be a start.'

She nodded, picked up her mug and sipped. 'I'm going through divorce,' she said suddenly. 'So I know how you feel, believe me. When I get the divorce behind me, I'll be all right. Right now . . . ' She bent her head over the mug.

I'd never seen any rings on her hand so I hadn't reckoned on her being married. But there was no reason why she shouldn't be.

'Is he another plod, I mean, police officer?'

She gave a rueful grin. 'No, he works for a bank. I'm rather sensitive about living space myself at the moment.' She jerked her head to indicate the room. 'Tom, my soon-to-be-ex, wants to sell up our house and split the proceeds. I'm damned if I'm going to lose my home! I decorated every room in that house! Up a ladder with a tin of emulsion every evening after I got in from work! While he sat in front of the telly or pushed off to play squash with his mates.'

She sounded really fierce. Tom obviously had a fight on his hands. I sympathised with her and made a few encouraging remarks.

We were getting on pretty well together by now. Then

Janice seemed to remember she was there on official business. She put the mug on the floor and sat up as straight as she could in the chair.

'Finding someone who could remember you and Porter in Camden has helped, Fran, but the superintendent still isn't happy. He can't believe that you knew so little about Theresa Monkton. Where she went during the day and other people she met. She lived with you. Even if she wasn't talkative, she must have let the odd comment slip. When you live with people you find out about them by a kind of osmosis. I found out plenty about Tom by living with him. Not because he told me, but because you can't hide from people you're with every day and night. You're either not trying to remember or you're holding out on us. Give yourself a break. Give me a break. Come up with something, can't you?'

I told her I would if I could, but as I'd told her before, even though I'd seen Theresa every day, I just hadn't known her. 'What about her family? They have to have known more about her than I did.'

'She hadn't been in touch with them in months. They had been trying to find her. You can imagine how distressed they are.'

I cast about desperately. 'How about Lucy? She brought Theresa along in the first place. Did you find her?'

'Lucy Ho? Yes. She met Theresa by chance in a pub and felt sorry for her.' Janice looked both irritated and depressed. 'There's a sort of vacuum around that girl and I'm beginning to think it was deliberately created.'

She saw I was about to deny responsibility and added quickly, 'I don't mean it was created by you or the others. I mean, she created it herself.'

Janice hesitated as if unsure whether to confide in me. Then she hunched forward on the chair edge and went on in a rush, 'Fran, think about this. No friends, no visitors, no background details about herself, no attempt to mix with the others and be friendly. To me that's someone trying to hide, terrified of giving clues.'

I did think about it and conceded she might be right.

'She was careful not to leave any trail for someone else to follow,' Janice insisted. I could see it was her pet theory.

I played devil's advocate. '*Someone* followed it. Because *someone* found her.'

I sounded hard-boiled but I wasn't feeling that way. I was feeling guilty. It had never occurred to me that Terry had been scared, living in fear all the time she was with us, and in need of help. None of us had offered it. I reasoned that she hadn't seemed afraid. But then, I hadn't tried looking beneath the surface of the front she'd put up. All right, she couldn't have expected much help from Nev or Squib, and Declan had his own problems and had left. But I could have listened. I could have tried to give her some support.

'I didn't want to know what made her tick,' I said. 'She lived with us, but she was a stranger.'

And that *was* the truth, although I was just beginning to see it myself for the first time.

Janice struggled out of the chair. 'Thanks for the coffee. I'll be in touch.'

I felt even more depressed when she'd left. I realised that I was feeling grief for Terry, something I hadn't felt before. I wasn't proud of myself. I should have felt it before.

Now I knew that I owed her. I hadn't helped her then, but I could still help now if I knew where to start. I gave it a lot of thought without coming up with an answer.

Ganesh came over in the van and took me to our old place, down by the river, where we sat on a chunk of concrete and looked across to the Crystal City and watched gulls picking over debris on the mudflats.

Gan said, 'I wrote a poem, about her, about Terry.'

Gan is a good poet. Generally he only shows his poetry to me, although he has been known to read out some of it to Mad Edna. The last time he did that, she said it was very good and had he thought of taking up the piano?

'I'm not bloody Nöel Coward!' Ganesh had told her.

So he read his poem to me now, the one about Terry. It was strange hearing him read it because he hadn't known her as well as I had, and had no reason to feel guilty as I did. But it was as if he felt what I felt and was able to express it better than I could in words.

When he'd finished, I said, 'Thanks, Gan.'

'Perhaps we aren't meant to know,' he said, tucking the paper away in his leather jacket. 'What happened to her really, I mean.'

'I want to know!' I retorted. 'But short of Edna recovering her sanity and backing up your story, I can't see where to begin!'

That must have been giving Fate a gentle hint. The next day, out of the blue, I had another visitor at the flat.

The doorbell rang as I was trying to block up some of the gaps round the bedroom window with ready-mixed filler.

I'm not much of a handyman but I was making a fair job of it and I was annoyed to be called away.

I peered through the little spyhole and saw a very smart, elderly gent outside. More out of curiosity than anything, I opened the door.

'Miss Varady?' he asked very politely, and raised his hat. 'I'm Alastair Monkton, Theresa's grandfather.' He held out his hand.

I apologised for having Tetrion smeared over me and suggested it would be better if we didn't shake hands.

He followed me into the sitting room, trying not to look too appalled. I invited him to take the notorious armchair, while I washed my hands and brushed my hair.

When I came back I asked him if he'd like a cup of coffee.

He probably didn't fancy coffee made in a place like that. He said, 'I don't want to impose, Miss Varady. You realise I want to talk about my granddaughter. Perhaps you'd allow me to take you to lunch?'

I wanted to talk about his granddaughter, too. He was hoping I could tell him something but I was hoping he'd tell me.

Moreover, any lunch he'd buy me had to be better than anything I had in my kitchen. I said 'yes' straight away.

Chapter Six

Monkton had a taxi waiting downstairs. It must have been building up a terrific fare on the clock but he didn't seem to mind. The taxi-driver certainly didn't, although you could see he didn't much like waiting around in that district.

We went to an Indian restaurant which Alastair Monkton said was very good. It certainly wasn't like the Indian take-aways I knew. It had a carpet on the floor and starched white damask tablecloths and the waiters wore white jackets.

The food on the other tables looked and smelled pretty good too, nearly as good as Ganesh's mother's. The menu was the size of *The Times* and it took nearly as long to read it. I settled for the special fish curry and he chose the lamb curry with ginger.

When we'd had time to settle down and size one another up across the Naan bread, he asked, 'I hope you won't take this amiss, Francesca. But may I ask how old you are?'

I told him, twenty-one. Also that I preferred to be called Fran.

'Twenty-one?' He looked for a moment as if his thoughts had drifted away somewhere. He said, more to himself than to me, 'No age, really. No age at all. Life before you. Everything to do. Everything to live for.'

He must have forgotten the flat we'd just left.

He turned his gaze back to me and rejoined the present. 'Then you're much of an age as Theresa, my granddaughter. She was just twenty. We had thought, hoped, she would have phoned home on her birthday, but she didn't. We didn't know where she was. We couldn't even send her a card. We couldn't help her at all and she obviously needed help so desperately.'

'We called her Terry. That was her idea.' I hesitated. 'She was doing what she wanted to do. I know that's hard to explain to you. She didn't want help. She wanted to be independent.'

I realised as I spoke how futile that sounded. Independence takes money. Not for nothing is it called 'independent means'. Money with no strings attached. Without it, you can forget independence. I realised I'd been deluding myself with notions of my own independence, when all I was, truly, was at a loose end. Nevertheless it was a freedom of sorts.

Alastair wouldn't have understood. He would have sent Terry money if she'd phoned home on her birthday or any other day. But it would have come with chains, not just strings, attached. For that reason alone, she would never have reached for that phone.

I knew he was going to ask me next if I had any idea how her death could have happened, and I didn't. He was so nice and obviously Terry's death had been such a dreadful blow to him, that I really wished I could help.

'She was very quiet,' I said. 'She didn't talk much about herself. I never saw her with a boyfriend.'

I knew she'd been keen on Declan but that didn't count because it didn't come to anything.

'I've been to Cheshire to talk to young Nevil Porter.'

That surprised me and I must have looked it. He smiled and said, 'I thought he seemed a pleasant young man. Sadly, it was obvious he'd been ill. You too, if I may say so, seem a pleasant, sensible young woman. I'm glad that Theresa wasn't in with a bad crowd, even if you were all living illegally in that condemned house. You and young Porter, you seem to be so, well, normal. A matter of – er – style, aside. Porter's people seemed very decent. I dare say yours, too. I admit I've been forced to reassess my earlier impressions.'

Obviously he hadn't met Squib. I rather hoped he didn't. He seemed to be thinking over something again. He was staring down at his plate and he looked very sad. I felt very sorry for him but a little embarrassed too. I looked away and saw that people at the next table were looking at us and whispering. We must have appeared a strange couple, Alastair and I. The woman at the table looked shocked. She probably thought Alastair had picked me up off the street for lunch followed by a session involving leather and bondage. I treated her to a stony glare and she flushed and looked away.

'Is something wrong?' I hadn't realised Alastair had come out of his reverie.

'No. We were getting funny looks from the next table so I gave them a funny look back.'

'Oh?' He almost smiled. 'I see, quite.'

There was an awkward little pause. The waiter brought

our food. I was feeling very hungry by now so I started on mine.

Alastair pushed a fork into his but didn't eat. 'Theresa first ran away from school when she was sixteen. She came home of her own accord but refused to return to the school. About six months after she came home, she ran away again. We traced her quite quickly and persuaded her to come back. When she was just eighteen she left again. We had more trouble finding her that time, because she was no longer under age and the authorities were less helpful. They pointed out she had a history of running away. There was no reason to suppose anything had happened to her. We tried every other way we knew to trace her. We even contacted the National Missing Persons Helpline and they managed to get that little magazine to show her photograph, the one the young people sell on the street.'

'You mean, *The Big Issue*?' I couldn't see Alastair poring over the magazine sold by and on behalf of the homeless, and it almost made me smile, the image was so incongruous. Luckily I managed to keep a straight face.

'We'd had no idea,' he was saying, 'until we contacted the helpline, just how many people go missing every year. Where are they all?' He sounded bewildered.

I could have replied that some of them were on the streets and some had turned to crime. A few were probably dead and some others, against all the odds, had made perfectly good lives for themselves elsewhere. But I didn't interrupt. He wanted to tell me about it. He was trying to explain what had happened, not just to me, but to himself.

'As it happened, she came home again by herself, just as she'd done the first time. She had been travelling with a sort of hippy convoy. New-Age travellers, they call themselves.

She was in a pitiful state and had developed a bad bronchial cough. She stayed with us until she was fit again and then, one day – it was so trivial . . . '

He was looking distressed so I finished for him. 'There was a family quarrel of some sort and she left again.'

'Oh, she told you?'

I shook my head and grimaced. It was always the same story.

'The last time I ever saw my granddaughter alive,' he said sadly, 'we exchanged harsh words. I'd give anything in the world to be able to take them back. To have her back. She was wilful and undisciplined. But I just don't understand how anyone could harm her. She was a beautiful girl.'

I mumbled that he wasn't the first person to feel that way after a bereavement. That he oughtn't to feel responsible for anything. Terry had been old enough to make her own decisions.

'I know things weren't easy for her.' He'd listened to me but I don't think anything I'd said had helped. He had to work it out for himself. 'Her parents divorced when she was thirteen. Neither of them was in a position to offer her a home, so naturally she came to live with me. Looking back, I realise she may have felt unwanted, although I assure you she wasn't! I did try, we all tried . . . '

His voice tailed away. I wondered, since Terry's parents had taken off somewhere, who 'we' were. 'We all'. That suggested more than two. I asked, 'What did her parents do? After they broke up, I mean? Since neither of them had room for Terry?'

He gave a little start as if his mind had been drifting off again. Conversation with him was a little difficult in more ways than one. He wasn't one of those elderly people who are confused. His mind was clear enough, but it didn't like focusing on one person, me, for more than five minutes.

'I do apologise!' he said, as if he'd realised what I was thinking. 'I suppose it's one of the drawbacks of age that one wool-gathers! My son, Theresa's father—' Alastair's voice had become stilted and it was obvious relations between father and son were cool. 'He works in America and has remarried there. Theresa's mother took up her former career which involved a great deal of travel. She's in the fashion business.'

I thought of that expensive knitted jacket of Terry's. A conscience-salving present from her mother?

Abruptly Alastair added, 'Marcia – that's my former daughter-in-law, Theresa's mother, has been to see me. She's naturally distressed and some harsh words were spoken. She was offensive. She seems to blame me for the way Theresa kept leaving home. I have taken the charitable view that Marcia's words were spoken in haste and grief. In the circumstances, I shall overlook the unpleasant nature of them!' He gave a snort. 'My belief is that Marcia feels guilty. So she damn well should! I hope she feels as guilty as hell!' He stopped short and muttered, 'Excuse me!'

I thought Marcia was lucky the old chap was so well bred. It now seemed Terry and I had had more in common than I'd thought. At least only my mother had dumped me – and my dad at the same time. Terry'd been effectively dumped by both her parents.

'When Philip and Marcia parted,' Alastair was saying, 'it seemed the only practical solution for Theresa to remain with me. It meant I had the melancholy task of informing both her parents of the dreadful tragedy.'

Unaware of what Janice had told me, he went on to explain, 'We saw it in the newspaper. That is, I didn't see it, but – someone else did. Only a small item, a young woman, police seeking next of kin. We all felt it would be Theresa. We'd been expecting something of the sort. Yet it was still a terrible blow.'

He raised his eyes to peer at me over the table. They were very pale blue, the whites discoloured, the rims watery. He looked frail, for all his neatness and upright bearing.

'She was an innocent. She thought she knew about the world, about life. But of course, she didn't. She didn't see the dangers. I tried to warn her that living as she did, she ran such risks. She wouldn't listen. I was just an old man who knew nothing about modern youth. But some things don't change. Human nature doesn't, more's the pity. Sooner or later she was going to find herself dealing with people who would be stronger, more ruthless, and I have to say, cleverer than she was. One wants to protect... one can't. That is the worst of it. I couldn't protect her. Too old. Just too old.'

He rubbed his hands together in a nervous gesture. The skin was thin over the back, paper-like, and the veins stood up corded and thick. I didn't know how old he was and wished I did. But I noticed a slight yellowness to the fingertips. He was a life-long smoker.

I remembered Edna and her golden packet and the matches, too. But this old man couldn't have done violence of the kind I'd seen done to Terry. Nor would he have wished to harm her. He had loved her.

He pulled himself together and began to speak again, more briskly. 'My son is flying over for the funeral. They –

the police – say, we'll be able to bury Theresa quite soon. They'll be finished – all they want to do.' He pushed his plate away and I didn't fancy eating any more, either.

When he spoke again, however, his voice was firmer. I guessed he thought out beforehand what he wanted to say and had it well rehearsed. He didn't look at me as he spoke, but kept his eyes fixed on his hands, clasped on the tablecloth.

'There is a strong possibility that her death came about through murder, not suicide or any other kind of mishap. The police have classed it as suspicious.' It must have cost him, but he went on, 'They believe she was knocked unconscious by someone who stood behind her and a little to one side. Almost certainly someone she knew and had admitted to the house.'

He cast me an apologetic look to show he wasn't accusing me. 'Whoever did it arranged her body afterwards to make it look as if she'd hanged herself. Even if she'd started to come round before he completed his task, it would have been too late to defend herself, to stop him . . . ' His voice faltered but he went on steadily enough, once he'd had a moment to pull himself together. He was a tough old fellow under the outward frailty. 'You saw the body.'

It was a statement, not a question. I nodded confirmation.

'The – ah – fixture in the ceiling from which she – the body – hung wasn't particularly secure. My granddaughter weighed very little. All the same, had she been conscious at any stage and thrashed around, she, the rope, everything, would've come crashing down. It leads the police to conclude that she was unconscious throughout. That, in turn, would seem to rule out suicide.'

It was true that Terry had been an anorexic seven-stoner. Anyone, virtually, could have lifted her. I could have done so in an emergency. To talk of 'he' might be jumping to conclusions. A woman might well have done it. But dead weights are more difficult to handle, or so I'd been led to believe. If Terry was unconscious, would that have made her necessarily easier to lift? I wasn't sure.

He had raised his eyes and was studying my face. I'd been lost in my own thoughts and must have looked startled. He gave a small, dry smile.

'I want to know for sure, Francesca. I want to know what happened. I want to know if it was, after all, suicide. The police have not completely ruled that out. Or if it was murder and if so, who killed her and why. I want your help.' He hesitated. 'This is an unpleasant subject to discuss with you. Perhaps I shouldn't have done so. But I came to you for a particular reason.'

'It's OK,' I told him, trying to disguise my unease.

'I have a proposition to make to you, Francesca.'

The people at the next table clearly thought he had, too. The murmured words, 'at his age . . . ' floated across. I hoped Alastair hadn't heard them.

'The police are working hard on this. I have no criticisms of them. However, they didn't know Theresa and you did. They didn't live in that house with her, and you did. They don't know the world she moved in – and you do. I want to ask you if you would undertake inquiries for me into her death.'

'Me?' I must just have gaped at him. It had been the last thing I'd been expecting. I began to stutter objections, that I didn't know how, hadn't the facilities, that there were private inquiry agencies better placed than I was to do as he wished.

He cut me short. 'Private detective agencies don't handle that kind of investigation. I've been in touch with a couple. They seem to spend their time serving summonses and following errant spouses around town. In any case, I've the same objection to them as to the police. They don't have the first-hand knowledge that you have.'

'The police won't like it,' I said. Janice's reaction didn't bear thinking about.

'They won't have to know.'

That took my breath away. He was a surprise, was old Alastair, in more ways than one. But he was right, the police would have to be unaware of my activities or they'd put a stop to them immediately. With or without a charge of obstruction.

'I'm sure you can be discreet.' He cleared his throat. 'I admit I had some reservations about asking a young woman to do this unpleasant task. But Nevil Porter was clearly in no state, when I saw him, to undertake anything. I understand the third member of your group might be unsuitable. I haven't met him, but from what I've heard, I fancy he would prove unreliable.'

'You think I'm reliable?' I had to ask.

His faded eyes fixed mine with disconcerting sharpness. 'Yes, I do. I thought you would be before we met, and now we have met and talked, I'm sure of it. I will, of course, meet all your expenses and – if you obtain any firm evidence of either suicide or murder – pay you a further sum. Oh, and should you get into trouble with the police over this, I shall naturally come forward and provide any legal representation you might need.'

That was a relief. Of a sort.

He put a hand to his inner breast pocket and took out an envelope which he put on the table, propped against a wine glass. 'Two hundred and fifty pounds on account. There will be a further two hundred and fifty on positive results. Does that seem fair to you?'

It sounded like a fortune to me, but I had to make it clear to him, that he might be throwing money away. 'I may turn up nothing.'

'I realise that. But I sense you are a determined young woman. Perhaps, if you turn up nothing, as you put it – it will be because there is nothing to find? In other words, perhaps my girl took her own life, after all. Will you do it?'

'You're crazy,' said Ganesh with such finality that I didn't feel like arguing with him about it. I'd already worked out for myself that I couldn't be in my right mind.

'It was difficult to refuse him, Gan. Poor old chap. Basically, he just wants to know what she'd been doing in the weeks before she died. He's desperate to fill in the gap between the last time he saw her and – when we found her.'

'It's occurred to you that grief might have unhinged the old fellow?'

'He seemed pretty sane. He gave me his card.' I took it out and put it on the greasy table in the café where we sat discussing Alastair's request. The proprietor was writing up the day's menu on a blackboard. He was having a little trouble.

Sosages and egs
Pissa with toping of choise

There was nothing to suggest that his cooking was an improvement on his spelling. Certainly not the smell of ancient grease coming from the kitchen.

'We're not eating here, are we?'

Gan grunted and shook his head. He was turning the card over and over, although nothing was written on the back. 'Abbotsfield near Basingstoke, Hampshire,' he read aloud. 'And what's this, Astara Stud?'

'Horses, I assume.'

'What sort of horses? Racehorses?'

'I don't know, do I? I've taken his two-fifty on account and I'm going to do my best to earn it, right?'

'Don't look at me,' he said discouragingly. 'I'm not going to help you.'

'Well, thanks. I'll manage on my own.'

We left the café and bought two foil boxes of special fried rice from the Chinese take-away. We sat by the river to eat, looking across at the Crystal City.

'Where are you going to start?' Gan asked.

'I'm going to talk to Edna.'

He tipped out the remains of his rice for the gulls. 'And that's going to be worth two hundred and fifty quid, is it?'

Needless to say, it wasn't. Edna had chosen to obliterate everything from her mind relating to the man she'd seen and the cigarette packet.

'Have you still got it, Edna? Or the packet of matches?'

She pushed her hands into the sleeves of her grubby coat and hunched on a tomb, sulking.

'Come on, Edna, I'll buy you a new packet.'

She wriggled away from me along the tomb. 'Don't want it.'

'Has something upset you, Edna?'

She raised furious eyes. 'They took them all away!'

I didn't understand at first and then I realised that there was a curious absence of cats around the place. My heart sank. 'Who, Edna?'

'Animal charity, called themselves. Came with little cages in a van. I told them, they didn't need any animal charity. They had me! I looked after them! She said—'

'She, Edna?'

'Skinny young woman in charge. Face like a ferret. She said, they'd find new homes for them. Don't believe it. Don't believe anyone. Don't want anyone. Don't want you!'

End of conversation.

I was more than disappointed because I'd already had thoughts I hadn't confided in Gan. The book of matches Edna had shown me had been printed with the name of a wine bar in Winchester. Winchester wasn't so far from Basingstoke, and that, in turn, was near Abbotsfield and the Astara Stud. That book of matches was evidence and it had gone.

It didn't change my mind. The police were looking in London for the answer to the mystery. I had an idea that was the wrong place. Down there in Hampshire was where the story started. And down there in Hampshire was where I might end up having to go.

Having a permanent address of my own now, even if it was only the flat, helped in one way and I was able to find another job. I still had Alastair's money, but it wasn't for day-to-day living. It was for my inquiries, and so far they hadn't cost me anything.

It was a pretty lousy job, waitressing in another café which sold nothing but fry-ups and slabs of bread pudding to truck-drivers and labourers from building sites. My clothes and hair stank of frying oil when I got home but the tips were good if the pay was meagre. I also got free food, which meant eating what was on the menu. I came out in spots but I saved money.

In between I trailed from pub to pub and squat to squat, trying to trace Terry. Sometimes my path crossed one left by the police. Generally they'd been ahead of me every time. I had to give them full marks. Whether they'd found out anything I didn't know, but I doubted it. No one had anything to tell me and they were more likely to talk to me than to the coppers. I even found Lucy again but she had nothing to tell me. She'd met Terry by chance and knew as little about her as I did. Lucy had a job now, child-minding. She seemed happy. I was glad.

this time, I'd heard nothing from Squib which didn't really surprise me. On the other hand I had been to the hostel and in theory, at least, he ought to know that. I wanted to know he was OK; I wanted to know what the police had been saying to him and he to them; and I wanted another talk about Terry. Squib was, after all, one of the few people other than myself who'd known her.

Accordingly, one evening after I'd finished my shift at the café, I went back to the hostel and settled myself on the stone wall outside. After a few minutes a woman came out, smiling, of course. Did they ever stop? She asked if I needed anything. I told her I was waiting for Henry and refused her offer of a nice, hot dinner which, from the smell oozing through the basement grill, was mostly cabbage.

She left me on my wall which was hard. The coldness of it seeped through my jeans. I wondered whether I'd get piles and kicked my dangling legs back and forth to generate a bit of heat. To occupy my mind, I listed my favourite films in order of preference. I'd done that before. It took me quite a long time and *The Good, The Bad and The Ugly* came out on top as it usually did.

As the evening wore on, the residents began to drift past me into the hostel and the boiled greens dinner. There were winos, who left their empty sherry bottles stacked by the door, dropouts and junkies, with the occasional out-and-out psycho, twitching and rolling his eyes, but no Squib. When it was nearly dark and I was about to give up, I saw a small white shape trotting towards me out of the gloom. Squib's dog.

Squib himself emerged from the shadows. I jumped up and nearly hugged him. I can't say he responded with equal enthusiasm.

'Hullo, Fran,' he said, trying to sidle past me.

I told him I'd been before and left a note, had he seen it? He mumbled and tried to get away again but I grabbed his sleeve.

'Listen, you don't want whatever they're dishing up in there. I'll buy you egg and chips. I've got the money.'

'Cafés don't let dogs in,' he muttered.

'Then I'll buy us all a burger from the van along the street there, the dog too.' The van had arrived about ten minutes earlier and was setting up in business, smoke belching from it. 'I've been sitting here waiting for you for ages and my backside's numb,' I added.

He gave in and we went to the van, first customers of the evening and the food hadn't yet got leathery. I bought Squib and myself a burger each with all the trimmings, and one for the dog without onions, mustard or pickle. We sat on a bench under a streetlight to eat them.

'How's it going, Squib?' I asked, licking my fingers.

'I'm going to be clearing out soon,' he said. 'I think I'll go travelling again.'

'They've told you to go?'

'Naw, but they don't like him.' He pointed at the dog which had gobbled up its burger and was eyeing mine. 'And I don't like them.'

'What about the police? They've been in my hair.'

'I gotta report in twice a week and stay at the friggin' hostel. Otherwise, they don't bother.'

I told him there was no justice. They didn't leave me alone. Why didn't they pester him in the same way?

'You're bright, ain'tcha?' said Squib. 'They ask you questions because they think you got answers. Me, I'm thick. They don't bother.'

'I don't know anything, Squib, but I'm trying to find out.'

'Whaffor?' He was getting bored, fidgeting and wanting to get up and walk off.

I wasn't going to tell him about Alastair. I told him, 'For my own sake. I want to know why she had to go and die in our house, like that. I want to know more about her.'

There was a silence. 'There was a bloke asking for her one time.'

It was Squib speaking but the words were so unexpected

I found myself looking round to see if someone else had joined us. 'What do you mean? At the house?'

'No, in the pub, couple of streets down, The Prince of Wales. He had her photo and was showing it around. He showed it me. I don't split on a mate, so I said I didn't know her. He said he was going round all the pubs. I wished him luck. Off he went. Flash feller.'

I suppressed a tingle of excitement. 'When was this, Squib?'

Asking him to be specific was a little like asking Edna. He looked vague. 'Couple of weeks before she topped herself.'

'And you didn't tell any of us?'

In the lamplight his face had an eerie sheen on it and his expression was aggrieved. 'Matter of fact, I did, see? I told her, told Terry. Reckoned she ought to know.'

'What did she say?' Keeping my own tone nonchalant was getting difficult. I had to try not to squeak.

Squib racked what passed for his memory. 'She was scared, I reckon. But I told her it would be all right, because I'd said nothing. She give me a fiver.'

'Five pounds? Terry did?'

'Yeah.' Squib frowned. 'It was more'n I expected. But he'd have given me that, wouldn't he? The bloke in the pub? If I'd told him. So it was fair.'

Both fair and shrewd. Squib hadn't given away information that time, but he might be tempted if the inquirer came back again, brandishing a fat wallet. Terry had been making sure. I was annoyed, though, remembering how she never had any money when it came to household expenses.

'I wish you'd told me,' I said.

He settled his woolly hat over his ears. 'Why should I? Wasn't nobody's business but hers.'

True – at the time. Now it was mine. 'Come on, Squib!' I ordered him firmly, 'what else did she say?'

'Nothing!' he protested. 'I forget.' After a moment, he added sulkily, 'She said her people must be trying to find her. That's where the bloke had come from.'

'Did she name a place?'

'Chuck it, Fran, will you? I forget!'

'Basingstoke?' I tried. 'Winchester? Abbotsfield? Ring any bells?'

'Horses,' mumbled Squib. 'It had something to do with nags.'

'Squib,' I said, 'was it called the Astara Stud?'

He muttered, 'Can't remember!' but he didn't mutter it fast enough. He remembered, all right.

I sat there, both excited and frustrated, because he was still holding out on me.

Suddenly he asked, sounding odd, sort of shy and hopeful mixed, 'Reckon her people got money?'

'Probably,' I said. 'Everyone's got more money than us.'

That seemed to make an impression on him and he sat thinking about it until, without warning, he stood up. The dog, which had been curled up under the bench, jumped up too.

'It's getting late,' he said. 'They close the doors nine o'clock. After that, you're locked out. It stops us staying down the pub late. They don't allow drink, no beer, nothing.'

He was already setting off down the street. I called after him, 'You can still set out your bedroll at my place!'

'Forget it!' he called back. 'I got plans.'

I dismissed that because Squib had never been known to have a plan of any kind, ever.

I should have paid more attention. Especially I should have realised that, being a novice where thinking was concerned, if Squib had finally got a plan, he was bound to screw it up.

Chapter Seven

My life continued on its usual doomed course. After two weeks of dishing out fry-ups by day and sleuthing around the less savoury parts of London by evening, someone left the fryer switched on overnight by mistake and my place of employment burned down. So I was out of work again. I sat in my highly undesirable residence and wondered where else I could go to ask about Terry. I'd reached the end of the road, as far as I could see.

By now I'd read nearly all Nev's books and reached the point where I couldn't stay in that flat another forty-eight hours. The estate's kids had taken to rampaging up and down the staircase. I had to lock and bar the door. The mould on the bathroom wall, despite my washing it down with bleach, was spreading and there were scuttling noises behind the rotten skirting boards which I was sure meant rats. I'd had enough.

Parry hadn't been to see me for a while, nor had Janice been in touch again. I felt a little hurt by that. I wondered if she was still on the case. Maybe she was having problems over the divorce and her mind was on that.

I knew I wasn't forgotten by the police in general. I'd

never be forgotten until they closed the file on Terry. But I didn't see how they ever would. No one knew what happened that Monday afternoon.

I was still thinking about Terry in the way I'd started to think after Janice's last visit. I still felt I owed her and there had to be something I could do. I'd made a start. I had what Ganesh and Edna had told me, added to Squib's story. I wished I also had Edna's packet of matches but, unfortunately, that was lost for ever.

I did go back to the hostel and try to see Squib again. But they told me, still smiling, that he'd cleared out, as he'd told me he meant to do. Everything was pointing me in one direction only.

I took myself to Victoria Coach station and asked about National buses down to Basingstoke. The return fare was cheap enough even for me. I went to see Ganesh and asked if I could borrow a camera. It seemed to me the sort of basic equipment a detective would need, although I wasn't sure what I would snap with it.

'Not an expensive one, just an ordinary one, easy to use. Nothing that it would be disastrous to lose or anything. Though I'll take great care of it.'

'What are you up to now?' he asked suspiciously.

I told him I intended going down to the country, to the Astara Stud, and seeing what I could find out.

He was aghast. 'You can't do that! The old fellow thinks you're investigating up here, scene of the crime. He doesn't expect you down there, stirring up trouble! If you ask me, it's time you called him and told him you're quitting. You have tried and you can't do more than that.'

'I've done nothing, Gan, except trail round in the

footsteps of the police, asking the same questions they asked and getting the same blank looks. I'm nowhere further on and frankly, it's a matter of pride! I *will* get to the bottom of this!'

'You're in enough trouble, already,' he argued. 'You don't know anything about this family except what the old man told you over lunch. Who's to know how accurate that was? You said his thoughts kept wandering off. He probably forgot half a dozen things. That woman inspector would throw a wobbly if she knew you meant to go there. You know sod all about being a detective. What have you found out so far? Nothing! You admit it yourself!'

'All the more reason to try somewhere else,' I growled.

He gave me a superior smile. 'What would you do if you turned up a murderer, down there in the sticks? On top of everything else, you don't know anything about the country.'

'What's to know?' I asked airily. 'It's got fields and cows and people saying *aarrh!*'

'It's different!' Ganesh snapped. 'You won't know your way around there, as you do here. You don't know those kind of people. Here in the city, people are too busy to bother what you do. Down there a stranger will attract attention. You will, that's for sure!'

'Why me?' I was insulted.

'Look at you!' he said unkindly. 'Jeans with holes in the knees and a black leather jacket, Doc Martens boots. They'll barricade the doors when they see you coming.'

I was sorry I'd asked to borrow the camera. But his attitude made me more than ever determined. 'Don't be so negative! Have a little faith in me, can't you? I took his money and I'm trying to earn it.'

'There's more to this than taking the old man's money!' he retorted suspiciously.

'All right! I have a stupid feeling that somehow I let Terry down, when she lived with us. I was mean to her.'

'No, you weren't. She was mean to everyone else. You used to moan about her all the time! And even if you were, there's nothing you can do about it now!'

I lost my temper. 'That's a cop-out of an attitude! I'm not just giving up!'

Ganesh yelled, 'This isn't about her at all, is it? Or old Alastair! This is really all about you and *your* father! You think you let him down. You just want to put this business of Terry right because you wish you could put right the way you think you failed your old man. Do you know what you're in danger of doing? You're in danger of adopting this Alastair Monkton as a substitute father-figure! That's a very dangerous thing to do. It's risky for you and him and it's unfair on him!'

I was in no mood to be psycho-analysed. 'Are you going to lend me a camera or not?'

He went upstairs and came down after some minutes with a really neat little camera in a leather case on a strap. 'Don't lose it! It's fool-proof. A six-year-old could work it. Don't put your finger over the lens.'

As he handed it to me, he muttered, 'I wish I could come with you. But we're busy in the shop and Dad's back is playing him up. He can't lift the crates. But promise me, you'll keep in touch.'

'Promise, Gan.'

Ganesh's remarks about my appearance had hit home. I

had to admit he was right. I'd stick out like a sore thumb around the Astara Stud. I had to look respectable. They were a traditional lot in the country or so I imagined.

I washed my hair and tried to style it. In the squat long hair wasn't practical because we only had hot water if we boiled a kettle. Although I kept it short, it was longer than I had it in my punk days when I wore it cropped down to a quarter-inch stubble and coloured it purple. Now it was back to its normal mid-brown.

At the time I'd been going through my purple phase, I had a gold ring put through the outer edge of my right nostril. I was still at school then. I think that was what finished the headmistress off as far as I was concerned, the day I walked in with my purple hair and nostril-ring. I just wasn't the image she wanted for the school. She told me so. They were trying to turn out ladies, even in these benighted days. She meant, of course, that well-heeled parents, arriving to visit the school with a view to sending their precious daughters there, didn't expect to see a purple-haired, nostril-ringed punk lounging along the corridor. There was a barney. I was told to take out the ring and grow my hair. I refused. About a week later, Dad got The Letter. Goodbye, Francesca. We tried to make you one of us, but you weren't suitable material. No one can make a silk purse out of a sow's ear. It was couched in more official phrases, the letter, but that's what they meant.

A little later, when I was on the drama course which I was also destined never to finish, I swopped the nostril-ring for a nostril-stud, gold with a diamond chip in it which twinkled in the sunlight. I still wear the stud. It fixes in with a fitting like a tiny Allen key. If I leave it out for any length of time, the hole in my right nostril fills up with soap. Sorry, but that's life, full of sordid details.

I sorted through my wardrobe. I'd got my best clean jeans with no holes in them, a clean shirt, a denim waistcoat and my Victorian-style lace-up ankle boots with little heels. All put together it didn't look bad when I studied myself in the bathroom mirror. Although that mirror didn't encourage confidence in your appearance. It had livid patches all over it. If you looked at yourself in the nude in it, the reflection made you look as if you had leprosy.

Apart from the nostril-stud, I'm not one for jewellery. But I have Grandma Varady's gold locket so I put that on. I used to babysit for Lucy while she was out job and flat hunting. When she left the squat, she gave me her good jacket because I'd always admired it. It was blue-grey loose weave with a pretty silver-grey satiny lining. She'd always kept it in a polythene bag away from the children so it was quite smart. It was a bit on the big side for me, so I turned the sleeves up and the satin lining showed on the outside but it looked quite good.

So that was what I would turn up in Abbotsfield wearing. I wasn't sure how long I'd be staying. (Or if I'd be thrown off the place as soon as I got there.) *Hope for the best and plan for the worst*, said William of Orange, or somebody. I got out my green and purple duffel bag and put in a towel with my toothbrush and soap. Then I put in three pairs of clean knickers and a spare pair of opaque black tights and spare shirt. There was still room so I added a sweater in case it turned chilly and finally my one blue cotton button-through skirt, because I wasn't sure quite where I'd end up and it might be somewhere that jeans didn't suit. That skirt was handy because it didn't need ironing, it was meant to look crumpled.

I managed to get it all in and just do up the zip. I've always carried my money in a purse on a cord round my neck under my shirt. The places I'd lived in, you kept your money on you and you didn't let anyone see it.

Amongst Nev's books was one called *Three Plays* by Turgenev. One of the plays was entitled *A Month in the Country*. That seemed an omen so I put the book in my pocket to read on the bus.

I'd got that far when the doorbell rang. It was Ganesh.

'I thought, if you hadn't left yet, I'd come to Victoria and see you off.' He picked up my duffel bag. 'What on earth have you got in here? A crowbar and a hammer?'

'Ha-ha! My overnight essentials. I might stay a few days.'

He was frowning at me, studying the outfit. But he didn't say anything and I asked, nettled, 'Something wrong?'

He shook his head but still didn't say anything.

I couldn't be bothered whether he approved or not and turned away to check I'd not left anything I'd need.

From behind me, Ganesh said very loudly, 'I wish you weren't going down there on your own. You don't know a thing about the place. Or who will be there.'

'It can't be worse than this flat!' I pointed out snappishly.

'Have you got my camera?'

'Here.' I picked it up and slung it across from one shoulder, bandolero fashion.

'Want me to show you again how it works?'

'Thanks, but I remember! I'm not totally simple! And you don't have to come to the coach station!'

'If I have to come looking for you,' he said. 'I want to know which bus you went on, where it was going, and what time it was supposed to get there. It'll give me something to go on when I report you missing to the police and we start tracing your last movements.'

It wasn't exactly an expression of confidence.

At Victoria I got a seat on a bus going to Basingstoke. Ganesh went off somewhere and came back with a plastic carrier containing two packets of crisps, a box of orange drink with a straw and a tuna sandwich in a triangular box.

'In case you don't get a chance to buy lunch.'

I knew Ganesh was the best friend I had, more than that really. But all I said was, 'Thanks!'

When I actually got on the bus, sat in my seat by the window, I found I was really suffering a bad case of butterflies. My stomach was just a quivering jelly mass.

I could see Ganesh standing by the side of the bus with his hands shoved in the pockets of his black leather jacket. His long black hair curled loose round his face. He has nice hair. I can understand why he doesn't want to cut it off, even if his dad does believe it would be the first step on the pathway to success. He looked worried. I smiled brightly and waved to him. He took one hand from his pocket, waved back and gave a thumbs-up sign.

Then we were off. I was on my own, just me and Turgenev.

I wondered if Ganesh was right and I would find a murderer down there in the country. And I wondered what I'd do, if I did.

I wondered if [illegible] would find a [illegible] [illegible] and [illegible] what I'd done.

Chapter Eight

The coach crawled through mid-morning traffic out of London. I'd brought along a little notebook and I thought I better start off straight away being organised, the way a proper detective would be. So I began to write down all I knew about Terry under the heading 'Lines of Inquiry'.

But it was difficult to write clearly as the bus wove in and out of traffic. There wasn't much room and an old woman next to me took out her knitting. She was doing some sort of complicated stitch which meant that every other minute she threw the wool over the needle with a flourish and her elbow stuck into my ribs. When this happened, she said, 'Sorry, dear!' But then she did it again.

I squashed myself up in the corner of my seat, which was by the window, put the notebook away and decided to think it through. But that didn't work, largely because I'd been sleeping so badly the last few nights. My brain was sluggish. It was the warmest day for weeks and it was really hot in the bus with the sun beating in through the window. We were stuck in a traffic jam. I decided perhaps

I'd better leave it for a while, and come back to it when I had my head together.

The jam was building up. The old lady next to me was unscrewing her vacuum flask. She was obviously a seasoned coach traveller and preparing to sit it out. I took Turgenev from my jacket pocket and made a start on *A Month in the Country*.

I wish I could have completed that college drama course. It was just getting interesting when I quit. I remember being told to think myself into a part as I read it. So I cast myself as Natalia and set myself the intellectual exercise trying to be her.

I admit the first thing which struck me was that it must take Russians ages to carry on even a brief conversation, what with calling each other by such complicated names all the time.

Leaving that aside, I found the play was about a group of people shut up in a country house in the wilds of Russia in the 1840s, all bored stiff and trying to get off with one another. Not very successfully, I might add, which considering how long it took one character to ask another character to go for a walk, wasn't surprising.

Was I going to find life like that when I got down to the country? The heat was overpowering. I closed up the book and I fell asleep with my head propped uncomfortably in the angle between the back of the seat and the window.

When I woke up we were belting along the motorway. I drank Ganesh's orange drink and ate a packet of crisps. I still hadn't worked out what I was going to do when I got to Abbotsfield. I hadn't planned this at all well. Just borrowing a camera wasn't enough. And now, before I knew it, we'd reached Basingstoke and I had to get off the coach.

Like most people, I suppose, I'd always vaguely thought that 'going abroad' or to a foreign country meant crossing the borders into another nation's territory. Some foreign countries appear more alien than others, to the mind. I, for example, have never thought of Hungary as a foreign country because Grandma Varady talked of it so much. Yet I've never been there and, were I to go now, it wouldn't be the Hungary Grandma remembered. It would be somewhere else, resembling nothing I'd ever imagined. Perhaps that's the reason I've never made a serious effort to get there. I want to keep my image of it intact.

The truth is subtler. It usually is. None of us has to travel very far to find a different tribal territory, certainly not outside the boundaries of your own country. You need only travel a few miles, or streets. A mere block away and hey presto, you're a foreigner. That's what Ganesh had been trying to tell me and he was right.

I realised that as soon as I set foot to the ground in Basingstoke. I didn't belong here. I didn't know where to begin. I pottered around for a while and bought a paper bag of vinegar-drenched chips and ate them in the street while I wondered whether to go on, or just find a coach back to London. It hardly seemed possible that only this morning I'd been in my familiar surroundings of boarded-up houses and crumbling blocks of flats.

Basingstoke, on the other hand, had an air of depressing respectability, a pleasantly dull sort of little place, busy enough. It must have been just a market town to start with but some years ago, the modern world had hit it and now it even had a couple of shiny office blocks, giving it a foot in both camps. The people scurried about, mostly looking ordinary and harassed. In the crowd was a scattering of women in calf-length skirts teamed with knitwear-over-a-blouse. Some of them wore headscarves, expensive headscarves, which made them look like off-duty Royals. Me, tie a headscarf on me and I look like a babushka.

Time was getting on. I still didn't know what I was going to do when I got to Abbotsfield, or how I was going to get there, or find the Astara Stud, or where I was going to sleep that night or anything.

I thought about telephoning Alastair Monkton and letting him know I was on my way, but I chickened out when I got to the callbox, and anyway, I didn't have the right change. Besides, if I rang, anyone might answer and whoever it was might be far less welcoming than I hoped Alastair would be. If Alastair were there. Suppose he was away? What did I do then?

By now I was muttering like Mad Edna as I talked myself out of going to the stud. But if I turned back now, after coming this far, I'd lose all self-respect. Ganesh would crow over me for weeks.

I got a grip on my nerves and went in search of a local bus to take me to Abbotsfield.

I was lucky to find a bus which went to Abbotsfield at all. It arrived there late afternoon, around five o'clock. A couple of women with shopping bags got off and disappeared quickly. I was left staring round me.

It had been a pleasant drive if you like countryside. It was pretty, I suppose, but it might just as well have been on the moon as far as I was concerned. I'm a townie, through and through, and was realising it with horrible clarity, even more so than in Basingstoke which had at least offered a jumble of streets and shops. I like bricks. You know where you are with bricks. You turn a corner and there are more of them. Turn a corner in the country and you never know what you're going to find. You can hide in a town. You can't hide in the country, or I couldn't. It was all too open. Miles of empty fields. On the other hand, you could bury a body out there and who'd find it?

From that it was only a step to thinking, who'd find *me*?

Abbotsfield was a sprawling place, bigger than I'd imagined. It had a centre of terraced cottages, a church, two pubs, a post office cum general store, a garage and *Lisa Marie, Ladies and Gents Hairdressing*. Beyond this was a sizeable estate of elderly council housing and a primary school. There was a newer estate of brick bungalows on the outskirts of town.

When I'd explored all this I made my way back to the general store which was still open. It looked the kind of place which stayed open as long as anyone was interested in buying anything. Mr Patel operated on the same principle. I went in and bought a carton of milk and asked the woman for directions to the Astara Stud.

She was obviously curious. She must have heard all about Terry's death. But she told me which way to walk, down the hill out of Abbotsfield, following the signpost for Winchester. Then to look for a turning which indicated Lords Farm.

I asked, puzzled, 'Is that the stud?'

She told me no, it was just a farm, but the stud wasn't marked on the main road. They didn't believe in making it easy for visitors down here.

I thanked her and made my way to the church. I couldn't get into the building itself, as it was locked. But the doorway was interesting, a rounded Norman arch carved with strange geometric designs, resting on corbel heads which had blunted with time and weather into faceless things. The tombs in the churchyard were also old, mossy, the lettering mostly obliterated, although in the far corner was a patch with newer headstones. The sun was going down and it was warm and pleasant here. I sat on a tombstone and ate the tuna sandwiches, feeling, and perhaps looking, a little like Edna. The sandwiches were threatening to go off by that time, they'd turned warm and squishy. Perhaps I'd get food poisoning. I drank the milk and decided what to do. In fact, I didn't have a lot of choice. I had to head for Alastair's place and see what turned up. Although I'd be the one turning up. Or, after the sandwiches, throwing up.

There's a general assumption these days that everyone has transport. I didn't, except my feet. By the time I started walking, it was six o'clock. I'd passed a public loo in a carpark on the way out of town and cleaned myself up, but I still felt sticky, dusty and a mess. The boots weren't made for walking, unlike the ones in the song. I was soon starting to hobble a bit.

I felt conspicuous going along the road, not only because of my increasingly dot-and-carry-one gait, but because no one else was walking. It wasn't like a London pavement where you're shoving or being shoved out of the way all the time. There wasn't any pavement, only a narrow beaten track along the verge. There weren't any houses so no obvious reason to be wandering along. You just weren't supposed to be walking here.

Cars passed, one or two slowing as the drivers – men – took a look at me. I realised I looked like a hitch-hiker. I stuck my hands resolutely in my pockets to show I wasn't thumbing. Grandma Varady used to read the *News of the World* and newspapers of that sort. They were great on tales of rape and murder of young girls. She would read the details out with gusto.

'You never do this, darr-link!' She'd peer over her spectacles at me, shaking the paper under my nose, and making hitching motions with her thumb. 'These men are out there – everywhere! Devils! They are lying in wait for young women!'

Despite this I have, on numerous occasions, hitched. I always applied the rule taught me by a chance acquaintance, a girl I met at a Salvation Army coffee stall near King's Cross one cold winter evening. She was working the area professionally. I was just passing through. She was a cheerful sort of girl, friendly once she'd established I really had just stopped for a hot drink and wasn't aiming to work her patch. She wanted to give up the game on account of her varicose veins but her boyfriend wasn't having it and beat her up when she complained.

'Standing about down here in the cold in a mini-skirt with your arse freezing is no joke!' she said. 'And it does in your legs and ankles.'

Her advice was, 'Never get in a car with any man under the age of thirty-five.'

I remembered that as I walked along the verge. I also remembered her other advice which was never wear a skirt so tight you can't run or kick. Also, have steel tips on your high heels so that you could kick out the windscreen if you did get in the wrong car and things got really tough. I never had to take that kind of action though I had a few wrestling matches with sweaty truckers. On the whole they weren't serious. They nearly all had wives and kids and just wanted company in the cab. The worst thing was being bored to death with tales of the kiddies and their photos taken on Spanish beaches.

I was thinking of all these things as I hobbled along that verge looking for the turning to Lords Farm. I was beginning to think I'd missed it and was about to retrace my steps and check, when one of the cars swooping past screeched to a halt. The driver got out and called to me, 'Want a lift?'

It was a big smart car, a Volvo. He was a big, smart bloke. He wore a shirt patterned in small green check and one of those sleeveless jackets with pouch pockets, coloured khaki. He looked self-confident and was clearly trying his luck.

I told him no thanks, I wasn't going far. I really hoped that last bit was true – I couldn't make it much further in these boots.

He smirked. 'Come on, girlie, hop in!'

No one, but no one, calls me 'girlie'.

I said sharply, 'You deaf or something, *laddie*? I said no!'

He pulled a face, still grinning. 'Oh, a feisty lady? Where do you want to go?'

'Shove off!' I said wearily. I couldn't be bothered with him.

'No need to be like that,' he said. 'I'll take you anywhere you want. We can stop off for a drink on the way.'

I couldn't believe it, that anyone could be that dim, to think I'd fall for a line like that.

'You must be off your trolley,' I said. I must have sounded as though I believed it because it annoyed him.

'Look!' he said nastily. 'You're walking here, hoping to be picked up, right?'

'Wrong! I'm going to call on someone.'

He glanced round in an exaggerated way, drawing attention to the dearth of dwellings. 'Where?'

I was wasting time. I started walking again and although my feet really hurt I was determined not to hobble while he was there to see. After all, if Chinese noblewomen could make it on bound feet, I could make it in pixie boots.

He got back in the car and drove alongside me with a practised ease which suggested to me he'd done his share of kerb-crawling. King's Cross is full of cars like his, doing slow motion manoeuvres, until they see a copper and then they speed off like it was Silverstone.

After we'd gone a little way like this he stopped the car again, just ahead of me and got out, confronting me on the verge.

'All right!' he said. 'You've made your point. What's the name of these people you're looking for?'

I suppressed the first retort to come to my lips. It occurred to me he was probably local and if I told him I was looking for the Astara Stud, he'd know where it was. So I told him where I was bound and added Alastair's name for good measure.

The reaction was extraordinary. It wiped the smirk right off his face. 'Then we're headed for the same place. I'm James Monkton.' He scowled and looked nonplussed. He wasn't sure what to do next.

Oh shit, I thought. It would be!

'But I don't know you,' he said doubtfully. His manner suggested that he was used to a better class of acquaintance.

I told him, 'I'm Fran Varady. I knew Terry – Theresa.'

For a moment he was reduced to silence. A couple of cars rocketed past. Then an ugly look crossed his face and he said, 'You're that girl Alastair talked to in London. You lived in that place where Theresa died! What the hell are you doing down here?'

'My business, all right?' The road was empty now and we were alone by the verge. I hoped I didn't look as nervous as I felt.

'And I'm making it mine!' he told me. 'You can just turn around and go right back where you came from!'

'Alastair told me to come and see him. He gave me his card!' I stood my ground and hoped the half-truth would work. James wasn't to know exactly what had passed between Alastair and me.

He thought about it for a moment, then decided to accept what I'd said. 'Then I'll take you to see him. And there'd better be no funny stuff. I'll be watching!' He gestured at the car and added sarcastically, 'Go on, get in. On the level!'

'Thank you!' I told him. I slung my holdall on to the back seat and we set off.

'Alastair didn't say anything about expecting you.' He glanced sideways at me.

I felt rather foolish. 'We hadn't fixed a date. He said to come when I – wanted. It was a spur-of-the-moment thing. I meant to phone from Basingstoke. But I hadn't any tenpence pieces.'

It sounded weak, not to say the height of bad manners.

But James wasn't worried about my lapse of etiquette. He didn't expect any better from me. His mind was running in a different line.

'So, you came down here without even tenpence for a phone call? Really up against it financially, are you?'

It was clear what he was thinking and I felt my face burn. 'I came to talk to Alastair. I told you that.'

'Not to touch him for a hand-out, by any chance?'

I said, very coldly, 'You don't have any right to suggest that. You don't know me. You don't know why I'm here and you don't have any business to know, as far as I can see.'

'Quite a little Daniel, aren't you? Running into a den of lions. Or did you think Alastair lived alone?'

As a matter of fact, I had assumed that. It had been stupid of me. Obviously he didn't. Indirectly he'd mentioned others. But I hadn't thought they all lived under one roof. What I wanted to know now was whether James here beside me was a permanent member of the household or, like me, a transient visitor.

When I didn't reply, he treated me to a smirk of satisfaction. I tried to pretend I hadn't seen it.

We'd reached the turning marked Lords Farm. James spun the wheel and we slewed off left and then right. We were now following a single-track road, very badly surfaced, and slowly climbing through rolling pastureland. Horses grazed peacefully behind the neat fencing. This must be part of the stud.

I sneaked another look at him. I supposed him to be in his late twenties. He was good-looking in a solid, healthy outdoor way. The solidity was muscle, not fat. I was pretty sure he could take care of himself and probably anyone who got in his way.

I could see he was thinking about me, too. I caught him giving me a couple of sidelong glances, just as I was doing to him, and there was a mean set to his mouth. Our glances collided at last and we both looked away. He was wondering what to do about me. For two pins, I think he'd have pushed me out of the car while rounding a corner at speed. But he *was* curious to know what I wanted.

Suddenly a wooden board appeared by the roadside. On it was painted a horse's head and the words ASTARA STUD. There were a couple of fir trees either side of an entrance. James turned into it with another flourish and roared down a long drive, bordered with overgrown purple-blossomed shrubs which I recognised as buddleia. Buddleia grows anywhere at the drop of a seed and has a liking for the sides of railway tracks in and out of London. James drew up in a shower of grit, before the principal block of a cluster of buildings.

'Here we are then!' he said.

I stared through the windscreen. This must be the main house directly before us. It was red-brick, with sash-windows in white-painted frames, and looked Georgian. A newer extension had been built to the left, forming a separate wing. The ground floor of that looked as though it might be kept for offices.

The really intriguing part lay on the other side of the house. What had been a stableyard had been considerably expanded. I could glimpse the stabling, built around a square yard. Between it and the drive a garage block had been added, standing by itself. Behind that I glimpsed a modern bungalow. In addition to the buddleia, rhododendrons had been planted, either to give the bungalow privacy or to shield the main house from the sight of the humbler dwelling.

James was watching me as I studied all this. He still thought I'd come to see if I could shake some money out of Alastair. He was sure he could take care of it, if so. I found myself wondering if they kept any dogs – the sort which could be set on unwelcome visitors.

I just said as sweetly as I could, 'Thanks for the lift! I didn't realise it was so far out of town.'

He just gave a dry little smile and got out of the car. I hopped out too, grabbing my holdall off the back seat. The front door of the house was on the latch which shows you how different it was to London. Leave your door on the latch where I came from and when you got back either all your belongings would have disappeared, or someone you'd never set eyes on before would be sitting in front of your fireplace drinking lager out of a can, all his kit stowed round the room.

James walked in, leaving me to lug the holdall in by myself which wasn't very gentlemanly. But I had the funny feeling James Monkton wasn't entirely the country gent he took so much trouble to appear.

We were in a wide hall with a polished parquet floor and a staircase running up to a landing. James pushed open a door to a room on the right.

'Why don't you go in and make yourself at home? I'll see if Alastair is anywhere about. He might be out back in the garden or over in the yard.'

The room was a sitting room. The evening sun was shining in the bay window and it looked very comfortable and pleasant. The chairs were old and chintzy and soft. There was a big new TV set in one corner and it gave me quite a surprise to see it there. I was beginning to imagine they'd sit round all evening playing the piano or cards or reading to one another out of leather-bound tomes, like all those characters in Turgenev. I sank down on a sofa and took another look around. If this was where Terry had lived, she must have found sharing the squat with us about as big a change as she could have made.

I guessed I had time to look around. James would want to find out from Alastair as much as he could before he let the old chap anywhere near me. He was probably trying to persuade Alastair to let him, James, send me off back to London forthwith.

There was a big marble fireplace and, over it, a shelf crowded with photos and knick-knacks. I got up and went to have a look. I didn't know most of the people in the photos. I recognised one of Alastair in tweeds at some sort of gymkhana or show. He looked as if he were judging. He had a rosette pinned on his jacket. There were a couple of women standing with him. They had weather-beaten faces and were grinning away at the camera with teeth which wouldn't have disgraced a respectable horse.

In one large silver frame was a studio portrait of a remarkably beautiful girl, all done up in a party dress and looking like a million dollars. It was with shock that I suddenly realised I was looking at a picture of Terry. For a moment, I doubted it and thought, perhaps a relative looking a bit like her? I took it off the shelf for a closer look and it was Terry. I was holding it in my hand still staring at it when I heard a footstep behind me. I just had time to put it back before Alastair came into the room. James was just behind him. I knew that he meant to hear for himself what I had to say, how I'd explain my being there.

But old Alastair forestalled us both. He came straight over to me, took my hand and said, 'Francesca! My dear, why didn't you let us know you were coming? I'm really so pleased to see you. What a good thing Jamie passed you on the road. This house isn't the easiest place to find.'

I could see James looking a bit miffed at all this. It made me feel quite cheerful to think his nose had been put out of joint. I apologised to Alastair for turning up unannounced and so late.

He asked where I was staying. That embarrassed me, and I mumbled that I'd have to go back to Basingstoke, unless there was anywhere in Abbotsfield which offered rooms, perhaps one of the pubs?

'Nonsense, you must stay here!' he said at once, ignoring negative signals from James. 'Stay as long as you like, my dear! I'll get Ruby to make up a bed for you. I dare say you could do with a cup of tea. Jamie, why don't you go along to the kitchen and see if you can rustle one up?'

James didn't like being dismissed, certainly not to fetch the tea, but he went. I think the phrase for it would be 'in high dudgeon'. It occurred to me he'd chalk it up against me as a score to settle. That stopped me feeling so chirpy about it. He was the sort who made sure he always got his own back on anyone who crossed him.

When the door had closed, Alastair leaned forward.

'Have you something to report, Francesca?' He looked anxious, but hopeful too.

I explained to him that to be honest, I'd discovered nothing in London and even worse, had found myself following the police around. 'They're doing a good job,' I said. 'If you want your money back, I've brought it, less my bus fare. But I've been thinking – and maybe you won't agree with this . . . ' I waited but he said nothing, forcing me to plunge on. 'I haven't had much luck following her backtrail in London, so perhaps I ought to start here, where she lived before she came to London. Or just seeing where she came from might give me some ideas. You see, I know she shared the house in Jubilee Street with us, but that doesn't mean any of us knew Terry well. To tell you the truth, we found her a bit of a pain and we tended to ignore her. I'm sorry.'

Alastair didn't seem to find that rude. He nodded. 'I quite understand. Frankly, Francesca, if you'd said you and Theresa were bosom pals I'd be sceptical. I know my granddaughter had difficulty in forming relationships. She didn't make friends. Or at least, not what I would have called real friends.'

'But I do want to know what happened,' I insisted. 'I wish I had talked to her more. I wish I'd been a better friend to her, someone she could have confided in. I promise, I mean to do my best by her now and by you. I don't want more money. That's not why I'm here. James thinks that's why I've come, but he's wrong.'

Alastair frowned. 'My dear, Jamie is not the arbiter of who may visit here and who not! Incidentally, although he knows I called on you in London, he doesn't know about our little arrangement and I see no reason to tell him. The money I gave you on account is yours to keep and, as I promised, I'll pay an equal amount upon result.'

'I may not get any results,' I pointed out.

'I feel sure you will!' he retorted optimistically. 'Now you're here, we'll put our heads together, eh? Work it out!'

He sounded quite enthusiastic and I began to feel a lot better. He was such a nice old boy. If there was a fly in the ointment now, it was Jamie Monkton who clearly thought I was up to no good.

Suddenly Alastair said, 'As for getting to know poor Theresa, I wonder if any of us ever did that?'

Before I could answer that one, the door opened and a middle-aged woman came in carrying a tray with teacups.

'There you are, my dear!' she said, putting it down on a little table. 'So you're Theresa's friend! Really nice to have you here. I'll make up her old room for you. I think you'll be comfortable there!'

Alastair said, 'Thank you, Ruby!'

I hadn't really expected to find a family retainer and I certainly hadn't reckoned on being given Terry's room. But if it still had some of her stuff in it, there might be a clue amongst it all.

Jamie had come back and looked more miffed than ever. He said sharply, 'Theresa's room? Isn't that a bit – a bit depressing for Fran?'

'No, it'll be fine, thanks!' I said quickly, which earned me a dirty look.

I decided to take the initiative and asked, 'Are you a cousin?' because that seemed the most likely.

'Sort of!' he said shortly. Or, at least, I think that's what he said.

'Jamie is actually the son of a cousin of mine,' Alastair said. 'Rather a complicated relationship. But cousin's a fair enough description. Theresa always called you a cousin, didn't she?'

Jamie grunted and began to hunt through his pockets. A tingle ran up my spine. He'd produced a familiar-looking gold packet of cigarettes. Relax! I ordered myself. It's a popular brand. It doesn't have to mean anything.

He'd looked up and saw how I stared. 'Do you mind if I smoke?'

'No,' I told him, honestly. I wanted to see if he also used a book of matches. But he didn't. He had a lighter, one of those disposal ones in coloured plastic. I resolved, at the earliest opportunity, to hunt through any waste-paper baskets in the house.

We drank our tea and made small-talk about the countryside and then Ruby appeared to take me up to my room.

As I passed by Jamie's chair he murmured so that only I could hear him, 'Don't make yourself too comfortable!'

Chapter Nine

I tried, as I followed Ruby upstairs, to get some idea of the layout of the house. Living in an old house, the squat, had given me an eye for the architectural features of yesteryear. They liked a lot of plaster moulding then, picture rails, arches, that sort of thing.

Even a quick glance round here told me that serious alteration had been made to this house, probably a century ago. To begin with, no one would be allowed to mess with the interior of a building as old as this one nowadays. Even the alterations had a permanent look. The tell-tale clues were the arches which began and never finished, chopped off by a partition wall. The rectangular uneven tracks across the plastering of walls marked where once doors had been blocked up. Other doors, and windows, were the wrong proportions, added later where they were never meant to be. There were hazardous drops in the level of the corridor, so that one suddenly had to step down a pair of flights, just to continue in the same direction. All this in the main part of the house, not the additional newer wing I'd noticed from outside. I mentioned it to Ruby.

'The house seems very old. Has it been much altered?'

'Not in my time,' she said, without turning her head, her broad rump plodding on ahead of me. 'But I do believe that originally it was two houses, back to back, as you might say. This corridor,' here she paused and pointed vaguely up and down the dusky passageway. 'This was where one house met the other, do you see? These doors were knocked through to make the two into one. Doesn't make it an easy place to clean, I can tell you!'

We'd reached our destination. She pressed down a polished brass doorhandle and light streamed into the corridor. 'Little Theresa's room,' she said. 'Can't seem to believe she'll never use it again. You'll be all right, then, will you, dear? Let me know if there's anything you need. The family usually eats at seven, but I'll hold up everything till seven-thirty to give you a chance to settle yourself. There's plenty of hot water if you want a bath.'

I understood immediately why Ruby couldn't believe that Terry wasn't ever coming back. The fact was, she had never left. I knew, as soon as I walked into the room, that Terry was there with me. I even glanced at the white-painted Lloyd Loom chair as though I would see her sitting there, in her grubby knitted jacket, peering at me through spaniel's ears of tangled blonde hair.

But there was one difference. Before, in life, she'd always appeared to resent me. But this had changed. This time, she didn't mind my being there. I had the even stranger feeling that she was pleased, that she knew why I'd come and approved. She expected me to do something. I hoped I didn't let her down again.

Alastair and Terry both pinning their hopes on me.

Ganesh was right. I'd bitten off more than I could chew.

The room itself was pretty, an adored little girl's room. A collection of stuffed toys, all rather worn and damaged, huddled together on the top of a white-painted chest of drawers. All the paintwork was white. There was a floral-patterned duvet and a kidney-shaped dressing table with a matching flounce round it. The curtains matched, too. Someone had taken a lot of trouble with this room. It was very feminine, just a bit twee, and definitely not my sort of scene. In fact it made me feel a tad uneasy. There was an obstinate clinging to childhood innocence in it. Terry, whatever else she'd been, couldn't have been described as innocent.

But that was my view of her. Alastair, in our talk over the Indian meal, had clearly clung to the view that his granddaughter had no idea of the wicked ways of this world. She'd been his little girl, she'd always be that. Death had done him a favour, did he but know it. It had preserved his image of her, always young, always beautiful. Not a human being with failings and the right to make her mistakes, but a doll, preserved in Cellophane so that her clothes would never get dirty and her hair never mussed. My unease increased.

I went to the window. I was at the back of the house here, which meant that, at some point, Ruby and I had stepped through what had once been the dividing wall between two dwellings, and I'd passed from the front one to the back one. It would be quieter here, away from the stableyard which would be a noisy, busy place from early in the day till last thing at night. The view from here was down the garden behind the house, a tangled, unkempt affair of grassy paths, overgrown shrubs, unpruned trees and uncut lawns. Attractive, though. A place to wander in. Kids would like that garden. A great place for hide-and-seek, cops and robbers, all the rest of it. Cops and murderers, even.

Someone could stand out there and watch the house from the shrubbery and no one here be any the wiser. He could stand only some fifteen or twenty feet away, invisible. He might be there now, looking up at this window, watching me.

I moved away. I did feel like a bath and, looking at my watch, I saw that it was already ten to seven. The bathroom had been pointed out to me, just along the corridor. I didn't have much time. A faded quilted dressing gown hung behind the door. I took it down.

There was a Cash's woven nametape sewn in the neckband. *T E Monkton.* It took me back to when I was eleven years old and just starting at the private school my father hoped would educate me into a success. Grandma Varady had sat sewing nametapes just like that into all my new school uniform, even on my socks. They were sticklers at that school for that sort of thing. I wondered who had sewn in Terry's nametapes. From what Alastair had told me of her mother, she hadn't sounded the type to do that, even if she was in the fashion business and ought to be able to manage a few stitches. This old dressing gown reminded me Terry had been at boarding school. Mine had been a day school. I was glad I hadn't been sent away to school. I'd hated the school I was at, but at least I got to come home at the end of each day.

I pulled the robe on and hurried along to the bathroom. I nearly fell headlong when I opened the door, because the bathroom marked one of those unexpected drops in level. I stepped in and plummeted down two steps, saving myself only by grabbing the door jamb and swinging on it, like a chimp. Ruby might have warned me.

The bathroom was the size of a bedroom and probably had once been one. Modern plumbing had come by degrees into this house. I ran three inches of water in a massive old-fashioned cast-iron tub standing on lion's paws. I hadn't time to run more. I'd taken my skirt with me and I hung it up so that the steam would help the creases fall out. Then I clambered up the side of the tub and down inside it into the water. I felt lost in depths of it, and began to wonder just how many people it was designed to accommodate at one go. I hadn't imagined the Victorians going in for merry jinks altogether in one bath. I wished I'd run more water. When I lay back, bits of me stuck up above the tide-line, knees pointed up like twin atolls, my stomach a low flat island which would be submerged at high tide and nipples lurking like coral reefs. I was splashing water over these dry-land bits of me, when I heard a curious noise outside the bathroom door.

It was a low whine accompanied by a faint rumbling. It sounded as though a very small milkfloat was going past. That was unlikely, but that's how it sounded. Then I heard a clang like a metal gate and – and there was no doubt about this – the noise of a lift.

A lift? In a private house? It looked as if the evening was going to be full of surprises.

I felt better as I climbed out of the tub, freshened up. I'd been afraid I'd discover my toes rubbed raw from the hike in the pixie boots but they were all right which was a relief. I couldn't afford to be laid up lame now. I let myself out of the bathroom, wrapped in the dressing gown, and turned to shut the door.

The corridor was dark here. As I fumbled with the handle I heard a step behind me and a hiss of indrawn breath. A man's voice whispered, 'Theresa?'

I turned. It was Jamie, white as a sheet as even I could see in the gloom.

When he saw who it was, colour flooded back into his face. He snapped, 'What the hell do you think you're doing wearing my cousin's clothes?'

'The robe?' I twitched at the dressing gown. 'I didn't bring one with me. It was hanging in the room. I didn't think anyone would mind.'

'Well, I mind!' He sounded really shaken.

I felt I ought to apologise. It must have given him a bit of a shock. I said I was sorry. 'I didn't think anyone would see me. I've only come along the corridor in it.'

'Don't let anyone else see you! The old people – Alastair. The old boy would have a heart attack! Even if he didn't, it would be distressing . . . '

He turned and strode off, still visibly shaken, and leaving me by the bathroom door. Something he'd said had lodged in my brain. Old people? Who else, then, other than Alastair?

Back in my – in Terry's – room, I opened the drawer in the kidney-shaped dressing table and found a jumble of odds and ends of makeup. There was a pink lipstick which wasn't too lurid. I smeared some on and rubbed the pad from a box of pancake powder over my nose, put on the skirt and my tights, polished up my dusty boots with a tissue from a box on the dressing table, and set off downstairs.

But first I went exploring up to the end of the corridor. Sure enough, just round a corner in a little nook, there was a lift. A lift in a private house? An old house, which didn't even have modern bathroom fittings? I thought about getting in and pressing the button but decided that might be thought presumptuous. I went back to the staircase.

As I walked down I could hear voices coming from the sitting room. Jamie was making a speech in a hectoring tone. I could hear Alastair murmuring some kind of protest. Then Jamie said quite clearly,

'But you don't know a thing about this girl! She says she knew Theresa. But we all know what kind of company Theresa kept! This girl is probably some heroin-shooting drop-out from God knows where! We'll be finding needles in the flowerbeds and we'll have to keep everything locked away!'

I thought it was time I made my entrance. I threw open the door and marched in. I was going to make a little speech about how I didn't do drugs and never had, nor was I a thief, so they needn't worry. I wasn't going to make off with the family silver. But before I could speak, a deep but female voice boomed out,

'So you are the young lady my brother met in London?'

I hadn't seen her when I first went in and so when she spoke it gave me quite a start. I fairly leapt round.

I saw a very stately old lady in a ruffled blouse and long skirt which covered her legs. Her hair was white, blue rinsed, and very neatly waved. Her eyes were deepset, but very large, dark and clear with a look which seemed to see right through me. She was in a wheelchair which explained the lift and the noise I'd heard outside the bathroom door. She was also so obviously Alastair's sister that even if she hadn't said 'brother' I'd have guessed it. She had the same large strong features but looked a year or two older than he was.

Alastair had risen to his feet as I came in but Jamie stayed seated, glowering at me. He knew I'd overheard what he'd said about me. He was glad. It saved him having to say it all to my face.

Alastair said courteously, 'Yes, this is Francesca, Ariadne. Fran, dear, this is my sister, Mrs Cameron.' Then, really throwing me, he added, 'This is her house.'

I'm not the sort of person who's easily embarrassed. But I felt really embarrassed then, because if this was her house, I ought to have been invited to stay by her and not by Alastair. I hadn't even known about her and here I was, a real gate-crasher, someone who had just marched in and wangled an invitation. I couldn't meet Jamie's eye. I must appear to be confirming every doubt he had about me.

However, Ariadne said, 'It's very nice to meet you, Francesca. I hope you'll be comfortable in that room. It was Theresa's, as I expect they told you.'

I mumbled 'Yes', adding, 'Please call me Fran. Only the teachers at school ever called me Francesca, so when I hear it, I always feel I'm in trouble.'

'Hear it often?' Jamie asked silkily.

Mrs Cameron gave him a look which would have stopped anyone in their tracks. But she spoke quite mildly. 'Now, Jamie, behave. Fran's made a long journey to come down here and visit us!'

She made it sound as though they'd really invited me and I was doing them some sort of favour so I was truly grateful to her. She must have noticed how red my face had turned. She and Alastair both seemed so nice, it hardly seemed possible that they and Jamie could be genetically connected.

Ruby came in and told us all to, 'Hurry up and get to the table, it's all going cold!'

The meal was traditional, grilled lamb chops with tomatoes, mushrooms and the best mashed potatoes I'd ever eaten, followed by treacle tart and custard. Mrs Cameron didn't have the pudding, only a small piece of cheese. The rest of us fell on the food and ate it all up. I hadn't realised I was so hungry.

We all went back to the sitting room afterwards and the coffee was there on a tray, ready for us. It was getting late so I asked, 'Would it be OK if I rang someone in London and let them know I've arrived? I'll pay for the call.'

'Of course you must ring and let your friends know you're safe!' Alastair said. 'The phone's in the hall.'

I went out into the empty hall. From somewhere in the distance I could hear crockery rattling. Ruby in the kitchen. There was a grandfather clock by the phone, ticking softly. But there wasn't anyone to overhear.

I rang the Patels. Ganesh answered. He said, 'Thank God, I've been worried sick! Where are you?'

I explained I was staying at the Monktons and he needn't worry.

'I'll be the judge of that!' he said grimly 'Look, don't hang around down there. You don't know those people!'

'They're dead respectable, Gan! Don't make a fuss. Look, I can't hang on the phone and run up a bill. I just wanted you to know I'm all right.'

'Fine, but if anything odd happens, anything, right? Get on the phone and I'll bring the van down and pick you up! Otherwise you might wind up very dead and not very respectable.'

'I promise. Cheers, Gan.'

I put the phone down and turned round. I was wrong about not being overheard. Jamie was lounging by the closed sitting-room door with his arms folded. He must have made an excuse to go out, just so he could eavesdrop on my conversation. I was furious.

'Heard enough?' I snarled.

'Who is Gan?' he countered.

'What's it to you? A friend.'

'Male or female?'

'Male. You don't mind asking questions, do you?' I stormed at him. 'How dare you snoop on me?'

'Not snooping, sweetie. Came out for a smoke. Ariadne doesn't like it. Makes her cough.' He produced his Benson and Hedges packet and held it out to me.

'I don't!' I said coldly.

'Got at least one virtue, have you? Lost the rest?' He lit up and grinned at me. 'As for snooping, I bet you're no shy violet when it comes to asking around, Fran! Isn't that what you came down here to do? Or one of the things you came here to do, anyway.'

He'd scored a point over me. I snapped, 'So what?'

'So mind your own business!' he snapped back. 'This Gan, is he a boyfriend?'

'Let's both mind our own business, shall we?'

I'd had enough of him. Besides my relationship with Ganesh was no concern of his.

Jamie and I locked stares but he backed down first. He opened the sitting-room door for me with mock politeness and I stalked past him to join the others.

Mrs Cameron didn't have coffee. There was a glass of water on the tray. Her brother handed her that and she took a couple of tablets with it. I wondered if they were painkillers. Her face had that drawn look which people have when the pain never quite goes away.

Directly after she'd taken the tablets she said she would 'go up now' and bid us all good night. That left me and the two men. Alastair opened a drinks cabinet, but I didn't want anything else. I was fit to drop with tiredness. I said goodnight too.

I was sure that, once I'd left, Jamie would start trying to persuade Alastair to get rid of me. They were going to have a whisky apiece and were clearly settling down for a talk. Alastair had produced a pipe and tobacco pouch and was fumbling with it. I waited hopefully to see if a book of matches would appear, but he got up, took a paper spill from a jar on the mantelshelf and lit it from the hearth. Jamie had produced his Benson and Hedges again together with his plastic disposable lighter. I was beginning to think the match booklet was going to prove a non-starter as a clue.

I wasn't worried about what Jamie would say in my absence. I was sure either of the old people could handle him. I did wonder, if he was such a distant relative, just what he was doing there.

But I was glad they were settled for a while. I knew that if I meant to do my detecting properly, I must lose no time making a search of Terry's room. I was well aware that if there was anything to be found there, which anyone in the house thought I oughtn't to see, tonight might be my only chance of finding it before it was removed.

But I just felt so sleepy. I knew I'd make a rotten job of

looking and probably would miss anything significant. I decided to get up early and search the room before breakfast. I pulled back the curtains so that the early morning sun would wake me.

It was pitch dark outside. Not the sort of darkness I was used to in the city where there's always a glow above the rooftops from the street lights in the main roads. This was just a solid wall of black night. If there was a moon up there, it was behind cloud.

It was so quiet. In the city there is always the faint background hum of traffic or trains. People stay up later and go out at night to have fun. Here it was only nine-forty-five, but Ariadne was already in bed. I was about to go to bed and, judging from the lack of any sign of life out there, everyone else round here, with the exception of the two men chatting over whisky downstairs, had also turned in early.

As a child, Grandma Varady had lived in a village out on the *puszta*, the great Hungarian plain. She'd described nights there as being like black velvet, dotted with the dancing orange fires of the herdsmen who tended the horses and cattle. Perhaps I will go to Hungary one day, if I ever have the money. There are lots of things I'd like to do if I ever have the money. I could seek out my roots. Not that I feel I have roots there. All my roots are in London. I don't even speak Hungarian. I've often wished I had learned when I was a child from Grandma Varady and Dad. Learning languages is a doddle to kids. But I hadn't. Another opportunity missed. The story of my life.

Nothing broke this darkness. We were an oasis in the middle of a sea of nothingness. I wished I could see the stableyard because that must have security lighting. But from here, nothing. I pulled myself together and told myself it was the lack of 'purple' in my eyes. Someone told me once that city-dwellers lack 'purple', whatever that is, and that's why they can't see so well in the dark. Country-dwellers are used to darker nights and manage better. I didn't know if that was true. And I didn't know whether someone who didn't mind the dark, as I did, was out there. The watcher, still watching. I had begun to believe in him by now, try as I might to convince myself he was only the figment of my imagination.

As if I didn't have enough worries about possible events inside the house. I turned the big old key in the door, locking myself in.

I fell asleep as soon as my head hit the pillow. I woke up just as suddenly. I'd no idea what time it was and, for a moment, didn't even know where I was. The moon had appeared to shine through the undraped window and the room was bathed in clear white light. I could see everything now, all the furniture, my clothes lying over a chair where I had thrown them, too tired to hang anything in the wardrobe, the battered collection of stuffed toys sitting on top of a chest of drawers, the pattern on the wallpaper.

And the door handle. I'd sat up and that made me stare directly at the door, and the handle which was twisting downwards ever so slowly as someone on the other side pressed it down. I watched it fascinated. I ought to have been scared but, in a way, I'd been expecting something like this, and in my own mind I was prepared for it. I wasn't altogether prepared for anyone actually getting into the room, but what I'd do then would depend on a lot of things.

Besides, I reasoned, the door was locked.

The handle went up again. The person outside was having a rethink. He – I was pretty sure it must be Jamie – realised I'd turned the key. The floor boards creaked. I thought he'd given up and relaxed.

I was wrong. After a moment or two, he was back. He had only gone to collect a sheet of cardboard. He slid this under the door where there was a sizeable gap. I guessed what was coming next but I watched, just to see if he could do it. The key rattled in the lock. He was pushing it through from the other side. It fell out and landed with a click on his cardboard. He began to inch it back, under the door.

The thing to do was leap out of bed, grab the key before it disappeared from sight and foil him. But I'd left it too late. It slithered under. The lock scraped. The doorhandle turned.

I was naked and didn't fancy offering Jamie Monkton a free show. I jumped out of bed and ran to snatch up the robe, pulling it on, as the door opened.

'Come in, why don't you?' I invited.

He walked in with as much composure as he could muster in the circumstances. He wore tennis shoes, jeans and a sweater. Burglar's kit and keeping burglar's hours.

I wasn't worried how to handle him because I was sure he wouldn't want to start a shouting match which would bring Alastair to investigate. But I did want to know what he was after. It wasn't my body, I was almost sure of that. I must have made it clear how I felt about him. But you never knew with men. They're loath to take no for an answer and big handsome Jack-the-lads like Jamie here can never get it into their thick heads that any girl doesn't fancy them, no matter what she says.

'If you're going to tell me I'm the sexiest thing you ever saw,' I told him sarcastically. 'Skip it.'

'You've got to be joking,' was his reply, expressed with considerable feeling. So much feeling that it really wasn't flattering and although I'd asked for that, I felt quite offended. He went on, 'I wouldn't touch you with a barge-pole with a rubber glove on it, as the saying goes.'

'Kinky!' I said.

He just gave me a disgusted look. 'As far as I'm concerned, you're just a piece of garbage which blew in here off the city streets. God knows what I'd catch. You might even be HIV positive, for all I know.'

'Thanks.' If nothing else, I really knew for sure now he hadn't come here looking for nookie. 'So what do you want?' I asked.

'You've got a confounded nerve!' His tone was almost one of wonder, as if he really couldn't understand it. 'You come here, get yourself invited to stay, run rings round the old people, even old Ruby, help yourself to my cousin's bathrobe, her room . . . anything else of hers you can find, I guess.'

Remembering the lipstick, I felt my cheeks burn and was glad of the moonlit room which meant, I hoped, he couldn't see it.

'I don't creep around at night trying to get into other people's rooms while they're asleep!' I snapped.

He just grinned, holding up the key and waving it slowly back and forth like a metronome beating time. 'Expecting me?'

He still laboured under the misapprehension that I must find him attractive and had been lying here hoping he'd appear. I suppressed the impulse to deny it, because he wouldn't have believed me, and would have taken my protest as proof.

'What do you want?' I asked as coldly as I could.

'A little talk, nice and private. And keep your voice down! I've taken care not to make a noise and disturb the household. You'll oblige by doing the same and not shouting your head off, as if you were still on your street corner!'

'Drop dead!' I invited him. 'You're out of your tiny mind if you think we've got anything to discuss. Right?'

Even in the pale light, I saw him glower. 'Wrong! We're going to straighten out this situation here and now, before you see Alastair at breakfast and get another chance to play little girl lost.'

That made me wild. But I realised that if I reacted to the jibe, I'd be playing this his way. It was time to set a condition of my own.

'You can do all the talking you want,' I told him. 'I'm not saying a word unless you give me that key.'

I saw him debate that with himself. It was no use his being my gaoler if I just heard him out in silence. No situation was ever 'straightened out' that way.

He didn't want it to look as though I'd won a point, however, so he decided to be amused by my request. 'Here!' He chucked the key at me. I just managed to catch it and, I have to admit, to have the small piece of metal pressing into my palm was comforting.

Preliminary negotiations settled, we moved to the next stage. Jamie swivelled the dressing-table chair and seated himself.

I took the Lloyd Loom chair, wrapping the bathrobe round me as much as I could. It was on the skimpy side, being tailored to fit, at a guess, a fourteen-year-old. I held it together over my thighs, but my boobs threatened to pop out the top which didn't quite wrap over enough.

He watched me wriggling uncomfortably and offered, 'If you want to put some clothes on, I'll turn my back. Although I'm surprised you're so shy.'

'Just a moment!' I snarled. I got up, sidled my way over to the bed, grabbed the duvet, wrapped that round me and returned to my chair, swathed like a chief attending a pow-wow.

When I was settled, he cut through any more ceremonial with, 'How much?'

'How much what?'

'How much do you want to go back to London, first thing in the morning? I'll pay a reasonable amount.'

'Why are you so keen for me to go?' I countered.

'Fifty quid? Eighty? That's my final offer.'

The man was determined to insult me. Not just by offering the money, but so little! I wasn't even worth a decent amount! But offering at all? He was worried.

'My, you're really keen for me to go! I'm just a bit of garbage, right? Why should you bother about me? Or have I got you rattled, Jamie?'

He couldn't take mockery.

He leaned forward, his face twisted in anger. 'Listen, you little bitch! Alastair doted on Theresa. Losing her was, for him, like losing an arm or a leg. He's been eaten up with guilt, too, poor old devil, because he believes he could have saved her, as he puts it. No one needs to be a shrink to work out what's going on now. You walked in and, as you no doubt hoped he would, he's seized the chance to work off some of his guilt and loss. But you're not going to play that little game. I won't let you. Think yourself lucky I'm offering to pay you off! I could just as easily take you out of the house and beat you to a pulp.'

I fought the instinct to flinch before the venom in his voice and managed to sit steady and meet his eye. 'You'd have a job explaining that to the old people, as you call them! And you'd have a job explaining to Alastair what you were doing in here if I screamed.'

'You? Scream? When did you last scream to defend your honour?' He gave a hoot of laughter. 'Go ahead. I'll tell Alastair it was all your idea. You invited me here, then tried to get money out of me for sex. He doesn't know you well, but he knows your background. He might just believe it.'

'He still wouldn't consider it gave you the right to be preparing to fornicate under his, or Ariadne's, roof. Alastair's old fashioned. He probably imagines you're a gentleman, Jamie, and somehow I don't think you want to disillusion him. As for money, forget it. I came all the way here after giving it a good deal of thought. I'll leave when I'm ready or Alastair tells me to go – whichever happens first. Either way, you don't come into it.'

He got up, towering over me. 'You're going to be sorry you turned down my offer,' he said. 'I won't make it again. You're a fool, Fran.'

He walked out. The door swung closed behind him, leaving me wondering if he wasn't right.

I didn't think he'd be back. I returned the duvet to the bed and clambered back under it. Thumping the pillow, I tried to settle down, but it was hopeless.

Detectives oughtn't to leap to conclusions. Just because I didn't like Jamie, didn't mean he was a complete villain. Perhaps he was just worried about the old people and wanted to protect them from me. Perhaps he had just come here tonight to offer me money to leave – or try and frighten me into leaving. But the more I thought about it, the more dissatisfied I became.

Was it my being in the house he didn't like? Or my being in this room in particular? If so, was it just sentiment? Or perhaps he feared there was something in here amongst all Terry's stuff, which might give me a clue. If so, a clue to what?

My earlier intention had been to search the room before anyone could tamper with the contents. Perhaps I oughtn't to put that off any longer.

Wide-awake now, I got out of bed and switched on a lamp. I didn't want to make a noise and waken the whole house so crept about barefoot, as sneakily as Jamie had done earlier.

First I went to close the curtains in case anyone *was* outside in the darkness. I could see a black frieze of tree-shapes moving in the night breeze against an indigo sky. The moon slid out for a moment and bathed the garden in a light which bleached out all the colours. My eyes, too, were becoming accustomed to the dark. Now I could see the outline of shrubs and paths. As I watched, the bushes moved, leaves shivering. The wind, I told myself. But I couldn't be sure. Was that a shadow down there, darker than the surrounding ones? Was it long and thin, not round and stubby like the shrubs? Did it stoop and shrink into the box hedges? Was it only shreds of cloud floating by the moon's face? Was I hallucinating? One thing was certain, I was clearly silhouetted against the lamplight.

I dragged the curtains to. This was a time to keep my imagination firmly under control. Detectives had to be businesslike. I began to work over the room systematically, slow and steady.

I tried the drawers of the dressing table. They contained the items I'd already seen there. Make-up, crumpled tissues, a manicure set. A couple of old bus tickets. They were similar to the one I'd bought to come from Basingstoke to Abbotsfield. So Terry had taken the bus into town a couple of times. I had to find something more significant than that. I abandoned the dressing table and turned my attention to the chest of drawers in the corner.

I took all the stuffed animals off the top and pulled it away from the wall. Nothing behind it. Nothing of interest in the top drawer, just a couple of sweaters. Second drawer empty. Third drawer filled with old schoolbooks and paperbacks. I took them all right out, each and every drawer, because there are good old reliable tricks like taping things to the reverse of the frame.

Declan told me that once, when a landlady threw him out of a furnished room he'd rented in Bayswater, he'd tacked a kipper to the reverse of a drawer frame before he left. He'd reckoned it would have stunk the place out before they found it.

But there was nothing behind any of these. I sorted through the books but I didn't see what relevance a bunch of old Agatha Christie's or *An Introduction to the Poets of the First World War* could have to any of this. One of the Agatha's had a picture of Hercule Poirot on the jacket. I fancied he was looking at me in a smug way, clearly thinking my 'little grey cells' were vastly inferior to his. No doubt he would have worked all this out in five minutes, assembled everyone downstairs and pointed at whom? It would be nice to think he'd point at Jamie.

I checked through all the other books to see if anything had been slipped inside, but there was nothing. I put them all away and turned my attention to the wardrobe. No luck. I looked under the bed, under the mattress, under the carpet. I remembered reading a book where the heroine had sewn love-letters into the lining of the curtains so that her wicked uncle couldn't find them. But these curtains didn't have any lining and who did that sort of thing these days, anyhow?

I sat down on the bed, discouraged. It was nearly five. It was light outside now and the birds were singing. Several times I heard a horse whinny. They were already at work over in the stableyard.

I'd forgotten to put back the stuffed toys which all sat on the carpet in a row gazing at me with their glass eyes. I felt that Terry's ghost was sitting with them, fixing me with the same reproachful look. I was supposed to have found it and I hadn't. I still didn't even know what it was!

'It's no use looking at me like that, you lot!' I told the toys. I got up and picked them up in one armful to replace them on the top of the chest of drawers. As I did, one of them crackled.

I thought: if I had to hide something small, I could do worse than hide it in one of these toys. If I couldn't sew it into the curtains like the heroine in that book, I could sew it in one of these animals.

I examined them all one by one. I ran a thumb along all the seams, tugged at their limbs and heads, prodded them all over.

Bingo! It was a blue and white rabbit and when I pushed its tummy it crackled again. Someone had definitely resewn the seam up his back, and not very well. The stitches were big and lumpy. I got a pair of nail scissors from the make-up drawer and snipped away at a few of them. It pulled apart easily and I pushed my fingers inside. They encountered a piece of paper, folded into a tiny wedge.

I eased it out, my palms sweating with excitement. It was two pieces of paper, not one. Two sheets of letter paper folded up together. After all, was this going to turn out to be an outpouring of purple passion? If so, I'd no right to read it.

I flattened it out and took a look at the signature.

It had been written by Ariadne Cameron.

Chapter Ten

I sat on the edge of the bed and placed the two rectangles of thick cream writing paper side by side beneath the bedside lamp. Each sheet was written on one side only and the letter was headed with the Astara Stud's address and dated three years previously. It began, *Dear Philip . . .*

The only Philip I'd heard mentioned so far was Terry's father, Philip Monkton. All I knew about him was that he was absent, unpopular and parted from Terry's mother. Why this letter to him from his Aunt Ariadne should be in Terry's possession and why she thought it necessary to hide it away, I'd only find out by reading it. I quashed any twinge of conscience at reading someone else's private correspondence and scanned it with indecent curiosity. The writing was cramped but clear, an educated hand but an elderly person's. Frankly, few younger people nowadays could write that beautiful even copper-plate. My handwriting looks like the tracks of a drunken spider.

The letter began with a general query after Philip's well-being and some remarks about Ariadne's own none-too-good state of health. Then came the nitty-gritty of the affair.

I am writing, Philip, to tell you that I've now settled details of my new will and Watkins, the solicitor, is drawing it up. I shall be signing it on Monday. The future of the Astara Stud is, naturally, my first consideration.

Until recently, my entire estate was bequeathed to my brother. But the passing of time and the corresponding change in circumstances has necessitated some different arrangement. Alastair is getting on in years, as I am, and would not wish the responsibility. Besides which, the Grim Reaper is as likely to call on him as on me! You have never shown any interest in the stud and you are, in any case, busy with your own very successful career. Neither you, nor Alastair, is in need of money. With the exception of a few personal bequests, therefore, I've left everything to Theresa. By everything, I encompass the stud, all property including this house, and the residue of my estate after the individual bequests and other outgoings have been settled. I've discussed it with Alastair, who thinks it the best decision. I hope you will also be happy with the arrangement. It will leave Theresa a wealthy young woman. That in turn will relieve you of any future financial burden in her regard. In view of your remarriage (which may in time produce a new young family for you), it will be, I'm sure, a great relief.

Theresa has been a little wild of late and caused us some anxiety. But it's to be expected of youth. God willing, I shall hang on for a few more years yet, so that by the time she inherits, she will be older and wiser, ready to settle down. She has a good head on her shoulders and I don't doubt she will cope.

I have told Jamie. He is perhaps disappointed, having worked so hard. But he is not so close a relative and, besides, he is one of those, I feel, who needs direction. Left entirely to his own devices and completely in charge, the temptation to realise a large sum of money could prove too much to resist. He might simply sell up. I don't believe Theresa would do that. She knows how much the Astara Stud has meant to me. It's a pity we are such a small family.

The letter concluded with a few more general phrases.

I sat back and thought hard. There was a waspish touch to the letter which rather appealed to me. Clearly Ariadne disapproved of Philip's remarriage and hadn't the slightest intention that a penny of hers should ever fall into the hands of the new wife and any children she might bring Philip. Poor old Phil had been cut off with the proverbial shilling. It was put more politely than that, but that's what had happened and he'd know it.

The letter was dynamite. It was reasonable to suppose Ariadne had no idea it had come into Terry's possession and that was why Terry had taken such trouble to hide it. How had she come by it? Had Philip shown it or sent it to her? Had she come across it by chance amongst her father's papers and simply taken it? Had Ariadne – or anyone else – ever told Terry openly that she would be heiress to Ariadne's entire fortune? And fortune it certainly must be. Or had Ariadne and Alastair deemed it unwise to tell such a young girl she was going to be very, very rich one day?

I pulled myself together. Speculation was dangerous. Nevertheless I was sure I had a valuable piece of information in my grasp. It opened a whole new aspect on the affair. Janice would certainly like to know about this letter.

I had to keep it safe. Above all, I had to keep it out of Jamie's hands.

Ah, Jamie! I thought. He, too, had been cut out of the will. Too unreliable, Ariadne thought him, though he'd 'worked hard'. Worked here, presumably, at the Astara. Someone must run the place. Neither Alastair nor Ariadne looked up to it. Nevertheless, she believed that given a chance, Jamie would sell up and blow the lot on a couple of years' fast living. She knew him better than I did, and nothing I'd seen of him so far, made me doubt her judgement.

I tried to make the rabbit look as if no one had touched him. I couldn't sew up the slit in his back but I pulled the cloth together and he looked intact. I folded the letter up as it had been in a tiny wad and put it in my purse. Then I thought, that was stupid, because if I had to open my purse in front of anyone, they'd see it. So I took it out again and smoothed both sheets out flat. The book of Turgenev plays was on the bedside table. I eased off the wrapper, smoothed the two sheets round the boards, and put the original wrapper back over it. It wasn't perfect, but it would have to do until I could think of something better.

I went back to bed quite satisfied and fell fast asleep.

When I went down to breakfast at eight-thirty in a clean shirt and jeans, only Alastair was there.

'Good morning, Fran! Sleep well? My sister breakfasts in her room. Jamie might join us later. He's been out since six in the yard.'

I sat down and Ruby bustled in and put bacon and eggs

in front of me. I hadn't had bacon and eggs for breakfast for so long, I'd forgotten what it was like.

'Glad to see you've got a decent appetite!' Alastair said, meaning it kindly. 'It's going to be a nice day. I'll take you out in the yard when you've finished and show you around. Do you ride?'

I confessed I only rode a bike.

'Well, we might be able to find a nice quiet animal to put you up on. I'll ask Kelly.'

I wasn't very keen but thanked him, adding, 'I thought I might try and get to Winchester and have a look round there, if that's all right with you. If I go back to Basingstoke, I'll be able to get a bus from there to Winchester, won't I?'

I'd two reasons for trying to reach Winchester. One was to try and track down the wine bar which had been the origin of the book of matches Edna showed me. The letter was important and suggested a motive for someone. But the match book was my only lead. My other reason was to phone Gan and get his opinion on my discovery. I'd already found I risked being overheard if I tried to phone from inside the house.

'Look at the shops, eh?' said Alastair cheerily. 'Or King Arthur's Round Table? They've got that in Winchester. Fake, of course.' He chuckled. 'They painted up an old table to please Henry the Eighth! I think Jamie is going in later this morning. He can give you a lift.'

My heart sank. I mumbled that I didn't want to bother him.

Alastair said heartily, 'Oh, it won't be any trouble for him!'

I'd have liked to hear what Jamie had to say about it. Later on, I probably would.

* * *

Alastair led me out to the stableyard after breakfast. Jamie hadn't appeared by the time we finished and although I looked for him in the yard, I didn't see him. With luck, he'd already left for Winchester. Perhaps I'd been wrong in assuming he ran the place for Ariadne. Perhaps Kelly, whoever Kelly was, ran it.

It was now about half past nine and clearly, most of the morning chores had already been completed. Lie-abeds like me wouldn't be much use around here where everyone was up with the lark, shovelling muck.

The yard was clean and tidy except for a stack of haybales in one corner. A girl was grooming a chestnut horse, working like a Trojan over it.

'Ah,' said Alastair, 'come and meet Kelly.'

I had been supposing Kelly to be a wizened Irish groom in a check cap. But Kelly was also a first name, a girl's name. I'd overlooked that.

She straightened up as we approached and came round the horse, holding a couple of brushes, one in either hand.

'Morning, Mr Alastair!' she said cheerfully, and gave me a curious look.

She was hefty in build, thighs like hams in tight jodhpurs and a bust like a ship's figurehead bouncing around beneath a knitted pullover. Her sleeves were pushed up over her thick forearms and wrists. She had bright ginger hair, plaited into a single long braid and, as often goes with such hair colour, a pale skin which had freckled alarmingly in the sun. Alastair performed introductions while she rubbed the two curry brushes one against the other to clean out the hairs. She wasn't hostile, but she didn't know what to make of me. She smiled a little uncertainly and when Alastair mentioned finding a quiet animal for me to ride, said, 'I'll see what we can do.'

At that moment a man I hadn't seen before came out of a loose-box and looked across at us. He was middle-aged, stocky and tweed-capped.

Alastair murmured, 'Lundy, I wanted a word with him. Excuse me, won't you?'

He set off towards the other man and left me with Kelly.

I took the opportunity to explain I wasn't all that keen on being turned adrift on horseback.

'If you've never ridden before,' she said, 'we might have a problem finding something suitable for you. There's old Dolly, she might do. She can be a bit moody, though, and on her off days she goes on strike. She'd realise you were a novice straight away and play up. We aren't a riding stables, you see. This is a breeding stud.'

'What are they, racehorses?' The question was probably foolish but not knowing one end of a horse from another, I could be allowed it.

Kelly shook her head. 'No, future competition animals. Show-jumpers, dressage, eventers . . . We've a good reputation. The top riders come here to look over our stock.'

'Who runs the stud?' I asked. 'I assume Alastair doesn't.'

'Oh no, Mr Jamie does. Has done for about six or seven years. Joey Lundy is head stud groom and I'm dogsbody. But Mr Jamie makes all the business decisions and does all the paperwork. Deals with buyers, that sort of thing. He's fantastic – and the only one who can use the computer. The place was starting to go downhill before he came but business has picked up terrifically.'

I thought about this. 'It's been here some time, then, the stud?'

The horse stamped a hoof and looked round inquiringly. Kelly patted its rump. 'The stud's been here thirty years.'

That surprised me and I must have shown it.

'Mr and Mrs Cameron founded it,' she explained. 'Then Mr Cameron died and Mrs Cameron carried on until her accident.'

It was beginning to fall into place. I asked, as tactfully as I could, whether the accident had put Ariadne in the wheelchair.

It had, said Kelly. But Mrs Cameron had continued to run the stud until just a few years ago. Then Mr Alastair, as she called him, had taken over for a few years. Then, as it got too much for him, Jamie Monkton had come along.

All this was fascinating but Kelly, as well as the horse, was getting restless. She wanted to get on with her work. I thanked her, apologised for taking up her time and for not being able to stay and lend a hand, and walked over to where Alastair talked with Lundy.

Lundy shook hands with me. He had a vice-like grip which mangled my fingers and he didn't smile. He looked an ugly sort of customer closer to, his eyes small with yellowed whites, as hard as pebbles. I decided I didn't want to tangle with him. He smelled strongly of horses and, I suspected, whisky, certainly not of cologne . . . but he looked just the sort of person to hang a body up as easily as a butcher does a side of beef. I wondered whether he smoked and resolved to look around the yard for the odd crushed packet or dog-end. But no doubt smoking was forbidden here for fire hazard reasons. All that hay and straw.

I told Alastair I was going back to the house. On the way I saw Kelly had finished grooming the chestnut and was walking towards a loose-box. She glanced across and waved. I returned the salute. She continued on her way, pausing only to stoop and heft a bale of hay which she carried before her into the box. I couldn't have lifted it, at least not without ricking my back. She was the first person I'd met who heartily approved of Jamie. And that might be significant.

I thought that if I was quick about it, seeing that Jamie hadn't yet shown his face, I might get out and catch the bus before he set out by car. But as I walked into my room, I knew Jamie was quicker off the mark than I'd been.

The reason he hadn't been anywhere I'd been that morning was because he'd been in here, going through the room. Don't ask me how I knew it had been Jamie, I just did. Well, it wasn't likely to have been anyone else.

I was mad with myself, aside from being mad with him, because I should have expected this.

My holdall had been turned inside out. I'd left Gan's camera in it and he'd found that and taken out the film. The celluloid reel sprawled in a tangle across the carpet. The film hadn't been used, but he wasn't taking any chances. I wondered what he'd been afraid I might have photo-ed. Himself, perhaps. It was a thought – another one which hadn't occurred to me before. I was a really lousy detective, that was for sure.

The wardrobe door, which I'd closed, swung open. My skirt had fallen off the hanger on to the floor. I picked it up, muttering what I'd like to do to the culprit. He'd even gone through the pockets of the jacket, leaving them pulled out.

He'd also searched around in the dressing table and the chest of drawers. But he hadn't touched the stuffed animals and – when I checked – I found he hadn't touched the Turgenev. The letter was as I'd left it, wrapped round the boards.

He was determined, was our Jamie, but skimped detail. He didn't know how much I knew and he wasn't sure exactly why I'd come down here. He wanted to get rid of me, but not before he found out. He wanted to know exactly what I planned to do. But there'd been nothing he could find to tell him except—

I gave a screech. My notebook! Yes, he found it. He'd sat on the bed and read it, I could see the dent in the duvet. Then he'd thrown it down. I picked it up and looked through it. I hadn't written much. Just a few key words with question marks. 'T's parents?' 'The last quarrel at home?' 'The man Gan saw?' That sort of thing.

It told him enough. It told him I was playing detective and 'playing' was the right word for it. Had I been half way competent I'd have made sure the notebook was where no one could lay his hands on it or at least invented some kind of code instead of writing it out so plainly.

I tidied up, muttering to myself, put on my jacket and went downstairs.

Jamie was in the hall, standing before a mirror and adjusting his cap to a rakish angle. He thought himself quite something, that was clear. He'd also splashed around aftershave, one with cologne scent. It was trapped in the hall, the same cologne scent I'd noticed when Nev and I had come back from Camden, and which had told me we'd had a visitor in the squat.

Reflected in the mirror, he could see me and see the furious glare I was giving him.

'Something wrong, Fran? Sleep badly?' He grinned and turned to face me. 'Bad conscience, perhaps.'

'Tell me about it,' I growled at him.

'My conscience is clear, sweetheart. Alastair told Ruby to tell me you want a lift into Winchester.'

'I don't. I'll go to Basingstoke and find another bus. Alastair had the idea I could go with you, but the bus seems much more attractive.'

'Bad-tempered little tyke, aren't you?' He shrugged. 'It'll take you all day to do it by bus both ways. Anyway, Alastair wants me to give you a lift. We need to keep him happy, don't we?' He gave that nasty grin again. 'Both of us.'

Alastair was walking back from the yard as we left. He waved at the car as it passed him. I waved back, trying to smile brightly.

'That's the ticket!' Jamie said.

He succeeded, as he probably intended, in irritating me. 'You think you've got all the answers, don't you?'

'Not all, Fran,' he retorted. 'Not as far as you're concerned, but I reckon I can make an informed guess.'

'Guess away, it won't do you any good. You wouldn't last five minutes where I come from, let me tell you that!'

'Spare me the tales of your seedy lifestyle, Fran. If you don't like it here, go on back to the smoke. Keep out of our way.'

'You mean, keep out of your way. Why did you search my room during breakfast?'

He glanced at me, eyebrows raised. 'Did I?'

'You know you did!' I snarled. 'Don't play stupid games! Ruby wouldn't need to sneak in. She could go in there openly to vacuum out or something, if she wanted an excuse. It wasn't likely to be Ariadne and Alastair was with me!'

'My, what a clever little sleuth! And that's what all this is about, isn't it? You fancy yourself as the great detective! Notebooks, camera, all the trimmings.'

He was laughing openly. Anything I said would only encourage his mirth so I seethed in silence.

I had another reason to keep quiet. I had remembered how Alastair had insisted on taking me to the yard after breakfast and talking to Kelly about finding me a horse to ride, even though I'd made it clear I wasn't keen on that idea. Was he giving Jamie time to go through my gear? I hoped not. But it was Alastair who'd suggested Jamie take me to Winchester. Was that so Jamie could keep an eye on me?

I was feeling miserable by now. I had trusted Alastair. But that was no attitude for a detective to have. From now on, I trusted nobody.

Jamie planned a cross-country route. We took the lane which had been sign-posted 'Lords Farm' and bumped along over its potholes. There were high banks to either side and no passing place that I could see. Jamie drove at a fair pace and I hoped we met nothing coming the other way, say a tractor.

Even as I worried about this, we rounded a corner and Jamie slammed on the brakes, cursing. I shot forward, was jerked back by my seat-belt, and grabbed the dashboard. The road ahead was filled with cows. They'd just come out of an open gate from a field on the right and were plodding down the narrow track ahead of us.

We inched forward but it was no good in this narrow defile. They'd more or less come to a stop and we had to stop, too. There were hairy bodies and big soulful eyes all around us. They peered in the windows and swung their mud-caked tails against the car's sides which obviously drove Jamie wild.

'Blasted animals! I only had the car cleaned two days ago! Who's in charge of them?'

'No one,' I said, slumping down in my seat. A huge bovine was investigating the door on my side. The creature's breath was misting up the outside of the window as it snuffled around trying, for all I knew, to get it open, and its gungy muzzle left yucky smears on the glass. You could understand Jamie being so mad.

'This is ridiculous!' He was building up a nice head of steam. 'Fran, get out and clear a way through the brutes!'

'What? You're out of your tiny mind!'

He glowered. 'Go on, you wanted to visit the country. All you have to do is chivvy them a bit. They'll move for you.'

'Forget it!'

'They're making a helluva mess of my car! What's the matter, afraid of them? I thought you were the tough sort. All that streetwise guff. I wouldn't last five minutes where you come from, eh? Well, you don't seem to be making out very well here!'

I know I should have ignored it. I shouldn't have risen to it. He was needling me into doing something I shouldn't. I knew all this but I still took the bait. 'All right!' I slipped off my jacket, I couldn't afford to get that messed up, and got out of the car.

I had a job even to get the door open because the cow which was so interested in it wouldn't move. I kept pushing the car against it, even though Jamie got very hot under the collar about making the mess on the outside worse, and at last the beast backed off.

Once I was out, I was marooned. The cows were all around me. There was one thing even I knew cows did a lot of, and it made me very careful where I put my feet. Have you any idea how large a cow is? It's enormous. Like a tank. You do not argue with a cow. It does what it wants and goes where it likes. Not only did they show no sign of moving out of my way, but they seemed to find me some sort of interesting novelty and they all wanted a closer look at me. I was pinned against the car by steaming, smelly, dribbling monsters.

It was a matter of honour, although it felt more like a matter of life and death. I couldn't get back in the car. Jamie'd never let me forget it. So I edged my way round to the front and clapped my hands.

Zilch. The cows ignored it but the flies which had been buzzing around the cows, now began to investigate me. I flailed my hands around my head to drive them away. When I looked behind me, Jamie was watching through the windscreen, laughing himself sick.

That made me mad. I slapped the nearest cow on the back. 'Come on, Bluebell, you've got to help me! It's you and me against him!'

It turned its head and gazed at me. There was a black and white one coming up on my left with a moody look in its eye. I had to act as though I was in charge and hope the bluff worked.

I gave a piercing whistle and yelled, 'Move it!' Cowboy stuff.

Funnily enough, they did try to move. They shuffled a bit sideways, bumped into one another and started lowing noisily. It was pretty clear to me by now, because I stopped panicking, that something up ahead was preventing them from going on. I shoved my way between them, and sure enough, just around the next bend was the farmyard and the gate was closed. They were all waiting for someone to open it.

I unhitched it and dragged it open. The cows began to plod through at quite a brisk pace and mill about in the yard.

Then a dog ran out and started barking at me. I was trapped between gate and cows so there was nothing I could do but get behind the gate as the dog ran up and began growling at me. The cows didn't like it much, either, and one of them put down its head and made a little rush at the dog. The dog backed off very sensibly and joined me behind the gate.

We were both rescued by a man in a pullover and gumboots who came out of a barn and shouted, 'What's the matter?'

'The gate was closed, they couldn't get in!' I yelled back.

'Oh, right!' He began to push the cows around and they ambled off towards the barn and disappeared inside. The cowman or farmer or whatever he was came towards me. He was a big fellow, built like a brick barn. He rested broad, calloused worker's hands on the top rung of the gate.

'Who're you, then?' he asked.

His voice was educated and he didn't ask it impolitely, just curious. The dog wasn't bothered about me now it saw the man didn't object to me. It sat down waiting, with its tongue lolling out.

I explained about being stuck in the car behind the herd. I'd just finished when there was a beep of a horn and we both looked round to see that Jamie had driven up as far as the gate and was gesticulating to me to get back in the car.

The farmer's friendly manner cooled distinctly. 'With him, are you?' The tone of his voice told that he'd met Jamie before and had much the same opinion of him I had.

'I'm not with him!' I denied. 'I mean, yes, he's giving me a lift. But that's as far as it goes. I'm staying at the Monktons as Alastair Monkton's guest.'

'Oh, yes?' He looked at me thoughtfully. His face was sunburned and he had rather nice blue eyes with little crow's-feet lines at the corner which crinkled up as he squinted into the light, studying me. He was wearing one of those tweed caps they all liked so much, but from beneath it escaped a mop of untidy light brown hair. There was something about him I liked. He was looking at me as though he rather liked the look of me, too.

'My name's Fran Varady,' I decided to establish the acquaintance on a formal basis. 'Is this Lords Farm? I saw the signpost further back.'

'Nice to meet you, Fran. Yes, this is Lords Farm. Welcome to it, if you take my meaning!'

He grinned and wiped one of his shovel-hands on the front of his sweater before offering it. 'I'm Nick Bryant.' It was pretty obvious he was deliberately ignoring Jamie who was grimacing at me and signalling I should rejoin him.

I tried turning my back on him. Jamie opened the car door and leaned out, yelling, 'Fran! Are you getting back in this car or are you going to stand there all day gossiping?'

At that point Jamie saw my companion and said loudly and sourly, 'Oh, it's you, Bryant? Your wretched beasts have made a mess of my car!'

'My, my,' said Nick amiably. 'So they have. You'll have to get the brush and bucket out, Jim!'

'Don't call me Jim!' yelled Jamie. He made an obvious effort to regain control. He looked at me and then back at Nick. 'And how is Mrs Bryant?'

Jamie's gaze slid maliciously towards me again as he asked. Damn, I thought. The nice ones are always married.

'She's fine. Old Mr Monkton and Mrs Cameron, they all right?'

Jamie told him ungraciously that they were, and as there appeared to be no more family members left between us to inquire after, conversation came to a natural end for the time being.

'I'd better go,' I said apologetically to Nick. I wanted to talk to him more than ever, now that it was clear he knew Jamie and the Monktons. 'Look,' I said quickly in a low voice. 'This may sound odd, but I need to come back and talk to you some time.'

Jamie squawked, 'If you don't get back in this car straight away, I'm going to drive on without you!'

'I've got to go!' I urged.

Nick glanced at Jamie in no very kindly way. 'Watch yourself!' he muttered. 'And come back any time you like.'

I got back into the car. Jamie was scowling and now he sniffed the air and said, 'You stink of cows! Open the window!'

'So, whose fault is that?'

He drove off with a squeal of tyres. I waved farewell to Nick who raised a hand in salute and set off towards the barn and his charges.

'Shouldn't have thought Farmer Giles there was your type!' said Jamie sarcastically.

'At least he was polite!'

Jamie muttered. After a little while he spoke again, quite calmly, sounding almost polite himself.

'Look, Fran. We can go on like this, sniping and snarling at each other or we can put our cards on the table, come clean. Last night was a mistake, I admit it. But we really do need to talk.'

He must have thought me simple. It was obvious that he'd realised that I'd made a possible ally in Nick Bryant and he was reformulating his own tactics accordingly. After trying to bully and frighten me, he was trying being nice to me.

'I don't have anything I want to talk to you about,' I told him. 'And there's no reason I should. Alastair came to see me in London. He sought me out. I returned the compliment. It's between him and me.'

Jamie gave a hiss and we swept round a corner. 'It concerns me too. I *am* family. In fact, I'm the only family they've got left apart from Alastair's son, Phil. I feel responsible for the old people. I am responsible for them. I carry the responsibility for everything round here and I take it seriously!'

I didn't want to give away anything I'd learned from the

letter. I asked casually, 'Why doesn't Phil run the stud?'

Jamie hooted. 'Phil? Hates horses, for a start! Anyway, he doesn't get on with Alastair. Alastair is a loyal old bird. He tries hard to welcome Phil whenever he shows up. But it's not easy. If you'd been here when they both – I mean Phil and Marcie, Theresa's mother – turned up for the funeral, you'd have understood. Talk about undercurrents. Of course, they divorced some time back and Phil's remarried. He didn't bring his second wife. I wondered whether he would. But even Phil didn't have that much nerve.'

That had given me a jolt because I hadn't realised that Terry had been buried in the time between Alastair coming to the flat and my coming down here. I said so and asked, rather miserably, whether she was buried in the churchyard at Abbotsfield. I'd sat there to eat my tuna sandwich and perhaps she'd been only a few feet away beneath the turf. I didn't tell Jamie that last bit.

He said she was buried there which made me feel pretty grim. The police had given permission, he said, especially as it was an interment and not a cremation. He didn't explain that but I guessed the reason. They could always dig her up again if they wanted to.

'What's Terry's mother like? Marcia, you said she's called?'

He nodded. 'She's a gold-plated bitch but I like Marcie. To be fair, she was genuinely cut up at the funeral, so was Phil. I don't want to give you the wrong impression about that. But neither of them could wait to get away afterwards. Phil back to the States and Marcia back to the new man in her life.' Jamie gave a short laugh. 'She probably doesn't trust him enough to leave him for too long.'

I gave it a minute or two, then asked, 'And that's the whole family, there's really no one else?'

'Not a soul.' We had reached a junction with a more important, busy road. Jamie drew up, waiting for a break in traffic.

'I don't want you down here asking questions. Ariadne's sick and Alastair is far more frail than he looks. Theresa's death knocked the stuffing out of both of them. Don't go making things worse.'

'I'm not thick!' I told him crossly. 'I'd be tactful.'

'I won't! If I find you've been talking to either of them about it, I'll break your grubby little neck!'

We didn't talk again until we reached Winchester. He parked in a public carpark near the town centre.

'If you want a lift back with me, be here at four. If you're not here, I'll assume you've caught, or mean to catch, the bus.'

'I'll take the bus!' I told him.

I hadn't put my jacket back on again when I'd got back in the car after talking to Nick. Now I picked it up. Loose change I'd kept in my pocket for phone calls spilled out and rolled over the well of the front passenger seat, most of it disappearing under the seat itself.

I cursed and scrabbled for it, watched impatiently by Jamie. I pushed my hand under the seat feeling for the coins and my fingertips touched something else, small, pyramid shaped and with a familiar, but momentarily unidentifiable, dusty feel to it. Instinctively, I scooped it up with the coins and withdrew my clasped fist and shoved the whole lot into my pocket.

Jamie slammed his door and locked up. We parted at the top of the road and I was able to look at my hand, the one I'd reached under the seat. The fingertips were smudged with blue colour. I reached in the pocket and took out the small, pyramid-shaped object.

It was an end of blue chalk. One of Squib's chalks, I was almost sure. And it tied Jamie into the squat along with the cologne smell and the fact that his general description was a match to that of the man seen by Ganesh. The chalk scrap must have been trapped in his shoe or maybe he'd worn trousers with turn-ups that day. Three things were too much for coincidence.

So it *was* you, Jamie! I thought and it was followed by a even more alarming thought. The note I'd stupidly made about 'the man Gan saw'. If I was right and Jamie was the man, that put Gan in real danger. It was quite possible Jamie was a killer, and I had kindly suggested his next victim. Supposing the next not to be myself.

Chapter Eleven

Winchester came as a surprise to me. I hadn't expected it to be so busy but it was obviously on the tourist trail. The pavements were crowded, the streets blocked with traffic. There were a number of expensive boutiques and any number of places to eat or drink. Seeking out one wine bar wasn't going to be so easy as I'd imagined.

Now that I had even less reason to trust Jamie, I had to make doubly sure he wasn't following me. In these crowds it wouldn't be difficult to do it unobserved. I dodged in and out of pedestrians, nipped across the road between cars risking my neck and getting a fair amount of abuse, and eventually decided that I must have given him the slip, if he had tried to trail me. If he saw me now, it would be just bad luck.

I couldn't remember the exact name of the wine bar on the match packet, but it had been something to do with ecclesiastical architecture, Crypt or Vault or Cloister, something of that sort. There had been a thumbnail sketch of a gothic arch on the packet. I decided it would be located centrally, where most tourist trade was. But it took me a while, trudging round (it goes without saying, that everyone I asked turned out to be a visitor). Eventually I stumbled across it in a narrow side alley. It had to be the one, not only because I was exhausted and there had to be a limit to the number of watering-holes in this place, but it was the only one so far with a name remotely in the category I sought. *Beneath the Arches*, it was called. I'd been near enough.

I went in. It looked old, and certainly had arches. It was nearing lunchtime and already pretty well packed out. I squeezed into a corner and ordered a glass of red wine and a cheese sandwich, that being the cheapest thing on the menu. There was an ashtray on the table and, propped in it, an identical packet of matches to the one Edna had so proudly displayed. I pocketed it. I was in the right place.

I wasn't quite sure how much further on that would take my investigations. The sandwich and wine arrived. As I ate, I reviewed what I'd learned so far and came up with several theories, each of which I discarded two minutes after deciding that it must be the right one.

I paid my bill and went along to the Ladies Room. I discovered, as I'd hoped, that just outside the toilets was a public pay-phone and, thank goodness, one which took coins, not cards. I rang the Patels.

As bad luck would have it Mr Patel answered and, although I asked him to fetch Ganesh, he started talking to me himself. I didn't want to upset him, but I did try and get across to him that public phones eat money and I didn't have that much loose change.

Eventually he fetched Ganesh when I was nearly out of coins.

'Listen!' I ordered Ganesh before he could start. 'I'm nearly out of money so can't waste time. I'm in Winchester in the wine bar which advertised with that book of matches Edna had.'

'What's this about a book of matches?' Ganesh asked. 'You told me it was a cigarette packet.'

Down the line came a tremendous crash of falling crates and voices upraised in dispute, somewhere behind Ganesh. I hoped he could hear me.

'There was a match book, too! Don't interrupt, Gan, please! I told you, I'll run out of money. I believe the man you saw in the street is down here and his name is Jamie Monkton. He's also the one who dropped the cigarette packet. I feel sure of it. And Gan – Jamie knows you saw him, so take care! He's a nasty bit of work. I've also found something else, a letter. I think all of this has to do with a will.'

Someone at Ganesh's end of things had now begun bashing some metal object with a hammer. 'Will who?' he shouted.

'A will!' I yelled. 'Testament! Saying who gets your goods and chattels!'

'Now you've found all this out, come back!' He didn't sound particularly impressed.

'Can't. Met someone today who might be able to tell me more. A farmer.'

'A what?'

'A farmer—' Peep-peep-peep. 'I've got no more money.'

'Fran—!'

The phone went dead.

I had a cup of coffee in order to collect more coins in change. This time I rang through to the police station and asked for Janice. They tried to stall me and find out what I wanted first, but I wasn't having that. I told them, either I'd talk to Janice or no one. If she wasn't there, I'd call back when she was.

Eventually they put me through to Janice.

'Fran!' Janice's voice, howling down the line, nearly dented my ear-drum. 'What on earth do you think you're playing at? You had no business to leave town without telling me of your intention and giving me your new address! Where are you?'

I'd learned something from my call to Ganesh. I told her I only had a few coins, so would she ring me back? I gave her the number of the pay-phone and hung up.

The phone buzzed almost at once. I picked it up. 'Janice, listen. Don't yell. You can yell at me when I get back to town.'

I told her what I'd told Gan and explained why I was in the wine bar, that Edna had shown me the match book, and had probably seen the same man as Ganesh had spotted. 'I smelled cologne in the squat when I got back that evening. Didn't I tell you that? Jamie Monkton uses a very similar cologne.'

She stopped shouting and became quiet and business-like. 'Fran, you could cause us all a tremendous amount of trouble. You're intelligent enough to know you shouldn't be blundering around in police investigations. As for the letter, you're not authorised to remove anything from that house and, if you do, it's theft.'

'I've got this gut feeling it's the key to the whole thing!' I was beginning to get exasperated. She really didn't have to be so dense. Was someone else listening in at the cop-shop? Yes, I thought, someone probably was.

'We need more than your gut feelings, Francesca. I've already got more than enough cause to charge you with obstructing the police. As for Jamie Monkton, I can't proceed on your flimsy evidence. The baglady's testimony is useless. She's certainly not mentally competent. As regards the so-called identification of an after-shave scent, all those male toiletries smell more or less the same. Tom uses them. They all stink.'

'Not like this one! How is dear old Tom, anyway?' I asked because she was being awkward and I wanted to needle her.

'Still being a shit. He wants to move back in.'

'You're going to let him?'

'He wants to rebuild our marriage. He's made an appointment for us to see a Relate counsellor.' She changed her tone. 'However, this is nothing to do with the matter in hand! I can't go by a smell you think you can identify. This isn't some party-game. As for a vague description made to you by your chum, Ganesh Patel! *You* didn't see this mystery man in the street! You don't know it was Jamie Monkton. You're *guessing*, Fran. That's all.'

She was beginning to give me doubts. I could be wrong.

'The chalk . . . ' I said desperately.

'Fell out of your jacket pocket with the coins.'

'It didn't! There was no chalk in the pockets, I know that!'

'Prove it. You can't. Look, I'm engaged on police work here, not kid's games. If you want to play detective, go and buy yourself a box of Cluedo.'

'But I may have put Ganesh in danger!' I bellowed into the receiver. Two women passing by on their way to the loo gave me alarmed glances.

'*You're* in danger,' Janice said silkily. 'You're in danger from *me*! Get yourself back here to London *pronto*? Understand? And no nonsense. If you try any more playing at detectives, I'll see you really are charged with obstructing police inquiries!'

'Stuff your police inquiries!' I said. Her ingratitude had really got to me. I hung up the receiver before she could reply.

I stomped back into the wine bar in a rage and it was nearly my undoing.

Jamie was there, sitting at a table, making a start on what looked like steak and kidney pie and talking to a pallid man in a business suit. The pallid man was sipping soup and looked as if he was making it his meal. A bottle of mineral water stood by his glass. Perhaps he had an ulcer. He looked depressed enough. Although having to sit in a cramped room full of tourists, watching Jamie munch through pie and chips and knock back half a bottle of plonk by himself would depress anyone. They must have come in just as I left to find the phone. It was a bit of luck because if I'd been at a table, they'd almost certainly have seen me. Equally, if I hadn't gone to find the phone, or if Mr Patel hadn't kept me talking, I might have left and missed them. But there he was, Jamie, large as life. This must be one of his favourite eating spots.

I wished I had the nerve to go back and call Janice again. Because here was another coincidence, and even she would have to admit it was one too many. If Jamie hadn't dropped that match book, someone else had, who'd been in this Winchester wine bar. The likelihood of that was nil.

I hadn't asked Jamie his reason for coming to Winchester

today, in any case it was unlikely he'd have told me. Clearly it was a business lunch of some kind. I wished dearly I knew what they were discussing. Jamie was doing most of the talking, the pallid man pushing the spoon around his bowl and crumbling a bread roll in gloomy silence as he listened. I hoped that Jamie was so intent on getting the point across that he'd be oblivious to all else around him. I had to walk past their table to get out into the street.

I edged past, trying not to look at them. If someone is looking at you, you sense it. I got to the door without anyone calling after me and glancing back, saw that Jamie was still talking away, and refilling his own glass at the same time. Even from the back, the man in the business suit looked depressed.

I reached the street. Safe. I set off. I had some shopping to do.

I went to the nearest chemist and bought a new film for the camera. I wanted to get back to Astara Stud quickly and the bus services would be too slow. Nothing for it but to hitch.

I was in luck. A middle-aged woman stopped for me, concern on her face as she peered at me through the window.

'My dear? You really shouldn't be doing this. It's very dangerous. Anyone could offer you a lift, just anyone!'

'I wouldn't go with just anyone, honestly,' I told her. 'And I wouldn't be doing this if I wasn't desperate. My boyfriend dumped me here. We had a quarrel. He'd pushed me out of his car on this road and just drove away and left me. I don't even know where I am. I need to get to a place just outside Basingstoke, Abbotsfield.'

She was shocked. 'How callous! What an irresponsible young man! Really, there can be no excuse for that sort of behaviour!' Indecision showed on her face. 'I don't normally give lifts to hitch-hikers. One never knows . . . '

She peered at me again and I tried to look innocent, harmless and hard done by.

'I suppose it's all right,' she said. 'I'm going near Basingstoke. I can drop you on the main road in.'

I hopped in the car before she had time to change her mind, thanking her profusely.

'What did you quarrel with your young man about?' she asked as we drove off.

This was a tricky one. But I noticed a mascot swinging from the key-ring holding the ignition key, a little plastic dachshund.

'He made me get rid of my dog,' I said. 'He wouldn't let me keep her.'

'What!' The car swerved. Perhaps I shouldn't have picked on something she felt so strongly about. 'What did you – he – do with your dog?' she demanded sharply.

I had to get this right. 'A friend took her. A good home, I know that. In the country and everything. It's not that any harm's come to my dog. It's just, I had to give her away. I was very fond of her. She used to sleep on my bed. That's what he didn't like. He said he was allergic to her. I don't think he was. He just wanted rid of her, you know.'

She sniffed. 'Couldn't you have compromised? Bought a dog basket?'

'He wouldn't,' I said firmly. 'He said she had to go.'

'What sort of dog is she?'

One can over-egg the pudding. I turned my eyes from

the dachshund mascot, bobbing on the key. 'Part retriever, part German shepherd.'

'Goodness, wasn't she rather large to sleep on your bed? I must admit, dear, I can see why your young man might object.'

'But she'd slept on my bed since she was a puppy,' I said pathetically. By now I'd begun to believe all this myself. I felt quite aggrieved.

She sighed. 'I know how it is with animals. It's so easy to spoil a puppy. Such adorable little creatures. Bad habits set in. And if it grows into a really big dog . . . You were rather unwise, dear.'

'Yes, I know that now,' I said meekly. 'I won't make the same mistake again.'

'You're going to get another dog?'

'Yes. And another boyfriend.'

'Perhaps you should get a smaller one,' she said thoughtfully.

'Yes, this one was a body-builder and it was hopeless arguing with him.'

'No, dear, I meant a smaller dog!' She frowned. 'A body-builder? Sharing a bed with a German shepherd-retriever cross and – er – and you? It really couldn't have been very comfortable.'

She had been intending to stop just outside of Basingstoke, but in view of my predicament, as she termed it, and the distress I was obviously feeling over parting with my dog, she insisted on taking me right into town and putting me down at the bus station.

'You are sure you've got money for the bus fare, dear?'

I promised her I had. I was feeling as guilty as sin by now, but the deception was in a good cause. Plus she drove off with the glow that comes from having done a good deed.

I jumped on the Abbotsfield bus, reckoning that I'd be home before Jamie. I knew he planned on leaving Winchester at four that afternoon and I knew how long it had taken us to drive there. Arithmetic told me what time to expect him home. And sure enough, there was no sign of his car at the Astara Stud. I looked in the garage. Empty. I'd cut it fine, but I'd done it.

I wanted to know who else was out and about in the vicinity because I didn't want to be observed when Jamie got back. I walked over to the stableyard. It had a sleepy late afternoon look about it. I wondered where Kelly was. As I stood at the entrance, looking around, a horse whinnied inside a loose-box near at hand, a male voice cursed it, and a moment later, Lundy came out.

He saw me and stopped. 'Can I help you?' The words contrasted markedly with the way they were expressed. The only help he wanted to give me was help on my way out, probably with his boot.

I told him, I was looking for Kelly. I didn't particularly want to find her and get into conversation, because I hadn't to miss Jamie's return, but I had to give Lundy a reason for hanging about there.

'She's not here.' He came closer and instinctively I took a step back. That was a bad tactical move because it encouraged him to think he'd got me at a disadvantage.

'I want a word with you,' he said ominously.

'What about?' I stood my ground although my instinct was to run. He couldn't harm me, I told myself. I was Alastair's guest.

'What are you doing here?'

'Looking for Kelly,' I repeated nonchalantly.

'Don't mess me about!' He pushed his ugly mug at me. 'I don't mean in the bloody yard. I mean here – at the Astara. What's your game, eh?'

'I'm a visitor!' I said grandly.

He spat to one side, expressing his opinion of that.

'Ask Mr Alastair if you've got doubts', I added.

His pebbly little eyes bored into me. 'Clever, think yourself, I dare say. Well, you be careful. I got my eye on you!' I was aware of it, both of them.

I chose to say nothing, largely because I couldn't think of anything. He seemed satisfied he'd delivered his warning and turned away, going back into the loose-box and cussing the unfortunate horse in it again.

I scurried away and hid in the tangle of buddleia bushes by the garage. The sweet smell was overpowering and reminded me of honey. There were any number of butterflies fluttering about the mauve blossoms and perched on them. A small bird of a kind I didn't recognise (I can only recognise sparrows) was darting about catching the butterflies and gobbling them up. I felt sorry for the butterflies but admired the agility of the bird.

He hunted. I waited, camera ready. I was a hunter, too.

Jamie didn't stand me up. He turned up about ten minutes later than I'd estimated. Perhaps he'd waited a few minutes in Winchester, at the carpark, to see if I was coming home with him. The car swept up to the garage and he got out. I took a snap of him closing the car door. Then he walked round the car to inspect the muddy marks left by our encounter with the cattle. That gave me a chance for another couple of shots. Then he looked back down the drive which gave me a beautiful profile.

I was getting careless by then and must have moved because the buddleia rustled and Jamie's head snapped round. I held my breath. But my little friend, the hunting bird, chose that moment to fly out. Jamie relaxed and set off towards the house, whistling.

I waited a few minutes and then followed, entering the house through the kitchen. Ruby was there, mixing batter. A woman I'd never seen before was tackling a pile of ironing in the corner.

'Hullo, my dear,' Ruby said. 'You came back with Mr Jamie, then?'

'No, I came earlier. I was finished in town.' I glanced curiously at the other woman, who hadn't looked up from her work or shown any sign she was aware I'd come in.

She was a shapeless sort of person, looking rather as if she were made of dough. Her straight grey hair was parted centrally and pinned back with a couple of kirby grips and she wore the sort of wrap-over apron I hadn't seen in years.

'Mrs Lundy,' said Ruby, nodding towards the woman. 'She comes over a couple of times a week to give me a hand.'

Assuming Mrs Lundy would acknowledge the introduction, I said hullo. But she carried on ironing without any reaction at all, although Ruby had spoken in a normal voice.

'Is she, I mean, is it—'

'Joey Lundy's wife,' Ruby anticipated me. 'They live in the bungalow, behind the yard.'

She still spoke quite normally, clearly audible to the

ironer, and still Mrs Lundy took not the slightest notice. She paused long enough to sprinkle water from a small basin on to her ironing, then carried on. It occurred to me she might be deaf.

As tactfully as I could, I lifted a hand, tapped my ear and raised my eyebrows.

'Oh, no,' said Ruby cheerfully. 'There's nothing wrong with her hearing. She's not one for chat. A bit slow on the uptake, but a good worker. Makes ironing a real art.'

An awful thought struck me. 'Kelly, the stablegirl, she's not their daughter, is she?'

'Oh goodness, no!' Ruby chuckled. 'She just lodges with them.'

Lodging with the Lundys must be about as comfortable as a Tudor traitor would have found himself in the Tower.

Ruby tapped her spoon on the edge of the mixing bowl. 'There, that's done!' She began to spoon the contents over a Pyrex dish part-filled with stewed fruit. Then she handed me the wooden spoon with batter smeared on it. 'Do you want to lick it clean, or are you too grown-up for that? Theresa, when she was little, she always did hang round to scrape out the bowl. And when she grew older, too!'

'I'm not too grown-up!' I took the spoon. 'I used to do this when my grandma made cakes. She used to make a wonderful chocolate cake.'

Ruby put the dish in the oven and began to clean the worktop. Mrs Lundy folded a pillowcase, put it on a pile of finished ironing and took another from a daunting pile of dampwash. Ironing might be an art with her but it appeared to have turned her into a zombie, or living with Lundy had. But she wasn't deaf and, despite what Ruby had said, she might understand more than expected, enough to repeat anything I said to her husband. On the other hand, it was a good opportunity to talk to Ruby. I just had to gamble.

'Ruby,' I said carefully, 'you know I shared a – a house with Terry, Theresa, don't you?'

'So they told me.' Ruby straightened up, expelling breath with an 'ouf!'. Her face was kind but her eyes were sharp. 'Was she in some kind of trouble, poor lass? Because seems to me, she must have been.'

'I don't know, Ruby. If she was, she didn't talk about it. Honestly, I'd tell Alastair if I knew.'

'She was headstrong,' Ruby shook her head. 'Mr Alastair and Mrs Cameron, they both doted on her. But she made life very difficult for them. They're getting on in years, you see. They couldn't cope with the sort of problems young people have. Not today's youngsters, anyway. It was beyond them. They wanted to help, but they didn't know how, most likely.'

'What sort of problems?' I asked guilelessly. Mrs Lundy splashed water and ironed on accompanied by a faint hiss of steam. It was a pity she was there, but it couldn't be helped.

Either Ruby had remembered Mrs Lundy or she wasn't going to gossip with a stranger, and that's what I was. 'Bless you, don't ask me!' was all she said.

She wasn't going to say any more. I thanked her for letting me finish the batter and walked past Mrs Lundy out of the kitchen. As I passed by her, she looked up. I had a fleeting impression of a flat, vacant face, heavily coated with face powder. But no lipstick or any other effort to make herself presentable. It seemed odd. I smiled at her and she looked down again at once, but not before I'd seen a momentary reaction in her eyes. Not any return of greeting. But fear.

I had plenty to think about as I went upstairs to my room. Once there, I set about adding to my photographic record. I snapped a view of the room, showing the toys on top of the chest of drawers. Then I snapped the rabbit, showing his back pulled open the way I'd done it to find the letter inside. Then I snapped both pages of the letter, although probably the writing wouldn't come out well enough to be legible, and returned it to its hiding place inside the book wrapper.

When I'd done all that, even though the film was far from finished, I ran it on to the end, took it out and rolled it up in some cottonwool from the make-up drawer. I wrote a note to Ganesh, telling him to get it developed by the one-hour service locally and take it straight away to Inspector Janice, because it would back up what I'd told them both on the phone. I especially wanted him to study the photos of Jamie to see if he could identify him as the man he saw hanging around the house the day Terry died.

When I'd done all that, I stepped out into the passage.

There was a gasp. Mrs Lundy was outside the room, standing by my door. I'd opened it suddenly and she stepped back, looking so confused and frightened that I automatically assured her, 'It's all right!'

She shuffled her feet. 'I been to the linen cupboard,' she said.

'Lots of ironing.' There wasn't much I could say to this poor creature.

She still seemed to think I was going to scold her for being in the wrong part of the house. 'I come upstairs to take it all to the linen cupboard,' she repeated. The flat face looked into mine, then she turned and hurried away.

But not before I'd had time to realise the reason for the layer of face powder. Beneath it, her doughy features were puffed and bruised. Joey Lundy was a wife-beater.

I walked slowly down to the kitchen. I knew I was very angry but I felt quite calm. Ruby was at the table, enjoying a quiet cup of tea and looking at cookery pages in a woman's magazine, waiting for her own fruit sponge pudding to be ready to come out of the oven.

'Joey knocks his wife around,' I said. 'Why doesn't anyone here do anything about it?'

She looked up from the brightly coloured pictures of perfect cakes and complicated desserts. 'One can't come between husband and wife,' she said reproachfully.

'Rot.'

She flushed. 'Mr Alastair has spoken to Lundy about it. Lundy's a good worker.' She leaned forward. 'Would you want Mr Alastair to sack Lundy?'

'I'd throw him off the premises!' I told her.

'Yes, you would. And then what? He'd blame that poor creature, take it out on her. She wouldn't leave him. Wherever he went, he'd drag her along with him. Away from here, it'd be worse. Mr Alastair, he keeps an eye on things. There's a limit. Lundy knows it. Leave it to Mr Alastair, dear.'

She was right, of course. Lucy had been bright, articulate, young, and she'd found it hard to break away from a violent husband. Mrs Lundy was never going to be able to make the break. Here the situation was controlled. It was the best to be hoped for. I hated to admit it but there didn't appear to be any way out of it.

I asked Ruby if she had any stamps and an envelope, preferably a strong manila one. It didn't have to be new. I could strike out the old address.

She did better. She found a little padded Jiffy bag. I bought two first-class stamps off her. Out of her sight, I put my letter to Ganesh and the roll of film in the bag and stuck it all down with Sellotape. Then I slipped out of the house and grounds and walked down the road to where I'd noticed a brick postbox by the roadside.

I posted the package with relief. Once it had left my fingers and fallen down inside the postbox, there was no way Jamie could get it back, even if he found out about it. It was on its way to Ganesh and, all going according to plan, from Ganesh to Inspector Janice.

As a detective, I was improving. I was at least getting a bit more organised.

Tomorrow, I'd tackle the farm. I knew now what time the cows pitched up for milking and I'd avoid that. I hoped Nick Bryant would be there at other times. I had an idea I could talk to Nick . . . and to his wife as well, of course.

There was an hour to go before dinner. I didn't want to go back into the house just yet and, anyway, there was something else I had to do.

I didn't really want to do it, but it had to be done. I walked on down the lane, turned into the main road and set off back to Abbotsfield. Now that I knew the way, it didn't seem so far. It took me a quarter of an hour. I went straight to the churchyard and sought out the corner where recent tombstones indicated the modern burials were taking place.

Theresa's was very recent and they hadn't got a stone fixed up yet. Instead there was a white-painted wooden cross with just her name and the date of her death. There were flowers on the grave, fresh ones.

It was getting late and the churchyard deserted and very quiet. Occasionally a car went past up on the road but it made little impression here. It was timeless. The white cross had slipped slightly to an angle. The soil was settling. That was partly why there was no stone yet. It seemed to be suggesting a time limit to me, as if I had to get this all worked out before the soil was finally packed down enough for the permanence of a marble slab. Right now the grave was neither one thing nor another, neither new nor established but half way in between. Unfinished business, I thought.

A curious feeling ran over me, as if I weren't alone. It felt as though someone stood behind me, had perhaps been behind me for some time, watching. I whirled round. But there was no one.

'Imagination again, Fran!' I said aloud. I glanced at my wristwatch. Time to go back.

'Don't worry about it, Terry,' I said to the white cross. 'I'll find out who it was and I'll see he gets what's due him!'

I hoped I could keep the promise. Even more now, because I couldn't do anything about Lundy's treatment of his wife. So many things were wrong and I had to be able to put at least one of them right.

Moreover, I was remembering the bruises on Terry's

body to which Janice had drawn my attention. Until this moment, I'd been concentrating on Jamie Monkton. But Joey Lundy liked beating up women.

Chapter Twelve

The best-laid plans of mice and men are apt to gang awry. My plan didn't go wrong but it did get unexpectedly delayed.

I was down promptly for breakfast the next morning, meaning to make an early visit to the farm. Alastair was already there, reading his newspaper, and after a few minutes Jamie walked in. This meant that at least he wasn't searching the room again and messing up my few possessions. We said 'good morning' to one another and exchanged frosty looks, just so that each of us knew nothing had changed.

'What are you planning today, Francesca?' Alastair asked, emerging from behind his newspaper. Jamie looked up from his chipolata sausages, mushrooms and tomato.

'I'll walk into the village,' I said casually. 'Just to take a look around.' I saw no reason to tell them I'd visited Terry's grave the previous evening.

'You'll need some different footwear,' Jamie said with a grin. He was remembering how I'd hobbled along the verge at our first meeting.

'Pair of wellies around somewhere, I dare say,' Alastair said. 'All kinds of odd pairs in the back porch. One of them should fit you.'

It was a good idea. I said I'd take it up. Jamie was still watching and listening and I wasn't sure whether he'd guessed I meant to go to the farm. He couldn't stop me, even if he did, but I didn't want him to know my plans, even so.

I went down to the kitchen after breakfast and dried up the breakfast dishes for Ruby before asking her about the boots.

'That shouldn't be a problem,' she said. 'Now, let's see—'

A bell above the door jangled. She glanced up. 'That'll be Mr Watkins, come to see Mrs Cameron. He said he'd be early but it's a little bit too early, I fancy. She mightn't be ready yet. Just wait a moment, will you, dear?'

She bustled out into the hall, heading for the front door.

Watkins was the name of the solicitor mentioned in the letter. It might be a coincidence, but I fancied not. I sneaked out after Ruby and lurked in a dark corner of the hall, behind a hat stand.

'Perhaps you'd just like to wait a moment, sir,' Ruby was saying. 'I'll run up and see if she's ready. Or Mr Alastair is about somewhere.'

'That's quite all right,' said a dry, gloomy voice. 'I'll just wait in the sitting room here, and if Mrs Cameron isn't ready to see me yet, I'll go and take a look round the stableyard.'

Ruby's feet pounded up the stairs. Faint shuffling and breathing told me Watkins was moving towards the room into which Jamie had shown me when I'd first arrived.

I peered out. The hall was empty, but the door to the sitting room was open. I crept out cautiously and peeked round it.

He was standing by the fireplace, his back to me, rearranging the photographs in the mantelshelf in a pernickety and, I thought, interfering way. Even from that angle he was clearly recognisable as the pallid man who'd been lunching with Jamie.

As bad luck would have it, he glanced up, having got everything neatly set out, and looked in the mirror above the mantelshelf. I jumped back behind the door jamb, but too late. His pale features froze and he turned.

'Who is that? Come!'

I trotted into the room as nonchalantly as I could. 'Sorry, I didn't mean to disturb you. I was coming in here to read the paper.'

He glanced round, sparse eyebrows lifted. 'I don't see any newspaper.'

'Alastair must still have it. He had it at breakfast.'

Watkins was still eyeing me with deep disapproval. Perhaps it was his normal expression. 'Are you the young woman who has come down from London?'

Jamie must have told him about me. I confirmed it.

He said, 'I see!' but looked puzzled. 'Have we by any chance met before?'

I told him I didn't think so, but I was cursing. Jamie may have been too intent on his lunch and his argument yesterday to notice me, creeping out of the wine bar. But Watkins was the sort of person who missed very little and no doubt owned a mental filing system. Lodged somewhere in his subconscious was a little card with my face on it and sooner or later, he'd connect it with a location.

'You seem, forgive me, familiar.'

'A lot of people look like me,' I said feebly.

'Indeed?' He had doubts about that. He took a watch from his waistcoat pocket and consulted it. His time was money.

'I am rather glad to have the opportunity of a word with you.' He tucked the watch away. 'You're not in a hurry?'

I began to explain that I was, actually, just on my way out. But there was something about his dry pale face and professional manner which overruled objections. I told him I had a few minutes to spare.

'Good, perhaps you'd be so good as to close the door.'

I closed it and perched on the edge of a chair. He had the kind of presence which made it impossible to sit back and relax.

He took his own seat in a cautious way, as if not sure the chair mightn't buckle beneath him, and hitching up the knees of his shiny trousers to reveal wash-shrunk wool socks and an expanse of dead white shin. He placed the tips of his bony fingers together. 'I understand that you were one of the young people who shared a house in London with Miss Monkton?'

'With Terry, yes, I did.'

'The police have spoken to you, of course.' His manner suggested I'd be the first one they'd haul in for questioning.

'Several times,' I assured him.

His features twitched. 'The police are aware that you are here?'

Thanks to my phone call to Janice, I was able to assure him heartily that Inspector Morgan was fully aware of my movements.

He tapped the tips of his fingers together and looked at me without speaking for so long that I began fidgeting.

'Were you a very close friend of Miss Monkton's?'

'I was one of the people closest to her in London,' I told him and had a fair idea it was true.

He didn't like that answer. The tapping hands were stilled. He pressed his thin lips and pinched his nostrils. 'Did she talk to you about her home? Her family?'

Fully aware he couldn't check on anything I told him, I said, 'Quite often.'

I wondered whether he played chess. He was watching me as if contemplating his next move and assessing my likely counter-move. I got the impression he'd be a good chess-player. He said delicately, 'However, I gather you told the police that you knew very little about Theresa.'

Yes, he'd be a good player, good at finding the opponent's weakness, while giving nothing away himself.

'Nothing relevant to her death, no. We thought she was out of the house, when in fact she—' I gestured at the ceiling. 'To think that we sat there while she – she was hanging there. To find her like that.'

'Yes, yes!' he said curtly. 'Quite. The whole affair is most distressing. She didn't, at any time, speak of the future? She didn't, for example, speak of the Astara Stud itself?'

'In the vaguest terms,' I said.

He wasn't sure what to make of that and sat staring at me with his gimlet eyes sunken in bags of unhealthy white skin like badly cooked poached eggs. 'And your own personal interest in this matter?'

I was spared having to find an answer which would satisfy this modern Torquemada by a welcome tap at the door, followed immediately by the appearance of Ruby.

'Mrs Cameron's ready to see you now, Mr Watkins. Would you like to go up?'

Watkins rose to his feet – I swear his knees creaked – and gathered up an ancient scuffed leather briefcase which he must have bought when he first joined the firm as junior clerk. He gave the barest nod and walked out.

'Right,' said Ruby, expressing no surprise at having found me there, tête-à-tête with the solicitor, when she'd left me in the kitchen. 'Let's see about those boots, shall we?'

Since she hadn't asked any explanation, I didn't offer one. I followed her back to the kitchen, feeling that I hadn't handled the interview very well. Watkins was suspicious of me. When he succeeded in placing me, as he surely would, he'd tell Jamie immediately.

Jamie would be furious to think I'd been spying on him. But he might not, I thought, be in a position to do much about it. It all depended on what he'd been discussing with Watkins. Watkins, too, might have something on his conscience. He wouldn't be the first solicitor to bend the rules and I had a funny feeling that's what had been happening in that wine bar yesterday.

I inspected the collection of ageing gumboots in the back porch to which Ruby directed me and found a smallish pair which I suspected had belonged to Terry. Ruby joined me as I was putting my foot alongside one of them, to check the size. I didn't put my foot inside it because of the cobwebs festooning it. If there's one thing I cannot stand, it's putting my foot into a shoe of any sort and encountering some kind of beastie. In the squat it happened fairly frequently. Woodlice mostly, and spiders with the occasional silverfish, my particular phobia because they slithered around so quickly. I'd got into the habit of tapping my shoes to see what fell out before I put them on.

Ruby was bearing a dreadful-looking waxed jacket 'in case it rained'. I accepted it gratefully, hoping that between the elderly Barbour and the wellies, I'd at least look more the part than I had yesterday.

I took the boots outside and bashed them against the wall to dislodge the creepie-crawlies. As I suspected, they were full of dust and dead spiders. When I was sure they were uninhabited, I tugged them on. They were on the tight side, I discovered, as I clumped round the front of the house. A blue Mercedes was parked there. Watkins's clients must pay well. Then, as I paused to admire it, another car drew into the drive and pulled up by me. The door opened and a blonde got out.

She was in her forties and wore an outfit even more out of place than mine had been when I'd first arrived here. It consisted of a short black skirt and sheer black tights, both a mistake because although the pins were shapely, the knees were on the knobbly side. Her fitted jacket was tangerine in colour with large ornate gold buttons and looked expensive. On her feet she had slip-on flatties, presumably for driving. The rest of the outfit called for stiletto heels. Her thick shoulder-length hair had faded slightly but she wore it brushed back and secured with an alice band. I guessed she dieted as a way of life. Her face was good-looking, but had that pared-down look. Her expression was sharp. In every way she so resembled Terry that I knew this must be Marcia Monkton.

She was giving me equally close scrutiny. 'Who are you?' she asked without preamble.

Since it was the second time I'd faced interrogation by a stranger that morning, I was quicker with my reply.

'Fran Varady,' I told her, adding, 'You're Terry's mother.'

She blinked. 'Theresa's mother!' she corrected icily.

'Sorry. We called her Terry because we never knew her as anything else.'

'Who are *we*?' Without pausing for breath she answered her own question. 'You're one of those awful drop-outs from that ghastly house!'

Even making allowances for her distress, I felt that was gratuitously rude. I tried to explain I, at least, had always struggled to hold on to some kind of a job, and the house had been our home and we'd liked it.

She shrugged. 'Perhaps it suited you and your friends. From what the police told us, it wasn't the sort of place I like to think my daughter lived in.'

I thought it was time to express some form of condolence. But it didn't go down well.

'Sorry? So you bloody well should be, all of you! God knows what went on there—'

There was a crunch on the gravel behind us and I turned. Jamie had appeared. 'Marcie?' He started forward. 'We didn't expect you!'

'Hullo, Jamie.' She walked past me and they exchanged a chaste kiss. 'I'm on my way down to the coast to catch the ferry. I thought I'd better call in on my way. Make my peace with the old chap. We had a bit of a barney when I was here for – for the funeral.'

'He understood, Marcie. Don't worry about it. He knows you were upset.'

Jamie looked from the Mercedes to Marcia and back

again. Her arrival had complicated things. He was no longer worried about me. Marcia was a bigger threat to upsetting whatever little applecart he and Watkins had been stacking in the wine bar. But he was putting a good face on it.

'You're staying for lunch, Marcie?'

The tangerine shoulders twitched. 'Can't, I'm afraid. I'm already pushed for time. All the same, I thought I ought to see him.' She glanced at me. 'What's she doing here?'

'Wouldn't we all like to know that,' Jamie sneered.

Suspicion, probably her natural expression, increased on her narrow features. 'Isn't that Sammy Watkins's Merc?'

'He's come to see Aunt Ariadne.' Jamie was looking uncomfortable.

'Are you pulling one of your stunts, Jamie?' She wasn't one to mess around. She was asking the question I'd have liked to put.

Jamie wasn't going to answer it in front of me. 'Family business, Marcie!' He jerked his head angrily in my direction.

'You carry on without me,' I said. 'I'm just going for a walk.'

It was working out rather well. If Jamie was busy with Marcia, he wouldn't have time to follow me. But Marcia had her own ideas.

'You're not going anywhere,' she said unpleasantly, 'until I've had a word with you!'

I was about to decline this pleasure when I recollected that a detective wouldn't pass up an opportunity to talk to her. I wouldn't get another. Jamie mumbled that he'd go and tell Alastair of Marcia's arrival. He set off indoors with such alacrity that I wondered whether he also meant to try and get the message to Watkins. It left Marcia and me facing each other like a couple of wary cats about to squabble over ownership of a stretch of pavement.

'What happened?' she demanded.

'I don't know.'

'Don't give me that crap!' she retorted. 'You must know. You were there!'

'Not when—' I broke off just in time. This was, after all, a woman whose daughter had been murdered. 'Not when it happened,' I finished.

Her features had become even more pinched with anger and the resemblance to Terry had increased. It gave me a strange feeling. It was like seeing Terry there, before me.

'How did she ever get to be there, with you?'

'She needed a place to live,' I pointed out.

Her voice rose to a wail, part rage and part, I realised, despair. 'She had a place to live!' She flung out a well-manicured hand to point at the house behind us. 'She lived here!'

'She didn't want to live here.'

'Why not?' she shouted furiously.

'Why ask me? Why didn't you ask her when you had the chance? Did you ever ask her if she wanted to be dumped here?'

'She wasn't dumped!' she practically spat.

'Wasn't she?' I ought to respect her grief, but she was a street-fighter, underneath that designer chic, and I recognised the type. She'd give no quarter and any attempt at niceness on my part, would be seized on as a weakness.

'You know nothing about it!' She'd moved slightly

towards me and looked as if she'd attack at any moment. Those manicured nails were long and pointed.

I got ready to get out of the way. 'Perhaps I know something about being dumped. My mother walked out on me. I know how it feels.'

She paused, looking me over, and thinking it out. When she spoke next it was more calmly but the voice was still steel-hard.

'I don't owe you any explanation. My marriage broke up. I needed to earn a living. I was offered an opportunity to get back into the only job I know. I couldn't turn it down. Theresa was well looked after. Her father paid the fees to send her to a good school. When she left school, I tried to get her to take up a place at art college. She turned it down and ran off somewhere. We were worried sick, and after a lot of trouble, found her and brought her home here. She did it again. More than once. On one occasion, she went traipsing across country with a band of hippies. I tried talking to her but I couldn't get through. She just seemed hell-bent-on—' Her voice wavered. 'She seemed hell-bent on her own destruction. We should have seen it coming, what happened.'

I realised that what she was telling me was true, but only partly so. There was a lot more she wasn't telling possibly because she considered it none of my business. She was right: it wasn't. But perhaps she was leaving out anything which didn't fit with the picture she was anxious to paint of a caring parent, who'd done her best, everything she possibly could in difficult circumstances. She wasn't painting that picture for my benefit, but for her own. She needed to believe it. How could I blame her for that? What would I have done in her place?

I still didn't like her but I'd begun to feel some sympathy for her and it hampered my side of the conversation. I mumbled something to the effect that not every runaway finished in such tragic circumstances.

She picked up the words as though they represented a foreign phrase she hadn't heard before, rolling them experimentally round her mouth.

'Tragic circumstances. Which, of all the utterly wretched circumstances, would you dignify as *tragic*? Her death? The waste of her talents? The miserable life she was leading in London? The sordid acquaintances who dragged her down with them – eventually to her death?'

She waited, as if I'd give some precise answer to this unanswerable list of woes.

I would've objected vigorously to the last, but I was beginning to understand Janice's dread of speaking 'to the family' in cases like this.

I floundered with, 'She didn't see her lifestyle the way you see it. The house in Jubilee Street was home to us and we were comfortable enough there. Terry was really very capable and knew what she was doing.'

She cut me short with a look which was pure vitriol. She didn't want to hear any of this.

I'd been a fool to try. Her grief had put her beyond reason. I compounded my errors by repeating my regrets. Since I didn't now know what to call it, I ended lamely with a reference to 'the accident'.

'Accident? You call it an accident?'

She was back on the offensive. 'My daughter was *murdered* and I'm by no means convinced that you and the others in that squat weren't involved! More to the point, right now, what are you doing here?'

'Alastair—' I began weakly.

'Don't bother!' She moved in close. 'Just pack your bags and get out! You're trouble. You were part of Theresa's problems and you've brought yourself and your street manners with you down here. Alastair and Ariadne don't need that. My hope is that, one day, someone will catch up with you. If not the police, then someone else, the sort of person who caught up with my daughter. My daughter's life was wasted. She could have done so much. No one would miss you. You're nothing.' Her voice rose again, wavering, 'Why couldn't it have been you? Who would have missed you? Why had it to be my lovely daughter? It's so unfair!'

She turned on her heel and almost staggered. I stepped forward to grab her elbow and steady her but she gave me a fierce look and made her own way indoors, head high.

Jamie had reappeared at some point during our talk. I hadn't noticed exactly when. He must have overheard a good part of it. He met my gaze now and chuckled.

'You think you're so tough, don't you, Fran? But you can't begin to match Marcie.'

'Get lost!' I told him. I tramped off towards the gate in my borrowed wellies, hearing him laugh behind me.

I knew he was wrong. Marcia was finding out she wasn't as tough as she'd thought she was. None of us is.

Chapter Thirteen

I had to admit that the conversation with Marcia had shaken me. Not just by her grief or her expressed wish I'd been the one found hanging from the light fitting. It had disturbed the way I'd felt until then about my own mother's desertion. Perhaps I'd also judged her too quickly. When she went, she must have had good reason. Much as I'd loved my father, obviously my mother and he had troubles which couldn't be resolved. If she hadn't taken me with her, possibly it was because she, like Marcia, had needed to begin her life over again from scratch, without the encumbrance of a young child, or had had nowhere to go remotely suitable for a kid.

Then I thought about Lucy and her children. Even reduced to living in the squat, Lucy had never once envisaged parting from the children. No matter how bad things got, she'd told me once, the three of them stayed together. No way would she ever let the kids be taken into care, and, as for the father having them, 'I'd kill him first!' she'd said. I think she meant it.

It was complicated and, to be fair, not having faced a similar situation myself, I was in no position to judge. But

I liked to think that, like Lucy, I'd have hung on to my children. Or at least tried.

The dog saw me coming as I walked into the farmyard and ran towards me. It barked once, then sniffed at my feet and wagged its tail. It was nice to be recognised. I hoped Nick remembered me and that he'd asked me to call.

He came out of a barn at that moment, dressed in grubby dungarees and wiping his hands on an oily rag. He looked more like a mechanic than a farmer.

'Old truck's just about given up the ghost,' he said. 'Have to be replaced. I just about manage to keep it ticking over from day to day. Nice to see you again. Have a good trip into town?'

'Fine, thanks. Nice place. I'm a true townie, as you can probably see.' I waved a hand around. 'Never been on a farm before in my life.'

'No? Really?' That seemed to puzzle him. He glanced at the buildings around. 'Not much to see. This is a working farm, not someone's tax dodge. Come inside and we'll have a cup of coffee or something. I could do with a drink.'

I hesitated. 'I don't want to trouble your wife.'

'Wife?' He looked surprised.

'Jamie asked after Mrs Bryant . . .'

'Oh, my mother!' he grinned. 'Not married. Haven't yet found a woman willing to take on the farm! It's a tough life.'

I hadn't counted on his mother and felt apprehensive. Respectable old mothers and I seldom saw eye to eye. I was glad I wore the boots and Barbour. At least I wouldn't be teetering along in my pixie boots.

As I followed Nick to the house, I tried to prepare myself. I imagined 'mother' as rosy-cheeked, in an apron, baking scones after a hard morning feeding chickens.

Nick took off his boots at the back door, using an ancient wooden device which I guessed was a 'boot-jack'. I followed suit and the pair of us padded indoors in our socks. The floor was stone-flagged and uneven, and the kitchen had an untidy, cluttered and comfortable look. Nick led me into an equally untidy sitting room where a woman sat at the desk, muttering to herself as she stabbed at the keyboard of a home computer. She swivelled round as we entered.

Nick's mother was surprisingly young. She had long hair, wore jeans and an old sweatshirt and I liked the look of her on sight.

'Hullo,' she said. She didn't seem surprised to see me. 'Do you know how these things work?'

'Sorry, no.' After all, I'd been living in a house which didn't even have electricity. When would I get to learn about computers?

'Never mind.' She sighed.

'This is Fran,' Nick told her. 'She's come to have a cup of coffee. She's staying with Mrs Cameron.'

'Penny,' she said.

I wondered if that was what she meant to charge me for the coffee, but even in the country things couldn't be that cheap.

'My name is Penny,' she explained. 'Let's go into the kitchen and I'll put the kettle on. I'm fed up with this machine. I want to get out of sight of it for a bit.'

Nick made an excuse and went off to clean up. In the kitchen, Penny rattled about in a cupboard and apologised for not having any proper coffee. 'Only this stuff in a jar. I've got to go shopping this week. I never seem to get any time. That machine in there—' She jabbed a finger viciously towards the distant computer. 'Is supposed to save me time. It takes me four times as long to do anything! Nick says I'll get the hang of it. Wish I felt sure.'

It seemed she didn't bake scones, either. She produced a tin, looked inside it, grimaced and said, 'And I haven't got any biscuits, either. You must think I'm a lousy hostess.'

I assured her I didn't need biscuits. I really appreciated being offered coffee. 'It's not just a social call. I'm – I'm on a sort of fishing trip, for information.'

I had decided that with Penny it would be best to be quite straightforward.

She clanged the empty biscuit tin back on the shelf. 'What about? Not computers, I hope? Farming? Ask Nick.'

'Do you and Nick farm here alone?' I asked, curious. I'd always thought farms abounded with dairymaids and shepherds and so on. I said as much and she burst out laughing.

'Not these days! Everyone has to be a Jack of all Trades! There's only Nick and myself and Jeff Biles who comes when an extra pair of hands is needed. He knows more about farming than either of us. My husband bought this place and had ideas.' She hesitated just fractionally. 'He didn't live to carry them out.'

'I'm sorry,' I said awkwardly.

'Yes, it was a pity. I wish I were more use. I can run the book-keeping side of it. Farming is a business, after all.

I'm used to that, dealing with the financial side of things. I've got a little antiques shop in Winchester. The trouble is that I have to spend a lot of time there and can't always be here.'

'Antiques?' I asked. That sounded interesting.

Very quickly she said, 'It isn't grand. It's more what once upon a time would have been called a junk shop. But I try to keep it looking decent and it doesn't do so badly, especially in the summer. The tourists, you know. A lot of people want a souvenir which isn't modern tat. They're happy to buy what, frankly, is often Edwardian tat. However, the deal leaves everyone happy.'

I remarked that it must be difficult, keeping the place stocked. She said she went to house sales, of which there was usually one somewhere in the area most weeks.

'Remember,' she said, 'I'm not after valuable stuff. Just old photo frames, odds and ends of china and ornaments, scrapbooks, period clothes which are still in good condition. Best of all, if I can get them, are toys. But old toys of all kinds are highly collectable and the dealers usually get there before me. There's a strict cash limit on how much I can pay for my stock because I have to price competitively when I sell on.'

'Who runs the shop when you're not there?'

'A friend. She's actually a partner who put up some of the original money. But she doesn't do any of the business side of it. She says she's got no head for it. She likes being in the shop, meeting people and selling things. Only she's been in poor health recently so I've had to spend a lot of time in town. I've hardly been out here at the farm at all the last few weeks.'

Penny looked glum. I realised she did have a lot of

worries and I felt badly about coming here and with the intention of pestering them about Terry.

But Nick's mother obviously wasn't one of those to brood on things. She dismissed her personal problems with a brisk shrug. 'I can offer you some tips on how to run a business on a shoestring!' She grinned at me.

Nick came back just then looking much more presentable, in fact, really rather handsome, in a clean sweater and jeans. We all sat round the table, very cosy. I didn't know why he had so much trouble finding a girl interested in the farm and in him. I was beginning to get quite interested myself.

'Everything all right at Mrs Cameron's?' Nick asked.

'That's it,' I said. 'I don't know.' They were watching me. Obviously they were both pretty bright and I felt I might as well tell them everything. One thing I'd already realised was that Nick didn't approve of Jamie Monkton. So I wasn't taking too much of a risk confiding in them. The fact was, I was too much on my own out here. I needed allies of some sort. The Bryants looked as if they were the sort of people to have on my side.

'You know the circumstances of Theresa Monkton's death?' I began and they nodded, both silent, both watching me and waiting.

'I knew her in London,' I said. 'We all shared a squat. We called her Terry, not Theresa. She preferred it.'

Penny stirred and sighed. 'Poor girl,' she said. 'She really had rotten luck. I used to urge her to call by here sometimes, when she was at home, just to have a chat and – I don't know – get away from the house. But she was a funny girl. She never came here. I don't know whether she was shy or it was just that she didn't want to talk. She was very – closed up. It was as if she was frightened to talk about herself.'

Nick asked, watching me, 'Did she talk much to you, Fran?'

I shook my head. 'No, it was just the way your mother described it. She didn't talk to anyone.'

I plunged in and told them all about the squat, the discovery of her body, Alastair's visit to my flat. I didn't tell them that just possibly Ganesh had seen Jamie hanging about outside the house before Terry died, or about the cologne smell or the scrap of chalk in the car. Nor did I tell them about Jamie's searching my things or my turning over the room and finding the will.

They were both of them clearly upset when I described finding the body. Penny looked quite pale and Nick got up to make some more coffee. He probably noticed that his mother was taking it badly and I hoped he wasn't annoyed with me for upsetting her. I apologised because I hadn't come to ruin anyone's day, just to find out if they could help.

Penny leaned across the table and patted my hand. 'Don't worry about it, Fran. Obviously it's not pleasant to hear about it. But it must have been even more unpleasant to be the person who found – who found her.'

Nick clashed the coffee mugs together and refilled them from the kettle.

'Don't take this wrongly,' he said, over his shoulder. 'But before we met you – well, we had a different idea about the people Theresa knew in London. We'd gathered she was living in a way Alastair and Ariadne Cameron wouldn't approve of. We imagined you all as down-and-outs. Obviously, you're not, weren't. Highly normal, I'd say.' He gave me a wry smile which quite made my heart hop.

'I can imagine what you've heard,' I told him. 'Believe me, she was safe enough with us! *We* didn't kill her!'

This time they both apologised, speaking at the same time. That made me feel I'd been rude so I apologised again and we all apologised together until it became funny and we all started to laugh.

When we stopped giggling, Penny said in a contrite voice, 'It's not something to be light-hearted about in any way, that's the worst of it. It's wicked and terrifying and – and it makes me so angry. What on earth happened to her? It must have been just—' She gave a gesture of despair. 'We can't imagine how awful it must have been during the last moments of her life.'

Nick grunted and buried his face in his coffee mug. I guessed he was upset too, but he had a different way of showing it. Strong, male, keeping it to yourself stuff.

They probably didn't know the details, how poor Terry had been knocked half unconscious and strung up, perhaps aware of what was happening, perhaps not. It was better they didn't know.

I just nodded. 'I want to know what happened to her. Alastair was nice to me and said to get in touch, so I did and here I am. I didn't know about Ariadne until I get here. I didn't know it was her house. It was embarrassing, I can tell you. I really wouldn't have barged in the way I did if I'd known about her.'

'Ariadne's fine!' Penny assured me. 'Just a bit formal in her ways. She's in a lot of pain most of the time. She hurt her spine some years ago in a riding accident. She was a very active woman before that. Being stuck in that chair must be unbearable for her.'

'Someone mentioned it to me. I understand her husband had died before that, so it must have been a terrible blow to find herself disabled as well.'

'It was more than that,' Nick said unexpectedly. 'She took the fall from his horse, Cameron's. The horse's name was Astara and they called the stud after him. Cameron had bought the horse with the intention of breeding good competition horses out of his bloodline. The horse was worth a packet to them. After Cameron died, Ariadne used to ride Astara around the place. Then she had the bad fall. You can understand it if she's a bit tetchy sometimes.'

'Basically she's a very kind-hearted woman!' Penny insisted. 'She gave a home to Theresa when her parents split. And to Alastair, come to that. He had nowhere to go so she took him in. He ran the place for a while for her, but he wasn't the ideal person. She could've taken on someone more efficient. Then there's Jamie. He was at a loose end until he came to the Astara Stud. Admittedly, he's turned things around there and made a go of it.'

'She took me in, too, in a manner of speaking.' I was thinking about it. Some people took in stray animals but Ariadne Cameron seemed to collect stray human beings.

At the mention of Jamie, however, a distinct *frisson* had been felt in the atmosphere.

I trailed a lure. 'I have to admit I don't like Jamie much.'

'Jamie Monkton cares about no one but himself!' Penny said crisply. 'I've known him since he was a boy. He was a little stinker as a kid and he's not improved.'

Nick was watching me carefully. 'Fran? Do you think Jamie had anything to do with Theresa's death?'

'Nick!' his mother exclaimed, shocked.

'Oh, come on, Ma! Fran's investigating. She told us so. And she's come all the way down here so she doesn't think the killer is in London, does she?'

He was right. I didn't. But this wasn't the moment to start making accusations I couldn't back.

Penny was going to argue about it. 'They were cousins, Theresa and Jamie. Near enough cousins, anyway. I know he's pretty well capable of most things but he wouldn't – not *family*, surely?'

It hadn't struck me that Jamie would let a relationship put him off his stride. But it would be undiplomatic to take sides in an argument between Penny and Nick. I stuck to my part of the conversation.

'I feel the more I know about Terry, the nearer I can get to *her*, then the nearer I get to the answer to all this. That's why I'm here. Alastair told me she'd run away several times before – before the time she came to London and ended up living with us. On one occasion she went off with some New-Age travellers. I know that's true because she did mention it once.'

The Bryants looked at one another uneasily.

'It didn't last long,' Penny said. 'A few months. Just during the summer. When the weather turned chilly and wet she came back. Her health had quite broken down, I think she was quite ill. I used to see her sometimes, wandering up and down the lane. She was as white as a sheet and I was worried she'd pass out somewhere and fall into a ditch, lie there for ages with no one any the wiser. Both Nick and I took her home a couple of times in the old pick-up after we'd found her wandering about. Her manner was always very odd, most unfriendly and withdrawn. I don't think either Ariadne or Alastair could cope with it. Poor child, she needed help, but there was none to be had at the Astara.'

I sipped at my coffee. 'She had parents. They could have been asked in to help. I met Marcia just this morning.'

'She's at the Astara? Theresa's mother?' Penny and Nick spoke together. Nick whistled.

'She doesn't lack nerve! There was a hell of a bust-up with Alastair at the funeral.'

'I think she's come to make up.' In fact, interesting though it had been to meet Marcia, I'd dismissed her from my investigations. Since her divorce and Terry's death, Marcia had no interest in what happened to the Astara Stud. But someone else did. I asked, 'What about Philip Monkton, Terry's father? If Terry was ill, shouldn't he have been told?'

Penny considered the question. 'He's a successful man in his own line of business, and I think there's some ill feeling between him and his relatives. He didn't come often to see his daughter. I fancy that if there'd been a problem, Phil wouldn't have wanted to know about it. He has remarried, too, and that always makes a difference. I understand his new wife is quite young – nearer his daughter's age, if you see what I mean, than his. It's not something he'd want to be reminded of.'

There was a silence. Into it came a clip-clop of horse's hoofs outside and a bark from the dog. A girl's voice called out.

'That sounds like Kelly,' Nick said. He raised his voice. 'In the kitchen, Kell!'

She came in a few moments later, her face flushed either from the exercise of having ridden over here, or from anticipation.

'Good morning!' she said happily. 'I thought I'd—'

At this point she saw me and broke off, an almost comical consternation on her freckled face.

'Another visitor!' said Penny hospitably. 'Join us, Kelly. I'll make another lot of coffee!'

Kelly came awkwardly into the room, her former exuberance evaporated. She sat down, her eyes still fixed on me. 'Hullo,' she said dully.

'Fran's seeing life on the farm at first hand,' Nick grinned. 'She's never been on a farm before, can you imagine it?'

'You've always lived in a town, I suppose,' Kelly sounded more resentful than curious.

She was casting covert looks at Nick and the situation was clear enough for me to read. She was sweet on him and in a big way. The thing was, did he even notice? She wasn't unattractive, in a healthy, outdoor way. In fact, I'd have thought she'd have been ideal if he really was looking for a wife on the farm here. But what people need, and what they want, are not always the same.

'I reckon', said Nick cheerfully, 'that she'd settle into a farming way of life in no time at all! You want to give it a try, Fran.'

Kelly was clearly startled and gave me a very unfriendly look. From now on, she'd see me as a rival. It was a pity, because I'd been getting along well with her and she might have been a valuable ally.

Rather too obviously, she turned her back to me. 'I

called by, Nick, because I missed you at the yard the other day. Lundy told me you'd been.'

'Only being neighbourly,' Nick looked momentarily embarrassed. 'I thought Alastair might be in the yard and I'd have a word to let him know Ma and I are thinking about them. But he wasn't there and I didn't want to call at the house in case I ran into Jamie. His car was parked by the garage so I knew he was there and didn't fancy chatting to him. Lundy was as tight as a tick, by the way. How does he get away with it?'

Kelly's features had become steadily more disconsolate as he spoke. She'd hoped he called by the yard to see her. 'I know Joey drinks, but it doesn't interfere with his work.'

'You oughtn't to be lodging with them,' said Penny severely. 'The man's not to be trusted.'

Kelly brightened, hoping, I was sure, for an invitation to lodge at the farm.

I decided the moment had come to make a tactful retreat.

I thanked Penny for the coffee and said I really must start back.

'Come again!' Penny urged.

'Show you around the place properly next time,' Nick chimed in.

Kelly's misery returned. Her day was ruined and I was the cause.

However, as I walked back, I had plenty to think about besides Kelly's troubled love-life.

Ariadne was a wealthy woman. Everyone depended on her. She was old and in poor health. She had no children and her brother, to whom she was close, was elderly. Her nephew Philip she disapproved of heartily and, in theory anyway, he was a successful man who didn't need to inherit wealth. Jamie had worked hard in the business, but she had doubts about him. Theresa, on the other hand, she had 'doted on' in Penny's words. Terry had been her heiress and Terry herself was dead. With no obvious alternative to Terry, Ariadne must have faced a dilemma over the future of the stud. Her choice had been restricted to plumping for one of several candidates, all of whom had less than her wholehearted support. But time wasn't on her side. She'd had to make a choice and make it quickly.

This morning, Watkins the solicitor had called on Ariadne with a briefcase containing, I'd bet my boots on it, a new will. And very likely, this morning, Ariadne had signed it.

But in whose favour? And would it mean that Ariadne herself was now in danger?

Chapter Fourteen

I needed to speak to Ariadne but realised it wouldn't be easy to get an answer to the question which mattered most. There was no way I could casually ask her about the provisions of her will. But I was convinced that the answer to that would provide the answer to everything else.

I set off back to the Astara Stud, turning over the problem all ways in my head as I tried to decide how to tackle it. I hadn't realised detectives had to be so versatile. A course in practical psychiatry might have helped but I didn't have it. All I knew was I had to deal with an iron-willed old lady of the old school, who was ill and on medication. No wonder I was so apprehensive at the thought. I juggled all kinds of approaches in my head, but none of them seemed realistic.

So buried in my thoughts had I been that I hadn't been aware of anything else. Belatedly I realised that a vehicle was following me along the narrow, single-track road. I'd been walking in the middle – there were no pavements and the verges to either side were treacherous obstacle courses of grass-concealed holes and drainage ditches. I assumed the vehicle behind me couldn't get past. Obligingly I moved over to the far side.

He didn't overtake. He seemed happy to crawl along at the same pace, just a few yards behind me. I glanced over my shoulder. It was an old van. The driver seemed to be peering through the windscreen at me. But the screen was yellowed with age and chipped where a flying stone had hit it. I couldn't make out the face behind the wheel. He was dawdling along, almost at a standstill. With a sick feeling in my stomach, I realised he hadn't been held up by me. He was following me!

I began to walk faster. What with all the ideas of family secrets and murderous plots running round my head, I succeeded in frightening myself considerably. Not only Ariadne was in danger. I was. Me. Fran Varady, the great detective. Imagining I was one of the Famous Five and putting my nose into Jamie Monkton's business.

I broke into a lumbering run, hampered by the gumboots which weren't designed for sprinting. Even the pixie boots would have been better. They, at least, belonged to me and were the right size.

The van increased its speed. I couldn't outrun a motor vehicle, even such an old one. Sweat poured off me. My feet were redhot and useless, my calf muscles ached. It was like running in thick mud, a nightmare of pursuit, as to lift one foot and put it in front of the other became increasingly impossible.

My heart was beating like a drum and I felt my isolation in this wilderness more than ever before. Why hadn't I stayed in London? In London I could have ducked down a side street, gone into a shop, jumped on a bus, anything. Out here I was marooned amongst empty fields. I'd have to scramble over a hedge or fencing before I could get into one of those and the driver would be out of his van and have grabbed me before I'd got ten yards.

The one hope was to reach the turning up to the stud. He wouldn't follow me on to the property, surely? Someone might see him from the house. I could see the turn ahead with the wooden sign, promising sanctuary. I made for it like a medieval fugitive, heading for the church door with the mob on his heels. But it was all uphill, very steep. An agonising stitch shot through my side. I doubled over. I couldn't make it. I had to halt.

The van had reached me and stopped. A door slammed. Footsteps grated on the road surface, approaching.

'This is it, Francesca!' I told myself between spasms of agony.

I tried to stand upright, groaning with the pain of the stitch. A hand gripped my shoulder. I wasn't going to give in without a fight, even in my state. If Terry had put up a fight, she mightn't have finished dangling from a light fitting. I struck back with my elbow and there was a yell of pain. Good! I thought. I'd got him where it hurt. I tried another jab and there was another howl.

'Fran! Stop it, will you? What are you trying to do?'

I could hear my name and the protesting voice was familiar. I twisted in his grip, peering up in my doubled-over state, hand clasped to my ribs, panting, sweating – a real sight.

'Have you gone completely crazy?' Ganesh panted. 'I tried to attract your attention and you took off like a rocket! What's is the big idea? Training for the Olympics? Then you tried to use me as a punch-bag. Country living has scrambled your brain – or what brain you've got left!'

* * *

'I thought you were a hit man,' I said.

We'd limped together to the van and driven past the house and down the hill on the other side until we reached a wooded dell. There we sat until the stitch in my side had gone and the pair of us had got our breath back.

Ganesh lounged sideways on the driver's seat, his back against the door, one arm propped on the seat and one on the wheel. His long black hair hung over his face and he was scowling ferociously at me through the tangles. He was probably still suffering from the two punches I'd aimed at him and what I had to say didn't make him any happier. In reality, I was delighted to see him, but at the moment could do no more than gawp at him.

Then he said in the tone which he reserves for pouring cold water on my ideas, 'Hit man?'

'Well—' I tried to sound as if it wasn't a daft idea. 'You might have been!'

'A hit man, in a van like this? Not built for getaways, is it? It only just got here from London! Why didn't you recognise the van, anyway? It's the one belonging to the shop. You've seen it enough times.'

This drew my attention to the fact that the inside of the van smelled of cabbages, potato earth and over-ripe bananas. There was a torn plastic net at my feet with a label reading 'Florida Pink Grapefruit'.

'I know I have!' I snapped, getting flustered. 'But in London, not here! You didn't say you were coming down here! What are you doing here, anyway?'

'Rescuing you,' he said. 'I've come to drive you back to town.'

'Not now! Not now I'm getting somewhere!'

I burst into a recap of my theories. 'Terry was going to inherit the lot. That would have left several people out in the cold. There's Philip, her father. Everyone says he was never interested in the stud and anyway, he's got his own successful business. And I don't really think he'd kill his own daughter. But what about Jamie? He was in London that day, I'm sure of it. You saw him and so did Edna. I found a piece of Squib's chalk in his car and he uses that cologne. He frequents that wine bar. He smokes Benson and Hedges. He's worked hard to rescue the stud from the slide in business while Alastair was in charge. He probably feels that if Ariadne left it to anyone, she should have left it to him. He is a family member, after all. He's probably resented bitterly her decision to leave it to Terry.'

'If he knew about it,' Ganesh pointed out. 'And even if he did, why didn't he just marry Terry?'

'That's the Indian way,' I said. 'Keep everything in the family. That hasn't been done in this country for a hundred years. What's more, I can't see Terry falling for Jamie.'

Ganesh didn't look convinced but I ploughed on. 'There's a very unpleasant groom, or stable manager, called Joey Lundy. He knocks his simple-minded wife around. Alastair and Jamie seem content to let him stay in his job and just drop a word from time to time when poor Mrs Lundy's bruises get too obvious. But Terry might have thought differently. She might have ordered Lundy off the place, once she owned it. So he would have a motive to kill Terry and he's the sort who'd do it.'

'Is there any evidence this Lundy fellow was ever in London in his entire life?' Ganesh punctured another theory.

'Evidence', I told him, 'is what I'm here to find. Maybe he and Jamie were working together. They both had an interest in removing poor Terry from the scene.'

'Only according to you and your theories.' Ganesh could, on occasion such as now, sound irritatingly smug.

'All right, there's something else,' I told him. 'I saw Jamie talking to the solicitor, Watkins, in that wine bar. I'm sure Jamie was trying to find out about Ariadne's new will. He might even have tried persuading Watkins to put pressure on her to make it out in Jamie's favour. Jamie had no business to be with Watkins there.'

Ganesh struck his hand against the steering wheel and swore vigorously, something he rarely, if ever, did. 'I've sometimes thought you were crazy, Fran, but I've never thought you were stupid. I'm beginning to change my mind! This is family business. Monkton family business. The last thing they want or need is a complete stranger like you prying into it! Besides which, you're putting up a load of theories without any proof! Why shouldn't Jamie Monkton meet Watkins? Watkins probably handles all the legal business to do with the stud. They needn't have been discussing the will at all!'

'Watkins came to the stud this morning. If Jamie wanted to talk business with him, he could have done it today, without traipsing into Winchester. He wanted to meet Watkins in Winchester, Gan, because he didn't want anyone at the stud knowing about it! Ariadne should be warned! Look, suppose—'

'You can't go about making accusations like this!' Ganesh broke in hoarsely. 'If you're wrong, you're going to be in a hell of a tight corner! And if you're right – it's not Ariadne you should be worrying about, it's you!' He leaned forward pugnaciously. 'You shouldn't stay here another minute. You've found out all you can. We'll drive back to London right now. We'll go to Morgan and tell her. She can sort it out, right? It's her job. Leave your stuff here. You can phone Monkton and ask him to send it on.'

'No way!' I told him indigantly. 'I've got your camera, amongst other things! Hey! Did you get that film developed?'

'What film?'

Dismay swept over me. 'You didn't get it?' Then I remembered. I'd only posted it the previous day and if he'd left London early this morning – 'It will be at your place now, unopened! Gan—' I grabbed his jacket. 'You've got to drive back, now, pick up that film and take it to the chemist's near your shop. He does one-hour processing!'

'If I drive back, does that mean you're coming with me?'

'No.' He was looking so furious I found myself almost pleading, 'I must stay just one more day. I've *got* to talk to Ariadne.'

'She'll tell you to mind your own business and I for one won't blame her!'

'I've still got to try! Right?'

He glared at me. 'Wrong! This isn't a game, Fran!'

'I know that! Look, I don't know why you have to come. I can look after myself!' I yelled.

It was getting pretty noisy inside the van. My ears were ringing. It was time to quieten down.

We both sat in silence for a few minutes until Ganesh began to speak again, using a reasonable tone which always infuriates me.

'You can't look after yourself, Fran, not this time. I know you can in normal circumstances, but there's nothing normal about this. You're in a strange part of the world, living among people you know very little about. These aren't your sort. They're rich. They've got big houses, land, horses and so on. They may quarrel among themselves but they'll close ranks against outsiders. You're the one who will be sacrificed. You do see that, don't you?'

He waited and when I didn't answer, went on more angrily, 'All right, look at it this way. Just now you thought you were being attacked. Suppose you'd been right? How tall are you? What do you weigh? I've seen twelve-year-old kids as big as you. You haven't got the strength, Fran, to save yourself in a struggle.'

'I know all this,' I told him. 'Because contrary to what you seem to think, I'm not stupid and not unaware of the risk. But I can't give up now, not just at this point. Not after I've come all the way down here and managed to find out so much.'

He sighed. 'How much longer do you think you'll need to stay on?'

'Twenty-four hours tops, I swear. Tonight and perhaps part of tomorrow. Then I'll go back to London. I realise I'm a fish out of water down here. But I don't like leaving something half-finished.'

He scratched his head and scowled. 'All right. One more night. I came prepared to doss down in the van in case I couldn't contact you at once. I've got a sleeping bag and some food. Tomorrow, right after breakfast, I'll come and collect you. If anything goes wrong before that, get out of the house, leg it down here and you'll find me.'

I felt a twinge of guilt at having yelled at him and I told him I really did appreciate his coming to help, and being worried, and all the rest of it.

'Yeah, yeah . . .' he said impatiently. 'Just remember, watch out! If anything – anything at all goes wrong – just start running as fast as you were running away from me just now!'

At the house, both Marcia's car and Watkins's Mercedes had gone. I limped round to the back porch to take off the wellies. They were jammed on my swollen feet by now and I could have done with a boot-jack, like the one they had at the farm. I managed to get them off and thankfully divested myself of the Barbour, inside which I was steaming like a steak and kidney pudding.

I staggered in my socks into the kitchen, carrying my pixie boots in my hand. I couldn't get them on.

Ruby was there mixing up batter again. She was an obsessive cook.

'Hullo,' she said without stopping the beating action. 'You look as if you've been running.'

'Brisk walk!' I told her. I drew a glass of water from the tap and drank it down in one long swig. She gave me a curious sideways glance. My purple face indicated more than a healthy stroll, but she didn't say anything else.

She poured batter into the cake tin and put the whole thing in the oven. This time she just handed me the bowl to scrape without asking.

The batter was sweet and sticky and made me feel about six years old.

'Ruby? Does Mrs Cameron come downstairs during the

day? She doesn't stay up there all day, does she?' I pointed my spoon at the ceiling.

Ariadne obviously had a private sitting room upstairs, but I hardly felt I'd be welcome if I just went up there uninvited and knocked on her door.

'Not generally,' Ruby said. 'You finished with that bowl? Not unless she's having a bad day. A nice day like today, she likes to go out in the garden. She's quite a fine artist. She's out there now with her drawing papers and pens. She's a very talented lady.'

I took off the socks and walked out barefoot into the garden. The grass was blessedly cool under my toes. Ariadne was at the far end in her chair under some appletrees which had seen better days. She had a board propped up on her lap and she was sketching. It must have been a little chilly there despite the sun, but she didn't seem to mind. She had a blanket over her legs and a gauzy scarf wrapped lightly round her throat, the ends trailing down her back *à la* Isadora Duncan. The breeze caught the ends of the scarf from time to time and lifted them gently, only to fall back again, pale turquoise tips trailing across the long grass.

It occurred to me that if anyone meant her any harm, she was about as vulnerable as she could be, sitting out here in her invalid chair, all alone and too far away from the house to shout for help.

'I wish I could draw or something,' I said, sitting on the grass by her.

'Have you ever tried?' She smiled down at me.

I had to confess I hadn't. She pointed to a satchel by her chair.

'Take a sheet of cartridge paper out of that and see what you can do. Try charcoal.'

I got myself a sheet of paper and a piece of charcoal and used the cardboard satchel to lean on. I could just see a corner of the house through the shrubs and old fruit trees so I had a go at drawing that but it looked lopsided when I'd finished, with all the windows too large.

Ariadne inspected it when I finally decided I couldn't manage any more.

'You're too worried about detail,' she said. 'You need to get down just a general impression first. Details can come later.'

That tied in rather neatly with what I was doing here. I wondered how I could get round to Watkins's visit that morning.

While I was thinking it out, she showed me what she'd done. It looked highly professional to me. I told her about Squib and his pavement reproductions. She seemed genuinely interested.

'If he's had no formal training, he must have an exceptionally keen eye,' she said.

I asked her if she'd had lessons and she said she'd had a few. She'd been at art college when she'd been young.

'Did Terry draw?' I asked. 'I never saw her do anything like that.'

'Theresa had no patience.' She began to put her work away. There was something final about the way she spoke. She didn't want to talk about Terry. I persevered, all the same.

'She never talked about her home, this house,' I told her. 'Or the stud. I was really surprised when I found out what was here.'

'Did she talk about anything else?' Ariadne's sharp eyes rested on my face.

I felt myself blush. 'No. She grumbled a lot. I don't think she was very happy with us. I'm not surprised, not if she was used to living here.'

'Obviously,' Ariadne said, 'she wasn't happy here, either, or she'd have stayed with us.' There was bitterness behind the words although her voice sounded calm enough.

I told her I was sure that Terry had simply been going through a phase. That she'd have come back eventually. It was such a beautiful place and there was so much here. The fact that she'd been so miserable in London showed how much she must have missed them all at the Astara.

She made no reply. It was as if I hadn't spoken. I felt horribly embarrassed.

We sat for a while. Ariadne just looked ahead of her at the view of the house. Though she was old her profile showed what a beauty she must once have been. Her skin was still fine, though wrinkled, and her nose, the line of her forehead and her deepset eyes were classical in form. Her hands, folded now in her lap, had long thin fingers and her rings were loose. But the hands were sinewy and I remembered that she'd been a horsewoman before her accident. I knew I was frightened of Ariadne. Not in the way I had been frightened when pursued, as I thought, in the lane. But frightened in a way more difficult to explain. There was no way I could talk to her without seeming crass, and in the presence of this poised former beauty, that appeared almost like a sin.

Nevertheless, I tried again. 'Look, I'm sorry, I know it sounds as though I'm interfering and making this worse for you all. But I shared a house with her. I want to know what happened to her. After all, we – I – found her!' I finished by blurting out.

I was beginning to feel a little aggrieved. After all, the police had grilled me and Nev and Squib and made us feel like assassins. They were still not satisfied now. When I got back to London, Janice would be round to my gungy flat the minute she heard I was there. Perhaps Ariadne didn't feel like talking about it to me. But she had no right to cut me out of the whole affair as if I were not already a part-player in it.

She seemed to be thinking it over. Eventually she said, 'Yes, you did, I was forgetting. How very difficult for you and your friends. I dare say the police were unpleasant.'

'Yes, they were.' Parry, at least. In case she was wondering, I added, 'She was *not* killed by anyone living in the house. I know I didn't do it and I know the others didn't. You must believe me, it's the truth.'

'I believe you, Francesca. I think I am a fair judge of character.'

There was no way I was going to finesse my way into saying what I wanted to say. I blundered in. 'Mrs Cameron, you know, you might be in danger? Whoever killed Terry, he – or she – it might be something to do with this house or the stud.'

She was watching me work up another sweat, this time of embarrassment. 'My dear,' she said, 'you really ought not to worry about me. I am quite capable of taking care of myself, you know.' She sounded faintly amused.

That's what I'd said to Ganesh, about myself. He hadn't believed me and I didn't believe Ariadne. But there was nothing I could do about it. I began to appreciate how frustrated Ganesh must feel about my obstinacy, and how useless. Ariadne didn't want to believe anyone could walk out here to this lonely corner of the garden and, quite unseen by anyone at the house, just reach out and tighten the gauzy scarf which encircled her neck.

As if she could read my mind, she said, 'It is my home, Francesca. I hope I'm safe in my own home!'

I hoped she was, too.

'Lunchtime, I fancy,' she went on. She reached down and released a catch on the side of the chair. She turned it manually with a push of her deceptively thin hands, preparing to return to the house. Only when it was in position, did she press the electric button and start up, whirring quietly as it juddered along the bumpy path. I walked a little behind her as there wasn't room alongside.

'I wish', Ariadne said conversationally, as if I were quite the ordinary sort of visitor to whom she was showing off the garden, 'that you could have seen the house when my husband was alive. The gardens were so much better kept then.' She raised her voice slightly so that I could hear, behind her.

I confessed I'd been told about the origins of the Astara Stud and how it had come by its name. I had no idea how long horses lived but it seemed unlikely she still had the original animal, Astara. I asked, instead, how many foals he'd sired and whether any of them had inherited his name. Were the horses here named like racehorses, which, as I understood it, got names based on their sire or dam's name?

'There has only been one Astara,' she said. 'And after the accident, he was shot.'

I was so startled, I stopped and let out a squawk of dismay.

She braked the chair and looked back at me, eyebrows raised quizzically.

'He was injured, too, unfortunately.'

'I see,' I said and asked whether he'd broken a leg. I had an idea that once horses broke legs, they were put down.

'No, but he was left permanently scarred and temperamentally uncertain. Why are you so shocked? Death isn't the worst thing.' She tapped the arms of her chair. 'There is worse. When one sees an animal which has been so beautiful and which one has cared for so long, reduced to a twitching wreck, would it be better to prolong its miserable life? No. Sometimes, a bullet is kinder. I've never feared death myself. I feel sometimes I've lived too long. The Greeks used to say that those whom the gods loved, died young. Death preserves beauty, strength, grace and innocence. Life has a way of destroying them. A beautiful thing, once damaged beyond recall, is better destroyed.'

The chair whirred into life and trundled on towards the house. I followed silently behind her. I wanted to cry out that she was wrong. That she misunderstood what life was about. That it wasn't a world just for the young and beautiful and rich. It was a world with a place in it for me, Squib and Mad Edna, too. That the faceless planners who had decided to demolish our squat had reasoned as she was reasoning. That it couldn't be saved, wasn't worth saving, was too far gone. But we'd loved that house with all its peeling plaster and leaking rooftiles, and given a chance, we'd have saved it.

But I knew, if I tried to tell her this, she wouldn't listen. I realised now why she scared me so. And was this why Terry had been afraid? Terry, the beautiful doll of a grandchild and great-niece, who had been destined to receive everything which Ariadne and Alastair had to give. But the doll had tumbled from her pedestal and broken, become a sharp-faced, shop-soiled, streetwise brat, 'temperamentally uncertain', unable to be restored.

'A beautiful thing, once damaged beyond recall, is better destroyed.' How terrible those words were. My head was filling with thoughts which froze me with such horror, that I thrust them away from me in revulsion.

Chapter Fifteen

Ariadne didn't lunch with the rest of us. I gathered she lunched in her room and rested until the evening.

Alastair and Jamie were whispering conspiratorially as I entered the dining room and greeted my appearance with an ill-subdued glee. There was absolutely no mention at all of Marcia's visit – and none of Watkins. Perhaps part of Alastair's good humour was due to Marcia having managed to smooth things over. I knew he'd been angry with her before. She must have said all the right things this time.

'Got a little surprise for you!' he chuckled.

I didn't like the sound of that. I looked inquiringly at Jamie. His bland expression made me feel worse. Their manner suggested they'd planned a jolly jape of the sort which generally leaves a third party humiliated and helpless. I couldn't quell the uneasy feeling I was to be the victim.

'After lunch,' crowed Alastair. 'Eat up.' The condemned man being presented with his last meal probably got that sort of grim encouragement.

They ate well at the Astara, three cooked meals a day,

including breakfast, and I was hungry. Lunch was Toad in the Hole, the sausages peeking coyly through the curled brown batter. It was followed by cheese and biscuits. Simple but substantial fare and, after it, I rather felt like going and taking a siesta myself. It wasn't to be.

Ruby appeared, obviously part of the plot, carrying a pair of riding breeches, a hard hat and soft-topped boots.

'They belonged to young Theresa,' she said. 'Seeing as you got her gumboots on this morning, you'll be able to get your feet in these and the jodhpurs will fit.'

My heart sank. It was clear where this was leading.

'Can't let you leave without getting you up on a horse,' said Alastair merrily. 'Kelly will saddle up old Dolly for you. Quiet as a lamb. Jamie is going to show you a bit of our countryside. The way to see it is from horseback.'

I didn't want to be shown the countryside by Jamie and I certainly didn't want to do my sightseeing from the back of a horse, but argument was clearly useless.

Togged up in my equestrian finery (the boots pinched and the jodhpurs fitted like second skin), I tottered out to the stableyard accompanied by my two supporters. Jamie looked the goods in his riding gear, very dashing. Grandma Varady and all those Hungarian hussar ancestors would've approved. I didn't know where Ganesh was. I hoped he wasn't wandering around the place, partly because he might be seen – and partly because he might see me in this ridiculous get-up.

Kelly was waiting in the yard, holding the bridle of a grey mare. She didn't smile. I was still the rival and it was possible she was about to be revenged.

I was slightly encouraged by the fact that Dolly herself appeared to be half-asleep, eyes closed and one hind hoof hitched up in rest position. But my relief, if any, was cancelled by the sight of Joey Lundy, lurking in the background with a smirk on his unlovely countenance.

'Here we are, my dear!' cried Alastair, slapping the nag on her neck. 'Give the lady a leg up, Lundy!' Dolly opened her eyes and twitched her ears. If ever a horse could be said to sneer, she did.

Lundy sidled over and stooped, cupping his hands. They all stood round me, blocking any escape. I had no choice but allow myself to be catapulted into the saddle.

The one and only time I'd ever sat on anything with four legs was when I was very small and was put on a donkey on the beach one summer. I must have been about four years old at the time and I yelled blue murder to be lifted down again. I felt the same way about it now. It seemed an inordinately long way up. Dolly's neck was very narrow and insubstantial, viewed from above, and it and the animal's head appeared way below me. I felt I was sitting up there in the saddle with nothing at all to prevent me pitching forward.

Kelly was fussing around me, giving instructions, showing the correct way to hold the reins and position my feet in the stirrups. Jamie, meantime, had swung into the saddle with the greatest of ease and looked as if he was about to lead the charge of the Light Brigade.

'We'll avoid roads,' he said kindly. 'So you won't have to worry about traffic. We'll cut over the fields.'

This reduced the likelihood that Ganesh would see us, which was a relief.

'You'll thoroughly enjoy yourself!' cried Alastair, waving us away. Kelly raised a hand in silent salute like a gladiator in the arena.

Lundy, I noticed from the corner of my eye, slipped away as we walked sedately out of the yard. His whole manner suggested someone up to no good.

For a while it went rather better than I'd expected. We crossed several fields of pasture, one of them with mares and foals in it. The youngsters were attractive with their spindly legs. I wasn't thoroughly enjoying it, but I was *almost* enjoying it.

Dolly behaved herself impeccably, despite having a novice aboard. She plodded along in her half-asleep way. Jamie, efficiently opening and closing gates as required, continued to play the gallant escort, pointing out local landmarks. I still wasn't quite sure what the purpose of this whole outing was and eventually I asked him, point blank.

'Alastair's idea,' he said briefly.

'I didn't expect you'd volunteered to give me the guided tour, Jamie. But I can't imagine why Alastair thought I'd be keen. He knows I'm no country girl.'

Jamie's horse snorted and tossed its head as emotion communicated itself from rider to mount. 'I hope to God he isn't trying to turn you into one!' Jamie growled. 'The idea's grotesque.'

He turned a direct stare on me. 'And just remember! You may be literally in Theresa's boots right now, but it's as near as you're going to get to taking her place. I've already warned you. No way will I allow you to insinuate yourself into the old people's favour.'

I was furious and told him what I felt about that suggestion. My anger bounced off him. I followed behind him as we progressed Indian file across a field towards distant trees. It occurred to me when I'd simmered down a little, that Jamie himself felt insecure in the old people's affections, or he wouldn't be worried about me. Perhaps, for all his assiduous attention to Watkins, the solicitor had refused to tell him the contents of Ariadne's new will. Until Jamie knew his name was on that document, he couldn't relax.

Sometimes the direct approach pays off.

'Jamie!' I called out. 'What will happen to the Astara Stud when Ariadne, say, decides to retire to Bournemouth?'

'That's Ariadne's business!' he shouted back. 'And of no possible concern to you, Fran!'

And sometimes, the direct approach doesn't.

Meanwhile, we'd reached a commercially planted plantation of conifers. A wide track skirted the edge of it. Now and again a wide swathe of clear ground ran off at right-angles between the trees.

'Firebreaks,' said Jamie, pointing up at a wooden watch-tower.

I asked if the plantation was privately owned, but he said it belonged to the forestry commission. He turned his horse's head into one of the broad firebreak tracks and I followed. The trees rustled darkly to either side. It was a sinister spot. Jamie informed me there were deer in the woodland, but we'd be unlikely to see any at this time of day.

At that moment, a shot rang out, closely followed by another. Something winged across the front of me, narrowly missing Dolly's ears. There was a crack and splintering of wood. A white scar appeared on the nearest tree-trunk. The next second, Dolly had taken off like a bat out of hell.

'Hang on!' yelled Jamie.

There was nothing I could do about it but hang on and we thudded headlong down the track. Hauling on the reins had no effect. I prayed Dolly was sure-footed as the ground was uneven and rutted with tractor tracks. I became aware Jamie was galloping after me, before Dolly swerved without warning and changed direction.

We nearly parted company at that moment. I slipped sideways and just managed to haul myself back. I'd seen cossacks in a circus doing stunts like that, and never felt the slightest urge to join them. Dolly now bolted down a narrow path, probably made by deer, between trees.

There was just about room for her. I grabbed the pommel of the saddle and Dolly's mane and crouched flat to avoid being swept to the ground by overhanging branches. I sensed, rather than heard, that I'd lost Jamie. He wasn't behind me, at any rate. The track must come out somewhere and perhaps he was riding round in an attempt to head me off at the other end.

Dolly plunged on. The ground was soft and uneven, in parts boggy so that Dolly's hoofs squelched in mud and came free with loud, sucking noises We came to a stream and she leapt it easily. By now I'd lost both stirrups and only a miracle kept me glued to her back. We hurtled across an open glade. Dolly took a new path, at a right-angle to the first. She seemed to know where she was going, but it was unlikely Jamie did and wherever he'd headed off to, he'd probably fail to connect up with me now Dolly had changed direction.

Without warning we shot out of the trees into another wide firebreak. There, bumping along towards us was an old pick-up truck. Dolly saw it, checked and wheeled round. I carried on, like the arrow from the bow in the poem, and fell to earth, literally, in a stretch of mud.

I lay there winded, a singing in my ears. I was vaguely aware of cold mud creeping over my outflung hands and dampness oozing through my clothing. Dimly, I heard a familiar voice calling, 'Fran! Are you all right?'

I opened my eyes. Nick Bryant was stooping over me.

Most of the breath had been knocked out of my body, but I managed to wheeze the unnecessary information that I'd fallen off.

'Take it easy, you may have broken something.' In concern, he began checking me over. 'Try and move your arms, one at a time, then your legs.'

I tried. Everything seemed to be in working order. He gave me a hand to sit up.

I rested my arms on my knees and concentrated on getting my breathing back in pattern. I was in a terrible mess, muddy from head to toe. Dolly had disappeared.

'I'll take you home,' Nick said. 'The mare will probably go back on her own.'

I told him Jamie was around somewhere. Nick expressed the opinion that Jamie could also find his own way home. I argued that I ought to try and find him. He wasn't likely to go back to the Astara without me. We were wrangling about this, when hoofbeats announced the arrival of Jamie himself.

He leapt from the saddle and pounded over the turf towards us.

'What the hell – what are you doing here, Bryant?'

'Taking a short cut – good thing I was here! Why didn't you take better care of her?'

I was still sitting in my patch of mud, getting my breath back. They stood either side of me, glowering at one another like a couple of dogs disputing ownership of a bone.

'Oy,' I called up to them. 'How about someone giving me a hand up?'

They hauled me upright between them.

'I'm taking her home in the pick-up,' Nick said, holding tightly to my right arm.

'I'll find the mare,' Jamie argued, gripping my left. 'She won't have gone far.'

'You can't expect Fran to ride back!' I was jerked to the right.

'I'll take care of her, all right?' A tug to the left.

'If you don't mind!' I protested.

They gave me surprised looks and both released me.

'I don't know where the horse is,' I told Jamie. 'But she went that-a-way.' I pointed. 'If you don't mind, I'll accept Nick's offer of a lift back.'

'Look,' Jamie urged. 'I don't want either of the old people seeing you in that state! Especially Ariadne. They mustn't know about your taking a fall.'

'So, I'll creep in the back door!'

Reluctantly, he let me clamber into the pick-up.

'He's a fool,' said Nick, as we bumped down the track with a grinding of gears. 'Taking a novice rider out on such a long hack across country.'

'It wasn't his fault. Someone fired a gun off and frightened Dolly, the mare. The shot only just missed me.'

'A gun?' He glanced at me, frowning. 'Might have been someone shooting pigeons or even a poacher after a deer. Venison fetches a good price nowadays. I'll phone the forest warden when we get back. He can send a couple of rangers out to check.'

I persuaded him to set me down in the lane leading to the stud. I hobbled the remaining stretch home and slipped into the house through the kitchen door.

Ruby was there and let out a squawk. I explained Jamie was following after, once he'd found the mare.

'You leave those muddy clothes with me,' she said. 'And go up and run yourself a good hot bath. Have a nice long soak in it. Oh, and you won't let Mr Alastair or Mrs Cameron know, it'd upset them to think you'd had any accident.'

I soaked in the bath feeling a hundred years old. Any plan I'd had of slipping out to find Ganesh was out of the question now. I limped along to my room and collapsed on the bed until dinner.

Ruby put her head round as I lay there, and informed me Mr James was safely back with Dolly.

I was more than aware that the person who'd come back safely, against all the odds, was myself. I wasn't meant to return in one piece. Whoever fired off those shots wasn't firing at pigeons or deer. He'd been firing at me. I remembered Lundy's expression as I rode out of the yard. But if it had been Lundy, had he been acting alone? Or had the whole thing been set up with Jamie?

I hoped neither Alastair nor Ariadne had been a part of it.

Chapter Sixteen

After dinner Alastair dug out some old family snapshot albums and insisted on showing them to me. They were interesting chiefly for the ones which showed Philip Monkton whom I hadn't had the opportunity to meet in the flesh. He appeared a heavily built, self-confident type of man, handsome in a florid way. In the couple of photographs in which he appeared with Terry, there was no appearance of closeness. The camera can lie, contrary to the saying. But attitudes don't. The pictures with father and daughter were obligatory family snaps. Looking closely at Philip, I decided he was a bully.

Meanwhile it started to rain heavily, beating against the windows.

'In for a nasty night,' said Alastair in the comfortable way of someone who hadn't to go out in the bad weather.

My mind was on Ganesh, sitting uncomfortably in the van, eating cold baked beans out of a tin, listening to the rain beat on the roof. I felt guilty. I had a warm bed upstairs. On the other hand, my bumps and bruises were coming out nicely and I was likely to be spending an equally uncomfortable night.

I limped to the window and peered out. It was tipping down.

'What's up?' Jamie asked, sounding suspicious. 'You've been fidgeting about for the last hour. What's out there?'

'Nothing,' I told him. 'I was just looking out at the weather.' Privately I muttered, 'I'm in agony!'

He scowled and glanced at Alastair, but he didn't ask again why I was so unsettled.

Poor old Ganesh. But it had been his idea to drive down here.

I awoke the next morning, hardly able to move a muscle. Every attempt was agony. Given free choice, I'd have remained where I was all day. But the choice wasn't mine. I got out of bed by sliding over the edge and finishing on my knees on the carpet. I hauled myself upright, yelping with pain, and I made my way down to the bathroom, hunched like Quasimodo. A hot bath helped a little and gave me the courage to tackle the stairs.

Making an entry into the breakfast room with the appearance of everything being all right, when everything hurt, took some doing. But Alastair didn't appear to notice anything amiss. Jamie wasn't there.

It had stopped raining. I managed to hide a toast and marmalade sandwich in my pocket and made my robotic way outside trying to look nonchalant. Gan probably had pneumonia by now. I'd find him coughing and expiring with just enough breath left to say 'I told you so!'

I took a deep breath. The air was filled with a wet-leaf smell. The overnight deluge had left deep puddles in the drive. The buddleia heads drooped and dripped moisture.

There was a rustle in the tangle of foliage. A voice whispered, 'Fran!'

I peered into the dripping jungle. 'Ganesh? Are you all right?'

He emerged, clearly anything but all right. He was in a dreadful mess, soaked, shivering and unshaven. But something more than physical discomfort troubled him as I could see from his drawn features and the look in his eyes.

I grabbed his hand. 'What happened, Ganesh?'

His fingers closed tightly on mine and then released them. 'Fran, we've got to get out of here. We've got to get back to London – we, I, have got to call the police!' He swallowed and looked nervously towards the house.

He was right to be cautious. 'Jamie snoops,' I told him. 'Back in the bushes, Gan!' I gave him a shove and we both retreated into the wet undergrowth. Water trickled down my neck and wet leaves slapped against my face. 'Just tell me,' I urged.

'The woods down there, where I parked the van.' He made an effort to pull himself together, pushing back his wet hair with both hands. 'I went into them to – well, the usual reason. Then I went wandering off further, just exploring.' His jaw wobbled. 'I found a grave, Fran.'

I couldn't say anything at first, only stare at him in growing horror and dismay. Somehow I managed to squeeze out, 'Are you sure about this, Ganesh? The terrain is pretty rough out there.'

'I tell you, it's a grave! The rain, it must have washed away the soil. It can't have been there long, you see. There – there was a hand sticking out among the leaves and brambles. I – I got a stick and just pushed aside a few more to uncover the face.' He paused and added in a choked voice, 'I'm so sorry, Fran. It's – it was someone we know.'

'Who?' I asked dully. But my guts, sickened with the knowledge of what he was going to say, heaved.

'It was Squib.' When I made no reply he added in a bewildered way, 'How's it possible, Fran? Down here? What was he doing—?'

'He had a plan!' I broke in miserably. 'Oh, Ganesh, this is my fault! I should have found out what was in his mind! But I didn't take him seriously. You know how he was—'

Ganesh grabbed my shoulders and shook me lightly. 'Yes, I know what Squib was like, but I don't know what you're talking about.'

'He knew about the Astara Stud. Terry had told him. He must have thought, somehow or other, he could get some money . . . He'd cleared out of the hostel and was on the run. He told me he was thick, poor sod, and he was thick! He hadn't worked out her killer could have come from here. If I'd only asked, I could have talked him out of it!'

'This isn't your fault!' Ganesh snapped.

I remembered the stub of chalk in Jamie's car. I'd thought it proved a visit to our house. But perhaps Squib had been in that car.

'The dog!' I exclaimed.

'No sign of it.'

'It wouldn't leave him and he wouldn't leave it. Squib thought the world of that dog.' So, somewhere in the woods would be a second, smaller grave. 'Take me there,' I said.

Ganesh shook his head. 'No, Fran,' he said gently.

'Squib was a friend!'

'Squib's dead. What's down there in the woods is a decomposing shell.' He paused. 'So, do we call the local cops?'

I struggled with my churning brain and shook my head. 'Not here. I don't want them swarming all over us here. I vote we go back to London and tell Janice. She'll be angry but she knows us. Here they don't know us, we're strangers. Gan, I suppose you couldn't tell how he died?'

That was asking a lot from a quick glimpse of a discoloured face and a hand.

Ganesh said fiercely, 'I didn't stay to find out! I couldn't *look* at it any longer, Fran!'

I gulped. 'Squib wouldn't have hurt *anyone*! It's foul – and fouler that you had to be the one to find him!'

'Someone had to find him. I wish it hadn't been me. Something, some animal, has been chewing at the fingers. The smell is indescribable, not foul exactly but sweet, like a mix of rotting fruit and disturbed stagnant water. It would have been bad enough even without knowing him. I threw up. If the police look around there, Fran, they'll find plenty of evidence to tell them I was there. The ground was soft. I must have left footprints. The van's tyre tracks. We have to go to the police before someone else stumbles over the body.'

I made a decision. The last thing I wanted was to be hauled away by the local police. They knew nothing about us, we were clearly out-of-towners and not the type of tourist a locality encourages. If, in addition, we told them the body was that of a friend of ours, they'd lock us up and toss away the key. I'd also be lying if I didn't admit to being afraid. It now seemed clear that what I'd suspected must be so, that someone at the Astara was involved in this whole blood-stained business.

I gripped Ganesh's hand. 'We'll go back to London right now. We'll tell Janice and she'll contact the locals here. I don't trust any coppers much but if I trust anyone, it's Janice.'

He mumbled, 'All right.'

He didn't need more problems, but I had to make a confession. 'I should tell you that someone took a potshot at me yesterday afternoon, while I was out riding, either hoping to hit me or spook the horse. But it couldn't have been Jamie who fired. He was with me. On the other hand, he was my guide and let me into the tree plantation. Or there's the groom, Lundy. He could have done it and would have done it, if Jamie ordered, I'm sure! I was set up. They set me up, dammit, between them!'

'What?' His confused look turned to surprise and then anger. 'I warned you, Fran!'

'All right, I know! I'll go indoors and—'

There was a screech of protesting metal followed by a grating sound, quite near at hand. Gan parted the undergrowth and we peered through the leaves. It was Jamie, over at the garage, pushing up the door.

'He's taking the car out,' I whispered. 'Can you see him? Is that the man you saw watching our house?'

'That's him!' Ganesh said firmly.

'Sure?'

'Absolutely positive.'

Jamie had gone into the garage and we could hear the engine being started up. The car slid out slowly backwards.

'Know where he's going?' Ganesh muttered.

'No idea.'

The car was coming towards us, still slowly. Jamie seemed to be looking about him. Looking for me, perhaps. He'd realised I wasn't in the house and he wanted to know where I was.

Just then something cold and wet fell off a branch and rolled down my neck. Stupidly I jumped. All the branches around me shook. Jamie saw it and slammed on the brake.

He was out of the car fast but I was quicker. I shot out of the shrubbery, hoping Ganesh was well hidden in the leaves behind me and hailed him brightly. 'Hullo, Jamie!'

'What were you doing in there?' he demanded. He tried to see past me but I moved to block him.

'Walking up and down trying to get some movement in my joints. I'm a wreck from that fall yesterday. There's not an inch of me which doesn't hurt.'

He wasted no sympathy on my ills. 'You've been creeping about in those shrubs. You're up to something! I damn well knew you were last night! What's in there?'

He shoved me aside roughly and pushed his way into the buddleias.

I held my breath. After a moment Jamie came out backwards, wet and furious.

'I want to know what you're doing, Fran!' He grabbed my arm. 'And if I have to shake it out of you, I will!'

I shrieked in agony as the sudden movement antagonised my aches and pains. The bushes further along rustled and Ganesh stepped out. I wondered briefly how he'd got down there without either Jamie or myself seeing him. Perhaps he had some mystic Eastern trick or two up his sleeve.

'Why don't you let go of her?' he asked unpleasantly.

Jamie released me and pushed me away. He stared disbelievingly at Ganesh and then burst out, 'I knew it! I knew you came out here to meet someone! You've been like a cat on hot bricks since yesterday.' He jabbed a finger at Ganesh and then whirled to face me. 'So, who the devil is that?'

'This is Ganesh Patel,' I said. 'He's a friend of mine and he's come to take me back to London.'

Jamie scowled at Ganesh. 'I've seen you somewhere before.'

This was bad. Gan had said that the man who had been watching the house the day Terry died, had noticed him. If Jamie now connected Gan up with that incident, he'd know Ganesh was the one who could finger him to the police. And he'd do something about it.

Very quickly I said, 'You'll be pleased I'm leaving, Jamie!'

That brought his attention back to me. 'Pleased! Yes, you could put it like that! You can't leave fast enough as far as I'm concerned. Is that your clapped-out old van parked down the road under the trees?' He turned to Ganesh.

'Yes,' said Gan shortly.

'If that gets all the way to London without breaking down, you'll be lucky!' Jamie said. 'You'll probably have to push it all the way!' He began to laugh.

I was afraid Gan was going to sock him so I jumped in with, 'I'm just going indoors to pack up my gear and say goodbye to everyone.'

Jamie had stopped laughing. He still wanted to have the last word. 'That's fine. I'm going down to Abbotsfield for half an hour. Try and be gone by the time I get back, right?'

I went indoors to pack my things and say goodbye to Alastair and Ariadne. I thanked them for everything. I really meant my thanks and they obviously realised it. They were both very nice and told me to come back again, although underneath it, I sensed they were relieved I was going. That, in turn, made me wonder if I'd been getting near the truth – and it was a truth they didn't want to hear.

'How will you travel?' Alastair asked.

I told them I had someone waiting outside for me. They immediately insisted I bring Ganesh indoors. They were clearly appalled when they saw the state of him. But Gan made a polite speech, apologising for his unkempt appearance, and they were very well bred about it.

Ruby wouldn't hear of us leaving before we'd had coffee and she'd cut some sandwiches for the journey.

This all took a little time and I kept expecting Jamie to return but he didn't. A niggle of worry formed at the back of my mind. What was he doing?

Time to go. Ruby and Alastair came out on to the drive to wave goodbye to us.

'I'll make your farewells to Jamie,' Alastair said. 'He'll be sorry to have missed you.'

He gripped my hand and addded quietly, 'And thank you, my dear, for caring. But to be honest with you, I'm beginning to have second thoughts about trying to do the work of the police for them. Sometimes it's better to let sleeping dogs lie.'

He sounded desperately sad. I guessed he was afraid my investigations might lead right back to the Astara and they'd had enough trouble. If someone here was a villain, they didn't want to know it.

I knew then we'd been right to keep stumm about Gan's

finding Squib's body. You had to take it a little at a time with someone of Alastair's age. I pressed his hand and thanked him again.

'They're nice people,' Ganesh said as we lurched down the drive. 'It's a pity you couldn't help them, Fran.'

'I've been trying to tell you that!' I knew I sounded exasperated. You can never tell men anything. They always have to work it out for themselves and then they pretend they thought of it first.

The van had reached the bottom of the drive. I looked at my watch. 'Where do you think Jamie is?'

'In the pub,' said Gan. He was probably right.

'Turn right!' He glanced at me surprised. He'd been about to turn left, taking the lane down to the main road.

'I just remembered,' I said. 'I need to call by a farm near here, say goodbye to the people there. Their name is Bryant.'

Nick was in the yard. The cows were bellowing in the shed behind him. There was an old chap in gumboots and a cloth cap squelching about in the mud in the background whom I supposed was Biles, the hired labourer.

Nick and Ganesh eyed one another like a pair of duellists, observing all the courtesies but waiting for a chance to jump in and gain advantage. Nick took us into the kitchen and offered us tea which we declined. We had a long drive ahead of us. Penny wasn't there, for which I was sorry.

'She's at the shop,' Nick told us. 'She'll be staying over in Winchester for the next couple of days. Her partner's sick again.'

Ganesh had been looking from me to Nick and back

again. Now he cheered up a bit because he knows all about running a shop. He and Nick had some conversation about that and afterwards, they seemed to get along better.

'If you find out anything,' Nick said. 'Give me a call, here, at the farm. Ma was fond of Theresa Monkton. She felt sorry for her. We all did, I guess. After you called the other morning, Fran, Ma talked about Theresa a lot. It's a really bad business.'

I had a similar request. 'If you find out anything, let me know, please.' I scribbled on a piece of paper. 'This is my address, my flat. I've no phone, but you can send me a letter.'

'He can phone the shop,' Ganesh said. 'Give him our number.'

So we did that and parted company. As I was getting into the car Nick put his hand on the door before I could close it and stooped to say, 'I hope you'll come down here again sometime.'

He sounded as though he meant it. I mumbled something because Ganesh was giving us funny looks again.

'You seem to have hit it off with him!' Ganesh said dourly as we drove off.

'They're nice people. He knew Terry and he's upset about her death. So is his mother. Don't fuss, Gan.'

Ganesh muttered, 'I've got more to worry about than him. I've got to explain to Morgan about finding Squib. I think we should have got in touch with the police here.'

'I don't. Believe me, Ganesh, I'm right on this one.'

'And what', he asked, 'if someone else finds Squib before we get to Morgan? Not only the body but my footprints and the marks left by the van, too? How do I talk my way out of that one?'

'Don't worry about things which haven't happened,' I advised. 'Just worry about the things which have.'

We sat silent for some miles after that, picking up the argument and rehashing it only when traffic on the motorway had slowed to a crawl. Ahead was London, the great magnet drawing it all inward. I could feel its power tugging me towards it.

We quit the motorway and negotiated the network of roads through suburbs which seemed never-ending, running into one another, linked by scraps of tired greenery, scrappy workshops and car-sale forecourts. At last respectability, or at least a façade of it, began to give way to a jumble of grimy streets. I was back where I belonged. I never thought I'd be so pleased to see grubby shops offering 'fire-damaged goods' or 'closing down sales', gutters filled with debris, vandalised telephone kiosks festooned with cards advertising the services of local prostitutes, spray-can graffiti from the hand of someone called Gaz. All the things which to me spelled home . . . with not a horse or a chicken or a cow in sight.

Home Sweet Home is what you want it to be.

Chapter Seventeen

'Just what did you think you were playing at? You can't just waltz off when you feel like it. How dare you tamper with other witnesses? Do you realise I could book you right here and now for obstructing the police and wasting my time?'

Janice had been rampaging around her office, hurling accusations and reproaches mixed with a variety of threats, until she appeared in danger of getting seriously overwrought.

You will have realised that our return hadn't been well received and when they heard about Ganesh's find in the woods, things got very nasty. They split us up, of course, as was their way. As Ganesh was marched off to give details of his discovery and for the Hampshire police to be alerted to go out and look for it, he managed to call to me.

'When I get out of here I'll have to go over and see my family. I'll get in touch later, Fran!'

'If he gets out of here!' said Janice unpleasantly. 'Nor am I overlooking your part in this latest development. When Mr Patel told you he'd found a body it was your duty to see the matter was reported at once to the local police. It wasn't just up to him. You knew. You share responsibility. After I've booked you for obstruction, I dare say the Hampshire force will do the same. You, Miss Varady, are in trouble!'

I wanted to reply, 'What's new?' But that wouldn't have been tactful. I realised at least a token apology was called for on my part. I'd had some stage training and if I couldn't put on a good show of abject regret, I had no talent at all. I hung my head, shuffled about on my chair and mumbled I was sorry for having caused any bother. As for reporting Squib's body, we had thought she ought to know about it first. We'd made an honest mistake. I wondered whether to squeeze out a few tears, but one can go over the top. She wasn't a fool.

I must have turned in quite a fair and well-judged performance because Janice calmed down considerably. She made a speech in which she said she realised that Ganesh and I had panicked. As for my going down to Abbotsfield, I probably thought I could help. But I was certainly intelligent enough to know that police investigations had to be conducted according to the rules. Apart from anything else, when a case got to court – if it did – defence lawyers would seize on any irregularity to get evidence thrown out. I didn't want that to happen, did I?

All of this was more or less a reprise of the kind of lecture my old headmistress used to deliver regularly to me. I'd long ago developed a technique for letting it flow over my head while keeping a reasonably alert expression on my face.

What I was really doing, as she droned on about responsibility and tax-payers' money (where did they get into it?), was studying her. I decided she was only about thirty-five. How did anyone get to be that institutionalised by the mid-thirties? She was dressed today as if she were sixty-five, in a grey flannel suit and a nylon crepe blouse with a tie-bow at the neck. Where on earth did she buy those clothes? The only place I'd ever seen them offered for sale was in newspaper ads aimed at the middle-aged, usually described as 'practical' and 'available direct from our warehouse'. She even had the round-toed shoes, low-heeled, with little tabs on the top, which are advertised with a promise that your feet will never hurt again. No store sells things like that now, surely? I felt a bit sorry for her. I realised that if she looked like a bimbo, she wouldn't be taken seriously as a police officer. But it seemed a shame that she had to make herself look like that. It was defensiveness, pure and simple. There had to be a compromise somewhere in between. I decided that if I ever got to know her better, and off-duty as it were, I'd have a quiet word with her about it.

'If you have anything else at all to tell me,' she was saying, 'let's hear it now. Be absolutely open, leave nothing out, and I might just overlook your behaviour. Don't hold out on me, Francesca. If you do, believe me, you're for the chop!'

Now, it seemed to me there was a touch of muddled thinking here, having her cake and eating it. I was being carpeted for interfering, but she wanted to know what I'd learned in the country. I gave her a stern look to let her know I'd rumbled her.

Then I settled down to tell her about the shot in the plantation, about Lundy and his habit of violence towards his wife, about the solicitor's visit to Ariadne and anything else I could.

'You can't just ignore Jamie Monkton!' I finished. 'He has a motive. He runs the stud and Lundy takes his orders from him. He took me out into that plantation and set me up. Get both his and Lundy's dabs off them. You must have prints from our house you haven't identified. Match up just one set with either Jamie or Lundy and it puts him in that house. Let whoever it is explain it away, if he can. Jamie says he never went there and I know he lies.'

'You don't know it,' she said coldly. 'I'll decide what's to be done about Mr James Monkton and, indeed, this other man, Lundy.' She turned her steely gaze on me. 'As for you, Francesca. Please go back to your flat and stay there. I want to be able to find you when I need you, OK?'

'OK!' I said meekly.

I took the bus home, as I laughingly thought of the place. It didn't appear any more welcoming than when I'd left it. Some new and more imaginative graffiti decorated the walls and a few more windows were boarded up. The lift was still broken and the electric light on the staircase was out. Perhaps there had been a general power failure.

It was getting dark by now and I'd have appreciated the electricity. Meagre light through broken windowpanes at each landing illuminated the lower three or four flights. The rest ran on into the gloom. The middle section had to be negotiated in the dark, until the light from the next landing cast grey comfort on my faltering footsteps. A chill wind was funnelled up the stairwell. I made as fast a progress as I could, promising myself a cup of tea when I got to the flat.

It wasn't possible to hurry too much. It was quite likely that someone had left an object on the staircase to trip up climbers. The kids here liked doing that sort of thing. So I made my way carefully up, keeping one hand on the greasy walls. Disgusting though it all was, each gloomy cold tread took me nearer my goal. Then, as I turned to face the last flight and began to climb up, out of the lighted lower portion into the murk, I became aware that I wasn't alone. Above me in the darkness, another human being was waiting in silence.

I stopped. I couldn't see a thing but I could hear the soft in- and out-take of breath. I was, presumably, about to be mugged.

I called up, 'I haven't got any money. If I had any, I wouldn't be living here!'

He moved. He was, possibly, just a jolly local rapist.

Or he was, and I didn't know why I hadn't thought of this at first, the person who had killed Terry, come to kill me.

Panic seized me. I whirled round and ran, heedless of breaking my neck as I plunged down the way I'd come up. Somehow, in my panic and my headlong flight, I became aware that someone called my name. It came from above, echoing down the stairwell.

'Fran! Wait! It's only me! It's Ganesh!'

I leaned panting against the wall, my heart leaping about in my chest like a yoyo. What on earth was he playing at? I crawled back up the stairs and found him at the top, on my landing. Or at least, a shadowy outline which turned out to be him. I did not feel kindly towards him.

'Are you mad?' I raged. 'I nearly had a heart-attack! I didn't know who was up there! The lights are out. Anyway, I thought you'd gone home.'

'I did but they all started on at me. I walked out. Besides, I was wondering about you. How did you get on?'

'Could have been worse. Let's go in and have a cup of tea. I'll tell you about it when we get into the flat.'

He moved to intercept me as I started off down the dark corridor towards my front door.

'You can't, Fran. You can't go to the flat.'

'Why ever not?' I'd had enough and the only thing I wanted was to get into my own place. 'Don't fool around out here, Gan. I'm desperate for a cuppa.' I gave him a shove, but he stood firm and gripped my arm.

'I've already been along there, Fran. While you've been away someone's broken in—'

I jerked my arm free and ran past him along the landing, fumbling for my key, although I no longer needed it.

My visitors had smashed in the front door completely so that it didn't lock any more. Even if it had locked, there was a hole in the middle of it.

I gave it a push. It swung inward. I put my hand round and fumbled for the light. It ought to be on a different circuit to the public staircase. It was. It came on, the yellow beam flooding out through the wrecked door and bathing Ganesh and me in its glare.

Ganesh took hold of my shoulders. 'Fran, don't go in. You don't want to go in there.' He sounded sympathetic but I didn't want sympathy. I wanted to know what had been going on.

'Yes, I do!' I said tightly. 'It's not much, but it's the only home I've got!'

'Fran—!' He tried to hold me back. I shrugged him off. He let me go.

It didn't take long to see what had happened in my absence. The block's kids, a small army of competent vandals, had broken in and had a field day. They'd rampaged through every room. Obscene graffiti covered the walls. All my furniture, including that got for me by Euan, was broken up. The armchair was ripped with a knife and all the stuffing pulled out. They'd tried to set fire to it but fortunately it hadn't burned, only smouldered. They'd stolen all my personal stuff. Nev's books had been left, but torn up and the pages scattered around the room. I think I minded more about Nev's books than losing my gear. Nev had really cared about his books and his giving them to me had meant a great deal to both of us.

All the mould I'd cleaned off with bleach had grown back again in the bathroom and the cistern had been pulled out of the wall and flooded the floor. The floorboards sagged in the middle and the water was probably leaking right through, down into the flat below which wasn't occupied.

On top of it all, as if anything more was needed, the place smelled foul, acrid from the singed chair stuffing, stale from the mould and damp, but mostly because one of the little charmers had crapped right in the middle of the sitting room floor.

'I tried to warn you,' Ganesh said. 'You can't stay here. You'll have to come back to our place. Mum will fix you up with a bed.'

'Thanks, but no,' I told him. 'I'd be answering their questions half the night and you know they wouldn't understand.'

'So where are you going to sleep?' He looked round in disgust. 'This is a pigsty – look at that filth! Come on, Fran. Even Morgan wouldn't expect you to stay here!'

I thought about it. 'I'll go back to the squat!'

He stared at me. 'You're crazy. It's boarded up.'

'So – unboard it. You're always opening crates of fruit. You ought to be able to prise a few boards off a window. We did it before, Squib and Nev and I, when we went back for our gear.'

He looked exasperated. 'But you can't stay there on your own! I'll stay with you. Always supposing we can get in and the place isn't already occupied by half a dozen winos.'

'No, you won't. You'll go home and make it up with your parents. That's what I want, Gan? OK? I'll be all right.'

I was glad to be going back to the squat. The flat had never been anything but a prison. The squat, with all its imperfections and despite the dreadful thing which had happened there, had been home. We'd been happy enough there. I knew the old house and it knew me. We'd keep each other company.

But by the time we got there it was dark and the street was deserted and sinister, like an old B-movie set. Every house had been emptied and only two street lights worked. The only sign of life came from the flat above the Patels' shop at the corner where they were obviously waiting up for Ganesh, probably with a deputation of aunts and uncles sitting around to lend weight. We stood outside and looked up at the windows.

'I didn't ask you how you got on with the police after they split us up,' I said. 'Sorry to be so self-centred. Did they give you a bad time?'

'Could've been worse.' He spoke absently. 'They phoned through to Hampshire who sent out a car right away to the woods. They must've found Squib. There was a lot of yakking on the phone between coppers which didn't include me. Then I was told I could go home but I have to report back in tomorrow first thing in the morning. I'll probably have to go back to Hampshire, under police escort. They'll want to talk to me down there.'

'Did you tell your family, I mean, about finding a body?'

'No – they've got enough troubles. Dad's had a letter,' Ganesh sighed. 'We've got to go, too. The shop's coming down. They've offered compensation. But where will we go?'

'I'm sorry,' I said again. 'I thought that would happen. I know your dad had plans about a different kind of shop for the new houses and flats that will come. But they were bound to want to clear the entire area.'

'When they rebuild, we won't be able to afford to rent, much less buy, around here.' Ganesh pushed his hands into his pockets. 'The family's very upset. It sounds selfish, but at least it takes the pressure off me. Really, they've got more to worry about than me.'

A sari-ed figure appeared at an upper window, outlined against the lamplight within. It looked out at us, and then shimmered away like a *peri* in an oriental fairy-tale. The curtain was drawn.

'Usha,' Gan said. 'Don't worry, even if she saw us, she won't give us away.'

We trailed down the dismal street to our old house. The council had repaired the breakage we'd made last time and nailed new boards over the windows and doors, stronger than before. Ganesh got a chisel from the toolbox in the van and we went round the back. The kitchen window was still the most promising. After Ganesh had levered at it for quite a while one of the wooden panels came loose. I swiveled it around and judged I could squeeze through.

'This', said Ganesh gloomily, 'is breaking and entering. We can get done for this. Do you realise that?'

'Entering what? Only a condemned house. Come on, Gan. There's nothing to pinch in there.'

There certainly wasn't. When we'd managed to scramble inside we found that the council had emptied it of any remaining furniture and only bare boards were left.

I tried the kitchen tap. The water was still running. But when I went upstairs to try the taps in the bathroom I found that the council had filled the loo with concrete as a deterrent to anyone else hoping to move into the place.

'You can't stay here,' Ganesh said. 'You couldn't even take a leak.'

'I'll go out in the garden, behind a bush. We've got enough bushes out there. It's like a jungle.'

'And where will you sleep? On the floorboards? It's going to be cold in here tonight. It's out of the question!'

'Look!' I said crossly. 'It's for one night and I'll manage. Tomorrow I'll go and see Euan at the council and ask them to clean up the flat for me and fix up another door. Or if they won't do that, they can move me into one of the other highly desirable residences they've got empty in that block.'

Ganesh looked miserable. 'You're crackers, Fran. How can I leave you here?'

I told him that he could quite easily, and if I was

crackers, then that was my problem. I said if he wanted to help he could lend me the sleeping bag from the van.

He went off to get it, muttering and mumbling.

I took a look round. To be quite honest, now it was really dark I was having second thoughts about staying here overnight, all alone. But I was too proud and obstinate to admit that to Ganesh when he'd get back. He'd given me a torch from the van. I flashed it around, telling myself that so long as I *was* alone, I was OK.

Ganesh had been gone some time, longer than just to fetch the sleeping bag. At last he reappeared and called to me to take the stuff he was going to push through the kitchen window. He'd been home and fetched a roll of plastic sheeting and an empty crate.

'For you to sit on.'

He'd also brought a Thermos of hot tea and a bag of peaches.

'Mum says', he panted as he climbed through the window after I'd collected all this stuff, 'why don't you come to our place? Honestly, Fran, they wouldn't mind. She's really worried about you down here.'

'Tell her thanks, but now I've got the sleeping bag and all the rest of it, I'll really be fine.'

'I've got this as well.' He was fumbling with the plastic sheeting. 'It's thin stuff but if we put it down on the floor boards under the sleeping bag, at least it will stop the damp rising. Otherwise you won't be able to get up tomorrow. Your joints will be set solid.'

They'd probably be set solid anyway. I was still suffering from my equestrian adventures.

He spread the plastic on the floor. I spread the sleeping bag on it and put the crate alongside like a bedside table, with the Thermos on the top. It didn't look so bad.

'Quite cosy,' I said.

'You're not just crazy,' he told me. 'You're weird.' He sat on the floor with his arms resting on his knees and frowned at me in the light from the torch. 'I'll come over in the morning before I go down to the station and turn myself in for interrogation by the Hampshire Constabulary. Sure you don't want me to stay here?'

'Sure, Gan. You should go home and sort things out. I'm really tired. I've got all I need and I'll sleep like a log.'

'Not a chance!' he said discouragingly.

'How are things at your place?' I asked.

'Bad, but I can handle that, don't worry about it. Worry about yourself.'

He didn't want to go but he went.

I didn't really want him to go, but the notice to quit must have come as a bombshell to his parents and they needed him there.

I settled down for the night. I drank the tea and ate a couple of peaches and told myself that morning would soon come and although I might be a bit stiff, I'd suffer nothing worse.

I couldn't get off to sleep. I ached. My mind ran on furiously. I began to imagine things. Right above me was what had been Terry's room. Every time I heard a creak, which happened every few minutes, I thought about her body dangling from the light fitting up there. I began to think about ghosts. I wondered if she'd turn up and accuse me of deserting the job, down there at the Astara. I felt I had deserted her. I hadn't established who had killed her, though I'd established a fair motive for Jamie and a lesser one for Lundy. The idea that Jamie and Lundy might've worked together was more and more feasible. Jamie would have been the planner and Lundy his executioner. I would go and see Janice in the morning and argue it through with her again. That had to be the way it had been. She had at least to talk to Jamie.

Not that it would do any good, not unless they did find any prints in the house and the more I thought about that, the more it seemed a long shot. Even the crassest amateur knows to wear gloves these days. As for Janice questioning Jamie, he'd be more than capable of fending off her queries. He'd be plausible. He'd sit there looking handsome and frank and turning on the charm. Janice, going through her divorce, was vulnerable. There'd she be in her crepe blouse and one of her dowdy suits, putty in Jamie's hands.

And why not? He wasn't a dropout who lived in a squat, but a respectable member of society with a clean record sheet and probably some influential friends.

'You're no good as a detective, Fran Varady,' I said to myself. 'You're full of big ideas but, when it comes down to it, you've accomplished zilch. A couple of fuzzy snapshots and an unprovable theory about a will.'

I'd just meddled, that's what I'd done. Made things worse. Meddlers make themselves unpopular. Jamie wouldn't just be satisfied with clearing his name with Janice. He'd want to drop me in it, Gan also, if he could. He'd counter my theory with another for Janice to consider. In his scenario, I'd be the villain.

At this gloomy point in my musings, exhaustion took over. Not even the hard floor could keep me awake. I drifted off into uneasy sleep.

I dreamed about Abbotsfield. I was standing just inside the churchyard, by the tomb on which I'd sat to eat my sandwich. The church was ahead of me and Terry was standing some distance off by her lopsided cross in a long white nightgown. Her long fair hair fluttered around her face.

She called to me and asked what I was doing there. I said I'd come to see her and began to walk towards her. She beckoned encouragingly. But when I got closer I saw that the grave stood open. I wasn't surprised. Obviously she'd climbed out. I saw now that her white gown was smeared with earth. I felt very cold but I knew she was colder.

She was smiling with her lips but not with her eyes, which were like the round glass eyes of the toy animals, quite expressionless and unblinking. She held out her hand for me to take, but I was afraid to take it, because I knew I could never free myself from her grip and she would drag me down with her into the open pit behind her.

I turned and ran blindly, until I found myself, with the strange logic of dreams, in Terry's room. All the plush toy animals which had been on top of her cupboard were there. They came to life and walked round, glaring at me with those accusing glass eyes, like Terry in the churchyard. I told them to leave me alone and they began to squeak at me, as soft toys do when you press their plush stomachs.

At that point I woke up. All the nightmare visions vanished, but not the cold, and not squeaks. I could still hear those.

It was pitch dark. Ganesh's plastic sheet hadn't kept out the damp. No wonder I'd dreamed as I had. I didn't know what time it was. Then I heard that shrill squeak again. Not floorboards or wainscoting, not this time. A different noise. Something outside in the garden? Something inside? A rat?

Oh God! I sat up in a panic, fumbling for the torch. Before I could find it, I heard a louder noise and I realised that what I could hear was someone manoeuvring the loosened board over the kitchen window. Someone was climbing in.

Chapter Eighteen

Even now, when I think of that moment, I get goose bumps. I can't tell you what it was like. That was something you'd have to experience although I hope you never do. Fear held me paralysed. My brain refused to send any messages to my limbs telling them to move. Even to breathe was an effort. My heart must have been beating, but to me it was as if it had stopped. Everything had stopped. The only thing which moved was out there and, very soon, would be coming this way.

There was a dull thud as whoever it was dropped to the floor inside the house. The sound broke the spell which held me frozen. I slid out of the sleeping bag and managed to find the torch, gripping it with clammy fingers and afraid it would slip from my grasp. At least I had the presence of mind not to switch it on yet. Its sudden beam would give me a powerful surprise weapon, throwing the intruder off track. Whoever it was couldn't know I was there. Like me, he was probably looking for a place to doss. The sudden beam of the torch would frighten him. For a moment I would be in charge. I had to stay in charge. With luck, we could come to some arrangement.

Even as I worked all this out, I knew I was grasping at straws. The surprise was on me and the advantage his. For all I knew he could be some psychopath or schizophrenic released into what's laughingly known as 'community care'. I could be shut in here with a madman.

Then I had a thought which was as bad or even more frightening. Perhaps he *did* know I was there. Perhaps he wasn't just some homeless wanderer of the streets or a junkie looking for a place to indulge his habit or a kid bent on sniffing glue. Perhaps he was looking for *me*. I remembered how scared I'd been on the staircase at the flats. Perhaps, whoever he was, he had been there too, waiting in the dark, and only the presence of Ganesh had thrown him off his stride.

I tried to tell myself that, just as back at the flats, it might turn out to be Ganesh again, come back to check on me.

But I knew with an awful sickening certitude, that it was Jamie Monkton – or Lundy – or both.

Of course Jamie wasn't going to leave me free to roam around poking and prying into Theresa's death. I'd left Abbotsfield suddenly and within hours, the police had been down at the dell, digging up Squib's remains. The two things couldn't be unconnected. He must have guessed that if I hadn't found Squib, then Ganesh had. He had seen Ganesh's van parked in the dell. He was going to do something about us both, something final to shut us up and he was beginning with me. He didn't know what else I'd found out. But he did know about this house.

If he'd been to the tower block and seen the smashed-up flat, he'd have worked out I'd come here. That I'd run like a hunted animal back to my den. He'd killed Terry and poor Squib, even Squib's dog, and he'd have not the slightest compunction about killing me. No one would ever know, because he'd be away by morning. Ganesh would find my body and it would be another unsolved crime.

I didn't have time to dwell on that now. Jamie – or his executioner – was moving down the hallway towards the front room where I had been sleeping. I started cautiously towards the door, hoping to get behind it as it opened. The idea was that I'd slip out behind him, make it to the kitchen and get out of the window before he could stop me. All very unlikely, but the only chance I'd got.

But the plastic sheeting Ganesh had put down was slippy under my feet in socks, and as I skidded and tried to keep my footing, the door opened.

At first I couldn't see him. I could hear his breathing, a laboured breath because he'd struggled through the forced window with difficulty. Then my eyes adjusted to the degree of moonlight which had entered with him through the kitchen window. I saw his silhouette. If I'd had any lingering hope that it would be Ganesh, it was dispelled. The silhouetted figure was too tall and bulky. Besides, after the mistake at the flats, he would have called out at once to let me know he was there. Both Jamie and Lundy were a lot bigger than Gan. The menacing figure in the doorway could be either.

I did the only thing I could think of. I switched on the torch and directed the beam straight at him, hoping to dazzle him so that I could run past.

But I didn't run. I just stood there transfixed. Because the face the torchlight picked up, making it shimmer and gleam yellow and unreal, wasn't that of Jamie Monkton or the unlovely Lundy. It was Nick Bryant's.

I asked stupidly, 'Nick? What are you doing here?'

His voice, in reply, sounded odd, as if some switch had been flicked, distorting it in pitch and tone. 'I thought I'd find you here.' No expression in the words, no satisfaction or enmity. Nothing at all. A crazy voice, belonging to someone with whom there could be no reasoning.

The paralysis of fear and horror threatened to return and I thrust it away. I didn't entirely understand all this, but I must not just fold in the face of it. He had moved into the room and I saw he was cradling something in his arms: a double-barrelled shotgun.

'What do you want?' Another silly question. My voice croaked it out, sounding in all probability as distorted as his.

All the time my brain was racing. Nick? *Nick*? It didn't seem possible. Had I got it all wrong? Nice was *nice*. He was a nice person. His mother was a nice person. And he *liked* me. Nick liked me. I knew he did. He wouldn't hurt me, would he?

Yes, he would. I knew it.

I must have moved because he swung up the shotgun and I found myself staring down the twin barrels.

'No!' he ordered. 'Just sit down, right there where you are.'

I sat down on the quilted sleeping bag, wrapped my arms round my knees and waited. He moved towards me and kicked the crate across the room. He sat on it, between me and the door, and rested the shotgun on his knees.

I was still holding the torch and he said, 'Put that down beside you and don't touch it again.'

I put it down. Its beam shone straight ahead along the floor and illuminated his feet. The rest of him was in dusk but the shotgun barrels gleamed.

I said, 'If you fire that, someone will hear.'

'Who? This street is nothing but empty houses. Nothing between here and that corner shop. Anyway, around here if anyone heard a gunshot they would pretend they hadn't. Or even if they rang the police, by the time the coppers got here, I'd be gone.'

There was a horrid logic about his argument. I hadn't an answer to that one. My father used to say that there was an answer to all our problems if we thought about things calmly. But I wasn't in a state to think calmly and I don't think it would have helped if I had been.

I said, 'You fired before at me. You fired in the plantation and made the horse bolt. Were you trying to hit me or just spook the mare?'

'Knew you couldn't ride,' he said. 'Thought you'd break your neck.' He moved slightly as he spoke and twitched as if that switch had been thrown again. When he next spoke, his voice sounded more reasonable. I realised he had hyped himself up to this. In his own way, he was as nervous as I was. He'd tried to kill in the plantation by stealth. This, face to face, was trickier.

'I'm sorry about this, Fran.' The gun barrels sank a little, no longer aimed at my chest but at my shins. He sounded as if he did regret it. But not enough to make him change his mind. 'You're a really nice girl. But you ask too many questions and you're too bright. I've just got to stop you.'

'I can't believe this,' I told him. 'How could you? How could you do what you did to Terry?'

'It was her fault!' The gun barrels quivered and pointed at my chest again. I should have kept my big mouth shut. I hoped his finger wasn't going to slip on the trigger.

'I loved her. I really did!' he said hoarsely.

That made me angry. I stopped being scared and snapped, 'You killed her! What kind of love is that?'

'I didn't mean to do it!' he shouted.

'Oh? You strung her up there from the light fitting by accident? And after trying to rape her, too, to go by the bruises!'

'Shut up!'

He was in a rage and a voice in my head told me I ought to shut up. The madder he got, the sooner he'd do something drastic. Another voice told me that he was going to do that, anyway. However, the longer I kept him talking and the calmer I kept us both, the longer I had to think of something, although I couldn't for the life of me imagine what. I made a superhuman effort. He was nervous, scared, dreading the moment when he was going to have to shoot me. He, too, might long to put it off for a minute or two. Just until he could get his nerves under control. Nervous people talk.

'Tell me about it,' I invited in a nice pleasant voice.

'You wouldn't understand.' He sounded sullen.

'Try me.'

He hesitated. 'She was so beautiful. You didn't see her when she was pretty. When she lived here, she'd changed. When I saw her here I could've cried, honestly. She looked so thin and dirty and as if no one cared. But I cared, even though she'd changed so much. If you'd known her a few years back, there was no one like her, she was perfect.'

Terry the pretty doll. Alastair, Ariadne and Nick had all wanted to preserve her like that, in Cellophane. No wonder she'd run away. I thought of Kelly in the stable-yard. She'd never stood a chance of capturing Nick's attention. Nick had eyes only for the pretty little girl with the fair hair like spaniel's ears. Galumphing Kelly with the ham-like thighs would've made a first-rate farmer's wife for Nick, capable and devoted. But we don't want what we can have – and we certainly never like what's good for us.

Nick had momentarily wandered away down memory lane. 'I'd watched her grow up. Every time she came home from school on holiday she was prettier. She'd chat to me too those days. She wasn't afraid. Things changed one evening. It was at a Young Farmers' Club Christmas dance. Her hair was pinned up on top of her head and she had a really nice dress. She looked – I can't describe it. Just beautiful, that's all.'

He spoke the words with an almost pathetic naïveté and I remembered the photograph I'd seen on Ariadne's mantelshelf, showing Terry in a ball gown, looking like a million dollars. I told him I'd seen the photo of her in her finery and I could imagine how she'd looked at the Young Farmers' bash. That pleased him and he smiled. But I spoiled it straight off, because I couldn't dismiss an incongruous image of all those red-faced, healthy country types, lumbering around the dance floor with the cream of the county crumpet in their arms.

'You're *laughing*!' Nick exclaimed and the shotgun barrels leapt again in a way I really didn't like.

'No, I'm not! Why on earth should I be laughing now, for goodness sake? In my situation?'

'OK,' he said grudgingly but he relaxed, I was pleased to see, and even turned the gun barrels away from my chest. 'I told her that night that I loved her. It was true. But the more I tried to tell her how I felt, the less I seemed able to make her understand. Sometimes she acted as if she was scared of me. But I only wanted to love her. She should have understood that.'

He looked up suddenly and I could see the craziness on his face. I had to keep him talking. It was the only thing I could do. Keep him talking until I thought of something.

'But I don't understand,' I said. 'What about Squib? And what about Jamie Monkton?'

Nick chuckled. It was a cold, mirthless sound and made my blood freeze. 'Jamie Monkton? He led me to her. I knew he was looking for her and all I had to do was watch him. He'd find her for me.' He leaned forward again, earnestness on his face and in his voice. 'I thought, I'll learn about it from Kelly. She's always dropping by the farm and chattering away. So I waited and one morning, bingo! I didn't need Kelly. I'd taken the old truck down to the garage in Abbotsfield. It was in the repair shop and I was in there talking to the mechanic about it, when I saw Jamie's car outside by the petrol pumps. He was standing by it, talking to the proprietor, Jepson. They were always pals, those two. Both driving around in flash cars. I could hear every word. He said he knew now where his cousin was living. He'd had a bit of luck. He'd been asking around in pubs and he met some rock guitarist or other—'

'Declan!' I muttered fiercely. By the worst mischance, Jamie, scouring the pubs, had come across Declan and

Declan, whom Terry had rather fancied, had betrayed her. Even Squib hadn't done that. I just hoped, if I survived this night, I'd run into Declan again. I had things I wanted very much to say to him.

'Jamie talked about the place and how the whole street, Jubilee Street, was due for demolition and most of it empty and boarded up. He'd been there but no one had been at home. He said he was going back the next day and was filling up the car with juice ready for the trip. He asked Jepson not to say anything to Alastair, if he came by. He wanted to get it all sorted out first.

'It was my chance. Ma was away from the farm, over at the shop in Winchester. I told Biles I was taking the next day off and gave him a tenner to stop him telling Ma. I went up to London, to Jubilee Street, broke into an empty house opposite and waited. I saw you all go out. The one with the dog first and then you and some other fellow. I hoped Theresa was on her own there. I saw Jamie arrive and go to the door. He knocked for some time and I was afraid he was out of luck again. Then an upstairs window was pushed up and Theresa put out her head. I'd found her.'

'Did she let Jamie in?' I wondered, if I was very quick, I could grab the shotgun. But he was too far away.

He nodded. 'Eventually she did, but he didn't stay long. He came out and she slammed the door on him. He went off down the road towards an old graveyard of some sort. He looked pretty wild. He'd asked her to go home, I guessed, and she'd refused. I waited a few minutes until he'd gone, then went across and knocked at the door. I thought she'd look out, as she'd done before. But she must have thought it was Jamie come back, because she opened the front door straight away, ready to yell at him again. And then she saw who it was, that it was me.'

The horror of that moment must have been complete. Terry had opened the door to the one person she feared more than any. The one she'd run away from and hidden from so successfully.

I'd remembered something and frowned. 'I found a piece of blue chalk in Jamie's car.'

Nick nodded. 'I put it there. But I didn't pick it up that day in London, I got it – later.'

'When you killed poor Squib,' I accused him. 'If you'd given him twenty quid, he'd have gone away happy. He was a simple soul.'

Nick began to look angry. 'I didn't know that, did I? He came to the farm. He said he was looking for the Astara Stud. I didn't know whether he'd really made a mistake, was looking for Jamie, or whether he was looking for me. I couldn't take the risk he'd mess things up. I was on my own at the farm when he came. I offered him a cup of tea. It was easy . . . '

How could he just say it like that? He might have been talking about someone else who had done this dreadful thing. He appeared to feel no guilt or responsibility.

'I got rid of the chalks,' he said, 'and all his gear. But I kept a small piece of blue chalk, hoping I'd get a chance to plant it on Jamie Monkton somehow. You see, I wanted the police to know he'd been to the house, just in case he continued to keep quiet about it. I wanted them to think that it was Jamie's finding her that had made her kill herself. It was already clear to me that old Alastair Monkton and Mrs Cameron knew nothing of Jamie's visit to Jubilee Street. It was as he'd told Jepson, he meant to drive up to the Astara one day in triumph with Theresa in his car, that was his idea. Then, when she was found dead, he panicked and decided to tell no one he'd been there. Jepson would've kept quiet. Like I said, he and Jamie Monkton were always as thick as thieves. But I wasn't lettting him get away with that!

'I went up to the Astara on the pretext of seeing Alastair. Only Lundy was in the yard. But Jamie's car was by the garage. I pushed the chalk under the front passenger seat. You found it, did you?' He scowled. 'You messed up all my plans, Fran. You shouldn't have done that.' He lifted the gun and the twin barrels swung to point their ugly mouths at my chest.

I knew I had to put on the best acting performance of my life. *For* my life. I had to act someone who was calm and in control when my every instinct was to start screaming. I started thinking, with a crazy vanity, what a mess that shotgun was going to make of me. He must have quite an armoury at home. In the plantation he'd shot at me with a rifle.

'Now, Nick,' I said, 'you really can't do this. You can't go round killing people. It's got to stop.'

'I'm only going to kill *you*,' he argued, 'and you'll be the last.' He added, rather to my surprise, 'I'm not going to shoot you. I'm going to make it look like an accident. Just like I tried to do before with Theresa, but this time I'll get it right. You're going to lie down again on that quilt. Only take that plastic wrap out from underneath it and drape it over the top. They'll think you did that for some reason and it got over your face and suffocated you.'

Oh, nice. This was the same person at whose kitchen table I'd sat, drinking coffee and talking to him and his mother. Telling them everything. I was angry with myself for being such a fool. I was angry with myself for telling Ganesh I'd be all right here, when obviously I wasn't and, if I'd thought it through properly, I'd have realised that.

But you never know what's going to happen, that's for sure. And right now I'd seen something he hadn't.

He was sitting with his back to the door. It had swung closed behind him but not clicked shut and now it was slowly and silently opening again.

Chapter Nineteen

I didn't know who it was out there in the hall. But unless they were lining up in turn to have a crack at killing me, it ought to mean help. The trouble was, I didn't know if whoever was out there, knew Nick had a gun.

Nick must have sensed something, either from my manner, or because a draught from the opened door brushed his neck. He swung round.

At the same moment the door opened wide and Ganesh stepped in.

I jumped up and yelled, 'He's got a gun!'

At the same time, I threw myself across the room at Nick and crashed into him, knocking him to one side.

There was a deafening explosion. Large chunks of ceiling fell down round our ears. Then Ganesh and Nick were wrestling for the gun which swerved terrifyingly back and forth between them as they lurched to and fro.

I was as sure as I'd ever been of anything that someone was going to get killed and it was more than likely to be me, because the ugly twin mouths of the barrels kept swinging round to point at me as I dodged around the room and the two men.

It's not my way to do nothing and, as usual, I acted on instinct. Lacking any weapon except the torch which was a small thing and useless, I grabbed the crate, swung it up and cracked it on the back of Nick's head. It might not have been the most sensible thing to do in the circumstances as I realised after I'd done it. He staggered forward and the gun went off again.

This time a whole section of the wall fell out. Plaster dust filled the air, getting into my eyes, nose and mouth. In the semi-darkness and dust, Ganesh yelled, 'What do you think you're doing, Fran?'

It was the most wonderful sound I'd ever heard because I thought he'd just had his head blown off.

Nick had regained his balance in the distraction and was trying to swing up the gunstock to use it as a club. Ganesh grabbed his arm and slammed him back against the wall, dislodging another lump of plaster.

I grasped the torch in both hands and held it out level, trained on them, because I couldn't see what was going on.

To my surprise, somehow Ganesh had got hold of the shotgun and had it pressed lengthways across Nick's throat. Nick's eyes bulged and he was uttering a strangled gargle.

Ganesh said very nastily, 'Right, my son! That's both barrels fired. Now it's just you and me!'

I have to say that – with all due respect to Ganesh – Nick was an awful lot bigger and even if he was pinned against the wall at the moment, I wouldn't have bet he couldn't get free. But just then, a massive great chunk of ornamental cornice fell out of the corner of the ceiling above them. It landed right on top of Nick's head and he went down like a skittle.

There was a silence. More plaster dust had filled the air and my nostrils, and I coughed. Gan stepped back, holding the shotgun.

'You all right?'

'Yes!' I croaked. 'Why did you come back?'

'I couldn't sleep, worried about you.' He pushed the still form of Nick with his foot. 'I started to climb through the window and I heard his voice. So I kept it as quiet as I could.'

'He was going to kill me. He killed Terry and Squib. He's nuts.'

'I gathered that.'

I said in a very small voice, 'Thank you, Ganesh.'

'Don't mention it. I'll sit here with him and you go up to my place and call the police.' He sat down on the crate. 'And don't mention the shotgun to my family because they'll go crazy.'

As it turned out, Ganesh was wasting his breath with his request. By the time I reached the shop, the entire Patel clan was going crazy. They'd heard the shots, of course. Mr Patel was standing in the doorway with a wicked-looking cleaver. Mrs Patel was already phoning the police and all the aunts and uncles were milling about. It was obvious the action wasn't over by any means.

They came very quickly, the boys in blue. In the quiet of the night, the shots had been heard, not just up at the shop, but in the surrounding streets from which the inhabitants hadn't yet been cleared. Everyone was phoning the police. Nick had certainly been wrong about that.

The police surrounded the area in double-quick time

and brought up an armed response unit, all kitted out in body armour.

I tried to tell them what had happened, that they didn't need all that weaponry, it was all over, but I couldn't get anyone to listen to me. The one in charge just kept bawling through a loud-hailer.

'Now, everyone keep back! You, too, love! There's an armed man holed up in that building down there!'

'No, there isn't!' I argued, and Ganesh's parents and all the aunts and uncles argued, too. 'The gun's been fired. It's a double-barrelled shotgun, both barrels are empty, and anyway, the gunman is unconscious.'

'No, he isn't. He's moving around in there and he's probably got another weapon or ammunition.'

'No, he hasn't! You don't understand. That's not the gunman, it's only Ganesh . . .'

I tried to get it across to them but they just wouldn't listen. I asked, I begged, them to fetch Inspector Morgan, to wake her up if she was at home asleep, and tell her it was me, Fran Varady, and Ganesh Patel.

Useless. They pushed us all back behind a barrier, me, the Patels, and all the people who'd come running from houses in the street behind to see what was going on. You never saw such a motley crowd in all your life, every kind of clothing from nightwear to daywear, Doc Martens, fluffy slippers, saris, the lot. One old lady in a dressing gown but with a felt hat stuck on her head, kept asking, 'Is it a bomb?'

'Tell them to go away,' whispered a voice by my ear and a familiar smell made itself known. Edna had been tempted out from her graveyard by curiosity and stood beside me. She was nursing the kittens which, safe in their tomb hideaway, must have escaped the charity cat-nappers.

'I don't like them,' she persisted. 'Tell them to go away.'

I explained, with feeling, that no one listened to me. I suggested she take both herself and the kits back to the graveyard, out of harm's way. She wasn't listening to me, either.

'What are they doing?' she began to sound frightened. The kittens mewled in her embrace, squirming as she clasped them tighter.

Frankly, I hadn't time to worry about her. The police had fixed up temporary lights, and marksmen were swarming down the side alley of the squat, and taking up positions in the garden behind, training their weapons on the kitchen window. Nick *was* being over-optimistic when he'd said no one would do anything if they heard the shots and he'd get away. It was like Custer's Last Stand down there.

The man with the loud-hailer was roaring, 'Come out with your hands up!'

Mr Patel and the uncles were shouting at them. Mrs Patel and the aunts were wailing. Usha was threatening to call a solicitor. (I suppose she and Jay knew one. I certainly didn't.) I was jumping up and down, yelling they should get hold of Inspector Janice. To put the finishing touch, Edna began to scream in a thin, high sound like some kind of radio signal. It went on and on, as if she didn't need to draw breath.

None of our efforts was achieving anything. I had to do something. At this rate, they would almost certainly shoot Ganesh in error. I couldn't get down the street now because they'd blocked it off. But I knew this area better than they did. I headed for Edna's graveyard.

Beside it stood the first house of the terrace. I scrambled

over the wall and dropped down into the garden. I landed on a stack of abandoned dustbins. There was a hideous clamour, but nobody heard it, or paid it any attention, in the general uproar.

I started across the adjacent gardens, one at a time, hauling myself over walls, getting my feet caught in old fruit netting and beanpole frames. It was like tackling one of those obstacle courses the Army sets up. I ricked my ankle and scraped my hands and just kept going, because I was getting nearer and nearer the back garden of the squat and the scene of the action.

I fell over the last wall and landed amongst the bushes just at the moment Ganesh threw the gun out of the kitchen window. Then he climbed out. All the coppers jumped him.

They had him pinned to the ground and I was convinced he'd suffocate under all that lot. They kept shouting things like, 'All right, sunshine, don't offer any resistance!' while I was still yelling that the man they wanted was inside the house under a lump of ceiling, unconscious. Although, for all I knew, he was coming round by now and would make his escape while all the attention was fixed on poor old Ganesh.

I tried to pull them off him, howling, 'You've got the wrong man, you idiots!' till I was hoarse. So they arrested me too and marched us both off to the station.

It was bedlam down there. They took our fingerprints. This gave me a definite feeling of *déjà vu*. I told them, they needn't bother to take mine, they already had mine, in connection with the murder enquiry at that house.

That really put the cat among the pigeons. They got so

excited I thought they'd have a collective fit. I think they thought they'd got a gang of urban terrorists.

Eventually, Inspector Janice turned up in jeans and a baggy sweater, with matching bags under her eyes, and rescued us.

I was really pleased to see her.

I jumped up, shouting, 'Did they find him? Did they find Nick Bryant? They didn't let him get away, did they?'

'No, Fran, they didn't let him get away,' she said soothingly. 'They searched the place and he was just coming round. He didn't give any trouble.'

I collapsed back on my chair. 'Thank God for that! So it's all over.'

'Now, I wouldn't want you to run away with that idea,' she said coolly. 'You've got an awful lot of explaining to do – to *me*!'

Chapter Twenty

'He's been telling us everything,' Janice said.

It was two days since 'The Siege of Jubilee Street' as the newspapers were calling it. Janice had calmed down considerably and even Parry had smiled at me as I'd arrived today and said, 'Hullo, it's Annie Oakley!' I was still so relieved, just to be alive, that I let him get away with that.

Ganesh and I were sitting in Morgan's office. We'd been offered tea straight away this time and some rather boring biscuits.

They were all being particularly nice to Ganesh because of the mistake they'd made. They had been dropping hints about a bravery award and all the swelling and bruises were clearing up.

Another bonus was that he could do no wrong in his family's eyes now. He was a hero. For the time being, anyway.

'I still can't believe it,' I told the inspector. 'I was so convinced Jamie or Lundy killed her and either of them could have come after me. I shone the torch at the intruder, fully expecting, in fact, prepared, to see either of them. I had hazy plans how I'd deal with the situation.

When I saw Nick, I just froze like an idiot. I couldn't believe my eyes. I thought I must still be dreaming. Most ridiculous of all, I still believed he liked me, as if that meant he wouldn't harm me! Huh! He loved Terry and he murdered her! What kind of a nutter is he anyway? He seemed so normal, too, down there on his farm. Sort of reassuring.'

'I told you you didn't know anything about the country,' said Ganesh, radiating smugness and glee. If we hadn't been in Janice's office, I'd have thrown something at him. He had been saying 'I told you so' in a dozen or more different ways, ever since the police had picked up Nick and released us.

All I could do for the moment was challenge him with, 'You met Nick yourself. If he struck you as a killer, you kept very quiet about it! You thought the same as me. He was fine.'

'I didn't think anything. I didn't make any judgement. You did. You decided he was Mr Nice Guy. And he wasn't.'

The tone of proceedings was becoming acrimonious and Janice hastened to break it up.

'Bryant isn't Mr Nice Guy but he isn't a regular villain, either. It's rather sad. He keeps insisting he loved Theresa. But it wasn't really love so much as obsession. He was truly obsessed with her.'

'You mean,' I said, 'he's a headcase.'

'Strong emotions', said Janice, sounding like an Agony Aunt, 'make people behave in unlooked-for ways.' She looked knowing and a bit glazed about the eyes at the same time. I supposed she knew what she was talking about, being a policewoman. But I also suspected she read those paperback romances in her spare time. 'He insists', she went on, 'that he didn't intend to kill her. But they argued and he had a sort of black-out. He doesn't remember what he did, but when he came out of it, she was lying on the floor. He thought she was dead. He decided, in a panic, to make it look like suicide. He rigged up the – well, you know what. His head was in a whirl, in a crazy state.'

'The man's a maniac,' I said firmly. 'He just went around killing people who got in his way. He killed poor Squib. I suppose no one thinks Squib matters, but I do. I suppose you didn't see any sign of Squib's dog?' I added without much hope.

Janice denied indignantly that they were not treating Squib's death as equally important and added that they'd found a dead dog in bushes near the body. She said she was sorry. She looked sorry as she said it and I suspected that she was more upset by the death of the dog than by Squib's death.

But she insisted again that I mustn't think they were giving Squib's murder anything less than full attention. 'It was a cold-blooded business,' she said. 'Bryant had no excuse of passion that time and he'd have killed you in the same calculated way.'

'Thank you,' I told her. 'I know.'

'Once he killed the girl,' Ganesh said unexpectedly, 'he was on the slippery slope. Couldn't stop. Had to keep on killing.'

'It all might have been avoided,' Janice mused, 'if only Theresa could have confided in someone, asked for some help in dealing with the problem of Bryant's obsession. Something might have been done about it to stop it right there, at the beginning. But I suppose she felt her grandfather and great-aunt were too elderly and frail to be bothered with it. And she didn't like or trust her cousin, Jamie Monkton. So she kept it to herself. She was already unhappy at home for other reasons, mostly connected with that will, as you rightly surmised, Francesca. Ariadne Cameron had named Theresa as sole beneficiary and expected her to behave as someone who was going to inherit a fortune and a thriving business. Alastair Monkton had the sentimental view that old gentlemen have of their grandchildren. He didn't want to hear about anything nasty. Jamie Monkton was stalking round the place, glowering because he'd been cut out of the will, despite the fact that he was doing all the work and had virtually saved the stud from bankruptcy. She hardly needed Bryant, half crazy with jealousy, lurking about the lanes waiting for her. She'd run away before and she did it again. Lord knows, who could blame her?' Janice concluded in heartfelt tones.

Neither of us could quarrel with that. I wasn't surprised she'd left. It only surprised me she'd gone back a couple of times before making the final break.

There was a long silence. Ganesh stared out of the window. I sat looking at the floor. Janice Morgan looked at me.

'We do realise, Francesca,' she said, 'that we would never have got to Bryant if it hadn't been for you. But you took a terrible risk, and you nearly came to grief.'

She was looking quite human and I decided she wasn't such a bad sort. But she had that pussy-cat bow blouse on again. When she'd turned up in the early hours to rescue Gan and me, she'd worn jeans and looked normal. Now she looked like an early version of the Iron Lady again.

I felt I ought to put her right on one thing. 'OK,' I said. 'But, as you said, you wouldn't have got him if I hadn't gone down there and found him . . . and got him worried enough to follow me to London. So the risk was worth it, I reckon.'

'I don't!' said Ganesh. 'I think it was daft. I always thought it was daft, from the beginning. I kept telling you so.'

'Listen to Mr Patel another time, will you?' Janice asked me.

Ganesh beamed at her.

But I'd got used to making my own decisions and I think she knew that.

Ganesh and I went back to the Astara to see Alastair and Ariadne.

It was strange returning there. The whole place looked so familiar this time, unlike when I'd first arrived there, out of the blue. I realise now I must have seemed to them rather like one of those evacuee kids from the East End who were pitched out into the villages during the Second World War. They'd welcomed me in much as they'd have done to the wartime children.

But familiarity didn't completely wipe away the awkwardness. I spotted Kelly in the yard. She gave me a despairing look and disappeared into the stables. Her world had ended with Nick's arrest. She probably still loved him and was indulging in some dream of his coming out of jail ready to recognise her devotion and let her help him rebuild his life. She was wasting her time.

Jamie wasn't there. He'd gone to Germany, it seemed, to see some horses bred at the stud, compete in some competition or other. I couldn't help wondering whether he, now, would be Ariadne's heir. It seemed to me she hadn't much choice. But it wasn't one of the things we discussed.

They told us that Penny Bryant was selling the farm. I felt sorry for Penny. I wished I could go and see her but obviously it was better I didn't. Both Alastair and Ariadne expressed concern at the danger I'd been in. Alastair said he felt responsible, since he'd come to see me in London and set me on the murderer's trail, as he put it.

I assured him he wasn't responsible, which was what he wanted to hear. He made an excuse to get me alone and handed over an envelope.

'As agreed,' he said.

I didn't want to take it, but beggars can't be choosers. I needed the money and I considered that I'd earned it.

Before we drove home we did make one more visit, Ganesh and I. We went down to the churchyard where Terry was buried. I felt I had to go. I wanted to tell her it was all right now. But perhaps she knew.

It was very pretty down there, the trees and nicely cut grass. A brand new white headstone had replaced the lopsided wooden cross and fresh flowers had been put in a marble vase. It felt calm and I thought she was at peace and probably glad it had all been sorted out. I didn't feel I owed her anything any more. In a way, I felt I knew her better now and liked her better . . . and if she still cared anything about me wherever she was now, she felt the same way about me. We were friends now, at last.

Ganesh has this idea about reincarnation and says Terry is somewhere else in the world in another body, probably a baby which has just been born somewhere. But I'm not keen on that idea. I like to know who I am.

I'm me, Fran Varady.

Oh, and I ran into Declan and did he hear from *me*!

Alastair says he thinks he knows of a flat I can rent. It's a basement flat in a house belonging to a retired lady librarian he knows in NW1. That sounds very upmarket to me. I'd like to talk to someone about books. As soon as I get any money to spare, I'm going to replace all Nev's which he gave me and got torn up by those wretched kids.

Ganesh is indulging in a monumental sulk because I'm talking of moving away.

'You won't like it, up north,' he said, as if I was headed for Hadrian's Wall, not NW1. 'They won't be friendly, like we are, round here.'

'Who is?' I retorted. 'Edna in the churchyard? Or the kids who did over my flat?'

'You know what I mean,' he said. 'At least everyone round here is skint. It sort of binds people together, having nothing.'

'Rubbish!' I told him firmly. 'It just makes them all better at nicking what anyone else does have.'

'You'll see,' he said smugly. And just to finish it off he added, 'And you won't be able to walk down to the river and look across at the Crystal City, as we do now.'

I told him, I wasn't leaving him behind, only getting a better address than the derelict flat Euan had found for me to replace the other one. Euan-speak described it as 'short-term accommodation' but it was just like the last. In the adjacent tower block, in fact. I'd had it with Euan's bright ideas. The pipes in the new place had started rattling all night long and I knew – I just *knew* – there were mice. They'd eaten a hole in my packet of cornflakes.

'So, it has to be better. Either of us would only have to get on a bus if we wanted to visit.'

'Better?' he snarled at me. 'What's better about it? I've been up there, you know, and seen them all poncing around. Have you seen the prices they charge for greens and fruit up there? Four times what Dad and I charge here.'

I pointed out that their shop was under the axe and why didn't they all think of moving too, to a classier area where people would have more money. 'You'd double your takings and your dad could do his speciality foods, the way he's always talked of doing.'

Ganesh said sourly, 'You may be getting somewhere at a cheap rent. We wouldn't.'

I gave up arguing with him about it because when he gets in a mood like that, the only thing to do is leave him until he comes round. He does eventually but he likes to take his time.

All in all, there's going to have to be something pretty horrendously wrong with lady librarian's flat to stop me taking it. Besides, I've got this idea. I didn't do so badly as a detective and I might start up in business. Nothing big, just small personal inquiries, because I haven't the organisation. I've only got Ganesh and his van (when he gets over his mood).

When he does – get over it – I'll tell him about my idea.

Keeping Bad Company

To friend and fellow writer
Angela Arney

Chapter One

I was sitting on one of those red metal benches on Marylebone Station concourse when I first met up with Alkie Albie Smith. Not that Alkie Albie would have been my choice of companion. A cup of coffee brought about our acquaintance.

I was miserably aware how cold it was that morning. I wasn't wearing my usual jeans, but a daft mini skirt and useless tights which wouldn't have kept out the mildest breeze, let alone the draught straight from Siberia that cut through the open-arched station entry to whistle around my ankles.

I was waiting for the train from High Wycombe to arrive, and for Ganesh Patel, who'd be on it. Just for the purpose, all the trains were running late. To fight off the cold, I'd bought coffee from the Quick Snack stall, and settled down to wait. The coffee was in one of those green-with-white-polka-dot polystyrene beakers and scalding hot, so I put it on the vacant seat beside me until it cooled down. A simple thing like that can cause so much trouble. If I'd kept hold of the beaker. If I'd worn warmer clothing. If the train hadn't been running late. When all these things come together and then events turn out as they do, you have to believe in Fate – or Sod's Law, as you may prefer to term it.

Ganesh, by the way, is a friend of mine. His family used to run the greengrocery that stood on the corner of the street in which was the house where I shared a squat. Redevelopment flattened our whole area and displaced us all. We straggled away like a bunch of refugees carrying our belongings to find somewhere else and start all over again. I had less to lose than the Patels. I'm an aspiring actress who has yet to get her Equity card and hasn't done anything yet but street theatre. But what little the squat was it had been a roof over my head, and then it wasn't there, captured by the council after a long, spirited and ultimately doomed defence.

Yet others fared worse. The Patels lost their shop, which was their livelihood, and the flat over it, which was their home. That's to say they pretty well lost everything. Compensation doesn't necessarily make that good. How do you compensate someone for years of hard work? For their plans and dreams for the future?

They hadn't been able to find another similar place to rent – or which they could afford to rent – in London and had moved out to High Wycombe. There they could stay with their married daughter, Usha, and her husband, Jay, while they searched for premises they could afford. That's why Ganesh was coming in on that particular train. He'd been to see how they were getting on.

Ganesh wasn't living in High Wycombe, as there wasn't room for him. He was lodging with and working for Uncle

Hari. Working for Hari had advantages and a rather greater number of disadvantages. The big advantage was that Hari's newsagent's and tobacconist's shop was just round the corner from where I lived. I'd just moved into a basement flat in Camden, of which I'll tell you more in a minute. The move was thanks to an old fellow called Alastair Monkton for whom I'd done some detective work. (And done it, I may say modestly, rather well.)

It was a bit of luck for me, having Ganesh nearby. Ganesh thinks clearly in straight lines. Sometimes it's irritating, but sometimes it helps. At least I knew he was there. I could count on Ganesh and we all need someone we can count on. It was good for him, too, because the job was cleaner and easier than the greengrocery – no hauling sacks of spuds and crates of fruit and veg around – and his family hadn't to worry about him.

But on the other hand, Uncle Hari was by way of a grade-one neurotic, one of those people who live on their nerves. Everyone who came into his shop was, in his mind, a potential shoplifter, which meant that after they'd left, he'd rush to count the remaining stock of Mars bars and peanut brittle. If anyone bought a magazine, he leafed through it suspiciously to make sure the customer hadn't slipped another mag inside it. Either that or he worried that some juvenile had got hold of one of the adult mags on the top shelf. If the customer asked for a packet of ciggies from the shelves behind his counter, Hari's head swivelled like an owl's, right round, to make sure the customer hadn't palmed something from the counter while his back was turned.

He was, in fact, the most worried man I'd ever met. He worried about everything, not just the business overheads and rates and things like that. He worried about the state of the pavement outside the store and the unreliability of the streetlighting and lack of litter baskets. He fretted about his health, Ganesh's health, my health, anyone's health . . . Chiefly, however, he lived in fear of some unpleasant surprise being sprung on him.

He did have reason for this. Ganesh told me Hari had had a traumatic experience that had marked him for life. A kid had come into the shop one day and bought twenty cigarettes. He was a big tough-looking kid, perhaps not quite sixteen, but big enough to be sixteen. Anyway, as Hari tried to explain to the magistrates, he was the sort of kid who, if he'd been refused the cigarettes, would've come back that night with his mates and kicked in the windows. So Hari sold them to him.

Only moments later, when he'd hardly had time to put the money in the till, a woman representing some trading standards agency rushed in, yelling at him for selling cigarettes to an underage customer. She was followed by a guy with a camera and another with sound equipment. The whole thing had been a setup by one of those TV programmes which like to make sure the consumer is being protected, or getting his rights. Never mind protecting poor Hari against that element of local youth which didn't care about anyone's rights. Hari found himself star of a show he hadn't volunteered to be in. He nearly had a nervous breakdown and was still swallowing a fearsome array of herbal remedy pills, all supposed to enable you to Cope.

Now he worried every time he sold a packet of ciggies to anyone who didn't qualify for a bus pass, and worried more when he didn't sell any, because business was down. Chief among his current crop of obsessions were: that the traffic going past the shop was shaking the foundations of a very old building; that the air pollution was bad for his sinus problems; that the new council parking regulations had put double yellow lines outside, which put people off pulling in to the kerb and nipping in to buy something.

Ganesh is a practical sort of person but even he was getting jumpy, being with Uncle Hari all the time. The way things were going, he would be trying the herbal pills soon. Visiting his parents that day would have given him a break, though not exactly a restful one. But even a change of problems is something, and the way life goes, sometimes it's the best you can hope for.

The display screens above the access to the platforms flickered and informed us that the delay, which was due to a unit failure at Wembley, was likely to last another half-hour. I wasn't going to sit there for thirty minutes more slowly petrifying. I'd take my drink and find somewhere warmer. So I reached for it and that's when I became aware that I had company.

The immediate impression was of a looming presence, hovering over me, and a whiff of sour booze dregs. There he was, no more than an arm's length away, with his eyes fixed on my coffee. He was wondering whether it belonged to me or whether some traveller had abandoned it to sprint for a train. He reached out tentatively and asked, 'That yours, dear?'

I told him it was and snatched it up protectively. Disappointment crumpled his face, which was already creased in folds like a bulldog's. He was a good sixty-five, or so I judged, with long greasy grey hair and pepper-and-salt stubble on his chin. He wore a tattered, dirty army greatcoat teamed oddly with clean, newish, stone-washed jeans. Some charity that hands out clothes to the homeless had probably given him those. It was a pity they hadn't also given him a pair of trainers as the ones he was wearing were about to fall apart. Inside all these clothes he was so thin he looked as if the keen breeze might bowl him over and back down the escalators to the tube, up which I guessed he'd just come.

Partly to get rid of him and partly because often enough myself I've not had the price of a cuppa, I took pity on him. I fished out a fifty-pence piece and told him to go and buy himself a coffee.

He brightened up. 'Thanks very much, dear!' He grabbed the money and padded off in a curiously light-footed way, actually making, rather to my surprise, for the coffee stall. I'd have guessed he'd have put my contribution towards something in a bottle, but it was a cold day.

I know I should have ignored him, but when have I ever acted wisely? I soon knew I'd been unwise on this occasion, because, having got his coffee, he came back and chummily sat down beside me.

'You're a good girl,' he said. 'Pity there ain't more like you.'

That was a first. I don't remember getting such generous, unqualified approval, not since Dad and Grandma Varady died. My mother walked out on us when I was only a kid, so I was brought up by my father and Hungarian Grandma Varady. They were the best family anyone could have asked for, so I didn't miss my mum. Things started to go wrong, as far as I was concerned, my first day at primary school. There was a mishap with the fingerpaint and the teacher stood over me – like a twenty-foot-tall ogre in a fairytale – shaking her finger and intoning, 'I see you're going to be a naughty little girl, Francesca Varady!'

She must have been a witch because that really put the kibosh on it. I never did get the hang of pleasing adults. After that, it was downhill all the way until the fatal day, just before I was sixteen, when I was asked to leave the private dayschool I attended.

That school was a meeting place for upwardly mobile entrepreneurial types and downwardly sliding impoverished professionals clinging on by their fingertips. The two groups collided there via their daughters. One group of pupils was collected by sharp-faced, bottle-blonde mothers driving flash cars. The other set of girls was collected by plain, vague women in sagging skirts, driving old motors. Occasionally, when it was raining hard, one of the first group would let down the car window and bawl at me as I stood at the bus stop, 'Jump in, love, and I'll run you home!' The others never offered me a lift and acted as if I were contagious.

I couldn't blame them. The fact was, I belonged to neither group. They didn't know what to make of me. I didn't have a mother in skin-tight designer wear nor in a Barbour. I had Grandma Varady, who'd turn up on Open

Day in a rusty black velvet dress and a crooked wig. They treated me like a freak so I began to behave like one and it stuck. My family had slaved and saved to send me to that school. I wasn't sorry to leave it but I was desperately sorry for Dad and Grandma, who sacrificed so much for me. I was also sorry I dropped out of the Dramatic Arts course at the local college which followed my swift removal from school. I did seem to fit in there. But my leaving was due to circumstances beyond my control, as they say: Grandma dying about a year after Dad died, and my becoming homeless and all the rest of it. One day I'll make it as an actress, you see if I don't.

In the meantime, even the approval of an old wino like my companion rang comfortingly on the ear. So easily are we flattered.

I said, 'Thanks.'

He was prising the plastic lid off the beaker and he had a touch of the shakes, so I added a warning that he should take care. I doubt he had much sensation left in his fingers, which were white beneath the dirt, due to lack of circulation, and tipped with ochre-coloured overgrown nails.

'It's all right, dear,' he said. 'What's your name, then?'

'Fran,' I told him.

'I'm Albert Antony Smith,' he announced with something of a flourish. 'Otherwise known as Alkie Albie. They call me that but it ain't true. Slander, that's what it is. I like a drink like anyone does, don't they? Dare say you like a drink, glass of wine, mebbe?' He belched and I was engulfed in a souvenir of his last encounter with the grape.

I shifted smartly along the metal bench and told him that yes, I liked a glass of wine, but this wasn't one of the occasions and if he thought I was going to buy him anything alcoholic, he could forget it. The coffee was as far as it went and he should make the most of it.

His crinkled, grey-stubbled face was a mesh of open-pored skin dotted with blackheads, which gave the impression he looked at you through a spotted veil, like the ones on hats worn by forties film actresses. These damaged features took on a shocked expression. He denied vehemently that he'd had any such idea in mind.

Then he slurped up the boiling coffee in a way that suggested he couldn't have much sensation left in his mouth either. I sipped mine cautiously and it was still almost unbearably hot. Why do they do that – serve it so hot? They know you're waiting for a train and have only got so much time to drink the stuff.

'I've been down the tube,' he said, confirming my guess. He indicated the entry to the Underground a little way off, by the ticket windows. 'It's nice and warm down there. I spend most of the day down the tube this time of year, till the transport coppers throw me out. They're miserable buggers, them coppers. I sleep rough mostly, in doorways and such. Bloody cold it is, too.'

I knew that. But I said nothing because I didn't want to encourage him, though I'd left it a bit late for that and he didn't need encouragement anyway.

He rubbed his nose on his sleeve and snorted noisily. 'Cold gets you terrible on the chest.'

'Have you tried the Salvation Army hostels?' I asked.

'I never go to hostels 'less I has to,' he said. 'They're very keen on baths in them places. Don't do you no good, bathing. Washes away the natural oils.' Slurp. Sniff. Snort. 'You got a job, dear? Or you on the dole?'

'I haven't got a job at the moment,' I said. 'I was waitressing but the café burnt down.'

'Shame,' he sympathised. 'Protection geezers, was it?'

'No, just the chip pan.'

'Nasty,' he said.

'I want to be an actress,' I told him, though goodness knows why. Perhaps to stop him sniffing.

'They always want girls in them bars in Soho. Bit of waitressing, bit of stripping. Do all right.'

'Acting, Albie!' I snapped. 'A-C-T-I-N-G, all right?'

'A thespian!' he said grandly. 'I know what that is. I ain't ignorant. Ter be or not ter be, that's the ticket!'

'That is the *question*, Albie!' I wasn't sure why I was bothering but I sensed there was a good-natured sociability under all that grime. It made me feel I couldn't just tell the poor old devil to push off.

'I had an act once.' He leaned back on the metal bench and gazed dreamily at the Quick Snack stall. People had cleared away from all around us and we sat there together in cosy isolation.

I thought he'd got a pretty good one now, considering how easily he'd conned me out of a cup of coffee. But his next words cut me down to size.

'I was on the halls,' he said. 'Don't have variety no more. All that tellyvision, that's what killed it. We had some marvellous acts on the halls.'

'Go on, Albie.' I was surprised and really interested. Poor old fellow, He'd been someone once. Just shows you shouldn't judge. And, oh God, look at him now. Was I going to end up like that? As a bag lady, mad as a hatter, and with all my belongings in a couple of sacks?

'I had some poodles,' he said. 'They're very intelligent, are poodles. They learn very quick. Three of 'em I had. Mimi, Chou-Chou and Fifi. They done tricks, you know. You wouldn't think how clever they were. They played football, walked on their hind legs, played dead. Mimi pushed Fifi along in a little cart, done up like a nursemaid in a frilly cap and Fifi with a kid's bonnet on. But Chou-Chou, he was the smartest. He could count numbers and read 'em. I'd hold up a card and he'd bark the right number of times. I had to give him a bit of signal, of course, but the audience never saw it. He was the best dog I ever had, Chou-Chou, and dead easy to train. He was very partial to a glass of stout. He'd have done anything for a nip of stout, would old Chou-Chou.'

'I'd have liked to have seen the act,' I said honestly. I didn't ask what happened to kill it off because I didn't want to know. Perhaps it had just been the down-turn in the variety scene, but I guess the bottle had done it. Albie'd shown up once too often, too drunk to do the act, or made a fool of himself on stage and that had been it. I wondered what happened to Mimi, Chou-Chou and Fifi.

As if he could read my mind, he added. 'I couldn't feed 'em, after that. I couldn't feed meself. They was clever little dawgs. Woman took them as said she could find 'em homes. I hope she found 'em good homes. I asked her to try and keep 'em together. They were used to being together. But I reckon she split 'em up. No one would want all three of them. Reckon they pined.'

Not only the poodles had pined, I thought.

He seemed to pull himself together with an effort. 'What else you do, then?' he asked. 'When you're resting, as we sez in the business?' Clearly he now saw us as fellow professionals.

'I look into things for people. I'm a sort of enquiry agent – unofficial.' I tried not to sound self-conscious.

He put down his beaker and stared at me. 'What, a private eye, like?'

'Not a proper one. No office or anything. I'd have to keep books and pay tax and stuff if I set up properly. I'm unofficial. Anything legal.'

'Are you now . . .' he said very slowly and, when I thought about it later, very seriously.

I should have got up and run then, but I didn't.

'You any good at it?'

'Not bad,' I said with just a twinge of conscience because I'd only had one case. But I'd managed it pretty well, so my failure rate was nil and there's not many detectives can say that, can they?

He was quiet for quite a while and I was just grateful for it. A few people had come through the gates from the platforms and it looked as if a train was in. They must have fixed the broken-down train or shunted it away.

'You see funny things when you sleep rough, like I do.'

What?' I was watching for Ganesh and only half heard Albie.

He obliged by repeating it. 'Only I keep my head down. I don't want no trouble. It's like anyone what's out and about at night, on the streets. You see a lot of things and you say nothing. Fellows what work on the dustcarts, going round the restaurants and so on, clearing away, early hours of the morning – they see all sorts, but they never say anything. That way, no one bothers the dustmen and it's the only way they can work safe, see?'

He peered into the bottom of his empty cup but I wasn't obliging with another fifty-pence piece. I'd just got my giro but it didn't stretch to supporting Albie as well as me in the style to which we had the misfortune to be accustomed.

But he had other things on his mind. 'I saw something the other night, though, and it's been really buggin' me ever since. I saw a girl. Nice young girl, she was, not a tart. She wore jeans and a little denim jacket over a big knitted sweater. She had long fair hair with one of them things what keeps it tidy.'

He put his hand to his head and drew a line from ear to ear over the top of his skull, meaning, I supposed, an Alice band. I knew about them. The daughters of the mothers with the baggy skirts had been keen on them.

'About your age, mebbe a year or two younger. Not very old. Pretty. Running like the clappers. She had a good turn of speed, too.'

'Running for the last train,' I said idly. I don't know why, perhaps because we were in a station.

'Naw . . . I told you. I was in the porch, over at St Agatha's church. You know St Agatha's?'

I did know it. It was a quarter of a mile or so from where I lived, a red-brick Gothic lookalike with wire over all the windows to protect them from missiles, like stones or Molotov cocktails. Churches attract that kind of attention these days.

'She wasn't running for no train. She was running from two fellers. Only they was in a car, so it didn't do her no good. They come screeching round the corner, pulls up by my porch. Out jumps these two blokes and grabs the girl. She starts kicking and yelling, but one of 'em put a hand over her mouth. They shove her in the car and whoosh, off they go.'

This story was beginning to worry me, always supposing that he hadn't simply made it up. But it had a ring of truth about it. I thought of a possible explanation, not nice, but possible.

'St Agatha's runs a refuge,' I said. 'For battered wives and so on. She might've come from there, or been on her way there, and her husband, or boyfriend, and one of his friends grabbed her.'

'She didn't look like no battered wife,' Albie said. 'She looked like one of the Sloanes, what they call 'em. I seen it clear. Right by me. Only they didn't see me. I squeezed in the back of the porch, outa the streetlight.' He paused. 'They weren't no amateurs,' he said. 'They were heavies. They weren't no husband or boyfriend. They knew what they were about. He'd got a bit of a cloth in his hand.'

'Who had?' I was getting more and more worried. At this rate I'd be needing some of Hari's pills.

'One of the fellers. He put it over her face. It smelled,

like a horspital. I could smell it, even from where I was. She stopped kicking, sagged a bit, and he shoved her in the back of the car. She went in limp and just lay there on the back seat in a heap. I could just see her shoulder in that woolly sweater. Knockout drops.'

'Did you report this, Albie?'

'Course I didn't!' He sounded reproachful as if I'd suggested something mildly indecent. 'Think I want my head bashed in? They'd come looking for me, they would, them fellers. I'd be a witness. I see their faces and their motor. It was blue, or I think it was. The lamplight plays tricks with colours. It was an old model, Cortina. It'd got a bit of damage along one side, a white scrape, like he'd had a run-in with a white car and it'd left its mark, know what I mean?'

I knew what he meant. I also reflected that the fact he'd noticed so much was remarkable. However, on the whole, I thought so many details made it unlikely he was making it all up.

'Albie, you're saying you witnessed a serious crime! That girl could be in real danger. You ought—'

'Fran?'

I'd been so engrossed with Albie's story that I'd failed to see that Ganesh had arrived. He was standing in front of me, hands shoved in the pockets of his black leather jacket, and frowning. The wind whipped up his long black hair. He took a hand from his pocket to point at Albie and asked, 'What does *he* want?'

'Who's this, then?' asked Albie, and it was clear he was offended. 'Friend of yours?'

'Yes, I was waiting—' But I didn't get any further.

Albie got up. 'Ta for the coffee, ducks.' He began to pad away in that surprisingly nimble way he had.

'Wait, Albie!' I called.

But he'd gone, through the main arch and out into the road.

'For goodness' sake, Fran!' (I could see Ganesh hadn't come back from High Wycombe in the merriest of moods.) 'What do you want to sit talking to him for?'

'He's a witness!' I exclaimed, jumping up.

'To what? How to live on an exclusive diet of whisky?' Ganesh asked, making an impatient move towards the exit.

'To a kidnapping!' I shouted and it was then, as the words left my mouth, that I fully realised what I'd said.

Ganesh was staring at me. With more than a touch of despair I repeated, 'He witnessed a kidnapping, Gan, and I'm the only person he's told or is ever likely to tell about it.'

Ganesh dropped his holdall to the ground and made a violent gesture of dismissal. 'Why must you always do this, Fran?'

'Do what?' I babbled, taken aback by the vehemence in his voice. Ganesh gets sarcastic and he gets censorious but he doesn't generally lose his cool.

'Mix in such bad company!' he retorted. 'You know it always brings you trouble!'

Chapter Two

Before I go any further, I ought to explain that, despite what you may be thinking, life wasn't going too badly for me at that time. At least I had a decent place to live and that was definitely an improvement on my previous situation.

Immediately before moving into my present flat I'd been living in short-term council accommodation in a tower block. The lets were short term because the whole building was scheduled to come down. Half of it already stood empty, boarded up and vandalised. Drug addicts broke in and indulged their various habits and insalubrious ways. Kids sniffed glue and various down-and-outs dossed. The council cleared them out at intervals and boarded the flats up again. Back came the junkies the next night and so it went on, with the occasional suicide plunging past the window on his way from the roof, muggers lurking in the entry hall, and Leslie, the neighbourhood pyromaniac, sneaking round trying to start his fires.

People like me were moved in there because the council had nowhere else to put us, or that it wanted to put us. We had low or nonexistent priority on the housing list and we were desperate enough to be prepared to put up with the squalor and the danger. It wasn't the first such place I'd lived in. I'd been vandalised out of an earlier one. That second one was even grottier than the first one, something I wouldn't have considered possible. But it's a fact that no matter how bad things are, they can always get worse. Beggars can't be choosers, they say, and I bet 'they' are comfortably housed.

There's only so long anyone can stand living like that and I'd got to the point where I was considering asking Leslie if I could borrow his matches. Things Had To Change. But if I walked out, the council would have said I'd made myself homeless intentionally, and they were under no further obligation towards me.

I'd have been prepared to settle for almost anything else. I had been enquiring without much hope about a place in another squat when Alastair Monkton got in touch.

The last time I'd seen Alastair he'd promised to see what he could do to help. I'd taken it as his polite way of saying farewell, like people you hear bawling 'we must have lunch' at someone they clearly mean to avoid like the plague.

But Alastair had come up trumps, being a gent of the old school, man of his word, etc., etc. Besides which, since I'd almost got killed trying to help *him* out, he owed me a favour. He told me about his friend in Camden. She was a retired lady librarian by the name of Daphne Knowles, whose house had a basement flat that she was willing to let to the right person.

I foresaw a problem in that. As you'll have gathered,

few people would consider me 'the right person' for anything, much less to have lodging under the same roof. Any lady librarian of advanced years, and certainly any known to Alastair, would, I imagined, be rather fussy about the company she kept and fussier still who lived in her basement flat. I knew Alastair had put in a good word for me, but I wasn't counting on it being enough.

Still, worrying what she might think of me was jumping the gun. Without money one can do nothing and I had to establish my financial position before I approached the librarian. Without much optimism. I set out for the council's benefits office. If I could at least persuade the woman I'd be able to pay the rent, it'd be something. Though what poor old Alastair and the lady librarian might consider a reasonable rent, would probably fall way outside my budget. I was undergoing one of my frequent jobless spells.

It was a quiet morning when I got to the benefits office, just a student with his head in a book, an out-of-work dancer, and a man with a cardboard box on his knees. The box was bound with string and had airholes punched in it. From time to time, a scrabbling sound came from inside it.

The student's number was called first, so off he went and I sat talking to the dancer who'd been out of work because of medical problems. She had consequently got behind with the rent and received notice to quit. She told me all about her stress fractures and asked me whether I thought she ought to accept a job she'd been offered abroad.

'Some of these overseas dancing jobs are a bit dodgy,'

she explained. 'When you get there, the sort of dancing they want isn't the sort of thing I trained for.'

I commiserated, knowing how hard it is to get a living from the performing arts, but suggested she check out the job offer carefully.

The student had gone off in a huff. It was the dancer's turn at the counter and that left me with the man with the cardboard box. By now, he was talking to it in a furtive whisper. I had to ask what was in it. I'm human.

He was happy enough to untie the string and open it up. It turned out to contain a large white Angora rabbit with pink eyes. It wouldn't have surprised me if the box had been completely empty or held an old boot, because you meet a lot of people like that out on the streets.

'I've got to leave the place we've living at,' he explained. 'It's got a rule, no animals. Plain stupid, I call it. I mean, it's not like a rabbit is a dog, is it? Winston's got his own little hutch and everything. I keep him clean. He don't smell. Cats is worse than rabbits. Cats go roaming around. Winston don't do that. But the landlord's downright unreasonable. He reckons if he lets me keep Winston there, next thing he'll have to allow pet snakes and things what more rightly oughta be in the zoo. So we've got to go. I mean, I couldn't part with Winston. He's all I've got.'

Winston twitched his nose and crouched quivering in his box. He looked like a nice enough rabbit, as they go, but it was a depressing thought that anyone could be left with no living friend but a rabbit. Whenever I get too smug about my own lack of strings attached, I try to remember people I've met like this.

The man leaned towards me, his face creased in worry. 'I never leave him behind when I go out. I always bring him with me in his box like this. He don't mind. He's used to it. There's people living where I am now that I wouldn't trust if I left Winston all alone. When I came back, I'd find the kids had got him out of his hutch, taken him round the back somewhere, and chucked him to a couple of dogs for a bit of fun. I've seen a couple of dogs with a good grip, one either end, tug a small creature like Winston here, clear in two. 'Course, that'd be if someone else hadn't turned him into rissoles first.'

I said sincerely that I hoped he found them both somewhere else safer to live.

After this, it was my turn at the counter.

I explained I'd been told of a vacant flat. Before committing myself, I needed to know what kind of help I might hope for with the rent, being out of work.

After I'd answered all the questions – and there were a lot of them – about my personal circumstances and where the flat was and what it was like (which I didn't yet know), there was good news and bad news.

The good news was that I would probably qualify for maximum benefit. The bad news, before I got too euphoric, was that in my case this would be based on what the council considered a reasonable rent for the sort of accommodation suitable for me in the area where I intended to live. Here we hit a snag. The accommodation the Rent Officer seemed likely to consider suitable for me was probably something a little bigger than Winston's hutch. Since Daphne's flat was likely to be quite a bit roomier, and was located in an area where vacant bedsits were as rare as hen's teeth, and landlords could name their price, whatever I got by way of benefit wouldn't nearly pay the rent. I'd have to find the difference myself.

'Or find a cheaper place,' suggested the woman behind the counter, smiling kindly at me.

It was much as I'd expected and I couldn't grumble. But it did seem that even going to view the flat would be a wasted journey. I went all the same, because I felt I owed it to Alastair.

I must say the first view of the area served to confirm my fears that I'd be considered the wrong person. It was depressingly genteel. Coming from where I was living, it was like being beamed down to another planet. The house itself was tall and narrow in a long curving terrace of such houses, all white-washed, with freshly painted doors and sparkling windows. One flight of steep steps ran from pavement to front door and another down into the basement. The road seemed unnaturally quiet. One or two householders had put shrubs in ornamental containers outside their doors.

That sort of thing wasn't recommended on the balconies of my tower block. The tub and plant would disappear inside five minutes, very likely pitched over in a light-hearted attempt to brain someone on the ground below. What I saw in Daphne's street was life, all right, but not as I knew it.

One oddity struck me. At intervals along the pavement,

before each house, was a round brass disc like a small manhole cover. Before Daphne's house the brass disc had been replaced by a circle of opaque toughened glass similar to the glass skylight in subterranean public toilets. Strange.

Before I announced myself, I crept down into the basement and took a look around. The entrance area was cramped because part of it was taken up with a newly constructed wall which ran between the house and the pavement above. I couldn't see the purpose of this and it had me puzzled. There was a window by the front door and taking a look through it I saw a large room brighter than many basements because additional light was admitted through a window at the far end, which appeared to be an outlet on the garden. It was furnished with quite decent furniture. Through a half-open door, I glimpsed a kitchenette. Even this first sight revealed the place to be clean, newly decorated and highly desirable. I was amazed it was still empty.

I was already certain I wasn't the sort of person who got to live in flats like this, even with the council's help. Daphne Knowles would probably press an alarm button or something the moment she set eyes on me. I might find a job, at some future date, that would pay a decent wage and enable me completely to transform myself and my life-style, but as of that moment I had neither job nor money and this place was right out of my league.

I'd come this far and Alastair would be asking Miss Knowles whether I'd been in touch, so I climbed back up both flights of steps, and rang her doorbell.

After a moment I heard a regular padding footfall. The

door opened and there stood a tall, very thin woman with wiry grey hair. She was wearing jogging pants and a sweat-shirt. On her feet were brightly patterned Fair Isle socks with soft leather soles attached. I was prepared for her to say, 'Go away, I don't give at the door!' But she didn't.

'Hullo,' she said cheerfully.

'I'm Fran Varady,' I introduced myself. 'Alastair sent me.'

'Of course you are,' she replied. 'Do come in.'

She shut the front door behind us and set off ahead of me down the hall at a brisk pace. I scurried along behind her, trying to get a look at the place as I went.

What I saw only convinced me more that I had no chance. The house oozed respectability. The furniture was old but polished and probably valuable. We were talking antiques here. Narrow stairs with carved wooden balusters ran up to unseen regions. The stair wall was lined with early French fashion prints. There was a lingering smell of coffee brewed fresh at breakfast time, lavender wax and fresh flowers.

We arrived in a large, airy sitting room overlooking a scrap of garden. The sun beamed in and lit up the spines of rows and rows of books. This was a librarian's home, all right. There was a table by the window and on it, a cumbersome old-fashioned manual typewriter. A sheet of paper was sticking out of the top and a pile of other paper was stacked beside it. It seemed I'd interrupted her at work. That would probably also count against me.

Daphne Knowles seated herself in a cane-framed rocking chair upholstered with bright green and pink flowered cretonne, and indicated I should take a seat on the sofa. I sank down into feather cushions and sprawled there, trapped, and feeling at a considerable disadvantage. Daphne, beaming at me, began to tip back and forth in her cane rocker, which groaned a teeth-grinding protest.

'So you're Alastair's girl!' she observed.

For one dreadful moment I thought there had been a mix-up, and she imagined I was Alastair's granddaughter, who was dead. I tried to lean forward as I hastened to explain, 'No, I'm only Fran who—'

'Yes, yes, I know that.'

She waved a hand at me and I sank back again. Getting out of this kind of sofa was always more difficult than collapsing down on it. I couldn't get leverage from my legs and it was a question of grabbing the arms and hauling oneself up and out.

'It was such a sad business, but life does go on. I'm a firm believer in reincarnation.' The rocker creaked and I could see why she preferred it to this sofa or either of the matching armchairs.

'I've a friend who believes in that,' I told her.

She leaned forward, serious. 'It isn't the dead, you see, who have the problem. The problem is for the living who have to go on, well, living when they've lost a dear one. I've told Alastair he mustn't worry about Theresa but he took it all very hard.' She sighed, then perked up. 'He tells me you want to be an actress.'

'It's what I dream about.' I added apologetically, 'We all dream about something. I did start a drama course, but I had to drop out.'

'Ah, yes,' she said and her eyes drifted towards the typewriter. I wondered whether it was in order to ask what she was working on. Before I had a chance, she asked, 'Would you like to see the flat?'

Jangling a bunch of keys she led me out of the house and down to the basement steps.

'As you see,' she said. 'It's completely separate down here, quite self-contained. There's no longer any communication through from my place. It's been bricked up.' She unlocked the front door and we went in.

She seemed to think I'd want to look around by myself, so she stayed by the door and waited.

I could see now that the furniture consisted of a pine rustic-style table and four chairs, and a large old-fashioned sofa covered in blue rep. There was a small television set on a low pine occasional table. The floor was newly carpeted wall to wall in dove grey.

I opened a door and found a small bathroom, also newly equipped. I inspected the kitchenette glimpsed from outside. Like the main room, it had a small window admitting light from the garden. It would be at ground level outside, but here it was halfway up the wall. There was a dinky little cooker and a fridge.

She must be asking the earth for this place. I was grateful to Alastair, but he just didn't realise. I knew I could never afford it.

Out of curiosity, I went back to the main room and asked, 'Where does the new brickwork you can see from outside come in?'

'It's a corridor leading to the bedroom.' Daphne led me

to a door to the left of the basement window. She opened it and sure enough, the new brick wall outside created a narrow corridor inside that led into a small square windowless room. Windowless, that was, in the normal sense. Light permeated through from a round skylight above and I realised that we stood beneath the pavement. Eureka!

'Victorian coal cellar,' explained Daphne. 'These houses had all the mod cons of their day. The coal was tipped down a chute through one of the brass manholes you probably saw in the pavement as you came along here. Straight into the cellar, no need for the coalman to invade the house. Most houses still use the cellars as junk rooms. One or two, like this one, have made an access from the basement flat. Previously the only access was in the well of the building, completely detached from the house.'

She switched on the light. A pine bedstead and wardrobe more or less filled the space. It gave you an odd sort of feeling in there and wouldn't do if you were at all claustrophobic. It was reinforced by the sound of footsteps passing over our heads. I wondered if this might be a bargaining point when it came to fixing the rent. Not everyone would fancy the setup.

'No one can see through the glass,' Daphne said reassuringly, perhaps thinking my silence meant I was worrying about that. 'And not many people go past. It's a very quiet street.'

It was confession time. I owned up. 'It's all very nice, but I couldn't afford it. I'm sorry. Thank you for taking time to show me around.'

She put her head on one side like a tall thin bird. 'If you really like it, and it would suit you,' she said delicately, 'we can discuss mutually convenient terms.'

My heart hopped. I sternly ordered it to calm down and not start getting excited about what wasn't going to happen.

Daphne led me back to the sitting room and we both sat down on the blue rep sofa.

'I should explain,' she began. 'I'm seventy-one now.'

I expressed surprise because she didn't look it. She waved my words away.

'My friends and relations, who mean well but *will* interfere, say I oughtn't to live quite alone. I can't see why not. I'm perfectly fit and not a bit gaga. They keep nagging at me. So I had the basement flat done up and the cellar turned into extra living space and joined on as you saw. I was playing for time with the alterations. I didn't really intend to let it. I hate the thought of strangers living in my house, even detached strangers down here. But eventually the work was finished and then they all began asking, when was I going to advertise the flat?

'Never, was what I told them. I'd wait until someone was recommended to me. So then they began recommending people and none of them was at all *sympathique*, as the French say. There was absolutely no rapport between us. My family said it didn't matter because I needn't ever see the tenants. But then, what was the point of them being down here? The idea was, if there was an emergency, I could get hold of someone quickly. But if there's an emergency you don't want to get hold of people you don't like, do you? So I kept making excuses not to let.'

She paused to look at me anxiously, her eyes asking whether I understood. I told her I did. It was her privacy and her independence all those well-meaning people were intent on chipping away at. Knowing how much I valued my independence, I knew exactly how she felt. I tried to explain this.

She beamed and nodded enthusiastically. 'I thought you'd understand. Alastair was pretty sure you'd be just the person but I was cautious. I wanted to wait and see. But I think you are *sympathique* and so, if the flat would suit you, we can fix a rent you can pay.'

I was in no position to turn the offer down. Besides which, it was far and away the best offer I was likely to get, probably in my entire life. I had a couple of qualms, I admit. One was that nothing comes without a price tag of some sort. It doesn't have to be money. The other doubt had to do with that strange little bedroom under the pavement. But I could worry about all that later. I told her the flat would suit me fine.

'Sure he saw a kidnapping,' said Ganesh. 'He also saw pink snakes, giant pandas and little men in green jackets playing fiddles.'

Ganesh can be difficult and he was being particularly so right now. We'd gone straight to my new flat from the station and had argued all the way there. Now we were sitting over plates of reheated dal and still arguing. (I'm not a cook. Ganesh had brought the dal from High

Wycombe in a plastic tub.) Not only the dal had been rehashed. We were picking over Alkie Albie's story for the umpteenth time.

'I believe him,' I said. 'Mostly because of the details, like the bit about the cloth with the knock-out drops on it.'

Gan put down his fork. 'Oh, come on, anyone could make that up!'

'And the Alice band.'

'The what?'

I explained what an Alice band was. 'He could have described her any way he liked, but a detail like that isn't something he'd imagine. He saw her. Besides, because he's down and out doesn't mean he isn't perfectly capable of observation.'

Gan pushed his plate away. 'You think I don't know anything about that old fellow, don't you? You're wrong. He's always around this part of town. You happen not to have run into him before. Let me tell you, you got him on a good day. He goes past the shop. Usually he's roaring drunk and the drunker he gets, the more aggressive he gets. He staggers along shaking his fist and leaping in front of perfect strangers, offering to fight them. Hari runs and shuts the door in case he tries to come in the shop.'

'I don't know why Hari even tries to run that shop,' I said, nettled. 'He doesn't trust anyone who goes in it. He's getting an ulcer. Why doesn't he go into another line of business which wouldn't attract the kids? We need a dry-cleaner's around here.'

Ganesh's face lit up. 'You and I could—'

'No, we couldn't, Gan!'

'It's a decent business.'

'I can't stand the chemical smell,' I said firmly.

This was also rehashing an old argument. We all have a dream, as I'd told Daphne. Gan's dream was that he and I could go into business somewhere. The idea of being tied to a shop didn't strike me so much as a dream as an out-and-out nightmare. I understood Hari's neuroses only too well. Put in charge of a business I'd end up just like Hari, swallowing the herbal pills and working myself towards early heart failure. Just thinking about being tied to anything fills me with strong negative emotions, as they say. Scares me witless, in other words.

I'd no present job and I'd no family. But I did, still do, have my independence and it's worth more and more to me as I see the price other people pay for giving theirs up. That's why I was in tune with Daphne. As for not owning anything, that doesn't have to be so bad. Not owning anything means nothing owns you. I have a decent place to live right now, but otherwise I don't have anything (except Gan as a friend but that's worth a lot).

But take Ganesh as an example. He has a close and loving family. But they have expectations of him. That's a terrible burden for anyone to bear. No one has expectations of me, not any longer. Grandma Varady and Dad had hopes of me once but I let them down. I'm sorry about that and always shall be, but there's nothing I can do about that now. There's never anything anyone can do about the past except, possibly, learn from it and that's not easy. 'Learn from your mistakes!' people say with varying degrees of smugness.

'Listen, chums!' I want to cry out. 'We make the sort of mistakes we make because we're the kind of people we are. We're poor judges of character, or easily influenced, too kind-hearted for our own good or just plain lazy. So we go on making the same mistakes over and over again.' I suppose you could say that in the end it gets to be a habit, a way of life.

This is not to say I don't have plans, hopes, expectations, dreams, call it what you will, for myself. I do. But as long as I don't owe anything to anyone but me, Fran Varady, I can't let anyone but myself down. That's the way I like it.

I stood up, collected the dishes and took them to my tiny kitchen. I was feeling rattled because perhaps, despite my earlier claim that no one has expectations of me, I realised it was possible Ganesh did. What's more, I could see now that Alastair did. They both expected me to make good somehow in some acceptable way. Which meant, rejoin the human rat-race. Now there was Daphne as well. If I wasn't careful, the pressure would get to me and if that ever happened I'd have to move on, walk away from them all.

Enough about me. I didn't want to get neurotic.

'How are your people getting on?' I called out as I filled the kettle for tea. 'Any luck with new premises?'

'They've found a couple of possibilities. Jay's sorting out what they can afford.'

Jay's an accountant. An accountant as a son-in-law is useful and the Patels were getting good advice. Ganesh, however, sounded depressed. I guessed that other things weren't going so well in High Wycombe. I went back into the sitting room. Gan had tidied up the table and was now wandering around tidying up the rest of the room.

'Look,' I said. 'They'll sort something out.'

'Yes. They'll either get a place in High Wycombe and expect me to move out there to run it with them. Or they won't get a place and I'll have to stay on here with Hari.'

'Why don't you tell them what *you* want?' I said, exasperated. 'You can't please everyone all the time.'

He grunted.

'In the meantime,' I went on briskly, because there was no point in letting him mope, 'what do we do about Albie?'

He expelled air between his teeth in a hiss and spun round, long black hair flying. 'We don't do anything! We'd have to get him to tell his story again to the police. He probably wouldn't even remember it. We don't even know where he is now.'

'You said yourself, he's always around here. We could find him. He's distinctive.'

'There I agree with you!' He jabbed a finger at me. 'He's also totally unreliable, Fran. When did this – or when was this snatch *supposed* to have taken place?'

'Quite recently.'

'*When*?' he persisted.

'Look, I don't know! We'd have to ask him again!'

So that's why we ended up spending the afternoon looking for Alkie Albie Smith.

Needless to say, we didn't find him. We went back to the station and asked the railway staff, the taxi-drivers outside, anyone who looked as if he might have been there earlier in the day. Surprisingly, a few people knew who we meant. Albie, it seemed, was quite a local character. But no one had a clue where he went when he wasn't hanging around Marylebone . . . or offering to punch passers-by outside Hari's newsagent's.

'That's it, then,' said Ganesh, sounding relieved. 'We tried. He'll have got hold of some booze and be sleeping it off somewhere. If you see him again, you can ask him again. Otherwise there's absolutely nothing we can do. I still think he dreamed it all up. You'd bought him coffee. You'd demonstrated you were a soft touch. He wanted a quid off you and was spinning an interesting tale. Look, I've got to get back to the shop or Hari will be worrying.'

'When isn't he? We should tell the police.'

'Give over, Fran. They'd chuck you out of the copshop before you finished your story. You didn't see anything. All you know is, Albie reckoned he saw something – and let's face it, the old chap isn't going to impress the police as a reliable witness!'

I wasn't going to argue with Ganesh. It's almost impossible at the best of times. Ganesh always makes perfect sense. The more sense he makes, the more I disagree with him. So I let him go. But I wasn't letting the matter go. I don't give up that easily. I could at least try to report it. So that's where I went, the nick.

Contrary to what some people might think of me, I don't have anything against our gallant constabulary. It does sometimes appear as if they've got something against *me*, but that's their problem. It was worse when I hadn't a regular address. But even now I've got a proper address, they treat me like I had a record as long as your arm, which I haven't, I may add. Gan says, what can I expect if I go around with holes in my jeans and a haircut that looks as if someone ran a lawnmower over it. Probably it doesn't help that my temper has rather a short fuse and the plods can be so frustratingly thick. We get into arguments and the Law doesn't like that. Generally, I leave them alone and hope they'll leave me alone.

Walking voluntarily into the local police station that afternoon felt all wrong. I was a fish out of water and probably looked as if I'd come to confess to being the Camden chainsaw killer.

It was a quiet period. A middle-aged desk sergeant was drinking tea from a mug with 'George' painted on it. A short distance away, down the counter, an intense woman in a red mac and black beret was making a formal complaint about a neighbour to an impatient woman officer who had probably heard it before.

'He exposes himself to me!' said the woman. 'Every evening at the bay window.'

'We made enquiries,' said the WPC. 'No one else has been bothered by him and he denies it.'

'Every evening!' persisted the woman. 'Wearing nothing but one of them baseball caps.'

The desk sergeant, seeing I'd become distracted, put down his mug and enquired, 'Yes?'

I apologised for my inattention and said I'd come to make a report.

'Sergeant Henderson,' he said. 'You wait over there, take a seat. And you're late. Should have been here this morning, ten sharp.'

'Why can't I report it to you?' All he was doing was drinking his tea and – I could now see – doing a crossword.

'If you're on bail and gotta report in daily,' he said, 'you see Sergeant Henderson. He deals with that.'

I explained, very patiently considering the insult, that I hadn't come to report myself but to *make* a report regarding an incident.

'An incident?' he asked suspiciously. 'Mugging? Traffic offence?'

'None of those. Much more serious.' He brightened up so I added quickly, 'Well, I didn't actually witness it myself.'

This didn't go down well. He'd picked up a Biro and now he put it down again and a scowl puckered his receding hairline. The suspicion began to grow in my heart that Ganesh had been right.

I started talking quickly before he could interrupt and managed to get out the gist of Albie's tale.

The woman with neighbour problem was interested at least. She'd left off telling her own tale and was watching me closely.

The desk sergeant looked as if pension day couldn't come soon enough as far as he was concerned. 'Now, let's get this straight,' he said. 'You were told by some old fellow who happened to sit down next to you on a public bench that he'd seen a snatch. Why didn't he report it himself?'

'He's living rough,' I said. 'He doesn't want trouble.'

He rolled his eyes upwards theatrically. 'Living rough? Oh well, yes, that makes it a whole lot easier! You wouldn't know his name, I suppose? Because, let's face it, dear, there's not a lot we can do with what you've just told me now. Half those old dossers are doolally. Live in a world of their own, you know. It comes of drinking anything they can find which is alcohol-based. You wouldn't credit what they'll knock back without a blink. Stuff which would poison you and me. They lose all contact with reality. Even if there's a grain of truth in it, the time scale's out. They tell you something like it happened yesterday and it turns out it took place forty years ago. If you knew his name, of course, we could check it out – if we could find him.'

In a general sense he was probably right. But I didn't believe that the drink had scuppered Alkie Albie, despite his nickname. I knew what had done for Albie. He'd dropped out of the regular world the day he'd had to part with Fifi, Mimi and Chou-Chou. The nice kind woman had taken them away to new good homes. But every day of his life since then he'd wondered what had really happened to those poodles (and one of them very likely a canine alcoholic, at that).

'As a matter of fact I can tell you his name,' I said proudly, confident of making an impression. 'It's Albert Antony Smith.'

It made an impression all right. The sergeant dropped his Biro and gave a yell of laughter. 'What? Old Alkie Albie? He's been spinning you one of his tales? Gorblimey, I've been listening to all this and it turns out to be one of

Alkie Albie's nightmares?' He leaned on the counter confidentially. 'Listen, we know old Albie here. He's never sober. He's just what you might call one degree more or less drunk. He never saw nothing, darling, believe me.'

'He wasn't on a bender at the time he talked to me,' I said. 'He was drinking coffee.'

'That'd be a bloomin' first! Old Alkie Albie drinking something which wouldn't go up in flames if you put a match near it?'

'I bought the coffee for him,' I insisted. 'I know what he was drinking. I believe he saw it all.'

He smiled at me in a kindly fashion as people do at the innocently deluded. 'Listen, dear. He believes he saw it. You believe he saw it. Perhaps the old git honestly believes he did see it. But then, he sees all sorts, does Albie, when he's had a skinful. Hallucinating, see? He mightn't have been puggled when you spoke to him, but believe me, the night he *saw* this incident, he would've been plastered. Don't you worry about it. Nothing happened.'

'That what they always say!' said the woman to me, in the tones of one who'd suffered long from the incredulity of the police force. 'And I saw him as clear as I see you, and him without a stitch on.'

The WPC said firmly, 'I think you're mistaken, Mrs Parrish, and this is the third time in a week you've been in here. We're very busy, you know! I'll have a word with the social worker.'

'Happens all the time, see?' the sergeant whispered hoarsely. 'In here reporting things every other day, she is. Loneliness is what causes it.'

Perhaps that did it, the notion that they classed me with a nutcase who saw naked men at every bay window. Or perhaps I had a sneaking feeling the sergeant might be right about Albie. I felt foolish and sought to rescue a shred of pride.

'Look,' I snapped. 'I only know what he told me and I'm reporting it. Kidnapping's a serious crime, right? You ought to check it out. At any rate, I've been a responsible citizen and told you and I want it logged into the daybook.'

I knew that much about police stations. They keep a record of reported incidents, day by day in the Occurrence Book.

His kindly smile vanished. 'If you knew the amount of paperwork we have to do, you wouldn't ask me to waste time writing up a report on one of Alkie Albie's meths-visions!'

I just stood there. He sighed. 'All right. Make meself a laughing stock. And your name is?'

I told him and also my address.

'And at least consider it might have happened!' I pleaded.

'Certainly, madam!' he said. 'And I'll ring round the press and tell 'em to hold the front page, and all.'

As I left, the woman was recommencing but about a different man, this time at a bus stop.

I was angry and frustrated – more than a little embarrassed, too – but most of all I was determined. I still believed Albie's story and I wanted to prove it true more than anything. I'm ashamed to say, the desire to wipe the superior look off the sergeant's face was a stronger motivation at that moment than rescuing the unfortunate kidnap victim. I'd almost forgotten about her. Not exactly, but she wasn't in the front of my mind, if you understand me.

But as I walked home, I calmed down more and remembered that behind all this was someone in real trouble and it seemed I was the only person who cared enough to try and do something about it. I might like to be free of commitments, but that doesn't mean I don't have a conscience. I had to find Albie and get him to tell his story again. He might dredge up some extra detail from his fuddled memory but the longer I let it go, the more likely it was he'd forget altogether.

After that, I had somehow to help the girl. But at the moment I had no idea how to find my witness, much less how I could secure the victim's freedom. But one problem at a time.

It was late afternoon and the wind had dropped. It was the nicest it had been all day. Perhaps tomorrow would be halfway decent. I'd want good weather if I was to be foot-slogging round the streets. I let myself into my flat. Good detective work starts with a cup of tea.

Chapter Three

Ganesh came by at eight-thirty that evening, rapping on the basement window in the familiar pattern that was his code.

'Hari was fidgeting about checking the till for ages but that's it, until tomorrow.' He slumped on the blue rep sofa, stretching out his legs towards the flickering little TV screen. He looked tired.

Hari opened up the shop early in the morning because of the newspapers but closed at eight sharp, usually on the dot. There's money to be made by staying open late, but there's always an increased risk of trouble from kids roaming in gangs looking for mischief and, later, from lager louts spilling out of the pubs. A small shopkeeper is a natural target. Hari played it safe.

Either because of the set's age or because of the subterranean location, the screen displayed poor picture reception, each frame showing two newscasters, one a ghostly *doppelgänger* hovering at the other's elbow. Ganesh didn't seem to mind. Perhaps he was just watching the moving shapes, not taking in any of it.

'I've just about had Hari,' he said. 'He's driving me

barmy. He had me counting rolls of Polo mints today. Not that they don't pinch Polo mints or anything else. Those kids take anything on principle. Just a game to half of 'em. Hauling sacks of spuds around was better.' That Ganesh had reached this conclusion was a measure of how depressed he was. 'No one shoplifts a potato.'

I told him I'd been to the police and the tone of my voice must have revealed with what success.

Ganesh muttered, 'I told you so.'

This didn't help and put me in aggressive mood. 'I'm not giving up. I'm going out again tomorrow looking for Albie. He has to be somewhere.'

Ganesh came awake. 'You can't wander round doorways, talking to winos and psychos, Fran!'

I pointed out to him that not everyone kipping rough was a maniac. There'd been an occasion, when things had been really bad for me, when I'd slept rough.

I'd been lucky because I'd only had to do it for one night. I'd been nothing but a kid at the time, not long after Grandma Varady went into a nursing home. She'd been my only relative since Dad's death and I'd been living with her. But the place we'd lived in had been rented in her name, not mine, and the landlord had wanted me out. So out I went, into the street, with my belongings in a rucksack. Not that the landlord cared about that.

It had been summer and I thought – being innocent or stupid, whichever word you prefer – that sleeping out under the stars might not be so bad if I did it in the local park. Before I left the house, I crept round the back without the landlord seeing me and filched a piece of tarpaulin from the garden shed, with the idea of making a tent. I probably saw myself like a character in a Famous Five story.

I'd forgotten they locked the park gates at night and that was just the first problem. I had to climb over the wall. Then I found I wasn't the only one to do that and every bench had a regular, settling himself down for the night. I hadn't reckoned on company, either.

Some of the company was distinctly unhealthy in more ways than one. Once the danger of it all was brought home to me, I gave up the idea of making a tent. Instead, I wrapped the tarpaulin round me like a sheet of armour, crawled into the centre of a large municipal rosebed, and spent a miserable, sleepless night among the floribundas. I kept telling myself that if anyone tried to come in there after me, he wouldn't be able to approach quietly and I'd know about it.

The next day I was lucky enough to meet up with someone I'd come across before, on the drama course, and he took me along to a squat where he was living and a place was found there for me. It was in a row of condemned terraced houses. The windows were broken and the floorboards rotted, but it was dry and safe. No one who hasn't been out on the streets can appreciate those words 'dry' and 'safe' as an ex-homeless person can, believe me.

That was the first of the many squats I've lived in. Sleeping rough was an experience I'm determined never to repeat. I look upon it as the lowest point of my career and from then on, no matter how bad things could get, they had to be better, and that meant I was on the way up.

Gan and I argued about it and in the end, he said, 'Look,

the old fellow told you himself he spends most of the day down the tube if it's cold, and it's been cold. Unless you want to ride round London Underground all day, you're not likely to find him.'

'He might go back to the railway station. Or if not that one, another one. Maybe over at Paddington? That's on the Bakerloo Line. If they throw him off Marylebone, he might just nip down the tube, ride two stops northbound and try again.'

'Check the railway stations, the lot if you like, but if he's not there, leave it until I can get here after work. I'll come round the doorways with you then. That's the best time to look for him. Fair enough?'

We agreed on that one. Ganesh had cheered up by now and suggested we went down the baked potato café for some supper.

The baked potato place was run by an exiled Scot called Reekie Jimmie. (The potatoes were from Cyprus.) If you wanted to know how Jimmie got his nickname you only had to look at his orange fingers and mahogany-coloured nails. But to his credit, Jimmie didn't smoke in the café. He smoked in the corridor accessed from the eating area by a narrow door behind the service counter.

The potatoes came with filling of your choice but the choice wasn't great: usually cheese, chilli or baked beans, and there was a suspicious similarity between the last two. Despite much talk of prime Scottish beef, I guessed that Jimmie created the chilli filling by adding an Oxo cube and a pinch of curry powder to the baked bean one.

This evening, when we got there, there was only one perplexed customer, crouched despondently over a corner table. He was dismembering the contents of his plate with painful intensity, setting it all out in small discoloured lumps of mash and baked beans. It was rather like watching a man who's afraid of swallowing the lucky silver coin with his Christmas pudding. He had probably ordered the chilli and was looking for the meat. I wished him luck.

Jimmie took our order and our money. Jimmie always wisely took your money first before you saw your baked potato. He gave us a numbered card despite the lack of competing custom and told us to sit where we liked.

We made our choice of the greasy tables, I put my numbered card on display, wiped the seat of the chair and sat down. Gan leaned his arms on the table, dislodging the number, and said: 'I've been thinking.'

'Yes?' I said.

'Let's say the old man did see a snatch. Then someone's missing, right? The snatch victim? It's just possible the police might not know about it but someone must know. She's got to have been missed.'

'Go on . . .' I encouraged.

We had time to talk it over. Jimmie had disappeared into the corridor and blue smoke curled through the open door into the area behind the counter. I was pleased Ganesh had changed his tune and was taking Albie seriously at last. It was always worth having Ganesh put his mind to a problem, because what he said generally made sense.

He made sense now. He was right. Someone who normally lived safely in the bosom of her respectable family couldn't disappear without it being noticed. No one would notice if I disappeared except Ganesh, and possibly Daphne, after a while. Though Daphne might think I'd just wandered off, and if Gan did go and live in High Wycombe, it'd be a long time before he found out. It was an unsettling thought. Fran Varady, the woman no one would miss.

'The kidnappers may have said to the family, don't call the cops or something nasty will happen. The family may be trying to handle this on their own.'

He had a point. It could explain the desk sergeant's indifference. If he knew of a kidnap in the district, Albie's story – no matter who was telling it – would have caused more of a stir.

The microwave pinged. Jimmie reappeared wreathed in swirling smoke like an alien in a low-budget film, extricated the spuds, and approached bearing two plates. He set them down before us with a flourish.

The potatoes were monsters of their species, overcooked to a pale brown all through, their skins dry, wrinkled and dull charcoal coloured, like a rhino's. My cheese had melted to a bright yellow waxy puddle, enveloping the side salad. I should have ordered the beans, like Ganesh.

'There you go, and I've put extra salad.' Jimmie pointed at it.

Yes, he had. There were two slices of unripe tomato and three of dehydrated cucumber nestling in the yellow sea with the crumpled, transparent lettuce leaf.

'And more filling!' he added with the kind of munificence the President of France probably shows when he's handing out the Legion of Honour.

We thanked him nervously. There had to be something behind this and there was.

Jimmie rested his fists and astonishingly hairy arms on the table and addressed me. 'I've been hoping you'd come in, hen. You're an actress, is that right?'

'Ye-es . . .' I said. 'But I haven't got my card yet.'

'You don't need a card for this. I've got a wee job for you.'

Ganesh asked jocularly, 'Has she got to dress up as a potato and run up and down outside advertising this place?'

I wished he hadn't said that because Jimmie obviously hadn't thought of it and began to think of it now. He frowned. 'You know, that's no' a bad idea there. Mebbe another time, eh?'

'Maybe another time, no!' I snapped. Not even for extra salad and cheese.

'But your friend here's not that far off the mark. How do you fancy being a model?'

'Does this involve taking off my clothes?' I asked, because this is what 'being a model' always seems to involve. Not that I'd be prudish in the case of true art. But getting my kit off on a small stage in front of a lunch-time crowd of boozy businessmen was not, to my mind, art. I told Jimmie if this was what he'd got lined up, forget it.

He looked offended. 'No, no, it's a young lad, Angus, an artist. He's a Scot like myself and seeing as he was a bit short of cash, I gave him a job here. He comes in mornings, early, and mops out the place, cleans the tables, that sort of thing. He doesna' make any money out of the art. But he's real serious about it and verra talented.' Jimmie nodded and paused to let all this sink in.

Ganesh twitched an eyebrow in disbelief and turned his attention to his food.

But Jimmie was concentrating on me. 'Now, you see, the thing is this. The lad needs a model. He had one but she let him down. She broke her leg, poor lassie, and is all laid up with a steel pin in her shin. He's got an exhibition all fixed up and he's really in a spot.'

I did see but, still suspicious, pointed out that there were plenty of professional artists' models. Jimmie said there was a little bit more to it than that. It wasn't a question of just sitting there and being painted. Wouldn't I like to come round to the café in the morning, around ten? Angus would be there, having finished his stint mopping out, to explain it all to me himself. Jimmie himself could promise me, hand on heart, that it was absolutely legit and a paying proposition.

I needed a job and money so I agreed to come back around ten in the morning, and meet the talented artist. I insisted I was promising nothing. I'd been offered paying propositions before. Besides, if Angus was reduced to cleaning out Jimmie's café, it was unlikely he had much dosh to spare and, it followed, not much to pay a model.

'Don't do it!' advised Ganesh when Jimmie had gone back to his counter.

It was good advice but as usual when Ganesh said don't, I did.

We set off slowly homewards – towards my place, that

was. It was half-past ten and the pubs were busy with drinkers getting in a last pint before eleven when most of the pubs locally turned out. The Rose at the end of the street had opened all its windows, despite the cool night, to let out the fug and steaming heat of bodies pressed together in its cramped bar.

The Rose is an unreconstructed bit of Old London Town. It has glazed brown tiles cladding the exterior and inside, although it's lost the spit and sawdust of its early days, it's kept the same atmosphere, resolutely downmarket. That's what its patrons like about it. Everywhere else around has been gentrified, yuppified or poncified. The term depends on whether you're an estate agent or one of The Rose's regulars.

There's plenty of life about the old pub. They had live music in there that night and either something was wrong with the sound equipment or the band was worse than usual. Discordant wails and amateurish guitar-playing escaped in bursts between shouts of laughter, roars of disapproval and the occasional crash of broken glass. All the usual sounds associated with The Rose, in fact. Despite what you might expect, serious trouble there is rare. The landlord pays a couple of bruisers disguised as bar staff to see things stay that way. They don't have women behind the bar at The Rose.

Another thing they don't do at The Rose is sell food, unless you want peanuts or potato crisps. They're a boozer, for Gawd's sake, and not a naffin' restaurant, as the landlord likes to explain if some stranger asks to see the bar menu. Anticipating the nightly exit of unfed but well-watered patrons, a van selling hot dogs had taken up position nearby. Puffs of acrid-smelling smoke wafted towards us. The proprietor was setting up a placard by his mobile eatery. It read: 'Three Hot Dogs for the Price of Two. Unbeatable value.'

I privately thought the mental gymnastics required to work that out were probably beyond the patrons of The Rose by the time they reeled out into what passes for fresh air around there.

'Hi there, Dilip,' Ganesh hailed the cook. 'How's it going?'

He straightened up. He was remarkable for being about as broad as he was tall, solid as a brick wall, with a walrus moustache. 'See that?' He pointed to the placard.

We duly admired it, Ganesh asking tentatively, 'What's with the special offer?'

'You gotta let 'em think they're getting something for nothing,' said Dilip. 'That's the only way you do any business these days.'

They fell to discussing the general slowness of business, whatever its nature. To illustrate the point, a couple of amateur-looking streetwalkers had appeared, both seeming depressed as if business had vanished altogether. One wore tight red leggings, not a good choice on spindly pins that lacked any discernible thighs or calves and were as sexy as two matchsticks. The other wore a short skirt revealing lace tights on legs that contrasted startlingly with her mate's, being bulbous about the calf and tapering to disproportionally narrow ankles. They looked like a couple of upturned beer bottles. She wore a silver blouson jacket.

At a guess I put Red Leggings' age at thirteen and her chum in the silver jacket's at fourteen.

They stationed themselves by the wall and Red Leggings took out a pocket mirror and began to examine a zit on her chin.

'Lookit that !' she moaned. 'They bloody know when I'm goin' to work!'

'You want to try that green make-up,' advised Silver Jacket.

'Who wants a green face?' retorted Red Leggings, offended.

'Honest, it's foundation, but it's green. You put your other make-up on top and it don't look green, not when you've finished.'

'You're havin' me on,' said the spotty one, still disbelieving.

I could've told them both a thing or two about stage make-up, but Silver Jacket was giving me a funny look. She thought I was on the game, too, and had strayed on to their pitch.

I wandered off a little way out of their range and out of earshot of the strangled sounds made by the musical group in the bar. There were cars parked here. Perhaps they belonged to people living in the flats above nearby shops, or perhaps to patrons of The Rose. Among them was a blue Cortina with a long white-ish scratch along one side. I wandered over to it

There were probably dozens of them. But not all in this one corner of London. I stooped to peer through the window and met Garfield's eyes peering back at me. Avoiding his outstretched paws, I made out what appeared to be a hole where there ought to have been a car radio. That wasn't unusual for city life anywhere. Windscreen wipers, aerials, chrome manufacturers' logos, radios . . . the absence, not the presence of these things, counts as standard if you leave your car unattended.

Despite the fact that the vehicle was in the old banger category and appeared to have been done over already, a little sticker in the window announced that it was protected by an alarm system. They didn't depend on Garfield alone.

Not all such stickers were genuine, I knew that. I wondered, if I rattled the door handle . . . I reached out my hand tentatively.

'Fran!' Ganesh called. 'What do you think you're doing hanging round that heap of scrap?'

I beckoned him over. Without speaking I indicated the car. When he'd had time to absorb the make and the scratch, I said, 'And it's the right colour.'

Gan was looking sceptical. 'It could belong to someone who lives up there.' He pointed at the upper windows of nearby buildings. 'And has it occurred to you that if it's parked here regularly, Albie could have seen it? When he needed to describe a car for the story he spun you, this is the one he chose. It doesn't mean it was used in a snatch.'

But I had that certain feeling. Certain, that is, this was the car. 'This is it, Gan. The one we're looking for.'

'No,' Ganesh said firmly. '*We* are *not* looking for it. You, possibly. Myself, absolutely not.'

'Your mate Dilip,' I said, 'does he work this pitch

regularly? If so, and the car's a regular, he'll have seen it, too. Go and ask him.'

Ganesh walked back to the van, hands in pockets. Dilip had clambered back inside and was getting his stock ready for the rush. There was an exchange of words and Ganesh came back.

'Dilip doesn't remember it.'

'Then he's in the pub, the driver. That means we can find out who he is.'

The wind was getting stronger. It tugged at Ganesh's long black hair and knocked over Dilip's placard, which landed face down on the pavement.

Gan went back to reposition it, wedging it between van wheel and kerb. He came back. 'So, what's your plan? We hang about here until chucking-out hour? We could be wasting our time and it's getting colder.'

I indicated the warning notice. 'If that's genuine, there's a quicker way of bringing him out here.'

'Are you crazy?' He was horrified. 'What do we say when he charges out with a couple of his mates and accuses us of trying to break into his motor?'

'We say we saw kids running off down the street. We were just standing by the hot dog van, chatting to Dilip. We didn't notice until we heard the noise, then we saw the kids.'

'No!' said Ganesh adamantly.

Do you know, that little warning notice wasn't fake? The old heap actually had an alarm and it went off. What I hadn't reckoned on was that with the noise going on in the pub, no one could hear it in there. Result, no one came out to switch the thing off.

What did happen was that lights began to appear in the windows of the flats above the shops. Soon irate tenants were hanging out in varying stages of dress or undress and yelling for someone to do something about that effing noise.

'You started it,' said Gan. 'Now what do we do?'

Dilip, behind his counter, opined, 'Run like hell, I should. I'll tell 'em it was kids.'

But we weren't likely to get another chance. I told Ganesh to wait and pushed open the door into The Rose.

The place was a pall of smoke, totally airless. You couldn't see across the bar. The stench of beer, cigs, cheap aftershave and sweat was awful. I stood there, gasping for breath and eyes smarting as blue clouds enveloped me.

Dimly, through the mist, I made out a raised stage at the far end of the room. The band was up there and had, thank goodness, finished their act. They were starting to dismantle their gear. The walls were yellowed with nicotine deposit and the net curtains (yes, net, no one could say The Rose didn't know what was nice) were greyish-brown. The carpet was so discoloured it was impossible to tell what its original design or shade might have been. Crushed cigarette stubs littered it but with so many holes burned in it already, that hardly mattered.

I edged over to the bar and tried to catch the eye of either of the beefy barmen. Both ignored me. They had a rush of last-minute orders and I was at the end of the queue. Besides, they don't like women going up to the bar at The Rose. They're traditional. There weren't so many women in the place. Those who were there were defiantly raucous, shouting to make themselves heard.

The first thing they teach you at any kind of voice production class is that if you yell, you distort. Voice projection, that's the thing. Breathing. The diaphragm. On the drama course they taught us all about that. Every word to be audible at the back of the gods.

'Who owns a blue Cortina with a scratch along one side?'

I'd given it the finest Shakespearean. Henry Irving would've been proud of me.

It worked. There was a fractional pause. Eyes turned my way. Faces were blank with shock. One of the barmen asked, 'What was that, darlin'?' Not because he hadn't heard, but because he couldn't believe he'd heard it – not from someone my size whose head was not much above the level of his bar.

I repeated my question in my normal voice, adding, 'Some kids are hanging around it.'

To back up my story, in the lull, the repetitive squeal of the car alarm could now be heard.

'Merv!' yelled someone. 'Ain't that your motor?'

The crowd heaved and parted like the Red Sea. Between the ranks, a figure appeared and came towards me. I felt like a very small Christian faced with a very large and hungry lion.

Merv was tall, pale, and rectangular like a slab of lard. He was one of those who think it obligatory to go around in sleeveless T-shirts in all weathers and his muscular arms were tattooed from shoulder to wrist. One displayed a morbid interest in coffins, skulls and daggers. The other showed an old-fashioned cannon and the word 'Gunners' in capital letters, indicating that if he knew what loyalty meant, which I doubted, he'd given his to the Arsenal Football Club. He had pale yellow hair trimmed to a stubble and his round slate-coloured eyes lacked lashes or brows. It wasn't the expression in them that worried me so much as the lack of it. Nothing. A pair of glass peepers would've had more life in them. No doubt about it: I was faced with one of the living dead.

It spoke. 'What about my motor?' it growled.

'Kids . . .' I faltered. 'Joyriders looking for a—'

He shoved me aside as he strode out. I staggered back against the bar and bounced off again painfully. The crowd reformed. The barmen went back to pulling pints and the band to unplugging the sound equipment. I trotted outside to see what was happening.

Ganesh had joined Dilip inside the van and was dispensing hot dogs to the tarts. The alarm was silent now but Merv, standing by the car, was exchanging insults with one of the flat dwellers.

'And you!' yelled the householder, slamming his window shut.

Merv, still ignoring me, padded along the pavement to the van, arms dangling, held away from his body and slightly bent, fists clenched.

'You seen 'em?' he croaked.

'No, mate, we've been busy,' said Ganesh. 'You want a hot dog? Buy two, get one free. That makes three,' he added.

He got a glassy stare.

'You see nothin', *no kids*?'

Merv wasn't as thick as he looked. He was suspicious.

Help came unexpectedly. The tart with the silver jacket said, 'I seen a bunch of kids. They was round our way earlier. Joyriders, that's what they are. They're always hot-rodding round there. Residents got a petition up to put them bumps in the road.' She eyed Merv. 'You on your own? Or you with a mate? 'Cos me and my friend, we know a nice little club.'

Merv gave his by now familiar growl and went back into the pub.

'Well, I didn't fancy him, anyway,' said Silver Jacket.

Red Leggings saved dripping mustard from her hot dog by curling her tongue lizard-fashion to catch it. 'He looked like a bloomin' nutter to me,' she said.

Ganesh was climbing down from the rear of the van.

'Are you satisfied?' he asked. 'Now can we go?'

Chapter Four

Somehow I couldn't get to sleep that night. I kept thinking about Merv, his bashed-up motor and Albie and all the rest of it. I had a bruise just below my left shoulder blade from my encounter with the bar and a personal debt to settle with Merv over that. It spurred my resolve but didn't help me get my ideas in order.

There was another problem. I'd been right to worry about that windowless little bedroom beneath the pavement. Try as I might, I couldn't relax in it. It was unnatural and there was no way I could come to terms with it. The air was stifling even though I'd left the door open. I also kept the door open because otherwise I was sealed in.

I tossed and turned as I stared into the darkness and juggled the oddly assorted scraps of information at my disposal. Like the kaleidoscope I'd had as a kid, each time I tapped my assembled facts, they reformed to make a different picture. The only thing the pictures had in common was that they were all lurid, all tangled and all vulnerable. There was no scenario that was simple, logical and unshakable. Nothing signposted the way to go with my investigations.

From time to time footsteps passed overhead and echoed eerily around my little room. The sense of being buried alive increased. Tomorrow, I decided, I'd make up a bed on the sofa in the living room. This was definitely the last time I'd sleep in a catacomb. Like a mantra, I began to mutter, over and over:

> 'Now I lay me down to sleep,
> I pray Thee, Lord, my soul to keep.
> If I should die before I wake,
> I pray Thee, Lord, my soul to take.'

That was keeping it simple and dealing with the basics. The words ran round and round inside my throbbing head. The feeling of being trapped and of being in danger increased. My brain was as scrambled as any kaleidoscope. I was afraid to go to sleep in case I dreamed. But despite that, eventually I must have dozed off.

I awoke with a start and a dreadful sense of claustrophobia, even worse than earlier. I didn't know what time it was but I knew it must be after midnight. Despite it being so late, someone was walking up there, above my head.

I'd heard feet earlier but this was different. These feet didn't march assertively or patter briskly past. This was a slow, even footfall and every so often, it paused. I wondered for a moment whether it could possibly be a copper on the beat. But coppers don't pound the beat the way they used to. They drive round, in pairs.

The man above was moving again. I knew it was a man.

The footfall was too heavy for a woman and men place their feet differently to the ground. He walked another few steps and stopped again, this time directly overhead, over the thick opaque glass of the skylight.

I knew he couldn't see me, any more than I could see him. But I knew he was up there and he – I had no doubt of it – knew I was down here, in my cell beneath the ground.

I sat up in bed, swung my feet to the ground and waited. There was a grille set in the door of the room so that I couldn't suffocate in here but there was no draught, just a still, warm smothering air. And quiet. So quiet I might, if I hadn't known better, have thought he'd gone away. But I did know better. I knew, because I could hear him thinking.

I saw a telepathy act once at an amateur variety night. I was also part of the night's programme. I was the drummer in the all-girl band. All right, I don't play the drums very well, but the others didn't play guitar very well. We were terrible. Anyhow, this act was good. We knew it was rigged, it had to be, but we none of us could see how the man rigged it and he wasn't telling. Otherwise, I didn't believe in telepathy. Or I hadn't done until that moment, when sitting on my bed and listening, I seemed to hear a kind of echo inside my brain. The sense of the unknown prowler's presence was overwhelming. I almost thought I could hear him breathing, though that would be impossible. But for a moment there, it was as if his mind and mine had touched.

Cold sweat trickled down my spine. I didn't dare switch on the light because that would've glowed up through the glass disc. I didn't move again. I forced myself to suggest explanations and knew that I was grasping at straws. He'd stopped to light a cigarette, I told myself. Less innocently, he could be a burglar, sizing up the house and contemplating entry. I ought to make a noise, let him know someone was awake and aware of him.

My brain rejected this feeble suggestion at once. 'No, he's not,' a pert little voice argued. 'He's looking for you, Fran. He wants to know where you live. He wants to know about you. He's looking around, compiling a dossier in his mind.'

Above my head, feet scraped and the footsteps began again, moving away, moving more quickly, as if he were satisfied and had found out what he wanted to know. He was gone. I knew he had left completely, and wouldn't be coming back, not that night at least. I was alone again.

I let out my breath with a long sigh, not having been aware I'd been holding it. I got up and padded to my kitchenette to make a cup of tea, switching on every light in the flat as I went.

I turned on my telly as well for a bit of company, longing to hear human voices. It was two in the morning and the reception was perfect, wouldn't you know it? No double-vision. No snow-storm. They were showing an ancient black-and-white film. I settled down to watch, nursing my mug of tea, returning to normal.

The film was about medieval villagers hunting out a witch who was saved in the last reel by the return of her crusader lover. They'd obviously been on a tight budget because they'd employed so few extras. There must have been lots of out-of-work actors like me who'd have given their eye-teeth just to be a bystander in the crowd with a chance to shake their fists at the camera. Yet whether dressed as peasants, or in saggy chainmail and partly disguised by helmets which looked as if they'd been fashioned from tin bowls and probably had, the same familiar few faces kept running past the cameras.

It distracted me for a while. But eventually the film finished and my worries came back. If you're a young woman and live alone, as I did, the risk of a stalker hanging around the place is always there. They see you around the area, follow you home. Sometimes it gets no further than that. They get bored and seek out other prey. Or they get frightened off.

If that was all he'd been, I could deal with it. But another possibility had occurred to me, that the visit had to do with Albie. If so, then logically the visitor had been Merv, yet I didn't believe it. I'd seen Merv walk. I recalled how he'd padded with dull muffled tread in his trainers towards Dilip's hot-dog stall. My man had worn stouter, heavy-heeled footwear. However, it was unlikely that Merv had been drinking alone and Albie himself had seen two men. So, had my visitor been the other man?

Ganesh had warned me about blundering into the pub but the opportunity had been too tempting to pass up. Had my rashness aroused suspicion and had Merv's companion decided to check me out?

It was a thought which sent my already jittery mind spinning off in several directions, conjuring up a variety of alarming possibilities. What if the two men seen by Albie to snatch the girl had realised they'd been observed? Once they'd got the girl away to a hiding place, they might have gone back with the intention of silencing the witness. Not finding him, had they, like Gan and me, gone looking for him? Suppose the other man had been following Albie on that fateful morning of our encounter at Marylebone? The stranger's intention had been to waylay the old fellow, but he'd been thwarted when Albie settled down to talk to me. Subsequently Ganesh had joined us. The follower might have decided at this point that three was a crowd and left, intending to await another occasion when Albie might be found alone. But before he'd left he'd had time to get a good look at me and had recognised me when I'd walked into The Rose the previous evening. If this was what had happened, then I'd really walked into trouble.

I cursed my rashness. It was all very well saying that I couldn't have known, but I ought to have thought more about it. Instead I had sought out Merv, an action too suspicious to overlook. I had truly become a player in the game. Until now, I could have reasoned that by reporting Albie's story to the police, I'd done all I could as a good citizen. But not now. Out there on the streets was an elderly, frail man who carried a dangerous memory in his fuddled brain. It was a memory I shared and someone suspected it.

I was yawning by now and nodding my head. It was beginning to get light outside and with the grey dawn, all my fears began to fade into foolish nightmares, probably induced by the extra cheese on my potato. Perhaps I was wrong about everything.

'Your trouble, Fran,' I told myself, 'is that you've got too much imagination!'

I went back to bed. It really wasn't so bad in the underground room with daylight seeping through the opaque glass overhead. With the new day, last night's walker became a man who'd stopped to light a cigarette. A Cortina parked outside The Rose had been coincidence. Albie's original tale could be dismissed as the rambling of an alcohol-ravaged brain. I could even choose to blame the railway, with everything stemming from a cold wait on Marylebone Station, which had led me to pay altogether too much attention to the incoherent mumblings of an old wino, building a regular house of cards on those poor foundations.

I couldn't allow myself to sleep late because I had to go over to Jimmie's and meet Angus the Artist. I crawled out, heavy-eyed, at around eight and got myself together, washed my hair, which doesn't take long because I keep it very short, and got into my comfy old jeans. If I was going to be an artist's model, I supposed I ought to make a bit of an effort so I dug out my turquoise silk shirt and quilted dark blue Indian waistcoat, both of which I'd found on a nearly new stall at Camden Market just after I'd moved in to the flat. I yawned and hoped Jimmie's coffee would wake me up.

So, there I was, more or less ready for the day, and just about to leave the flat when someone rang the doorbell. One thing I wasn't ready for was visitors. To begin with, normally I didn't get any, other than Ganesh and occasionally Daphne from upstairs. It was too early for Ganesh and a bit on the early side for Daphne. She knew I tended to sleep late. And no one sends me parcels.

I went to the window that gave on to the basement well and peered out. A man was standing before my front door, his back to me. His jacket, which was a sort of sage green overlaid with a grille of white squares, was unknown to me. But the solid build of the wearer and his cropped ginger hair rang a bell – a warning bell. While I was trying to place him, he turned round. Either he had eyes in the back of his head or he'd sensed I was scrutinising him through the window. He came to rest his palms on the outer sill and stared at me through the glass.

Eyeball to eyeball, there was no mistaking him. It was my old adversary, Sergeant Parry.

'Can I come in?' he mouthed, words muffled by the glass and the echo off the basement walls.

My heart sank. I had no idea what he wanted, or why he was even lurking in this neck of the woods. I would find out, no doubt, very soon.

'Surprise!' he said when I opened the door. He grinned at me evilly.

'Hullo,' I said in what I hoped was a deflating tone. 'I'm just going out.'

'Won't take a moment, Fran,' he lied.

'Miss Varady to you,' I told him. 'Come in, then.'

He came marching in and made himself at home, settling down on the sofa. 'Got a cup of tea to spare, then, *Miss Varady*?'

'No. What do you want?' I asked him. 'And what are you doing around here, anyway?'

'I work out of the local nick now,' he informed me. 'And you've been down there, Fran, I hear. Now that interests me. Fran Varady going to the police? Gotta be a story worth hearing.'

He'd read the daybook, that's what he'd done, and seen the entry. It was just my luck that he was now gracing the local CID with his unlovely presence. He was still trying to grow a moustache and still having little luck with it.

'Ask the desk sergeant,' I said. 'He can tell you all about it.'

Parry shook his head. 'You tell me all about it, eh?'

He didn't sound so much encouraging as minatory. He'd never been my friend and I doubt he was anyone's friend. He had what Grandma Varady would have described as a nasty, suspicious mind, and no social skills. Neither, looking at that jacket, did he have any dress sense. He did have a shaving rash, though, on his throat. Red hair and sensitive skins go together. But if his skin was sensitive to soap, it was as thick as an elephant's in other respects. DS Parry wasn't New Man. He was an old-style bullyboy armed with a police ID, and he was sitting on my sofa, resentful at being refused the tea. But at least he'd arrived in broad daylight and rung the bell. Parry's style was to barge in, not prowl around outside. Nothing subtle about him.

I repeated my tale about Albie and hoped that he'd get up and go away satisfied. I should have known better. Nothing satisfies Parry except getting the better of you, preferably in sadistic fashion.

I told you I don't feel this way about all policemen. Mostly I don't have any opinion about them. It's just that I didn't like Parry and accepted he didn't like me. But at least we understood one another.

He listened in silence, mouth turned down disapprovingly beneath the mangy ginger moustache.

'And you took this load of cobblers seriously?' he asked at last, when I'd finished.

'Yes, that's why I went and reported it. Not that it did any good. I'm not surprised we've got the crime rate we have. People take the trouble to go and tell you someone's been snatched off the street and no one takes it seriously.'

Even as I spoke the words, I realised I was wrong. Lack of sleep and surprise at seeing Parry had momentarily clouded my thought processes. Now the truth hit me, as they say, in a blinding flash. Parry wouldn't waste time on me if someone wasn't taking something seriously.

It wasn't that they were inclined to pay an awful lot of attention to me. They wouldn't be interested in anything I had to say in the normal run of affairs. The only reason they were conceivably interested enough in what I'd reported to bring Parry over here was because what I'd told them tied in with something they already knew.

I settled back in my chair and smiled at Parry, which gave me the added satisfaction of seeing him look startled. 'There's been a snatch,' I said. 'Albie's right. I'm right. And you lot are keeping it quiet for some reason.'

So under wraps were they keeping it that not even the desk plod knew. This was a CID special.

It was taking him a moment to adjust to the fact that he'd lost the initiative. He played for time. 'Go on, make us that cuppa, love.'

The words were wheedling but the tone wasn't. It was a mix of peremptory and patronising. I stifled my instinctive reaction and got up to make him his tea. I'd won one round and letting him have this little victory was bearable. Besides, it was a sacrifice in a greater cause. I wanted to keep him happy, because I wanted him to relax, and tell me a bit more than he probably intended.

'To begin with,' he said, when we restarted and he'd slurped at his hot tea, 'you've got it wrong. There's been no snatch.'

'No, of course not,' I agreed.

'Don't be clever, Fran.' Parry put down his mug. 'Not with me. You've got a smart mouth and you don't mind using it. It even impresses some people, but it doesn't impress me, right? I'm not going to sit here and tell you there's been a kidnapping on the manor. So I'm telling you there hasn't been one, right?'

'Right, sergeant,' I said meekly.

He gave me a suspicious look. 'But if there had been one, right? Only *if* . . .' he paused but I said nothing, 'then it'd have to be handled very carefully and professionally by the police. There's procedures for handling kidnappings. A technique, if you like. We wouldn't want publicity, Fran. We wouldn't want you wandering around shooting off that mouth of yours about things.'

Making him tea was one thing. Allowing him to sit there and insult me was altogether different and I'd no intention of letting him get away with it.

'I don't shoot my mouth off!' I said coldly. 'Nor do you have any reason to harass me, which is what I reckon you're doing. I'm a member of the public and you're the one with the attitude problem.' He didn't like that and I pressed on with, 'Incidentally, since all this is hypothetical, have you told Albie Smith the same thing? That he isn't to tell people he saw what he saw?'

He relaxed. 'Alkie Albie Smith is an old soak who spends most of his time paralytic and the rest of it hallucinating.' Parry's mouth twisted in the rictus that is what passes for a smile with him. 'No one's going to listen to anything he's got to say.'

'But they might listen to me?' I sighed elaborately. 'Oh, come on, sergeant. Who'm I going to tell? And who'd listen?'

'How do I know?' he retorted sourly. 'You've got a funny way of getting yourself into places where you've no business to be. You get people to listen to you who should know better. Keep out from under our feet, Fran. This is police business and if you go interfering, it could spell disaster. I mean that. A life could be at risk. Leave it alone, right? If you don't, you'll be in trouble.'

Being in trouble was as permanent a state with me as being drunk was with Albie. Parry's threats didn't worry me. But his dismissal of Albie did.

'Albie's your witness,' I said. 'Have you spoken to him? You ought to, urgently.'

Parry hesitated. 'We're looking for him. He's lying low, probably sleeping it off. But we'll find him and find out if he really did see something suspicious – though if you ask me, he dreamed it all up while under the influence.'

'Not everyone might think so!' I snapped. 'Someone

might want to make sure, just in case. Someone might want to shut him up.'

'Leave it. No one's going to worry about an old soak.' Parry drained his mug and got up. 'Nice place you've got here, Fran. Better than the dump you were living in last time we met. Fallen on your feet, haven't you?'

'No,' I said. 'A friend helped me out.'

'Yeah, I know,' he sneered. 'Alastair Monkton. That's what I mean with you, see? You sweet-talk people who normally wouldn't dream of mixing with lowlife like you and your mates. You get 'em eating out of your hand and blowed if I can see how or why. Respectable lady like the one who owns this house and lives up there . . .' He pointed at the ceiling. 'Oh yes, I've had a word with her. She thinks you're a nice girl. "Resourceful" was the word she used. I've a better word for it but I didn't like to disillusion her. Even a nice old bloke like Monkton . . . Tsk, tsk!' He shook his head.

I pointed to the door. 'Out!' I said crisply.

'Keep your hair on, Fran. Just remember, I don't want to have to come and see you again about this, *right*?'

'Next time you come, bring a warrant,' I said. 'I've got nothing more to say to you, right?'

'I might just do that, bring a warrant. Just remember, Fran, meddle in this and I'll charge you with obstructing police enquiries.'

He hadn't changed since we last met. He was still a graceless thug. But he wasn't stupid. It was just my luck to have him hovering in the background on this.

* * *

I was late setting out for Jimmie's café, thanks to my visitor. I hurried there feeling hot and bothered; angry with Parry for upsetting me right at the beginning of my day, and with myself for letting him do it.

There were few people about today, just some women with grizzling toddlers in tow and the usual drifters. I passed Hari's shop and paused to peer inside to see if I could spot Ganesh. He wasn't there but Hari was and saw me, so I had to go inside and ask him how he was and listen to his latest troubles.

'Ganesh has gone to the wholesaler's,' he said. 'I suspect they are cheating me.' His face, small-featured and lined, crumpled up with distress.

I assured him this was highly unlikely, even though I had no way of knowing. But even if they were, Ganesh would deal with it, I added.

'Ganesh,' I said with perfect honesty, 'is very hard to fool.'

It was what Hari wanted to hear and cheered him up. He nodded furiously and said, 'Yes, yes, my dear, you are perfectly right!' and offered me a cup of tea.

'Sorry, I've got a meeting,' I told him, and hurried out.

When I got to Jimmie's it was well after ten and they were open for business. A few people sat around drinking coffee. Generally speaking, it didn't get busy till around lunch-time. Jimmie was leaning on the counter and talking about football with a short, thickset, freckled young man with red hair to vie with Parry's. By his feet rested a large cardboard folder tied with ribbon. This had to be Angus.

Jimmie had spotted me. 'Here she is,' he told his

companion. Then he called out to me, 'Go and sit yourself down, hen. I'll bring you and Michelangelo here a couple of coffees!'

Angus came towards me, holding out his hand. He wore ancient jeans and a dark blue Scottish national football squad shirt.

'Hullo.' He appraised me through narrowed eyes, as if literally measuring me up, which was a tad disconcerting. I hoped none of his part-time jobs had been in an undertaker's. 'Thanks for coming,' he said.

His accent was milder than Jimmie's. I guessed that, young though he was, he'd left Scotland some years ago. I shook his hand and apologised for being late. I also noted that he was in exceptionally good physical condition. Perhaps he spent time in the gym or perhaps his line of creative work involved hauling chunks of stone around.

Whereas Parry's red hair and sharp features made him look like a predatory fox, Angus was a friendly lion with round face, blunt features and a mop of copper curls. His eyes were bright blue and, now he'd sized me up, had reverted to a slightly preoccupied expression which I guessed was normal. I'd lived in a creative artists' commune, over at Jubilee Street, before the council razed it all to the ground. I knew that look in the eyes. It meant a mind on higher things, and went with unrecognised talent and, usually, no money. Angus, however, had plans regarding the recognition aspect of his talents, and I was part of them. He didn't waste time getting down to business.

'No sweat,' he said, dismissing my apology. 'Jimmie's

explained it all to you, has he?'

Jimmie arrived with the coffees at that point, and answered for himself.

'Only in a general way. I thought you do the explaining better yourself.'

He padded off and disappeared through the door behind the counter into the corridor that was his refuge. Within seconds, a curl of blue cigarette smoke coiled through the crack.

'Right,' said Angus, pushing his coffee cup to one side with a careless gesture, which caused the contents to slop into the saucer. 'It's to do with the Save Our World Resources Arts Festival at the Community Hall on Saturday next.'

I was obliged to admit I hadn't paid much attention to this forthcoming event, although I recalled seeing a few flyposters around.

'That's the one!' he said impatiently. 'Local artists were asked to contribute one work apiece. The theme's the world's vanishing resources, Well, first of all I was going to create a tower of significant objects representing the natural world under threat. Then I thought, no one's going to take any notice of that! It's boring. I want at least to get a picture of my work in the *Camden Journal*.'

He paused to look wistful and I sipped my coffee. 'It'd be nice,' he said, 'if the national press would take an interest but I don't suppose they will. Or local TV . . .' He shook his mop of red curls and sighed. 'But it's not likely. Anyhow, I thought, it's got to be eye-catching. Then I thought, natural world means life, right? So what I'd create would be a living sculpture. It'll just last the one day, and symbolise the ephemeral nature of the world's resources which we're destroying and wasting at a devastating rate. So you see, apart from the chance to get my work on public view, it's all in a good cause, too.'

He stopped on this confident note and looked at me expectantly. Well, I hadn't thought it'd be for the Tate. I realised I was supposed to comment. I assured him I liked the idea. But, I added hesitantly, although living sculptures had worked very well elsewhere, say, the Hayward Gallery, I wasn't sure about trying the same thing in our local Community Hall.

'You're likely to get a load of kids and weirdos in there,' I said, 'making the model's life a misery. I'm not on for that.'

Since I was clearly intended to be the basis of the living sculpture I was going to insist on such practical details being hammered out first. It's not the sort of thing an artist, with his mind on saving the world and creating a masterpiece that would gain him media recognition, would think about. But I had no intention of standing there to be pelted with wads of wet paper propelled by an elastic band. Much less being propositioned with offers that had no place in the natural world at all.

'You'll be absolutely safe!' he promised. 'The organisers have got a couple of doormen lined up to watch out for troublemakers and I'll be there to protect you. After all, you'll be my contribution to the show. I won't want it – I mean, you – damaged.'

It was an unflattering but valid point. Angus himself,

moreover, from the look of him, ought to be a competent minder. He saw me weaken.

'Let me show you!' he urged. 'This'll blow your mind!'

He hoisted the cardboard folder and undid the ribbon. Opening it out, he turned it towards me. 'There!' he said proudly, but just a touch anxiously. 'I decided to concentrate on the vanishing rain forests.' His eyes searched my face, waiting for my response.

If I'd have told him the plain truth, I'd have said it looked like nothing so much as an overladen Christmas tree. The human body around which it was built had virtually disappeared beneath festoons of greenery, trailing lianas, and birdlife, which, I trusted, would be made of fabric. I really didn't fancy being turned into a full-length version of an Edwardian lady's Sunday hat. But he was the design expert and I was just the model. I concentrated, instead, on the practical problems.

'How's it all fixed to me?' I'd had a vision of something painful involving pins or, even worse, instant glue.

'You wear a body stocking, dark green. It's very strong and absolutely decent. I sew the other materials to the body suit.'

Sew? A handy chap to have around.

'How do I hold the pose? I mean, I can hold it for so long, but there's a limit before I get cramp.'

'No problem. I've made this.'

He whipped away the picture of the tree and displayed a sketch of what looked remarkably like a medieval torture instrument. It was a big steel coil, rather like a basketball hoop without the net, fixed upright with an opening on one side.

'You stand inside it,' Angus explained. 'On this platform. The ring supports you at waist level, against the small of your back, and you rest your right arm along it. Basically it takes your weight. Once I've arranged all the materials, foliage and so forth, the viewer won't be able to see it – well, hardly.'

So far, so good. One important question remained. 'I'm not a camel.'

'You'll get comfort breaks,' he promised earnestly.

'I see, and do I get to practise beforehand? To get used to the feel and weight of the body suit?'

He folded up the cardboard case and looked a little embarrassed. 'Unfortunately, we can't do that. I've run into one or two hiccups getting hold of all the materials and some of them have to be fresh on the day or they'll wilt. But it'll be all right by Saturday. You turn up early at the hall, put on the leotard and get into the frame. Then I attach all the other bits and pieces to you – I mean, to the body suit.'

He leaned across the table and entreated. 'Please say you'll do it. The girl who was lined up has her leg pinned together and had to cry off. I know it'll work perfectly.'

Of course I'd do it. I was a would-be actress being offered a role, albeit static, before a live audience. If we struck really lucky, the local press would print a pic, which meant I'd get my face – and my name – in the paper along with Angus.

'All right,' I said.

Relief glowed in his blue eyes. 'Thirty quid, OK? It's all I can afford and it's a fair rate.'

A *paid* live performance. 'It's a deal,' I told him.

'Fine, then. See you Saturday at the hall, eight thirty, right? Gives us time to get everything fixed up before the public's let in at ten thirty. Exhibition closes four thirty.'

Six hours' legitimate work. It couldn't be bad. At the same time, I privately resolved not to tell Ganesh anything more about it, not unless he actually asked outright. He'd be much happier not knowing.

My mind straying from art, I hoped Ganesh wouldn't drop out of our planned expedition that evening in further search of Albie.

'You look a bit worried,' said Angus solicitously. 'It will be all right.'

That's what they always say.

Chapter Five

I walked over to the shop that evening to meet Ganesh, as agreed, outside at eight thirty. A light rain spotted my face and I hoped it stayed at that and we weren't in for a downpour. I'd pulled on my black leather jacket as a precaution.

The shop was closed and in darkness. I pressed my nose to the glass all the same, because sometimes someone's in there stacking shelves or doing odd jobs, but it was empty. I moved to the street door alongside, which gives independent access to the upstairs flat and was about to press the bell when without any warning it was jerked open from inside. Ganesh appeared, bolted out, yelling a farewell up the staircase, and slammed the door shut behind him.

I was relieved to see him. After my brief conversation with Hari earlier, I'd more than half expected the problem with the wholesaler to have led to lengthy arguments after work and midnight studying of the accounts. It had happened before that Hari had found some last-minute problem to delay Ganesh and I'd been left hanging about out here in the street, exchanging banter with passing local sex maniacs.

I opened my mouth to ask him how the visit to the wholesaler had gone, but a glance at his expression told me this wouldn't be a good idea. So I just said. 'Hi. All ready to go?'

'Where first?' he asked, zipping up his jacket to the chin and glancing nervously up at the first-floor bay window in case it was flung open and Hari put his head out to call him back. 'Let's go,' he added before I could answer.

I was happy to move off. A stiff breeze now gusted unimpeded down the street, bowling rubbish and increasingly heavy rain squalls ahead of it and moving had to be better than standing around. It wasn't so late in the year, only September, and it really oughtn't to have turned so cold yet. Another thing affecting our expedition was the shortening of the daylight hours. It was already beginning to get dark. Gan thrust his hands into the pouch pockets of his blouson and we set off in the general direction of The Rose.

'Just to check it out,' I said. 'See if Merv's there. If he is involved then I'd like to know where he is.'

'He's going to get suspicious if we start hanging around, Fran,' Ganesh mumbled, chin down inside his upturned jacket collar.

'It's a pub! People hang round pubs. Anyhow, I don't think he's that observant. He wouldn't remember me. I'm just some woman he shoved back against the bar.'

'You shouldn't have gone in there,' Gan picked up the vengeful note in my voice. 'What did you expect? By the way, did you go round to—'

He was going to ask about Jimmie's artist friend and I didn't want to explain all that, not just now.

I broke in with, 'By the way, I've had a visit from the Monster from the Black Lagoon. Sergeant Parry dropped round to see me.'

Ganesh stopped and turned to me, incredulous. 'What did he want?'

I told him about Parry's visit. Ganesh thought about it, lips pressed tightly together. 'Well, you could be right. Something brought him running over to your place to warn you off.' He paused. 'It *would* be him, wouldn't it?'

'Yes,' I agreed. 'It would.'

We went on our way in a thoughtful silence. I reflected that Parry had, in a way, done me a good turn because Ganesh had temporarily forgotten my modelling job. Only temporarily. He'd remember.

Despite it being a fairly early hour, the homeless had already staked out their pitches if they were begging, or bedded themselves down for the night beneath whatever sleeping equipment they possessed. We stopped and made brief enquiries of anyone we came across on our way to The Rose. We were greeted either with colourful abuse or the request 'Got any change?' Asked about Albie, they replied, 'Who's he?' or 'Never heard of 'im.' It wasn't a good start.

We also drew a blank at the pub, much to Gan's obvious relief – no beat-up old wreck parked outside and no Merv inside.

The patrons' musical ears were being given a rest tonight in the absence of a live band. But their tolerance was being tested in another way by a stand-up comedian. He was young, very nervous, and dying on his feet up there on the tiny stage. He'd misjudged his audience and prepared all the wrong material, trying for the witty and satirical when what they wanted was blue jokes, the more politically incorrect the better. At the moment the drinkers were in a fairly good mood and ignoring him. Later, when their tolerance wore thin, they'd start barracking him. The landlord was casting the performer uneasy glances. I could see that at any minute the perspiring jester would be requested to cut short the act, such as it was, and go while the going was good. I wondered if he'd get paid and doubted it. I was sorry for him because he was probably a struggling wannabee, like me, trying to get himself an Equity card.

'Come on,' said Ganesh, rightly judging the mood. 'Before they start throwing things.'

We set off again, seeking information in earnest. I fully realised it wasn't polite, to say the least, to disturb someone who had cocooned himself in a sleeping bag or gone to earth under a pile of old clothes or newspapers, but I quickly discovered it was also hazardous. Shaking a sleeper's shoulder usually resulted in a fist punching out of the huddled shape. We'd also forgotten that the homeless often keep a dog for protection. A close encounter with a large and very unfriendly Dobermann reminded us. The animal chose to go for Gan and not for me, rather to my relief though not to his. Gan escaped with minor damage to his jeans but became especially sensitive to a canine presence after that. He'd exclaim, 'Dog!' as soon as we got anywhere near, long before I spotted the mutt in question.

It was best, in fact, to stand well away from the doorway or alley and call out my request. Sadly, but understandably, street dwellers don't like being asked for information, especially about one another. My polite questions about Albie's whereabouts got me nowhere. 'Never heard of him!' was still the usual reply, followed by, 'Bugger off!' or some variant of same. Frequently we were spat at, and on one occasion the occupant of a doorway shied an empty lager can at us. It missed me by a hair's breadth, hit the pavement with a clang, and rolled noisily away into the gutter.

'Could've been worse,' I said, determined to look on the bright side. Ganesh hadn't been enthusiastic to begin with and noticeably less so since the dog episode. It was up to me to keep the momentum going. 'Could've been a bottle.'

'Could've been a knife,' said Ganesh, who prefers to look on the downside, and had begun to hang back, happy to let me go first as we approached each new doorway. 'Or hadn't you thought of that?'

I hadn't, but I did from now on.

I approached the next likely place with more caution. It was a narrow passage, floored with black and white chequerboard tiles, and running back towards some kind of business entry. It was pitch-dark in there, despite the streetlighting, which had now come on and buzzed fitfully behind me, casting a murky yellow glow on the wet pavement. There was something at the far end of the entry because I could hear movement. Paper rustled.

'Hullo?' I called. 'Is someone there? I'm sorry to disturb you but I'm looking for someone . . .'

There was no reply. The rustling stopped and then recommenced in a flurry. There was a scattering noise across the glazed tiles that made the hair on my neck bristle. A car drove past and its headlights cast a sudden ray of brighter light into the doorway. I had a brief sighting of a shape, raised on hind legs, nose snuffling the air in my direction. Evil little eyes gleamed in the reflected glare of the headlights.

I leaped back with a strangled squeak of horror and cannoned into Ganesh, who yelped and exclaimed. 'What is it?'

'Rat . . .' I whispered, gripping his arm.

I had to admit that was something else I hadn't thought about. There was another reason for sharing your sleeping place with a dog if you were out on the streets. Rats don't like dogs.

I don't like rats. I'd face any street-dweller, with or without dog, bottle or knife, and in any state of mind or out of it, sooner than face a rat.

'We'll give this doorway a miss,' I said.

After that I was more rat-conscious than Ganesh was of slavering hounds. I saw rodents more than once. A pair of them scurried round a plastic rubbish sack in which they'd gnawed a hole. Worst of all, I spotted a real monster crouched on a windowsill, his scaly tail hanging down by the brickwork. That did it. From now on, no matter how hot it got, I'd keep all the windows of my flat closed!

All this time we were getting nearer and nearer to St Agatha's church where I knew, from his own account, Albie was occasionally to be found at night in the porch. So although it had begun to rain steadily and promised to be an unpleasant night, I wasn't yet ready to give up.

Ganesh felt differently. 'I'm getting fed up with this,' he said. 'And I'm hungry.' Rain had plastered his long black hair to his face and he was examining the rip made in the leg of his jeans by the Dobermann.

But I had high hopes of finding Albie at St Agatha's. Enquiries on the way there had only been on the off chance and I hadn't really expected anyone to tell me anything.

'We must check out the porch,' I said. 'This is the last. Then we'll find a place to eat, promise.'

'All right,' he muttered.

I suggested kindly that if he preferred, he could go home. He pointed out that for him this meant returning to Hari's flat above the shop. Seeing as he'd put up with Hari since returning from the wholesalers, he could do with a break, thanks very much. Even if it was only traipsing round the streets with me, risking life and limb disturbing the disturbed.

'You'll see, at the very least we'll pick up fleas!' he concluded.

I'm often grateful to Ganesh for being there, but there are occasions when I wonder if his kind of support is what I really need.

St Agatha's is in a quiet residential area – quiet at night, at least. It wasn't too well lit around there. The mock-Gothic building reared up against the sky like a part of the set in that old film I'd been watching the previous night, all pinnacles and arched tracery, half veiled in shadows. The line of sight was further impeded by trees planted along the frontage. One of the nearby streetlamps had gone out. Iron railings divided the property from the pavement. There was a gate, now secured with chain and padlock.

'That's that, then,' said Ganesh with relief, rattling the gate and turning away.

'Are you kidding?' I asked. 'If you're sleeping rough, you look for somewhere secure. There must be a way in.'

There was, just a short distance down, and disguised by a rampant buddleia bush. The railings had been damaged and two of them removed. We squeezed through and approached the porch, which extended some eight feet out from the building and was doorless. I turned round when we got there to survey the road and work out just what had been in Albie's range of vision when he saw the snatch. Actually, not a great deal, due to the trees. A moment's doubt struck me. Had it all been, after all, an alcoholic nightmare?

Ganesh whispered, 'There's someone in the porch . . .'

I'd realised that as soon as I'd poked my head through the arched entry. A sour stew of unwashed human body, filthy rags, booze dregs and nicotine combined in a stench fit to make you gag. Albie hadn't smelled that bad. But I hadn't seen Albie since Marylebone Station and had no idea what he'd been doing meantime. For all I knew, he'd spent the time in a massive drinking session.

I called out tentatively, 'Albie, is that you?'

Whoever it was moved, rustling about like a larger version of the rat we'd discovered earlier, recalling my fears.

'It's Fran,' I called more loudly. 'Fran, the private detective.'

'Who?' asked Ganesh incredulously.

'And actress!' I added, determined to jolt Albie's memory. 'We met at the railway station.'

'Do I know this woman?' Ganesh was asking rhetorically. 'Private eye star of stage and screen? I know a Fran who's usually out of work between spells waitressing or mail-order dispatch packaging.'

'And you might remember my friend,' I explained to the darkness. 'He was at the station, too.' To Ganesh, I added, 'And the word "friend" is variable!'

A wheezing cough came from within the porch. 'Go away . . .' quavered an elderly voice. 'I gotta dog, a big 'un . . . wiv rabies.'

'That doesn't sound like Albie,' I whispered.

'He hasn't got a dog,' said Ganesh, the expert. 'It would've had us by now.'

I ventured into the porch. My eyes were adjusting to the gloom and I could make out the occupant, huddled in the far corner by the church door.

'I ain't got nuffin'!' His old voice was tremulous and terror made him smell even worse. 'Why don't you leave me alone? You ain't gonna hurt me?'

'Of course not, I swear. Don't be scared, please. I just want a talk—' I began.

'You ain't goin' to throw me out?' he whined, less afraid

and ready to defend his space. 'It's raining. I got me bronchitis again.' He wheezed and spluttered and sounded pretty bronchial to me.

He oughtn't to have been sleeping here. None of the people we'd seen should have been existing like they were. 'If you're ill,' I said, 'perhaps we can get you into a shelter somewhere.'

He spluttered. 'I ain't goin'! You one of them do-gooders, ain'tcha? You Sally Army or what? Well, you can go and shake your bloody tambourine somewhere else . . .' He began to cough, wheeze and hawk in a frenzy. I stepped back sharpish because there was a lot of saliva flying around. Eventually he subsided, like a dying volcano, and mumbled, 'Used to make a living, good living . . .'

'I'm looking,' I said loudly, hoping to penetrate the haze that fogged his brain, 'for Alkie Albie Smith. Do you know him?'

'No . . .' he croaked.

'Oh, come on, he kips here sometimes. If you come here as well you must have run into him. I'm a friend. I've got a message for Albie. It's important.'

Gan, edging into the porch behind me, pressed a couple of coins in my hand. 'How much?' I whispered.

'Coupla quid. Go on, tell him. Then we can get out of here if he doesn't know anything. I'll throw up if we stay any longer and he's probably got half a dozen notifiable diseases!'

'Who's that feller?' quavered the old bloke, taking fright again at the sight of Ganesh. 'Why ain't he got his uniform on if he's Sally Army?'

I pushed Ganesh back outside again. 'I'll pay for information about Albie, right? A quid or two quid if it's special.'

The mound in the corner heaved and another waft of foul air engulfed me. I clapped my hand over my nose and retreated. 'You can stay there and tell me,' I said hurriedly.

From somewhere in the heap of rags and the gloom, a hand emerged, palm uppermost. It looked like something you'd find if you unwrapped a mummy's bandages. 'Give us the two quid!'

I put one pound coin in the withered palm. 'Tell me and you can have the other.'

His claw closed on the coin and was drawn back into the darkness. 'Sometimes,' he grumbled, 'they play jokes. Sometimes they chucks me them tokens what go in the slot machines.'

I waited for him to satisfy himself that the coin was real. 'I ain't seen him fer a week or more,' he said suddenly. 'I know 'im, yes. Known 'im for years. I come here tonight, thinking 'e'd be 'ere. But he wasn't. So I settled meself down to wait for 'im. Cause he usually comes 'ere sooner or later, see? This is where he kips.'

This much I knew already. A week. I wondered how well the old man was able to keep track of time. 'When you saw Albie last, did he mention anything special? Like he'd seen something unusual happen, outside here, at night?'

'Nothing much round 'ere, ducks. Gotta a hostel fer wimmin down the road. Bit of trouble there sometimes.'

The battered women's refuge. Somehow, it seemed to

me, we kept coming back to that.

'Did he tell you he'd seen some sort of dust-up relating to the refuge?'

'No . . . he don't take no notice. None of us does. What you don't see don't get you into no trouble.'

But Albie had seen something and I was afraid it was yet going to get him into trouble. There was no more to be learned from the old bloke. I gave him the remaining pound coin.

'Thanks, ducks,' he said, and wheezed again.

'Satisfied?' asked Ganesh when I rejoined him.

Angry, I snapped, 'That's hardly the word!' Ganesh was silent. I added, 'Sorry, you know what I mean.'

'I know what you mean,' he said. 'But there's nothing you can do about it, Fran.'

We set off back up the street. The air out here was crystal clear and clean compared to the fug in the porch. The remains of it lingered in my nostrils. I wondered why the church hadn't put an outer door on the porch. Perhaps they were sick of it being broken open, and calculated that it was better to let wanderers sleep in the porch than to have them break into the church itself in search of shelter. It was fully night-time now but the rain, which had contributed to the freshness, had eased. The lamplight glittered on puddles and the wet road surfaces. Our feet echoed off the pavement flags. A solitary car splattered past, showering spray from the gutters. As the old chap had said, there was nothing much around there. It was a respectable area and at night people barred their doors and didn't go out. Not on foot, at any rate.

But there was someone about. Ganesh touched my arm and pointed ahead.

A dishevelled figure had turned the corner up ahead and was padding down the pavement towards us, clad in an oversized greatcoat, which flapped like bats' wings as he moved.

I drew in a sharp breath. 'Albie?'

Then it happened.

A car rounded the same corner and screeched to a halt by the lone figure. Two men jumped out, one tall, one shorter, both wearing dark clothing and knitted hats pulled well down over their ears. They grabbed the pedestrian and began to hustle him efficiently into the car. Their victim set up a voluble protest, familiar enough to identify him for sure as Albie to me. He began to thresh about wildly in his captors' grip, kicking out with his feet, but he was already half way through the open car door and in another few seconds would have disappeared inside completely.

Ganesh and I came to life at the same time and yelled out, 'Hey!'

We set off up the pavement, waving our arms and screaming anything we could think of, just to make sufficient noise. Noise is a weapon. If you can't do anything else, yell. It disorientates, frightens and above all, attracts outside attention.

The two thugs by the car paused and looked towards us. Despite the poor light and the little that could be seen of either of their faces, I felt sure the taller one was Merv. In reality, there was no way Gan and I would have been a match for them, whoever they were, but just at that moment, someone pulled back a curtain from an upper window overlooking the road and a beam spotlighted the scene below on the pavement.

The would-be snatchers released Albie, jumped back in their motor and roared off with a squeal of gears and smell of scorched rubber. I did manage to get a better look at the car as it swerved and rounded a corner to the right.

'It's Merv's Cortina,' I gasped.

'I don't know what sort of engine they've got in it,' Ganesh retorted. 'But it's either been souped up out of recognition or replaced. It didn't leave the production line with that one under the hood, that's for sure!'

The beam was abruptly cut off as the person at the window above dragged the curtains together, not wanting to be a witness.

Ganesh and I turned our attention to Albie who was propped against the nearest lamppost, panting and wheezing.

'Are you all right?' Ganesh asked anxiously. An incoherent gurgle responded, followed by a feeble flailing of Albie's hands meant to indicate, I supposed, that he couldn't speak for the moment.

We waited and eventually the poor old devil got his breath back, or most of it. 'You see that?' he croaked indignantly. 'You see what them geezers tried to do?'

'Yes, we did. You remember me, Albie?' I peered into his face, which glowed eerily in the light from the lamp overhead.

Recognition dawned. 'I do, indeed, my dear! You're the actress.'

'And private detective,' said Ganesh, a trifle maliciously, I thought.

'That's it, I remember!' Albie nodded. 'Thanks, dear, for giving a hand and frightening them two off!' He nodded at Ganesh, 'You, too, son.'

I moved away a little and whispered to Gan, 'What are we going to do with him?'

'You're asking me? Nothing.' said Ganesh.

'We can't just leave him out here on the street! You saw what happened. They'll come back, try to snatch him again.'

Albie was searching in one pocket of the greatcoat, his face anxious. 'I bet them buggers have broke it.'

'What's that?' I asked.

'A bottle. I gotta bottle. The good stuff.' He pulled out a half-bottle of Bell's and examined it. 'No, it's all right.' He gave it a tender pat as to a baby.

'You've got more to worry about than a bottle of booze, Albie!' I told him sharply. 'I – we've – been looking everywhere for you. I've just been down to the church. There's a friend of yours down there, dossing. He's been looking for you as well.'

Albie nodded. 'That'll be Jonty. Thought he might turn up tonight. I was just on me way to share this with him. Either of you care for a nip?' he added hospitably.

'No!' we exclaimed in joint frustration.

'Please yourselves, then.' He returned the bottle to his pocket.

'Albie,' I said, 'you remember the story you told me? About seeing the young girl snatched by two fellows, perhaps those two?' I pointed down the road in the direction of the would-be kidnappers' car.

Albie looked shifty. 'I may've said something. Don't recall.'

'Yes, you do!' I wasn't going to let him get away with that, not after all the trouble we'd had finding him. 'Albie, I think you saw a kidnapping. I think the police are looking for the girl. You've got to come with me and tell—'

'I'm not going near no coppers!' interrupted Albie.

'I'll come with you, I promise. You're a very important witness, and after what happened tonight you could be in danger. Those two obviously know about you. The police will put you somewhere safe—'

'Not in the cells.' Albie shook his head. 'These snotty young coppers they got nowadays don't let you sleep it off in the cells the way the old-timers used to. Was a time when the cells were always a good bet on a cold night. All you had to do was shout a bit of colourful language at a few old ladies and chuck a bottle or two in the gutter. After that, you just had to sit on the kerb waiting for 'em to collect you. Then it was off to a nice warm cell and a proper breakfast in the morning. Like a bloomin' taxi service it was. Now they just tells you to bugger off and you're lucky if they don't kick your head in.'

'Not a cell, in a hostel.'

'I don't like hostels!' he retorted immediately. 'On account of the baths. They're fixed on baths.' He patted my arm. 'You're a good girl, like I said. Fact is, you're a very nice young woman, and bright. It's a pity I don't still have the act because you'd have fitted in there very well.

You ever work with animals? You'd have picked it up in no time. We could've fixed you up with a costume – nothing gaudy, just to catch the eye. Audience would've liked you.' His voice grew sad. 'The dogs would've liked you. They're good judges of character, are poodles.'

He took out the bottle, unscrewed the top and put it to his lips.

'Look, Ganesh,' I hissed, 'he's at risk! We can't just leave him here! Besides, if we let him go, we'll be ages finding him again, if we ever do. I want Parry to hear his story.'

'Take him to your flat then,' Ganesh suggested drily, 'if you're so keen. Then you can go over to see Parry with him in the morning.'

There were limits. I couldn't cope with Albie for twelve hours. Certainly not once he'd drunk the rest of the whisky. Besides, whilst he didn't smell as bad as Jonty, he didn't smell that good either. I'd have to fumigate the flat afterwards.

'I can't do that!' I snapped. 'What'd I do once the whisky got to his brain? Besides, there's my landlady. If she got to know I'd brought him in, she'd throw a fit. I'd be out.' An idea struck me. 'What about the lock-up garages behind the shop? Hari's got a place there, hasn't he? Couldn't Albie bed down there tonight?'

'Come off it, Fran! You know Hari!'

Albie had been paying closer attention than I'd supposed. 'It's very kind of you to worry about me,' he said grandly. 'But I've got plans for the evening, as they says. I'll be all right. Them fellers won't come back tonight.'

I made a decision. 'Albie, listen to me. I want you to get away from this area round the church. I'm not so sure those two goons won't come back. Go and collect Jonty if you must, but I really believe the pair of you should stay away from St Agatha's, right? I worked out I might find you here and our friends with the Cortina thought the same. I'll meet you in the morning where we first met, on Marylebone Station, understand? Just by the Quick Snack stall. I'll come along early, around eight o'clock. Can you be there? It's very important.' I reached out and took his hand. 'Promise me, Albie.'

'My dear,' he said, 'I'd promise you anything. Putty in a woman's hands, that's me.'

'*Please*, Albie . . .'

'And for a lovely girl like you, what wouldn't I do? All right, dear. I'll be there, early, like you said.' He raised my hand and made a kissing sound, thankfully well clear of contact.

Ganesh and I watched him lurch off down the road on his way to share the whisky with Jonty. I just hoped they could keep from opening it up until they'd left the porch. I had my doubts. Nor could I blame them. At least the whisky dulled the misery for a few hours. In their shoes, I'd probably take to the bottle. I wondered where he'd got the bottle from, if he'd pinched it or paid for it and if the last, what with? But confirmed drinkers always manage to get hold of their favourite tipple somehow.

'He might be at the station tomorrow,' Ganesh said, 'but I wouldn't count on it. It's like I said, Fran. There's no talking sense with him. Still, there's nothing you can do except trust the old soak, I suppose.'

'You saw what happened! You must've recognised that Cortina. You can hardly blame me for worrying!' I said bitterly.

Chapter Six

I was absolutely whacked when I got home that night, but still curiously reluctant to go to bed. The memory of a footstep above my head nagged at me.

I fell on the sofa before the TV set, thinking that a burst of mindless late-night entertainment, or even a serious political discussion, anything, might distract me. It's a funny thing, but you do without something for years and don't miss it. Then you find yourself unexpectedly presented with whatever it is. After that, you wonder how you managed before and can't imagine life again without it. That's how it is with me and the telly.

The last squat I lived in, we didn't have telly, but then we didn't have electricity either. The council had disconnected us, not because we were unwilling to pay the bill, but because they wanted us out of the place.

Then I came here and sitting in the corner was the little television, with its blurred focus and crackling sound, and I was hooked. I know it's a time-waster. But it's also a time-filler and when you're out of a job, it's a sort of cackling companion, rabbiting on about trivia of all sorts and throwing up endless pictures to amuse the eye. I understand only too well why so many old people, especially those living alone, switch on first thing in the morning and don't switch off until they go to bed.

But tonight I only stared at the blank screen, lacking the will or the strength to turn the thing on, even for my regular old film fix.

It wasn't surprising I was dog-tired. It'd been a long day, what with not having slept very well the night before, getting up early and finding myself involved in an unexpected skirmish with DS Parry. Then there was arranging with Angus about the forthcoming Saturday, and traipsing around looking for Albie, plus rescuing him from Merv and his pal.

I was worried about Albie, where he'd gone after I'd left him and whether he'd turn up on time in the morning. I was also having serious second thoughts about having committed myself to Angus's loony art project. I was only thankful I'd hadn't told Ganesh any more about it. To top it all off, I kept thinking about rats. My brain churned. I was developing a full-scale panic attack. 'Stop it, Fran!' I ordered myself aloud.

Ganesh and I had found a pizza place after leaving Albie, so I wasn't hungry. I *was* thirsty but making tea was beyond me. I hauled myself upright, staggered to the kitchen and drank two glasses of water. Then I went to the subterranean bedroom, removed the duvet and pillow from the bed and brought them back to the living room and the sofa. A brief expedition to clean my teeth and I fell on the sofa, tugging the duvet around my ears.

Tired as I was, I lay awake for quite some time,

wondering whether my visitor of the previous night would return. At first I quivered with tension at the sound of every passer-by and that night, just for the purpose, everyone seemed to be taking a short cut home down our street. As time wore on, the pedestrians were fewer. That was worse. Now each one was a possibility. Anyone walking slowly set my nerves jangling and had me sitting up on the sofa, alert to jump up and be ready, though for what I didn't know.

But no one stopped or even paused by the house. Last of all, the next-door neighbours arrived home by car, headlights sweeping the front of our house like air-raid search beams. They – a carload of them by the sound of it, perhaps they had houseguests – staggered out on to the pavement, the women's voices shrill and excited with drink, the men hoarse, incoherent with that drunken bonhomie that can so quickly turn sour. They giggled, guffawed and swore as someone, stumbling up the steps, had trouble with the key. Eventually, they too had gone indoors with a final echoing slam of the front door. I was left to myself, my imagination, and the ever-present distant rumble of London traffic.

I began to be angry with the absentee. How dare he keep me from my well-earned sleep like this? *If you're going to come, come!* I addressed him silently. But he didn't oblige and eventually I ordered myself to put him on one side, like a half-read book, and go to sleep. At least, I told myself, I wasn't in that tomblike bedroom. Out here, in my living room, I felt safer. I wasn't, but I felt it.

* * *

When I eventually passed out, it was completely. I didn't dream, not even in the circumstances. I was too far gone for that. It was a wonder my old-fashioned wind-up alarm clock woke me at seven. Thinking I must have been barmy to have arranged such an early rendezvous with Albie, I staggered around the flat getting myself dressed, and set off for Marylebone.

I hopped on a bus that took me there by a more direct route and made it to the Quick Snack stall by about ten past eight. If Albie had been prompter, he wasn't to be seen. But I didn't think he'd have given me up already.

Looking around, I realised I'd forgotten how busy railway stations are at that hour of the morning. Commuters poured off every train and swept by me, a solid sea of determined faces. The concourse had the appearance of a disturbed ants' nest as people scurried towards the main exit or the Underground entry within the station precincts. To spot even Albie's distinctive figure in the throng would be difficult. I got myself a coffee and sat down, as I had before, on the metal seat, with a definite sense of *déjà vu* or at least *déjà* been there.

From here I could watch the entry to the Underground, over to my left as I faced the coffee stall. It was clogged with office workers pushing through the barriers. There was a notice informing them the down escalator was out of action and that there were 121 steps to negotiate. That would add to the poor souls' enjoyment. When I worry, as I occasionally do, that I haven't a regular job, sights like that cheer me up no end.

Fewer people were coming up from the tube and through the barrier into the station, and none of them looked remotely like Albie. I began to wonder if he'd taken my advice and moved away from the streets around St Agatha's. I knew that, on the whole, it was unlikely. He and Jonty would have started on the whisky, and after that they wouldn't have bothered to move on.

The seat seemed to get harder and harder as if there were no flesh padding my bum at all and my joints rested directly on the metal. I'd drunk the first coffee and another one. The commuting crowd had thinned out. Eventually the last of them vanished. A different sort of passenger was arriving off the trains now. Not workers, but shoppers and people coming up for the day for one reason or another, who had no reason to fight for the early train, or could take advantage of cheaper tickets by travelling later. It was well after ten. I'd been here two and a half hours and I knew Albie wasn't coming. Perhaps I'd always known it. I stood up and eased my cramped legs.

Damn it! I thought. He probably hadn't even remembered. He was sleeping it off somewhere. I quelled the fear that some other reason detained him. I simply should have known better than to attempt to make any kind of firm arrangement with someone like Alkie Albie Smith. Ganesh and I would have to go out tonight and try to find him again. Ganesh would love that.

I went home. I'd had nothing to eat with my coffee and it was getting on for lunch time. I set about making toast in my kitchen and was debating whether to scramble a couple of eggs, *haute cuisine* as far as I was concerned, when I was interrupted by the ring of the doorbell followed by the noise of someone hammering on the front door.

Footsteps scuffed outside in the basement and as I walked out of the kitchenette into the main room, a face appeared at the window and a hand tapped urgently on the glass. Faintly I could hear my name being called. It was Parry.

'Go away!' I shouted.

'Let – me – in!' he mouthed back.

'Get a warrant!'

'I – need – to – talk – to – you!'

I unlocked the front door and he stepped in, uninvited.

'I'm just getting my lunch,' I groused. To back me up, a strong smell of burning toast wafted into the room. I belted back to the kitchen and whipped two charred squares from beneath the grill. Cursing, I hurled them into the bin.

Parry appeared behind me. 'Here,' he said, 'I'll do that. You make us a cup of coffee or something.'

His offer of help convinced me more than anything else could have done that he was the bearer of bad news. There were only two people he could have come about. Ganesh or Albie.

I asked, 'Is it Gan?' because when all was said and done, Ganesh mattered more. I felt cold and my heart gave a little hop of fear.

'No,' he said, his back to me. 'As far as I know, your Indian mate is still selling bars of chocolate and girlie mags in that shop. You putting anything on this toast?'

He obviously wasn't going to blurt it out. But so long as it wasn't Ganesh, it could wait five minutes and I wanted that five minutes. Whatever Parry had come about, I wanted to be ready to deal with it.

'Eggs,' I said. If the man liked to cook, I'd let him.

Well, he wasn't a great cook but who am I to criticise? I sat at my table and ate my lunch and he lounged on the sofa, drinking his coffee and smoking. He didn't ask, as he took out the ciggies, whether I minded. When I'd finished, I picked up my coffee mug and swivelled round on my chair to face him.

'All right,' I said. 'Let's hear it.'

He squashed out the cigarette stub in a saucer he'd found in the kitchen to serve as an ashtray. The man was certainly making himself at home but I was too worried to care.

'I'm really sorry, Fran,' he said. 'It's your mate Albie Smith. We fished the old bloke out of the canal this morning, half seven. Early morning jogger along the towpath spotted him.'

It's possible to be shocked without being surprised. The niggling fear I'd first felt at Marylebone when Albie'd failed to appear had remained with me and now it was proven well-founded. But being to some extent prepared was no protection against the feeling of horror and dismay. I stared at Parry in silence, unable to find words. All I could think was that, all the time I'd been waiting on the station bench, down by the canal Albie's waterlogged corpse had been laid out on the towpath, surrounded by the coppers he'd mistrusted so much.

I knew if Parry wasn't sure he wouldn't have told me, yet I still played for a few moments to come to terms with the news. I managed to ask, 'You've identified him, definitely?' My voice sounded unnatural, hardly mine at all.

'Yes.' Parry waved vaguely at the table. 'I thought you ought to get some food inside you before I told you. I know you took a liking to the old devil. But let's face it, he had no kind of life. Maybe he's better off wherever he is now, eh?'

I could have argued but lacked the will to do so for the moment. Parry, with a rare lapse into niceness, was attempting to console. But he was making the mistake generally made by people whose lives fall into the category of mortgage, car and two point four children.

They see life as being one of those questionnaires with little boxes that you tick or cross according to your circumstances. Tick enough of them and you are Doing All Right. Too many crosses and you're seriously disadvantaged. They assume we all want the things our consumer society reckons essential to health and happiness. But what about the ability to find hope and happiness in little things? Some people would look at me and say my life wasn't worth much. They say it about the severely disabled, the mentally ill and drink-sodden old dossers like Albie. I'm not saying Albie's life-style couldn't have been improved. But the last I'd seen of him, he'd been making for the porch with a half-bottle of Bell's and the prospect of finding his mate Jonty. He'd been quite happy. True, he'd just had a nasty experience from which Gan and I had saved him, but he'd forgotten it already. It was a pity he'd done that. He might be alive now if he'd scared more easily or if the prospect of a drink hadn't numbed his brain to more important things.

Unwarily, I said, 'He must've stayed around the church.'

'Whazzat?' I swear Parry's nose and ears quivered.

So I had to tell him all about the previous evening's adventures. 'I wanted to persuade him to come with me to see you,' I concluded. 'I wasn't interfering. I was trying to help.'

I suppose I sounded defiant. He grunted and said, 'We were looking for the stupid old git as well. I sent a man I could ill-afford to spare to check out Marylebone and Paddington railway stations and every tube station between there and Oxford Circus. I even went myself to that old church, the one he reckoned saw the snatch from. He wasn't there. There was another bloke hanging around, stank to high heaven. It wasn't Albie and he scurried off when he saw me. They're never so far gone they don't recognise the police!'

'Probably,' I muttered, 'because you're so obvious! You were there too early. He came later and so did the two men looking for him. Albie saw the snatch from the porch of St Agatha's, just the way he said. But the kidnappers realised he'd seen them, so they came back last night to silence him. I'm pretty sure I recognised one of them. He's called Merv, a big bloke with an Arsenal supporters' tattoo and nearly white hair. He drinks at the Rose and drives a scratched blue Cortina. The Cortina Albie saw the girl bundled into – and I saw last night when they tried to grab Albie!'

'A burned-out Cortina was reported last night,' Parry

said, a tad thoughtfully. 'Alongside the park. Fire engines called out to it at four in the morning. No sign of anyone in it. Firecrew reckoned it might've been joyriders who torched the motor when they'd finished with it.'

'Merv and his chum knew Ganesh and I saw the car,' I explained as patiently as I could. 'So they got rid of it.'

Parry was still in an argumentative mood. 'If you're right, and they came back to take out a witness, why didn't they leave his body in the car before they torched it? That way they'd have got rid of him altogether, give or take a few charred bones.'

No wonder our crime rate is what it is.

'If the firecrew discovered a charred body in the car, the police would set about identifying it,' I pointed out. 'If, in some way, it was found to be Albie's – and Merv couldn't be sure it wouldn't be – then you'd want to know what the hell Albie was doing in a car. They wanted Albie dead, but it had to be in some way that'd look like an accident. Unfortunately for them, Gan and I saw them earlier, trying to grab Albie off the street!'

Parry fixed me with his bloodshot gaze. 'That's right,' he said. 'They know *you* saw them – and *they* saw you.'

That shut me up. They had seen me. They might even come looking for both Ganesh and me. I remembered the incident two nights before. That had been bad enough. Just a solitary stroller had got my imagination working overtime with creating scary scenarios. Now there was a real possibility of flesh and blood thugs on my trail. I wondered briefly if it were worth telling Parry about the man out there on the pavement, above my head as I lay in my dungeon bedroom. But there was nothing to tell. No facts. The police like facts although when presented with them they seemed, in Albie's case, to have made precious little effort to follow them up.

I glowered at Parry and saw that he'd lit another cigarette. I was badly upset by what I'd learned and the sight of him sitting there quite at home was the last straw.

I lost my temper with the frustration of it all and yelled, 'If you'd tried harder, you'd have found Albie and he'd be alive now! I spent all morning sitting on Marylebone Station hoping he'd turn up! And all on your behalf! So that he could tell his story to you! What's up? Don't you want to find the snatched person, whoever it is?'

'Come on, Fran, be reasonable!' he wheedled. 'We don't pass up any lead. You were quite right to report what he'd told you. But even if we'd found him, we'd always have had to take any testimony he gave with a big pinch of salt. Even you can't say he'd strike a jury as reliable. We always knew we couldn't ever have put him on the witness stand and no identification he made would've stood up for two minutes if challenged! The most we could've hoped for was that he'd have given us a further lead and that was doubtful, too. Look, his brains were as scrambled as those eggs I made you.'

It was not a nice simile and made me distinctly queasy. 'He was still your witness! You didn't worry about him, but they did, Merv and his mate! They kept looking until they found him and they killed him!'

He leaned forward, foxy features sharp. 'So you keep telling me, Fran. But just hold on a minute. You're talking murder, here, and the fact remains that you don't know what happened after you left Albie. He had a bottle, for crying out loud! He was all set to drink himself senseless. You've got at least to consider that he reeled off and fell in the canal, full of whisky. He drowned, Fran, and despite what you tell me you saw earlier, he didn't need any help in doing it. He fell in, poor old sod. Couldn't get out – finish. There's no *evidence*, Fran, to show otherwise. Evidence points to accidental death.'

'What was he doing down there by the canal?' I snapped. 'I left him heading for the porch.' With a stab of guilt, I remembered I'd urged him to move elsewhere. Perhaps he had, perhaps the canal path had seemed safer. 'Did anyone see him go in?' I asked.

'No one's come forward to report hearing a splash or a cry,' Parry said unwillingly. 'But that's not surprising, is it, at that hour of the morning? Give it time. We're asking around.'

'Did *you* see his body? Did you see Albie in the water?' I couldn't believe he was taking it so calmly. They'd lost their only witness, and now had a murder on their hands. All Parry could say was that Albie was better off where he was now.

'No. I got down there after they'd dragged him out. I understand he was found floating face down with an empty whisky bottle in his pocket.' He made sure I took that point in.

I sat back and asked, 'So where's Jonty?'

'Jonty?' His nose quivered again.

'The old man he was going to share the booze with.

The old man you saw scurrying away! Look, there were two of them going to drink a half-bottle of Scotch. That makes a quarter-bottle each and that wouldn't be enough to send Albie tumbling into the canal!'

Parry was shaking his head. 'Naw, he had a whole bottle. He was wearing that big old coat he always had on. When he fell in, that coat would've made it impossible for him to clamber out. The bottle was still in his pocket, Fran, just like I said. It was empty and I saw it with my own eyes.'

'No, *I* saw it,' I told him triumphantly. 'I saw it last night. He offered me a nip from it. A *half*-bottle of Bell's whisky. A half-bottle, sergeant! You can check that out with Ganesh Patel. If there was a full-size bottle in his pocket this morning, someone put it there. And hey, why on earth should he return an empty bottle to his pocket, anyway? Once it was empty he'd have chucked it away. It was a plant!' Sarcastically, I added, 'I'd have thought you'd know enough to recognise a plant when you saw it!'

Parry didn't like that. His mouth pursed up tight and his little eyes glared at me, but he didn't say anything. I'd got him. He couldn't ignore a significant discrepancy.

'No signs of violence on the body,' he said at last, sulkily, I fancied.

'What do you expect?' I asked. 'Albie said they weren't amateurs. I saw them hustling him into their motor. They nearly got him inside for all his kicking and yelling. They're a couple of professional heavies. They waited around until the coast was clear and went looking for him again. They found him.'

My voice quavered unexpectedly on the last word and I was horrified to realise I was near to breaking down. Only determination not to give way in front of Parry stopped me.

'They found him in the porch,' I went on, 'and gave him another bottle of whisky. Maybe they took him elsewhere first. They made him drink it, which wouldn't've been difficult. *Stopping* him might have been. When he'd passed out drunk, they put him in the car, drove over to the canal and heaved him in. The car had become a liability, too reçognisable, so they drove it to the park and torched it.'

Parry's cigarette had smouldered to a spray of ash, which suddenly collapsed and dropped on to the sofa. He started, swore and brushed the ash quickly to the floor. 'You say Albie was on his way to meet up with the old geezer I spotted, the one who smelled like he'd been dead himself a month?'

'His name's Jonty and I'm not surprised he ran away from you. He's terrified of everyone. He could never have fended off an attack. I hope they didn't get him too!'

Parry chewed his thumbnail for a moment before taking his hand from his mouth and heaving a sigh. 'So what you're telling me is, I've got to go out looking for yet another deadbeat? All right, you got a closer look at him than I did. Can you give me a more detailed description? To me he just looked a moving pile of rags. Got any idea of his surname or where he hangs out during the day?'

'No idea,' I confessed. 'I reckon he must be as thin as a skeleton to go by his hand which was the only bit of him I really saw.' Something occurred to me. 'He mumbled about making a good living once,' I said. 'I thought he was rambling but—'

'Probably made a good living begging,' Parry interrupted, 'until the smell put people off!'

'I was going to say, perhaps he was on the halls, like Albie. Perhaps that's why they were friendly.'

He thought that over and shrugged. 'We'll never find him,' he said, and something about the way he said it made me shiver.

Jonty had either run away in terror and wouldn't come back to this part of London, or Merv and his pals had got rid of Jonty too, somewhere else. Just one more old man dead in a doorway. What's new?

Parry got to his feet. 'Merv, you say, and drinks at The Rose?'

'That's right. People there knew him. They called out his name when I asked about the car.'

Parry was staring down at me thoughtfully. 'You and your pal, what's his name, Patel? You both stay away from that pub, you hear me? In fact, from now on, you stay right out of this altogether, Fran. Remember, the two blokes saw you and there's something about you, Miss Varady, that people remember!'

I watched his legs and feet disappear up the basement steps and after a moment or two, I went upstairs too, to call on Daphne.

'I just wanted to talk to someone,' I explained.

She peered into my face. 'My dear,' she said. 'You've

clearly had a terrible shock. You need a drop of brandy.'

I hadn't realised my face betrayed so much or just how shocked I was. The brandy was welcome, though it's not something I drink much of. I spluttered over it a bit and said I was sorry to have disturbed her. The large, old-fashioned sit-up-and-beg manual typewriter still stood on the table with what appeared to be a fresh pile of paper beside it.

She shook her head vigorously. 'No, not at all! What's happened?'

I couldn't tell her everything, so I just said, 'An old man I knew died. His name was Albie Smith. He was just an old tramp, but he used to have a variety act, years ago. He had a troupe of performing poodles. He—' I hesitated. 'A jogger spotted him in the canal and called the police.'

'Oh dear.' Daphne leaned forward, her hands clasped and resting on her bony knees, which were outlined through her jogging pants. She had a different pair of hand-knitted sock-slippers on today. 'Years ago,' she said, 'I remember seeing some performing dogs at, let me see, oh, at the Theatre Royal in Portsmouth. They were very clever. One of them pushed another one along in a little pram.'

'That might have been Albie's act,' I said. But she couldn't remember the name of the turn and anyway, he'd probably had a stage name.

'Why did he fall in the canal?' she asked.

'The police think he was drunk. That's to say, he probably was drunk.'

How he got drunk was another matter, but it didn't concern Daphne.

It concerned me. I should have made sure Albie spent the previous night in a place of safety. At the very least I could have gone with him to collect Jonty and chivvied them both elsewhere, somewhere they could have drunk themselves into a stupor hidden from Merv.

'What are you thinking?' Daphne asked.

'I saw him last night. I wanted to take him to a hostel, but he didn't want to go.'

'There might not have been a place free for him,' she said. 'And if he didn't want to go, you couldn't make him.'

I was grateful to her for that. 'Do you think,' I asked, 'that poodles have souls?'

I'd have felt foolish asking anyone else but Daphne. She didn't bat an eyelid. She thought about it and then said, 'I don't know. Nobody knows, do they?'

'Sergeant Parry, who came to tell me about Albie, said that wherever Albie is now, he's probably better off.'

'Ah,' said Daphne, 'we don't know that, either. Because he was a tramp, doesn't mean he wouldn't rather be here than there, wherever there is. On the other hand, there's no reason to suppose he isn't perfectly all right there now. Why shouldn't he be? Personally I believe in reincarnation. If I'm right, then Albie's got the chance to start all over again. On the other hand, if the heaven theory is right, then it seems logical to me that if there's a heaven, it's a sight better organised than we've made our world down here. There might not have been a place for him here, but there should be there, wherever heaven is. I imagine heaven is what we want it to be. In your friend's case, a sort of ever-open hostel, perhaps, with unlimited beds.'

'Hope they don't make him take a bath,' I said wryly.

'Because our bodies may be dirty doesn't mean our souls aren't clean.' Daphne gave a deprecating cough. 'I don't lay any claim to that burst of wisdom. It was something I was taught in Sunday school, aeons ago. The children used to sing, "And your souls shall be whiter than the whitewash on the wall!" I've no idea if those are the correct words. It's what we sang, anyway.'

'I like to think,' I said, 'that we've all got souls, the animals, too. Wherever Albie is now, I hope that Chou-Chou, Mimi and Fifi are all there with him, that they're together again.'

'Why not?' asked Daphne. 'Because we can't be sure of anything, doesn't mean it isn't so. We just haven't got any proof.'

Bingo! I thought. I couldn't be sure what happened to Albie, but that didn't mean my suspicions weren't correct. I just needed proof. Parry was wrong, quite wrong, if he thought I was going to give up as easily as that. Just because he'd warned me off? Never. And because of Merv and his mate? Even less. Now I really had matters to settle with Merv.

I thanked Daphne for the talk and the brandy and told her I felt better now.

'Any time,' she said. Then as I was leaving she added, 'You won't do anything hasty, will you, Fran?'

She understood me a lot better than I'd imagined. It gave me something to think about.

I went down to the canal. It was a visit I had to make.

Albie's body had long been removed, of course. All that remained to mark his demise at that spot was a fluttering blue and white tape that had cordoned off the area. And even that was broken down.

The strip of mud and straggly grass beside the concrete towpath was strewn with cigarette stubs and sweet wrappers and trampled by police-issue boots. But the visitors, both official and simply ghoulish, had all gone for the moment and I was alone. I was glad of it, because I had a little ceremony to perform and I didn't want an audience. I placed the spray of carnations I'd brought with me neatly in the middle of the wet, flattened grass. The next person to come that way would probably pinch my floral tribute, but I wanted to do the right thing and mark the spot of Albie's passing in a decent manner, if only for minutes. I stood back, like they do at the Cenotaph, and remained with bowed head as I said a brief prayer for Albie.

As I came to the end of my short act of memorial, it seemed to me I wasn't alone after all. I looked up quickly, thinking someone might be watching me from the railings atop the steep bank, or had come along the towpath unheard, or was even in one of the quiet houseboats.

But there was no one. The canal itself was covered with a scum of debris, everything from waste paper to discarded condoms. Water slapped against the houseboats as they groaned and creaked. Yet I still felt that tingling between the shoulder blades that you get when someone is watching. I wondered for a moment whether it was Albie's ghost. Except that Albie's spirit would have been well disposed towards me and what I felt was alarm, some age-old instinct, as if an unfriendly presence had manifested itself and prowled about me.

The mood was broken as, with a whirr of wheels, a cyclist appeared at the far end of the towpath and pedalled determinedly towards me. He was all kitted out in a special helmet, goggles, thigh-hugging black cycling shorts and a tight jersey. I had to clamber up on the bank, almost trampling my flowers, to let him past. The ignorant oaf just cycled on without so much as a nod of thanks, not even slowing down. Yet I was pleased to see him because just then any sign of another human life was welcome.

I didn't agree with Parry that there would have been absolutely no one around down here in the early hours of the morning. There's a whole world out there that seeks the darkness and the lonely places. But if there'd been anyone and if they had seen anything, they would be keeping quiet. It was as Albie'd said. Those who move about the city streets by night see and hear a lot, but they say very little about any of it. It's one of the laws of survival out there.

But Albie had seen something and, against all the rules, had told me. He'd put confidence in me because we both hankered after the theatre: he, because he'd lost the life, and I, because it shimmered before me like a mirage, vanishing whenever I tried to grab at it.

He'd trusted me and I wasn't about to let him down.

Chapter Seven

It was after four when I left the canal and started to walk home. My mind was busy planning how to go about my enquiries. There were two lines of approach, as I saw it. One was Jonty, assuming I could find him again, and the other was the women's refuge run by St Agatha's.

The refuge had cropped up a couple of times and the more I thought about it, the more I felt it tied in somehow. In fact, St Agatha's church seemed to feature large in all of this, one way and another. It would only be a slight detour to call in there on my way home. I turned my steps in that direction.

In daylight St Agatha's mock-Gothic looked less like a backdrop for a *Hammer House of Horror* special. The gate in the fencing around the place was unlocked and pushed open wide. The porch was empty and clean and reeked of extra-strength commercial disinfectant. The church door also stood open and from within came the whine of a vacuum cleaner. I put my head through the gap.

I'd never been inside but I could have made an educated guess and been more or less right. It was a fairly typical late-Victorian church, with oak pews and pillars bearing wooden boards for hymn numbers, and brass memorials to local worthies. There were a lot of flowers around, either in free-standing arrangements or attached as posies to bits of the architecture or fittings. It suggested that recently the church had seen either a wedding or a funeral. A woman was standing on one of the pews, tin of metal polish in hand, rubbing energetically at one of the brass plaques with a rag. Further away, up in the chancel, another woman pushed an ancient upright Hoover back and forth. Both were intent on their tasks. I walked in, up to the brass polisher and cleared my throat loudly.

She turned and looked down at me from her vantage point on the pew. 'Oh, hullo,' she said. 'Can I help?'

I apologized for disturbing her and indicated I just had a couple of questions, which wouldn't take a moment.

She seemed glad of the chance to stop work and chat, and clambered down from her pew, puffing. She was a little on the heavy side to be climbing up and down furniture. Her companion in the chancel had switched off the machine and was struggling to extricate the full inner paper sack from the outer bag.

'It's our turn on the cleaning rota, Muriel's and mine,' my new friend explained. 'I'm Valia Prescott. My husband is captain of the bell-ringers. If you want the vicar, I'm afraid it's his afternoon off. There's an emergency number on the notice board. If it's a baptism or a wedding, that's not emergency, I'm afraid, and you'll have to get in touch with him tomorrow.' She paused for breath.

It can't be helped, but some given names don't age with their owners. I suppose it will be odd being called

Francesca when I'm eighty. Perhaps one ought to be able to change one's name as one goes along, to suit one's years – turn into a Maud, Doris, or a Muriel like the wielder of the vacuum cleaner. The name Valia, to me, suggested some sort of wood nymph cavorting about veiled in nothing but her long hair. But this Valia was sixty something, grey hair set rigidly in a tight perm, and she wore a hand-knitted tangerine-coloured pullover, which clashed nicely with her flushed rosy complexion. None of the information she'd so kindly reeled off for me was of any use. I nodded brightly to show I'd taken it all in and then explained my business.

'My name's Fran Varady. I'm trying to find an elderly homeless man who might have been sleeping in the porch out there last night. His name is Jonty.'

She first looked a little startled, this being an out-of-the-ordinary request, then her good-natured expression became grimmer. 'Someone was there last night, all right! The smell out there was still dreadful when I got here with Muriel around two. It's difficult to get cleaners for a place this size and paying someone's out of the question, so the Mothers' Union got up a rota. I don't mind doing it – I quite like cleaning brass.'

She paused to glance up complacently at her work. The memorial was to a 'physician in this parish', paying tribute to his observance of his 'duty as a Christian and as a man of healing'. His patients had lost his services in 1894. His testimonial gleamed like gold, testifying to Valia's efforts. I complimented her and she beamed at me as brightly as the brass plaque.

'I don't mind doing anything, really, but anyone would draw the line at having to clean out the porch. Not that I had to clear away the worst of the mess. Ben, our caretaker, had done that this morning. But the smell was such that we just had to throw a bucket of Jeyes down there and brush it well out. It's the vicar, you see.'

Fortunately I was able to decipher her meaning. 'You mean the vicar lets the homeless sleep out there?'

'Not exactly *allows* it, but doesn't stop them. We used to have a wire mesh outer door but vandals broke it down. Then this vicar got the idea that we ought not to refuse shelter to a homeless person, even if it meant letting him sleep in our porch. Of course, one wants to be charitable . . .' she drew a deep breath, her ample bosom filling like a pair of water wings, 'but there are limits! As I say, the vicar doesn't have to clear up after those people. Sometimes – well, I won't tell you what kind of disgusting mess they make out there.'

'This Ben, the caretaker,' I asked. 'Would he still be around the place?'

She looked vague. 'He might,' she said. 'If so, he'd be seeing to the furnace. We've had a lot of problems with it. It's very old. It's in the basement, entry outside the church. If you go out of the door there where you came in, turn right and make your way along, you'll see the door, down a couple of steps.'

I thanked her and went to find Ben the furnaceman. If he had been the one to clear up the porch first thing, it was just possible he'd seen or found something that might give a clue to what happened here last night.

I made my way along the outside wall of the church. The area between building and street was untidily planted with shrubs and might once have been a garden. Someone, perhaps Ben, had cut the grass, but otherwise the shrubs had been left to grow straggly and misshapen. As I approached one clump, from behind it came a metallic clang and rather to my surprise, Muriel, the wizard with the vacuum, appeared. She was holding the crumpled emptied paper liner. St Agatha's cleaning rota, economical souls, reused them. She started on seeing me and stopped, clasping the bag to her flat chest.

'Sorry,' I said. 'I'm looking for the furnace room. Valia said it was along here.'

'Oh,' she looked relieved. 'Yes, just behind there.' She hurried past me, back to the safety of the church.

I saw now that the bushes served both to hide a row of refuse bins and the steps down to a low door in the side of the church. I wondered whether St Agatha's had a proper crypt. Probably not, but possibly some cellars, one of which now housed the furnace.

I paused by the refuse bins and eyed them. If Ben, or anyone else, had found anything, it might have been tossed into one of these. Gingerly, I took off the nearest lid. A layer of grey dust, fluff and unidentifiable scraps covered the top. The contents of Muriel's dust bag, no doubt. I peered at them.

'What're you looking for, then?'

The voice came from behind me, male, hoarse and suspicious. I jumped round.

He was elderly, red-faced beneath a greasy cap, and

stout. He wore dark blue overalls and carried a folded tabloid newspaper.

'Ben?' I asked.

'That's me. Who're you, then?' He wheezed as he spoke and I saw the redness of his skin was accentuated by purple threads.

I explained who I was, what I wanted, and that Valia had directed me to him.

He snorted and went past me down the steps to unlock the door. He disappeared inside, but left it open, and I assumed I was meant to follow.

Once inside, I saw I was in Ben's personal sanctum. Most of it was taken up with the furnace, an ancient and alarmingly rusty-looking monster. Just enough room was left for a small table, a wooden kitchen chair, a small paraffin heater and a billycan. Ben had placed his newspaper on the table and added to it a packet of cigarettes and a box of matches. He indicated I should take the chair.

'You belong to one of them charities, then?' he rasped.

'No, it's – it's personal. Ben, do you ever see any of the men who sleep in the porch or have they always gone by the time you get here in the morning?'

He prised a cigarette from the packet and lit it. Shaking both the match to extinguish the flame, and his head at the same time, he said, 'No – not hardly ever. They clear out before they see me because they know I'd help 'em on their way with me boot.'

So much for the vicar's charity. It wasn't shared by his staff.

'So you wouldn't know an old man, rather smelly, called

Jonty? Or another, a bit cleaner, called Albie Smith? I think Albie slept here regularly.'

'Journalist?' Ben asked, ignoring my question.

'No, not a journalist. I told you, it's private.'

He looked disappointed. It occurred to me that journalists have been known to pay. But I didn't have any money. All I could do was stand my ground and wait.

'It smelled bloody awful this morning,' Ben observed. He didn't seem to hold it against me that I'd not offered any money. It'd been worth a try. 'I wish I did know who done it because if I'd got hold of the bugger I'd have made him clean it up! Gawd knows what they were doing in there last night.'

God probably did know. I was trying to find out. 'Was there anything left behind like clothing or blankets?'

'Just a few rags. I slung 'em in the furnace there.' He pointed. 'Not that it's lit. But if I find anything what burns, I sling it in the furnace. It's all fuel.'

Hesitantly I asked, 'Is it possible to get them out again?'

He looked at me in amazement. 'Think I got nothing better to do than to spend my time raking rubbish out of the furnace just to amuse you, whoever you are?'

I glanced down at the table, the newspaper and the cigarettes. He scowled but took the point.

'It's my tea-break,' he said sulkily.

'What time do you go home, Ben? I mean, what time do you lock up?'

He pointed to the ceiling. 'When them women finish their polishing. They generally goes off around five. I lock up at six and that's it. Can't leave the place open.

Sometimes the vicar wants it of an evening and then he lets me know. He's got his own keys, of course.' He shuffled about and curiosity got the better of him. 'These rags, what do you want 'em for?'

'Just to see them, in case I recognise any of them.'

Ben expelled his breath in a hiss between his yellowish stubs of teeth. Then he picked up a long metal rod fashioned into a hook at one end. Alarmed, I wondered if he meant to drive me off, but he inserted the hook into the handle of the furnace door and tugged it. The round metal door swung open. Ben reached in with the useful hook and poked around, eventually emerging and turning toward me. A grimy and tattered piece of gabardine, once the skirts of a raincoat, hung from the rod.

'This 'ere's part of it. Make you happy?' He raised his eyebrows. 'There was a bit of blanket as well. I can try and find it.'

It meant nothing to me. I shook my head. Ben pushed the rag back into the furnace. He swung the door shut and tapped the metal behemoth with the rod. It replied with a cavernous echoing groan. 'Pipes is buggered,' he said. 'Whole lot wants replacing.'

'And that's it?' I asked. 'You found nothing else?'

'Only what you'd expect,' he said. 'Whisky bottle. Live on alcohol, them old blokes. No matter how badly off they are, they always manage to get themselves a drink. A bottle and a fag packet. I put the packet in the furnace and the bottle in the dustbin, one of the bins outside there.'

Crossing my fingers, I asked, 'Would it still be there? Could I look?'

'Course it's still there. Haven't been emptied, have they? Take a look if you want. Leave it all tidy, that's all I ask. Don't go chucking stuff around.'

'Which dustbin?' I'd remembered there were three of them.

He frowned. 'End one, as I recall. Where you was looking just now.'

I thanked him again and left him settling down to read his paper as I climbed up the short flight of steps to the outer air and the lines of refuse bins behind the bushes.

I took the lid off the bin in question and stared down at the grey mix of dirt. I didn't fancy putting my hands in that. What I needed was something like Ben's furnace hook. I retraced my steps. He was reading the football page and looked up crossly.

'What d'you want now? No, you can't borrow it. I needs it.'

'You're not using it now,' I pointed out.

'Ah, and if you go running off with it, I won't never be using it again, will I?'

I promised faithfully I wouldn't leave the premises with the poker. He picked it up and gazed at it as if it were made of precious metal, before handing it over to me, laid ceremonially across his two hands, like a symbol of office. Perhaps, to him, it was.

I lugged it back up the steps and began to scrape little trial trenches in the dirt. At first I turned up only crumpled sweet wrappers and other assorted scrap paper. But eventually, after much diligent probing, the metal poker chinked against the glass and the round neck of a bottle appeared. I picked it out carefully – an empty Bell's whisky half-bottle.

I replaced the lid of the bin and made my way down to the furnace room. Ben, who evidently read his newspaper from back to front, had progressed from the sports news to the indiscretions of a politician on page two. I propped the poker against the furnace and thanked him for the loan of it.

He glanced down at it sternly, checking it was undamaged. I held out the Bell's bottle.

'Is this the bottle you found?'

'That's it.' He nodded and lost interest. He turned over the last sheet of newsprint so that now he'd reached the front page. It was nearly filled with a photograph of the erring politician arm in arm with a leggy bimbo. Ben, sucking his teeth, studied the picture carefully and gave his verdict.

'Oh well, good luck to 'im, anyway. I didn't vote for 'im.'

'You don't mind,' I asked, 'if I take it away?'

'What? That empty old bottle? Blimey, you got some funny ideas, ain't you?'

'Yes,' I said simply. 'Have you got a bit of paper I can wrap the bottle in?' I didn't want to walk along the street holding an empty bottle. I had my standards.

Ben had decided I was a joke. He got up chuckling and began to rummage in a black plastic bin-liner in the corner. He emerged with a crumpled and grubby plastic carrier bag. 'Here, take this. I find 'em floating around the place and I keep 'em because they come in handy.'

'Thanks,' I told him.

'Just don't come back again,' he bade me kindly as we parted.

I set off with my plastic carrier containing the Bell's bottle. Much as I disliked the idea of dealing with Parry again, he'd have to know about it. It supported what I'd told him, that Albie had had a half-bottle of whisky last night in the porch and not a large bottle.

Of course it wasn't proof unless they could get Albie's fingerprints off it. I wondered, uncomfortably, where Albie's body was. Lying in a morgue? Would they carry out a post-mortem? I thought they probably would. Stray deaths have to be accounted for. They'd confirm he'd died by drowning and we'd be no further forward. I glanced down at the plastic bag with the bottle. Jonty would've handled it and after that Ben handled it and lastly I picked it up, though I'd been careful. Other rubbish had rubbed against it in the bin, unfortunately, and Ben's hands had been like shovels. If there had been prints, they would've been smudged or obliterated by now.

I realised at this point that I wasn't walking towards my flat. I was walking the other way, towards St Agatha's refuge. It seemed I was meant to go there.

The refuge looked like a quiet, respectable house not unlike Daphne's and in a similar street. The only real sign that anything unusual ever happened there was a wooden board temporarily nailed over the lower half of the window to the left of the door, signifying a breakage. That, and the tiniest, most discreet of notices beside the bell push, reading 'Women's Refuge'. I stood on the step and wondered what I could say that would sound convincing. No story came to mind so I rang the bell anyway and trusted to luck and inspiration.

The door was opened by a thin-faced woman with a wary expression. Her hair, cut in an old-fashioned, dead straight page-boy bob and dyed an unlikely reddish colour without variation in texture or shade, had to be a budget wig.

'Come in,' she said, without preamble, and I found myself standing in a narrow hallway that smelled of cooked vegetables. From the rear of the hall, through a half-open door, came the rattle of crockery as if someone were laying the table for the evening meal. Upstairs a baby wailed, and a sudden burst of shrill voices was cut short by the slam of a door. The air of tension about the place was palpable. I'd been surprised by the way the woman had hurried me inside without question and then I realised that possibly they didn't like leaving the front door open. I remembered the boarded window panes. They had a bit of trouble here sometimes, so Jonty had said.

'You want a bed, I suppose?' The woman sounded partly resentful and partly resigned. Her gaze took in the plastic carrier. 'Is that all the stuff you've brought with you? Just as well, we've got very little room to store personal effects.'

Embarrassed I explained that actually I didn't want a bed, I'd only come to ask a couple of questions.

Her thin features reddened. 'Oh for goodness' sake!' she snapped. 'If you want to do a story, you might at least phone first! And in any case, we don't want too much publicity. We get more people coming here than we can cope with as it is.'

It was the second time that day I'd been mistaken for a journalist. I explained to her that I wasn't from the media.

'So what do you want?' Her temper was getting shorter by the second.

I told her my story. 'The old man said he saw a girl running away from somewhere around here. So I wondered whether you'd missed any of your – ' I wasn't sure what to call the women who came here, so ended up, 'clients.'

She pressed her lips together. 'We don't discuss anything which happens here with anyone outside. We don't discuss the circumstances of any of the women here nor do we give out any names or details which might allow them to be identified. They come here knowing that all their problems will be heard with sympathy and the information received in complete confidence. I don't know who you are, but it's clear you have no valid reason for being here at all. Please leave.'

She moved past me and opened the front door.

'Look,' I pleaded, 'perhaps this girl meant to come here but never reached you? She may have been snatched on the way. You might not know about her but she knew about you! Wherever she is, she still needs your help!'

'If you refuse to leave,' she said, 'I shall fetch help to put you out.'

She meant it. I left.

I walked home thinking that I'd handled that particularly

badly. It would be difficult for me now to go back there again. But the woman I'd seen couldn't be on duty all the time. If I returned tomorrow at a different time, say in the morning, there was a chance someone else might answer the door. Provided the first woman hadn't passed on a warning message about me, another refuge worker might be more helpful.

I turned into my street. I didn't know what time it was but the meal-time activity at the refuge had reminded my stomach I hadn't eaten since Parry cooked scrambled eggs for me at lunchtime.

I hurried towards my flat. Daylight was failing and it was that peculiar hour of the day when objects begin to blend into their surrounds. What with the poor light and my mind being occupied with food, I failed at first to realise that a large car was parked opposite the house, shielded by a gnarled, unhealthy city tree and the gathering dusk.

My attention was called to it by a slam of the driver's door. He'd got out, a big solid bloke in a pale grey uniform-type suit and a dark tie, and was walking towards me.

I cast a despairing glance at my basement steps. No way could I get down them and indoors before the hulk reached me.

'Miss Varady?' he asked in a flat, unemotional voice.

I had a choice of answers. 'No' would be pointless because he'd already identified me. I said, 'Yes?' and looked up at Daphne's windows, hoping against hope she was looking out. But there was no sign of her.

'Mr Szabo would like to talk to you,' the hulk said. He nodded towards the parked car.

I took a look at it. It had tinted windows.

'I don't know him,' I quavered.

'He's waiting in the car.' The hulk's voice grew slightly reproachful. 'He's had a long wait. You're late coming home tonight, Miss Varady.'

'Look, this has to be a mistake . . .' I began. But I got no further. He took hold of my arm, not roughly, just firmly, and guided me across the road with gentle persuasion.

The rear passenger door swung open and with it the interior light came on. But I still couldn't quite make out who sat in the back seat because he was leaning away from me into his corner. But I heard his voice.

'Miss Varady? Please don't be alarmed. My name is Vincent Szabo. I believe I knew your father.'

The tone was precise, a touch old-maidish. As a chat-up line, it was different.

Chapter Eight

When I was a kid I was told, as kids are, never to get into a car with a strange man. I've hitchhiked a few times and broken the rule, but the choice had always been mine. Get into the car or not. This time, given any kind of choice, I'd have decided not. This wasn't the sort of lift I'd have accepted. Nevertheless, before I knew it, there I was sitting in the back of Szabo's plush motor. I was torn between wondering whether I was ever going to be allowed to get out of it again and a curiosity to see the owner of the voice.

The chauffeur hadn't joined us. He was hanging about outside somewhere, making sure we weren't disturbed. Szabo had asked the man to set the interior light to 'on', so that we shouldn't be left in the gloom when the door was shut again. Now we eyed each other in the resultant cosy intimacy.

I'd had no time to imagine what he'd be like but even if I had done, I wouldn't have been anywhere near the mark. He was a small man with a round head and a halo of grey curls. His face was pale, lined with worry, and his eyes – blue or grey, I couldn't be sure which – anxious. He was about as frightening as your average lollipop lady. I began to understand the chauffeur. If you haven't got muscles of your own, you have to hire 'em.

Szabo's appearance was further undermined by his clothes, which were expensive and stylish but looked too big for him. He seemed to be sitting inside his overcoat as in a tent, and his shirt collar stood away from his neck. Something about it all niggled briefly at my memory, but I couldn't put a finger on what he reminded me of, other than a white mouse. The coat rustled as he leaned forward and his hand, small as a woman's, emerged from a sleeve to reach over and pat mine.

'Don't be alarmed, my dear,' he said again, reassuringly. They really were more suited to be a woman's hands, tiny, and the fingertips very soft with nails professionally manicured. He took his hand away, not letting his fingers linger, but I still didn't like the gesture or the velvety feel of his skin. The guy was a toucher. There's the paternal kind and the groping kind, but it adds up to the same thing in my book. They want to get their grubby mitts on you.

Perhaps he sensed he'd made a wrong move. He made a vague, deprecating movement of the hand in question and withdrew it into the baggy sleeve of the overcoat. Then he folded both hands tightly, after the fashion of an imperial Chinese mandarin, to show he had them under control. I wondered what else he had up his sleeve, in both senses.

Urgently he repeated, 'I really do mean I knew your dad.'

'My dad's dead.' I managed to make icicles form on the words, and squeezed up in the corner as far away from him as I could, just to let him know the touching hadn't gone unremarked and sitting there with his hands clasped like a mother superior didn't fool me.

I supposed him to be about fifty, which is what my dad would have been if he were still alive, or forty-seven, to be exact. Though Szabo in no way resembled my father, who'd been stockily built, there was something in his cast of features that was identifiably Central European. Szabo was a Hungarian name as common as Smith, and I supposed it was just possible he was telling the truth.

'I was very sorry when I heard Bondi had died,' he went on.

My father's first name had been Stephen but Grandma Varady had always called him Bondi. No one else to my knowledge had even done so until this man. I knew then that somehow, though I'd no idea how, he might well have known Dad. Nevertheless, I said, 'He never mentioned you.'

'Why should he?' Szabo unfolded his fingers and pressed the well-manicured tips together. The sleeves of his coat still came halfway up his palms. 'We were boys at the time. Let's see, we'd have been ten, eleven years old? We played in the local Catholic boys' football team. How time flies. My parents moved to Manchester and took me with them. I lost touch with Bondi. I've always regretted it. We were good friends for several years. Happy days . . .' He sighed.

I wondered what line of business he was in. Whatever else had happened after their lives diverged, Szabo would appear to have made money. Dad hadn't. Or rather, Dad had made fair amounts from time to time, but always had trouble keeping it.

Hungarians have a name for being good at business, highly entrepreneurial, hard workers, quick to learn, and are usually welcome as immigrants anywhere. 'A Hungarian,' so the saying goes, 'is a man who goes into a revolving door behind you, and comes out of it ahead of you.' Szabo was probably a perfect living example of this.

My dad had been the exception that proves the rule. The one who'd somehow got stuck in the door's workings and gone round and round, always heading somewhere and never arriving anywhere.

'You're wondering about me,' Szabo was saying, 'wondering how I got to you, what I'm doing here. What I want, I dare say.'

'Yes, I am.' The only thing I was fairly sure of was that Vinnie here wasn't just kerb-crawling. I might still be wrong about that, of course. On the other hand he was being so damn polite, looking so worried, was so anxious not to offend. What did he need from me?

'Of course you are!' Szabo nodded. 'I'm sorry there wasn't a – a less alarming way of introducing myself. But now I have, I'd better explain myself.'

I settled back. I could have scrambled out of the car, I suppose, and set up a yell if the chauffeur had tried to grab me. But I wanted to hear what Vincent Szabo, self-styled friend of my father's youth, had to say. After all, the man would have appeared to have gone to a lot of trouble to meet me.

'You don't mind if we talk in the car?' he asked. I didn't point out I'd not been given any choice in the matter. He was watching me anxiously, as if my agreement mattered.

'Go ahead,' I said.

After all, I might learn something. There had to be a reason for all this. Besides which, what can't be cured must be endured, as Mrs Worran, who'd lived next door to us when Dad had been alive, had been fond of saying. I'd heard her say it to Grandma after my mother walked out. Later, when Dad died, she'd said it to me. There was something in her grim acceptance of Fate that had struck me then as worse than despair. I still found it irksome as a philosophy, but sometimes, like now, it described the situation perfectly.

'You see,' Szabo was saying, 'I like my privacy. I'm essentially a private man, a family man, you'd say. I don't care to discuss my affairs in a public place or to think that others might be discussing me in that way, for all and sundry to hear. I find it distressing. That's why I find this meeting distressing and I've chosen to conduct it in this way. I hope you'll understand.'

I waited. He had paused as if he expected me to speak and when I didn't, he rubbed his small neat hands together and began again, his voice staccato, the words chopped into broken phrases.

'What I have to say is particularly sensitive. Oh dear, this is quite— You see, I hardly know how to begin. To have to talk of it at all. And of course, I shouldn't, shouldn't be talking to you or to anyone. But then, when I realised you were Bondi's girl . . . I thought, that would be different. Almost as if I were talking to him. He was a dear friend.'

'Excuse me,' I said, irked by this continual dropping of Dad's name, 'but I honestly don't remember my father mentioning your name.'

'Why should he?' For a moment Szabo seemed even more downcast, if that were possible. 'Life took us in different directions.' Suddenly his manner changed, becoming all at once confident and almost cheerful. 'Oh, those were the days! He was a real scrapper of a kid, your dad. Always getting into fights with bigger kids and coming off worst. Never learned.' He gave a rusty chuckle as if he'd got out of the habit of laughing of late. Then amusement faded. 'He should have learned, but he never did. It doesn't always pay to go straight in there with fists flailing.' He tapped his forehead with a manicured nail. 'Use this.'

Well, I already knew *that*. If I hadn't got in the way of using my brains before this, I wouldn't have survived as long as I had. Before now I'd have been one of those bodies they find in the canal, like Albie's, all shot up with booze and drugs. I knew enough to keep clear of trouble. I can't help it if sometimes trouble seeks me out.

I glanced at the little man in the opposite corner and wondered if Vinnie had early learned to use his brains because he wasn't built for the rough stuff. Undersized children sometimes tag along with a tough kid for protection, like a moon orbiting a powerful planet. Had that been the nature of the link between Dad and this man? Had Dad protected him from the playground bullies? The football team story could still be right. A small kid like Szabo could still have been nippy about the football field and a nifty player, despite his present unathletic appearance.

'I'm here because of something so – appalling, something which has quite, I don't exaggerate, turned my world upside down,' Szabo said earnestly. 'My dear, you're confused. I'm confusing you. It'd be best, perhaps, if I explained events in the order in which they happened. You'll soon see why I want – why I need – to talk to you.'

His manner had changed. Now he'd made up his mind to tell me his story, he began speaking briskly and in a coherent way. I was relieved because his manner had been making me jumpy. I'd even begun to wonder if he wasn't on something.

'As I was saying, my parents took me away from London to Manchester.' He sounded brighter, as if the change had been a turn of luck for the better. 'I went into the soft furnishing business, wholesale, not retail, supplying upholstery fabrics to the trade. It's a good business – or it was before the recession set in. The housing boom did me a power of good. Everyone buying a new home and each new home filled with nice new furniture and curtains.'

He sounded cheerful again, remembering his successes. 'Oh, I didn't forget your dad,' he said. 'Even if, as you suggest, he might've forgotten me! No, I remembered him and when I started to do well, I wrote suggesting he come up North and join me in business. He wrote back refusing. Felt it wasn't his style. That was the last time we communicated. I'd no idea what he did after that.' He raised his eyebrows questioningly and paused for me to fill in the detail.

'Not very well,' I admitted. 'Although sometimes better than others.'

He shrugged. 'I was afraid of that. If he'd joined forces with me, I'd have guided him. Oh his own, Bondi was always – erratic. However, I did well for a long time and then we had a few setbacks. The bottom fell out of the housing market and it hit me as it hit a lot of suppliers to the trade. Carpets, housepaints, bathroom fittings, you name it. The whole shebang took a hell of a knock. Saddled with negative equity, who buys a new three-piece suite? But I'd made my money by then and besides, I'd got a good export business going. Speciality fabrics to the Middle East.'

He gave a coy, old lady's giggle, indicating he was about to make a joke. 'Many a harem's fitted out using my fabrics. They're mad about velvets.'

'Great,' I said vaguely.

'I've also diversified into other interests,' he went on. 'It doesn't do to keep all the eggs in one basket, as they say.'

He didn't explain what these other interests were and I didn't ask.

His manner, which had continued to veer between the depressed and the almost hilarious, changed again. His state of mind was beginning to worry me. He was either under intolerable stress and barely coping, or seriously nuts. I wasn't sure which.

'I was married for twelve years and I count myself blessed to have had an extraordinarily happy marriage. My wife was a widow at the time we met. She had a little girl, Lauren, aged just six. It's difficult for a woman on her own, bringing up a child, especially with the world being like it is today,' he concluded earnestly, leaning forward slightly to impart this wisdom.

Within a stone's throw of where we sat we could've found half a dozen single mums who could tell him a thing or two about how tough it was. But this prissy little fellow, with his success hanging smugly about him, seemed to think he'd made the discovery.

'I adopted Lauren and brought her up as my own,' he said, emphasising the last word just a little. 'I'm as proud of her as *any* father. I've done my best for her. Good school, dancing lessons, elocution classes, cordon bleu cookery course . . .' He rattled off the list with simple pride.

I nearly told him *I'd* been to a good school and had acting lessons, and look at me! But I didn't.

'My responsibilities towards Lauren increased after my wife died.' His blue eyes rested on my face, watching for my reaction. 'She had cancer.' His gaze moistened and I felt an awful lurch in the diaphragm and hoped he wasn't going to snivel. Poor little guy. Perhaps he'd lost weight when his wife fell ill and died. That could be why the wretched overcoat was too large.

'After that I had a double duty towards Lauren. I had to play the role of both father and mother. I owed it to my late wife to take every possible care of her and see she wanted for nothing. I did make sure she lacked nothing. Like I said, she's had everything, the best money could buy. I made sure of it. Anything she wanted, she only had to ask.' He leaned towards me again and I guessed it was a substitute for touching. He'd realised I didn't like the hand-patting, but he couldn't help himself. He had at least to imitate a physical contact.

Well, all right, all right, I believed him. But I'd got control of my emotions, and was thinking straighter. If he'd done his homework on my background, as he surely had, he'd know that my father had been left with the care of me after my mum cleared out. Szabo was making a bid for sympathy, assuming I'd appreciate his problems and the effort he'd made to tackle them.

He'd probably done his best, just like he'd said. But I don't know whether spoiling a kid rotten is the kindest thing to do in the long run. I also wondered if he'd been there to listen when Lauren burbled about her dreams, as my dad had been for me. But perhaps I was misjudging him. Maybe he idolised Lauren.

As if he sensed my thoughts, he burst out emotionally, 'She's a lovely girl, a beautiful girl, with a sweet nature!'

Well, there have to be a few examples of pure young womanhood around like that, even in this wicked world. Perhaps he'd kept Lauren locked up in a tower, like Rapunzel. Lauren, he said, had been aged six at the time of her mother's marriage to Szabo and the marriage had lasted twelve years. I didn't know how long his wife had been dead. 'How old is Lauren now?'

'Nineteen,' he said. 'So a little younger than you.'

He obviously knew I was twenty-one. The man probably had the equivalent of a *Who's Who?* entry on me.

He drew a deep breath, as if he'd surprised himself by the outburst, and resettled himself in his corner of the back seat. 'I'm successful. It's attracted jealousy and resentment in some quarters,' he went on. 'It's inevitable. I can live with that. Unfortunately money also attracts another kind of attention.' Emotion entered his voice again. 'What I'm about to tell you isn't to be repeated to anyone, you understand? No gossiping among your friends.'

'You're sure you want to tell me?' I asked, since he was getting het up again and the muscles around his mouth were wobbling.

'Not particularly, to be truthful. But I'm in an unusual and unexpected difficulty. My daughter has been kidnapped.'

He broke off and seemed to be waiting for my reaction. It was blunt enough as a statement and was meant to shock. But I couldn't sound surprised. I knew that a snatch had taken place. That an identity had at last been given to the snatch victim came almost as a relief. I said I was sorry.

'Sorry?' He picked up my word and shook his head. 'You can have no idea what it means. Oh, kidnap – everyone thinks he knows! But when it happens to you, when someone you love, someone you've cared for, watched grow from a young child to a lovely woman, is taken from you . . .' He twitched. 'Not to know where she is, if she's well or hurt, who has her prisoner, in what circumstances they're keeping her, what kind of people— ' He broke off and twitched again. I hoped he wasn't going to break down. Instead, he rushed on, 'I say, what kind of people? But I know what kind. Only depravity of the worst sort could do this, only a mind dulled to any human emotion could even contemplate it!'

I felt I ought to say something so I said, 'They have no reason to harm her.'

'They don't reason like you or me. What's happened is

worse than death,' he said quietly. 'You can mourn a death and bury a body. I don't know whether I'll ever see Lauren alive again, or whether it's a body they'll bring back to me. Or neither. It could be that I'll never know. At least they are still sending their messages and while there's contact, I have hope.'

'They've named a ransom?'

He nodded. 'I've received a ransom note for a quite exorbitant sum. I'm a wealthy man but I'm not a millionaire. Perhaps, given time, I might raise the money but even if I did, there is no guarantee Lauren would be returned. I am not a fool. Until I pay, they need Lauren. She is their security as well as their hostage. We're hampered in everything we do, knowing she's in their hands. But once they have the money, they don't need her any longer. She's an embarrassment and worse, a weak link in their armour. They will be taking precautions so that she can't identify them. They probably have her blindfolded, or keep her in a dark room. She'll be distraught, terrified. But she may still have heard a voice, smelled some distinctive odour, caught the sound of something unusual out in the street, recognised some peculiar feature of the house . . . any of these things could lead to their capture and conviction. So why shouldn't they kill her, once they have the money? After that, all that will matter to them will be their safety.'

I was following this as best I could and trying to deduce what I could from it. Some of what he was saying sounded semi-official. Before, he'd said 'I', but now he was saying 'we'.

'You've been to the police,' I said, not a question.

'I knew I had no choice but to go to the police!' he retorted vehemently. 'They have their procedures. The first thing they organised was a blanket ban on news reporting. Despite the fact that I'm not accustomed to following orders, I've been following their instructions in negotiations with the kidnappers to the letter. Meantime, the police have been trying to locate my girl. They've not done so and I'm beginning to become impatient, not to say out of my mind with worry. One can't know what those creatures who hold my daughter will do. My confidence in the police is dwindling. In fact, it seems to me they're floundering, with no more idea what to do than you would have, if I gave the job of finding Lauren to you.'

I thought that he underestimated my ingenuity, but it wasn't the time to argue. I nodded.

It seemed to encourage him. He began to sound more determined. 'I think it's time I took a more active hand. Now, I understand from Sergeant Parry that you had some conversation with an elderly vagrant who claimed to have seen a girl, answering Lauren's description, snatched from the street?'

So that was it. That's how Szabo knew about me and I came to be sitting here, listening to all this. Parry had grassed.

'That's right,' I said. 'I did. And if you've seen Parry today, you'll know the old man's body was found floating in the canal this morning. Parry declares there is no evidence to suggest it was anything other than an accident but I don't think so.'

'I've spoken with Sergeant Parry and with his superiors. Like you, I feel it's unlikely the death was accidental. And if those men killed the old man, why shouldn't they kill my girl? I can no longer afford to sit back and leave it to the authorities! Tell me what the vagrant told you, all of it, exactly as he said it.'

I told him, but only that, not what I had seen. Szabo listened intently, looked dissatisfied and tapped his pale fingers on the knees of his quality worsted pants.

'And the two men?' he asked. 'Did the tramp describe them?'

I was being manoeuvred rapidly into a no-win corner here. If I answered all these questions, I was likely to end up on the receiving end of aggro from Parry. If I didn't, Szabo could turn awkward. He might look harmless but I'd an idea he was used to getting his own way and I hadn't forgotten the beefy chauffeur. 'Look,' I said, 'do the police know you're talking to me?'

'Naturally,' he said, sounding rather starchy. 'Recognising a Hungarian name, I asked the police what they knew about you and Sergeant Parry appeared to know your background quite well. I informed him that you were almost certainly the daughter of my boyhood friend Stephen Varady and that I'd seek you out as a matter of courtesy, if nothing else.' He sniffed vengefully. 'The police didn't like it, perhaps. But since they've come up with absolutely nothing so far, they were hardly in a position to argue with me. I've put through some tough business deals in my time. I know when to call someone's bluff!'

So take that, he might have added.

'All right,' I said. 'He didn't describe the men. He described their car.' I gave him the description and told him a car like that had been torched during the previous night.

'And the men?' Szabo practically bounced in his seat with excitement. 'Perhaps the old man didn't describe them, but I understand you can give a description of at least one of them?'

I cursed Parry and wondered what on earth he was playing at, putting Szabo on to me. I wasn't sure how much I was supposed to tell him. But if the police had wanted to keep Vinnie from questioning me, Parry should have kept his mouth shut. I wondered why Parry had given out the information. It could be that Szabo was a difficult man to refuse, or that the sergeant thought I was holding out and might tell Vinnie here more than I'd told the plods.

'I saw one of them, I think,' I said. 'Very tall, possibly a body builder, all muscles and tattoos. Ugly mug. Not nice.'

He leaned forward intently. 'Tattoos? What kind of tattoos? Any special marks?'

'Gunners' supporter,' I said. 'Arsenal Football Team, that is. Got it tattooed on one arm.'

'You've told the police?'

'Of course I have,' I said sharply. 'I don't keep things like that from the coppers!'

I might do if I thought it advisable, but I wanted Szabo to think I was a law-abiding type. I didn't want him to get the idea he could use me in some way with Parry none the wiser.

My companion was searching in his inner breast pocket and took out a little silver case and a silver pen. From the case he took a business card and with the pen wrote a phone number on the back. He handed it to me.

'I can always be reached on this number,' he said. 'If you see this man again, I want you to get in touch with me immediately, do you understand? Whether or not you tell the police, I want you to tell me directly. Or if you come across anything else, or remember anything, however insignificant it might be, which the old man said, you understand? Get in touch with me!'

'I understand,' I said, pocketing the card. I hadn't said I'd do it, but he took that as read. His mistake.

He'd put away the card case and pen and brought out his wallet. 'Look, my dear, I hope you won't take this wrongly. Obviously things have been difficult for you since your father died. I know if the situations had been reversed, Bondi would have tried to look after any daughter of mine who was in need. I'd like to help. If I'd known about you, I'd have offered my help before this.'

'It's not necessary,' I said sharply. 'I can manage.'

'Please!' he urged. 'I'm not offering charity! I understand you're proud, like your dad, but look at it this way. Let me pay you for your time this evening. You've been more than patient and I do appreciate it. I apologise again for any alarm you may have felt. Matson, my driver, lacks, er, tact. Call it compensation?'

He took out several twenty-pound notes and fanned them out like a magician, inviting me to pick a card, any one. The notes were all crisp and new. I nearly asked him, jokingly, if he'd printed them himself, but he was probably deficient in a sense of humour right now, and if they were duds, he wouldn't be passing them himself.

There were five of them. 'One hundred pounds,' he emphasised, peering at me in the poor light. 'Do you feel that's adequate?'

There are moralists among you reading this who would feel I should have refused the money. But I took it because, fair's fair, he *had* taken up my time and originally given me a heck of a fright. Nor would he have liked being refused. Besides, I was broke, and it wasn't like he hadn't known Dad.

'And you won't forget what we agreed?' he asked.

As I recalled it, we hadn't actually agreed anything, but there was only one answer. 'No, Mr Szabo,' I said meekly, pocketing the readies.

He smiled and nodded and almost patted my hand again, but remembered just in time. 'You know, I feel as though I've managed to do something to help Lauren at last. It's been so frustrating with the police, they always reckon to know best – though I've begun to doubt it. Just talking to you, telling you, it's been such a help. I want to thank you. You're a good girl. You're like your father. I knew I couldn't go wrong seeking out Bondi's daughter.'

I'd been going to give him a nice bright smile back, but it faded. The last person to call me a good girl had been poor old Albie.

'Can I go now?' I asked.

'Of course!' He looked stricken and tapped on the

smoky window. 'I've held you up, such a long time, I'm so sorry . . .'

The door beside me opened and the chauffeur waited outside on the pavement, hand outstretched to help the little lady out.

Halfway out, I made a mistake. Curiosity got the better of me. I turned back and asked, 'Why was Lauren walking around at night on her own, near St Agatha's church?'

I don't know if Szabo heard the question or not. The chauffeur's deferential touch turned to an ungentle grip. I was hoicked smartly out of the motor and deposited on the pavement. The car sped away, leaving me rubbing my upper arm.

Bruise on my shoulder from Merv and bruises on my arm from Szabo's minder. I was keeping the wrong sort of company.

Chapter Nine

Ganesh came over in the evening with a bag of takeaway food and a bottle of wine. I was glad we hadn't to go out to eat, not least because I wanted to avoid Jimmie's until the art show was over. It was already Thursday, which meant I'd only one clear day left before my debut as a living work of art. I still hadn't told Gan about it and wasn't keen to.

So when he asked, 'What's been happening?' I concentrated on telling him about Albie, St Agatha's and an edited account of my meeting with Szabo.

'I'm sorry about the old fellow,' Ganesh said, 'even if he was a disgusting old drunk. I'd like for the two thugs to get caught. But it's a job for the police, Fran. You should hand that whisky bottle over to Parry at once. I remember it. I mean, I remember that Albie definitely had a half-bottle of Bell's.'

'That's handy,' I said. 'You can tell Parry, back my story.'

But Ganesh was frowning, his mind running on something else. 'This Szabo, you reckon he really knew your family?'

'Yes, I do. I don't think he'd claim he had if he didn't and he seemed to know all about them. I know my dad never mentioned him, but why should he? Vinnie was sitting up there in Manchester turning out the quality loose covers and making a fortune out of the chintz and cretonne business generally. Dad was down here making one bad business decision after the other, probably regretting he hadn't joined Vinnie when he had the chance. But then, I don't know what capacity Szabo had in mind when he asked Dad up to Manchester to join the business. I don't somehow think he was intending to make him a partner. Dad might've ended up driving his old footballing pal around town, wearing a chauffeur's suit like Matson. Perhaps that's why he declined the offer!'

'He sounds a bit dodgy,' said Ganesh, who said that about pretty well everybody.

'Szabo? He's a funny little guy. Lots of brains and a dab hand at business, that's for sure. Thought the world of his wife and of course, the kid, Lauren. I don't know, but it's occurred to me . . .'

'Go on,' Ganesh urged when I stopped, embarrassed.

I put into words something I'd been mulling over. 'All right. It's occurred to me that perhaps Vinnie married a widow with a child because it seemed a good deal businesswise. I don't mean he wasn't nuts about them both – but it took some of the uncertainty out of getting married. She'd been married before. She already had a kid. He didn't mention any other children so I don't think they had any together. It was like, well, buying a package holiday. You know exactly what you're getting.'

'Hah!' said Ganesh with feeling. 'Usha and Jay bought a package holiday and got food poisoning.'

'So there's always a risk in any business! I'm just saying, Vinnie took the best option. I don't imagine he's ever been the type to sweep women off their feet! There was this young woman with a child, looking for a nice home and there was Vinnie, looking for a family. It worked out well. Everyone got what they wanted.'

Ganesh was looking dissatisfied. Chewing and waving a piece of naan bread at me to emphasise his words, he said indistinctly, 'I still don't see why he had to turn up like that and nab you. I understand the man's desperate, but – don't get me wrong – talking to you was really grabbing at straws.'

'I think he only came to find me when he realised whose daughter I was. Szabo's getting tired of waiting about for the police to pull the chestnuts out of the fire. He wants Lauren found, fair enough, and found quickly. And he's used to doing things himself, his way, calling all the shots. More than that, he's isolated. He's come down from Manchester. London's a place he left as a kid. He doesn't know people here. This isn't a situation where he can call in business favours and get things done. Suddenly, there I am, Bondi's daughter. I'm almost family!'

'I understand how he feels, but he could screw up the whole investigation,' Ganesh said, still disapproving and scraping the rest of the chicken korma out of the foil tray on to my plate. It was kind of him to think of bringing meat for me. He's vegetarian himself. 'And *how* did he learn that you were a friend's daughter? I mean, what made Parry send Szabo to you?'

'Hah!' I said darkly. 'Wouldn't we all like to know what Sergeant Parry's up to? He's got a nerve, setting Szabo on me! What did Parry expect me to tell Vinnie I haven't already told the police? Does Parry think I'm holding out on him? I've already told them all I know and a fat lot they've done with the information.'

We sat in silence eating. Ganesh was deep in thought and I didn't disturb the process because generally he's good at figuring things out and exceptionally good at finding weak links in arguments, especially my arguments.

'It seems to me,' he said at last, 'that you're looking at this from the wrong point of view. That's to say, from your point of view when you ought to be looking at it from Parry's. What I mean is, I don't think Parry thinks you're not telling all you know. I think he thinks *Szabo* isn't telling all he knows. I'm not saying Szabo is a crook. He probably just sails a little close to the wind sometimes and it's not in his interest to tell the coppers all his business, right? At the very least, he's probably got money offshore and the tax people are sniffing round.'

'He likes privacy, he told me so,' I informed him.

'Exactly. Normally he'd probably go a hundred miles out of his way to keep the police or any other official authority out of his hair. Who's to blame him? Look what happened to Hari. But now this girl, Lauren, has been kidnapped. Szabo's had to open up and let the cops put their big feet over his threshold. But no more than he's got to. He's not letting them into the front room and offering them cups of tea. The police would like to know more about

Szabo and just how it's come about that his daughter's locked in a cupboard somewhere while a couple of thugs put the squeeze on her family. Perhaps there's a lead or a connection which is slipping by Parry because Szabo's trying to be clever. The man wants his daughter found, but he's a businessman, and he's trying to cut a sort of deal with the police. He wants Lauren back but to give away as little as possible in return. Parry's not using Szabo to shake you loose. He's using *you* to shake up Szabo.'

'Poor kid,' I said. 'As if she's not in enough trouble, Szabo and Parry are playing silly games instead of getting together. I hope she's not having too rough a time. She must be scared out of her wits.'

We sat in silence for a while, both of us aware of the brutal reality of Lauren's situation. Some kidnappers, according to press reports of past cases I'd read, kept their victims prisoner in Dark Age squalor, locked in airless cupboards as Ganesh had just suggested, or even worse, boxed in coffin-like horror, possibly underground. No wonder Szabo was half out of his mind with worry. Even if they got her back in one piece, what sort of mental state would she be in?

I pushed all this gruesome speculation from my mind. It didn't help Lauren and rescuing her was what we all ought to be concentrating on, that and nothing else.

What Gan had said made sense to me. I ought to know enough about Parry to realise he hadn't sent Vinnie along to me without some dastardly plan behind it all. Never mind if I get the fright of my life, abducted by a goon into a motor with tinted windows, to be faced with someone I never saw before but who knows all about me.

Just you wait, Sergeant Parry, I promised myself. I can be very awkward about this. You weren't told to do things this way at Hendon Police College. Or perhaps you were. Come to think of it, Parry had been rather clever for once. He couldn't bully Szabo in the way he liked to bully people, so he had to manipulate the situation. Neat, Sergeant P., but, from my point of view, nasty. The boys in blue are a devious bunch.

'God, Parry's a creep,' I said fervently.

'Sure he is,' said Ganesh. 'But he fancies you something rotten.'

That startled me so much I dropped my plastic fork. 'You're barmy!' I yelped.

'No, I'm a bloke and I can read the signs. He gets that gleam in his eye when he sees you. Now he knows where you are, he'll be back.'

'Thanks for nothing,' I said.

'Let me know if you want me to rush round and defend your honour.' He started chortling away happily to himself.

'I'll have you know I can look after myself!' I snapped. 'Parry? *Parry?* Parry waltzing round my bedroom reeking of aftershave and lust? I'd sooner face a firing squad!'

'Well, they used to call it a fate worse than death!' said Ganesh. He laughed so much he choked on a cashew. I had to thump his back until he yelled out for me to stop before I fractured his spine.

My unknown visitor came back that night.

Before going to bed, I had managed to convince myself

that I'd imagined it all two nights ago. It was that sealed little bedroom, I'd told myself. Now I was sleeping out here in the living room, my mind wouldn't be tempted to create wandering ghouls. Anyone lying in the subterranean room, listening to footsteps overhead, would be bound to start making up scary tales. In this way, a late-night, homeward-bound stroller had stopped for a quiet ciggie and in my imagination I'd built it up into a Gothic novel.

Whereupon he proved me wrong. He came back. He even ventured a little closer. He came down the basement steps into the well and stood by the window. He couldn't see in because I'd drawn the curtains and all the lights were out.

I woke up with a start and a sick feeling in my stomach that was fear, not indigestion. Even in my sleep I must have been aware of his approach. Now, as I sat up on the sofa hugging the duvet around me, I saw him.

To be exact, I saw his silhouette on the curtain, slightly distorted by a fold in the curtain. The lamplight outside the house shone down into the basement well and there he was. Not a tall man, not Merv certainly. A squat figure, burly, and somehow familiar. He stood still and silent for a moment or two and then he moved away. I heard his heavy footstep, wearing strong boots of some kind I guessed, as he reclimbed the steps. Then he must have walked off in the other direction, and not back past the basement well, because I heard only the faintest footfall and then, very distantly, a revving motorbike engine. But traffic noise out on the main road travelled at night and the two last things needn't have been connected.

I went into the kitchen, got the bottle from the fridge and drank what remained of the wine Ganesh had brought. With the Dutch courage it provided, I wished I'd had the presence of mind to jump out of bed, snatch back the curtains and glare at him, eyeball to eyeball. Ten to one, it'd have scared him off. He was a prowler, a creeper in the shadows. He played out his fantasies in secret. He didn't like to face his victim.

Victim? I tipped up the bottle but it was empty. Was I indeed to be a victim? If so, what sort? He could just be a nutter. There were people like that who went out at night and roamed about. They had given rise to tales of werewolves and vampires in ages past. Now we just knew them for psychos. But what could he want?

I ran through the possible variations on this theme. He might be a rapist. Basement flats were notoriously vulnerable to break-in. But I had a chain on the door and bolts on the windows.

Or he might be a burglar. But surely he didn't think my place worth robbing? I ought to tell Daphne, though. He might think she had valuables around the place, or money. But I didn't want to frighten her, that was the thing. If he were interested in the rest of the house, why hang about in the basement? If I were the sole object of his attentions, why trouble poor Daphne?

Did he know, I wondered, that I was aware of him? Tonight had he known that I'd woken and seen his shadow on my curtain? He hadn't rattled at the window, trying it. So what the hell was he playing at? To frighten me? Was that his aim?

I raised the empty bottle to him in salute. 'You're doing a good job, friend,' I said. 'I'm frightened.'

I could tell Ganesh. But Ganesh would go berserk. I could tell Parry. No, things weren't that bad.

I crawled back beneath the duvet, but I didn't sleep much.

Dawn came at last and I fell asleep for a restless hour. I reawoke around six thirty and jumped off the sofa. I couldn't afford to waste daylight. Not now. One thing not on my side was time – amongst all the other things which weren't on my side, of course. Come to think of it, *nothing* was on my side.

If you added to that The Shadow hanging round the place at night, I didn't lack good reason to get moving. But at least I now knew where to start looking. I showered, dragged on jeans and a sweater, and trotted off to St Agatha's women's refuge.

I can't say I was feeling very chipper. But once away from the flat, the sheer normality of daily life all around encouraged me to believe I'd sort it all out somehow. Besides which, I had Szabo's hundred quid in my pocket and being in funds is guaranteed to brighten the outlook. I hadn't told Ganesh about the money. I knew he'd say I shouldn't have taken it. He'd probably argue that I'd implicitly put myself under some sort of obligation to Szabo and that's certainly what Vinnie intended. But I make my own rules.

There was some activity at the refuge this morning. They'd had a visitor of their own since I'd been there. Not content with just heavy breathing like my nocturnal caller, this one had kicked in the front door, which was off its hinges and leaning against the wall. A couple of carpenters were replacing the wooden panel. A skin-headed glazier, half his shaven skull tattooed with a spider's web, was fixing the broken window, getting everything shipshape till the next time. Fixing up St Agatha's must be like painting that Scottish bridge.

There was a transistor radio on the pavement blaring out pop music, and what with that and the sawing and hammering and the workmen all shouting at each other about football, it was bedlam.

I couldn't get past the carpenters so I had to stand next to them and shout. 'Excuse me!'

'My pleasure, darlin'!' said the younger one, all purple singlet, muscles, body odour and dirty blond locks tied back with a bit of ribbon.

'He lives in 'opes, he does,' said his mate to me, winking. 'You want to go in there, do you?'

Oh yes, we'd got a quick thinker here! I was only standing on the step, trying to get past.

'What's up?' enquired Purple Singlet. 'Your old man give you a thick ear?'

'I've just come to see a friend,' I explained, hoping to shut him up. I edged past them both.

The radio had stopped blasting out pop and a presenter was waffling on about something. The shaven glazier burst out unmelodiously into song, informing the world he was forever blowing bubbles.

'You don't want to go in there,' said the second

carpenter. 'Right funny lot in there.'

'I wouldn't mind getting in there,' said Purple Singlet.

''E's sex-obsessed!' shouted the West Ham supporter from the windowsill.

'Well, 'oo in't?' Purple Singlet justified his interests.

I left them arguing it out and managed to get past the damaged door into the hall.

The door to the dining room was shut, as was a door to my left. But the door to the right marked 'Office' was ajar and the rattle of a keyboard could be heard. I knocked.

As I'd been hoping, the dragon with the fright wig wasn't on duty this morning. She'd been replaced by a motherly but competent-looking woman wearing a silk shirt, a drooping skirt and, yes, an Alice band securing faded fair hair. I knew where I was with this one. It was time to polish up the legacy of a good education (in my case, gone wrong, but that didn't matter).

'I'm terribly sorry to bother you,' I said with a diffident smile.

'Not at all,' she said cheerfully. 'Come in and do sit down. Just a moment, I'll make a space.' She swept a pile of papers from a chair. 'We're all at sixes and sevens this morning, I'm afraid.'

'Gosh, yes,' I burbled. 'I saw the damage. Frightful.'

'Nothing to worry about,' she reassured me. 'Just a bit of a nuisance.' She lowered her voice. 'They *will* play that music.'

I sat on the chair, keeping my knees together as taught. 'The reason I've come is that I've been terribly worried about a friend, well, an old schoolfriend, actually. I hadn't seen much of her since I left school but I bumped into her a little while ago and we had a coffee and a sort of catch-up talk, you know?'

She was smiling and nodding, but her eyes were watchful.

I plunged on. 'She didn't seem to be awfully happy. She had some sort of man problem which she wouldn't talk about. The thing is, she's rather disappeared. I've asked for her all over the place and no one's seen her. So I've started looking anywhere the least bit likely. That's why I came here. Her name's Lauren Szabo. She's got longish hair and the last time I saw her she was wearing jeans and a sloppy sweater and had a hairband like yours.'

'Oh dear,' said the woman. 'You understand we don't give out names or personal details. We just can't. We operate here on a principle of trust.'

'Oh yes!' I breathed earnestly. 'I mean, I wouldn't expect you to! I just would be happy if I knew she'd been here and was safe.'

'Well, yes . . . I do see your problem. The trouble is—'

There was a rap at the door and Purple Singlet put his head round. 'You know your frame isn't square?' he demanded.

I cursed him silently and tried telepathy to get him to clear off and sort out the crooked frame for himself. After all, he was the carpenter. But telepathy didn't work.

'We'll have to plane the door down or it's gonna stick, otherwise. All right?'

She looked flustered. 'I'll come and see.' She turned to me. 'Could you just wait a moment? Oh, um, not in here.

Just come this way, would you?'

She led me past the carpenter, who winked at me and asked, 'All right, then darlin'?'

'Thank you!' retorted my guide for me before I could answer. She scurried down the hall and opened the door to the dining room. 'Please, if you don't mind?' She gestured at me to enter. 'Back in two ticks!' she promised, and shut me in.

The room smelled of stale vegetable water and old grease mixed with the vinegary aroma that scouring powder manufacturers call 'lemon-scented'. I sat down at the table wondering what they were all going to have for dinner that evening and glad I wasn't going to be eating it myself.

The door creaked and I turned my head. It opened slowly. I waited. There was a scuffle on the other side and a child put her head round.

'Hullo,' I said.

'What are you doing?' asked the child suspiciously.

'I was told to wait in here,' I said truthfully.

It seemed a satisfactory explanation. She came in and closed the door. She appeared to be about nine, with a round, wary, tough little face and straggling brown hair. She wore a sleeveless denim pinafore dress, which was too big, crumpled off-white socks and black PE plimsolls. She climbed up on the dining chair at the head of the table, leaned her elbows on the scarred table-top and surveyed me closely.

'You've got no bruises,' she said reproachfully, as if I'd failed some test.

'Yes, I have,' I said, 'I've got a bruise on my back and

on my arm, as it happens.' I pushed up my sleeve to display the imprint of Szabo's chauffeur's fingers.

But it wasn't judged good enough. She sniffed scornfully. 'That's nuffin'. My mum's got a broken arm. Gary, her boyfriend, he bust it.'

'I'm sorry,' I said. 'What's your name? I'm Fran.'

'My name's Samantha,' she said with dignity. 'I was named after a Page Three girl.'

'It's a pretty name. So you and your mum, you're here because of your mum's friend.'

'I never liked him, I never liked Gary,' she confided. 'I liked the boyfriend she had before. He was called Gus. He could make all his fingers crack, like this . . .' She tugged fiercely at her small fingers but, disappointingly, they refused to crack. 'She should've stayed with Gus. He had a job and everythin'.'

Clearly we had here a budding Agony Aunt. And perhaps she was right, at that. Being able to crack your fingers is an achievement of sorts. Not everyone can do it, after all. Throw in a steady job and I was inclined to agree that Samantha's mum had been unwise to leave Gus for violent, workshy Gary.

Then I remembered the brief discussion between the workmen. Gary probably had the charisma of a pop star and, when he wasn't belting the living daylights out of a girlfriend, was the life and soul of the party. While poor old Gus had sat there evening after evening, cracking his fingers, before turning in early because he had to get up to go to work in the morning.

I just hoped Samantha here remembered all this when

she grew up. It might be better to phrase that 'when she grew older' since she appeared to have grown up already.

'Whatya doing here?' she asked shrewdly. I wasn't battered enough to be a genuine refuge-seeker. I had to be after something else.

I glanced at the door. It was taking the woman a long time to sort out the carpentry problem, but this might be to my advantage.

'I'm looking for a friend,' I said. 'Have you been living here long, Samantha?'

'For a bit.' She looked vague. 'We bin here before, lots of times. I don't know how long we're staying this time.'

'My friend's name,' I prompted, 'is Lauren.'

'Oh, she's not here no more,' Samantha said immediately.

I fairly jumped off the chair in triumph. So Lauren had been here! But there might be more than one Lauren.

I said tentatively, 'My friend's got long hair and an Alice – hairband – like that woman in the office wears on her hair.'

'That's Miriam in the office,' said my informant. 'Lauren had one of them on her hair. I'd like one too,' she added, her gaze growing thoughtful. 'Do you think my hair's long enough?'

'Yes, I should think so,' I assured her. 'When did Lauren leave?'

'Dunno,' she said vaguely.

'Did she stay long?'

Samantha frowned. 'She didn't stay. She didn't live here. She used to come in and help out—'

The door opened and Miriam reappeared. Seeing Samantha she halted and exclaimed, 'Oh!' Then she rallied. 'What are you doing in here, Sam? Your mum's looking for you. Go on, run along, dear!'

Samantha slid off her chair. 'Goodbye,' she said to me politely. She trotted past Miriam into the hall and could be heard there, equally politely greeting someone else. 'Hullo. What you doing here? They don't let no men in here! You a boyfriend?'

'No,' said a familiar voice. 'I'm a policeman.'

'Oh, one of *them*,' chirped my small pal dismissively.

I couldn't have put it better myself.

Chapter Ten

They taught us all about entrances and exits when I was a student of the dramatic arts. A good entrance is important, but a good exit is *really* something. Shakespeare's '*Exit, pursued by a bear*' is a good one. But on balance, and without boasting, I'd say not as good as the exit made by Sergeant Parry and me from St Agatha's refuge. That was exceptionally dramatic. That would've had 'em on the edge of their seats and without a pantomime animal in sight.

Once he'd caught sight of me chatting peaceably to my little friend Samantha, Parry had stormed into the dining room in fouler than usual mood.

'Get the kid out of here!' he'd snapped. Unnecessarily, as it happened. Poor little Samantha had already learned when it was time to disappear and had nipped down the hall and scuttled away upstairs out of reach of his anger.

'All right, Fran!' he'd continued. 'I might've guessed it'd be you. You're leaving now, right?'

'I've not concluded my business here,' I said with dignity because one shouldn't lower one's standards to match this sort of thing. They taught us that at school. A lady acts with calm and poise no matter what the circumstances. She doesn't descend to exchanging vulgar abuse, not even with the police.

The woman with the drooping skirt, who'd been through the same kind of social schooling only in her case with better result, was looking equally askance at his manners. She stood ramrod straight by the door, her bosom quivering while she made little disapproving clucking noises, just as if she hadn't phoned him to come over, which she clearly had.

'Oh yes, you have!' Parry snarled to me.

'Oh no, I haven't!' I couldn't resist.

But Parry has no sense of humour. He grabbed my elbow in the manner recommended for arresting officers. He then frogmarched me past the snitch in the doorway, down the hall and through the gap where the front door had been removed. Out into the street we shot, linked like Siamese twins, and there the fun really started.

The workmen, all three of them, must have marked Parry down as a copper when he arrived. I think it's the purposeful way they walk that betrays plainclothes officers. Either that or the fact that no one but a plod in mufti would emerge in daylight wearing a sports jacket like the one Parry had. So they were curious, and ready for us, when we emerged.

'Oy! Whatcha doin' with the little lady?' demanded Purple Singlet aggressively, barring our way.

The older carpenter asked sternly, 'You got a warrant, mate, or what?'

The skinhead glazier hopped from his ladder in happy anticipation of a chance to put the boot in. I noticed he'd also slipped a chisel in his back pocket and this worried me. I foresaw having to throw myself across the wretched Parry to save him. The picture didn't appeal.

Parry turned a clashing red to his moustache and yapped, 'Out of the way, please!'

All three stayed put. 'What's she done?' asked Purple Singlet. 'You taking her down the nick, or what? Here, let go of the poor little mare's arm before you dislocate her perishing shoulder. Pick on someone your own size.'

The glazier didn't quite jump up and down and shout 'Me, me!' but his expression grew more eager.

'The lady's not under arrest!' growled Parry. 'But you all will be if you persist in causing an obstruction and hindering a law officer in the performance of his duty.'

'Ooh!' cried the glazier in a shrill falsetto and stamping one of his Doc Martens. 'He's getting angry!'

'Watch it!' ordered Parry, nearly as purple as the carpenter's singlet.

'Isn't he masterful?' admired the glazier. He'd obviously got tormenting the constabulary down to a fine art.

The older carpenter was proving himself a saloon bar lawyer. 'If she's not committed an offence, she don't have to go with you.'

He then turned to me. 'You don't have to say nothing, ducks, right? You tell 'em you want a lawyer. And mind they get you a proper one and not some pensioned-off old geezer they got in their pocket. If you don't know a lawyer, Mr Eftimakis in Dollis Hill's very good. You give him a ring and tell him Harry Porter recommended him.'

'You're going to need him yourself,' squawked Parry,

'if you don't get out of my way! She's not under arrest. I'm escorting her home!' He immediately lived to regret this indiscretion.

'Aha!' chorused all three of my knights champion with varying degrees of ribaldry.

The glazier leered and enquired, 'Goin' to show her your handcuffs, are you?'

'One more word,' panted Parry, 'and you're nicked!'

'Goin' to arrest us all?' asked Purple Singlet with interest, eyeing the car parked at the kerb. 'Goin' to squeeze all five of us in that motor? Cosy.'

'If necessary,' said Parry, clearly meaning it. 'I'll call backup and we'll get you all to the nick in style!'

It was time for me to cool things down. 'Thanks for the support, fellers,' I said. 'But the sergeant and I are old acquaintances. I can manage. No grief, OK?'

They parted reluctantly to let us through, the older carpenter calling out final advice to ring Mr Eftimakis in Dollis Hill.

'Nice to think chivalry's not dead in England!' I piped as Parry gunned the accelerator and we roared away from the refuge.

'Bloody yobbos!' he muttered, crouched white-knuckled over the wheel.

'No, they're not, they're British craftsmen!' I defended my new friends. It seemed only fair to return the favour.

'British ruddy football hooligans more like. I don't care what they do on a weekday. Come Saturday afternoon that lot'll be rampaging round the terraces, when they're not kicking in shop windows or chucking one another off trains!

I know your common or garden yob when I see him!'

'They were only trying to look after me,' I said placatingly because I was afraid Parry might collapse at the wheel with an aneurysm. His neck had swollen up and bulged over his collar and his eyes popped out of his head.

He rolled a red-veined eyeball at me. 'Strange as it may seem, Miss Varady, I am also trying to look after you!'

It was a pity he said that because up to that moment I hadn't been too worried by his appearing. I'd been confident of dealing with the situation and secretly pleased he'd not wanted to talk in the dining room, because it gave me more time to think up a reasonable excuse for my being there. But now I remembered Ganesh's loony notion that Parry fancied me. My presence of mind completely deserted me.

'Where are we going?' I quavered.

'Where I said, I'm taking you home. Then we're going to have a little chat.'

'I don't mind going to the station. I'll come and talk about it at the station, if you like.'

He glanced at me in puzzled annoyance. 'What's the matter with you all of a sudden?'

'Nothing!' I cried unconvincingly.

He was normally of a suspicious disposition and now he demanded, 'What's back at your place you don't want me to see?'

'Nothing! I've already told you.'

'We'll go there then, right?'

We went there.

* * *

When we got out of the car I made a last-ditch stand to prevent him following me down the basement steps. Custer had better luck.

'We can talk here!' I began on the pavement, lolling nonchalantly on the gate like a cut-price tart.

'Whaffor? We can talk in your flat, private.'

That's what I didn't want, privacy with Parry. I changed tactics.

'Whatever you've got to say, say it here!' I now declared in ringing tones, barring access to the basement steps by gripping the iron railings with one hand and bracing myself against the house wall with the other.

'You're hiding something, you are!' He stood over me, glowering.

A window above our heads was pushed up and Daphne's head appeared. 'All right below there? Fran? Is that man harassing you?'

'It's fine, thanks, Daphne!' I called back. 'I can manage.'

'I can easily fetch help!' cried my landlady. 'Who is that strange man?'

'He's a police officer, Daphne. Sorry and all that.'

'Are you sure, Fran dear? Ask to see his identification. There are a lot of confidence tricksters about, always pretending to be policemen or that they've come to read the electricity meter. Why isn't he in uniform? Why's he dressed like that?'

'It's plainclothes, madam!' howled Parry. He waved his identity card up at her. 'I called to see you the other day, if you remember? Sergeant Parry?'

'Oh yes, so you did. I haven't got my glasses on. But now I recall the jacket. Is there something wrong?'

'No, madam, just checking out something.'

'Well, please do it quietly!' she ordered him, and slammed down the window.

'That's right,' I grumbled. 'Get me thrown out of my flat. Come down if you must.'

I led him down to the flat and let us both in. He pushed past me and marched into the living room, eyeballs swivelling all over the place like bagatelle balls.

Not seeing anything likely to cause a breach of the peace, he whirled round. 'All right, what are you playing at now? What's your little game, eh? Why were you at the refuge asking about Lauren Szabo? What d'you know about her?'

'Only what Vincent Szabo told me, after you'd so kindly told him all about me, including where I lived,' I informed him crisply.

It threw him off balance slightly, but not for long. 'Well, he's a respectable businessman, isn't he? Drivin' round in a Roller with a chauffeur and all. Thought you might like to move up a class for company. Anyway, he reckons he knew your dad.'

'He probably did. Not that my father ever mentioned him.'

Parry sat down uninvited on the sofa. 'So he did turn up, did he? I wondered if he would. He didn't lose time. What did he say to you?'

'Private conversation,' I told him. 'None of your business. But if you want to put something in your report, put down that I don't like being used.'

'Don't come the injured party with me. You're always keen to stick your nose in. What did Szabo have to say?'

I sat down too. It was, after all, my flat. 'He told me his stepdaughter has been snatched. He's not happy with the lack of progress being made by the police. If I heard anything, I was to tell him. So I told him more or less everything I told you.'

He chewed at the end of the mangy moustache. 'Why did you go to the refuge?'

'I'm not sure,' I confessed. 'Probably because when I asked Vinnie if she was likely to have been walking back from there when she was picked up, his tame gorilla tossed me out of the car.'

'She helped out there,' said Parry. 'She's one of them wealthy girls with nothing else to do, so they go round doing good works. No need to earn any money. Daddy makes 'em an allowance.'

'Why shouldn't he want me to know that?' I asked, puzzled.

'He disapproved. She was doing it behind his back, the voluntary work there. The impression I got of him, he's on the overprotective side. On the other hand, he might've feared something would happen to her, mixing with the wrong sort. Perhaps he was afraid she'd fall for some sandal-wearing social worker with long hair and granny glasses. You know, fortune-hunter. How do I know? He's rich, for Gawd's sake. Rich people have to worry about things like that. The kid's the apple of his eye. His wife's dead. She's all he's got left. He's a worried man.'

I reflected that we'd come a long way since Parry had

sat on that sofa, pretending there was no snatch and poor old Albie hadn't seen anything. I said as much.

Parry had the grace to look sheepish. 'Yes, well, that was when I still hoped you'd keep your nose outa things. I should've known better. Stay quiet about all this, right?'

'You told them at the refuge to call you if anyone came asking about Lauren Szabo. Were you thinking of me?'

'Routine,' said Parry, which is what they always say when they don't want to answer.

'Or were you expecting someone else to be asking after her? Has she got a boyfriend?' That was a new idea to strike me. 'You said Vinnie was afraid she'd meet someone unsuitable. Did she?'

'We've followed that line up and got nowhere,' Parry said, tugging at the sleeve of his jacket with a frown. 'She's been dating some Hooray Henry what works in his own family's firm. Suppose they had to give him a job. Strictly between you and me, he hasn't got the brains to organise a teddy bears' tea-party. Anyway, he's got an alibi for the night she was snatched.'

'Of course he has,' I said patiently. 'He would, wouldn't he? He wouldn't do it himself. What's his name and where can I find him?'

'Forget it!' Parry snapped.

'All right,' I said, to keep him happy. 'Have you tried looking for Merv? He can't be that difficult to find.'

'We've got your description of him,' he said. 'Give us time. We'll pick him up. But we won't necessarily be able to link him with the old man.'

'Of course you can! Ganesh and I saw Merv and his mate try to snatch Albie!'

'So you say, but that's not good enough,' Parry retorted aggravatingly. 'It was late at night. Poor streetlighting. All over in a few seconds. Can you describe the second man?'

Unfortunately I couldn't. Merv I'd recognised, but in the circumstances all I'd noticed about his pal was that he was shorter, broader and either dark-haired or wearing a dark woolly hat. I told Parry this.

'There you are then,' he said. 'I can't haul anyone in on the basis of a description like that. Adds up to mistaken identity, doesn't it?' He shrugged. 'Your word and Patel's against his. Not good enough, like I said.' He crouched aggressively on the edge of the sofa, flexing his mitts, which were sprinkled with long red hair like an orang-utan's.

A thought had occurred to me. 'If you want to know what Szabo and I talked about, ask Szabo himself. Or doesn't he talk to you? What *was* the big idea sending him along to me?'

Parry scratched his chin. The shaving rash was clearing up, but if he carried on rubbing it like that, it'd come back. Serve him right. I hoped he came out in boils like those people in the Bible.

'You're near enough his daughter's age. He knew your dad. He might've said something to you he – he overlooked when talking to us.'

'I'm two years older than his daughter and I don't think Szabo would draw any comparison between me and his Lauren. Szabo's gone out of his way to protect her from life's nastiness until now, whereas he sees me as someone who can be bundled into a strange car by a minder and asked a lot of nosy questions.' A new idea leapt into my head. 'Have you got a picture of her, of Lauren?'

'The girl? Sure.' He fumbled in a wallet and produced a couple of snapshots. One showed a young girl with long fair hair, apparently sitting at a pavement café table. The background looked continental and big city, probably Paris. The labels on the bottles of soft drink were French. The girl in the photo leaned on her elbows and stared at the camera with a cool challenge in her eyes. She was a good-looker.

The other picture was a studio portrait, one of those little polyphotos, all varying poses, which the photographer gives the client for him to make his choice. Her hair was tidier and she wore a lot more make-up for this one but I was more taken by the difference in her expression. In the café picture she looked as if she were in charge. In the polyphoto she looked trapped and angry. She hadn't wanted that picture taken. I wondered who had taken the informal snap. Looking at Lauren's picture made me uneasy. Before, she'd been a name, and a vague description by Albie. Now she was a real person, a prisoner somewhere, frightened and in danger. I handed them both back to Parry who put them away.

'So,' he said, 'what else you got to tell me, Fran? Now's your chance. Withholding evidence is a criminal offence.'

I got up and fetched the empty Bell's bottle and put it down on the coffee table in front of him.

'What's all this?' His eyes began to turn pink again.

I told him. 'I was going to bring it to you, right? You know as well as I do that Albie saw Lauren snatched and this –' I pointed at the bottle – 'this shows he didn't just fall in the canal unaided.'

'It doesn't show anything of the sort,' he retorted.

I hadn't expected thanks, but this annoyed me. 'No wonder Szabo's fed up with the slow progress you're making!' I snapped. 'You lose your one witness and now you've got tangible evidence you don't know what to do with it. Can't you fingerprint it or something?'

'I told you before,' he said, 'that you're a mouthy little madam. I remember when you lived in that squat with all those other dropouts. You were a right bossy little piece then, issuing orders right, left and centre. Don't try it with me. You're sailing close to the wind, Miss Varady. You say you were going to hand over the bottle to us, but you did your damnedest to stop me coming down here.'

'That wasn't because of the bottle,' I began. 'It was because—'

But I couldn't tell him it was because Ganesh reckoned Parry lusted after me. I didn't know where Gan had got that idea from. If the sergeant here fancied me, he'd got a funny way of showing it. I finished lamely, quoting Szabo, 'I like my privacy. This is my home. I don't want you marching in and out just as you like.'

'Actually,' he said. 'I don't like it. Think I've got nothing better to do? I'm a busy man investigating a serious crime. Don't mess me about, Fran. If you do, I'll get you on a charge, right?'

'Oh, will you?' I challenged. 'I could make a formal

complaint against you for sending Szabo to me.'

He treated me to a wintry smile. 'You overlook that, Fran, and I'll overlook the fact that you didn't hand the bottle over at once, also that you went to the refuge, causing trouble—'

I opened my mouth to protest because he'd caused the trouble there, not me.

He overrode my objection. 'So keep out from under my feet, right? That way we can stay friends.'

'We are not friends,' I told him coldly.

I was treated to another of those gargoyle grimaces. 'Oh, come on, Fran. I think you and I could get along rather well!'

'In your dreams!' I corrected him icily.

'Please yourself. I'm taking the whisky bottle, right? Got a paper bag?'

I gave him Ben's plastic bag. He stood up. 'So find yourself something else to do, leave the sleuthing to the professionals. Weekend coming up. Go away somewhere nice. Go to Margate and get some sea air.'

'As it happens,' I informed him, 'I have a job this weekend as an artist's model.'

His ginger eyebrows shot up to meet his hairline. 'What? In the buff?'

Simple soul that he was, I hastened to disappoint him.

'No! In costume.'

'What sort of costume?' he asked with interest, his limited mind running on bare-breasted bimbos hiding the essentials behind a pair of unzipped jeans lodged at crotch level.

'A tree,' I told him. 'I shall be dressed to symbolise the threatened Amazonian rainforest.'

He burst out laughing and made a pretty good exit of his own, warbling about talking to the trees in a surprisingly good baritone.

I was fed up so I ran myself a bath to wash away all contact with the law. The hot water steamed up the bathroom mirror. I wrote I HATE PARRY on it so that I could meditate on it as I lay in the bath. But the moisture on the mirror began to trickle and changed my slogan to I HAVE HAPPY. Sometimes nothing works.

Chapter Eleven

The long soak in the tub, a grilled cheese sandwich and three cups of coffee succeeded in erasing the tainted air of Parry's presence from the flat. A single ray of sun, angled down through the basement window, told me it was after two o'clock and encouraged me to go out and try something else. My brain was working again, If at first you don't succeed and all the rest of it. Thanks to Parry, I now knew Lauren had a steady boyfriend. The first thing to do was to find out if Szabo had known about this and what he'd felt about it.

Dressed in clean jeans and my best silk shirt and quilted waistcoat, I ran up the steps to Daphne's front door and rang the bell.

She must have seen me coming and the door was opened almost at once. 'You are all right, aren't you, dear? What *is* going on?' she demanded breathlessly.

'Sorry about the bit of bother earlier,' I said.

'There was no need to come up and apologise for that!' she returned, and fixed me with a reproachful gaze. 'If that was the same police officer who came to see me the other day, I thought him uncouth.'

'He is uncouth,' I said. 'But he can't help it. May I use the phone?'

'Help yourself!' She waved at the instrument and trotted back to her ever-growing pile of manuscript. I was momentarily distracted enough to wonder again what it represented, but it seemed rude to ask.

I punched the number Szabo had given me and after a moment, his high-pitched, nervy voice asked, 'Hullo? Yes?'

'Mr Szabo?' I said. 'It's Francesca Varady.'

'You've seen the tattooed man again?' He quavered with eagerness and I imagined him standing there, the mobile phone pressed to his ear.

There was a sound of movement in the background and Szabo, his voice fading slightly as he turned his head, snapped, 'Yes, yes, just leave it there!'

I deduced he was sitting in a probably expensive hotel room and the room service had just delivered something. I had felt sorry for the man, because after all, there was nothing he could do but sit there all a-jitter and wait. But my sympathy was tempered by the thought that at least he was doing it in comfort.

I had to disappoint him. 'Sorry, no, I haven't seen the man again. But I've been thinking and I wondered whether anyone has talked to Lauren's friends.'

'Why?' He sounded edgy and a little annoyed that I'd falsely raised his hopes for a moment.

Trying not to antagonise him further, I began, 'Suppose she'd noticed that someone appeared to be watching or following her—'

He broke in with a terse, 'She'd have reported a stalker.'

'I wasn't thinking of anyone so obvious as a stalker. Just a face which seemed to be turning up more often than coincidentally, but not often enough or aggressively enough to make her report it to the police. If no one made an actual approach or spoke to her, what could she have reported? She might not have told you either, not wanting to worry you, or thinking she might sound neurotic. But she might have mentioned it to a friend.'

A pause. 'The police have already followed up this line of enquiry,' he said discouragingly. 'Naturally they've spoken to all her close friends.'

'Oh, the police . . .' I let my voice tail away.

He thawed. 'Well, yes, I do see that a casual approach might turn up some little, overlooked fact, something which appeared too trivial to be mentioned to the police.'

'Or too embarrassing,' I pursued. 'A situation like that can be awkward for a woman.'

'I take your word for that,' he said, terse again. Perhaps he'd made the connection between this and his own cautious fencing with the police. I had to be careful not to tip Parry's hand.

Silently cursing the sergeant, I asked, 'I wondered whether your daughter had a particular boyfriend, someone in London?'

'I fail to see the relevance,' Szabo's voice had grown icy. 'You mean, I take it, that she might have confided her fears to Jeremy. But Jeremy would have reported anything like that to me at once. He'd know I'd want to be informed of anyone annoying my daughter!'

'She might have asked him not to.'

'Jeremy is a thoroughly reliable young man,' he replied, apparently unaware that the word might mean something different to him than it did to Lauren. 'I've no reason to doubt his judgement. He's extremely fond of Lauren and would have insisted she went to the police immediately if there were the hint of any threat.'

I said nothing, letting him think it over.

'Very well,' he said at last. 'I'll call him and tell him to expect you. I'm willing to try any avenue which might get my daughter back safely and soon.' His voice broke and trembled. 'You can't imagine what the uncertainty is doing to us, to me and to Jeremy, what it's like . . . I'll ring him at once.'

The last thing I wanted was to appear to Jeremy as Szabo's stooge. 'No!' I said hastily. 'Don't do that. Far better if I drop by and tell him I've been trying to get in touch with Lauren. That we had a lunch date or something and she didn't show. As you said, we want to keep it casual.'

It was important to make him think this was basically his idea. It worked. Though I still expected him to put up more argument, he folded almost at once, went along with the plan without any fuss, and told me Jeremy's full name and where to find his business. Really, handling him was a doddle.

I replaced the receiver, put a fifty-pence piece by the phone, called my thanks to Daphne, and set out.

Thais Fine Arts was located in a narrow blind alley in the New Bond Street area. The alley looked as if its original purpose had been to provide a back entrance to the block, for removal of garbage, that sort of thing. It had been spruced up since those days and the dustbins taken away. But it wasn't the sort of place you'd ever find if you didn't know it was there, which meant the business wouldn't attract the casual passer-by. Perhaps it dealt with recommended customers only. There were places like that. Or perhaps it dealt in export and import.

Further investigation confirmed my suspicions. This was by no stretch of imagination a shop, gallery, showroom, call it what you like. The premises consisted of offices at the top of a narrow flight of stairs. The name appeared on a discreet but well-polished plate on the outer door by a bell. I pressed. It buzzed and the door uttered a disgruntled click as the locking mechanism was released. I pushed it open, thinking that the person within hadn't bothered to check who rang.

Then, as I went through, my eye caught the tiny camera up in the corner of the stairwell, trained on the door. The person inside knew exactly who was out here and had watched me climb the last stairs, peer at the doorplate and fidget about making up my mind to ring. I didn't like that and marched in belligerently.

I found myself in a reception area, a large square room decorated predominantly white like a hospital ward. White walls, white leather chairs, oatmeal carpet. The only splashes of colour were provided by a tall green plant in a white pot and the dark blue of the business suit worn by the receptionist. Above her head flickered the screen on which she'd seen me arrive and on her stainless-steel and glass desk stood a dinky little wooden nameplate with the gold-painted legend 'Jane Stratton'. This was a nice place to work, all right. It must be really neat to have your name in gold, stuck there in front of you for all to see. Ms Stratton rose to intercept me. Greet was not the word.

'Yes?' she asked.

She was a human version of an Afghan hound, long, lean, thoroughbred. Her narrow face was perfectly made up and her long blonde hair sculpted and lacquered into rigid waves and curls. The overall effect was intended to be glamorous but failed for lack of warmth or personality. She had eyes like twin lasers.

I ignored the permafrost welcome and asked cheerfully if I might see Mr Copperfield.

'You have an appointment?' she enquired, faintly incredulous.

'No, it's personal. I'm a friend of Lauren Szabo.'

She hesitated then pressed a switch on the intercom and relayed the information. It squawked a distorted reply.

'Do take a seat,' she said to me, marginally more gracious. 'Mr Copperfield will be out to see you shortly.'

I sat on one of the white leather chairs and studied my surrounds, wondering what constituted fine art. I also wondered whether I was to be interviewed by Copperfield out here, or whether I'd be admitted to some inner sanctum. It depended how much he wanted the chilly receptionist to overhear, although she could overhear whatever she wanted through the intercom system.

There were two doors in the walls facing the reception desk but neither carried a nameplate. The only example of a fine art object stood near me atop a plinth perched on a glass-topped table. It was a marble bust of a cherub and would, to my mind, have been more suited to a monumental mason's showroom than an art dealer's. It was an extraordinary ugly thing. Its fat cheeks bulged and rosebud lips were pursed as if it ought to be blowing a trumpet, but someone had taken away the musical instrument. This meant the overall effect was that it blew a raucous raspberry towards the entrance door.

I wouldn't have fancied it around the home, but then it was unlikely I could ever have afforded it so the problem didn't arise. It didn't carry anything so vulgar as a price tag.

I caught the Ice Queen's eye, nodded towards the cherub and asked, 'How much?'

'Fifteen hundred,' she said, and allowed herself a smirk of satisfaction when she saw my mouth fall open.

She returned to her work, rattling a keyboard with scarlet talons. At her elbow, a red light suddenly glowed on the telephone. She ignored it. After a few moments, the light went out. I wondered if it signified an outside line was in use.

Without warning, one of the twin inner doors opened and a bulky figure filled the aperture.

'Miss Varady?' He moved solidly towards me, spectacle lenses glinting, hand outstretched. 'Jeremy Copperfield. I'm sorry to have kept you waiting. Do come through. Would you like some tea or coffee?'

The receptionist paused in her work and raised a forbidding eye.

'No thank you,' I said. 'I won't take up much of your time.'

I followed Copperfield to his office, which closely resembled the outer room in colour scheme and general furnishings. He invited me to sit on one of the ubiquitous white leather chairs, and eased himself into a beige leather executive chair with stainless-steel arms. He placed his fingertips together and swivelled gently to and fro before me, all the while watching my face over the top of his specs.

Fighting the impression that I'd strayed into some private sanatorium and was facing an expensive medical consultant, I forced myself to relax on my chair, and studied him back. There was silence while we eyed one another in polite antagonism.

Lauren's boyfriend was about twenty-eight and had a weight problem which, if he hadn't got to grips with it by now, he never would. His belly bulged over his waistband. His jawline was lost in the cushion of double chins, which in turn made his mouth, with its pink pouty lips like those of the cherub, look too small. It struck me that he showed little sign of the distress he ought to be suffering. But perhaps he was good at hiding his feelings.

'I don't recall,' he broke our silence to say, 'that Lauren ever mentioned your name to me.' He stopped swivelling the chair and rested his hand on the steel arms, raising his head so that his eyes were still fixed on me but this time through, not over, his glasses. The lenses were thick and made his eyes appear piggy. He wasn't my cup of tea, but then I wasn't Lauren, and the choice was hers.

I'd already decided to use the story that had worked

well at the refuge until I'd mentioned Lauren's name.

'We hadn't seen each other for a while when we bumped into one another. We fixed up a reunion lunch but she didn't show. I did think she seemed worried about something, so that made me concerned. I've been trying to get in touch with her.'

Behind the jam-jar-bottom lenses, his eyes blinked at me. As if I hadn't spoken, his voice flowed on, 'So I took the precaution of phoning her father. He says it's in order to talk to you. You know there is a possibility she's being held somewhere against her will and the police are involved. You understand all this is highly sensitive and mustn't become public knowledge.'

So it *had* been an outside line. So much for the approach I thought I'd agreed with Szabo. Now I was left looking foolish. But I had to admit that without Szabo's go-ahead, Copperfield wouldn't be talking to me.

'That's fine,' I said, abandoning that line. 'I understand the circumstances and believe me, I'm very sorry. You're all under a terrible strain.'

'Yes,' he said, 'we are.'

But he still didn't look it, not to me. Curiously, I asked, 'Have you been dating Lauren very long?'

Blink. 'We've known each other several years,' he said, pursing his fat little lips and suddenly looking so like the marble head out there in reception that I had a job not to grin.

'Is Mr Szabo also involved in the art market?' I asked, 'I thought he was in loose covers.'

Copperfield ignored the question and his stare informed

me that he considered it improper. Worse, he suspected me of mockery. His opinion of me wasn't high. But there again, neither was my opinion of him. It was clear to me already that far from being the love of Lauren's life, this man was her Malcolm Tring.

I should explain. Obviously, Jeremy here was Szabo's choice for Lauren, a man who saw things his way and could be relied upon to report back to her stepfather at the first sign of trouble. Szabo himself would deny this was the reason for his selecting Copperfield. He'd roll out a whole list of Jeremy's virtues. Personal charisma wouldn't figure among them, but neither would Szabo see it as a disadvantage. If anything, he'd see it as an irrelevance.

That's the way it goes. Families judge by a whole different set of criteria to that favoured by their offspring. Which is where Malcolm Tring comes in.

Malcolm figured briefly in my life when I'd just turned fourteen, and all because Grandma Varady liked a game of cards. She belonged to a whist club and there she met a fellow fanatic called Mrs Emma Tring, a well-to-do widow. Mrs Tring, it soon turned out, had a grandson, one Malcolm.

'A really nice boy,' enthused Grandma V. to me, as she ladled out the goulash soup one evening. 'Just a year older than you, fifteen, and doing very well at school. He escorts his grandmother to the whist club regularly, such a kind boy. Not many his age would give up the time! He's always polite and so well spoken, and the family has a pine furniture business in the High Street. I understand from Emma it's doing very well, and my goodness, she has some beautiful pearls.'

Grandma paused for dramatic effect and chinked the ladle on the soup tureen. 'And he's an only child!' she whispered.

'I want to be an actress,' I said, correctly divining the drift of all this. 'I don't want to spend my life selling pine furniture.'

'Actors starve,' she said, correctly as it happens. 'A business is handy to fall back on.'

'Especially if it's furniture!' I quipped, and was rapped on the knuckles with the ladle for not taking the matter seriously. But how could I take seriously anyone connected with a business that advertised itself as selling 'FURNITURE TO MAKE YOUR HEART TRING'?

Grandma did take it seriously and needless to say, I was eventually dragooned into accompanying her to the whist club, there to meet Malcolm Tring. Also needless to say, he was awful, and I'd have had to be out of my skull to want to fall back on him. Nor did I think his grandmother's pearls all that great. They looked fake to me. I was already something of an expert on stage props by then.

Malcolm reciprocated my feelings. It was mutual dislike on sight. Grandmothers Tring and Varady engineered one more meeting and then, a stroke of luck, Malcolm had to go into hospital for his adenoids, and that was that.

I don't think Grandma V. ever quite forgave me. Not even when the furniture business burned down eighteen months later. It was in the *Standard*, and arson was suspected. So perhaps it hadn't been doing all that well. I always knew those pearls were false.

Jeremy offered the kind of reassurance to concerned

families that Malcolm had appeared to offer. No doubt the marble cherub business was doing well. Every home should have one. Szabo probably saw in this young entrepreneur something of himself when younger. Jeremy would guarantee Lauren a nice big house and a generous personal spending allowance. Jeremy wouldn't stray and he wouldn't ask where Lauren spent her money or her afternoons. Business would always come first with him, women a long way back second. I was even prepared to bet Jeremy Copperfield was an only child.

The scepticism in my face succeeded in rattling Copperfield. He flushed and said loudly, 'We were about to announce our engagement!'

By 'we' he meant himself and his prospective father-in-law. I doubt Lauren was in full agreement.

'Then you'll want to find her,' I said.

The flush turned to beetroot. 'I would feel any other suggestion to be insulting, Miss Varady!'

'I want to find her too.' I ignored the huffing and puffing. I wasn't here to listen to Copperfield's bluster. I was here on business.

My voice must have told him so and it was an attitude he respected. His own manner changed. The flush faded, he sat up straighter in the executive chair, folded his plump hands and asked crisply, 'And what would be your interest? You don't know Lauren personally. Is Szabo paying you?'

It was possible Szabo thought he was. I didn't. 'My interest,' I said, 'is in what happened to an elderly man whose body was taken from the canal yesterday morning early.'

Copperfield's small sharp eyes gleamed behind the lenses. 'Has this any bearing on what's happened to Lauren?'

'I think so.'

'I'd appreciate your reasons,' Copperfield said.

'Fair enough. I believe he saw Lauren snatched off the street. The men involved knew he'd been a witness. They arranged his death.'

There was a silence. Then Copperfield said carefully, as if picking his way through a verbal minefield, 'You are suggesting murder. That's a very serious matter. Where do the police stand in all this?'

'You'd better ask them,' I retorted.

'I shall, believe me.' He unfolded his podgy paws and tapped the armrests of his chair. 'And what do you think I can tell you, Miss Varady, that the police or, indeed, Vincent Szabo can't?'

'I had wondered,' I confessed, 'whether Lauren had told you of anything unusual that had happened to her lately, during the time leading up to her disappearance. Had either of you made any new acquaintances? Started going to new places? Had anyone been asking about her, making some excuse or other?'

'Much as you are doing?' His cheeks shuddered as a sarcastic smile rippled away from the edges of his mouth.

'OK then, much as I'm doing. Was there anyone?'

'If she'd told me any such thing,' he said, 'I'd have insisted she report it to the police.'

Time to shake him up a little. 'Did you know,' I asked innocently, 'that she was a regular volunteer helper at a refuge for battered women in the area where she was snatched?'

I was wrong in fancying that would bother him. He looked annoyed, but not surprised. 'The police have already investigated that angle, as I understand it. I'll be frank with you, Miss Varady. I didn't approve of such good works, laudable though they might have been. The simple fact is that when a young woman stands to be heiress one day to, well, not exactly a fortune perhaps, but certainly a comfortable amount, she has to accept the risks that go with having money. She becomes a prey for spongers, spinners of hard-luck tales, penniless young men and unsavoury elements in society of all kinds. Her family and friends will try to protect her but she must also protect herself.

'I knew she gave her time to the refuge, amongst other similar hostels. I tried to dissuade her. The very nature of such a place is that she must meet all kinds of riffraff there and that sooner or later, one of them may try to gain advantage from the situation.'

I couldn't let that pass. I nearly jumped out of my chair to remind this well-heeled slob that the women at the refuge had received horrendous treatment. They weren't there by choice. They were there often because their very lives were in danger. To describe them as 'riffraff' was unacceptable and I'd be glad to hear him withdraw it.

'On the contrary,' he said. 'What you've just said confirms my view. The women in those places are there because of violence. They are associated with violent men. So it follows that anyone associated with those women is also likely to become the target of violent men.'

I remembered the broken window and damaged door at the refuge and reluctantly conceded he had a point. 'So you're saying,' I said, 'that it's through her voluntary work that Lauren became known to her eventual snatchers?'

'I think it's highly likely, don't you? I fancy the police think so too. Look, Miss Varady . . .' he consulted an expensive-looking wristwatch, 'I've given you quite a lot of my time this afternoon and frankly, I can't see to what purpose. There is nothing I can tell you that isn't more properly learned from the police. In fact, I suspect the police would be strongly opposed to my talking to you at all.'

He wasn't going to talk to me any further, he was saying. So I could just get out. I got up and prepared to go, but I had one last query.

'Tell me,' I said, 'that cherub thing out there,' I pointed at the door and the reception area beyond. 'Is it really worth fifteen hundred smackers?'

'Cherub?' He looked puzzled. 'Oh, you mean the zephyr! Yes, a lovely piece. Exquisite. Italian Renaissance and established provenance. It was salvaged from the ruins of a pleasure villa on Lake Garda at the close of the Second World War.'

'Salvaged', I suspected, might be a euphemism. 'Trophy of war?' I asked.

'Certainly not!' His full lips pressed together and disappeared into a thin line. The flesh around them had turned white with anger. 'Good day, Miss Varady,' he said, opening the door.

There was a motorcycle courier in the outer office. It was a tribute to the soundproof quality of the office doors here that I hadn't heard him arrive. Leather-jacketed, metal-helmeted and high-booted, he was a space-age vision, even more out of place in these surroundings than I was, even though he was here on proper business, not part-time detecting.

The Ice Queen handed him a package. He growled, 'Right!' and clumped away, casting me no more than a dismissive glance. If he wondered about my presence, he didn't show it. Perhaps I hadn't even registered with him. A man who spent his days weaving in and out of London's packed traffic probably didn't worry much about anything except staying upright.

The receptionist gave me a glance that was only marginally more aware than the courier's.

'Mr Szabo is waiting for you downstairs,' she said, and returned to her work, wiping my presence from her mental screen.

Vinnie Szabo was standing in the doorway, sheltering from the draught that cut through the alley. Perhaps he also wanted to avoid the scrutiny of any passer-by who might glance down the narrow way and wonder what he was doing lurking there.

'Hi,' I said dourly, because I was cross with him.

We left the alley awkwardly, obliged to walk in single file. I went first. The courier had made it out into the main road, mounted his machine and was already zigzagging away. There was no sign of Szabo's car or the muscular driver. He wouldn't have found it easy to park around here. Perhaps Szabo had wisely taken a cab. He edged out of the narrow entry behind me, and stood unhappily on the pavement. He was wearing his overcoat and it looked even more oversize than it had in the car. His small hands barely poked out of the sleeves and the skirts nearly reached to the pavement.

He peered up at me, Mole from *The Wind in the Willows*. 'You've seen Jeremy? Did he— Was there anything?'

'No,' I said. 'But then he knew exactly who I was and why I was there. I thought we'd agreed I'd say I was a friend of Lauren's?'

'But he phoned me,' he protested in dismay. 'I had to tell him.'

'I might have got more out of him if you hadn't,' I said, still feeling sour about it.

'He wouldn't have spoken to you at all,' Szabo defended himself. 'When he phoned me, he was worried you might be an emissary of the kidnappers.'

That certainly hadn't occurred to me!

'Never mind,' I said, conceding the point. 'He wouldn't have believed the other story anyway. He doesn't know anything. I don't think Lauren would've told him if she'd had anything on her mind.'

'She certainly wouldn't have wished to worry poor Jeremy. He is devoted to her.' We'd fallen into step and he spoke these words confidently as he scurried beside me.

I wasn't getting into an argument over that one. I'd have been surprised if Lauren spoke much to Jeremy about anything.

We'd reached the corner of the street and parted with a minimum exchanged of farewell words. I promised to ring Vinnie if I learned anything but it was clear from his expression he no longer held out any hopes of my turning up any information of value. He'd been desperate when he'd contacted me. That I'd failed him hardly made any difference. He hadn't really expected much.

He headed off in the direction of Mayfair, a small dejected figure in a too large coat, padding along the centre of the pavement. An air of loneliness and loss hovered around him and I knew what it was that niggled at me whenever I looked at Szabo. In his own way, he reminded me of Albie, a lost soul, someone out of whose life the heart has been wrenched.

I set off in the opposite direction, making for the Underground and home.

Back on home turf, there didn't seem to be anything else I could do. But I hadn't forgotten Jonty and, wanting to do something, even if I knew I was wasting my time, I went looking for him again.

Unsurprisingly, I didn't see any sign of him. I hoped the poor old fellow was all right and polluting the environment somewhere safer for him than around here. I was in two minds whether to go to the shop and talk to Gan, but I remembered that tomorrow was the day of the art exhibition in which I was to figure, literally. It would be best to avoid Ganesh until it was all over.

Suffering from severe doubts about the whole project myself, I went to Reekie Jimmie's instead. I was hoping unrealistically that I'd be told Angus had unexpectedly been called back to Scotland and the proposed display was off. Suddenly even the prospect of thirty quid didn't compensate for looking an idiot all day.

Chapter Twelve

As a hope, it'd only been an outsider and not surprisingly, it never got out of the starting traps. Angus, apparently, had been in that morning doing his mopping out stint, and was all keyed up and worrying about keeping the vegetables fresh.

'Can't talk about anything else but tomorrow, the lad is that excited,' said Jimmie. 'He reckons it's his big chance. He's counting on you, hen. We all are, eh? Ah, we'll show the auld enemy where he gets off!'

He beamed at me fondly. Somehow or other I'd become the focus of Scottish aspirations, in this part of London, anyway. But something he'd said sounded an ominous note.

'Veg?' I asked hollowly.

'Aye, to pin on your wee costume. Would you like a cup of tea or coffee, on the house? It's bottomless cup tonight, you'll have seen the notice.'

He pointed to the wall behind him where, above the microwave, was a poster showing a steaming coffee cup and emblazoned 'Special Promotion. One night only. Pay for first cup! Refills on us!'

I accepted a bottomless cup of tea and began to wonder

how Angus was proposing to fix a couple of pounds of mixed veg to a body stocking without making it sag disastrously. I hoped Jimmie had got it wrong. I didn't think we got our vegetables from the rain forests.

Jimmie had left me to take some orders. The café was filling up and trade threatened to become a rush. This couldn't be, surely, because of the special promotion?

'Friday night,' he told me when he rejoined me. 'Lot of 'em got paid and the weekend starts here!'

He began slicing a cucumber at a furious rate, the knife flashing wickedly near his fingers, missing by a miracle. 'Would you happen to be free for the rest of the evening?' He swept the cucumber slices into a bowl and reached for some greeny-orange tomatoes. 'I know you've a busy day tomorrow, but as you can see, I'm fair rushed off my feet here. The cashier's not turned up. You wouldn't fancy lending me a hand? I can manage the till and taking the orders if you keep the spuds coming. It's not difficult. There's plenty of salad done ready, see?' He waved the knife under my nose. 'Just put a bit out on the plates beforehand. Then all you need to do is pop the spuds in the microwave. When they're ready, add a filling. We've got another one now, tuna and sweetcorn, going very well. It's all mixed up in a bowl over there.'

I followed the line indicated by the point of his knife and saw a huge plastic bowl of unappetising beige and yellow gunge.

'That's all there is to it. Put a few quid in your pocket,' he concluded artfully.

Why not? I couldn't do anything about Lauren tonight

and though it mightn't be *haute cuisine*, it would stop me brooding on the next day. 'Sure,' I said.

'You'll find the uniform on the coat rack in the corridor,' he told me. 'And go easy with the cheese.'

By the time I left Jimmie's at ten, I was whacked. Business had been nonstop all evening, to Jimmie's joy and my despair. I burned my fingers trying to keep the spuds coming along. As for the 'bottomless cup', that had proved a nightmare. The patrons, unused to being offered anything free here, had seen it as a challenge. They'd kept coming back and holding out empty cups, determined to take full advantage. The coffee percolator hissed, gurgled and spat dementedly and the tea urn ran dry. But at the end of it all, I had a tenner in my pocket and half a pound of left-over grated cheese in a washed margarine tub.

'Make yourself Welsh rarebit for your supper,' suggested Jimmie. 'Save a few pennies.'

'Tomorrow, perhaps,' I said. Food had temporarily lost its appeal. I never wanted to see another potato in my life. The smell of melted cheese, singed potato skins and baked beans clung to me even after I'd peeled off the rayon overall that Jimmie called staff uniform. My hair must stink of it. But provided Angus paid up the next day as promised, I was doing all right this weekend on the financial front.

It had rained while I'd been juggling hot spuds and ladling out the beans. Surfaces gleamed in the lamplight. There were comparatively few people about and not much traffic, but as I walked away I heard a motorcycle engine cough and splutter into life a short distance behind me.

Enjoying the cool damp air on my perspiring face, I took little notice.

With a low growl the machine caught up and passed me. It wasn't travelling fast and that did strike me as odd. Most bikers like to take advantage of an empty road. I remembered then that I'd heard a bike before, revving up in the distance on the occasion of my night visitor's second call.

I didn't want to end up seeing and hearing things every time I stuck my head out of doors. But I decided to take a different route home, just in case. I turned the corner and left behind the lighted main road with its pubs, cafés, and security-lit store windows.

I was walking through deserted residential roads now. Curtains were drawn and doors locked against the night and its dangers. The only sign of life within was the flickering phosphorescent glow of television screens, playing on the blinds. My footsteps echoed on the pavement. I'd ceased to enjoy the coolness, and shivered as a cold draught whistled uncomfortably round my neck. Greasy paper wrappings from fried food and empty foil trays, discarded back there in the main shopping area, had been scooped up by the wind and diverted into this side street. They bowled past me, rattling and fluttering along the uneven flags. Occasionally one wrapped itself unpleasantly round the back of my legs. I pulled up my collar, shoved my hands into my pockets, in one of which I'd wedged the tub of cheese, and head down, hurried on.

The motorcycle roar, coming from directly behind me, broke into the quiet solitude like a wild animal let loose.

Had I stopped and turned to face it, I'd have been a goner. As it was, instinct made me leap first without waiting to see. I scrambled up someone's front steps as the machine raced past along the pavement. The tug of air as it swept by almost knocked me off my feet. The rider was crouched low over the handlebars, a dark helmeted faceless shape.

'Maniac!' I yelled after him. 'What're you trying to do?'

The margarine box of cheese fell out of my pocket and bounced away down the pavement.

My question had been both stupid and unnecessary. What he was trying to do was run me down. His speed carried him on to the end of the street. I hammered frantically on the door behind me, knowing it was useless. No one, hearing any kind of fracas outside, would open up at this time of night.

I jumped down the steps and began to run back towards the main road. Behind me, the biker had skidded round in a U-turn and the engine snarled as he began the run back. I couldn't make it to the lights and safety ahead. There was a side turning and I dived into it. The machine swept past. He was faster than me but less mobile. He had to slow and turn again before making his third and possibly successful attempt.

I had no option but to run and no time to think where I might be running to. All I knew was that I had to find a hiding place. I pounded round the next corner and found myself in a broader street but even more poorly lit and not residential like the one I'd left. One side of it was entirely taken up with a large building, which, judging from the general architecture, had probably once been a warehouse.

Despite that, a peeling sign advertised it for rent and specified a large amount of office space. The sign looked to have been there a long time. The building was in complete darkness and its windows stared down at me like so many blind eyes. Nothing suggested a security patrol or even a caretaker was there to look out and see my predicament.

The other side of the road was bordered by iron railings and bushes. It was eerily empty of all life. I couldn't have chosen worse.

Since the commercial building offered nothing but a solid wall and ground-floor windows barred with iron grilles, I crossed to the fenced side of the street. I raced down the line of metal posts, hoping for a gap or at least a place where the spikes were broken and I might climb over. And there was a gap! I leaped into it just as the motorcycle's headlight swept around the corner of the street.

I'd hoped to be able to scramble away among the bushes, but in my haste I'd miscalculated. The gap was the entry to a flight of steps leading downwards. I lost my footing and rolled and bounced to the bottom, where I landed face down in the dirt. I was bruised and my hands scraped but I had no time to worry about injuries. I crawled into the nearest bushes and crouched there. My heart was thudding and my breathing sounded so loud I thought my hunter must hear it. The machine was put-putting slowing along the street above. He was looking for me. He'd see the gap in the railings and he'd guess I'd gone down here.

The machine moved on. Had he missed the gap? Cautiously I put my head out and, for the first time, took note of where I was. A fresh breeze rippled past my face. Water lapped and nearby somewhere there was a creak of some wooden object. A pungent, tarry, muddy, faintly stagnant smell pervaded the air. It was familiar. I was on the canal towpath, not far from where poor Albie's body had been taken from the water. I edged out and stood up. There was a bridge some way down and about fifteen feet from me, the same two houseboats were moored. I began to move towards them and then let out a yell as I stubbed my toe painfully against some hard projecting object.

It was a metal ring set in a lump of concrete. Attached to it was a length of coiled rope. The houseboat it was presumably meant to secure was missing from its mooring.

I cursed myself for having given away my position by the shout, and stood, straining my ears for my pursuer. Faintly, some distance ahead of me, I heard the splutter of an engine. Then almost at the furthest point of visibility along the towpath from where I stood, a sudden bright beam flashed and swept across the bank, path and water like a searchlight. A menacing engine cough told me it was the headlamp of the motorbike.

Dear Lord! I thought, my heart leaping sickeningly into my throat. He did see the gap and realise where I am. Now he's found a way down on to the path! He's coming down here!

I had to get rid of him. I could only elude him so long before our cat-and-mouse game finished suddenly, messily and horrifically. I looked down by my bruised foot and saw the coil of rope. I snatched it up and leaped into the tangle of shrubbery and nettles on the bank, hauling the rope behind me. As fast as I could I pulled it taut and secured it to a stump of tree-trunk. Then I poked out my head.

The biker was waiting at the far end of the towpath. Cunningly he'd switched off the headlight. But I knew he was there, watching for a movement in the shadows or an outlined figure in the pale towpath lights. I remembered the cyclist who'd sped past me as I placed flowers in Albie's memory. There was no telling if it had been the same man, come to see what was happening. A murderer returning to the scene of his crime. But if it had been the same man, he knew this towpath, access points, width, evenness of surface, everything. He was on home ground. I was playing his game.

So I obliged him further, stepping out on to the path. When he'd had time to spot me, I turned to run back the way I'd come.

He spotted me. The engine roared triumphantly. The headlight, leaping back into life, flung its long white beam the length of the path as he charged down it towards me – and the rope, drawn tightly a few inches above the ground.

I don't know whether he saw it before he hit it or not. It wouldn't have made much difference the speed he was going. I didn't wait. Behind me a deafening crash shattered my ears, a final screaming roar from the engine, which was abruptly cut off and followed almost at once by a mini tidal wave as the surface of the canal lurched and splashed up over the towpath and my fleeing feet. I'd reached the steps leading back up to the road. I stopped briefly and looked back.

There was no sign of my pursuer on the towpath nor in the heaving water. Then a head popped up, an arm followed, waving frantically and he was splashing about in the canal shouting out for help. All at once, a light beamed out as the hatch of one of the houseboats was opened. A figure emerged and began flashing a torch around. It picked up the figure struggling in the water.

I heard the boat-owner shouting, 'What the devil is going on?' as I ran up the steps to the road.

I was scarcely aware how I managed the rest of the way home. Only when I'd stumbled down the basement steps and got inside my own flat could I even begin to take stock and organise my thoughts.

First aid was a priority. I went into the bathroom and took a look at myself in the mirror. I'd cut my chin, and blood was trickling down. The palms of both hands were badly grazed and grit was embedded in the weeping flesh. I wriggled out of my jacket. Using my elbow, I turned on the cold tap and ran the water over the raw area of my palms until the grit had washed out. The injuries burned like a million wasp stings. I smeared on antiseptic cream, yelping and swearing, because I'm a total coward when it comes to medical treatment of any kind.

My jeans were torn but had largely saved my knees from being skinned as well. My toe was red and swelling badly where it had struck the mooring ring. I hoped it wasn't broken.

It all hardly mattered. I was alive.

So was he, my pursuer. I supposed they'd got him out of the canal by now. He'd lost his bike. Serve him right! I tried to be pleased he hadn't drowned and I hadn't his death on my conscience. But in truth my conscience was untroubled. He'd been luckier than Albie. If he was connected with Albie's death then justice *hadn't* been done. He ought to have drowned.

I hobbled into the kitchen and boiled the kettle. I don't normally take sugar in drinks but it was supposed to be good for shock so I put two spoonfuls in my instant coffee. I retreated to my living room and settled on the sofa, the duvet pulled round my shoulders, and sipped the hot sweet brew. My toe pulsated painfully in the flip-flops I'd donned and my hands still felt as though they were on fire.

Who was he? And why the murderous assault? He might have been drunk or high. But he'd handled the machine too well. It might've been mistaken identity. He'd wanted to get someone else. But no, he'd been waiting outside Jimmie's, I remembered, and he'd moved the moment I'd left the café.

He'd been out to get me. It had to be someone to do with either Lauren's kidnapping or Albie's murder or both, supposing the two to be connected as I was sure they were. Had it been Merv? If Merv had torched his car the other night, he might have taken to a motorcycle.

Otherwise I'd only come across one motorcyclist lately. That had been the courier in the offices of Thais Fine Arts. The possibilities opened up by that were endless. I'd no way of knowing if it had been the same man, of course, and mustn't jump to conclusions.

'Well, anyway, you've got 'em worried,' I told myself aloud in a poor attempt at comfort.

And they had me worried. They were unlikely to give up. They'd try again.

Much as it went against the grain to appeal to the police, and little faith though I had in them, I knew I had to report this.

I finished the coffee, reluctantly got off the sofa, found another pair of jeans, and let myself out of the flat. I felt distinctly unsafe out here in the street but I knew Daphne went to bed fairly late and there was still a light at an upper window. I hobbled briskly up the steps and pressed the bell. Then I opened the letter box and called through it. The hall light went on within a couple of minutes.

'Fran?' She peered through the chained door. 'Just a sec!' The door was shut again, the chain rattled, and the door reopened, wide enough to let me in.

Daphne was wrapped in an ancient dressing gown and her grey fringe was secured in a row of pin curls. She cut short my apologies, took my arm and guided me straight to her warm, cheerful kitchen, where she switched on the coffee-maker for a proper brew, and produced a bottle of brandy.

'What happened, dear?' Her eyes crinkled up with concern and the low-level lighting from the worktop made the row of aluminium pins across her forehead gleam like a silver tiara.

I told her I'd had a near miss in a traffic accident. I thought I ought to phone the police.

'I'll phone them,' she said firmly. 'That's a nasty cut on your chin. Perhaps you ought to get it stitched.'

The very idea made me feel faint. 'It'll be fine,' I said

hastily. 'And I'd better speak to the police myself. You know, for the details.'

She was giving me a look that clearly said she guessed there was a lot more to this 'traffic accident' than I was saying.

The deeply unimpressed police voice at the other end of the line promised that they'd look into it and would send someone round in the morning to get a statement. I told them I was working in the morning and suggested they get a message to Sergeant Parry tonight.

'He's gone off duty,' said the voice disapprovingly.

'Listen!' I snapped. 'Someone tried to kill me! Get hold of Parry! Tell him I want protection!'

If I hadn't had such a stressful evening I wouldn't have said that, the bit about protection. It was asking for trouble.

I'd sat with Daphne for a few minutes and then made my way back to my flat. It felt chilly and I lit the gas fire in the grate. I didn't feel much like going to bed. It hardly seemed likely I'd sleep. But I had to be at the Community Hall first thing in the morning ready for a full day being a tree. I hoped I wouldn't fall asleep tomorrow, wedged in that frame Angus had constructed.

A car drew up outside, a door slammed, footsteps clattered down the steps and someone rang the doorbell.

I froze with fear. Was it my hunter? Now that he'd quitted the shadows for open attack, had he decided on the direct approach here, at my home?

'Fran?' A fist beat on the door. 'You all right in there?'

It was Parry, galloping over like a knight on a white

horse at the first shriek from the damsel in distress. I told myself forcefully that I was an idiot and opened the door.

Parry bounded in clad in a sweat-stained tracksuit. 'You all right, Fran? Bloody hell, what happened to your face? What's been going on?'

'I didn't mean for you to come round here,' I told him.

'They said you'd asked for me to come. You asked for protection. I was over at the sports club. Lucky I had my mobile with me. You mightn't have got me otherwise.'

I should've been so lucky. He had found himself a chair as he spoke and now sat there, looking at me with concern.

'That's a nasty cut. You oughta get that stitched.'

I ignored that suggestion and told him what had happened that day. I told him about my night-time prowler too, and that I was sure he and my murderous biker were one and the same.

Parry's face got redder and redder as I spoke and when I finished, he threw both arms in the air. 'I can't understand you,' he bawled. 'You're not daft. You're bright enough. You just act thick. Didn't I tell you to leave well alone? Why didn't you tell me you had this herbert creeping about at night? Who did you think he was? Father Christmas? You think he was just going to be content with hanging around by moonlight? He was bound to move in on you sooner or later. He's a perishing psycho.'

I informed Parry I wasn't in the mood to be lectured. 'What's more,' I added, 'I arranged my visit to Copperfield with Szabo and if he didn't mind, you've got no reason to whinge on about it.'

Parry leaned forward, pale blue eyes protruding with a

righteous anger. 'Oh, haven't I? Just to remind you, this is a police matter and highly sensitive. What do you want, you and Szabo? For that kid Lauren to turn up dead? Buried out in the country somewhere? Divided up between half a dozen black plastic sacks on a rubbish tip? Pulled out of the canal like old Albie?'

'Don't be stupid!' I snapped.

'Take a leaf out of your own book,' he retorted. 'Don't tell me your going round to see Copperfield didn't do any harm! Caused you plenty of trouble, didn't it? Chased all round the streets by a lunatic on a motorbike. Like dicing with death, do you?'

We sat scowling at one another. I decided there was nothing to be gained by pursuing this argument.

'What about Copperfield?' I asked. 'I didn't like him. He didn't strike me as the slightest bit upset about Lauren's disappearance.'

'What you mean,' Parry said offensively, 'is that he didn't choose to talk to you about it. Not the same thing.'

'But what about him?' I persisted. 'Is he on the level? Is it worth checking him out? What about that fine arts business of his? Does it make any money?'

He chewed the ends of his ragged ginger moustache as he worked out how much, if anything, he could tell me. He was sitting near the gas fire and the sweat patches on his clothing had dried out with a resultant lingering aroma of BO. He made a decision.

'As it happens,' he said, 'and strictly between us, he's on the PNC.'

'What?' He'd thrown the initials at me casually and in

my blurred state, they became confused with PCC, the parochial church council. As a fact, it seemed possible but hardly relevant.

'The Police National Computer,' he explained kindly, putting me right. 'Out at Hendon.'

That made a lot more sense. 'You mean, he's got form?' I gasped, and jumped up, forgetting my sore foot and other aches and bruises. My whole body twanged in painful protest and I sat down quickly.

Parry coughed discreetly behind his hand as if I'd said something risqué.

'Well, hardly what you'd call real form. A few years back the Fine Art and Antiques Squad took a bit of interest in him. They broke a setup dealing in dodgy export licences. A lot of people were pulled in for questioning, Copperfield among them. He got a suspended sentence. He'd never committed an offence before – or not been found out if he had – and the court took the view he'd been the pawn of cleverer blokes than himself. Seeing as he's a first-class, grade A prat, that means just about the rest of the world! The worst you could say about the poor sod was that he'd been foolish in some of his business relationships. More sinned against than sinning, as the maiden said.'

He uttered a hawking sound that was probably intended as a chuckle. 'As for that firm of his, trade suffered what you'd call a temporary setback while he was under a cloud. He got into financial difficulties but he's pulled out of it. After all, a lot of businessmen these days have had the odd embarrassment with the law, and it don't do 'em no harm. Now he's dealing straight, although word is, he owes big money to the banks.'

I thought this over. 'How about Szabo?' I asked. 'Is he as rich as the kidnappers think he is?'

'You bet he is,' said Parry, and chuckled. 'And the kidnappers must know what he's worth because—' He broke off and looked momentarily embarrassed.

'Go on,' I encouraged him. 'You might as well. You've started.'

'Well . . .' He fidgeted. 'The first ransom demand was fairly modest – as ransoms go. Then, the next demand, the price had gone up stiffly. Szabo reckons it's because he didn't pay the first price. See, he's afraid it'll go on increasing the longer they hold her. We're having trouble keeping tabs on him, making sure he doesn't go behind our backs and try to make a deal with the villains.'

'Is that why you sent him to me?' A thought struck me, which, until now, would've seemed incredible but suddenly seemed quite likely. 'Hey!' I said indignantly. 'Did you think he might try to use me as a go-between?'

'He'd have to use someone.' Parry sounded defiant and truculent in equal parts. 'He might've thought you'd fit the role.'

'Well, he didn't – he hasn't suggested it!' I told him. 'And if he did, I'd tell him to forget it!'

'What you do,' said Parry, 'if he does suggest it, is tell me, right? Me or someone else on the case. Straight away, no delays, no trying to be clever, no attempts at fancy footwork.'

'This is a really lovely setup,' I said. 'No one trusts anyone else. Szabo doesn't trust the police or the kidnappers. You don't trust him. I don't trust you or Vinnie or the kidnappers or Jeremy Copperfield or anyone! And by the way, have you found Merv and has he got a motorbike?'

'We found him.' Parry folded his arms and looked smug. 'He's got an alibi for the night the old man fell in the canal. He was watching telly with a bunch of his mates. Football, international match. They all swear to it. They'd stocked up with a few crates of beer and didn't leave the flat they were in. And what d'you mean, you don't trust *me*?'

'Alibi?' I couldn't believe my ears.

'That's right. And he can discuss the match. Not, I realise, that that means anything because edited highlights were repeated the following night. But four other blokes saying he was there does carry weight.'

'I saw him – Ganesh and I both saw him – try to snatch Albie off the street. Merv and another man!' I protested.

'Poor lighting, difficult circumstances – you can't swear it was him, Fran.'

'Who can't? And what about his car? Was it his car torched up by the park that night?'

'Yes, it was. But he says it was taken earlier by joyriders. He'd had trouble with joyriders hanging around it before.' Parry's eyes gleamed. 'Seems one evening he was having a quiet drink in the pub when in comes a young woman and warns him that kids are hanging around the motor, and the alarm's gone off. He describes her as having short brown hair, skinny figure and a voice like a foghorn. She'd been hanging about outside talking to a couple of Asian guys by a junk food van. Anyone you know?'

'Can't imagine. Do you want me to give you a statement about the attack on me or what?'

'Fair enough. I've got nothing with me, coming here straight from the club. Got a bit of paper?'

I told him my story again. He wrote it down and I signed it.

'Thank you very much, madam,' he said formally.

'That's all right, officer. Thank you for coming round. You can go now. I'm all right.'

'I was going to offer,' he said, 'to doss down here on a chair tonight. Protect you, like you asked.'

'It won't be necessary!' I informed him.

He looked almost wistful. Even his moustache drooped. 'You did send for me.'

'Correction. I asked them to tell you. Not the same thing.'

'But you did request protection,' he insisted, clinging to his hopes.

I dashed them. 'Just to have the area patrol car include the house on their route a couple of times would do the trick. Or a uniformed officer calling in once a day to see if I'm all right.'

'How much spare manpower do you think we've got?' he retorted disagreeably. 'Not a chance.'

'How about moving me to a place of safety, then, a hotel?' I suggested.

'Who do you think you are?' he asked. 'Prime witness in a matter of national security? Forget it.'

In the end, he checked the safety catches on my windows

and the lock and chain on the door and pronounced me secure.

'Only you ought to have a phone. I can't leave you my mobile. I need it. But that's what you ought to get, a mobile. Every woman on her own ought to have one.'

I promised I'd look into it. By this time it was nearly one in the morning and I finally persuaded him to go home.

At least his visit had dealt with my overwrought wakefulness. I collapsed on the sofa. Oblivious of my bruises, I slept, as they say, like the dead.

Chapter Thirteen

I arrived early at the Community Hall the following morning, as requested. I'd spent some time and my theatrical make-up skills disguising the cut on my chin. I'd washed my hair and knew I looked fine, not like someone who'd been fleeing for her life only hours before. Despite this, I was feeling highly nervous. A persuasive little Mephisto in the corner of my mind kept whispering, 'Hey! You'd rather be anywhere else than here! Why don't you just turn and run?'

But I'm not one to break a promise. Angus was depending on me. If I let him down, I'd feel bad about it, and I'd never be able to eat at Jimmie's again. Though the last thought was more an inducement to defect than to stay, I ordered the tempter to be silent and looked around.

At least I wasn't alone. People were arriving from all directions. Beneath a banner proclaiming 'Art for a Cleaner Safer World', artists working in every medium were struggling through the doors with exhibits. As I watched, a thin man with a neatly trimmed beard, and a red neckerchief knotted fancily around his scraggy throat, staggered past. His arms clasped a scrap-metal sculpture to his bosom as if it were a dancing partner.

'Fran! Fran, over here!' I heard Angus's voice as my eye caught a waving arm.

He was sitting between the open doors at the rear of an ancient rust-pitted Transit van, drinking milk from a carton. He put it down as I approached.

'Just having my breakfast,' he explained. 'Thanks for being on time. You know, we're really in with a chance. I've seen most of the other stuff. Talk about unimaginative, run-of-the-mill junk. We'll knock 'em into next week!'

Trying hard to share his enthusiasm, I peered past him into the van. 'Jimmie said something about vegetables,' I mumbled.

The interior of the van, as far as I could see, was littered with foliage of various sorts. A pineapple poked its fronds from a Tesco bag.

'Veg?' Angus looked puzzled. 'No, he's got it wrong. Fruit.'

'Oh.' I supposed that was better. 'Where's the thing, you know, the frame.'

'Already taken it in.' He stood up. 'Right, you take the bag there and this one . . .' he thrust another plastic carrier at me, 'I'll bring the lianas.'

Inside the hall, chaos reigned. A shrill woman in a long purple skirt and a patchwork jacket was shouting instructions at anyone who cared to listen, though most people were ignoring her. She clasped a sheaf of cards to her flat bosom.

'All the individual areas are marked in chalk on the floor!' she shrieked. 'Newcomers please get a number from me!' She held the sheaf of cards up in the air but no one took the slightest bit of notice.

'They're not doing it properly, Reg!' she wailed to a gloomy, middle-aged individual standing nearby.

'Let 'em sort themselves out,' advised Reg.

'But it'll be a dreadful mess. Do something, Reg!'

Two girls trotted past, bearing between them a lurid canvas splashed with lime green and red.

'Come and get your number!' begged the woman.

The girls, like everyone else, took no notice and carried straight on to the back of the hall.

The woman caught my eye. 'Have you got your number?' she asked dispiritedly.

I explained I was an exhibit, not an exhibitor.

'You've still got to have a number,' she said obstinately.

Reg edged over and peered into my Tesco bags. 'Blimey, brought your lunch with you, love?'

Hearing I was going to wear it, not eat it, he chuckled. 'Cor! Carmen bloomin' Miranda!'

I recalled that Angus had promised a couple of minders on the door to stop troublemakers disrupting our festival of culture. Apparently, all we had was Reg. He was in his fifties and overweight. He may once have been a fine figure of a man, but not since it had all settled round his midriff. I enquired tentatively about the door attendants.

'They cost money, do professional bouncers,' said Reg. 'Shouldn't need them. Not in broad daylight.'

'It's an arts festival,' put in the purple-skirted woman. 'One couldn't have a couple of heavyweights on the door, scowling at people. It would put the visitors off.'

Well, we mustn't frighten the horses. But the news did nothing for my already fragile nerves.

Angus appeared, his arms filled with strands of greenery. 'We're over on the right,' he informed me.

'Your number!' shrilled the woman.

'Don't worry, I've got it,' he told her.

'Then you're the only bloody one who has!' she snapped. She pushed the sheaf of cards into Reg's hand. 'You carry on, I'm going to find a coffee. My head is splitting!'

Angus and I progressed to a chalked area on the floor where the frame stood waiting for us, looking more than ever like something from a castle dungeon. The thin man had set up his scrap-metal sculpture alongside us in the next chalked area.

Its creator stood back and squinted at it. 'Does that look straight to you?'

Given the nature of the exhibit, it was hard to tell. I said it looked more or less straight to me.

'We are reducing the world to a mountain of debris, the legacy of our life-style,' he informed me. 'And in doing so, we are reducing ourselves to mere accumulation of debris. Junk in. Junk out.'

Hence the scrap metal figure, I deduced. The thin man was staring fiercely at the frame created by Angus for my support. 'I see your friend is a minimalist,' he said. 'The pure spiral, representing man's spiritual search, guiding him to the heavens or dragging him inexorably earthwards, am I right?'

I was saved replying by one of the girls who had carried

in the lurid canvas. She approached. 'Oy!' she hailed the thin man. 'You're in our square.' She brandished a numbered card at him.

'Find yourself another one,' he retorted.

'You find your own square!'

'I can't use my own square. Someone's already in it!'

'Reg!' screeched the girl down the hall. 'Come 'n' tell this silly sod he's in our square!'

Avoid other people's fights is my motto. The bystander always gets hurt. I returned to Angus. 'Where's my costume?'

He handed me yet another plastic bag. I peered into it. It was the body stocking, dyed a fetching sludge green. It did, however, look reassuringly robust.

'You'll have to change in the women's loo,' he said. 'But if you bring your clothes back here, I'll lock 'em in the van till it's over.'

A little later I emerged hesitantly from the washroom clad in the green body stocking. But I needn't have worried that anyone would take any notice of me. They were all too busy arguing over floor space and setting up their exhibits. The woman with the purple skirt was running up and down in increasing hysteria. Her cries of, 'No, no, you can't *do* that!' were alternated with appeals of, 'Reg, do *something*!' I had to admit there was a real air of excitement, just like the last minutes before a first night. I began to cheer up.

Nevertheless, things didn't start too well, with Angus and I having a serious disagreement over the pineapple.

To my horror, he intended this to go on my head, fixed with a wire crown. I flatly refused to consider it.

'Look here,' he said, getting truculent, 'I'm the artist and you're the model, right? We'll get nowhere if you're going to carp at everything. You agreed.'

'I'll model the rest, but not that thing, certainly not on top of my head! I've already heard one Carmen Miranda joke. I mean it. You'll have no model at all if you insist.'

'But it finishes the whole thing off,' he protested.

'Too right, it'll finish it off. It'll finish me off for a start. It's naff, Angus. Forget it.'

He said crossly that it had cost a lot. I told him to take it over to Jimmie's and sell it on to him. 'He can chop it up, mix it with cottage cheese and stick it in the potatoes.'

He gave way with bad grace. Miraculously things sorted themselves out and we were all just about ready at ten thirty when the doors were opened to the public. The frame wasn't that comfortable but it wasn't actively uncomfortable. Angus, working from a diagram, had attached all the bits of greenery and some flowers, together with some large and beautifully painted paper butterflies and birds. Reg came along to watch. He looked impressed.

Angus positioned me facing the scrap-metal man next door and I felt it and I would be good friends by the end of the day.

The atmosphere, as Reg approached the doors, quivered with the vibrations from artistic nerves strung like violin strings. The first members of the public to drift in were clearly friends and supporters of the different artists. They clutched leaflets pressed on them by the organisers. In addition, they all had a private brief, which was to stand in front of their friend's chalk square and express loud admiration, before moving on to the other squares and pronouncing all the other work rubbish.

Before our square they fell silent. I wasn't sure whether this was because they were struck with awe or because, with Angus being brawny and wearing his Scottish football shirt, they didn't feel it was wise to make the sort of sarcastic comments they were firing at other exhibits. They were rude about the scrap-metal man instead.

The thin man was soon pale with emotion. 'Philistines!' he howled. 'Cultural cretins!'

After a while, genuine punters began to arrive – only a few at first, some carrying bags of Saturday shopping, but all of them seemed strangely attracted to our square. Angus had been right about the living sculpture. It – I – exerted a weird fascination over observers.

Word must have got around because a lot of people began to arrive and they all made for our corner where it became very congested. I concentrated on keeping still and soon realised how the Buckingham Palace guards must suffer.

Comments floated towards me. 'She must be real, you can see her eyes blinking.' 'Poor girl, she'll get terrible cramp.' More mysteriously, I heard, 'I expect she's used to this sort of thing.'

Cameras began to flash. Angus was in seventh heaven and even the thin man brightened up, probably hoping that the photographers would include his sculpture in the picture.

The show closed for a lunch break between one and two. Angus helped me out of the frame and removed some of the less firmly fixed greenery and artwork.

'You were right about the pineapple,' he said generously.

'Of course I was,' I said.

I nipped along to the loo to struggle out of the rest and answer Nature's call. There was a chair in the washroom. I sat on it in my bra and pants to drink a cup of coffee and eat a sandwich, which Angus had sent in care of the woman in the purple skirt.

'It's going awfully well,' she enthused. 'I do think you're terribly brave.' She hovered over me. 'You won't catch cold, will you? We have got the heating on.'

I promised her I wasn't cold. In fact, inside the body stocking and all the attachments, it had been very warm in the hall. She told me again that I was brave and she wouldn't have done it, not for the world.

I had to get back to my stand well before two so that Angus could reattach everything. The crowd was thinner after lunch. People had other ways of spending their Saturday afternoons. The exhibition was due to close at four thirty anyway, and by three fifteen I was beginning to think we might be able to knock off early. Even as I thought this, I became aware of fresh eyes staring at me.

I had quite got used to the gawpers, but this was a gaze so intent, it made my skin tingle. Worse than that, it sent out signals of recognition and of menace. It conjured up fear such as I'd felt in my underground bedroom. My night visitor – it had to be.

A bead of sweat trickled from my shoulders, down inside

the clammy body stocking, running along my spine like the touch of a finger. I eased my head round just a little.

There were two of them, standing side by side: Merv and his mate. Merv, tall, pale and slab-like as ever, chewed gum impassively. I no longer cared about Merv. I was interested in the other. I was seeing him face to face for the first time. No smoky-visored biker's helmet, no curtained window, no thick piece of opaque glass veiled him from my sight. I saw my ogre, fair and square.

In appearance he was disappointing, short, squat, olive-complexioned and losing his hair. His build was that of the glimpsed silhouette against my curtains. I realised, too, that this was the man Ganesh and I had seen with Merv the fateful evening they'd tried to bundle Albie into Merv's car.

Hats or helmets, the man liked to cover his head. It could either be from vanity or because baldness is quickly identifiable, something even a confused witness would remember.

We'd foiled their attempt at a snatch that night, but later they'd found their quarry. This man, I knew, had killed Albie.

I expected to feel a surge of hate yet somehow it eluded me. The baldness remained disconcerting, a mark of human frailty. I don't quite know what I'd expected of Merv's partner. Whatever it had been, it hadn't been ordinariness, even dullness. Yet everyone, they say, has one striking feature. With this man, it was the eyes. Enormous eyes, it seemed to me, like the eyes in an oil painting, and very slightly protuberant. In colour they were very dark brown, almost black, so that they seemed not to consist of iris and pupil, but just a large dark luminous disc in the surrounding whiteness of the eyeball.

I knew him and he knew I knew him. As I met his gaze of those unnaturally large dark eyes, they laughed at me, matching a mocking curve of his fleshy lips. My mind picked up his message clear as a bell. *I had you running scared, gal . . . Now you see me face to face. Still scared?*

You bet I was scared. Ordinary thugs are simple souls. This one was a nutter. Merv's interest in me, I supposed, was professional. I'd got in the way of a job and he would remove me as any other obstacle in his path, animate or inanimate. It made no difference.

This other one's interest was different, personal. To begin with, I'd cost him a valuable motorbike and with it, I supposed, his employment as a courier. Even if I hadn't, his attitude would still be different to Merv's. He'd enjoyed prowling outside my flat, or chasing me on that bike, as he enjoyed staring at me here. He was doing it for kicks.

Well, I didn't for a moment suppose that either of them was an art lover. Nor did I think they'd give up an afternoon normally spent on the football terraces unless they had urgent business. The business, I was miserably certain, was finding me. Now they'd found me.

I didn't how they'd tracked me down. Possibly Jimmie, meaning to advertise Angus's work, had put the word around and by bad luck, it had reached Merv's ear. Merv caught my eye and his chewing mouth stilled and then twitched nastily. My balding adversary continued to stare, eyes bulging with lewd interest, laughing himself sick inside as he watched me squirm there on my stand, dressed in my ridiculous costume, unable to escape. I must have looked like a butterfly impaled on a pin. It was an uncomfortable image. I could imagine this man as a child, pulling the wings off living insects, tying cans to dogs' tails, interfering with the neighbourhood's little girls. A really nice sort.

'Angus . . .' I hissed, as loudly as I dared.

But Angus was busy explaining what I represented to an interested audience of two middle-aged women and a girl with a baby in a buggy. The balding man shook his head at me chidingly. Merv was chewing again and studying me with puzzled care, as if he couldn't work out what the hell I was supposed to be or why I was dressed like it. I was wondering myself.

When his questioners had moved on to the scrap-metal man, I tried again to attract Angus.

This time he heard my hoarse whisper and came over. 'What's the matter, Fran? You don't need to go to the loo again? Can't you hang on till the end? It's only another three-quarters of an hour.'

'Ring the police . . .' I breathed huskily. My voice seemed clogged in my throat.

'What?' He put his ear closer. Merv and his chum began to move away.

'Ring the police. Ask for Sergeant Parry. Tell him Merv and – and another man are here and have seen me.'

'Can't it wait till four o'clock? It's going well and I don't want to leave the stand.'

'No!' I found my voice and it emerged in a strange

squawk. The scrap-metal sculptor looked across at us in surprise and some concern. Perhaps he thought some part of my anatomy had been pierced by a pin securing a liana.

'Go and ring them now!' I urged. 'There must be a phone in this hall somewhere.'

Some more people had arrived and stopped to study me. 'Excuse me . . .' one of them said diffidently to Angus.

'I'll ring in a minute, when I get a chance!' Angus promised me hurriedly.

There wasn't much I could do. I couldn't see either Merv or his pal. My field of vision was restricted so I had no way of knowing whether they had left the hall altogether. Perhaps they'd heard my request for the police and decided to make themselves scarce. I hoped so.

There was a flurry of new visitors in the last ten minutes. Angus was fully employed and didn't leave me, or not for long enough to have phoned. Then, miraculously, the public had gone and clearly weren't coming back. Merv and the other had also vanished to my great relief. At four thirty, or just after, Reg closed the doors.

The woman in the purple skirt clapped her hands and shrilled, 'Oh, well done, everybody!'

There was a huge combined sigh of relief from the various exhibitors. They turned to one another, offering congratulations or, in a few cases, recriminations. The two girls with the painting had fallen out over something. The thin man produced a hip flask and saluted his scrap-metal creation before taking a swig. I climbed down from the stand unaided.

'Gimme my clothes!' I gasped as I began to divest

myself of paper birds and strings of greenery.

'Hey!' Angus yelped. 'You'll damage everything! Wait, let me do it!'

'You can untangle the bits later. I just want to get out of this suit. Look, fetch my gear, will you?'

'It's all right,' he said, realisation dawning on his face. 'Those two blokes have gone. They went ages ago. I don't know what they were doing in here. Just a couple of creeps, I suppose, hoping for a free boob show. I didn't ring the police, I'm afraid. I didn't get time. Reg was supposed to keep the weirdos out. But it didn't matter. They didn't cause any trouble. You didn't know them, did you?'

'Believe me,' I wailed, 'they were very bad news. I've got to get out of here, Angus!'

It finally dawned on him that this was a genuine emergency. His forehead crinkled in decent dismay. 'Sorry, Fran, didn't realise you were really worried about them. I thought you just thought they were kinky. I'll get your gear from the van,' he promised. 'Hang on.'

Back in the loo, I transferred myself into my own things in record time and emerged holding the body stocking, which was still festooned with birds and greenery. The corridor was empty. From the hall came noisy scraping and bumpings as the exhibits were dismantled. I started forward with the intention of returning the body stocking to Angus, who would be worried about it, and then making for the nearest phone.

I was vaguely aware that the door of the men's washroom opposite was opening, but paid no attention. That was a big mistake but I was barely given time to realise it. There was a scuffling behind me and the next thing I knew, someone had enveloped my head and shoulders in a musty-smelling piece of cloth.

I dropped the body stocking and tried to shout for help and disentangle myself at the same time. My voice was muffled by the cloth and my arms were neatly pinned to my sides. I was trussed up as neatly as an oven-ready chicken with some kind of belt or rope, then hoisted by feet and shoulders. I was carried away full length and at a cracking pace, with no more control over what was happening than one of the exhibits in the hall might have had. (Amongst which, as I had time to reflect, I'd recently featured with such distinction.)

I was aware that we'd left the hall. We bumped down some steps and I could hear traffic. Without warning I was dropped, landing with a painful wallop that knocked the breath out of me. Doors slammed. An engine revved. My world, wherever it was, began to move around me, lurching and rattling. I'd been slung into the back of a van and was being driven away.

Chapter Fourteen

It wasn't easy to keep my wits about me in the circumstances, but I did my best.

I reasoned with glum realism that no one would have paid any attention to my plight, even if they'd seen me thrown in the van. Everyone was busy with their own valued works of art, intent on dismantling and moving them out of the hall without damage. Oddly shaped articles of every kind were being lugged into the car park and a body form wrapped in a cloth wouldn't attract even a cursory glance.

Angus would worry, though, if I didn't come back. He'd go looking for me and the body stocking. I'd dropped that on the floor when my captors grabbed me and unless they'd had the presence of mind to scoop it up, it still lay where it fell and Angus would find it.

He would be bright enough to connect this with my earlier plea to call the police and with luck, he'd belatedly do just that. Whether this would help me or not was debatable. Lauren Szabo had been missing two weeks with the police hunting high and low and no one had found her.

I considered trying to bump my way along to the rear

doors of the van and kick them open. On telly, captives do that kind of thing all the time. Believe me, it's not so easy. I was being thrown around all over the place as it was, and organising myself to move in a controlled fashion quickly proved hopeless.

I was sweating profusely and my mouth was parched with thirst and fear. It was increasingly difficult to breathe. The cloth wrapped itself tightly over my face and loose fibres forced their way into my nose and mouth. It stank. Since there was no point in struggling and getting exhausted, I concentrated on not suffocating and conserving my strength for when we should arrive. Always assuming, of course, they didn't intend simply to wait till nightfall and drop me off the nearest bridge. They'd already shown a tendency to dispose of inconvenient individuals in water. I tried not to think about that option.

I couldn't judge time well. In my situation minutes had to feel like hours. I certainly seemed to be thrown around in my prison for some time, but in London traffic, that didn't necessarily mean we'd travelled a vast distance. As far as I could tell, we'd not spent more than a third of the journey time stuck in one spot. I was sure we were still in London and probably not more than a couple of miles or so from where we'd started. Merv and his mate had tribal instincts. They wouldn't move far off their own patch where they knew every alley and bolt hole. (And where a phone call to an obliging pal would fix up an alibi if need be, as they'd demonstrated on the night Albie died.)

At last we stopped altogether. Doors slammed again. Footsteps approached. Though I still couldn't see anything, the darkness had lifted. The van doors had been opened. Hands grabbed me and I was unceremoniously but highly efficiently carried, as before, into a building.

They were careless now, manhandling me with less regard than would've been shown by a couple of piano-shifters for a pub's beat-up set of ivories. They were talking to each other and in normal voices, arguing about where to put me. A voice I identified as Merv's suggested taking me upstairs. The other man was against this as getting me around the corners would be difficult. It wasn't as if the lifts were working, he grumbled. What's more, for such a skinny little cow I was beginning to weigh effing heavy. He refused point-blank to carry me any further. They put me down, upright this time, while they argued it out. The second man, I'd been able to gather, went by the name of Baz.

To me all this meant they felt themselves secure wherever they were. There was no one to see or hear them and they had complete freedom of the place, choosing where to put me and able to bawl at one another to their hearts' delight. In the end, they decided I could walk up a flight of stairs if guided.

I was shoved along and then ordered to start climbing. I don't know if you've ever tried going upstairs with your arms pinned to your sides and a cloth over your head. Try it as a party game, if you want to get rid of your friends. I stumbled repeatedly and fell headlong twice, bruising my shins badly and cracking my forehead on the stairs above. Even Merv and Baz seemed relieved when we reached the next landing and there was no talk, even from Merv, of moving up another flight.

All this told me we were in some large, or at least tall, building. Their voices had an echoing quality suggesting emptiness, and together with their attitude indicated a deserted block of condemned flats, or possibly of office units that had failed to attract tenants. There were such places, and small industrial units sporting sun-faded 'To rent' signs, all over London.

We moved forward again on the level. A door was opened.

'In here,' said Merv, as if I could see.

I moved forward. A chair scraped and hit the back of my legs.

'Siddown!' he invited.

I sat down. There was movement and the door creaked. One of them went out. The other hesitated by my chair before stooping to whisper in my ear.

'I'll be back, darlin'.'

I had no doubt of it. But for the moment, blessedly, he left too. They muttered together some distance away, I guessed outside the room in a hall or corridor.

I strained my ears but they kept their voices low and the cloth muffled their words. For a brief moment Baz raised his voice: 'The little cow cost me my bike!'

Merv swore at him.

'. . . got it coming to her.' That was Baz again. He sounded like a man looking forward to having fun. Not very pleasant fun for someone. Me.

More mumblings from Merv and Baz subsided like a grumbling volcano. It wasn't a nice thought that I depended on someone like Merv to protect me from Baz and whatever perverted ideas he might dream up by way of vengeance.

There was a rattle and scraping noise and my heart leaped in panic. Were they coming back? No, the door was slammed and a key turned. Faintly I caught the sound of retreating footsteps, then there was silence.

My relief at their departure was soon eclipsed by the grim knowledge that I had very little time to get out of here, wherever here was. Wrapped up as I was like Pharaoh's mummy, I couldn't do a thing, so my first task was to get out of my bindings. Apart from being unable to see, breathe properly or move my arms, the material smelled evil. God knew where it'd been.

I managed to wriggle one arm to the front and by dint of breathing in and ignoring the pressure on my ribs, I dragged the arm up and free. That enabled me to grab the cloth from inside and heave it. I pulled it off my head with a sigh of relief, taking a deep breath. The air was marginally fresher but still whiffy.

The room I was in was gloomy but I was able to see that I'd been enveloped in an old curtain, blue and dirty, very dirty, cream. It had been held in place by a leather belt. I was soon able to deal with that and release my other arm. I stepped out of the whole lot, kicked it away across the floor, and looked around me.

Though I hadn't time to feel smug about it, I'd guessed remarkably accurately to what type of building I'd been taken: a disused office block. The walls were bare and pitted with holes where shelving had been dismantled. The only furniture consisted of my seat, which proved to be an ancient typist's chair with foam stuffing coming out of the padded back, and a metal filing cabinet with a massive dent caving in one side. The floor was covered with worn and filthy carpeting and scrap paper. The stale air was imprinted with traces of a lost way of life, of cigarette smoke, dispenser coffee, 3-In-One oil, and more recently, mouse droppings.

There were no external windows. Light filtered in through a glass transom above the door from the corridor outside. I went over to the light switch and flicked it but nothing happened. I rattled the door handle, despite having heard the key turned in the lock as they left. I didn't know for how long Merv and Baz would be gone, but I guessed not for long. They'd dumped me here while they worked out what to do with me, or went for orders from someone else. I wondered if the unknown controller was Copperfield.

Finding out could come later. In the meantime, I had to get out of here. I looked up at the dusty glass transom. It was hinged.

Standing on the chair didn't raise me high enough. My eye fell on the filing cabinet. It wasn't easy to move, too awkward and heavy to slide across the carpet. On the other hand, the carpet muffled the sound it made as I manhandled it clumsily toward the door. Sweating and puffing, I finally managed to get it into place and scrambled on top of it.

Now I could reach the transom catch which was on the inside and although it was stiff from disuse, I was able to twist it up. I pushed at the frame and it moved protestingly. I fixed it with its metal arm. The resultant space was narrow, but it was the only way out and fortunately, I was slim or, as Baz had opined, skinny.

I had to disconnect the arm and let the transom fall back again, because in the fixed position the arm barred my exit. Gripping the frame with both hands, I hauled myself up and swivelled over it on my stomach, pushing the glass open with my body and trying to anchor myself with my right leg while my left leg hung down on the other side of the door.

So far, so good. Painful and insecure, but progress. The next bit was worse. While teetering dangerously, I had to get my right leg over the frame and at the same time try to turn my body so that I could drop down straight into the corridor without being decapitated by the loose transom frame, which would fall back as soon as I released pressure on it.

I almost did it neatly. But at the last moment my sweaty hands slipped on the metal frame. I couldn't hold on and support my own weight and I plummeted to the corridor floor below. I hit my chin and nose on the frame edge as I went down and landed crunchingly on the unyielding floor tiles. Had I not been taught on the drama course to take a stage fall, I should almost certainly have broken something. As it was the breath was knocked out of my body and my jaw felt as though a mule had kicked it, taking in the bridge of my nose at the same time. The cut on my chin, which I'd received when fleeing from Baz the biker, had reopened and was bleeding. I discovered my nose was trickling blood, too. I hoped I hadn't broken it.

The transom had fallen back into place with a metallic clang that echoed down the corridor. I had no time to hang about here, although other office doors along either side stood ajar and revealed only empty rooms.

I rubbed the stream of gore away with my sleeve and scurried along the corridor to the staircase at the far end. At some stage this place had been adapted from warehouse to office premises, I guessed in the late fifties or early sixties. Most of the internal walls were gimcrack, forming endless tiny airless rooms out of what had been an open floor. Hence the lack of windows. The outer shell appeared more solid and even older.

The surrounding air smelled foul, of damp, dust, crumbling plaster and vermin, a fetid miasma redolent of failure. The building was clearly redundant because it'd been built when the welfare of employees hadn't been considered important and even the later attempt at modernisation had fallen lamentably short of its goal. It was antiquated in every way, including the cobwebby exposed iron heating pipes that had been fixed along the base of the walls, probably at the time of the conversion to offices, and which were big enough to serve a power plant.

But here at least was a large window, one of the originals, through which light beamed down the passageway and illuminated the graffiti-decorated stairwell. Peering through the grimy glass, I saw that it overlooked a deserted yard and a chained and padlocked pair of high gates. There was a row of brick outhouses, which had lost their roofs and looked remarkably like old-fashioned privies. Visits to those had probably been rationed in the good old days.

I tried the window catch but it'd been painted over and stuck fast. Even if I'd been able to open it, I wouldn't have fancied another dead drop, this time from the upper floor where I was. Apart from its other many disadvantages, this place was a fire trap and certainly wouldn't conform to any modern regulations. No wonder it was abandoned.

I wondered how many floors were above me. There was at least one other, because the staircase ran upwards as well as down. I hesitated. Self-preservation indicated immediate descent to the ground floor and discovery of an exit. But I'd had an idea.

If this place was used by Merv and Baz as a sort of safe house to which they could bring me with no fear that I'd be discovered, then might they not have brought Lauren here, too? I'd never get another chance to find out. For an unspecified length of time I had the place to myself unless there was another prisoner.

I crept up the staircase and emerged on the floor above and as I did so, it seemed to me that the silence was broken by the muffled sound of voices. Was I not alone? I paused and half turned to run. Then the voices were interrupted by a burst of music and a squeal of car tyres. Somewhere in this apparently deserted pile was a television set.

I realised that if I investigated, I might simply walk in on Merv and Baz, taking a tea-break. But that was a risk I had to take. The initial floorplan up here was on the same pattern as below. The office doors to either side gaped open to reveal dismal abandoned interiors. But one opened on to a washroom and on the shelf above the basins stood a jumble of toiletry items, soap, handcream, toothpaste.

At the far end of the corridor and facing me was a door with a narrow panel of reinforced glass set in it. It was shut but there was no doubt that from behind that came the sound of the television.

I crept down the corridor towards it. Luckily whoever watched the telly was a fan of the noisier kind of car-chase movie. The squealing of tyres and the frantic music had both increased and now were interspersed with shots. The viewer or viewers wouldn't hear me.

I'd reached the door and there I stopped to work out my next move. I couldn't just open it, not knowing what lay beyond. I might not even be able to open it. There was no key in the lock.

I put my eye to the glass strip. The crisscross wire reinforcing and the grime obscured my view. I ventured to breath on it and rub. A clearer patch emerged.

The first thing I saw was the TV screen. It flickered wildly and the music was deafening. The film was coming to an end in a final pile-up of vehicles and lots of running bodies. The credits began to roll up the screen.

There was a scrape as of a chair and a shape moved across my spyhole. My view of the TV screen was blocked by a body as someone, jeans-clad, stooped to switch it off. The figure was neither Merv or Baz, of that I was sure. It was too small and slightly built.

The noise of the set silenced, the person in the room straightened up and turned towards the door. I ducked down in the nick of time before she saw my silhouette on the glass.

Because 'it' was definitely 'she'. I'd only had a brief

glimpse but it was enough. I'd seen Lauren Szabo.

I stepped away from the door and wondered what to do. Escape from the building and contact Parry would make sense. But if Merv or Baz came back and found me gone, they'd move Lauren at once. I had to take her with me.

I could hear her moving about the room. I put my eye back against the clear patch. I couldn't see her now, but neither could I see anyone else. I was pretty sure she was on her own in there.

I raised my hand, tapped on the glass panel and called as loudly as I dared, 'Lauren?'

From inside the room came a quick intake of breath and a muttered exclamation. She came back into view, darting towards the door, long hair flying, and with an expression on her face that told me everything. Dismay, surprise, anger were there, but not relief, not hope or delight at being found, at the arrival of a friend.

I hadn't time to tell myself how stupid I'd been, but I knew it at once. The door was jerked open from inside. Yes, Fran, I thought miserably, it wasn't locked. You are a class-one idiot. You might at least have tried the handle before you starting calling out her name.

She stood in the doorway, red-faced and staring at me in fury. I stared back, no less angry.

She spoke first. 'How the hell did you get out?' she asked.

I wasn't here to answer her questions. I had questions of my own. I launched myself at her, catching her in the midriff and knocking her backwards. She sprawled on the floor, but rolled over and grabbed my ankle. I kicked out and she released me, swearing in a way no nice girl should.

Behind, the door had clicked shut and as I turned towards it, I saw the key was in the lock on the inside. I twisted it and snatched it out of the key hole. She dived for it, but I shoved it down my shirt where, in time-honoured fashion, it lodged in my bra.

'Right, Lauren,' I panted. 'I think we'd both better stay here so you can tell me exactly what's been going on!'

'You stupid cow!' she yelled. 'Give me the key! You don't know what you're doing!'

'I thought,' I said, 'that I was rescuing you. But I'm not, am I? Because you're not a prisoner?'

She hesitated before saying sulkily, 'Merv told me they'd picked up the girl who was hanging around, poking her nose in. He said you were tied up safe, downstairs.'

'That'll teach you,' I retorted, 'to believe everything you're told by someone like Merv. What's going on here?'

She blinked at me, reddening. 'You shouldn't have meddled and you can damn well stop doing it now. This is none of your business. You're not involved.'

'Excuse me,' I said. 'I've been grabbed, trussed up, chucked in a van and driven over here like a sack of spuds, slung in a filthy disused office and left there, locked in. I feel very involved.'

'It's your own fault!' she shouted, before she realised this wouldn't get her anywhere and it might be better to be reasonable with me. 'Your own fault,' she repeated more calmly. 'We had to do it, to keep you quiet for a bit. We weren't going to hurt you. We'd have let you go once – once everything was settled. Right now, you must stay here.

You're going to spoil it all, don't you see?'

Her voice rose passionately. 'Look, I've gone through a hell of a lot here! You don't think it's been easy for me, do you? I mean, since they grabbed me off the street? You don't know what happened! You don't know the trouble I've had managing those two nutters, Merv and Baz! Getting them to do what I wanted. Even now, I still can't trust them! Apart from anything else, they're so bloody incompetent! Everything is – is just balanced on a knife edge! If it goes wrong, we're both in real trouble, you and me!'

This was all very well and interesting, but missing the point. 'If you're on the level at all, you'll walk out of here with me now,' I argued.

'But I can't!' she wailed, throwing out her hands despairingly. 'I'll explain it if you want, if it'll satisfy you. Once you see how it is, you'll understand why you mustn't interfere!'

She was genuinely distraught. I didn't know what all this was about, but there was enough agony in her voice to make me hesitate.

'You've got five minutes to convince me,' I told her sceptically. 'And then I'm getting out of here, with or without you. But talk fast. No playing for time until your two muscle-bounds chums come back!'

'All right, all right!' she promised breathlessly. 'It's like this . . .'

Chapter Fifteen

An expression of relief had crossed Lauren's face as she spoke and it irritated me. She'd made the offer to explain grudgingly, as if it were something on which I'd been insisting, suggesting I'd won a point. But I realised too late that, on the contrary, it was what she wanted. I'd been in full flow bawling her out. She'd got me to shut up and listen while she put her spin on whatever was going on here.

Ruefully I told myself that Vinnie's pride and joy wasn't the wide-eyed innocent he believed her to be. She was a quick-thinker and had certainly shown herself smarter than me. Now that rankled because, let's be honest, I fancied myself as fairly streetwise and not one to fall for a sob story or a neat line in manipulation. Yet here I was, taking the bait, hook, line and sinker.

Of course I knew I didn't have to do as she wanted. Especially as a sentence she'd let slip about getting Merv and Baz to do her bidding had lodged in my brain. The clear implication was that I was being lumped together with those two. This I did not like one bit.

My mulish expression must have warned her. 'Look,' she said persuasively, 'why don't we sit down? There's no point standing here shouting at each other.'

I've learned over the years to trust my instinct with people and it's kept me safe till now. Instinct warned me not to trust Lauren Szabo. Instinct said, run like the clappers out of there.

But there were so many questions I wanted answered that I actually wanted to hear what she had to say. To begin with, there had to be some really strong reason why she was sitting here watching telly behind an unlocked door when all she had to do was walk out. Albie *had* seen her snatched. She'd been genuinely upset moments before. By not listening I could miss something vital. For the first time in my life, I told instinct to shut up for a minute and I sat down.

The chair she'd offered me was an old-fashioned wooden kitchen type. Lauren herself made a dive for a ropy armchair, which looked as if it'd come from a dump, but offered far more comfort. She sat well back in it with her hands resting on the scabby moquette arms. She looked as pleased with herself as a boxer who knows he's won the first round and anticipates finishing off his opponent easily before too long.

All the alarm bells were ringing frantically in my brain, telling me this supposed kidnap victim was actually a shrewd manipulator, one who always got her own way. But somehow, despite that, I still sat there, waiting for her to speak. Annoyed by my own unquenchable curiosity that kept me there, I was also struck by how very impolite it was of her to have grabbed the only comfortable chair like that.

Irritation stops you thinking. I stopped being irritated and kick-started my brain. When I did, I realised it wasn't her lack of manners that was bothering me.

There was something about that chair and her smug expression now she was sitting in it that was highly suspicious. She'd not only got me physically where she wanted me, she was also physically where *she* wanted to be, which was in that rickety old armchair. I couldn't understand its significance and my unease increased, if that were possible.

I took a quick look around the rest of the room. The window was like the one I'd looked out of before, large and old-fashioned. Juggling the geography of the place in my head, I worked out that if the window from which I'd seen the yard with the privies had overlooked the back of the building, this one overlooked the front.

The furnishings were spare. The portable telly on a wooden crate. A Put-u-up bed with a crumpled duvet and pillow thrown on it. The armchair and the chair I sat on. One of those tin trays on collapsible legs that come in handy if someone is bedridden, or to take on picnics. There were a paper plate and an emptied foil carton on the tray, both smeared with the remains of takeaway food, Chinese, by the look of the dried rice grains welded to the surface. A battered tin fork didn't looks as if it'd been washed through several meals. This place was the pits and I couldn't think what made her sit here, patiently waiting. For what?

'Is it for the money?' I asked the obvious first. 'Doesn't your father give you enough of that without you have to try to cheat him out of more?'

Her face thinned with tension. She snapped, 'He's not my father. He's my stepfather. There's a world of difference.'

'But you've taken his name.'

'I got given it whether I wanted it or not. He adopted me after he married my mother. He didn't do that because he wanted me or loved me. He did that because it gave him a hold over Mummy.'

I said carefully, 'I've met Vincent Szabo. It seems he knew my father when they were kids.'

Surprise flashed into her eyes, which mirrored the mental gymnastics within as she adjusted to the new facts. She got them sorted out and filed away.

'Nice,' she said rudely, adding, 'What did you think of him, my *stepdaddy*, when you met him?'

I considered my reply. I recalled the little man in his too-big clothes, sitting in his outsize car, driven by a hulking chauffeur. It had been like watching a child trying on grown-up clothes in play, shuffling perilously in overlarge shoes while lugging a parent's briefcase along with both hands. Yet it would be foolish to dismiss such a successful man as a mere player. Whatever else he might be, he wasn't that. There was something about the little man that made on cautious. The truth was, I hadn't known, and still didn't, what to make of Szabo. All I could remember was his pain at the thought of the torments he had imagined his daughter was suffering at this very moment. That same daughter, however, would appear to be cruelly indifferent to his feelings.

I said cautiously, 'He's really distressed about all this,

Lauren. He's imagining all sorts. He thinks you're terrified, starved, locked in a cupboard or something. Even dead.'

'Good,' she said viciously. 'Let him sweat.'

'Why?' I asked her simply.

She took her hands from the moquette arms of the chair and rested them on her thighs. 'What you've got to know about Vinnie Szabo,' she said, 'is that he's just an old-fashioned wife beater. A plausible and clever one when it came to covering up the evidence. But a nasty, cruel, sadistic little monster all the same.'

'The women's refuge!' It suddenly dawned on me. 'That's why you helped out there.'

'Sure. Mummy and I even lived there for a couple of weeks when I was eight. She ran away and came down to London because she thought he wouldn't find us. But you don't shake off Vincent Szabo that easily. He tracked us down and persuaded Mummy to come home with him. He promised he was going to change, all that sort of crap. He didn't. He was OK for about a month and then it started again. It's a sex thing with him, you see. He can't do it unless he beats the woman around first. It gives him a thrill, gets him going.'

'Did he hit you too?' I asked.

She shook her head, long hair falling around her face. She raised her right hand to push it back and when she let the hand fall again, it rested between her thigh and the side of the chair.

'He knew that would be the one thing Mummy wouldn't put up with. He didn't need to hit me, though. He could use me to frighten Mummy in quite a different way. He was paying for expensive schools, for ballet lessons, piano lessons. He bought me a pony. We had a nice big comfortable house. All he had to say to Mummy was that if she left and took me, I'd be the loser because I'd lose all that. My mother wanted the best for me and he'd persuaded her all those things added up to the best. That a house full of violence and fear went with them didn't make them seem less desirable.'

Aggressively, Lauren added, 'Don't get my mother wrong! She didn't want material advantages for herself, she wanted them for me. She'd been at a really low point when she met him. She'd lost everything and she was desperate. She'd even feared she might have to put me into care. He appeared like the answer to a prayer and he'd seemed all right. Not one to set the world on fire, but a nice man who'd offer a comfortable home and security to us both.

'She couldn't have been more wrong. He wasn't a nice man. There was no security – not from fear. Only the comfortable home was real. She clung to it, salvaging it, if you like, from the wreck of her dreams.'

Lauren's gaze had grown absent, staring back into memory. 'I tried to tell her that all I wanted was to see her free of him and happy. But she only told me I didn't understand how important it was for me to be well educated, to move in good company, make nice friends, meet nice boys. She was trying to make the best of a bad job. If I got something out of the whole rotten deal, then at least she hadn't failed completely.'

She sniffed in derision. 'Those nice boys and their nice

parents would've run a mile if they'd known the truth. Mummy wasn't a fool but she was a sick woman and she worried about the future. She knew she was going to die and leave me. If she left me with Vinnie at least I'd be comfortable. "I'm not going to make old bones, Lauren," was how she put it.'

I ventured to interrupt: 'But she did run away at least once.'

'Yes. At the bottom of her heart she knew she ought to get out. She was confused, I suppose. She got into a situation which was bad but she didn't know how to change it. Vinnie had got the upper hand. She was sort of conditioned to accept whatever he dealt out. I can't explain it. It happens. It happens all the time.'

'I understand, believe it or not,' I said. 'But after your mother died, you could have left Szabo's house.'

She gave an odd tight little smile. 'Sure I could. I could have walked out and let Vinnie get away with it. Get away with all those years of misery my mother suffered. Well, I'd long ago made up my mind he wasn't going to do that! I'd make him pay somehow. I wasn't sure how, but I knew I'd do it one day. So I stayed around and watched for an opportunity.'

She shrugged. 'The funny thing is, I think that after Mummy died, Vinnie began to be scared of me. I definitely have the edge over him in our relationship. Perhaps he's got a guilty conscience over Mummy. I started doing voluntary work at the hostel, just to let him know I hadn't forgotten. I didn't need to say anything. All I had to do was keep going to that hostel, rubbing his nose in it. He hated it but he couldn't stop me. He's frightened to let me go and frightened of me when I stay. I think the roles have got reversed somehow. He can't do without me, even though he's on hot coals all the time I'm around.' She gave an unexpected giggle.

'What about Copperfield?' I asked, puncturing her self-congratulation.

'What about him?' She raised her eyebrows and stared straight at me. 'He's Vinnie's stooge. I played along, but you don't think for a minute I've ever seriously considered marrying Jeremy, do you?'

'I had my doubts,' I confessed. 'All right, suppose you tell me about the kidnap.'

'It wasn't my idea,' she said quickly. 'It's – it was – a real kidnap. Those two dumbclucks Merv and Baz thought it up. Baz works as a motorcycle messenger. Jeremy's business uses him. Baz saw me at Jeremy's office and I suppose he worked out, wrongly, that we were engaged. He nosed around and found out a bit more about me.'

I couldn't help interrupting at this point to remark that Baz seemed to like prowling around finding out about people. Lauren looked mildly puzzled so I explained that Baz had made a habit of hanging about outside my flat in the middle of the night. 'He's dangerous,' I said. 'He's not just hired muscle like Merv. Something else makes him tick.'

'He's a weirdo,' she said, as if that explained everything. 'They lurk about,' she continued, kindly explaining the nature of the animal to me. 'They get a kick out of the daftest things.' She tapped her forehead. 'It's all in here.

Not that he's shown any interest in me.' She paused to survey me with a critical eye. 'I wonder why he took a fancy to you.'

I told her I appreciated the plain speaking and had no more idea than she did why Baz had taken an interest in me. She should think herself lucky he hadn't taken an interest in *her*. 'And please,' I begged, 'don't say I must be his type.'

Lauren wasn't really interested in Baz's sexual preferences. 'Does it matter?' She shrugged before briskly getting on with her story. 'He decided there was easy money to be got. So he and Merv hatched their little plan. They grabbed me off the street by St Agatha's church!' She started getting worked up as the insult of the snatch was relived in her mind. 'They doped me and brought me here, the bastards.'

'Yes, they're good at snatching people,' I said. 'I know. But at what point did the rules of the game change?'

'When they started talking money, boasting what they'd do when they got the paltry thousand or two they hoped to make.' Lauren's eyes opened wide. 'God, they hadn't a clue. They had no idea how much real money they could make out of this. They thought if they got enough –' here Lauren's voice changed, mimicking the two men's speech – '"*to buy a flash motor, some new gear, pull a few birds* –"' she resumed her normal tones and finished – 'and drink themselves senseless too, I suppose. Well, that was it. That was living it up! Talk about pathetic. I said, "Look, fellers, we can play it your way. You keep me here against my will, which I guarantee will be a lot of hard work and cut into your drinking time, and if you're lucky you get a minuscule payoff at the end of it all. Or we all work together. You don't have to guard me because I'll stay put. We ask for a hell of a lot more, and we split it three ways." I worked out just how much I thought we could sting Vinnie for. You should've seen their faces, Merv's and the other one's. They were awe-struck. They stood here in this room, staring at me as if I was a holy vision, dispensing salvation. After that, it was easy. They did everything I suggested. They're simple souls.'

'Just in case you're under the impression,' I said coldly, 'I am not a simple soul.'

She leaned forward. 'I know that! Look, my share of the money will go to the women's refuge. They need the cash and I'll make it an anonymous donation, once Vinnie's paid up. You see why you mustn't rock the boat. Vinnie's got the money. He's got it piled up in offshore investment companies, numbered Swiss accounts, you name it.'

I looked at her while I thought about it. If all she'd told me was true, and I guessed it was, then Szabo certainly ought to pay up. I oughtn't to feel pity for him. But I still felt uneasy. I think it was Lauren herself, her intensity and the deep hatred she nursed for the man. It had been eating away at her for years, and somehow I didn't think this one act of vengeance would appease it. I began to wonder if she wasn't just a bit unhinged on this point. She certainly seemed focused on her immediate revenge to the exclusion of all else.

I began, 'Supposing it had worked, this scheme of yours—'

'It will work,' she interrupted. 'If you don't screw it up!'

'All right, let's assume it all goes according to your plans. What then?'

She goggled at me and then snapped, 'What do you mean, what then?'

I was right. She hadn't thought any of it through. 'What do you do next?' I asked. 'Do you just go home?'

She shrugged. 'It doesn't matter what I do next.'

'Of course it does!' I argued. 'Are you going to feel better about Szabo when this is over? Will you be ready to call it quits?'

She stared at me, her face showing something of the hatred infesting her. 'Call it quits? Are you out of your mind? Of course I'll never forgive him!'

'I didn't say forgive,' I pointed out. 'I wouldn't expect that. But are you going to just go on trying to get even with him, for years and years, the rest of your life? Because if you do, you're letting him win. You're throwing your life away worrying about Vincent Szabo. That doesn't seem very clever to me.'

She explained pithily that my opinion was of no value where she was concerned. She wasn't doing it for herself, she was doing it for her mother.

'Your mother's dead, Lauren. She went through all those years of hell for one reason – so that you could have what she saw as opportunity. You're throwing away all her sacrifice, aren't you?'

'Shut up!' she said in a low, cold voice.

I tried another tack. I told her how my mother had walked

out on us when I was seven. It still hurt if I thought about it. So I'd learned not to think about it. 'You've got to put it behind you,' I argue, 'or you'll go nowhere.'

She told me to stop preaching. Right, I would. What did I care whether she messed up the rest of her life? Besides, who was I to tell people how to live? My life hadn't been a spectacular success to date. But at least I wasn't carrying the burden of old resentments around with me. I'd be kidding myself if I pretended I wasn't carrying any left-over baggage from the past. We all do that to some extent or other. But I was doing my level best not to let it screw up my future.

It occurred to me that she'd succeeded, through the intensity of this single obsession of hers, in excluding everything but herself from the situation. She'd even hijacked me into addressing her personal problems. It meant there was something I'd been in danger of forgetting, and which she was overlooking completely. I wasn't there just because of her. There was someone else and I was his advocate. If he didn't speak through me, he had no voice.

'What about Albie?' I asked.

My question appeared to puzzle her. Her face went blank and then her eyebrows rose. 'Who's he?'

'He's the down-and-out who saw you snatched. Only he's dead now, which is convenient. The one and only witness.'

She looked at me as if I were mad. 'There wasn't anyone to see. The street was empty.'

I told her Albie had been in the church porch.

She thought about it, shrugged and dismissed it. 'I didn't

see anyone. I don't know anything about him. Does it matter? I mean, if he's dead now?'

I lost my temper. 'Matter? Of course it matters! If he's dead, it's because of you, because of what he saw!'

Her features tightened again. She was a pretty girl but when she looked like that, she appeared shrewish. She was wearing jeans, a pullover and a jeans jacket, basically the same gear she'd been wearing the night Albie saw her grabbed off the street. Missing was the Alice band.

The accusation in my voice made her restless. She blurted out, 'Look, I'm sorry if he's dead, and if what you say is true. But I don't know that it is true, and I don't know a damn thing about any old drunk!'

'You didn't send Merv and Baz out to take care of him, by any chance?' I asked. I was so angry with her by now, I was ready to accuse her of anything.

'Of course I bloody didn't!' she shouted. She leaned forward in the chair in emotion but fell back again into place immediately.

'Right!' I snapped. 'Out of that chair, now!'

She stayed put, pushing herself right back into the well of the chair and grabbing the arms defensively. 'Why?'

'Because I say so!' I dived at her and grabbed her.

We were about evenly matched in build but she'd never had to take care of herself physically as I had. She was no street-fighter. I got her out of the chair and down on the floor, and planted a boot on her neck.

'Let me go!' she gurgled, threshing about. She seized my leg but pressure on her throat soon changed her mind.

'All I want to see,' I said, 'is what's hidden in this chair that you're so keen I don't find.'

Well, would you know? It was a mobile phone, pushed down between the cushioned seat and the arm. I picked it up and waved it at her.

'Control line to your heavies?'

She spluttered and swore at me from the floor. I pulled out the aerial and punched in 999.

Lauren twisted beneath my foot and threw me off balance. I staggered and fell backwards into the armchair. She launched herself at me and I kicked out. She stumbled and landed on her backside on the floor. Her eyes blazed through the tumbled mess of her long fair hair. If she could have done it, she'd have torn me limb from limb. I jumped out of the chair and got clear of her.

I was through to the operator. I asked for the police, but as soon as I was connected Lauren took advantage of my momentary distraction and threw herself at me, screeching, 'No!'

We were by the tin table and her wild lunge tipped it over. The paper plate fell on the floor and with it, the fork. I snatched it up a split second before she did and darted back with it held out ready to jab her.

'This is about the Szabo kidnapping!' I panted into the phone. 'I'm Fran Varady and I've found Lauren Szabo. We're in an empty office block.'

Hell's teeth, I didn't know where the block was! I scurried to the window at the end of the room, still holding the fork as a weapon, and keeping my eye on Lauren, who stood, panting and waiting her chance. I took the briefest possible glance out of the window.

What I saw gave me a shock. A road, railings, bushes and – the canal. My God, I thought, I ran past this place the night Baz chased me on his bike. Perhaps Lauren had even been standing here at this window, in a darkened room, watching me run for my life. Any lingering feeling I might have had that she and I were basically on the same side was scotched by the thought.

'It's a disused warehouse opposite the Grand Union Canal. Converted into offices inside but Victorian-looking outside. It's about two or three blocks from—'

Lauren flew at me screaming like a banshee. She struck the fork from my hand and grabbed at the phone. I was forced to release the mobile. It shot up in the air, crashed through the window pane and disappeared down into the street below.

We glared at each other.

'You stupid bitch!' Lauren hissed. Her face was twisted in anger and all her prettiness vanished. 'You've spoiled everything!'

'You should've left Albie alone!' I riposted. 'I don't give a tinker's cuss about Szabo, or you, come to that. But someone has to care about Albie and it seems it has to be me.'

'I don't know anything about your blasted Albie!' she yelled. 'You keep yammering on about him but I don't give a damn, whoever he is! All I know is I'm getting out of here! Hand over that key!' She held out her hand. 'If you don't,' she added nastily, 'you're holding me against my will.'

She had brass neck, give her that. But she had convinced

me she really didn't know about Albie. Perhaps the two men had taken care of that little business all by themselves. I scrabbled in my bra for the key and handed it to her in silence.

She grabbed it with smirk of triumph and made for the door. But as she turned the key in the lock, I asked, 'Where are you going, Lauren? You don't have anywhere to go. The police have kept all this quiet until now because you were presumed an innocent victim of kidnap. Now they'll go public, pull out all the stops looking for you. Your face will be flashed on the nation's television screens. How long do you think you can last out there?' I indicated the window. 'Someone will recognise you and turn you in within twenty-four hours. I dare say there'll be a reward.'

She froze, then turned back to face me and I had to give her credit for nimbleness of mind. 'Right,' she said. 'You're right. So I'll stay here and when the police get here, it'll be my word against yours. All I need to say is, you found the key on the outside of the door. I was locked in here.'

'Don't be too sure of yourself,' I snapped. 'Not only will I tell them the key was on the inside and you were free to walk out, but Merv and Baz, when they pick them up – which they will do – will say the same.'

'They can say what they like.' She smiled at me serenely. 'So can you. Tell them about the key, it doesn't matter. You forget, I know about victims conspiring with their tormentors in their own oppression. Vinnie showed me how it was done, with Mummy. Anyway, it's a classic hostage situation. Stockholm syndrome. The prisoner ends up doing voluntarily whatever the captor wants, even to outright helping, in a weird partnership. As for me, I'll claim I was too scared to try to escape, and later, too brain-washed to try anything independent.'

Crazy as it seemed, I wasn't sure she couldn't make that work for her. She was clever, manipulative, and I was certain she'd prove no mean actress. No one would take Merv's word, or Baz's. Parry might take mine, but in a witness box, a clever lawyer would destroy my credibility with the jury in minutes. It was all so neat and credible, except for one thing – something we'd both overlooked.

Merv and Baz. That's what couldn't be made to make sense. They didn't have an original thought between them. Look how easily they'd been swayed by Lauren's arguments and had handed over all the advantages so meekly to her, putting themselves under her control. Could that pair really have worked out the original kidnap plan? Just to abandon it? Why had they been expecting so little money from the deal? Was it because they were not in charge of the haggling? Not prime movers, in fact, but mere hired heavies?

It was so obvious, I almost smiled. They had been paid cash to seize and hold Lauren. They had not been intended to share in any ransom. Not until Lauren came up with her own deal. Yes, that made a lot more sense.

'Lauren,' I said, 'it's not going to be that easy.'

'Oh, why?' she sneered.

I explained briefly how I reasoned it. 'You thought you were running things because the only people you saw were Merv and Baz, and you had that pair of lowlifes eating out of your hand. But if you think it through, there has to be someone else behind all this.'

She began to look uncertain. I pressed home my argument.

'For goodness' sake, Lauren! The only thing you can be sure about with Merv and Baz is that they're foot soldiers. They take orders from people they perceive as having brains. They even took orders from you. The one thing that motivates them is the thought of money. When they snatched you, they were following the orders of someone who planned it. That person was paying them what looked like a lot to them at the time. It was a flat rate for their services, not a cut of the ransom money. You said yourself, they had no idea how high a ransom could be asked.

'But when you offered them a three-way split in a new deal, they decided to double-cross whoever was employing them. Whoever masterminded the kidnap still thinks they have you tied up here with a bag over your head. Because the organiser daren't risk coming here himself to check. It's far too dangerous. He has to accept Merv or Baz's reports. Merv says you're a prisoner here and Mr Unknown can only accept it.'

Lauren's confidence was evaporating visibly as I spoke. 'But who could it be?' she asked.

'How about Copperfield?' I suggested. 'He owes money to the banks.'

She shook her head vehemently. 'Forget it. No way is Jeremy behind this. He's terrified of blotting his copybook again. He had some trouble a couple of years ago when he got involved in some dodgy deals. He got off with a suspended sentence but it scared the wits out of him. He wants to continue in the art and antiques business. He can't afford any more damage to his reputation. He wouldn't touch anything crooked. He breaks out in a sweat whenever he sees a police uniform. Anyway,' she concluded firmly, 'not only hasn't he got the nerve to organise anything like this, he hasn't got the brains. It has to be someone else.'

Before I could answer, the sound of approaching motor vehicles became audible. We both hurried to peer out of the window.

'The police have found us already!' Lauren exclaimed disbelievingly.

I wish she'd been right. But it wasn't the police. It was a private car, one I didn't recognise, and following it an old van.

Both vehicles stopped. The van doors opened and Merv and Baz jumped down into the street. They went to the driver's side of the car. At their approach, the window was wound down. Then two men stooped and put their heads close to it. An animated conversation began.

'What are they all talking about?' Lauren whispered, and for the first time she seemed scared.

'Your pals are getting their final orders,' I said. Merv and Baz were still huddled over the car window. 'Getting the details right.'

'What do you mean?' Now she'd lost all her self-assurance. She looked at me helplessly.

'Triple-cross,' I explained. 'Now they're double-crossing you, Lauren. You had them seeing pound signs with your offer, but it's all getting too complicated and they can't handle it themselves. Suddenly a flat payment and no strings looks awfully attractive to them. Let someone else sweat over extorting a ransom, arranging the drop and all the rest of it. It's way out of their league. Maybe it's just occurred to them that, even if they did get their hands on a really large sum of money, they'd have no way of laundering it. Word would get round in hours and reach the police.'

She blinked at me. 'How?' she argued, but without her former spirit.

This was not the time for me to give her a detailed rundown on the criminal world. I said irritably, 'It's called informing, Lauren, in case you haven't heard of it. Merv and Baz know that if they show up with more than the average windfall in used notes, someone will grass. So they've gone to their original employer with a highly edited version of recent events. They're ditching you and your grand scheme, and taking orders from their former boss.'

Lauren was staring down in morbid fascination at the car below and the huddled figures. She put a finger to her mouth and chewed nervously at the nail.

'Down there?' she mumbled. 'He's really down there in that car?'

'You bet he is!' I told her heartlessly. 'He's been under the impression he's been giving them orders all along, of course! But now he's smelled a rat, or in this case, two rats. He's not sure how far he can trust them any longer. He's down there, in that car, come to see for himself what's going on here and to make sure Merv and Baz do the job they've been sent to do.'

'What's that?' she faltered.

There was no point in hiding the truth from her. 'This whole thing's got in such a mess, I don't think any of them can let either of us leave here alive,' I said. 'They've come here on a damage-limitation exercise. Remember, they all think I'm locked in a room on the floor below. The big chief thinks you're locked up here. None of them has any way of knowing I've called the police.

'The man in the car is badly rattled by being told he's now got two prisoners, but he still believes he can shake the money out of Szabo. He doesn't realise that his two henchmen have tried to cut a deal with you and –' I allowed myself a nasty smile – 'provided you and he never meet face to face, there's no reason he'll find out. So Merv and Baz will make sure you never do meet him.

'From Mr Unknown's point of view, you and I are just too much of a nuisance. All three of them, for different reasons, want us permanently out of the way. On that they're well agreed.'

Merv and Baz straightened up and began to walk towards the building where we were. Lauren gripped my arm.

'But who is he?' she whispered desperately. 'He can't just order them to kill us!'

'Why not? They killed Albie.'

Below us, without warning, the car door opened. There was a flash of long blonde hair as the driver leaned out and called to Merv and Baz. They went back to the car and there was another brief exchange. The two men eventually nodded and started off again towards the building. The driver got out of the car and stood by the door, watching them go.

'There you are,' I said. 'Not a he but a she after all.'

Beside me, Lauren gasped, 'That's Jane Stratton, Jeremy's receptionist.'

Chapter Sixteen

Recognising Jane Stratton effectively disposed of Lauren's temporary nervousness. In a flash she was back to her old dictatorial self.

'Bitch!' she yelled at the window panes. 'Wait till I get my hands on you!'

'You're not going to get the chance,' I reminded her crisply. 'Because the way things are going, Merv and Baz'll reach us first if we don't get out of here! Baz, for one, will be looking forward to it! Come on!'

I made for the door, but she stayed by the window. Would you believe it? She was still intent on yelling abuse at the blissfully unaware Ice Queen below. I ran back to her, glancing out to see how things were going below. Stratton stood elegantly by her motor, waiting for her two thugs to return and report they'd dealt with us.

'She can't hear you, you idiot!' I snarled and grabbed Lauren's wrist. I could've left her there, but I'd come this far in finding her, and losing her now made little sense. I hauled her away from the scene, with me through the door and down the corridor.

She was still spluttering with rage as she ran, obsessed,

even at a moment like this, with the wrongs done her.

'Would you believe it? I should've known – I should've guessed! She fancied her chances with Jeremy before I came on the scene, you know. She thought she'd be Mrs Copperfield, heaven help us! Not that she had the hots for him – but she always thought she could run that business better than he could . . .'

We'd reached the end of the corridor and the stairwell. From the floor below came a hoarse yell and a burst of profanity as Merv and Baz discovered I wasn't where they'd left me. Baz sounded particularly enraged, cheated of whatever fun he'd promised himself. I needed no further encouragement to make myself scarce. We couldn't go down so we had to go up. Stairs indicated another floor and we took them.

'He dumped her for me because he thought he could get his hands on Szabo money!' Lauren panted as she pounded up the staircase beside me. 'So I suppose she thought she'd get her own back on him *and* get her own hands on Szabo money—'

'Will you shut up for a minute!' I gasped as we stumbled out on to the next landing. 'Just concentrate on finding somewhere to hide!'

Fat chance, was what was I was thinking. This floor mirrored the ones below, a corridor of stripped rabbit hutches. It offered no hiding place safe from the vengeful Merv and Baz who, from the sound of it, had reached the floor we'd just quit and any minute now, would find that Lauren was also missing.

A painted sign on the wall read 'FIRE EXIT' and an

arrow pointed upwards. This staircase was unlike the others, narrow and dimly lit. It was Hobson's choice. I raced up it, Lauren on my heels.

At the top our way was barred by a steel emergency door. 'Give me a hand!' I gasped.

We wrestled with the bar and managed to release it. The door scraped open outwards and a blast of fresh air hit us as we stumbled through to find ourselves on the roof.

I hadn't realised, until we came out into the open, how late it had got. The daylight was fading fast and a grey pall hung over the skyline. The roof itself was flat, with a surrounding waist-high parapet. We'd exited through a square concrete hut-like affair. It was the only thing up here apart from a similar locked hut which was probably the housing for the immobilised lift machinery. Dotted around were some metal hoods crowning ventilation shafts. In the gloom, they looked eerily like giant mushrooms. The wind gusted around freely up here and it was very cold. There had to be a way down. It wasn't a fire exit otherwise.

I raced round the parapet and finally spotted a short flight of metal rungs running up the inside of the low wall to a pair of hooped handgrips bolted to the rim. I looked over.

The malicious wind grabbed my hair and blew it across my face. The world swam unpleasantly from side to side. I shut my eyes and opened them again. Over the parapet was a straightforward metal rung ladder leading down to the floor below. An encircling metal cage offered the escapee some protection from falling as he/she climbed out on to the ladder and negotiated the top rungs. The cage looked anything but reliable. Its effect would be purely psychological. The lower rungs lacked even this nominal safety device. The ladder terminated at a metal platform opposite a window on the floor below. From there on downwards there was an iron staircase, running in sections from floor to floor, window landing to window landing, to touch down in a deserted shadowy alley at the side of the building.

I felt sick at the thought of clambering down there, but sicker still at the idea of falling into Baz's hands. The bolts fastening the top of the ladder to the parapet had leached orange stain into the concrete, but when I shook the handgrips they seemed firm enough. We had to chance it. I showed it to Lauren.

'Shit,' she said. 'I'm not going down there.'

'Please yourself,' I told her. I was more than fed up with her by now. 'Stay here and let Merv throw you over the edge, why don't you?'

'I might just as well,' she retorted. 'Look,' she pointed at the cage, 'if a cat climbed out on to that rickety old thing the whole lot would fall off the wall.'

'That's dodgy, but the ladder's OK. All you've got to do is climb down to that platform, see? From there on down it's a proper iron staircase.'

'I don't much like the look of that either,' she grumbled.

Nor did I, to be honest, and the longer I stood here arguing with her, the less I liked it. It was either climb down there now, straight away, or lose my nerve.

I grabbed the handles, fixed my eyes resolutely on the

concrete wall and climbed over. My toes felt for the rungs. They were thin and insubstantial and my feet teetered on them, seesawing as I attempted to find balance. The wind whipped past me fiercer and even colder than up on the roof. It took my breath away, snatching it from my nostrils and mouth. I had a terrible sensation of being suspended in space and for a split second I froze, unable to move at all. I didn't want to look down, but I couldn't avoid looking sideways.

I wished I hadn't. What I saw made things worse. There in the gap, where the alley met the road, was Jane Stratton, pacing up and down in the twilight beneath a flickering streetlamp. She kept looking at her wristwatch, perhaps wondering why her two goons were taking so long. If she looked down the alley and up, it was likely that even in the poor light, she'd see me clinging to the side of the building.

'Sst!' That was Lauren. I looked up and she was leaning over, glaring at me. 'Well, go on, then,' she said. 'I can't climb down till you get going.'

I managed to avoid pointing out she'd only just said she wasn't going to try. Instead I told her I could see Jane Stratton.

'So we'll have to keep it as quiet as possible!' I warned, hoping I could count on her to control her desire to shout insults. I wouldn't put it past her.

I left her to make up her mind and got my feet moving, creeping downwards. My heart was pounding, I felt sick, and my hands sweated, but somehow my foot touched the landing at last.

The ladder quivered and creaked ominously. Lauren was scrambling down. She managed pretty well. That girl just liked making the maximum fuss.

'Now what?' she said, as she joined me.

'We carry on down,' I said. 'And do shut up and try not to make the metal treads rattle. The Stratton woman will hear us.'

Jane had her back to the alley at the moment, which was all to the good. This slight plus was immediately wiped out by the sound of voices from above. Merv and Baz had found their way out on to the roof.

They would certainly see the top of the fire escape ladder and take a look over the parapet. I made a quick inspection of the window alongside the landing, but it only opened from the inside.

'For God's sake, get going!' Lauren poked me painfully in the back. 'Why're you hesitating?'

With Lauren so close behind me that she threatened to dislodge me and send me plummeting down, I began to descent of the metal stair to the landing below.

We reached that all right but then such luck as we'd had ran out. What hadn't been discernible in the dull light was that a complete section of the next staircase down was missing, about four treads in all, leaving a space too big to bridge with an outstretched leg.

'We'll have to let ourselves drop down,' I said. 'From here, down through the gap to the landing below.'

'You first,' she said, running true to form. Somehow, even if we succeeded in getting out of this, I was never going to be able to take a shine to this girl.

I lowered myself to the landing and sat there with my legs dangling through the hole left by the missing treads as I tried to judge it. The absence of good light made it tricky. The gap seemed to fluctuate in width and the metal platform below alternatively rose towards me and fell away. I couldn't see what kind of condition it was in, and what worried me most – always supposing I didn't fall off the side of the platform when I hit it – was that the sudden impact of my weight on a long-unmaintained structure might be enough to shake the whole thing loose.

The exercise would, moreover, make a heck of a noise and was likely to attract attention.

I glanced over my shoulder towards the spot where the alley below debouched into the road, looking for Jane Stratton. She was still there, wandering up and down in a fidgety manner. Her blonde hair gleaming in the lamplight, she suggested a sort of latter-day Lili Marlene. But then I saw something very odd.

Without warning she turned and ran past the alley entrance in an attitude of complete panic, blonde mane flying.

Seconds later an engine roared and headlights swept the street. Her car lurched past but the moment it went out of sight, there was a screech of brakes, then more engine noise and more protesting metal. Something had caused her get out of her car again, because she reappeared, racing back towards the building. Hard on her stiletto heels came several uniformed figures, pounding along on their size twelves.

'We haven't got to jump it,' I told Lauren in relief. 'The

police are here. Thank God for that!'

And it's not often you hear me say that when the boys in blue pop into view.

'About time too,' she grumbled, always the happy little soul.

From our windswept perch where we crouched like a pair of dispossessed eagles, we watched figures scurry back and forth. Two brawny uniformed figures emerged, holding Baz between them. He glanced back and up as they shoved him into the police van, and even at that distance and in twilight, I felt the stare of those bulbous dark eyes.

'They've got Baz,' I said to Lauren, unable to disguise the relief in my voice. 'I hope they put him away for a long time.'

I didn't add that if they failed to do that, and the law does funny things sometimes, I would have to quit the flat. Probably quit the country. I fully expected to see two more coppers frogmarching Merv away in similar fashion, but although there seemed to be a good deal of activity within the building, no one came out for several minutes. Then a movement caught my eye in the dusk away to my right. Here the wall around the building's rear yard bordered the alley. To my surprise, a man had appeared, perched astride the top with one leg dangling down on the alley side, the other still on the yard side. Even as I watched in dismay, he completed the movement he'd begun, slipping over the wall and dropping down into the alley.

'Hey,' I yelled desperately. 'Hey! Stop him!' I rattled the nearest iron stanchion in an attempt to attract attention. 'Hey, you lot in there, he's getting away!'

'What do you think you're doing?' Lauren's fingers gripped my arm like a vice. 'Leave it alone, look, the bolts are coming out of the brickwork! Are you crazy or something?'

'Merv!' I gasped, pointing.

She released me and peered in the direction I indicated. He hadn't run down the alley, but crossed it to the buildings on the other side and we were just in time to see him squeeze his bulk into a narrow gap between them. Rats know their bolt-holes and Merv had found his.

I cursed fruitlessly while Lauren wittered about the danger I had put us in by shaking the rickety stair.

'It's all right, we don't have to stay here now!' I snapped back in exasperation. 'We can go on back up.'

'I can't,' she objected. 'It was bad enough coming down that wretched rung affair. Now you've loosened it even more. It's got too dark now and I can't see.'

'We haven't got any choice!' I yelled at her. 'Start climbing!'

'Don't shout at me!' she snapped, hoity-toity.

'Shout at you? If you don't watch it, I'll push you off!' I bellowed.

'Oy! You down there!' a male voice shouted from above.

Torchlight bathed us. We looked up. A familiar head had appeared over the parapet, festooned with hair that looked colourless in the torchbeam and a mangy moustache.

'For Gawd's sake, Fran,' Parry called. 'How did you get down there?'

If it'd been only me stuck down there they'd have told me

to start climbing. But then they realised the kidnapped Szabo heiress, as they probably thought of her, was with me. They started talking about sending for the fire brigade and a turntable ladder.

I'd no intention of sitting there for another fifteen minutes waiting for Captain Flack. I told Lauren she could wait on her own. I was climbing back up the ladder.

'I'm not staying here on my own,' she snivelled. With that, she shoved me out of the way and shinned up the ladder like the boy in the Indian rope trick. Metropolitan Police arms lifted her the last part of the way and over the parapet to safety.

Then they all disappeared, taking their torches with them, leaving me to struggle up the vertical rungs in semi-darkness, under my own steam.

'Oy!' I called up. 'What about me?'

Parry reappeared. He handed the torch to a uniformed man who directed it at me in a haphazard way as I crawled upwards. Parry seized my arms and dragged me unceremoniously the last few inches over the concrete wall.

'You've let Merv get away!' I gasped as my feet touched the flat roof. 'He ran over there, between those buildings!' I pointed out the crack into which Merv had scurried, hardly visible now in the dusk.

Parry swore, abandoned me and went to yell instructions to others. Reaction had set in. My legs began to quiver and nausea swept over me. I sat down on the roof with my back against the parapet and rested my head on my bent knees.

A few minutes later heavy footsteps crunched towards

me. 'All right, there, Fran? Not going to throw up, are you?'

I looked up into Parry's face, looming over me. 'No, I'll be fine,' I managed to say weakly. 'How did you manage to lose him?'

'He must have got down into the basement here and hid up among the pipes. Slipped out behind our backs, but we'll pick him, don't worry.' He dropped on to his heels before me and went on. 'By the way, your Jock boyfriend rang us up, the artist. He said he thought you'd been kidnapped.'

'I was kidnapped,' I told him. 'I've been tied up, hooded, driven around, dumped in a locked room . . .'

'Well, you're all right now,' he interrupted. 'No harm done, eh? You've even got your clothes on.'

Not for the first time, Parry's reasoning eluded me. As it stood, his remark sounded highly insulting but at least it cured my temporary weakness. 'Clothes?' I snarled. 'Why not?'

'Rabbie Burns said he found your costume on the floor. He thought you might be in your frillies.' He grinned. 'Oh well, next time, eh?'

'Just turn it in, will you?' I groaned. 'I've suffered enough.'

He frowned at me. 'Yeah. Someone smash your face again?'

I'd forgotten the blood smears. 'I hit a door,' I said, 'climbing through a transom window.'

'Sounds like you,' he said. 'You don't ever learn, do you?'

I looked over his shoulder to where a sympathetic group was still gathered around Lauren. They were dispensing TLC by the bucketful and I wondered why no one, not even Parry, ever gave me so much as a reassuring pat on the shoulder.

'About her,' I said. 'About Lauren Szabo. There are one or two things you ought to know . . .'

Lauren looked up at that point and saw me and Parry huddled together by the parapet. She met my eye, swayed, and crumpled realistically to the ground in a dead faint.

Immediate pandemonium, of course, and summoning of an ambulance with paramedics and all the rest of it.

'Poor kid,' said Parry, jumping to his feet. 'Gawd knows what's been happening to her.'

I let it go for the time being. I've seen some stage faints and Lauren's was a good one. But she was going to have to put on a better act than that to get out of this.

Chapter Seventeen

Lauren was borne away in the ambulance for a hospital checkup. I was taken to the nick and asked to make a statement.

An inspector appeared, a thin, pale man. He looked resentful, as though he'd been called in on his day off, probably in the middle of a dinner party, if the smudge of tomato on his tie was anything to go by. If so, he clearly blamed me for his bad luck and incipient indigestion. I had foolishly imagined he – all of them – would be crowding around, vying for the chance to congratulate me and thank me grovellingly for doing their job for them.

Instead I was seated on a hard chair, presented with a mug of tarry tea, and invited to relate my adventures into a tape recorder.

In the less than comfortable surrounds of the interview room, I told them everything. I didn't leave anything out. A policewoman had joined us.The inspector took a packet of indigestion tablets from his pocket and chewed on them. Apart from that, he sighed a few times in an irritable way but he didn't say anything. Even Parry didn't interrupt more than twice. The policewoman began to show signs of restiveness as my account progressed but Parry silenced her with a look. By the time I'd finished, they all looked thoroughly glum and it was dawning on me that far from being the heroine of the hour, I'd upset the police applecart well and truly.

I'd done what they hate most. I'd introduced a whole new aspect to things and it would result in paperwork.

The inspector rose to his feet, put his tube of pastilles in his pocket, dusted himself down and announced that he would leave everything in the hands of the sergeant. He nodded to me as he left but avoided my eyes in a decidedly shifty manner.

With his departure, the atmosphere changed but not for the better. I wondered whether the senior man had left because if anything irregular was going to take place here, he didn't want to know about it. Perhaps he was just hurrying off in hopes of getting back in time for the pudding.

Parry looked up at the fly-speckled neon strip in the ceiling and chewed the ends of his moustache. The policewoman found her voice and asked if I wanted to add to or change anything in my statement. I said no, I didn't, that was it.

'Play the tape back,' Parry ordered.

She played it back. I thought I sounded coherent enough. In fact, all things considered, I thought I sounded pretty good.

'You're sure about all that, then?' Parry asked.

'Sergeant,' I said, 'I am absolutely sure. I will, if necessary, go into a witness box and swear to it.'

They still looked down in the mouth – more so, if anything. They offered me another cup of tea and said, perhaps we could go through it again later?

I was awash with tea by now, tired and just wanted to go home. In considerable bad temper, I told them all this and added that if they would just get the statement typed up, I'd sign it.

The pair of them exchanged glances. The policewoman switched off the tape recorder. Parry leaned forward earnestly.

'Look, Fran,' he said. 'You're making a serious accusation here. For God's sake, unless you're absolutely one hundred per cent sure, tone it down now, before anything's signed. You don't want to go on record with some wild tale you can't back up.'

'The point is,' the policewoman chimed in, 'that you can hardly expect Miss Szabo to support what you've told us about her part in things. You've accused her of plotting to extort money from her own father.'

'I'm not accusing her,' I pointed out. 'She told me.'

The policewoman gave me a gargoyle grimace. 'Was there any witness to this confession of hers?'

'It wasn't a confession. She told me because she was trying to get me on her side. He's her stepfather, incidentally, not her father, and I told you what she told me, about how he used to knock her mother around and she and her mother ran away to the refuge. Actually, you can check all that. The refuge must have records.' I knew I was beginning to sound exasperated but that always happens when I deal with the police.

'We'll check,' Parry said grimly. 'But Szabo's not going to take kindly to this.'

It seemed to me it didn't matter whether Szabo took kindly to it or went into a red rage. If that's the way it had been, then his misdeeds had caught up with him, and he oughtn't to grumble about it. Chickens come home to roost and all the rest of it.

'You're making a lot of trouble for the girl, you know,' said the policewoman accusingly.

'And for us,' said Parry, who had his priorities in strict order with himself first.

I felt the tiniest twinge of compunction. Why drop Lauren in it? Hadn't she and her late mother suffered enough? It wouldn't take much. Hints were being dropped here with resounding thuds. I couldn't ignore them so why not listen?

All I had to do was murmur apologetically that perhaps I'd misunderstood and they'd all be happy. It was what Parry and his steely-eyed female partner here wanted. The dyspeptic DI would be mightily relieved. In Lauren's place, wouldn't I have done as she did? Hadn't she some right to try to make Szabo suffer a little in his turn? I owed him nothing.

But neither, I told my overcharitable conscience, did I owe Lauren anything. If she could have got the better of me in our scrap for the mobile phone, it was unlikely we'd be here now. Come to that, she had known Merv and Baz had locked me in a room on the floor below and hadn't even had the decency to come down and check whether I was still breathing. Self-centred little madam.

She had wanted to play dirty and she had to take the consequences.

Nor was I going to oblige the police, who were playing their own dirty game, pressuring me to change my story while I was tired and shocked. Justice was in danger in slipping out of the window here, just to save everyone inconvenience.

But I had justice firmly by the coat-tails and wasn't letting go. There was another issue, one that mattered an awful lot more to me than anything we'd discussed here so far. I hadn't forgotten how casually Lauren had dismissed Albie's death. I wasn't dismissing it and neither was I going to allow the police to sweep it aside.

'Look,' I said, 'I'm fed up with the entire Szabo family. I've told you all I know and you can sort it out. You've got her back all in one piece. No ransom paid. You can take the credit for all of that. I suppose you'll do that anyway and not think to share any of it with me! But I don't care about that. What concerns me is that we're in danger of forgetting Albie.'

Parry glowered and the policewoman looked vague. She shuffled some papers in the hope of her memory being jogged. That annoyed me more than anything. As I feared, they'd just forgotten the poor old blighter.

'Albert Antony Smith, deceased!' I said loudly. 'The murder victim you fished out of the canal.'

'Alkie Albie?' Parry's sparse ginger eyelashes fluttered in alarm. 'You're not going to accuse Lauren Szabo of sending a couple of killers after a witness?'

'No, not her,' I said wearily. 'Stratton did that. Lauren

Szabo didn't know about Alkie Albie and had no reason to tell the men to get rid of him. Stratton is the efficient type. She'd eliminate any loose ends. You want to know what I think happened?'

Neither of them looked as though they did, but they were going to hear it anyhow. 'I think you told Szabo there was a witness to the kidnap, a homeless man. The witness had spoken to me. Szabo hurried off to find out what I knew. But he also told Copperfield the police were looking for the vagrant, as I expect you called him. Copperfield, in turn, confided in his receptionist. She had probably been holding his hand and making soothing noises during this stressful time, and he'd obligingly kept her up to date on the progress the police were making, or lack of it.'

Parry glowered, but he was on weak ground where setting Szabo on to me was concerned, so he didn't interrupt.

'Mind you,' I added, 'Merv and Baz might have decided off their own bat to eliminate Albie. But for my money, Stratton told them to do it.'

Parry thought it over. 'Leave it with us, Fran,' he said. 'We're not overlooking the old man's death, whatever you think. But we need more to go on than your theories. Right now we can't prove either of the two men was ever in that church porch.'

'They're going to get away with it, aren't they?' I asked, exasperated. 'They killed poor Albie and are going to get clean away with it.'

'Have a bit of faith in us,' coaxed the woman officer.

But I'd lost faith in them. I said, 'I want to go home.'

* * *

They drove me home in a police car. Although by now it was very late, both Daphne and Ganesh were waiting for me. They'd been sitting in Daphne's warm, comfortable kitchen, which smelled strongly of coffee.

They greeted me with relief tinged, on Ganesh's part, with disapprobation.

'If you had told me,' he said, 'that you were going to accept to be a model for that crazy artist, I should have advised you very strongly against it.'

'I know,' I said. 'That's why I didn't tell you.'

I collapsed on to a chair. Daphne took charge.

'Don't scold her now,' she ordered Ganesh. 'She needs some hot food and lots of rest.'

She proceeded to feed me homemade soup and crusty bread, and brewed up a hot toddy to finish it – and me – off.

In between mouthfuls of soup, I told them all about everything, what had happened to me at the community hall, at the office block, on the fire escape, and at the police station.

Daphne clicked her tongue disapprovingly. 'That girl's certainly caused a lot of people a lot of trouble, much of it unnecessary by the sound of it. To think she could simply have walked out of there! If you ask me . . .'

Daphne was fair-minded. She searched for some form of condemnation which would make allowance for Lauren's unhappy childhood and well-intentioned if warped scheme for raising money for the refuge, all of which I'd explained.

'If you ask me,' she concluded, 'that young woman needs straightening out.'

I thought, good luck to anyone rash enough to try.

Ganesh said unexpectedly, 'You can't expect her, Lauren, to be a nice person.'

We stared at him.

'Where would she learn about niceness?' he asked. 'She was a young child when her mother married Szabo. From then on, all she saw was violence and betrayal, not only in her own home, but at the refuge, listening to the stories of the other women there.'

'And yet,' I said unwillingly, because it was hard to speak up on behalf of anyone in this whole business, 'and yet Szabo did seem so fond of her when he talked to me. When he spoke of her being in the hands of criminals, he was nearly in tears.'

'People cry for all sorts of reasons,' was Ganesh's response to this. 'Half the time, they're crying for themselves. How do you know Szabo wasn't just feeling sorry for himself?'

Daphne cleared her throat delicately. 'I've always been fascinated by the story of Elizabeth Barrett,' she said. 'You know, the Barretts of Wimpole Street? She was a poetess and ran away with Robert Browning?'

'I know it,' I said. 'But sorry, Daphne, I don't see the connection. I don't see Lauren lying on a sofa writing verse.'

Daphne leaned forward. 'But there was no need for Elizabeth to lie on her sofa, day in and day out, in Wimpole Street, was there? She wasn't an invalid. Her father had persuaded her that she was, to keep her there. By all accounts he treated his children abominably, yet had he been asked to defend his actions, he would have insisted he'd acted out of love.'

'I don't know these Barretts,' said Ganesh. 'But I do know that when something's really badly wrong in a family, you often find that every member of it swears blind everything is just fine. You read it in the papers every day. Women married to murderers swear the bloke was a perfect husband and father. Families,' added Ganesh with some emotion, 'no one understands them, only the family members.'

This was all getting beyond me. I wasn't in the mood for subtle argument. I'd had a very packed day, and the toddy and the soup combined were making me drowsy. The kitchen was very warm. Exhaustion took over.

'You know,' I mumbled. 'I told Parry no one trusted anyone else in this business. I was right. Even Stratton didn't know her two goons were cutting a separate deal with the kidnap victim.'

'You need to go to bed,' Daphne said firmly. 'A good night's sleep will set you right.'

'Is that the time?' Ganesh looked at his watch and leaped up with a hunted expression. 'I've got to go! Hari will have locked up the place and I'll have to get him out of bed to let me in. I'll never hear the last of it.'

'You can doss down in my place till morning,' I mumbled, 'and go back when he opens the shop.'

'Or I've got a spare bed,' offered Daphne.

'Thanks but no,' he said. 'Hari will've been on the phone to High Wycombe by then. Dad'll be on the first train up to town.'

Let him sort it out. Not for the first time, I appreciated the fact that I had no one. I propped my head in my hands. I knew I ought to go but was too tired to move.

'Don't be depressed, dear,' Daphne said, returning from showing Ganesh out. 'I think you've been a heroine.'

I thanked her, but said I felt a failure. 'All I wanted to do was get justice for Albie. I also wanted to find the missing girl and I did find her. But justice for Albie seems as far away as ever. On top of all that, they've lost Merv.'

Daphne sighed and joined me at the table. 'Things will work out, Fran. Give the police a chance. They've only just got the girl back. They'll go into it all very thoroughly, I'm sure.' With slightly less assurance she added, 'They'll find out the truth about your friend, Albie.'

'Truth is no good without evidence,' I told her. I hauled myself to my feet, because I was going to fall asleep where I sat if I didn't make a move right there and then. I apologised for keeping her and thanked her for the soup.

'Nonsense,' she said. 'I'm just so glad you're safe. You're sure you wouldn't like to sleep here tonight? I can make up a bed in a jiff.'

'Thanks, but I've only got to go down to the basement, after all,' I told her.

She led me down the hall and opened the front door. A blast of cool air swept in, shaking me out of the mist of tiredness. The street was bathed in murky lamplight and empty – no!

It wasn't empty. Coming towards us along the pavement was an extraordinary sight.

Two figures lurched along in a disorganised fashion as

if arguing with one another. The taller one, who urged the other on, I recognised at once as Ganesh. The smaller one, who was protesting and grumbling as he scurried spider-fashion alongside, was invisible beneath a motley assortment of old clothes bound round with string. One of those old-fashioned Balaclava knitted hoods covered his head and in his arms he was clasping some sort of bundle. The pair of them reached the bottom of the steps to Daphne's door.

'Fran!' Ganesh called up excitedly. 'I've found him! I mean, he found me! He was waiting for me at the shop!'

The mobile pile of rags emerged from behind Ganesh into the light flooding down the steps from Daphne's hall.

'Good gracious!' muttered Daphne as a powerful odour enveloped us.

Only one person smelled that bad.

'Jonty!' I cried. 'I – we – thought you were dead!'

'Dead?' He snorted, coughed and wheezed, then spat to one side.

Ganesh leaped back. 'Hey!'

'If I ain't dead,' Jonty croaked, 'it's because I was bloody lucky. I got out, I did. I run like I never run before or since! They was busy nabbing poor old Albie and they hadn't time to grab me. I got away and I've kept away till now.'

He moved up a step, closer to us, still clasping the sack with his assorted possessions. Daphne retreated hastily.

Jonty peered up at me. I hadn't seen his face before. Framed in the filthy knitted hood, it resembled some sort of monkey's, creased in deep lines and sprinkled with grey whiskers. His eyes were small and bloodshot and fixed me with a ferocious expression. Spittle dribbled from his mouth as he spoke and he appeared to have very few teeth.

'Go on, tell her!' urged Ganesh from behind him. 'Tell her why you came back.'

Jonty cast him a look of mixed surprise and disapproval. 'Course I come back, soon as it was safe. He was my mate, was Albie. I couldn't have helped him. I couldn't have done nothing to save him, but I want ter see right done by Albie. By his memory, like.' He took one hand from the bundle and poked a yellowed forefinger at me. 'You're a do-gooder, you are. Well, do a bit of good, then. Go and tell the coppers what I told him!' Jonty jerked his thumb over his shoulder at Ganesh.

'Yes, I know you've told me!' Ganesh said testily. 'But I want you to tell Fran!'

'All right, then.' Jonty cleared his throat again and I waited apprehensively for him to spit. But after taking a brief look round, he seemed to decide this wasn't the place, and just began, 'When you come and found me that night in the porch, I told you, didn't I, I was waiting for old Albie to turn up? Expected him, I did. Sure enough, a bit later he come along. He brought a bottle of whisky. Half-bottle of Bell's it was. He said, he'd seen you two and you wanted to take him along to talk to the police the next day. You wanted him to tell 'em what he saw, about that girl being snatched. He said, he'd fixed to meet the young lady there at Marylebone Station. He said that he –' Jonty's blackened thumbnail hooked towards Ganesh again – 'that feller there worked in that newsagent's, up near the traffic lights, a bit down from that spud caff. So when I reckoned things might've quietened down a bit and those two fellers weren't looking for me no more, that's where I went.'

'He was waiting for me,' said Ganesh. 'In a doorway near the shop. He jumped out as I went past. I couldn't believe my eyes.'

'Jonty,' I whispered, all trace of tiredness gone, 'are you saying you saw the two men take Albie away? That you can remember what they looked like and can identify them?'

'That's what I'm telling you, isn't it?' Jonty was getting irritated at my obtuseness. 'I saw them two blokes. I was there when they grabbed old Albie. One was a big slab of a feller, all pale, pale hair, eyes, like a walkin' stick of lard. The other was a little dark feller wearing one of them leather motorcyclist's jackets. They drove up in an old Cortina. They hadn't reckoned on finding me there too, and they'd have taken me along with Albie, I reckon, only Albie was putting up a good scrap and it took the two of 'em to drag him away. So that's when I scarpered. Remember 'em? I'll never forget 'em.'

I could've kissed him. I didn't because of the smell. But I could've done.

We weren't going to make the mistake with Jonty we'd made with Albie. Now we'd got him, we weren't going to lose him. We marched him down to the police station right away.

They weren't too pleased to see us. They complained about the smell. But when we got them to understand what it was all about, they changed their minds.

When I finally got home again, it was one in the morning. I fell on the sofa and slept through till noon the following day.

Chapter Eighteen

I was woken by the ringing of my doorbell. It gave me quite a start and for a moment I was disorientated, then I pushed my head out of the duvet, squinted at the alarm clock and saw it was one in the afternoon.

Someone was outside the window and tapping on the pane. I hoped it wasn't Parry. I couldn't face the police in any form just at the moment, even if they'd come to tell me they'd caught Merv. For a nasty moment I wondered whether it could be Merv, bent on revenge. But he was unlikely to tap politely at the window. Chuck a brick through it, more likely. I trailed over there and saw Ganesh gesturing at me.

I let him in. He was carrying a plastic bag filled with something that clinked as he set it down.

'I just dashed round to see how you are today,' he said. 'In my lunch-break,' he added sounding martyred.

I said I was fine. I had a slight headache and was also hungry.

Ganesh fished a large block of milk chocolate from inside his jacket. 'Hari sends this and is glad you're safe.' He pushed the plastic carrier with his foot. 'And I've brought these from the chilled cupboard. Half a dozen iced teas. Good for you. I'll put 'em in your fridge.'

I could hear him rattling around in the fridge and in my kitchen generally. He came back to announce. 'All you've got is a tin of tomato soup and some stale sliced bread. I can make toast and heat the soup, if you like.'

I told him to carry on while I went to shower. A little later, sharing the soup, accompanied by iced tea, with milk chocolate squares for dessert, I listened while he told me that word of my heroism had spread locally.

'Hari's telling everyone,' he said. 'You're famous.'

'That'll please Parry,' I said. 'You haven't heard whether they've picked up Merv, I suppose?'

'No, but they'll find him. He's a local villain. He won't go far. Off his home turf he'd be lost.' He nodded confidently and broke off another square of chocolate. 'They'll pick him up in no time.'

I was glad Ganesh was so certain, but had I been in Merv's boots, I'd be putting as much distance as I could between London and myself. Lost in the grey underworld of any large city, Merv could be at liberty indefinitely, not a pleasant thought.

'To think I handed the whole gang to them on a plate,' I said bitterly, 'and still the coppers managed to lose one of them.'

'They ought to give you a reward,' Ganesh insisted indistinctly through the chocolate. 'They owe everything to you.'

I put down my spoon. 'Listen, I just want to forget it for a few hours, right? It's going to be bad enough reliving it when the case gets to court. I only ever wanted to achieve two things and I managed both. I wanted to find Lauren and I found her. I wanted to see justice done by Albie. With luck we'll get that now Jonty's turned up again.'

Ganesh looked as if he'd just remembered something. 'That Scotsman's been into the shop,' he said. 'The artist. He left this for you.' He delved into his pocket again and produced a grubby envelope.

It contained twenty quid and a note promising to pay me the remaining ten pounds when Angus should have it.

'That's legal,' said Ganesh, who had read the note upside-down. 'That's an IOU. Make him pay you. You earned it.'

'He'll pay me,' I said. 'He's the honest type.'

'And you're too trusting,' he said sententiously.

'Me? I'll never trust anyone again. Not after all I've been through. But Angus will pay me. I'll keep nagging Reekie Jimmie if he doesn't and Jimmie will make him pay.'

'You know,' Ganesh said, 'I really don't think you ought to do anything like that again. That modelling business, it wasn't decent.'

I told him it had been more than decent. But I wouldn't be offering my services to Angus again. Not because I was suddenly prudish or was having to wait for the balance of my money – I was sure Angus would pay me – but because I didn't dare think what Angus's next project might be.

It was all very well talking airily to Ganesh of my resolve to keep well away from the aftermath of the whole business.

I knew I'd have to give evidence at some future point when Stratton and her henchmen came to trial. I also knew in my bones that I hadn't seen the last of Vinnie Szabo. I'd come across him eventually in court, but he wouldn't wait that long. By the time it got to court, it'd be too late. He'd be round before that. Even so, I didn't expect him to turn up quite so soon as he did.

He came that very day. Ganesh hadn't been gone long. It was about two thirty and I was in the kitchenette, washing up the soup bowls. The doorbell rang again. When I looked out of the window, fearing this time it would be Parry, I saw Szabo, standing in the basement well. I think I'd have preferred Parry.

I couldn't see the chauffeur. I supposed he was waiting with the car nearby. I opened the door.

Szabo bustled in, rubbing his hands together, his fringe of hair standing up like a halo round his bald crown.

'My dear,' he said with patently false solicitude, 'are you all right?'

I told him I was fine.

He shifted about from foot to foot and looked uneasily around the room. 'You're alone? I was hoping to have a confidential word . . .'

I said I was alone and asked him if he wanted to sit down. He was making me nervous fidgeting about like that.

He sat on the edge of my blue rep sofa and it was a bad choice because being a little fellow, the big old sofa dwarfed him. His feet, I noticed for the first time, were as tiny as a woman's and neatly shod in highly polished black shoes with pointed toes and built-up heels. Handmade at a guess and very expensive. He looked so ill at ease that I had to start the conversation off.

'How's Lauren?' I asked, trying to sound neutral.

'Oh, recovering. It was a terrible ordeal . . .' He blinked. 'About the circumstances in which she was held – in which you found her. I am, of course, more than grateful that you did! I can't express my thanks enough. But there, er, there does seem to have been some misunderstanding, about the *exact* circumstances, I mean . . .'

'Oh?' I asked coolly, and waited for what I knew was coming.

'It's quite understandable,' he said quickly, 'that you were unable to think clearly by the time the police arrived last night at that dreadful warehouse. You may be misremembering some things as a result.'

'Me not thinking clearly?' I interrupted indignantly. 'I got your precious Lauren out of there!'

He held up both hands palms outward to stem my protest. 'My dear, my dear! I'm not accusing you of anything! I'm not blaming you, please believe me! In no way at all am I criticising, not in the slightest! Without you, I wouldn't have my girl back again. Forgive me if I've phrased this badly. I'll start again. Let me put it another way. Perhaps you didn't lack presence of mind. But Lauren had been imprisoned in that place at the mercy of those thugs and as a result, she was confused and frightened. She may have said things to you which – well, which were not quite correct.'

'About her time at the refuge with her mother, you mean?' I asked.

The muscles round his mouth twitched and the skin turned white. 'She was rambling, almost delirious. She'd been held prisoner, mistreated, starved. You should pay no attention either to that story or anything else she may have said regarding her relationship with the two scoundrels who held her captive.'

'Look,' I told him, 'you've got to sort this out with her, not with me.'

'But you are the only reason the police have heard these – these ramblings. They've been asking questions. It's highly embarrassing for a man in my position. You really shouldn't have repeated what my poor girl said. Not without checking it with me first. Most importantly, you obviously made a mistake in one significant detail, a very significant detail. There is one clear mistake in the story you told the police and it must be put right without delay.'

'What's that, then?' I asked.

'The key. You said the key to the room in which my daughter was held prisoner was in the lock on the inside. But obviously it was on the outside and you turned it to open the door – and found her.'

'No,' I said. 'She opened the door, from the inside, and found me, if you like.'

Szabo stopped fidgeting and in a cold little voice said, 'That is impossible.'

'I'm sorry,' I said, because after all, it was hard for him to accept the humiliation he must be suffering, now that the whole story had come out. Not that I had any real reason to be sorry for him, but we all do things we're ashamed of from time to time. Supposing Vinnie to be ashamed, which I'd no reason to believe he was. But I gave him the benefit of the doubt.

'You were mistaken,' he repeated in the same cold little voice. 'You had hit your head. Lauren said you were covered in blood when she first set eyes on you.'

'I hit my nose and chin,' I said. 'I wasn't concussed, if that's what you're suggesting. I know what I saw, what I did, and what Lauren told me.'

He sat back in his chair and fixing his grey pebble eyes on me, said flatly, 'I want you to change your story.'

I pointed out I couldn't if I wanted to. I'd already made a statement to the police.

'The police were remiss,' he said. 'They should have asked a doctor to examine you. Despite what you say, I believe you were concussed and confused. Indeed, you still are. So much is obvious. No blame will attach to you if you go back to the police and say you've thought it all through, and you want to amend your statement. If necessary, I can get a doctor to certify that you are suffering from a head injury received last night and no statement made by you can be taken as it stands. It was wrong of the police even to question you at that time, before—'

'Before you'd had this chat with me?' I suggested.

'Before,' he said coldly, 'before you'd had a good night's rest and time to think things over.'

His voice grew louder. 'It is unthinkable,' he said, 'that a foolish rumour should be allowed to take root and grow. It is, at the very least, highly speculative, fanciful. At the worst, it is slanderous. I cannot allow it. I'm a well-known businessman. I have friends, not only in Manchester but throughout the soft-furnishing trade. They respect me. I've got influence, connections in local government who are important men. This story you've told, if it became public knowledge, would be damaging, very damaging. It could ruin my standing, lose me their respect, I'd be finished!' He was breathing heavily, his voice shaking. Tears filled his eyes and he blinked them away and he leaned towards me, 'It must be stopped. I've come here to stop it and I shall stop it.' Behind the tears his eyes gleamed with frightening intensity.

I forced back the instinct to flinch and managed to hold that almost maniacal gaze. I wondered why, a few minutes before, I'd been feeling sorry for him. Here he was asking me to swear to lies. Not to protect Lauren from any charge of conspiracy to impede police enquiries or to extort money, or whatever she might be guilty of. No, he feared for himself, for his reputation socially, his business contacts, the cosy little deals with his influential friends and his personal self-esteem.

'Forget it,' I told him. 'Ganesh was right. You don't care about Lauren, you only care about yourself. You want to keep her under your thumb, at home where you can keep an eye on her or married to Copperfield which would be the next best thing, because you don't trust her not to blab out the truth. You're just a control freak, that's what you are, and a nasty little sadistic one!'

His mouth twitched. The tears had dried. For a moment I almost thought he might hit me. Instead, he turned to another method of settling opposition, one which he'd probably found effective in the past.

He put a hand to his inside coat pocket and said silkily, 'If it's a question of money . . .'

'It's not a question of money!' I snapped.

He hastened to rephrase the offer he'd been about to make. 'I mean, I had been intending to offer a reward to anyone leading us to Lauren. I would have done so if the police hadn't insisted on a media ban. It's quite allowable in the circumstances and you are more than entitled to that reward. It's a considerable amount.'

He might be able to buy a doctor's certificate, but he wasn't going to buy me.

'There are other things beside money,' I told him.

His hand dropped from his lapel. 'Such as?' He stared at me with his mouth twisted scornfully. 'I'd have thought that in your situation money was of prime importance. What else could there be?'

'Honour,' I said. 'Honour, Mr Szabo. My father understood honour. He was an honourable man. Which is why, although you may have known him as a boy, I don't believe you and he were ever friends.'

His mouth opened and closed soundlessly. For a moment there was such fury in his eyes that this time I really thought he was going to attack me and I cast my eye round for some sort of weapon with which I could fend him off. But instead he got to his feet.

'I see you are indeed your father's daughter,' he said nastily. 'Bondi could also be very stupid.'

I watched him leave. I'd made an enemy, but it couldn't be helped. You can't go through life without treading on a few toes. I hoped I'd trodden hard on Vinnie Szabo's polished handmades.

The next few days passed off uneventfully, for which I was grateful. They were busy, however. Some kind of family crisis blew up in High Wycombe which meant Ganesh had to go there and stay over to help settle it. So I went to help out Hari in the shop. I was still basking in glory in Hari's eyes so he was over the moon to have me there and kept pointing me out to customers, which was embarrassing. It was also good business, of course. They hung around to gawp at me and generally bought some extra item to excuse their curiosity.

Hari appeared quite sorry when the last day of my temporary employment came. When he shut up shop at eight, he invited me into his back parlour for a cup of tea and told me his medical history in amazing detail. Hari cheers up when he talks about illness. I've come to the conclusion it's a sort of hobby with him. He probably got little encouragement from Ganesh, but in me he had a fresh audience, so I got the complete works including the time he fell off a ladder while stacking the top shelf and chipped two vertebrae. Poor Hari does seem accident-prone.

It was nearly nine when I left. It was that moment before dusk settles properly when your eyes play tricks because it seems as if it ought to be light enough to distinguish objects, but it isn't. As I turned into the street where I lived, I thought I glimpsed something whisk into a doorway a little down from my place. People came and went all the time and it was an hour at which quite a lot of people are about so I didn't pay too much attention. Nevertheless, some little warning signal must have rung in my brain because I paused at the top of the basement steps to look up and down the street.

Had I done what I usually did, which was just swing round the railing post and clatter down into the basement well, I'd have had a bad accident. Perhaps, too, I had Hari's story of his fall from the ladder still ringing in my head. So as it turned out, when I moved forward again, I did so more cautiously than usual.

Even so I almost fell. My ankle snagged some resistance and I stumbled and for a dreadful moment I thought I would plunge headfirst down the stone steps to the concreted floor below. I just managed to clasp the railings and hang on desperately until I found my footing. It was very gloomy now, even though the street lighting had come on. I reached down and felt around and my fingers found the wire. It was stretched across the second step down. That was clever. It was also the trick I'd played on Baz on the tow-path so I didn't need to guess who'd played it on me now. Merv was still around all right. Ganesh was again proved right. Even hunted, Merv still felt safer on his own territory. I glanced down the street. Was he still in the doorway, waiting to see if I fell? Or had he slipped out while I was disengaging the wire?

I went back up again and rang Daphne's doorbell.

I told her not to worry but I needed to ring the police. They came quickly this time. Parry wasn't with them, off-shift it seemed, but the two who came knew about me and about Merv. They searched up and down the street but he'd made off. One of them went back to their car and radioed in while the other checked my flat before I was allowed to return to it.

As it proved, letting us know he was around and active was Merv's big mistake. It established that he was holed up locally somewhere. The radio message the copper had sent resulted in an immediate raid on Merv's mother's house.

It was hard to think of Merv with a devoted mum but apparently he'd been known to hide up at her place before. They had checked it out right after he'd given them the slip at the office building, but now they went back there in force and sure enough, he'd scuttled there with the intention of packing up a few things and clearing out. But the police arrived before he could leave and he was trapped.

Dear old Mum barricaded the front door against the forces of law and order and hurled abuse and kitchenware at them from an upper window, while her darling boy tried to escape out the back. But the police were waiting for him so Mum had sacrificed her nonstick saucepans in vain.

Jonty later picked out Merv and Baz at an identity parade. Faced with a witness, they started gabbing. They blamed each other and both of them blamed Stratton.

Parry came round and told me the police had searched Stratton's flat, which he described admiringly as 'a real tart's boo-dwar, all satin sheets and white fur rugs'.

The police also checked out Baz's home. I wasn't surprised to learn he'd been living in a single filthy room stacked high with mouldy junk food cartons and women's underwear.

'Knickers,' said Parry with relish. 'Hundreds of pairs. He must've pinched them off washing-lines. We had to bring 'em away in umpteen boxes, filled a squad car. We can't charge him because we can't prove he stole them. No one's been down to complain they lost any and I don't suppose anyone will come in to identify 'em. You've not lost anything off your washing-line, have you?' He raised his foxy eyebrows hopefully.

I told him I hadn't got a washing line, not outdoors. 'What does he do with them all?' I asked naïvely.

'He collects them,' said Parry. 'You know, like people collect dolls in national costumes or old football programmes. He collects ladies' panties.'

He seemed to think this was a logical explanation, which not only told me something about Baz, but quite a lot about Parry.

In the end, and not surprising anyone, no charges were brought against Lauren Szabo. Vinnie got a top medical man to give his highly paid opinion that she'd been brainwashed during her time in that deserted block. As the official version went, the two men had put ideas in her head and she'd gone along with what they'd suggested. She'd been living a kind of fantasy whilst in captivity. Szabo sent her off to an expensive Swiss nursing home to recuperate and get her side of the story right before she met the general public again. I hoped she remembered to take her skis along.

As far as I know, she and her stepfather are still together as a family unit. I imagine them, Szabo trying to buy her goodwill and silence with endless presents, terrified of what she might do if she leaves and frightened of her when she's there: she circling round him like a shark waiting for a chance to dive in and destroy him, and all the time letting bitterness eat away at her. There's a name for that sort of relationship. Mutually destructive.

I bought two Alice bands, one in black velvet and one in pink satin, put them in a Jiffy bag, addressed it to Samantha and took it over to the refuge. I approached the place with some caution in view of my ignominious exit on the last occasion I was there. But this time it was all smiles because news of my part in Lauren's rescue had given me something akin to celebrity status. This couldn't last, but I might as well enjoy it while it did. Miriam even made me a cup of coffee and showed me the newspaper clipping recounting my exploits.

'It's nice to have some good news for a change,' she said. 'Generally we hear nothing but bad news here.'

She told me Samantha and her mum weren't there at the moment, but they would keep my gift safe until they returned. 'Because they're bound to be back,' Miriam added with depressed certainty.

Angus paid me the ten pounds two weeks later. I'd been sure he would and so made a point of telling Ganesh and reminding him of my confidence. Ganesh retorted that Angus was the type who would happily give you his last fiver, if he wasn't trying to borrow your last tenner.

'Spend it before he asks for it back!' he advised.

Thanks to all the excitement and being involved in a front-page rescue story, the photos taken of me at the community hall art show not only got into the local press, but into the *Standard* and two of the national tabloids.

But it hasn't led to any more offers of modelling work for me. Nor, as far as I know, has anyone expressed any interest in any other work by Angus. He's still swabbing out Reekie Jimmie's spud bar of a morning.

The world just isn't ready for either of us.

Running Scared

To my son, Tim, who gave up his free time
to help me in my research, with thanks

Chapter One

I'm not the sort of person who goes out of her way to find trouble. It's just that trouble always seems to find me. Generally, I just try to make it from one day to the next and avoid hassle. I don't know why it never works out like that. It's so unfair, and especially as Christmas approaches and everyone's looking forward to the holiday. But my luck being what it is, that's when I ran into my latest set of problems. Because if you can be certain of anything in this world, it's that you never know what life's going to hit you with next.

It was a cold, rainy morning and I was helping out my friend Ganesh in his uncle's newsagent's shop when disaster struck. Ganesh not only works for his Uncle Hari, he also lodges with him over the shop. I don't know whether Hari really is an uncle or some other kind of relative, but uncle's what everyone calls him, even me. Hari is a nice man but nervous and fidgety and that gets Ganesh down. So when Hari announced he was going on an extended family visit to India, and in his absence Ganesh was to be left in sole charge of the shop in Camden, Gan just about danced round the place for joy.

I was pleased for Ganesh too, because it was high time he had a chance to run something without interference from his family. All his life he's helped out in shops run by relatives. He'd helped his parents in their Rotherhithe greengrocery until they'd been dispossessed by the council, who were redeveloping. Now they run a fruit and veg place out of town at High Wycombe. It's very small and they don't need Ganesh, nor is there any accommodation for him, so that's why he's currently with Hari. I sometimes ask Ganesh why he puts up with being passed round the family like this, filling in where needed, but he always says I don't understand. Too right, I tell him, I don't. Explain it to me. Then he says, what's the point?

He's really capable and if he could just get his own place, he'd be fine. I wish he'd give up the dream of being in charge of a dry-cleaner's, though. He has a crazy idea he and I could run something like that together. Not a chance, I tell him. I don't want to spend my life handling other people's dirty clothes and I hate the chemical smell of those places, and the steam.

However, I didn't mind giving Ganesh a hand in the newsagent's while Hari was away, especially in the mornings, which is always the busiest time, though with Christmas coming up things would start getting really hectic pretty soon. Hari had given Ganesh authority to hire me as a part-timer and I needed the money. But I want to make it clear that one day I'm going to be an actress – I nearly finished a course on the Dramatic Arts and everything once – but in the meantime I take any legitimate work going, including being an informal enquiry agent.

So, off went Hari, leaving Ganesh three pages of minutely detailed instructions in a curly alphabet and I turned up on my first day bright and early at eight o'clock. Ganesh had been there since six, but I have my limits. Everything went swimmingly for a bit and I was enjoying being a genuinely employed person. It was quite interesting in the shop and at the end of the first week I got my pay packet and felt I was a regular member of the public at last. Only 'last' was what it wasn't going to do. I should've known.

It was on the following Tuesday that things started to go wrong. The week had begun all right. Gan and I had spent Sunday putting up Christmas decorations in the shop. Ganesh's idea of a decorative colour scheme is red, lots of it, and gold, even more of that, enlivened by an occasional flash of hot pink or vibrant turquoise. When we'd finished with the shop it looked fantastic – perhaps rather more Diwali than Christmas, but Gan and I were really chuffed with it.

All Monday we gloried in the compliments from customers. Then, on Tuesday, a postcard of the Taj Mahal arrived from Uncle Hari and the atmosphere changed. Ganesh stopped buzzing cheerfully and skulked around beneath the crepe paper chains. He'd propped the card on the gold tinsel-trimmed shelves behind the counter along with the cigarettes, and kept giving it hunted glances.

I'd already guessed that Ganesh was up to something because he'd been making furtive phone calls over the previous week and looking pleased with himself. I knew it wasn't just the approach of festivities and seasonal sales. I could see he was dying to tell me, especially during Sunday when we'd been pinning up the decorations, but I wasn't going to encourage him although I was longing to know. With the arrival of the postcard, he stopped looking smug and became clearly worried. Eventually, he came clean.

We were having our coffee-break. The early morning rush had thinned, there was no one in the shop for the moment, and the emptiness of the rainswept pavement outside suggested things might stay quiet all day until the usual early evening flurry of trade. We didn't have to go upstairs to the flat to make the coffee because we had an electric kettle downstairs which I filled with water in the washroom.

The building's old and long ago converted from what must once have been quite a nice house. There are two ways up to the flat, one from the shop, using the former back stairs, and a separate one from the street. The downstairs washroom was at that time a museum of antiquated plumbing and fixtures, tacked on to the back of the building in what must have seemed at the time the height of modernity. It was all as clean as it could be kept given its general state, but that was terminal. The washbasin was hanging off the wall. The tap dripped. Any wall tiles were loose and cracked and the floor tiles had gaps between them. The vent for the extractor fan was clogged with dust and dead flies. The lavatory cistern was operated by a chain which had lost its handle. It clanked furiously whenever it was flushed and the cistern lid was loose so if you didn't watch out, there was always a chance it would fall down and brain you. The loo itself was the *pièce de résistance*. An original, no kidding, patterned all over with blue forget-me-nots. It had a wooden seat with a crack in it which pinched your bum. I tell you, anyone ventured into that washroom at his peril. I called it the Chamber of Horrors.

Ganesh, to be fair, had been grumbling to Hari about the state of the washroom ever since he'd moved there. But whenever Hari was tackled, he always replied that he wasn't a rich man who could afford to replace everything just like that. 'Besides,' he'd declare, 'look at such a beautiful lavatory pan. Where would I again get such a wonderful object?' He usually ended up by promising to get a new tapwasher, but even that got put off indefinitely.

On this particular morning, I steered my way to the counter carrying a mug of coffee in either hand and said crossly, 'The least you can do, Gan, while Hari's away, is fix that dripping tap.'

At that, Ganesh, who since the postcard's arrival had been brooding darkly in a corner like Mr Rochester on a bad day, brightened up. He chortled, rapped out a rhythm on the counter with his palms and, just as I was deciding he'd gone bonkers, let me into his secret.

'I can do better than that, Fran. I'm going to get the whole thing done out, ripped out, fixed up, everything brand-new, while the old bloke's away.'

He beamed at me. I stood there, slopping coffee and gawping. I'd only set my sights on the new washer. Ganesh must have got *Homes and Gardens* down from the shelf and let it go to his head.

'Hari won't agree,' I said.

'Hari won't know, not until he gets back and by then it'll be a whatsit, *fait accompli*, that's what they call it.'

'They call it a screaming hysterics,' I said. 'That's what Hari will have when he sees the bill.'

Ganesh took his coffee from me, stopped looking smug, and started to look obstinate. 'He left me in charge, right? I'm empowered to sign cheques on the business and everything, right? So I'm going to get it done and he can make as much fuss as he likes. What's he going to do, sack me? I'm family. He can't. Anyway, I know the stingy old blighter. He always carps at spending money, but once it's gone, he shrugs it off. When he sees how good it looks and how reasonable the cost was, he'll get over it. It's improving the property. That has to be good. And if he still argues, I'll tell him Health and Safety at Work rules didn't allow the old one. They probably don't.'

'It'll cost a bomb,' I said, playing devil's advocate. Someone had to. He was too full of it.

'No, it won't. I've got a really reasonable quote. Dead cheap. Bloke can start work on Friday and he'll be done, finished, gone in days, by the end of next week, certain.'

I perched on the stool behind the counter and sipped my coffee. It all sounded a bit too easy to me. 'How come it's going to be so cheap?' I asked. 'All the existing fittings will have to go, new ones put in. The extractor fan has never worked to my knowledge so that's got to be replaced. The plumbing's knackered. The walls will have to be painted, the floor retiled . . .'

'It's all taken care of,' said Ganesh airily. 'And he'll take away the old fittings and rubbish for me and everything.'

'Who will?' I asked suspiciously.

Ganesh's air of confidence slipped just a tad. 'Hitch,' he said.

I spilled my coffee. 'Hitch? Are you mad?'

'Hitch does a good job,' Ganesh said obstinately. 'And he's cheap.'

'He's cheap,' I said, 'because all the stuff he uses has been knocked off from a builder's yard somewhere.'

'No, it hasn't – or this won't be. I checked that with him first. Think I'm daft? It's all on the level. He's given me the name of his supplier and everything. I can ring them up – and I will, before he starts. I'm not daft, Fran.'

I could have argued, and perhaps I should have done, but in the end, it wasn't any of my business. I didn't doubt Hitch had given Ganesh the phone number of a 'supplier'. But I'd be willing to bet that, if Gan rang up, on the other end of the line would be some mate of Hitch's, sitting in a lock-up garage filled with dodgy goods. Ganesh is stubborn and always wants to know best. He wouldn't listen to anything I had to say. So why not let him get on with it? A new washroom would be nice. But that Ganesh, of all people, should behave like this took me aback. He was usually so sensible, never did anything without examining it from all sides first, never acted rashly, never gambled and never did anything which would upset his family (other than befriend me, an act which had them dead worried).

I let it go and concentrated on my coffee. Ganesh obviously thought he'd won the argument so that put him in a good mood. An air of truce hung over the shop.

That's when the door opened. At first the only thing I was aware of was a cold draught which ruffled all the magazines on their shelves and sent the crepe chains threshing. A red one and a turquoise, twisted together, fell down. A squall of rain spattered the tiled floor. More tinsel fell off the shelves. We both looked up. Silhouetted in the open door was the figure of a man. He stood there briefly, steadying himself with one hand on the doorjamb, then staggered towards the counter and grabbed at it for support. Ganesh stretched out a hand towards the jemmy he keeps under the counter for opening boxes and fending off drunks. I stood there rooted to the spot, horrified and fascinated.

I faced a Halloween mask – gaping mouth, bulging eyes, streaked scarlet with gore which poured from a cut above one eyebrow, filling the eye-socket beneath. More blood dribbled from both nostrils. I knew I should do something, but I couldn't move. The clutching fingers scrabbled at the wooden surface, inarticulate sounds issued from the mouth and, with a last throaty gurgle, the intruder slid beneath the counter and disappeared from sight. A strand of silvery fronds floated after him, undulating gracefully in the disturbed air currents.

His disappearance jolted both of us into action and we raced round the other side. He was sitting on the floor, back to the counter, legs splayed, bloodied head grotesquely crowned with the tinsel strand.

'Cripes,' said Ganesh. 'Get a cloth, Fran.' He ran to the door, looked up and down the street, twisted the notice on the glass to 'Closed' and locked us in. Whoever had done that to the man on the floor, we didn't want them joining us.

We divested our visitor of his tinsel crown, got him to his feet and propelled him into the storeroom. He stumbled along between us, gasping, but, apart from the obvious, apparently not otherwise injured. We propped him on a chair and I ripped open a box of Kleenex to mop up the blood.

'Haven't you got something else?' hissed Ganesh, who even in a time of stress realised he had to write off that box of tissues as no-sale. 'Couldn't you have used loo paper?'

'Make him some tea!' I snapped.

Our patient gurgled and seemed to be regaining his wits. His nose wouldn't stop trickling blood so I wedged wads of tissue in both nostrils and told him he had to breathe through his mouth.

Ganesh came back with a mug of tea.

'Thag you,' mumbled whoever-he-was.

'What happened, mate?' asked Ganesh. 'Was it a mugging? You want me to call the cops?'

'Doh!' cried the other in great alarm, sloshing tea around.

'Keep still!' I ordered. 'You'll start bleeding again. Perhaps he ought to go to casualty, Gan. He could have broken his nose.'

'Doh, doh! I dode want dat!' The stranger decided he couldn't communicate with both nostrils bunged up, so removed the blood-sodden wads and threw them in the waste-paper basket. I waited for a fresh scarlet waterfall, but it didn't come. My first aid had worked.

'No police,' he said firmly. 'No hospital. I'm all right now.'

'Please yourself,' said Gan in some relief. He didn't want the law in his shop. That sort of thing puts customers off. Nor did he want to take time to drive the guy to the nearest casualty unit. 'So long as you're OK, right? You were unlucky. It's safe enough round here in daylight, usually.'

The victim mumbled agreement. 'Yeah, I had a bit of bad luck.'

I wondered if he was going to give us any details, but apparently not. He was patting the inside pocket of his coat and progressed from there to the side pockets. Eventually he pulled out a handkerchief and passed it gingerly over his bashed features. When he took it away, it was freely smeared red. He studied it with interest.

Ganesh was getting restive. 'Look, mate, I've got to reopen the shop. I can't stay closed much longer. I'm losing trade. You can sit here as long as you need. Take your time, right?'

'I'm really sorry about this.' Our visitor looked stricken. He thrust away the handkerchief and began to fumble again at the inner pocket of his overcoat. 'I realise this is costing you money. Let me make it up.'

Now up to that moment, neither Gan nor I had doubted our friend had been mugged. So we were a tad surprised when out of the pocket came a wallet and out of that came a tenner. It wasn't alone in the wallet. It had some company, as I could see – a couple of fivers and a twenty at least.

I met Ganesh's eye. He was thinking what I was thinking. This wasn't a mugging. If muggers had had time to dish out that amount of facial decoration, they'd have got the guy's wallet for sure. Come to that, he still had his wristwatch and a gold signet ring. I couldn't make out the initials on the ring, which was a pity. They were sort of swirly and tangled up but one might have been C.

Our visitor was looking anxiously from one to the other of us. He'd misunderstood our exchange of glances. 'Not enough?' he asked and made to add another note.

'No, I mean yes, that's fine!' Ganesh took the tenner. We had shut up shop, after all.

I took a more critical look at our guest, who'd suddenly become very interesting. He was in his thirties, a biggish chap, wearing a dark suit under that charcoal-coloured overcoat. His white shirt was blood-spattered and his tie askew. The damaged eye was swelling shut. He wasn't looking his best, but even so, he wasn't bad-looking. Still, there was something about him I couldn't quite fit together. He was dressed like a business type but didn't look like a man who spent his life in an office. There was a faint odour of nicotine about him which suggested he was a heavy smoker and offices tend to be smoke-free zones these days. You see the exiles, lurking unhappily in the doorways at street level, puffing furtively as they try to keep out of the rain.

On the other hand, he wasn't particularly an outdoor type, though he sported a recently acquired tan. Perhaps he'd been on holiday. It wasn't fair to judge in the circumstances, but to my eye his suit and coat weren't quite right. They were too well worn and unfashionable, the sort of clothes someone might keep in the wardrobe for the odd occasion when he needed to impress, but didn't wear day to day. His trousers weren't kept up with the snazzy braces they hand out to high-fliers with their business diplomas, but by a tooled leather belt with a fancy brass buckle which was definitely leisure-wear.

You see why I consider myself to be quite a good detective. I notice these things. *You know my methods, Watson*. Here, I deduced, was a youngish, fit man who normally dressed casually but left home today tricked out to look prosperous and businesslike. Why? To impress someone. Not a woman. Not in that coat. No, a bloke, the sort who'd be wearing a snappy suit and wouldn't be impressed by chinos and a leather jacket. He'd set off to do a bit of serious business, but whoever he'd met had duffed him up. It suggested more than one person, because our new friend here looked well able to handle one assailant. For my money, he had set up a meeting with someone dodgy, perhaps even someone who'd had a minder with him, and it hadn't turned out as he'd wished. He shouldn't have gone alone. Unless, of course, he had good reason for keeping his business private.

Eat your heart out, my old violin-scraper.

'I don't want trouble,' Ganesh was saying. 'So, whoever's after you, do you think they're still out there, looking around? Will they come in here?' Before the other could speak, he added, 'Look, I'm not prying, but it wasn't a mugging, was it?'

I chimed in with, 'One mugger would've thumped you while the other grabbed your jewellery and dosh. Ganesh and I mean, if you've got a private fight that's your affair. But we don't want the shop damaged.'

'Don't suppose the insurance would cover it,' Ganesh added, 'seeing as we didn't call the police.'

The stranger took his time thinking about his answer to all that and I didn't blame him. 'Take your point,' he said at last. 'Truth is, I don't know who's out there, if anyone. I'm pretty sure they don't know I came in here. They might be still scouting around for me, I suppose.'

He began to struggle up out of his chair. 'Don't worry about me,' he said. 'I'll take my chances.'

He sounded brave and doomed, like that chap who went with Scott to the Antarctic and walked out into the snow when the rations ran low. It seemed to call for some responding gesture on our part. Not for the first time I spoke up when I should've kept quiet.

'I tell you what,' I said, 'I'll slip out the back way, stroll round to the front as if I was coming here to buy something, and see if anyone's hanging around.'

'Take care,' Ganesh said, worried.

I had a question for the man. 'Who should I be looking for?' (Yes, I know it should be 'whom' – I went to a good school where they fussed about that kind of thing – but I was under pressure.)

'They're in a car,' he said. 'A silver-grey Mercedes. They stopped at the traffic lights down the block. I got the door open and rolled out into the road.'

'They', were careless, I thought, and they'd lost their man. Whoever was paying them wouldn't be pleased. They'd be moving heaven and earth to get him back.

'Nearly got run over by a bloody bus,' said our visitor, aggrieved.

'Is that when you smashed your nose?' Ganesh asked sharply.

'Do me a favour. Look, if you can see the car, two guys in it, one small, one big with a ponytail, that'll be them. But I reckon they don't know I came in here. My bet is, once they saw I'd got away, they burned rubber getting out of here.' He was quite perking up. I had a suspicion this wasn't the first tight corner he'd been in and squeezed out of. Curiouser and curiouser.

I had to ask. 'Why'd they do it?'

'Misunderstanding,' he said, and that was as much as I was going to get. I hadn't really expected more.

'You watch yourself,' muttered Ganesh to me.

'It'll be all right,' said our guest, not altogether gallantly. 'They won't be expecting a girl.'

I hoped they weren't as I let myself out of the back door. I pulled up the collar of my fleece-lined denim jacket to keep out the rain and hide my face, made my way along the alley at the back of the shop, into the side street and back to the main road again.

There was a bus stop there, so I lingered by it, scrutinising the traffic as if waiting for my bus. The street was fairly busy – taxis, vans, cars, one or two motorcyclists. No Mercedes. Double yellow lines precluded legal parking for most of its length and the only stationary vehicle was a red Post Office van.

I turned round and leaned nonchalantly on the metal post. The people passing along the pavement were the usual mob, mostly women at this time of day, some with kids. One or two of the men who passed looked scruffy but none of them like a minder. No ponytails. This was an open bus stop without a shelter and I was getting wet. I put up a hand to wipe water from my hair. A split second later, there was a growl of tyres behind me. Intent on the pavement, I'd failed to observe the arrival of a double-decker. A woman got off. The bus throbbed expectantly and I realised I was meant to board it.

'You getting on or what?' the driver shouted at me. I waved a negative at him. 'You hailed me!' he bellowed.

'No, I didn't!' I shouted back.

'You bloody did. You put your hand out.'

'No, I didn't. I was rubbing my head.'

'I gotta schedule to keep, you know!' he informed me.

'Well, go on and keep it, then!' I'd had enough of this.

He gave me a dirty look as he accelerated away. There was a man who lacked the Christmas spirit.

If anyone had been watching, that would have blown my cover, so I might as well go back and report all clear as far as I could see.

I strolled up to the shop. Ganesh, framed in gold, was standing on the other side of the glass door, peering between a sticker advertising Mars bars and one advertising Rizla cigarette papers. At my nod, he flipped the closed sign to open, and unlocked the door.

'Can't see anyone,' I said, wiping trickling raindrops from my face. 'All I got was into a barney with a bus driver. Where's our friend?'

'Cleaning himself up in the washroom.'

'Hope he doesn't leave it smeared all over with blood. Just think, when Hitch has done it all up for you, you'll be more fussy who you let go in there.' (Yes, 'whom', same excuse.) 'Did you warn him about the loose top on the cistern? It'd be a pity if he came out more injured than he went in. He might sue. He'd want his tenner back.'

'I told him!' said Ganesh testily.

There was a clanking from distant plumbing and the stranger reappeared. He'd got rid of all the blood, brushed his coat, and, swelling apart, no one would have noticed at a casual glance that he'd been in very recent trouble. I told him I'd been unable to see any Mercedes or ponytailed heavy.

'That's all right, then,' he said. 'I thought they'd have cleared off. They wouldn't have seen me come in here. I shouldn't worry.'

He'd now completely regained composure and was well up to dealing with his problems. I still wished I knew what they were.

'Thank you very much,' he said to me, nice and polite. 'I appreciate everything.'

With that, he opened the door and slipped out. He looked quickly in either direction and then set off rapidly.

Another crepe paper chain fell down.

'So much for that,' said Ganesh. 'Breaks up the morning, I suppose.'

'I wish I knew what it was all about,' I said wistfully. I gave Ganesh a quick rundown of my ideas about the visitor, adding, 'It's all very well deducing things, but you like to know if you got it right.'

'*You* would. Leave me out of it. I'm sure it's better we don't know anything.' Ganesh opened the till, extricated two fives, put in the tenner and closed the till. He handed one of the fives to me and tucked the other in his pocket.

'We earned it,' he said.

We? As I recalled, I was the one who went outside in the rain and made myself a possible target for aggro. Ganesh stayed inside and made the tea. But never argue with the man who's holding the money.

'I don't suppose we'll ever know,' I said, pocketing my fiver.

But I was wrong and Ganesh, as usual, was right. I mean, we *were* to find out what it was all about – and it would have been better if we hadn't.

Chapter Two

I walked out of the shop at just gone one o'clock. Things had stayed quiet after our visitor left, the rain either keeping people indoors or sending them scurrying past, anxious to reach dry destinations. As we pinned our now somewhat battered decorations back into place, Ganesh and I had rehashed the morning's main event. It remained a riddle and we went on to talk about Hari, whose postcard seemed to watch us accusingly from behind the counter. We wrangled about the washroom and Hitch's imminent arrival on the premises and half a dozen other things. Just as I was leaving for home, Ganesh presented me with a Mars bar. Perhaps he thought I was owed a bonus for going out in the rain to spy out the land, or possibly he felt guilty for letting me do it. I put the chocolate in my pocket.

There was a supermarket on my way. I called in there and used some of my fiver to buy a packet of tea and some pasta and a jar of pesto. Memories of the morning's events were beginning to fade. It had been just one of those spurts of activity which occur from time to time. Like a pebble thrown into a pond, they disturb the surface, create a few ripples, and then everything settles down again.

'Have you got any change?'

I heard the voice, though the question wasn't addressed to me. The voice came from a doorway just ahead of me and the request was made of a prosperous-looking elderly gent.

'Have you got any change, sir?' She emphasised the last word. She sounded pathetic. The old guy wavered, wanting to stick to his principles and walk on. But he couldn't do it, not with that childish desperate voice echoing in his ears, a young girl's voice. If that had been a man begging, he'd have told him to go and get a job. What he did now, as I knew he was going to do, was give too much. A small blue note changed hands.

The old gent huffed a bit and said, 'You know, my dear, you really oughtn't—' But he couldn't finish the sentence because he hadn't a clue what to say. He hurried away, distressed and angry, already regretting parting with the five-pound note.

I approached the doorway carefully. There had been something about that voice which rang a bell. I peered in.

She looked wet, cold and miserable, and was stick-insect thin. No wonder the old fellow had coughed up. Talk about Little Nell. Rain had plastered her straight fair hair to her head. Her eyes were huge and tragic in a face which had the matt, pale complexion of the heroin user.

I said, 'Hullo, Tig.' Truth was, I'd hardly have known her if I hadn't heard her voice first, she was so changed from our last meeting.

She jumped and her eyes blazed in her waif's features. I thought she was going to take a swing at me.

'Take it easy,' I said hastily. Those frail-looking ones can catch you a nasty swipe. 'It's Fran, remember me?'

I hadn't seen her for the best part of a year. She'd passed through the Jubilee Street squat when I'd been living there. I'd got to know her as well as you get to know anyone in that sort of setup, which is always as well as they'll let you. She hadn't stayed long, a week or two, and had been no trouble. A cheerful, plump, happy-go-lucky fifteen-year-old who hadn't long been in London, she'd hailed from somewhere in the Midlands. She'd left home, she said, as a result of some family dispute, the old story. We'd rather missed her when she'd moved on, but I hadn't expected her to stay long. The feeling I'd had then was that she was trying to give her parents a scare, get back at them for some real or imagined injustice. When she reckoned she'd done that, she'd go home. If asked, I'd have guessed she'd have returned there long before now, when cold, hunger and street violence ceased to sound adventurous and just got real and frightening.

But I was clearly wrong. The change in her shocked me deeply, even though I'd seen kids like Tig before. They arrived from out of town, full of optimism, although I couldn't think why. What did they think they were going to find in London? Other than a whole community of people like themselves with nowhere to go and a host of sharks ready to prey on them? They learned quickly if they were lucky. The unlucky ones came to grief before they'd time to learn.

The thing that really stuck in my mind about her from Jubilee Street days was that she'd brushed her teeth after every meal, even if she didn't have toothpaste. There are a lot of people who think that being homeless means being dirty. That isn't true. Whatever the practical difficulties, homeless people try to keep themselves clean. Cleanliness means there's still fight in you, circumstances haven't ground you down. You still care about yourself, even if others appear to have written you off. When a cat ceases to groom itself, you know it's sick. People are no different. With them it's also a sign of a sickness, either in body or in spirit. The sickness in spirit is the more difficult to deal with. Looking at Tig now, I wondered which kind of sickness afflicted her.

We'd had a no-drugs rule in the squat and if she'd had the habit then, she'd concealed it very cleverly. But I didn't think that was the case. She couldn't have been that smart. I guessed the habit was recent. Actually, she wasn't that smart. Belatedly, I remembered that, too. Naïve, perhaps, but a bit dim also.

'Yeah, Fran,' she said eventually. Her eyes slid sideways, past me. I remembered her gaze as it had been, bright, full of good nature. Now it was dull and hard. 'Got any spare change, madam?' she wheedled of a motherly woman with a bulging plastic carrier. The woman looked concerned and parted with twenty pence. Tig put it in her pocket.

'How are things?' She seemed to be doing well begging, but there was a quiet desperation about her which made me wary because when they reach that stage, they can really freak out.

'All right,' she said. Her gaze shifted past me again, this time nervously.

I still had two pounds left from my fiver and I gave her one of them. She looked surprised and then suspicious.

'It's OK,' I said. 'I had a bit of luck.'

At those words, misery welled up in her face, and was immediately wiped away. Luck had been avoiding her. She no longer expected any. But on the streets you hide your feelings. They make you vulnerable and God knows, you're vulnerable enough without the enemy within.

'Good for you,' she said bitchily and shoved the pound coin away in her pocket with the rest.

I persevered nevertheless – the memory of the old Tig made me do it. 'You heard what happened to the Jubilee Street house? They knocked it down.'

'Yeah, I heard. It was going to fall down anyway.'

That hurt. I'd been fond of that house and it had sheltered

her, as well as me, for a time. She owed it better than that.

'It was a good place!' I said crossly.

'Look,' Tig said, 'you're really in my way here, you know? How'm I supposed to ask people for bloody change with you standing there nattering about sod all?' Her voice was aggressive but her eyes were flickering nervously past me again. She hissed, 'For Chrissake, get lost, Fran!'

I got the message. 'Here,' I said, and handed her my Mars bar. She needed it more than me.

She snatched it away and I walked on without looking back. I was too busy looking elsewhere and sure enough, I spotted him almost at once. He was a big bearded bloke, in his twenties, wearing a plaid wool jacket, jeans and a woolly hat. He was loafing in the angle formed by a building which jutted out on to the pavement and under the shelter of an overhanging first-floor balcony. It kept him nice and dry and out of the draught. That dark little corner would be a mugger's haven in the evening and I wouldn't have seen him if I hadn't been looking for him. He wasn't a mugger, of course. He was Tig's protection, amongst other things.

I'd come across these street partnerships before and as far as I was concerned, the woman was scarcely better off in them than out of them. Don't get me wrong. I've known some really good partnerships which have started out there on the street, but it's rare for them to last, even the good ones. The fact is, you can't let yourself become dependent on anyone out there. You've got to stand alone, be able to take care of yourself, sort out your own problems. The street's a family of sorts, but it's a family of loners. Once you can't hack it any more on your own, you're lost.

Still, couples form, split, make new partners, just as they do in the world of the nine-to-fivers. There's the old man/

woman thing, of course. But there's also a practical side to it. Tig's man might be an idle lout who hung around in warm corners while she stood out in the cold wind. But he was on hand if things got rough, either while she was begging, or at any other time. Mind you, he probably also took most of the money, if not all. He'd see she had enough to keep the drug habit going because as long as she was on that, she'd have to beg, steal, sell her body, do whatever was necessary to get the money to feed it. He might even have got her on to it in the first place. He'd look on it as a business investment. People were far less likely to give him money had he been standing in that doorway with his hand out. From the brief glimpse I'd had of him, he didn't look as if he'd been going hungry lately. Unlike Tig, who looked as if she hadn't had a square meal in days. But the worse she looked, the more she earned. He couldn't lose, really.

I felt a spurt of hatred for him, whoever he was. I'd never let myself be used like that, but then perhaps Tig's situation had got so bad that whoever he was he'd seemed like a good idea at the time.

I was feeling pretty angry by now. One morning can only hold so much hassle. I stomped on homewards, ready to take on the next person to cross my path. Fortunately, no one did, at least not until I got there and then the encounter made me more inclined to laugh than spit fire.

At that time I was living in a basement flat in a house owned by a retired lady librarian called Daphne Knowles. I'd come by the flat through the intervention of an old gent called Alastair Monkton, whom I'd helped once. The flat had given me more security than I'd had in years. I've been on my own since I was sixteen and I'm twenty-one now. The trouble with security, when you're not used to having it, is that you don't really believe in it. I somehow knew that flat wasn't going to be permanent, but I meant to make it last as long as possible. I was never going to get so lucky again, that was for sure.

It had stopped drizzling by the time I got to the street where I lived, and a feeble sun had crept out. The pavements looked clean and washed. As I passed the basement railings of the house next door, I saw coming towards me a sight which made me grin.

There were two of them, alike as peas in a pod, walking side by side, in step. Both were short, tubby, middle-aged and smug-looking. The one on the left wore a green tweed jacket and the one on the right a brown tweed jacket. Both had pale fawn trousers and polished brogue shoes. The green jacket carried a bunch of flowers and the brown jacket a bottle wrapped in paper. Tweedledee and Tweedledum, I thought, and wondered who they were, where they were going and what on earth they were going to do when they got there. They looked, with their gifts, as if they were going courting according to some out-dated ritual. I hadn't seen them around before.

Perhaps they were wondering the same thing about me, because they inclined their heads together, keeping their eyes on me, and whispered. We reached the steps to Daphne's front door at the same time and stopped by mutual consent.

'Well, well,' said Green Jacket. 'What have we here, eh?' He gave me a jovial smile which was so fake I could have ripped it off his face like a piece of Elastoplast.

I could have made a number of pithy replies but instinct told me to avoid this encounter.

'Excuse me!' I said, and made to pass them and run down the steps to my basement door.

I wasn't to get away so easily. Brown Jacket chimed in with

his pennyworth. 'Now, let's see, eh? I believe you must be the young woman who lives in Aunt Daphne's basement flat.' He shook a podgy forefinger at me and looked pleased with himself.

Aunt Daphne? Were these two fat creeps Daphne's family? I felt sorry for her and glad, not for the first time, I didn't have anyone. I suppose my mother might be alive somewhere, probably is, but since she walked out on Dad and me when I was seven, I'd long since cut her out of the picture. I was brought up perfectly well by Dad and my Hungarian Grandma Varady but they're both dead now. No one could replace them.

'Yes,' I said bleakly, eyeing the pair. I'd never seen them call on Daphne but that didn't mean they hadn't been to the house. The basement flat was totally independent. There was no reason why Daphne should know who visited me, nor I who visited her, unless – as now – we met on the pavement.

'Our young friend is a trifle *farouche*, Bertie,' said Brown Jacket. 'A product of our unsettled society.'

That was asking for a punch on the nose and he might have got one if there hadn't been an interruption.

Daphne must have been watching out for their arrival from a window, because now the front door opened and she stood at the top of the steps, peering down at our small group. She wore, as usual, jogging trousers and hand-knitted Fair Isle socks with leather soles attached. But she sported a new sweater and had been to the hairdresser. Her grey hair was waved and primped, and from beneath two sausage curls over her ears dangled long earrings. Daphne had dressed up.

My landlady is in her seventies but is twice as alert as many younger people. I'd got to know her quite well and felt rather protective towards her. Not that she normally needed protecting. She could look after herself. But she appeared anything but sure of herself just now, unhappy and perplexed, as if she didn't know what to do about the situation.

'Oh, Bertie – Charlie . . .' she said unenthusiastically. 'How nice. Oh, hullo, Fran dear.' She brightened when she saw me.

Bertie and Charlie climbed the steps as if they were joined at the hip, and threw out their free (outer edge) arms in a sort of token joint embrace, Bertie (the green jacket) his left, Charlie his right. At the same time they clasped their gifts to their chests with their other hands. 'Aunt Daphne!' they cried. Bertie thrust out his flowers and Charlie, at the exact same moment, his bottle of wine. You'd have thought they'd rehearsed it.

'How kind,' said Daphne without enthusiasm. 'Do come in, boys.'

Boys? But perhaps it wasn't so unsuitable a term. There was something about them which suggested a bad double case of arrested development. I suppose it's cute to dress twin babies alike. It's just about permissible to dress toddlers so. But middle-aged men ought to have outgrown the desire to look exactly like someone else. If you couldn't help it – i.e. you were identical twins – you could at least develop an individual clothes style. But there's no accounting for the way people behave. I went downstairs and let myself into the flat.

I still hadn't got used to coming home and knowing that this was my place and it was private, I hadn't to share it with anyone and I hadn't to defend it against intruders who wanted to take it from me or the council who wanted to throw everyone out. It was early afternoon and I hadn't had any lunch. I put on a pan of water for the pasta and when it boiled, and before I put the salt in, poured off enough to make coffee.

I took my coffee into the living area and sat down on my old blue rep sofa. I started thinking again about the man who'd come into the shop. I don't like puzzles I can't solve and this time I had a strange feeling we hadn't seen the last of him. The pasta was ready. I strained it, stirred in the jar of pesto, and sat eating it before my aged, flickering TV set. The ghosted picture, as wasn't unusual, gave the viewer a sense of double vision and I couldn't help being reminded of Daphne's 'boys'.

There wasn't much to watch, no old film this afternoon, always my favourite viewing. I must have dozed off. I was awoken suddenly by the sound of voices and the clatter of feet on the front steps above my head. It was already dark on this wintry evening and the blue light from the screen was the only thing illuminating the room.

I ran to the window and peered out and upwards. I was just in time. A taxi had parked outside and the footsteps which had awoken me had been those of the driver, running up to the front door. Now he came back and in his wake came two pairs of pale trousers and some very thin female legs beneath a drooping skirt, all lit by the yellow lamplight. I'd never seen Daphne in anything but jogging pants, but obviously, wherever they were going, it was the sort of place you dressed up for. I wished I could have felt pleased for Daphne, having a night out. But I didn't. Wherever it was to be, I was sure she didn't want to go – at least not in that company.

I returned to my sofa and wished I knew where they'd taken her. I recalled the unhappy look on her face as she'd greeted them earlier. It made me feel uneasy and fuelled my misgivings about the tweeded pair. No decent restaurant would admit me nor could I have afforded its prices, but I could've lurked outside and kept an eye on things. I looked out of the window and saw that rain pattered down again on the pavement up there. I'd done enough hanging around in bad weather today. Daphne was with her family and if you can't trust your family . . . Let's face it, I thought. You can't. You can't trust anyone, it's a fact.

The taxi came back at about nine thirty. The headlights strafed the front of the house; there was a slam of a car door. I was still watching TV in the dark. It was the film version of *Death on the Nile* with Peter Ustinov. I liked the scenes of hot sands and sun-baked temples, a contrast to the cold dank outdoors. I hoped Daphne had taken her coat. Voices called out 'Good night!' One set of lightweight footsteps began to climb the front steps, hesitated, turned and came back down again. They began to make a tentative descent of my basement steps. I hurried to switch on the light and open my door, letting the glow flood out into the basement well. I didn't want Daphne crashing head first down the rain-wet steps.

But she'd already negotiated her way safely to the bottom and was standing outside, clutching her coat lapels together against the chill air and peering at me.

'Oh, Fran,' she said, 'I'm sorry to bother you, but I thought there was a chance you might be in. I thought I could see the TV screen flickering. I wondered, if you're not doing anything, whether you'd like to come upstairs and join me in a glass of wine?'

'My nephews brought this,' she said a little later in her kitchen. She was wrestling with the corkscrew and eventually surrendered the task to me. The cork came out with a satisfying pop.

'The one good thing you can say for Charlie,' said Daphne, 'is that he brings a decent bottle when he comes. He fancies himself as a bit of a wine buff, you know.'

Wine bore, more likely. 'I haven't seen them before,' I said, pouring us out a glass.

Daphne rooted about in a cupboard and produced some savoury biscuits which she shook out on to a dish on the table. 'Help yourself.' She raised her glass. 'Cheers!' She was beginning to look much happier than she had when her visitors had arrived. A couple of curls in the brand-new hairdo had come adrift and her lipstick was smudged. She'd kicked off her smart shoes and donned her Fair Isle sock-slippers and looked much more the old Daphne.

'I don't encourage them,' she said, sounding rather as though she was talking of stray cats. 'They mean well, you know. I don't want to be unkind. But I don't like being bothered by people who know better than I do what I want. They think I need looking after.' An indignant note entered her voice and her long purple glass earrings bobbed in sympathy. 'Me! Do I look as if I need looking after?'

'You're fine,' I said robustly. 'And if you need anything, I'm here.'

'Yes, dear, I know. But Bertie and Charlie don't see it like that. They're my brother, Arnold's, sons. Arnold was older than me and he's been dead twenty years. He was a solicitor. The boys joined the firm as soon as they were able and took over when Arnold retired. Neither of them is married.'

That didn't surprise me. 'Are they retired now?' I asked.

'Oh no, dear. They're only fifty-one. I think they look older and they've always been quaint. I mustn't be nasty about them. They took me out for a slap-up dinner. Of course,' she sighed, 'they really wanted to talk business. They always do.'

She took off the purple earrings and laid them neatly side by side on the table, next to her wine glass. 'My mother's,' she said. 'Amethyst.'

I should have known they wouldn't be purple glass. But then, Daphne was probably fairly well off and it sparked an unpleasant notion.

I asked, rather alarmed, whether Bertie and Charlie handled her business, i.e. financial affairs, because I wouldn't have liked that idea at all. But fortunately it seemed not.

'Oh no, because they're my principal heirs, you see. It wouldn't be proper. But naturally, they have an interest. They're worried about death duties.'

It was unlikely I'd ever have anything to leave but the clothes on my back and who'd want those? However, the thought that the duo stood to gain by her death made me, if possible, even more uneasy than the idea they might handle her money during her life. I knew I wasn't being fanciful because Sergeant Parry, my old CID foe, once told me that a person's still most likely to be murdered by a relative or close acquaintance. 'And it's pretty always sex or money,' he'd added. I didn't want to pry into Daphne's affairs but perhaps some outsider without an axe to grind ought to know more about what was going on. Besides, she obviously wanted to talk to someone.

She leaned forward. 'It makes sense, you see, for me to give money or even things away now. To avoid the tax when I drop off the twig. I mean, the house is left to the boys already. But if I, well, made it over to them now . . .'

'They want you to give them this house?' I cried tactlessly.

'I'd go on living here,' she assured me. 'It'd be a formality, that's all, to avoid the tax.'

She might trust them, I certainly didn't. They might or might not let her go on living there. It was more likely they'd try and bundle her into some sort of home. As for me, they'd certainly have me off the premises p.d.q. Really, there was no difference between those two and Tig's boyfriend. Both were after the woman's hard-earned cash.

'You aren't going to do it, Daphne?' I couldn't but sound appalled.

She took a long deep swig of Charlie's wine. 'I don't want to, but when I'm with them, they do seem to make such good sense.'

'You ought to talk to your own solicitor,' I said firmly.

'Yes, I shall do so. I won't be pushed, don't worry.'

'Look,' I said, leaning over the table. 'You know how you value your independence. That's what they want you to give up. You'll be their tenant, Daphne! I mean, even if you're not paying, you'll be living here on sufferance. You don't know how the future will pan out. You might change your mind.'

She was nodding but sighing. 'It's so difficult when it's family. One ought to *like* one's relations.'

Not if they were like Bertie and Charlie Knowles, I thought, but managed by biting my tongue not to say it. I was fast forming the idea that the Knowles twins were very bad news.

Daphne was looking downhearted so, to divert her, I told her about the man who'd burst into the shop that morning.

'Dear me,' she said, and brightened up. Daphne likes a mystery. I'd seen plenty of them on her bookshelves and she sometimes lent me one, usually an Agatha Christie or a Ngaio Marsh. I liked best the Ngaio Marsh books about the theatre. Ever since I'd first met her, Daphne had been tapping away at a great lumbering old manual typewriter, piling up sheets and sheets of densely typed manuscript. I'd never plucked up the courage to ask her what it represented, but it wouldn't have surprised me if it had been a great novel, something on the model of *The Woman in White*. That's a book she likes very much, she told me.

'Perhaps he owes someone money,' she suggested.

But I said, not quite knowing why, 'Or perhaps he's got something to sell.'

'Ah . . .' said Daphne, reaching for the wine. 'But what could it be?'

'Something he ought to get rid of quick,' I said. Not knowing, of course, that he'd done just that.

Chapter Three

Hitch's Transit van rattled to a stop outside the shop three days later, at eight in the morning, minutes after I'd arrived for work. Along the side of the van was printed in tipsy capitals 'PROPERTY MAINTENANCE COMPANY'. The van itself was no great advert for the firm's skills, being distinctly unmaintained and showing evidence of rust and minor collisions. The rear doors were tied together with string.

Ganesh and I stood in the doorway of the shop like a reception committee for royals as Hitch, with a bit of trouble, extricated himself from the front seat. There seemed to be something wrong with the door catch and several bits of pipe, tools, paintbrushes, etc. fell out with him.

'Morning!' he greeted us cheerily, adding for my benefit, 'All right, darling?' He picked up the things which had fallen out, slung them back inside and slammed the van door. Something in the interior fell down with a clatter.

Hitch addresses all women as 'darling' and it doesn't signify any affection or even recognition. It's no use turning PC on him and asking him not to do it. He doesn't even realise he has done it. Still, I tried.

'I'm fine,' I said. 'But I'm not your darling.'

'Right you are, darling,' he replied, walking past me into the shop. 'Where's this boghole you want tarting up, then?'

'Oy!' I called as he and Gan disappeared towards the back of the building. 'You can't leave the van there! You'll get a ticket. Double yellow lines.'

'That's all right, darling!' floated back to me. 'You stay by it and tell anyone who asks I'm just dropping off some gear. I'll be back in a tick.'

I stood there in drizzling rain for one minute and decided that that was enough. It wasn't my problem. I hoped they clamped the thing. I retreated inside and almost at once a customer came in, so I had an excuse.

I listened as Ganesh and Hitch, unseen, shouted at one another in the washroom, their voices echoing off the walls. Hitch only has one voice pitch – loud. It's infectious. After a few moments you find yourself yelling back.

The thing about Hitch is that, until he opens his mouth, he's Mr Anonymous. Not only would you not pick him out in a crowd, you wouldn't notice him if he was the only person walking along the pavement. He's of middle height and I couldn't even guess his age. He's slim, but wiry from all that heaving around of knocked-off building supplies, and going bald. Hitch refers to this last feature as a receding hairline. It's receded to the back of his head, leaving the top domed and shiny. To compensate, he's grown what's left long so that it hangs round the bare patch like the fringe on an old-fashioned table-lamp. He always wears worn jeans and a washed-out navy-blue tee shirt. I've never seen him in anything else so he must have a wardrobe of these items. He's always cheerful and always on the fiddle. He misses nothing.

He came back as the customer left. 'Gonna move the van, darling,' he said. 'You'll be pleased to hear. And ah—' He fished in his jeans back pocket and took out a grubby wallet. He opened it up, revealing a wodge of notes and some small white cards, one of which he peeled off and handed to me.

'There you go, darling. Stick that up on your board, all right?'

I looked at the card. On it was printed: 'JEFFERSON HITCHENS. ALL PROPERTY MAINTENANCE AND HOME IMPROVEMENTS. PATIOS A SPECIALITY. ESTIMATES FREE. NO OBLIGATION. BEST TERMS.'

I said, 'Ha!' loudly.

Hari keeps a corkboard in the window and, for a pound a week, anyone can leave a notice up there. I added Hitch's. Ganesh came back while I was doing this. I pointed out that Hitch hadn't paid the required pound.

'Don't worry,' said Ganesh. 'I'll knock it off his bill. Don't go upsetting him, for goodness' sake.'

'Me?' I protested.

'Yes, you. You glare at him as if he's just insulted you and that weird haircut of yours bristles even more. Can't you do something about it?' He frowned. 'It looks like a mangy hedgehog.'

'Join the club, why don't you? Let's all insult Fran. I don't like being called darling. If he's going to do it all the time he's here, he's going to get a flea in his ear.'

'Oh, don't make such a fuss,' said Ganesh.

For all he was acting in control, I guessed Ganesh was nervous. It was one thing plotting to go behind Hari's back and get the washroom fixed up. The reality of Hitch on the premises had reminded him that he hadn't Hari's authority and if anything went wrong, the buck stopped there with Gan.

I appreciated his fragile state of mind, but he'd got himself into this and he could get himself out of it. Likewise, he had no cause to be rude about my hair, although by the same token,

I'd no right to be rude about Hitch's baldness. A few weeks back, when the weather had still been mild, I'd decided to go for a new look. So I had my hair shaved off at the sides and kept a short brush top and a thin layer at the nape of the neck. I quickly decided I'd chosen the wrong time of year. In the summer, the shaved sides would've been all right. But now, at the onset of winter, it was a chilly style, so I was growing it all out. The result was a bit of a mess, the sides were fuzzy and the brush top was going all ways, some of it sticking up, some falling over. I'd done my best to tidy it up, using gel, and I didn't need reminding I looked as if I'd just had an electric shock. It'd grow out. The sooner the better. Haven't you ever made a mistake like that?

Hitch came back, whistling happily. He was carrying a colour chart. 'If you was to decide on the magnolia,' he said, 'I've got a few tins of that on special offer. Left over from a job.'

I glared at Ganesh but he was refusing to look at me. He took Hitch through to the storeroom so that they could discuss colour schemes in private without my help.

I leaned on the counter and leafed idly through one of the tabloids until my attention was taken by the ting of the bell above the door.

The man who came in was short and Mediterranean-looking. His hair was dark and tightly curled, his features small, his skin olive. He stared at me and said, 'Twenty Benson and Hedges.'

I fetched them off the shelf behind me and turned back to find he'd moved. He'd wandered over to the magazine rack and was studying the titles. I put the cigarettes on the counter and waited. I didn't have anything else to do so I watched him. Gan had told me to watch out for loiterers at the mag stand. They sometimes slipped one magazine inside another and tried to get away with paying for one only. Then there are the ones who're coy about taking down the girlie mags from the top shelf. They spend ages looking through titles on woodwork and computer graphics and finally reach up for one of the dirty dozen with a start of surprise, as if they'd just noticed them and hadn't a clue what they contained.

Somehow, I felt this man wasn't interested in any of the magazines. He was looking all round the shop and I started to get apprehensive. When he started back towards the counter, I glanced down to make sure I knew where the jemmy was in case I had to grab it.

He sought through a handful of coins in his palm. 'Business quiet,' he observed.

'Comes and goes,' I replied. I took his money and rang up the till.

He tucked the packet of cigarettes inside his blouson. 'Nothing exciting ever happens, eh?' He was smiling at me in a way he probably thought charming. He had small white pointed teeth.

'Not since I've worked here,' I said.

'Friend of mine,' he said, 'came by here the other day.'

'Oh, yes?'

'He said there was a bit of a dust-up outside. A chap got roughed up. He came in here.' His English was good enough but heavily accented, with a lisp and Rs which stuck in his throat.

'No one came in here,' I said coldly.

'Perhaps you weren't here, then.' His eyes slid round the store again. 'Anyone else work here?'

'I'm always here mornings,' I said just as icily, 'and I saw nothing.'

The little white teeth flashed. 'That's right, it happened during the morning.'

Ouch. I'd slipped up there.

He was smiling with his mouth but his eyes watched me like a vicious dog waiting for a chance to snap. 'Sure you didn't see anything?' His hand slid into the jacket and came out holding a note. 'Fact is, the man might've dropped something and my friend would like to give it back to him. He thinks he knows where to find him.'

He was offering me twenty quid. Offering any money was clumsy, offering so much was plain stupid. If I'd not been interested before, I'd be fascinated now to know just what he was after. Actually, I was interested – but I wasn't going to let him know it.

'You're wasting your time,' I told him.

There was movement at the back of the shop floor. Ganesh and Hitch emerged from the storeroom, causing me to glance their way. At the same time the doorbell tinged again. I looked round and found the customer had slipped out. I wondered whether to tell Ganesh and decided against it. No point in worrying him.

'All right, darling?' asked Hitch cheerfully. 'No problems? I'll come in tomorrow early, bring along a mate to give me a hand. We'll carry on over the weekend, have it all finished by Monday afternoon.'

'You owe a pound,' I said, 'for pinning up your card in the window.'

'Wish I had you keeping my books,' he said, fishing in his pocket and producing fifty pence. 'Here you are, on account. Give you the other fifty tomorrow.'

'What did you do that for?' asked Gan when Hitch had left.

'Because I don't trust him.'

'I don't know what you've got against Hitch,' Ganesh said. 'You've never liked him.'

'Instinct,' I told him. But truth to tell I had other things on my mind than the washroom. Ganesh could tell Hitch to paint the place purple and put in gold taps for all I cared.

'You haven't found anything in the shop, have you, Gan? Dropped on the floor?'

'What like?'

'Like lost property. I don't know.'

'What've you lost?'

'I haven't lost anything. Oh, forget it.'

'Sometimes,' said Ganesh, 'the way you ramble on, I wonder about you.'

'That's it!' I said crossly. 'I'm quitting for the day.'

'It's not eleven!' he protested.

'It's quiet. You can manage. I'll come in tomorrow.'

'I'm only paying you for the hours you've worked, not for the whole morning.' He sounded pompous and indignant in equal measure.

'On what you pay me, that's no great loss!' I stormed out.

I don't like quarrelling with Ganesh but the row had been brewing up over the last few days and now it was out and by tomorrow the air would've cleared. I was still annoyed with him, though. To tell the truth, I was feeling annoyed with myself. I really didn't need to get involved in anything. I hoped the little foreign guy asking the questions wouldn't come back. Perhaps I should've told Ganesh about him.

When you're fending for yourself in the city, you develop all your senses like an animal. You get to smell danger and I smelled it now. Nevertheless, I must have been getting careless, because it wasn't until I was almost home that I became aware of a tingle between the shoulder blades which told me someone was following me. Not walking behind me, following me.

I wheeled round. People were surging along, faces set and purposeful, on many the strain of the approaching festive season already showing. I wondered which one it was. None of them looked a likely candidate. Perhaps my nerves were overstretched, firing my imagination. Or perhaps the tracker had been quicker than me and, a split second before I turned, had nipped into a doorway or wheeled round and started back away from me. I moved on, thoughtful.

The rain had packed in during the previous night and a fitful sun had shone all morning, drying up the pavements and streets. Despite that, a puddle had formed in the road outside my flat. Water doesn't usually collect there but the rains had been heavy. I didn't pay it too much attention.

I hadn't seen anything of Daphne since our chat over the bottle of wine. As far as I knew the brothers Knowles hadn't returned, but I was keeping an eye open. Daphne wasn't the only person on my mind. There was Tig. I should let that situation alone; it wasn't my business. But I decided to give it a try. The day was fairly bright, but it wouldn't last long. By four darkness would've drawn in again. If I wanted to find Tig, I had to set out now. I had a quick cup of tea and went in search of her.

I returned to the entrance near to the supermarket where I'd found her, but she wasn't there. I widened out my hunt in slowly increasing circles because I thought it likely she and her partner were working this area. But they appeared to have moved on. Maybe they'd been warned off, either by the law or because they'd trespassed on someone else's turf. At any rate, neither Tig nor the man in the plaid jacket were to be seen.

I decided to give up and for something to do in the remaining short space of daylight, set off for Camden High Street.

Trotting down the Chalk Farm Road, I felt my spirits rise. I like this patch. To my mind, it's the nearest thing to Dickensian London, alive and kicking in all its variety and vulgarity. So, it's getting a tad gentrified with middle-class stores and antiques shops setting up, but it is still reassuringly eccentric and clinging to its pleb roots.

The recent rains had washed it clean. The black horses with glaring red eyes which leaped out from the façade of the Round House gleamed as if some infernal groom had buffed them up. I was lured by the promises of the Circus of Horrors and the Terrordome, but they were closed at the moment. So I went on, revelling in the used-car outlets, cheap clothes shops, the fast food dispensaries and street pedlars. I smiled up at the huge painted figures decorating the upper floor façades of the shops, the giant wooden boots, camouflaged tank, leather-jacketed rocker, silver skull and, why oh why, above the tattoo parlour, a sea of scarlet flames?

I knew that the Stables and the canalside markets wouldn't be open now, but remnants of Inverness Street market could still be in progress and I might pick up something cheap and cheerful there. As stallholders closed up, they were often happy to let you have something virtually at cost. But before I ever got there, I glimpsed a plaid jacket ahead of me and there he was, Tig's boyfriend. I was just in time. Seconds later, he turned into The Man in The Moon pub.

He wasn't likely to be out in a hurry. Tig wasn't with him, but ten to one, she wasn't far away. I guessed they'd staked out a pitch and he'd left her begging while he spent the money on lager. I hunted in earnest now, casting about below the railway bridge and in the environs of the big drive-by supermarket which lay behind the main road, round by the bridge over the canal and at last ran her to earth in the entrance to Camden Town tube station.

She wasn't pleased to see me. 'You again!' she exclaimed, and her pinched face blenched with fury. It emphasised the greenish-black patch on one cheekbone. 'You following me around or what?'

'Time for a coffee-break, Tig,' I said. 'And don't worry about him. He's in the pub.'

We took our polystyrene cups of coffee down by the dark olive-green canal and found a seat. Tig hunched on her end of the bench, sipping the coffee, eyes fixed on the water swirling sluggishly past, thick as treacle.

'What's his name?' I asked.

'Jo Jo.'

'He the one who beat you up?'

Despite herself, she took one hand from the cup to touch the bruise on her face. 'No one beat me up,' she said. 'It was just a slap.' She straightened up and became belligerent, her eyes, through the rat's tails of greasy fair hair, as cold as the canal's waters. Since the Jubilee Street days, she'd acquired a ring through the outer edge of her left eyebrow. Speaking as one who wears a nose-stud, I'm not criticising, you understand. It was just one more detail about Tig different to the old days. 'Anyway, it was your fault,' she said.

'Mine?' I wanted to know how she'd worked that out.

'The chocolate bar you gave me,' she said. 'He found it in my pocket. He said I'd been siphoning off the takings and spending them on stuff. I wasn't.'

'One lousy sweet?' I gasped. 'He thumped you because you'd bought one chocolate bar?'

'I didn't buy it,' she argued. 'You gave it to me.'

'Oh, sorry, excuse me!' I retorted sarcastically. 'I didn't realise that made it all right for him. Yes, my fault, why didn't I think of that?'

There was a silence. She looked away. 'Well, anyway, Fran . . . I didn't mean it wasn't nice of you. But when people try and help they nearly always foul you up more, you know that.'

I let her simmer. We finished our coffee and she slung her cup into the canal where it bobbed away. The old Tig, who'd arrived bright-eyed and bushy-tailed from the Heart of England, wouldn't have dreamed of littering up the place like that.

'Why'd you take up with him?'

'Why do you think?' She shrugged. 'He's not so bad.' She glanced sideways at me. 'If you want to know, I had – a bad experience. I was raped.' She spoke the last words with an awful blankness of voice and expression.

I waited. After a moment, she went on, 'I was on the game at the time, but I hadn't bargained for that. I was stupid. I should have realised – I mean, a regular working prostitute would've sized up the situation and got out of there, but I walked into it, didn't I?'

'It was a punter, then?' I prompted her.

'Yes, or I thought so. I thought he was on his own. He came up to me, youngish guy, bit drunk, City type. It was a Friday evening. He'd been celebrating the end of the week, I thought, and now he was looking for a cheap lay. I went with him to his car – I told you I was stupid – and the next thing I knew, there were two other guys, pals of his. They bundled me into the car and drove me to a house. They were just like him, hooray Henrys, red braces, Italian suits, the lot. Drunk as skunks. They kept me there for, I suppose, a couple of hours while they had their pervy fun. I don't know exactly how long, I just wanted to get it all over with and get out of there alive. My biggest fear was they wouldn't let me leave. But they did in the end.'

'Do you know where this house is?' I asked angrily.

'No, it was dark. I was too scared to take notice, I was watching them, not watching the surroundings. I didn't know what they were going to do next. There were the three of them and I didn't know which one of them to watch. They laughed all the time. One of them was sick, threw up on the floor and the first one swore at him so I guess it was his house and his carpet. Perhaps that's what made him think the time had come to call a halt to the fun and games. At any rate, he told me to get dressed. They got to arguing a bit while I scrambled into my gear as fast as I could. I knew they were arguing about what to do with me. I thought perhaps I could run while they were distracted, and get outside. They wouldn't want a scene in the street.

'But then the first one – I don't know any of their names – he grabbed my arm and shoved me along ahead of him down the hall, out and back into the car. He told me not to say a word or he'd take me straight down to the river and hold my head under till I drowned. The river police pull out bodies every day, he said. I'd just be one more, floating past. I believed him. I sat there almost too frightened to breathe. He drove me back to King's Cross, which was where he'd picked me up. He gave me eighty quid and said, "Don't try telling anyone it was rape, sweetheart. You offered and I paid."'

'Eighty quid,' I said, 'would hardly have covered it even if you'd agreed. That's under thirty quid each.'

'What was I going to do, argue? He tossed me out and drove off. I told you, Fran, I thought they'd kill me. I was just so pleased when he drove off . . . Afterwards, though, I couldn't put the whole business out of my mind. I was too scared for the meat trade. So I took up with Jo Jo and we do all right, with me begging and Jo Jo watching out for me. I've had no more trouble with men since Jo Jo's been around.'

'What about the habit?' I asked.

A dull flush stained her pale cheeks. 'I'm clean now, Fran, I swear. That was when I was turning tricks to get the money for a fix. After the rape, I knew I had to break the habit because as long as I was on it, I'd take any risk to get the money. I went on to methadone and now I'm clean.'

I told her that was great, because it was. It had taken courage and perseverance but most of all, it showed that Tig hadn't slid so far down the ladder that she no longer realised how bad things were.

'What about you, Fran?' she asked. 'You seem to be doing all right.'

I explained that I was working temporarily at the newsagent's, just while Hari was in India.

'You haven't cracked it as an actress, then?' She gave a little smile.

'Not yet,' I said. 'I will.'

'Sure,' she said. It niggled.

'I also,' I said, 'look into things for people.'

That made her suspicious. 'What sort of things? What sort of people?'

'Mostly people who can't get help anywhere else. Like a private detective, you know, only I'm not official. I'm not fixed up with a proper organisation or the tax and insurance people would get me. Anyway, I don't do enough work for that. But what I have done has been all right.'

I suppose simple pride must have echoed in my voice, but why not? I'd been reasonably successful, considering.

Tig looked impressed but persisted, 'But what *sort* of things do you do? Say, if someone came to you and told you they wanted something arranged but they couldn't do it themselves, would you do that?'

'I do anything legal,' I said, perhaps not as cautiously as I might've done.

'Should've thought that cramped your style a bit,' said Tig. 'Sticking to the law, I mean. Don't the coppers get in your way?'

'Yes,' I said, adding airily, 'but I can handle them.'

You know what they say about pride coming before a fall, don't you? Tig didn't ask anything else but sat scowling at the canal water and twisting one finger in a lank strand of hair.

'You know,' I said, breaking in on whatever deep thoughts she was having, 'I was really surprised to see you the other day. I thought you'd have gone home long before now, back to where you came from.'

She gave a strangled little laugh. 'I can't go back, not now, not like I am. Can you imagine their faces if they saw me now? No, of course you can't. You don't know them.'

'You mean your parents?'

'They're really respectable people,' she said dully. 'Really decent. My mother's so houseproud she can't even bear to see the streaks the rain makes on the windows. She's out there polishing them off as soon as the rain stops. She's always polishing everything up. A perfect house, that's what she runs, because that's what he likes, my dad. Everything just so. I can't go back, Fran.'

'You could try.' I leaned forward. 'Listen, Tig, sooner or later Jo Jo's going to get tired of you, right? You're certainly going to want to get away from him. Where are you going from here?'

'Don't!' There was so much pain in her voice that I was conscience-stricken at my question. 'What do you think, Fran? What do you imagine *I* think about, day in, day out? How do you think I like facing another Christmas on the streets? Even if Jo Jo and I find a place in a hostel, it'll be for a few days only – and then going back out is worse. I can't get along with these charities and I'm not like you, Fran, a survivor.'

'Pull yourself together!' I said sharply. 'That isn't true and you know it. It took guts to get yourself off drugs and you wouldn't have done that if you hadn't had some other vision for yourself, some idea of getting away from all this—'

Suddenly she struck out at me wildly, sobbing in dry gasps, her fists clenched into rock-hard little mallets. She caught me a couple of times, but I fended off most blows because she was too disorganised and angry to think about targeting them. At last they became weaker and finally stopped. Her hands dropped back in her lap.

For a moment she was still, then she sat up, tossed back her hair, and turned a stony face to me. 'I've got to go,' she said. 'I'm not making any money sitting here chewing the fat with you.'

'Write to your family!' I urged. 'A postcard, that's all. Call them!'

'How can I? Don't be stupid, Fran.' She sounded weary and exasperated. 'I don't even know what the situation is back home now. Maybe they don't live in that house any more. Perhaps they were so ashamed when I left that they couldn't face the neighbours. Perhaps they've moved. It's the sort of thing they'd do.'

'And perhaps they're still there, hoping that the next time the phone rings—'

'Shut up!' she hissed.

She'd jumped to her feet with the last words and was making to walk off. I knew that if I lost her now, I'd lost her for good. She'd never sit and talk to me again. She was several yards away already, at the foot of the stone steps up to the bridge.

'What have you got to lose?' I yelled desperately.

I thought she mightn't have heard me but she stopped and turned. The light was fading very fast and I couldn't make out her face, only her dark spindly form. Her voice, eerily thin, came through the gloom. It gave me goosebumps. 'They hope I'm dead, Fran. For them, I am dead. Soon I will be dead. We both know that.'

'Rubbish!' I bellowed back. 'You're giving up! This isn't the time to give up!'

'Why not?' She sounded calm, too calm. I had to keep her there, keep her talking.

'Perhaps together we can think of something.'

'You're crazy, Fran. You always were. Don't try and help me. I told you, do-gooders always foul you up.'

'You're already fouled up,' I retorted. 'But you want to get out of this and I might be able to help. Or I can try.' I hadn't a clue how, mind you, and probably I shouldn't be sticking my neck out like that, but I could feel her slipping away, not just physically, but mentally. A few moments back, just for an instant, I'd made contact. 'Isn't it worth it?' I shouted. 'Or do you want to wait until Jo Jo knocks out your front teeth and then goes off with some other girl?'

She swore at me and turned on her heel. I shouted after her, 'You can find me mornings at the newsagent's by the traffic lights, just down from where I saw you the other day. Or leave a message for me there with Ganesh Patel.'

A brief abusive reply drifted back to me through the evening shades.

I let her go and wondered if I'd see her again. I told myself it didn't matter if I didn't. That was life on the streets. People came and went. If anyone vanished it might be because they wanted to. Everyone had that right – to be anonymous, to be spared probing questions, needing to give an account of oneself. It was up to Tig to decide how she wanted to live. In the end, it mattered to no one but herself.

'Not to you, Fran, at any rate,' I told myself aloud. I went home.

The chap was wrong who said no man was an island. That's what each of us is, an island.

Chapter Four

'Morning, darling!'

'Hullo, Hitch,' I returned unenthusiastically.

He was on time, I'd give him that. It was just a little after eight. I'd arrived ten minutes earlier and found Ganesh in subdued mood. I fancied he looked relieved to see me. I went to take a last look at the old washroom and I had to admit, it badly needed doing up. Hari really shouldn't complain. I just wished, somehow, it wasn't Hitch carrying out the work. There's always a snag where he's concerned, something he hasn't told you. But for the life of me, looking around the small area involved and the basic fittings, I couldn't see what it was here.

'Go and tell him to open up the back gate, will you, darling?' Hitch wheedled now. It must have got through his thick skull that he wasn't my favourite person and he was wary of me. 'So's Marco and I can bring the new stuff in and take the old out, right? You don't want it coming through here, do you?'

Ganesh came out of the storeroom at that moment so I said, 'Tell him yourself.'

'I'll go and open up,' said Ganesh, who'd obviously overheard. He gave me a very direct look which meant, I knew, don't antagonise the workforce.

Ganesh disappeared to open up the small yard out back and

Hitch followed, taking a good look round him as he went. I hoped he kept his fingers to himself in the storeroom.

I was on my own. I fiddled around, tidying the mags and papers, replenishing the bins of packeted snacks and the sweet trays until the bell jingled, the paper chains and tinsel rustled, heralding a newcomer in the shop.

I emerged from behind the rack of Christmas cards and gaped. He was six foot tall and beautiful. His long blond hair was tied back with a ribbon and contrasted with large dark eyes and eyebrows in an oval face with a long narrow nose. His expression was dreamy and serene, suggesting behind it was a mind concentrating on higher spiritual matters. It was as if the Angel Gabriel had just stepped off one of the cards. Perhaps the hair was bleached – I didn't care. He wore an old dark quilted jacket and clean but paint-stained jeans and trainers. He hadn't, alas, brought a message from on high.

'Hitch around somewhere?' he asked. He had a nice voice and was altogether my idea of a Christmas present.

'Out back in the yard,' I croaked, adding in, I hoped, a more normal if incredulous voice, 'You're Marco? I'm Fran.' If he looked like any kind of painter, he ought to be one knocking out some entry for the Turner Prize.

'Oh, right. Can I get through here? Or have I got to go round?'

'You can go through, I'll show you.' I led the way to the storeroom. Perhaps having the Jefferson Hitchens Property Maintenance Company on the premises wasn't going to be so bad, after all.

Oh yes, it was. The rest of the morning was dominated by a deafening banging and clattering from the washroom as the old fittings were torn out. Every customer who came in asked what was going on and I soon had a headache. Brief respite came roughly every hour when Hitch and Marco took a tea-break in the storeroom.

'You know,' I said to Gan, 'not that it's any of my business, but you ought to keep an eye on them in there.'

'I can't spy on them,' said Gan nervously.

'We'll take it in turns,' I said. 'I'll go first.'

I opened the storeroom door and peered in. Hitch was sitting on a plastic chair, reading the *Sun* and drinking from a large souvenir mug celebrating West Ham Football Club. There was an empty crisp packet on the table together with the crumpled wrappings from a bar of turkish delight. Marco was drinking Coca-Cola from the can and reading a Terry Pratchett novel. They glanced up.

'Need some more KitKats!' I excused my presence hastily and grabbed a carton.

'Just the job,' said Hitch, brightening. 'Cheers, darling.'

I handed them out a KitKat each and went back.

'Price of two KitKats, a can of Coke, a turkish delight and a packet of crisps to be knocked off the final bill,' I said. 'You'd better keep a tally. Has he given you the fifty pence owing from yesterday?'

Ganesh looked at me in wonder and reproach. 'I've never known you so stingy, Fran.'

'It's like Aladdin's cave in there as far as Hitch is concerned,' I warned.

Ganesh looked worried and the next time the workers took a break, he was in there like a shot, checking on them.

At eleven, I made coffee for us all, using water from the kettle I'd filled before they started work. Needless to say, the water supply was now switched off. They were quick workers, at least on the demolition side. They'd pulled out the washbasin and the loo and cistern. I'd had to go next door to the petfood shop and ask to use the loo there. This time, as I carried my offerings of coffee to our two creative builders in the storeroom, my nostrils were assailed by a distinctive sickly scent as I opened the door.

'I don't want to worry you,' I said to Ganesh, 'but Marco's smoking a joint in there.'

'What? For God's sake, stop him!' Ganesh looked as if he was going to have a heart attack. 'Anyone coming in the shop will be able to smell it!'

'You stop him,' I suggested. But in the end I was the one who went back in there and informed Marco that smoking – of whatever kind – on the premises was strictly forbidden owing to the high fire risk.

'Sure,' he said, smiling serenely up at me. I found myself smiling back, mesmerised.

'You mean, you gotta shop full of fags and you can't light up?' demanded Hitch, shocked.

'That's it,' I said. With Hitch playing gooseberry, what chance romance? 'The insurance company insists.'

'We'll have a couple of them Mars bars over there, then.' He pointed airily at the box.

By now, I didn't have to tell Ganesh to keep a tally. He was feverishly jotting it all down on a scrap of paper by the till.

'Here,' said Hitch suddenly, 'we found something when we pulled the old basin out, didn't we, Marco? You got it?'

'Yeah.' Marco fished in his pocket and handed me one of those small padded envelopes. 'Jammed down behind the pipes underneath.'

'Thanks,' I said, taking it. I turned it over. It was stuck down with Sellotape. I pressed it cautiously and felt something small, cylindrical, and solid inside. I didn't recognise the shape but the envelope looked clean and fresh. Whatever it was, it couldn't have been there long.

'Dunno what it is,' prompted Hitch, adding virtuously, 'We didn't open it, Marco and me. It's stuck down.'

I forbore remarking that it was a pity the contents of the storeroom weren't stuck down. I retreated into the shop, followed by our workers, and handed the package to Ganesh.

'They found it hidden behind the pipes.'

'What is it?' asked Gan suspiciously.

'How do I know? Open it, you're the manager.'

'I'm not going to open it,' he said. 'It might explode. You read about these things in the papers. Nutters go round shops hiding incendiary devices.' Hitch and Marco backed off a little.

'What would be the point of it going off in the washroom?' I asked. 'It wouldn't set fire to anything in there. Besides, how would he get into the washroom to hide it? The public never goes in there and no one could get past whoever is working in the shop without being seen.'

'You open it, then,' he said.

'All right, I will!'

Hitch and Marco watched with interest and from a safe distance, as I tore open the envelope and shook out what appeared to be a small roll of film on to the counter top. We looked at it. Ganesh put out his hand.

'Wouldn't touch it if I was you,' said Hitch. 'Might be dodgy. You don't want your dabs on it, do you?'

That will tell you quite a bit about Hitch.

'What's it doing in the washroom?' asked Ganesh, bewildered. 'Why should anyone put it there?'

'It might be mucky,' suggested Hitch brightly. 'You know, some feller and girl getting up to things. I mean, things like in that Indian book what tells you how to do it all kinds of funny ways.' Both he and Marco gazed at Gan and myself with a new interest and some respect. 'Never read it myself,' added Hitch with regret.

This irritated Ganesh who snapped, 'Don't talk such nonsense! The *Kama Sutra* is a serious work of great beauty.'

Hitch opened his mouth to ask for further enlightenment but the look on Ganesh's face made him change his mind.

I knew why Ganesh was ratty. It wasn't just that he doesn't like to hear his culture misunderstood (although he grumbles enough about it himself), it was because that's not how things are between him and me. Some people get the wrong idea about that. Hitch wasn't the first. But Ganesh is my friend, not my lover. Not that I couldn't fancy Ganesh, or that he couldn't fancy me. There have been times when we've come awfully close to moving beyond the friendship scenario. But we both know it wouldn't work out if we did. Sex complicates things, in my experience, and for us it'd make life more than difficult. His parents have other plans for him, and I'm not part of them. They like me, or I think they do, even though they obviously fear I'm a bad influence on him and give him dangerous ideas of independence. Ganesh says they like me and they've always acted as if they do. But they simply don't understand me or my life-style, my lack of family or the way I exist from day to day. It's one of those situations. Nothing can be done about it and you just have to lump it. Still, I'm glad to have Gan as a friend because that means an awful lot.

Ganesh went on now in tones clearly meant to dash any remaining fantasies Hitch might have, 'In any case, this doesn't belong to me. Is it yours, Fran?'

'Course not!' I protested. 'I'd have said so. Why on earth should I hide it in the washroom, even if it was mine? Besides, I haven't even got a camera.'

'Well, Hari wouldn't hide it there, would he?' argued Ganesh. 'If he wanted to tuck it away somewhere, he'd put it upstairs. So it isn't his.'

'That makes it no one's,' I pointed out. 'And that's daft. It has to belong to someone.'

'Oh well,' said Hitch, losing interest. 'Makes no difference to me and Marco. It's all yours whatever it is.'

The two of them drifted back to the storeroom. I took Ganesh's arm and propelled him nearer the entrance to the shop, out of earshot.

'It belongs to that bloke!' I whispered excitedly. 'It must do, Gan. You know, the one who stumbled in here the other morning? It must be his and he hid it there. You let him use the washroom to clean up. Someone was after him – after *this* – and he stashed it there to pick up later.'

'Don't be daft, Fran,' said Ganesh, but he looked uncomfortable. 'Anyone could've put it there. Even Hari, though I don't know why.'

'Of course Hari didn't put it there! Why on earth should he? Look, Gan, I didn't tell you this, but someone came in yesterday morning, asking about the guy – and wanting to know if we'd found anything dropped on the floor. He told a stupid tale about a friend of his losing something – and he offered me twenty quid.'

'Fran!' cried Ganesh, agonised. 'You didn't take it?'

'Course I didn't! I didn't say anything, either. Think I'm daft?'

Ganesh glanced at the counter and the roll of film lying on it. 'What do we do with it? Give it to the police? It really doesn't look like it's anything, but if you think someone's after it—'

'We could get it developed first.' I tried to make the idea

sound as tempting as possible. 'You know, just to make sure. I mean, we can't go to the police with a blank film or someone's holiday snaps, can we? I'll take it along to Joleen at the chemist's down the road. They've got a one-hour service.'

Hitch and Marco had recommenced the labours in the washroom. Hitch was whistling piercingly as they hammered the old tiles off the walls. As each tile came loose, it fell to the ground with a shattering of ceramic.

'I can't stand much more of this,' I said. 'I'll nip along to the chemist's, anyway. I need some headache pills.'

'We sell 'em here,' said Gan, not losing his business instincts, even in the circumstances.

I nipped back to the chemist for the developed reel at lunchtime. It was Saturday and the place was packed. Joleen, to whom I'd given the film, was dealing with a customer. Another woman in the shop fetched them for me.

'It says here,' she read from a note stapled to the yellow envelope, 'that most of the film was unused and there were only four snaps on it.' She stared at me curiously.

'Right,' I said jauntily, as if I knew. I paid her and scuttled outside with them.

I couldn't resist taking a peek on my way back to Ganesh, but they weren't very interesting. They showed three men sitting at a table in some kind of garden or possibly a planted area surrounding a swimming pool at a posh hotel. Exotic-looking flowers bloomed on a creeper growing over a whitewashed wall. To the extreme right of the picture, beyond the wall, could be glimpsed a small area of coastline, a beach of sorts, some hinterland and a smidgen of sea. One of the men was mustachioed and swarthy in appearance, one had his back to camera and I could see only dark hair and a sweat-stained grey-blue shirt. The third man, in early middle age, was either fair or grey-haired, it was hard to tell. He looked plump and prosperous, but tough, and wore a multi-coloured leisure shirt. Dark glasses hung on a safety chain round his neck. Holiday snaps, after all, I thought, and felt really disappointed. I don't know what I'd expected.

'Here,' I said, pushing them under Ganesh's nose in a gap between customers. 'What do you make of them?'

'Nothing,' said Ganesh, glancing at them.

'They've got to mean something,' I persisted.

'No, they haven't. Don't tell me that bloke who was in here the other day went to the trouble of hiding those! Four pictures of him and his mates on the Costa Brava?'

'He's not in them,' I objected. 'Not even this guy with his back to camera is him, I'm sure of it.'

'So, he was the photographer. Only he wasn't, because I don't believe they belong to him, Fran. It doesn't make any sense.'

I was peering at the snaps more closely. There was a bottle of beer on the table, label towards the camera.

'If we got this blown up,' I said, 'we could read that label and it'd give us a clue.'

'They are someone's holiday snaps,' said Ganesh patiently. 'And even you can't make out differently. Look at that chap's shirt.'

'It's somewhere warm and holiday-ish,' I mused.

'It might be the Canary Islands,' said Ganesh thoughtfully. Despite his dismissive attitude, I could see he was gradually getting as hooked on this as I was. 'Usha and Jay went there on holiday and this could easily be one of their snaps.'

Usha is his sister and Jay her accountant husband. Jay is doing spectacularly well and now Usha's studying accountancy at evening classes so she can work in his office. The better they do, the more depressed Ganesh gets. I tell him that's nobody's fault but his own. He's got to get out of the retail business.

This wasn't the moment to bring up that delicate subject. Right now the photos had priority. I didn't go along with the Canary Islands theory and said so.

'Well, it's not Bournemouth, is it?' argued Ganesh.

'That doesn't mean it has to be some other obvious holiday spot. Look, see that bit of beach? It hasn't got any parasols or sunbathers on it. And look at the landscape behind the beach. You can only see a bit of it, but it looks as if it's in the middle of nowhere, scrubby-looking trees and dried-up grass. There aren't any skyscraper hotels. The beaches in most tourist resorts are lined with hotels and bars.'

'Ever been to the Canaries?' retorted Ganesh.

I had to admit I hadn't. 'But I've seen pictures. Come to that, I've seen Usha's holiday snaps and they don't look a bit like this.'

Ganesh straightened up. 'So, what do we do with them?'

'If that bloke hid the film,' I reasoned, 'he wanted to keep it safe and my guess is, he'll come back for it. But not until he knows the coast is clear. If he thinks the men who were after him are watching this shop, he won't come here yet. He'll wait. The least we can do is keep the pics and negatives safe until he comes. So I think you should put them somewhere safe while *we* wait.'

'OK,' said Ganesh resignedly. 'I'll keep them for a week and if he hasn't come back for them in that time, I'm going to bin them, right?' He shoved the yellow packet under the till. 'Look, are you going out anywhere tonight? I've been thinking, every other business round here is having a staff Christmas dinner. So I don't see why you and I can't go out and have a decent meal at the expense of the shop.'

'Hari—' I began. I thought it only fair to remind him.

He interrupted. 'I'm the manager while Hari's away and it's my decision that the staff can have a Christmas outing. We're entitled. We've worked hard.'

'Fair enough,' I agreed. 'I'm not doing anything else.'

Ganesh nodded. 'Come back here around eight-fifteen – gives me time to lock up.' He hesitated. 'See if you can fix up your hair before then, can't you? It does look awful, Fran.'

I overlooked renewed criticism as I was being offered dinner.

Chapter Five

On my way home, however, I caught sight of myself reflected in a window and Ganesh was right. My hair looked awful. A little further along, on the corner, was a small hairdressing salon. I peered in. It didn't look particularly busy. I pushed open the door.

A ferocious-looking woman, who was assaulting a customer with an outsize can of spray, looked up through a cloud of chemicals and exclaimed, 'Gawd, what scissor-happy maniac done that?'

Everyone in the shop, staff and customers, stopped their conversations, magazine-reading, cutting, washing, etc. and stared at me.

Before I could answer, she went on just as fiercely, 'You didn't get that cut here. She didn't get it done here!' she repeated more loudly for the benefit of anyone who hadn't heard.

'No, I didn't,' I said meekly. 'Can you fix it?'

'I dunno . . .' She looked at the clock on the wall.

'I'm going out tonight,' I said pathetically.

'Make the date over the phone, did he?' asked the charmer with the hairspray. 'He'll have a fit when he sees that. Oh well, sit down a tick and I'll have a go when I'm finished here. That hedge on the top will have to come off.'

When I emerged, some time later, I looked like Joan of Arc about to go to the stake. My hair resembled a reddish-brown bathing cap. She'd trimmed the spikes on top back to little longer than the bits at the sides and brushed it all forward to a little wispy fringe on the forehead. I have to admit, though, it looked quite good, certainly better than before.

Because of this I didn't get home until three-thirty and the light had a dirty greyness to it presaging the early dark. But I could see the puddle in front of the house still hadn't dried up. It hadn't rained again and I wondered vaguely about it before my attention was distracted.

The lights were on in Daphne's front window, a room she seldom used, and the curtains hadn't been drawn. Through it I could see, brightly lit, Bertie and Charlie standing close together in deep discussion. Charlie was leaning on the marble mantelshelf and Bertie was puffing on a pipe. They looked the perfect pair of crooks. I couldn't see Daphne. She was probably making the unspeakable duo tea.

I resisted the urge to knock on the door and ask to see her. If she wanted to tell me what they were up to now, she'd tell me in her own good time. But the sight of them there, looking so at home as if they already owned the place, made my new haircut bristle.

I went down to the basement and my own flat, put on the kettle and sorted through my meagre wardrobe. Since I hadn't acquired any new clothes in the past three months – apart from a pair of sock-slippers kindly knitted for me by Daphne and hardly suitable for the 'staff dinner' – it looked like the ankle-length purple skirt I'd got from Oxfam and the ethnic Indian waistcoat again (Camden Lock Market), teamed with a black polo-neck sweater (BHS sale) and my Doc Marten boots, because they were the only footwear I had at that time, apart from a pair of ancient trainers with holes in both soles.

Later, when I'd showered and put it all on, I stood in front of the bathroom mirror to study the effect. I looked a real ragbag. When I was studying drama, we did a production of *Blithe Spirit* and I got to read for the part of the batty medium, Madame Arcati. Now I looked as if I was dressed for the role. I was distracted by a loud ring on my doorbell.

It wasn't even a quarter to eight yet and I didn't think it could be Ganesh. Besides, the arrangement was I meet him at the shop. As I went towards the door, I noticed an envelope lying on the mat just inside. Either someone had delivered it since I'd come home – and I hadn't heard the letter box – or I'd stepped over it in the gloom when I'd walked in. I stooped and picked it up, tucking it in my pocket, before opening the door on the chain and peering through.

It was one of the Knowleses – going by the brown jacket, Charlie. 'Good evening!' he crowed, and simpered at me in a sickly fashion. 'Can I come in for a little chat, my dear?'

'I don't know what about and I'm not your dear,' I said to the crack in the door. It was worse than being called 'darling' by Hitch. At least Hitch did it unconsciously.

'Won't take a mo,' he fluted in a coaxing voice.

I opened my mouth to tell him to get lost, but I remembered this was Daphne's nephew. So I slipped the chain and let him in. He nipped over the threshold and toddled past me, uninvited, into the living room. There he stood, dead centre, with his eyes darting all over the place. He might be related to my landlady, but he was making pretty free here, just as he and his brother had been doing upstairs when glimpsed by me through the window. Only he wasn't anything to me and I objected. Before I could let him know this, however, he added insult to injury.

'You're keeping it very tidy, I see,' he said. 'Quite a little homemaker, eh?'

The sheer rudeness of all this rather took my breath away. But I rallied. 'That what you came to check on?' I still couldn't get over the patronising old git's attitude but I kept telling myself this was Daphne's nephew. Be nice to him, Fran, even if it kills you.

He had slipped his hand into his jacket pocket and took out a small notebook. 'As a matter of fact, I have come to check – not on your housekeeping, dear, oh my, no. Purely a technical point, you might say. I understand from Aunt Daphne that when you moved in no inventory was made.'

I was starting to hyperventilate. I made myself count to ten. 'I signed an agreement with Daphne. The flat was furnished, just as you see it now.'

'Yes, but no detailed inventory was done, no actual list of items. You didn't sign for the individual contents, did you? I thought not. Aunt Daphne isn't a businesswoman, I'm afraid. It does mean that when you leave – ' a faint smile hovered on his plump cheeks. He couldn't hide his hope that would be soon – 'it will be very difficult to establish that everything's in order. Now, don't be offended, my dear. This is as much in your interest as in ours. You understand that? So I thought, while Aunt Daphne . . . I thought I'd just nip down and check them off. You've got time, have you, mmn? It won't take us long. For your own protection, you know.' He gave a sickly grin.

There was something more than rotten in the state of Denmark here. But he had already flicked open the notebook and produced a gold pencil. He began to walk round the room. 'Is anything here yours? This little table? No?' He scribbled industriously. 'I see the carpet appears to be new. No marks or stains.' Scribble. 'Now, how about the kitchen? Pots and pans? These mugs?'

'Those are mine!' I snarled.

He crossed them out reluctantly. 'Now what about the bedroom?'

He was sidling towards the door which led into the little windowless bedroom beneath the pavement, formed from a Victorian coal cellar. I didn't follow but stayed where I was in the living room. He hesitated.

'Perhaps you ought to come too, dear. I don't want to list any *personal* items . . .' He was breathing, I fancied, rather more heavily than he'd been doing earlier. I was beginning to get the drift of this. I mean, I'm not that thick.

More interested to see how far he'd commit himself than anything else, I followed him into the bedroom. After all, if it came to fumble and grapple, I could take care of Charlie with one hand – or a knee in the groin.

He was standing by the bed and there wasn't much room for more than one person. He wrote something in his notebook and then leered at me, eyes bulging. 'My brother and I were a little concerned when Aunt Daphne took you in.'

'She didn't take me in. I rent the flat,' I said.

'I don't somehow think you pay the full rent,' he retorted silkily.

'What I pay's between me and Daphne. Ask her.'

He moved up against me, his face as red as beetroot. I hoped the build-up of lust in his creaking loins wasn't going to lead to some kind of seizure. If he keeled over on my bed, it wouldn't be a good situation at all.

'Things may change,' he wheezed, sweating profusely. He had open pores all over his nose. It looked like a pumice stone.

'I'm going to meet a friend of mine in fifteen minutes,' I said. 'Have you listed everything?'

'Now, then,' he said. 'Not so fast, eh? Let's say, for the sake of argument, my brother and I take over control of this house, including this flat. We might want to reconsider your position.' I said nothing and he went on, 'You are aware of your legal position with regard to fully furnished accommodation?'

'Get on with it!' I said crossly.

Unfortunately, the silly old goat misunderstood.

'I knew you'd see reason!' he yelped, dropped the notebook on the bed, and threw his pudgy arms round me.

My knee came up in automatic reaction. He let out a shriek, a gasp, and tottered back, doubled over. I scooped up his notebook and then I grabbed him by his collar. He spluttered and coughed and looked terrified.

'Look, Charlie boy,' I said, 'no fun and games. No deals. Got that? Now take your notebook and go back upstairs. And if I see you down here again, or if you try anything silly now, you're going to come off very much the worse, got it?'

'You little cow!' he gurgled. 'You assaulted me!'

'No, you assaulted me, and if you try anything like that again, I'll scream blue murder and make sure the whole street knows. Now get out!'

He staggered as far as the front door where he turned, straightened up as much as he could, and spat, 'Street is where you belong and I'll see you back out there before you can say knife, you – you trollop!'

Then he bolted before I could reply.

I slammed the door after him. Trollop? I didn't know whether to be angry or laugh. Perhaps I ought to be worried. I thought Daphne would resist their bright idea that she make over the house to the twins. But she was elderly, there were two of them to her one, and blood was notoriously thicker than water.

No time to brood over it now. Thanks to Charlie, I was running late. I pulled on my jacket and dashed out of the house.

'You choose,' said Ganesh. 'Indian or Chinese?'

'Greek,' I said. 'That nice new taverna. The shop's paying, isn't it?'

The taverna was busy and we were lucky to get a table without booking. What they call the chattering classes were well represented in the crowded room, together with well-heeled City types. The general atmosphere was just that bit noisier, the customers just that bit more jovial, more slap-happy, because Christmas was coming. They all felt they had a licence to go out and make merry, even an obligation to. After all, that's what Gan and I were doing there. The Greek staff were taking it in their stride. It was all good business. But since their Christmas wasn't due until January, they were keeping their heads about it.

'Why do people do it?' I asked Ganesh, as I looked around the crowded room. 'I mean, years ago, I suppose people didn't take many holidays or go out for a good blow-out so often and once a year was special. But this lot – half of them are on expense-account lunches all the year round and eat pretty well even when they aren't. They party all year. They take holidays, sailing round the Caribbean or skiing or pretending to be Tuscan peasants or what-have-you. But just look at them. You'd think they'd been let out of the workhouse for a binge.'

'It's truce time,' said Gan. 'You know, bury the hatchet in the ground and not in each other. It doesn't happen often. It's like the old Greeks. They used to call a halt to their wars during the period of the Olympic Games. I read that in a Sunday supplement.'

I had noticed, that since working at the newsagent's, Gan had become a mine of odd information gleaned from a variety of magazines. He could tell you the top restaurants, the season's fashion colour, how much it would cost you to go camel-trekking across the Gobi desert, the world's ten best-dressed men and the best-kept secrets of the stars. None of this was of the slightest use to him, but he just liked knowing it and, if the opportunity offered, telling me.

Over the meal, I told him about Charlie's visit and his grotesque advances. 'I couldn't believe what I was seeing and hearing,' I said. 'Did he honestly think—'

'Course he did,' said Ganesh indistinctly, chewing.

'What's that supposed to mean?' I demanded.

He swallowed. 'Keep your hair on.' This struck him as funny and he fell about giggling for a bit. When he'd calmed down, he went on, 'He doesn't know you. He thought he'd try his luck.'

'Well, his luck ran out.'

Ganesh wiped his mouth with his napkin and pronounced, 'He and his brother won't rest till they've got you out, Fran.'

'Tell me something I don't know,' I muttered.

'Be careful.'

'Am I ever anything else?' At this point, I put my hand in my pocket for my hanky and my fingers encountered the envelope I'd put there earlier and quite forgotten during my encounter with the rampant Charlie.

I pulled it out and put it on the table. Ganesh squinted at it and asked, 'What's that?'

'I don't know. Someone must have put it through my door

and I didn't see it when I went into the flat. I hadn't switched on the light and it was pretty gloomy down there. Besides, I was thinking about the twins and how pleased with themselves they looked up there in Daphne's drawing room. I didn't see the envelope until I went to let Charlie in.'

'Well, open it!' he prompted impatiently. 'What does it say?'

'It might be private,' I pointed out, but my fingers were tearing at the seal.

Inside was a single sheet of paper, torn from a pad, and folded over. On it was scribbled:

> You were kind enough to render first aid at the newsagent's recently. I need to talk to you. I'll call back tonight at ten, if that isn't too late.
>
> Yours,
>
> Gray Coverdale

'Look, look!' I squeaked, jabbing a finger at the note. 'You said that reel of film didn't belong to him! I told you it did. It must do. What else would he want to see me about? I thought someone was following me yesterday. It must've been Coverdale spying out where I lived.'

Ganesh looked at his wristwatch. 'It's gone half-past nine.'

'Then what are we waiting for?' I jumped to my feet. 'Ask for the bill!'

We hurried to the flat as fast as we could make it, but it was still going to be after ten by the time we got there. I hoped Coverdale would wait. As we turned into the street I searched the pavements but there was no one about and no strange cars waited at the kerb. The wind whistled chilly round my shaven head and Ganesh hunched his shoulders, sinking his chin into his upturned jacket collar.

'Looks like he's been and gone, Fran.'

'He mightn't have arrived yet. It can't be more than ten minutes past. He might be in the basement.'

The front of the house was in darkness. That didn't mean Daphne was out or in bed, but that she was probably in her preferred sitting room overlooking the back garden. At least Bertie and Charlie would appear to have left.

I began to clatter down the steps to the basement well, Ganesh at my heels, when suddenly his hand gripped my shoulder. 'Hang on, Fran!' he said sharply.

On mid steps we both paused and peered down. The well was gloomy, the yellow sulphurous gleam of the streetlamps only touching the far corner. Yet in the near corner, right up by the flat entrance, the darkness seemed oddly different, blacker and thicker. As I stared, I began to make out a shape, huddled against the door. It didn't move and I tried to tell myself it was only a trick of the shadows.

Ganesh had no such doubts. 'Someone's there, Fran.' His voice breathed the words into my ear. I shivered and leaned over the railing.

'Mr Coverdale, is that you? It's Fran Varady, the girl from the newsagent's. I got your note.'

There was no reply. The shape – I didn't doubt now Ganesh was right that it was human – didn't move. There was something horrible about its stillness. Even a sleeping body in a doorway radiates a kind of life. This gave out nothing.

I moved slowly to the bottom of the steps and waited there, unwilling to investigate any further. Uncertainly I said, 'I'm sorry we're late.' I spoke because I wanted to hear a human voice, even my own, not because I expected an answer. None came. The wind rattled the railings and the streetlamp's yellow pool of light quivered. A few late-falling leaves rustled at my feet.

'Do you think it's a drunk or a down-and-out?' I whispered to Ganesh. 'You know, just thought he'd found a good place to sleep it off?'

Ganesh squeezed past me and walked up to the huddled form. 'Hey, mate?' He stooped. 'You all right, there? Come on, wake up. Can't sleep outside the lady's front door.'

He put his hand on the shape's shoulder and shook gently. Slowly, with a scrape of clothing against the brick wall, the shape tilted sideways, uncoiled and collapsed. No longer a huddle in the shadows, it became a human being, sprawled across the basement pavement at our feet. The man's head, previously tucked into his chest, fell into the patch of streetlight. It shone down on a livid but recognisable face.

'That's Coverdale!' I gasped.

Ganesh dropped on his knees and, his long black hair veiling his face as he crouched over the body, put his fingers to Coverdale's neck. Then he tore at the front of the prone figure's overcoat, trying to locate the heart.

Suddenly he muttered, jerked back his exploring fingers and raised his hand for my inspection. Even in the gloom, I could see Ganesh's palm was smeared with streaks which, though they looked black rather than scarlet in this light, I knew were blood.

'He's dead, Fran,' Ganesh said, his voice shaking. 'Looks like he's been stabbed.'

Chapter Six

We didn't panic, Ganesh and I, but the situation did develop rapidly into semi-controlled chaos. I raced up the steps to Daphne's front door where I rang the bell and shouted through her letter box until she opened up in visible alarm. I was glad to see she hadn't gone to bed but wore her reading glasses and clutched a rainbow-striped knitted cardigan about her thin frame.

'Fran? What's happened?'

Bearing in mind she was elderly, I knew I should break it gently. But a body in the basement isn't the kind of news which lends itself to being wrapped up in soothing words. I did my best and told her there'd been an accident and I needed to use the phone.

'An ambulance?' she cried, snatching off the reading glasses to see me better. 'Who's hurt, Fran? Not you? I hope it isn't that nice young man from the newsagent's.'

'No, it's not Gan and I don't need an ambulance – I need the police.'

I had to tell her about the dead man, there was no way out of it. She reeled back but, true to form, she rallied fast. Daphne is tough.

'You are quite sure he's dead, Fran? You're not a doctor. Perhaps you should send for an ambulance as well.' She patted the cardigan pockets wildly. 'So silly, I ought to have my other glasses. Perhaps I should come and have a look? I did a first-aid course once. I know how to put him in the recovery position and that sort of thing. We should wrap him in a blanket, but not give him anything to drink.'

All this sounded so sensible that for a moment I even hoped that after all, Coverdale might only be unconscious. But even before the hope took root, I knew it was no more than a desperate wish unlikely to be fulfilled. The recovery position, I explained to Daphne, wasn't going to help Coverdale. Nor was he in need of a blanket. He was dead, all right, and I didn't think it a good idea if she came downstairs to view the body. But I asked for an ambulance anyway.

The paramedics confirmed the diagnosis the moment they arrived. Or as one of them murmured to his mate, 'No rush, this one's a stiff.'

During the few minutes' wait before the ambulance arrived at the door, Daphne had provided tea and brandy in her kitchen for myself and Ganesh. We sat miserably avoiding one another's eye until Daphne, perhaps desperate to talk, took the opportunity to make an apology for which she'd no reason at all.

'This gives me a chance, Fran dear, to say how sorry I was to learn how badly my nephew Charlie behaved earlier today.'

Even with my mind on other things, I was startled. Had Charlie confessed his amorous advances? No.

'He had no right whatsoever to come downstairs without even mentioning it to me and ask you to agree an inventory. He did it entirely off his own bat and I'm very annoyed with him. I told him so. It's absolutely none of his business and I shouldn't have allowed it, if I'd known what was in his mind.'

She hadn't known all that was in Charlie's mind and he

certainly hadn't told her about the scuffle in the bedroom. But he had told her about the inventory in case I complained. He could deny the little episode in the bedroom, but he couldn't deny he'd been in the flat. It went without saying that Daphne must guess that Charlie had crept down to the basement without mentioning it to her, because he'd known full well she'd have forbidden it.

'I realised you had nothing to do with it, Daphne,' I said. 'You don't have to say sorry. Forget it.'

Nevertheless, I hoped she didn't, and that it'd have demonstrated to her that Charlie and Bertie were already counting their chickens, and she must be on the watch for further tricks on their part.

'Well, at least we know who the poor bugger was,' said DS Parry.

On the heels of the ambulance, a patrol car of uniformed men turned up. Swiftly after that, CID moved in, in the person of Parry, also the police doctor and a posse of photographers.

I had hoped that after my last run-in with Sergeant Parry, I'd seen the last of him. But no, here he was again, sitting in Daphne's kitchen, drinking coffee, still trying unsuccessfully to grow that moustache, still suffering from a shaving rash and with a haircut even worse than mine. His resembled a ginger coir mat.

You wouldn't think, would you, with disadvantages like that, and lacking any kind of charm, Parry could possibly imagine I might be brought round to fancying him? But deep in what passes for his heart, or more likely in what passes for his brain, it seems he fantasises about me. It was Ganesh who pointed this out to me and at first I wouldn't – couldn't – believe it. But I've been brought round to the horrid conclusion Gan is right about this, as about so much else.

Outside, men measured and photographed and crawled round under their arc-lights for clues to put in their plastic bags. The remaining population of the street had turned out to watch and speculate, but were kept back behind a blue and white plastic tape tied across the thoroughfare. Behind the crowd, indignant motorists had got out of their cars to demand why they were being denied access.

Inside this cordon, like a set of plague victims sealed off from normal humanity, we were at Parry's mercy.

He took Daphne's statement first, rightly surmising whatever she had to say would be less interesting than anything he could bully out of Ganesh and me. Daphne hadn't heard or seen anything because she'd been in her sitting room at the back of the house. Parry thanked her with a politeness he never wasted on me, before dismissing her from her own kitchen and turning his attention to Ganesh and me, his preferred prey. Daphne was the starter, we were the main course.

'All right, then, let's have it,' he said. 'You first, Miss Varady, being as it's your flat where the bloke copped it.'

'Not *in* my flat,' I protested vigorously, '*outside* my flat!'

'In your basement,' said Parry, unimpressed.

I told him my version and Ganesh told him his, which was virtually the same. We also had to tell him about the business at the shop when Coverdale – as we now knew him to be – staggered in and I told him about the man who'd come enquiring later.

The *bombe surprise* was Hitch's discovery of the packet behind the pipes of the washroom and the roll of film it contained. This had Parry scribbling like a man possessed, all the while chewing one straggling corner of his moustache, his expression steadily more disapproving.

When he heard that I'd taken the film to be developed, he stopped scribbling and turned puce. 'You did what? Don't tell me, I can guess. You were playing detective again, Fran? Right? How many times have I told you? You got anything suspicious to report, you bring it to us.'

'It wasn't suspicious,' I argued.

'You still oughta have reported it. Where are these snaps now?'

'At the shop, stuck under the till,' Ganesh said.

'Then we'll have to go over there and collect 'em, won't we, son? If they're still there – which I hope they are. If they're not, you two are in a spot of trouble. They're material evidence, they are.'

'Look!' I said sharply. 'We didn't know he was going to get murdered, did we? We offered to call the police when he was beaten up and he didn't want it. What else could we do?'

'You are certain, are you,' Ganesh asked in a very formal voice, 'of your identification? The only reason we're calling him Coverdale, as I see it, is because a note signed in that name was pushed through Fran's letter box.'

Parry gave Ganesh a dirty look. 'Well, no one's identified him yet, if that's what you mean. But he'd got business cards in that name in his pocket and a press pass with his phizog on it. He's – was – a journalist, Graeme Coverdale. Don't worry, we'll track down someone who knew him to take a look at him in the morgue.' Nice.

Parry was tucking away his notebook. 'I think the best thing would be if a constable accompanied you to the shop, Mr Patel, to get those photos and negatives. You'd better stay here, Fran – Miss Varady – until Inspector Harford arrives. He'll want to talk to you, both of you.' Parry gave a sinister leer.

'Who's he?' I asked. Obviously this was a serious crime

and they weren't leaving it entirely to Parry, but there was a relish in Parry's voice which suggested Harford would prove some sort of ogre. Parry, by contrast, would be a regular Peter Pan.

'Harford? Oh, he's the blue-eyed boy, he is. Graduate intake, fast-track promotion. He's been to university, has Inspector Harford.' Parry oozed rancour. Even the ginger hair in his ears seemed to bristle. Then he rolled his bloodshot gaze in my direction and added, 'So don't you try giving him any lip, Fran. He's not tolerant, like me.'

On this breath-taking misstatement, he ushered Ganesh out of the door and left me in the kitchen.

Daphne put her head round. 'All right, Fran?'

'Wonderful,' I said gloomily. 'I'm waiting for an Inspector Harford, apparently the Met's finest.'

'A car's just drawn up outside,' she said. 'I'll go and spy out the land.'

She pottered off quite cheerfully. Daphne never fails to amaze me and I realised that far from being terrified at the thought of gory death in her basement, Daphne was enjoying all the hullabaloo. This must beat reading about murder in one of the whodunits lining her shelves. This was the real thing.

There was much conversation going on in her hallway. I could hear Parry's voice and another man's, more of a tenor to Parry's bass growl. Daphne scurried back.

'He's here!' she announced, eyes shining. 'And he's awfully young. I suppose policemen do get younger as one gets older, but really, this one looks like a schoolboy. I suppose he's got enough experience for this sort of thing. It hardly seems possible.'

Unfortunately, as she spoke the last words, a new figure loomed up behind her.

'Good evening.' The voice had a noticeable edge to it. He'd overheard. 'My name is Harford. Excuse me, madam,' the newcomer sidestepped Daphne, 'I'd like a word with Miss Varady, if she's up to it.'

He didn't look like a schoolboy, but also he didn't look all that much older than me, though I suppose he must be. He was chunkily built, with a shock of light brown hair, parted on the side and brushed straight with a ruthless hand. Add to that, a wide mouth, good complexion, blue eyes and, most striking of all, an air of arrogant self-possession. He was wearing an expensive-looking suit and a clean shirt, all pressed and starched, even at this time of night. I wondered if he'd jumped into his car when he'd got the summons, or taken time to shower and change first.

His voice matched his looks, with clean-cut vowels which must have made him something of a novelty at our local nick. In fact, I shouldn't have thought they knew what to make of him at all. I'd have loved to be a fly on the canteen wall.

I met his gaze and found it was studying me in no very generous way. By comparison, my own appearance was distinctly at fault. Harford's gaze suggested he classed me with something brought in by the cat. I was glad I'd had my hair trimmed, but wished I wasn't wearing the assembled contents of a jumble sale stall. If I'd been sitting here in a power suit and stilettos I might have stood a chance. As it was, he'd clearly labelled me riffraff.

'Right, let's get started, shall we?' he said bossily, taking his place at Daphne's table. I felt a fleeting sympathy for Parry.

'The coffee's cold,' I said, to make amends for Daphne getting us off on the wrong foot. 'I can make some more.'

'We won't worry about coffee.' His tone put me firmly in my place. 'Now, I've had a quick word with Sergeant Parry and glanced over your statement and Mr Patel's. But I'd like to hear it from you.'

'Starting from when?' I asked.

'From the incident at the shop where I believe you're employed.' He made it sound as though I sold sex aids and porno videos.

'It's just a newsagent's,' I said. 'And I work mornings only.' He said nothing, only sat there looking fit, sharp and unpredictable, like a police dog. So I went through it all again, about the stranger, whom I now knew to be Coverdale, how someone had come to the shop enquiring about him, how Marco and Hitch had found the envelope containing the film and how I'd taken it to be developed. This last, as expected, proved the stickiest bit.

'Why did you take the film to be developed?' he asked.

'There might have been something on it to tell us whose it was.'

'But you realised it had been hidden by a total stranger. Why did you think you'd recognise anything on the film?'

'I supposed – we supposed – it'd been hidden. We didn't know it for sure. We didn't know what sort of pics they were. They looked like holiday snaps.'

'Why should someone want to hide holiday snaps?'

'How should I know? I'm not the detective, you are!' I retorted unwisely.

He froze. The blue eyes bored into me. 'Just answer the questions, Miss Varady, if you don't mind.'

'I do mind. I've been through this already for Parry.' I realised I was doing badly but his attitude was niggling me. He was managing to make it sound as if I was hiding something.

'Tell me about this evening.'

I told him how I'd found the note but hadn't read it until I was in the restaurant with Ganesh.

'Ah, yes, your boss, Mr Patel, had taken you out to dinner. Does he often do that?'

'It was our staff Christmas dinner,' I said tightly. Now it was my friendship with Ganesh he was managing to make sound seedy. 'We went to a Greek restaurant.'

'Food any good?' he asked suddenly.

He must think I was stupid. 'I had the moussaka and Ganesh had something which was mostly chickpeas. He's a vegetarian. You can check at the restaurant. The waiter's name was Stavros. He had it on a label pinned to his shirt.'

Harford's face twitched. He leaned forward slightly. 'You still have this note?'

'I gave it to Parry.'

'Ah—' He paused and straightened up. 'You're something of an old acquaintance of Sergeant Parry's, I understand.'

'We've met. Strictly official.'

'Yes . . .' Harford tugged at his crisp white cuffs. 'You do seem to attract trouble, Miss Varady. I made a few enquiries before I came over here. Not your first brush with murder, is it? Or three murders, to be exact, not to mention a kidnapping.'

'I don't go around collecting corpses,' I said wearily. 'I wasn't involved in the others. I just happened to be around and got drawn in.'

'The bodies just drop in your vicinity?'

Was this meant to be a joke? He wasn't smiling although there was a sort of rictus round his mouth. If he was joking, it was at my expense.

'I can't tell you anything else,' I snapped. 'Go and enquire about Coverdale, if that's his real name. That's your lead, for goodness' sake. Parry says he was a journalist. Find out what story he was working on. I bet it's connected with that.'

'I think we can manage our own investigations, thank you!' His face had reddened. 'I – we don't need advice from you.'

'It seems to me you're wasting time, sitting here with me,' I countered. 'Look, Coverdale said in his note he'd come back at ten o'clock. Ganesh and I were here by quarter past ten, but Coverdale was already dead. So he couldn't have been dead long. What does the doctor say?'

'That's police information.' The red flush had now crept up his throat. He looked about to explode.

'Well, I reckon it couldn't have been more than fifteen – twenty minutes. Someone followed him here.'

'That's supposition.'

'Or was waiting for him when he arrived,' I mused. 'It's dark in the well. Someone could have been hiding down there.'

And Ganesh and I had just missed him. It was an eerie thought. A few minutes earlier and we could have met the killer coming back up the basement steps, knife in hand.

'We've thought of that!' Harford was getting really annoyed. 'Just leave the detection to us, will you? Don't start pretending you're Miss Marple.'

'Miss Marple? *Miss Marple!*' I fairly bounced in my chair with rage. 'Do I look like some old girl who snoops on her neighbours? How about a murder weapon? Have you found it?'

'Look, I'm asking the questions.' He was getting flustered now. That 'I'm-in-charge' air was slipping. Now it was more 'it's-my-cricket-bat-and-I-say-who's-out!' 'Let's get back to Coverdale.'

'That's what I was telling you to do,' I muttered.

'Thank you!' he retorted sarcastically. 'Did you see anyone else in the street when you arrived? Anyone walking, driving, anyone apparently going into a house.'

I said we hadn't. I was sure. I'd been scanning the scene for Coverdale and I'd have noticed anyone else.

'How,' asked Harford, 'did the killer know he'd find Coverdale here?'

'He followed him,' I said patiently.

'All right, so how did Coverdale learn your address?'

'Someone followed *me* from the shop yesterday, I'm fairly sure of it. It could've been him.'

'But you didn't see him? He didn't approach you?'

'Of course he didn't. Someone else might have been watching me. He had to be careful.'

'Not careful enough, it seems,' said Harford as if the whole thing was entirely my fault.

Luckily we were interrupted. A tap at the door heralded Parry, looking pleased with himself. He brandished a yellow envelope.

'Got 'em, sir. Got the snaps and the negs.'

Harford rose to his feet with dignity. I got the impression he wasn't sorry for the interruption either.

'Good man,' he said. 'Thank you for your time, Miss Varady. We'll talk again.'

Parry gave me a triumphant wink.

'Do you know, Daphne,' I said, when they'd left, 'I never thought I'd say it, but I think I'd rather deal with Parry than with Inspector Harford.'

'He's a very handsome young man, isn't he?' said Daphne sentimentally.

I'd noticed that, but I wasn't going to let it influence me. Women of Daphne's age, I told myself, were susceptible to young men of Harford's ilk. Not so yours truly.

Eventually, after all the photographs were taken, everything measured up, and documented, they dismantled their lights and Coverdale's body was removed, leaving behind a sinister chalked outline, over which I had to step to return to the flat at one in the morning. They really didn't want me returning to the flat at all. They said I'd be interfering with a scene of crime. I pointed out I wasn't going to sleep in the basement well, but in my flat, in my bed – and Coverdale hadn't crossed my doorstep. I can't say I relished the idea of going into the flat, let alone sleeping there alone that night, but I insisted as a matter of principle, even though Daphne offered me a bed.

'Don't touch anything, right?' Parry warned.

'He wasn't ever in my flat,' I repeated, I don't know for what number of times.

'We'll just check, shall we?'

Parry followed me into the flat, also stepping over the chalk outline, and stared around. 'It don't look touched,' he admitted.

'It's not. Now can I be left in peace in my own home? I've had a very trying evening.'

'Just mind how you go in and out. Don't touch anything in the stairwell. Although we'll want your dabs for elimination. Bloke will come round tomorrow for 'em.'

'Where've I heard that before?' I muttered.

They were still scurrying around out there when I went to bed, and in a way that was comforting. I still went to sleep with the light on.

'Hitch looked in this morning and turned the water off again,' said Ganesh plaintively. 'He said he and Marco will come over later and install the new loo and washbasin ready for tomorrow morning.'

It was Sunday morning and he'd arrived around nine. That's classed as daybreak on a Sunday in my book at the best of times and after a disturbed night, I'd hoped for a lie-in. I wasn't dressed or ready for visitors and had to open the door in my Snoopy nightshirt.

'Turn it on again,' I said grumpily, padding back inside.

'I did and it spurted out the hole in the wall where the washroom tap used to be.'

'But you must be able to turn off the washroom plumbing separately.'

'Well, I haven't found a way to do it. Can I use your shower?'

'How much are they charging you to come in on a Sunday?' I asked. 'Or haven't they said?'

'Hitch is a mate,' Ganesh defended him. 'He's doing it so's we don't have to keep running round to the petshop on Monday morning every time we want to take a leak. You know how you grumbled about that.'

'That's right, blame me. Go and take your shower.'

I trailed back to the bedroom and tugged on jeans and a sweater. Ganesh was still locked in the bathroom when I came back, and outside the window, in the basement, the police were back and still searching around. There was a guy fingerprinting the doorway and the windowsill. Like it or not, I was living on a scene of crime. I made coffee against the splashing of water from the bathroom and handed Ganesh a mug as he emerged, his long black hair dripping. I could've made coffee for SOCO outside, but I drew the line at that. They were causing me enough disruption.

'Got a hair dryer?' Ganesh asked.

'Do me a favour,' I said. 'With a haircut like mine? What'd I do with a hair dryer?'

'I'll catch cold,' he said sulkily.

'I'll turn up the gas fire. Gimme that towel.'

He sat in front of the gas fire grumbling as I towel-dried his long hair briskly. 'Ouch! Ow! That's my ear, Fran!'

'Oh, shut up or do it yourself!'

'He grilled me again, too, you know,' said Ganesh, emerging from the towel. 'Harford, I mean. He went bananas over those negatives. Said we should've turned them in straight away. But there wasn't anything on them for us to need to do that.'

'Conceited snooty prat.'

'Got your back up, then, I see. I thought he seemed bright enough. He's probably worried you won't take him seriously.'

'I do take him seriously. He's set to be a real pain. What else did he ask you?'

'Kept making me go over the same thing over and over again. I began to wish we'd just chucked those photos away.'

'Harford would love that,' I said. 'I wish I knew who the rich-looking guy in them is. He must be the one who was after Coverdale to get them back. Why is he so worried about them? They don't show anything criminal, just three guys having a drink.'

'Perhaps it's to do with the other two men in the pictures? I know you can only see one's face. Perhaps this other man is the one who wants the negatives back.'

I shook my head. 'No, the dark one is just a regular thug. The light-haired man with the bright shirt is the important figure. He's the one we've got to worry about.'

Ganesh put down the towel and stared at me in concern. 'We've got to worry?'

'Yes, of course we have. He doesn't know where the film is and he's still looking, right? I bet whoever killed Coverdale went through his pockets and didn't find it. They know Coverdale ran into the shop to escape his pursuers the other day. They'll find out pretty quick I work there. Coverdale was ringing my doorbell when his killer found him. What would you make of it all, if you were him?'

Ganesh looked unhappy. 'I should've warned Dilip. He's looking after the shop this morning.' They were open for the Sunday newspapers until noon.

'Dilip's built like a brick barn,' I reassured him. 'He can look after himself.'

A ring at the bell announced that the fingerprint guy whose visit Parry had promised me, was ready for me. He took my prints. 'Are you the bloke who was with her last night?' he asked Ganesh. 'Right, let's be having yours as well.'

'My father,' said Ganesh emotionally, scrubbing black ink from his fingertips when the man had gone, 'must never know about this.'

'It's routine, calm down,' I said, old hand at this sort of thing as I was by now.

But Ganesh carried on fretting and said he ought to go back to the shop and make sure Dilip was still in one piece. I walked out of the flat with him, through the SOCO, and up to pavement level, ducking under the police tape which still cordoned off my basement. Across the road, someone was taking photographs of the front of the house. He didn't look like a copper and I suspected he was press.

The road was open to traffic again and, as we emerged, a taxi drew up and out popped the Knowles brothers. They were wearing identical blazers today, with some badge or other on the breast pocket, but by now I could tell them apart, having had the chance to view Charlie so close at hand in my flat. He had the coarser skin and slightly less hair, but he did have his own teeth. Bertie, I noticed now as he bared them at me in rage, didn't.

'We knew it!' they cried in unison. 'Nothing but trouble! Poor Aunt Daphne! A victim of her own kind heart.'

'What are you talking about?' snapped Ganesh, who was in

no mood for this sort of thing. 'Who are these people, Fran?'

'Oh,' I said with a sigh, because this was all I needed. 'Allow me to introduce Bertie and Charlie Knowles, Daphne's nephews. I did mention them to you before.'

'And who,' asked Bertie icily, 'is this gentleman?'

'He's Mr Patel. I work for him.'

'Work? Indeed?' said Bertie nastily.

'Murder!' Charlie moved in, practically salivating with revenge. He flung out a hand towards the basement and the boiler-suited figures down there. 'To think poor Aunt Daphne, a solitary, defenceless lady of mature years, could have had her throat cut. And all because of you.'

'We shall insist,' said Bertie, 'that you leave these premises at once! Aunt Daphne cannot be left at risk.'

'Hey!' said Ganesh indignantly. 'She didn't do anything. It was all a bit of bad luck.'

'Luck?' Charlie sneered. 'I'd say it was your seedy life-style and unsavoury connections leading to violence, crime and God knows what else. From the start we told Aunt Daphne she should never have taken in a person like you, straight from the street.'

'I wasn't living on the street, I was in a council flat,' I told them. I was glad they hadn't seen the flat in question, a condemned high-rise in a block from hell. It was the second of such flats I'd had. The first had been trashed by neighbourhood kids. Before that, I'd always lived in squats. I have what the council likes to call 'low priority' on the housing list, i.e., no clout at all.

'We shall, if necessary, take legal steps,' chimed in Bertie. 'Aunt Daphne must be protected.'

At this juncture, the door at the top of the steps flew open and Daphne appeared. She might be frail and in her seventies, incongruously clad in jogging pants and Fair Isle socks, but she radiated authority.

'Charles, Bertram!' she called. 'Stop that at once!'

The twins fell silent and shuffled, shamefaced, like a pair of five-year-olds caught throwing stones.

'I will not permit you to harass Francesca,' went on Daphne majestically. 'She has had a frightening experience for such a young girl. I apologise, Fran. Bertie and Charlie – inside!'

She withdrew and the Knowles brothers scuttled up the steps after her, their voices chiming in duet.

'Horrified to hear – so pleased to see you unharmed – a dreadful experience – not safe in your own home – warned you about that girl – change all the locks . . .'

The door shut on them, cutting off further accusations against me and lurid scenarios of what might have happened.

'Weird,' said Ganesh.

'I just hope they don't frighten Daphne,' I said. 'She's been fine till now.' I glanced down at my feet where the puddle in the gutter still hadn't dried out and seemed to my eye to have got bigger, spreading out into the road.

'It didn't rain last night, did it, Gan?'

'No,' said Ganesh. 'Does it matter?'

'I was just wondering,' I said.

'I'd have thought you got something more to wonder about than the weather!' was his reply.

Chapter Seven

I walked round to the shop at lunchtime, mainly to avoid having to watch the SOCO scrabbling around in my basement. What's more, I had a feeling Parry was going to turn up at some point and I really couldn't cope with him again so soon. Parry's best taken in small doses.

Outside the house, a notice had appeared, tied on the lamppost. It informed passers-by that a serious incident had occurred, giving time and date, and requested anyone who'd seen anything unusual in the vicinity to notify the local nick. I doubt anyone could've seen what was going on in a dark basement well. It made a nice, ironic touch, though, considering the yellow Neighbourhood Watch notices which sprouted in several windows up and down the street. Since none of the neighbours had called the police last night, they'd all been confining their watching to their television screens, presumably.

Two of the local good citizens were standing before the notice, looking serious. 'Time for a meeting, Simon,' said one.

That was par for the neighbourhood. Not good on action, but dab hands at meetings.

They were just closing up the newsagent's when I arrived at twelve, as was normal for a Sunday. Dilip was standing in the doorway with Ganesh.

You can't miss Dilip. The impression he gives is that he's as broad as he's tall. He has a walrus moustache and immensely powerful shoulders. His normal job is running a hot-dog stall and he never has any backchat from the punters.

'No trouble?' I asked hopefully.

'No trouble,' growled Dilip. 'But a kid came round asking for you.'

'For me?' I was startled.

'Young girl, skinny, looked like she was going to peg out at any minute.' Dilip doesn't approve of skinny people. He thinks everyone ought to be built on the same lines as himself.

It had to be Tig and I was taken aback. I really hadn't thought she'd get in touch with me. I wondered what had happened to prompt her change of heart and asked if she'd left a note.

He shook his head. 'She said she'd come in again some time.'

It was a pity and might prove an opportunity missed for good. When someone's in Tig's situation, there may only be the one moment when they're prepared to allow anyone to help. Miss it and it's gone. From within the shop came a loud clatter and clang and the sound of Hitch swearing.

'Got the workers in, I see?' I observed.

''Sall right,' said Dilip. 'I locked them out of the storeroom and they didn't argue.'

He took himself off. I followed Ganesh back inside in time to see Marco stagger in from the back yard carrying a lavatory pan. In his arms, it looked like a piece of modern sculpture. 'Hi!' he said, smiling serenely at me. I smiled back, all silly.

'See,' said Ganesh. 'It'll be all fixed up by tomorrow. All they'll have to do is slap a bit of paint round and finish fixing the wall tiles. It's going to look really good. Come and see what they've done already.'

They'd put in the washbasin and new extractor fan and I had to admit the place was shaping up very well. I still felt a niggle of unease, though about what specifically I couldn't say, but dismissed it, telling myself it wasn't my problem.

'Where's the old stuff?' I asked.

'Taken that to the dump, darling,' said Hitch. 'Don't you worry about that. I've taken care of it.'

Ganesh and I went upstairs to the flat over the shop and made sandwiches. We'd talked ourselves to a standstill about Coverdale, so we talked about Tig instead. I explained her situation and why I was worried about her.

'She ought to go home,' said Ganesh.

'It's not as easy as that.'

'Still the best chance she's got.'

I set off back to the flat when I judged the SOCO team would've left. They had, and taken away the plastic tape, but I'd forgotten the press. A couple of bored guys in raincoats, sharing a Thermos, leaped into action as I appeared and cornered me at the top of the steps down into the basement.

'Fran, is it? Could we have a word?'

'No,' I said, trying to get past.

Fat chance. 'We understand you found the body. Did you know him? Why was he in your basement? Had you arranged to meet him? What's his connection—'

'For crying out loud,' I said wearily. 'How the hell do I know? I met him once. I don't know how he wound up dead in my basement.'

They exchanged glances. 'Look,' one of them said confidentially. 'He was a journo, right? Like us. He had to be on a story.'

'If he was,' I said, 'I don't know what it was.' A thought struck me. 'Here,' I said. 'You'd know which paper he worked for. It must know what he was up to.'

'Forget it,' said one of them. 'He was freelance, was Gray. He had quite a reputation.'

'Oh?' I said encouragingly. 'What sort of reputation?'

'For news,' said the other. 'He dug up some great stories. He could smell 'em out. Knew how to sell 'em, too, to the highest bidder. Editors were ready to give their eye-teeth for some of the stories Gray Coverdale ran to earth.'

He sounded wistful. The thought seemed to have slipped him by that digging out another great story might just have got Coverdale killed. It did seem to occur to them both, however, that they were giving out more information than they were getting.

'Come on,' they wheedled. 'At least tell us how you met him. Go on, it can't hurt.' Two false smiles beamed down on me.

'Are you crazy? The police would go ballistic if I talked to you.'

'Just general background, you know, something we can take back to our editors. Give us a break.'

They sounded pathetic, ill-used, at imminent risk of the sack if I didn't give them any information.

I was rescued, if that was the word, by a car drawing up. They swung round eagerly.

'Right,' said Inspector Harford. 'The lady's got nothing to say. Got that? Nothing.'

I had to ask him in. I had little choice. Watched by the two presshawks, we descended the basement steps and I conducted him into the living area of my flat, a largish room with the tiny kitchenette and bathroom off it.

'Nice place,' he said, taking a good look. 'You're lucky. How did you find it? I'm trying to find a new place. Where I live now means too much time lost travelling.'

'I wasn't just lucky,' I said. 'I helped someone out – and later he helped me out. He's a friend of Daphne's.'

'That wouldn't be Monkton, would it? The old guy whose granddaughter was found hanged in a squat over by the river, Rotherhithe way?'

'Well, you seem to know all about it,' I said sourly. But he must do, of course. He'd mentioned it in passing the first time we'd met. This wasn't my first encounter with violent death and he wouldn't forget it.

Through the small window at the far end of the living room could be glimpsed Daphne's back lawn. Due to the sloping topography, it was at eyelevel. Immediately outside the window was a sort of ditch, enabling light to get in. So I shouldn't look out on to the bare earth wall of the ditch, Daphne had disguised it, not very well, as a rockery. Unfortunately, the plants hadn't flourished in the sunless, damp ravine. All to be seen were lumps of rocks jutting through mud and suggesting a half-hearted archeological excavation. Sparrows hopped about on them, searching. I was in the habit of chucking crumbs out through the window for them.

Inspector Harford had moved to this window and was studying the uninspiring view.

'You've got no door out into the garden, then?' He peered through the glass, craning his neck upwards at an unnatural angle which is what you had to do to see anything more of the garden.

'Not as such. My landlady's told me that if I want to sit out there in summer I can. But I'd have to go through her place. I could climb through that window, I suppose, by way of a short cut.'

I really shouldn't have said that bit about climbing through the window. It was just a casual remark, a feeble joke, but he took it very seriously. He rattled at the catch, pushed open the window, which had hinges at the top of the frame and appeared to be making calculations. Eventually he let it drop back into place and secured the latch before turning round.

'I didn't,' I said sarcastically, 'stab Gray Coverdale on the doorstep, shut myself in and lock the door, go through this room, out that window, climb over all the garden walls between here and the end of the street, come back along the pavement and "find" his body.'

He sat in my pine-framed easy chair, rested his hands on the wooden arms, and said, 'I didn't suggest that.'

'You looked as if you were working on it.' I stared at him resentfully. To be truthful I was surprised to see him. I'd expected Parry. I'd imagined Harford would be at home recovering from a roast Sunday lunch, or doing something healthy and outdoor. He wasn't wearing his suit today, but M & S chinos, peacock-blue Puma sweatshirt and navy suede Nike trainers. He obviously wasn't a man who held much truck with brand loyalty.

'Why should you kill Coverdale? He was a man you'd hardly met, so you said,' he asked, managing to imply I'd been economical with the truth the last time we'd met.

'That's right, I scarcely knew the man. On the one occasion I did meet him, I didn't know his name.' I paused. 'He definitely is Coverdale, then?'

He nodded. 'A relative was found to make the identification.'

I imagined the scene and it was a gruesome picture. Then I

wondered who'd potter down to the morgue to identify me if I turned up dead. I didn't fancy Daphne being asked to do it. I supposed it might be Ganesh. I don't have any relatives. After my mother walked out when I was seven, Grandma Varady moved in and looked after Dad and me. Dad died first, which was odd because he wasn't old and he didn't think he was ill. He'd long had what Grandma called 'a delicate stomach' but the list of foods he couldn't digest got steadily longer. It turned out he had stomach cancer and by the time that was found out, it was inoperable. Grandma and I soldiered on pretty well for a year or so, but Dad's death had hit her hard and she never came to terms with it. Her mind grappled with it in vain until she descended rapidly into a half-world. She didn't so much die as fade out, and then I was on my own – out on the street because the landlord didn't want me in the property. I was sixteen and alone. I've been on my own ever since.

My mind had been drifting, thinking all this. I realised Harford was watching me closely.

'Well, go on then,' I said.

He frowned. 'You didn't answer my question.'

'You didn't ask a question,' I said, and realised straight away that of course, he must have done, but I hadn't heard it.

I apologised. 'Sorry, I was thinking – you know about someone having to look at his body and say they recognised him. That's a pretty lousy job.'

'Yes, it is.' He glanced towards the curtain of plastic strips covering the entry to the kitchenette. 'Shall I make us some tea?'

I supposed I should have offered him some. I started to get to my feet, but he waved me back and took himself off and returned minutes later with tea in two mugs. 'Do you take sugar? I couldn't find any.'

'I probably haven't got any.'

He sat down again. 'How are you feeling today?' He'd changed tactics. I was getting tea and the bedside manner now.

'OK.' I thought about it and decided to unburden myself of the thought which had been nagging at me since Coverdale's death. 'I can't help feeling a bit responsible for what happened, because I didn't read his note straight away when I found it. If I had, I'd have been here at ten when he came back – and not turned up with Gan, late. Too late.'

'Why didn't you read it?' He sipped from his mug, his eyes watching me.

'I was distracted. Someone else was here.' He raised his eyebrows so I told him. 'One of Daphne's nephews.'

'Mr Charles Knowles or Mr Bertram Knowles?' he asked unexpectedly.

'You've met 'em, then.' I was surprised, but really oughtn't to have been. We couldn't have something like this happen without the brothers scurrying round to put in their fourpenn'orth. 'It was Charlie.' I wondered if he'd ask what Charlie had wanted.

He nodded. 'They sought me out to express their concern about the murder and their aunt's safety and, frankly, about your presence on the premises.'

The miserable pair of shysters. They didn't lack brass neck. I leaned forward, slopping tea, and declared, 'Well, let me tell you something about Charlie and Bertie, they're creeps and they're con men. They're trying to persuade Daphne to give them this house. *Give* it to them! Just like that. They've told her some spiel about letting her stay on, which has to be a load of rot. I don't believe them. Is it illegal for them to suggest that to her? If it isn't, it ought to be. Can you stop them?'

He shook his head and put his empty mug on the carpet by

his feet. 'That's a family matter. Naturally they're concerned about an elderly relative. They're partners in a firm of solicitors, I understand, so I'm sure they know the law. I wouldn't, if I were you, go about suggesting that they had ulterior motives. Not unless you have concrete evidence. If they got to hear of it, you could be in trouble.'

'I thought,' I said bitterly, 'one was supposed to report anything suspicious.'

'There's nothing suspicious in suggesting she think about avoiding inheritance tax. Anyone would do it.'

People with the sort of background he no doubt had did it. People like me, who had nothing to leave and no chance of inheriting so much as a rusty watch chain, had no such worries.

'As a matter of pure hypothesis,' he was saying, 'if anyone who wasn't a registered financial adviser were to urge Miss Knowles to invest money somehow or other, that might be a different matter. But as it is, I wouldn't meddle, Fran. You'd probably end up burning your fingers.'

I felt my face flame as I told him that I wasn't meddling. I was concerned for my landlady. His attitude made me angry. I didn't like his familiar use of my Christian name and I was doubly infuriated to think the brothers had been complaining about me to him. Then it occurred to me that here I was, complaining to him about *them*.

'However,' he was going on, 'since you're so keen to report anything suspicious, I'm surprised you didn't report the incident at the newsagent's when Coverdale came into the place, injured.'

So we were back to that again. 'We explained all that. He didn't want us to do it.' I decided it was time I took charge of this conversation. We were in my flat, after all. 'Have you studied the pics? Do they mean anything to you?'

I hadn't expected much of a reply to this, just an official brushoff, but it had an extraordinary effect. 'I don't want you talking to anyone about those photographs!' he snapped. 'That's one reason I'm here today, to make that absolutely clear to you. I don't want you even to mention finding them. Their existence has to be kept secret, right?'

Hold on, here. I'd hit a nerve. 'They do mean something to you!' I gasped.

He'd reddened. 'We're investigating. But I mean what I said, Fran. You're not to talk about those pictures to anyone at all, not the press, not your landlady, not to your friends. You're not to say what's in them or describe the people they show. It is standard practice not to reveal everything in a murder investigation,' he added belatedly.

'All right, all right, keep your hair on.'

He simmered down and looked a tad embarrassed. 'It's important, that's all. Police investigations can get completely buggered by gossip.'

'You'd better speak to the builders, then. They found the packet with the film in it. Hitch – Jefferson Hitchens – and one of his—' What was Marco? Hardly a registered employee with all the paperwork, National Insurance contributions, tax and all the rest of it, involved. 'Some chap who was helping him out,' I finished.

'We're on to that, thank you,' Harford said primly. 'Someone's gone to see them.'

Parry, ten to one. Harford had wisely left it to someone who'd fare better on that territory. Now he sat back in the chair and changed the subject completely. 'Parry tells me you trained as an actress, Fran.'

It seemed like he knew so much about me, he could've written my biography. Didn't they have anything else to chat about down the nick? 'You keep calling me Fran,' I said coldly. 'I don't remember telling you that was OK.'

He flushed. 'Sorry,' he said stiffly.

'And I don't see how my having been on a Dramatic Arts course matters to you, either. I was – but I didn't finish it.'

'Why did you drop out?' he countered.

I could have explained about Grandma Varady dying and the landlord throwing me out and all the rest of it, but I didn't see why I should. 'I just did,' I said.

'Pity you didn't stick to it.' He had that superior note in his voice again.

'My business, not yours.' I was getting more and more fed up. But as I spoke, it occurred to me that if he knew I'd had stage training, he might be wondering how convincingly I could lie. 'Did you come here just to tell me not to talk about the photos?' I asked icily.

He hesitated. 'That – and to ask you not to talk to the press at all.' He held up his hand to stem any indignant rebuttal I might make. 'Yes, I know – they were pestering you and you were refusing to be drawn, which was quite right. They'll hang around for a couple of days but they'll soon get bored and move on if you don't help them out. If they get no news story here they'll go and find something else.'

'Unless,' I said, 'they've got wind of what Coverdale was up to.'

He started to get worked up again, flushing to crimson. 'If you, or your pal Patel, screw this up for me, I'll throw the book at you both, remember that.'

There was no reason why I had to sit here and let him insult me. 'If you've finished,' I told him, 'I think you'd better go.'

He hesitated but got to his feet and made towards the door. Determined to see him well off the premises, I accompanied him up the basement steps to street level. The two pressmen had gone – or were hiding in a doorway until he went.

Harford looked up and down the street, perhaps checking it out for the missing reporters. Then he said unexpectedly, 'Someone been washing a car out here?'

'Not that I know of.'

'Just, there's a lot of water in the road here.'

He'd noticed it too. Perhaps I ought to mention it to Daphne. Harford was sliding behind the wheel of his own car. I'd imagined he'd be driving some powerful flash motor, but he'd climbed into an elderly Renault. I watched him drive off and decided not to bother Daphne about the growing damp patch outside. She had enough on her plate.

The rest of the day passed off without incident. I didn't see either of the Knowles twins nor did any more coppers decide to make nuisances of themselves. I turned in early. I had to be at work the next day.

It was a pleasant Monday morning, quite mild, with pale sunshine lending quite a cheerful air to everything. Even with all the outstanding unsolved problems, I felt quite cheerful too, until I turned the corner into the street where the newsagent's stood – and saw the police car parked outside the shop.

It wasn't quite eight. I wondered how much hassle of witnesses constituted police harassment. We must be getting near the dividing line. Geared up for battle, I threw open the door and marched into the shop, ready to defend Ganesh's rights. What I saw stopped me in my tracks.

Ganesh sat on a chair in the middle of the shop. His head was bound in thick white bandages and he looked badly shaken. Nevertheless, he was doing his best to answer the questions of a policewoman who hovered over him, notebook in hand.

'Gan!' I shrieked.

The policewoman jumped round as if stung and nearly dropped her notebook. She was a strapping blonde with legs like a footballer's in her black stockings. She jammed her hat back on her head and scowled at me.

A second copper, who'd been prowling round behind the counter, came rushing out and tried to bundle me back out of the door on to the pavement. I resisted.

'Shop's closed, miss. Didn't you see the notice on the door?' He took my elbow in the approved manner.

'Leggo!' I snapped, wedging myself in the doorframe, my back against one upright and my boots braced against the other. 'I work here. What's happened to Ganesh, to Mr Patel?'

He was unwilling to let me back inside but was obliged to check my claim. He looked over his shoulder. 'That right?' he called towards Ganesh. 'She work here?'

'Yes . . .' said Gan faintly.

The copper reluctantly stood back to let me in.

I hurried over to Ganesh. 'What's happened, Gan? Who did that?' Had someone tried to hold up the shop? First thing Monday morning was a hell of a time to try it. So little business would've been done, the takings would be negligible. But thieves weren't always logical. The culprit might've been a psycho or desperate for just enough money for a fix. I felt sick with rage and anger.

'Last night,' Ganesh mumbled. 'Intruder . . . down here. Heard a noise. Went down to see what was going on, got laid out by some joker, whoever he was, and ended up in casualty.'

'We think an attempt was made to burgle the shop,' the policewoman said. 'Perhaps you could take a look round, if you work here, and see if you notice anything missing. What's your name?'

She didn't like me, I could tell. I told her my name.

Ganesh, fidgeting, said, 'I don't think anything's gone. I looked in the storeroom and the cigarettes are still up there behind the counter. There wasn't any money in the till.' He met my eye as he spoke. I knew what he was telegraphing. Don't mention the photos or Coverdale's death. These were ordinary uniformed coppers and they might not know.

The male officer walked through the shop and disappeared out back somewhere. The woman asked, 'Shop alarm in order, sir, as far as you know? Only it appears not to have gone off. Isn't that odd?'

I fancied Ganesh looked shifty, and had just decided it must be a look of pain, when he said, 'Fact is, I might've forgotten to set it.'

'Forgotten?' She was both surprised and suspicious. So was I.

Luckily she was distracted by the return of her partner, bare-headed and breathless. 'I reckon he climbed over the rear wall. Back door's open, but not forced. Who's got a key?' He stared at Ganesh.

'No one,' said Ganesh indignantly, and then put a hand to his injured head. 'Ow! Look, no one has a key but me.'

'You ever have the key?' The copper turned an accusing eye on me.

'Never!' I told him.

The law looked at one another. 'Chummy might've been clever with locks,' said the one who'd come in from the yard. 'But if he was, he wasn't your run-of-the-mill break-in artist. Force entry, grab goods, get out. That's the usual style. You say he never took nothing?'

Now they were both looking at Ganesh and disbelief was written all over their mugs.

'You say, sir,' said the policewoman, 'that you collided with this intruder on the stairs?'

'I was coming down,' Ganesh said. 'And he was hanging about there, right by the bottom step.' He pointed towards the door which opened on to the staircase leading up to the flat overhead. 'I started to say something like – I dunno – who're you? Then he lashed out.'

'He'd got that door open, then?' The male copper scratched his head. 'Like he was going to come upstairs?'

'He might've been.' Ganesh sounded wary.

'And how long did you say you were unconscious?' The copper was consulting his notebook in a theatrical manner.

Ganesh told him he hadn't said because he didn't know. He hadn't looked at the clock before coming downstairs. He thought he must have been out some time and then it had taken a while before he was *compos mentis* enough to ring for an ambulance. 'Because I realised I'd been hurt,' he said. 'I was bleeding.'

'Yes, sir. Your call was logged by the ambulance service at ten minutes to five this morning. You must have been unconscious a long time. What do you suppose the intruder was doing in that time?'

'How,' muttered Ganesh, 'should I know? I was out cold. Perhaps he'd left.'

The woman took up the questioning. 'You've got to see it looks a bit odd, at least to us. I mean, more chance of his being caught if he went upstairs to the living accommodation, wasn't there? You might've come round and rung us, or got out of the shop and raised the alarm. Easy enough for him to help himself to a few thousand ciggies and a load of first-class stamps down here, wasn't it? But he's not touched a thing, either here or upstairs.'

'He could've printed himself out a few lottery tickets for nothing, while he was about it,' said her partner. Must have been the canteen comedian.

'Oy!' I said, thinking it was time I took a hand. 'It's not funny.'

It wasn't. They didn't believe Ganesh's version of the night's events, that was clear. They'd turned their steely gaze on me. The male officer smirked.

The woman said in a cajoling voice, 'Now, sir, you're sure this wasn't a domestic?'

'I'm not married!' Ganesh's voice rose and again his words turned into a yelp and he put a hand to his bandages.

'You live nearby, do you?' The man gave me the sort of look they give you when they're trying to convince you they know the truth and you might as well speak up and save time. It usually means they know sod all and are hoping you'll be stupid enough to tell them. 'Weren't here at all last night, were you, miss?'

I gave them my address and informed them I'd been at home all night, thank you. Unfortunately, I couldn't give them a name of a witness who'd verify that. I lived alone. Yes, alone.

They received all this with a world-weary air. 'We know it's embarrassing,' said the policewoman, 'but best to tell us exactly what happened. Wasting police time is an offence. Now, you had a bit of a quarrel, did you?'

'We didn't quarrel!' I yelled, losing my cool. 'I wasn't here and I certainly didn't bash Gan over the head!'

'Well, if it isn't our own Calamity Jane! In trouble again, Fran? Can't leave you for five minutes, can I?'

We all turned to the door. Sergeant Parry stood there,

grinning like the Cheshire Cat, the pale sun playing on his ginger stubble.

'Nothing here for plainclothes,' said the policewoman. 'Who sent you over? Just a break-in, nothing taken, so he says.' She glanced at me. 'Possible domestic.'

''Sall right,' said Parry. 'You let me take care of this one. I'm already on this case.'

They exchanged glances. The policewoman shrugged, closed her notebook and gave me a dirty look. They took themselves off.

Parry shut the door, checked that the closed sign was showing, and came back into the room.

'Right,' he said. 'What's been going on here?'

Before Ganesh could begin to tell his story again, there was an interruption. From the back yard came a loud but tuneless whistling followed by the clatter of noisy entry. Hitch arrived and stopped, surveying the scene. Marco appeared behind him, saw Parry, and melted back out of sight again, probably to shove his private grass supply down the nearest drain.

Hitch had also identified Parry. 'Got the strong arm of the law here, I see. Sergeant Parry, I do believe. What's up? Can't keep away from us?' He turned his attention to Ganesh in his bandages and then to me. 'Hullo, darling. Been knocking the poor bloke around again, have you?'

Chapter Eight

'It was a joke,' I said wearily. 'It's Hitch's idea of a joke.'

We were sitting upstairs in the flat, Parry, Ganesh and myself. Ganesh was drinking tea and swallowing aspirin, and looked as if he ought to be lying down quietly in a darkened room. Parry was walking round the place examining everything, and I was sitting in the basketwork chair suspended from the ceiling, a sort of Indian equivalent of a rocker.

Hitch had been sent home, Parry warning him yet again to keep his mouth shut or else. Marco had vanished without being sent.

'That's all right,' said Parry. 'I didn't think you and him –' he nodded at Ganesh – 'had had a barney. Or at least, I didn't think you'd taken up GBH. Give it time, eh?' He grinned at me. He needed to see a dentist and get a scale and polish.

I decided that if ever I were tempted by a spot of grievous bodily harm, it'd be directed at Parry.

'By the way,' I said, 'before we start on any other business, I'd be glad if you'd stop telling everyone my private history. I'm not some villain whose past form is everyone's to know.'

'Ah,' he returned, unabashed. 'You've had a visit from his nibs, haven't you? How'd you get on with the boy wonder?'

'He was making a lot of fuss about those photos, but he wouldn't tell anything about them.'

'Nothing to tell,' said Parry unconvincingly.

'Do me a favour. Why tell us all to shut up about them, then? Me, Gan here, Hitch, Marco . . . Last night's intruder was looking for that film they found in the washroom, wasn't he? Don't say you can't be sure. *I'm* sure. Who *is* the guy in the prints?'

Parry grinned mockingly. 'That's for us to know and you—'

'To find out,' I finished.

He glowered and shook a sausage-like finger at me. 'No! No detective work this time, Fran! I mean it. You've already interfered and messed up enough. You had no business getting that film printed up. You could screw things up badly for us. What I was going to say was, for you to keep quiet about.'

'I'll have to keep quiet, won't I?' I said sarcastically. 'Seeing as I don't know anything and you won't tell me.'

He nodded. 'And that's the way it stays. You keep your trap shut – unless, of course, there's anything you've forgotten to tell us. Now's your chance if there's something you want to get off your chest.'

Here Parry appeared sidetracked and allowed his bloodshot gaze to rest on the front of my sweater. Dream on, I thought. That's as far as you're ever going to get.

Parry caught my eye, flushed and turned to Ganesh. 'All right, then, let's have your story again, from the top.'

'He ought to be lying down,' I protested. 'He can't keep going over it again and again. He's concussed. Anyone can see that.'

'He can go and lie down all day, once he's told me his story.'

'No I can't!' mumbled Ganesh, whose eyes were beginning to look distinctly unfocused. 'I gotta open up the shop.'

'Shop's closed for the day,' said Parry. 'Fingerprint guy is coming over to dust the back door and all around. Your visitor last night was a professional. He knew all the wrinkles and he had help. Of course, if you hadn't forgot to set that alarm . . .' Parry oozed suspicion. 'Funny coincidence, that.'

'Listen,' muttered Ganesh, propping his head in his hands. He sounded deeply despondent. 'There's something I've got to tell you about the alarm.'

'Oh, yes?' Parry sounded ominous. 'What's that, then?'

I saw Ganesh take a deep breath and wondered what on earth he was going to say. My heart sank. It had to be bad news.

It was. I couldn't believe my ears.

'A fake?' yelled Parry, when Ganesh had stopped speaking. He wrestled for control, gave up and, breathing heavily, glared at us both in a way which made me seriously alarmed for his mental and physical health.

Ganesh, totally dejected, mumbled, 'Not my fault. My uncle—'

'Your uncle is a bloody idiot!' yelled Parry.

'Hey, wait a minute!' I broke in. I was really worried about Ganesh by now. I'd never seen him look so ill. 'I don't know what's gone on here, but yelling at Gan won't help. He's not fit, right? He's got to go and lie down.'

Before Parry could object, I grabbed Ganesh by the arm, hauled him up from the chair and propelled him into the bedroom.

'Lie down, right?' I ordered. 'And stay there until Parry's gone. I'll handle it. I'll see to everything. I'll open up the shop when the cops are out of the way and everything. *You are sick!*' I gave him a shove in the direction of the bed and retreated, closing the door firmly behind me.

Back in the sitting room, Parry was waiting and now having only one person to vent his fury on, advanced on me, flecks of spittle flying as he spoke.

'Of course it didn't go off last night, did it? Because it wasn't set? No. Because the sodding thing's a dummy, a phoney! The bloke who owns this crummy shop is too damn mean to pay for proper security, so what does he do? He rigs up what he hopes will fool a burglar. Does it? Does it hell. A professional break-in artist was always going to rumble it straight away – and one did, didn't he?'

Silently I cursed Hari. One positive thing came out of this, however, I thought. I no longer had to worry that Ganesh was going to get it in the neck for having the washroom done up. Hari deserved to be made to pay. He could hardly grumble, however much Hitch charged for whatever kind of job he did. If Hari hadn't been so penny-pinching, Gan wouldn't have got knocked cold.

But that was for the future. Right now, I had to calm down Parry. Things were looking bad for Ganesh. I let myself drop into the chair vacated by Gan near the table, and rested my elbows on the red chenille tablecloth. 'OK, I agree with you, for what it's worth. But making a fuss about it now isn't going to get us anywhere, is it?'

Reason was wasted on Parry who stormed over, put both palms on the table and loomed over me.

'You can't dismiss it just like that, you know. When I got here, Patel had already reported the break-in to the uniformed boys. I don't think – correct me if I'm wrong – he told them that all he'd got out there on the wall was a painted tin box without a perishing bit of wiring anywhere near it! That's wasting police time, that is. That's withholding essential information. That's actively misleading police enquiries, that's—'

'Oh, shut up!' I snapped. 'He'd been bashed on the bonce. He wasn't thinking straight. He was dozy—'

'There,' Parry interrupted sarcastically, 'I agree with you. Dozy is one word for it. I can think of others. If he's lucky, that bang on the head will have knocked some sense into it.' He paused. 'Here,' he said at a new thought, 'I bet the insurance company doesn't know about that little setup. That could be an attempt to defraud. Strikes me, your mate is in a lot of trouble.'

'He isn't,' I insisted. 'Hari is. You can't blame Ganesh. It's not his fault. He only works here. He's not stupid, he's in a difficult situation. Hari is his uncle. He couldn't shop a family member to the insurance company, could he?'

'Why're you so bloody loyal to him?' Parry demanded.

Taken aback, I retorted, 'Because he's my friend, and everything I said is true.'

'Yeah, yeah.' Parry chewed the end of his ragged moustache. 'I've been a good friend to you and all, seems to me. Fat lot of thanks I've got for it.'

'When?' I gasped.

'I've stood between you and a lot of trouble. You could've been charged with interference in investigations before now, if it weren't for me.' He managed a sickly leer. 'And you're going to need me again, this time, aren't you, if your pal Patel isn't to be dropped in the brown stuff? I don't have to put this dummy alarm business in my report, you know. You think about it. Only don't take too long. I'll be filing the report as soon as I get back to base.'

I met his bloodshot gaze and held it. 'Do you know,' I told

him, 'I don't know which of you makes me want to throw up more – you or Charlie Knowles.'

Parry flushed, then grinned evilly. 'That old feller been patting your bum?'

'Something like that.'

'Dirty old devil.'

'Well, he's not the only one living in hopes, is he?' I snapped back.

Parry straightened up and shook a yellowed fingernail at me. 'One of these days, you'll wish you'd been nicer to me, you'll see.'

'At your funeral,' I told him.

'Very funny. We'll see who laughs last, eh?'

'Listen,' I'd had enough of this, 'why can't you and Harford let it be known you've got the negs and pics? That would take the heat off the rest of us.'

He shook his head. 'No way.'

'Oh great,' I muttered. 'Ganesh gets laid out senseless. I could be next, or Hitch or Marco as well, I suppose.'

'We've warned the two cowboys fixing up the washroom. But to lay it on the line, if chummy approaches either of them, they'll pass the buck so fast, it'll be a blur. All they did was find a sealed package. They gave it to you and Sleeping Beauty in there.' He nodded towards the bedroom door. 'They saw nothing, no negatives, no prints. Not like you, eh? You went running along to the chemist and got the film developed, didn't you? Not smart, Fran. Take my advice – it's official – don't go opening the door to anyone you don't know, right? If anyone comes here to the shop, or to your flat, or makes any kind of approach, phone call, anything, you let us know straight away. It's in your interest, remember. Do yourself a favour, Fran. Wise up.'

'I told you, someone already came to the shop, asking.'

'Yeah, well, you didn't give him the right answer, did you? He came back last night. He didn't get any joy then, either, so he's got to keep trying.' Parry leaned forward again. 'He needs that film.'

'Who does?' I countered.

The only reply to that was a spiteful grin. Parry walked to the door. 'Oh,' he said, 'I'm still not sure whether to put that dummy alarm in my report. Let's say, I'm holding that as a sort of guarantee of your future behaviour, Fran.'

I told him to get out, but he'd already gone.

I didn't get the shop open until after three in the afternoon, just in time to sell the day's *Evening Standard*, a few packets of ciggies and a couple of girlie mags. In between, I had to keep nipping upstairs to check on Ganesh, who was sleeping so soundly I began to worry if I ought to wake him up. He might be in a coma for all I knew.

Everyone who came in the shop wanted to know why we'd been closed earlier. Since several of them had seen the police cars outside first thing, I had to put out some kind of story. I said there'd been an attempted break-in, but the intruders had been disturbed and fled empty-handed. That was true, as it happened.

Every listener to this story told me we'd been bloody lucky. They were right.

At six, I shot the bolts across and went upstairs to check on the invalid. Ganesh, to my great relief, had woken up and was moving around the kitchen in slow motion. I opened up a tin of soup and made toast, but he wasn't very interested.

'You ought to see a doctor,' I said.

But he wasn't having that. 'I'll be fine tomorrow.'

'Gan?' I had to mention it. 'About that dummy alarm.'

He waved both hands, fending off the question and the look on my face. 'I know, I know.'

'I'm not blaming you. But you ought to get your family on to Hari. He had no right to leave you here with nothing but an empty mock-up on a wall for protection.'

A hunted look crossed Ganesh's face. 'You haven't let my family know about this, have you?'

'Relax, of course I haven't.'

'Only they'd write to Hari and he'd be back from India on the next flight. He'd say it was my fault. He'd never leave me in charge again. He must never know anything about any of this, Fran!'

'All right, all right!' What with the coppers telling me not to talk and Ganesh joining in, I might as well take some kind of Trappist vow and be done with it. I went back downstairs and reopened for business.

I left around eight. Ganesh had promised to go to bed early and I'd promised to be at the shop at seven the next morning to help with the papers. I hoped my rusty old alarm clock did its stuff. Sometimes it just sat sullen and silent. I ought to get a new one, but normally I had no need of a morning alarm. I never seemed to stay in employment long enough.

A thin drizzle was falling. The pavements were wet and the light from bar and café windows threw yellow strips across them. Through the windows I could see the Christmas decorations strung around walls and ceilings, lots of glittering tinsel, paper bells and plastic holly. It looked really festive and made me feel sad. Everyone was getting into holiday mood. People were going out for the evening, hurrying past me, chattering and laughing. They'd stop, study a menu fixed up outside a place perhaps, decide against it and move on, or go in, whichever. They were out to enjoy themselves.

I never went out in the evening. I never went anywhere and the one recent time I had gone, for our staff Christmas dinner, I'd come home and found a body in the basement. Why does this happen to me? Why doesn't it happen to other people?

I began to think about Coverdale and his unfulfilled wish to talk to me. The more I thought about it, the more uneasy I became. His killers would want to know why he'd been keen to see me. They'd checked the shop because they were thorough. But what they'd decide in the end was that either Coverdale had given me the film – or I'd found it and Coverdale had come round to see me and get it back. This was what probably had happened. Either that, or he'd come to tell me where he'd hidden it and to ask me to get it for him. He wouldn't have risked returning to the shop in case the guys after him were watching. They were watching him, as it happened, rather more successfully than he'd realised.

So, whichever way you cared to look at it, the villains were sure to reckon I was the link to the negs. The police had embargoed the news that they had them. I was left, staked out like a goat in a clearing, waiting for the tiger. Or even several tigers.

It wasn't a cheery thought and it made me highly nervous. I kept looking over my shoulder and wondered if I ought to go straight home, or adopt some devious route, designed to throw anyone following off the trail. But if they'd killed Coverdale outside my front door, they didn't need to follow me to find out where I lived. They knew.

I still kept looking back on principle. So busy was I doing it, that when someone stepped out of a doorway in front of me, I almost collided with them and just about jumped out of my skin when a voice said, 'Fran?'

'Oh God, Tig,' I gurgled. 'I nearly had a perishing heart attack.'

'What's the matter with you, then?' asked Tig.

I hadn't wanted to hang about in the street and neither had she, so we took refuge in a nearby café, a narrow-fronted establishment that ran back a long way like a tunnel. It was crammed with marble-topped tables. In the summer, they moved some of the tables out on to the pavement, but this time of year, only a lunatic or a polar bear would sit outside.

Tig and I had retreated to the furthermost end of the room from the door with our espressos.

'I'm scared Jo Jo will look in and see me,' Tig had explained, leading the way. She now gave me curious scrutiny. 'Who're you trying to avoid?'

'Don't ask,' I said. 'I'm not allowed to say.'

She shrugged. She didn't care anyway. She didn't look any better or healthier since I'd last seen her. The dark shadows under her eyes were worse, the pinched look more pronounced and there was more than fear of Jo Jo in her eyes. There was a deeper fear and it had driven her to seek me out. I waited for her to tell me what it was.

She went at it a roundabout way. 'I came to the shop yesterday, where you work, Sunday morning. There was an Indian guy there, big bloke. He said you weren't working, not Sunday. They'd got the builders in. They were working Sunday. They moonlighting?'

'No, self-employed. Dilip told me you'd been. I hoped you'd get in touch again. Sorry I missed you.' I sipped the coffee. I was glad of it. My nerves needed settling.

Tig shifted on her wooden chair and it scraped on the tiled

floor. 'Yeah, well, I'm sorry I gave you an earful last time.' She rubbed her thin hands together. The fingertips were blue and the nails dirty. She needed a bath.

I asked, 'You sleeping rough, Tig?'

She twitched. 'Look, did you mean what you said? About doing anything legal?'

'Ye-es,' I said, not at all happy.

'OK, then, I'm hiring you.' I must have looked as if I'd been hit with a sock full of wet sand because she added irritably, 'Well, you said you were a private detective and you worked for people who couldn't get help anywhere else. That's me. I can't go anywhere else, so I've come to you. I want you to get in touch with my family for me. Like, act as go-between.'

I knew I could only blame myself for this. I'd urged her to go home. I'd offered to help if I could. It had been a spur-of-the-moment thing. If I'd given it any thought afterwards, which I hadn't, I would've decided, with relief, that she wouldn't take me up on it. And I'd also told her I took on jobs for people. I'd boasted about it, to be frank. Which just goes to show you've got to be ready for the unexpected, and if you don't want to be reminded of something you've said, keep your mouth shut.

'Well?' She was leaning across the table, her pinched face flushed in anger and her whole attitude a bad case of aggro. People at a nearby table gave us alarmed looks. They probably thought we were about to start a fight on the floor. 'Or was it just a load of crap?' she went on. 'All that what you told me? You made it all up? You've never done any jobs for no one.'

'Yes, I have!' I was moved to defend myself. 'I was surprised when you asked, that's all.'

'Are you going to do it?' She leaned back now, fixing me with a very direct stare.

'All right,' I said. 'What do you want me to do? Phone them?'

'No, go and see them.' She was fumbling inside her jacket and pulled out a roll of dirty notes secured with an elastic band. 'See this? It's my emergency cash. All I've got. Jo Jo knows nothing about it. There's enough there to buy you a day return ticket, rail, from Marylebone to Dorridge. That's where they live. There's a train every hour – I checked it out for you. Leaves Marylebone quarter to the hour. Coming back, leaves Dorridge at forty-eight minutes past the hour. Any money left over you can keep for your fee. I don't know what you usually charge, but this is all I've got, so take it or leave it.'

She was going too fast for me and my fee was the least of my worries. 'Who lives there, your parents? Where's Dorridge, for crying out loud? It sounds like porridge.'

'It's on the way to Birmingham, before you get to Birmingham, just before Solihull. It'll take just over two hours to get there and the same back, so you'll have to go early in the morning.'

'Hey, hold on.' She'd got it all planned, it seemed, but I had questions to ask.

A streetwalker came in out of the cold. She was just starting the evening stint and was all dressed up nice in a fake fur coat and patent leather stilettos. She wasn't young, in her forties, a bit blowsy with bottle-blonde hair and too much make-up. The Italian waiter evidently recognised her because he gave her a secretive sort of smile and, without her having to ask, yelled down the café to the guy on the espresso machine, 'Hey, give the lady a coffee!'

She didn't pay for it. I guess she'd already paid.

Tig, watching the same scene, said scornfully, 'Why'd guys

pay her? They can pay someone like me half the money and I'm half her age.'

'Then watch out for the pimps,' I said. 'They don't like competition on the same patch.' I didn't mention that the professional tart had certainly taken the trouble to shower before she went to work. Some punters, though admittedly not all, might be put off by Tig's appearance and the whiff of street doorway.

My companion shrugged again. 'Well, I'm not on the game now, anyhow. I told you, I don't do it any more, not unless I'm really skint, you know, and some old feller comes up and asks. They bloody well nearly always are old, the ones who like really young girls.'

'I know,' I said, memory of Charlie still fresh.

'Still – that sort don't give no trouble.' Her gaze darkened. She was thinking of her treatment at the hands of the City types who'd gang-raped her.

My mind was working overtime. If I went on this errand for Tig, it'd take me out of London for a whole day. That would mean, in present circumstances, a whole day without having to look over my shoulder and jump at shadows. I liked the idea of that. On the other hand, with Ganesh in his fragile state of health, I couldn't leave him to manage on his own in the shop. I'd have to go on a Sunday when Dilip could help out doing the morning papers.

'We need to talk serious business,' I said. 'If, and it is only *if*, I do this for you, there are things I need to know. For starters, why you left home in the first place and why, all of a sudden, you want to go back. And it's no use clamming up on me. I'm not going into a situation like that blind, OK? Another thing, I can't just get on a train and go to this Dorridge place. Suppose I turned up and your parents had gone out for the day? Or like you said before, they might've moved. I'd have to phone first and make an appointment. They're going to ask questions. Also, does Jo Jo know what you're planning and what's he likely to do when you take off? Follow?'

'He can't,' she said quickly. 'He doesn't know what I'm going to do or where my family lives. I've never told him where I come from and he hasn't asked. You don't, do you?'

She was right. The homeless respect one another's privacy and the right to keep stum about an individual's past. If you want to tell everyone, fine. If you don't, they don't press you. It's a rule.

She hunched over her empty coffee cup. 'If I tell you, you'll do it?'

'I'm not bargaining,' I told her. 'I'm telling you my terms. Take it or leave it.'

The waiter was giving us funny looks. I told Tig to wait and went up to the counter to get us another couple of coffees. Thanks to the lay-out of the place, it would be difficult for her to slip past me and out while I was away from the table. But I kept an eye on her, in case.

She'd taken the time given by my absence to think it over and had reached a decision. 'All right, I'll tell you anything you want to know. I'll give you the phone number and you can ring them. But if you do, you're not to say where they can find me, right? The last bloody thing I want is them driving down here.'

'Understood.'

'I'll write their names and address and phone number down for you.'

Neither of us had a bit of paper though I had a stub of pencil. There was a card on the table telling customers of some Christmas offer the café was running – coffee, choice of sandwich and a cake for £2.50, something like that. Tig turned it over and wrote on the back.

'Their name is Quayle, Colin and Sheila. My name's Jane, really. That's what you'll have to call me when you talk to them.' She pushed the card towards me. She'd written it all down, with address and phone number.

A thought had struck me. 'You need to send a personal message, or tell me something that I couldn't know about you or them unless I knew you well. I mean, I've got to convince them I really am speaking on your behalf.'

She gave an odd little smile. 'All right. Wish my mum a happy birthday. It's her birthday tomorrow.'

It was personal, all right, but I wished she'd thought of something else.

Tig found giving out the practical details easier than the next thing she had to tell me. I could see her bracing herself. 'Jo Jo and I,' she said, 'we had a place to doss but we lost it. The last few nights, we've been sleeping over Waterloo way, in an underpass. You know the place? It's under the road system, a big empty space. There used to be lots of people sleeping there. Most of them have gone now, moved out. They're building there now. But there's still space to doss if you haven't got anywhere else. They try and move you on, of course.'

I nodded. I knew the place she meant. It had been the site of Cardboard City, that squatters' camp in the maze of subterranean walkways between Waterloo and the South Bank complex. I'd never slept there but I'd been there in its heyday, looking for someone or just passing through. Each inhabitant had had his space, with his sleeping bag and plastic carriers of personal belongings, his dog, his transistor radio – some even had a scrap of dirty carpet down and a broken old armchair or two. Some were young, some old, some in sound mind and some way out of theirs. Some had been there years. When I was at school, our art teacher had been keen on the painting of a guy called Bosch who'd turned out stuff which looked as if it had all been painted when he was as high as a kite – but which she reckoned was symbolic. The old Cardboard City had put me in mind of one of those paintings by Bosch – a world of weird things which were normal to those caught up in the nightmare.

But even down there the homeless hadn't been secure. The area was being developed, as Tig said – luxury flats and a monster cinema going up. The debris of the streets was being swept up and moved elsewhere as the men in the hard hats and their equipment moved in.

Tig was avoiding my eye, her face turned down, her stringy fair hair falling forward. Her voice was muffled. 'Coupla nights ago,' she said, 'someone died there.'

People do die on the streets. I waited. There had to be more.

'It was a girl, about the same age as me. She was sleeping right near us. She'd got a little dog. Nice dog, friendly. Some people have those big dogs that go for you. Jo Jo had one once and I was glad when he sold it on to someone. You had to watch it all the time or it'd have you. Anyhow, this girl, I didn't know her name or anything, but I'd talked a bit to her that evening. I'd made friends with the dog and that's mostly what we talked about, the dog. Later she went off somewhere and she didn't come back until after midnight. She'd had a couple of drinks, I could smell the booze – and I guess she might've got hold of some stuff and been shooting up somewhere. Sunday morning, she never got up. Never stirred. No one bothered much at first. But then the dog started whining and sniffing at her. I got a really bad feeling. I went over and shook her shoulder. She was cold already. Her eyes were open and bulging and her jaw had fallen open and stiffened like that. She looked horrible. It was the scariest thing I ever saw in my life. Like a horror film only worse, because it was real.'

Tig shook back her hair and looked up, meeting my gaze firmly. 'And I thought, that's me. That's how I'm going to end up and pretty soon. It's true, isn't it?' She stared at me defiantly.

'Unless you do something about it,' I said.

'Right. That's what I thought. I won't like it, I won't like going home and facing them. Perhaps they won't even have me. But I've got to try because it's the only way out I've got. Some people get out of it other ways. They get a permanent place to live and they get a job. Like you, you've got out of it. You always were smart. But that's not going to work for me. I haven't time enough for that. I get out now or by spring, I'm dead.'

'Don't worry,' I said. 'I'll do it.'

She relaxed and I felt a stab of unease. She'd be relying on me. Supposing I messed the whole thing up? Said the wrong thing on the phone? It'd be Tig's lifeline snapping. I forced the worry away but I did venture, 'You could ring them yourself and then I could go up—'

'No!' Her voice was fierce. 'I won't talk to them until— They'd ask too many questions.'

They were going to ask me questions, but I took her point. 'So, why'd you leave in the first place?' I asked. 'Just general.'

She shook her head. 'I told you what my mum's like, everything so perfect. Dad's worse. It didn't matter how hard I tried at school, he'd find some subject I'd done poorly at, and ask, what about that? I went to a good school, they paid – private.'

'So did I,' I said glumly. 'Until it threw me out.'

'Well, then, you know how it is. Parents have spent money and they want results, don't they?'

She was turning the knife in my conscience, though she didn't know it. Her parents had probably found the money without too much difficulty, but Dad and Grandma Varady had really scrimped to send me. When I'd been expelled, they hadn't moaned, just sympathised and rallied round. But I knew I'd let them down and would have it on my conscience to my dying day. For Tig, it was different, however. She'd worked hard, apparently, but it hadn't been enough.

'He – my father – kept talking about university,' Tig was saying. 'But I didn't want to go to university. He said I'd never get a really good job without a degree. He kept on and on. Then there was Mum with her "you-can't-go-out-looking-like-that" and "be-careful-to-make-nice-friends"! And, of course, "you-don't-want-to-be-thinking-about-boys-you've-got-your-studies".'

Tig shook her head and leaned forward, her pale face flushed. 'Look, I know it doesn't sound so bad, talking to you now. They weren't beating me up. Dad hadn't got his hand in my knickers, there was nothing like that. It was just day in, day out, pressure. I couldn't get away from it, not there. So – I left.'

Everyone's got their reasons. It doesn't matter whether they sound good or bad reasons to anyone else. They're good enough for the person concerned.

'You see,' Tig said sadly, 'how hard it is to talk about going back. How disappointed they'll be, how shocked, horrified. I don't know if they can cope with it. That's why you've got to find out first.'

'I'll really do my best, Tig,' I promised. 'Honestly, I will.' I hoped I hadn't bitten off more than I could chew.

Chapter Nine

With all the trouble I was causing Daphne at the moment, I didn't feel I could ask to phone long-distance to Dorridge from her place. I don't mean I wouldn't pay her. I always paid for my calls from Daphne's. But I might find myself explaining about Tig. Daphne would be interested and I was pretty sure, sympathetic, but she'd worry about it. Besides, I needed time to think out what I'd say. The more I thought, the less I liked the whole idea.

The next morning, I explained it all to Ganesh. He was feeling better and had got rid of the bandages, but still had a large plaster on his head. I told him to sit on a stool behind the counter and stay there. I'd do any running around and would stay all day till closing time. At least I was spared Hitch and Marco creating havoc in the washroom. It seemed they couldn't come in and finish today.

'He's got a problem with his supplier over the floortiles,' said Ganesh.

I made no comment on this, but privately decided they were both keeping clear of the place while there was any chance of running into the police on the premises. Neither of them, I fancied, liked answering questions. Instead, over our coffee-break, I explained about Tig.

'You ought to have steered clear of that,' said Ganesh. 'No

way are you going to come out a winner. Tell her you've changed your mind.'

'You told me you thought she ought to go home,' I protested.

'I know I did. I still do. But I didn't mean you should set it up. Families,' said Ganesh, who knew about these things, 'are tricky.'

'It's her only chance, Gan. She's right. She's not really a survivor. She looks sick. She's had to take up with the awful Jo Jo just to get protection. She's got to get out fast.' I added sadly, 'And I did offer to help.'

'More fool you,' said Ganesh. His sore head was making him grumpy. But his thinking was still clearer than mine. 'Look at it from the point of view of her people,' he went on. 'They will have been waiting to hear from Tig for months. Suddenly, out of the blue, they get a call from a complete stranger who claims to know their missing daughter. The stranger wants to come and see them and arrange the daughter's return home. What does that sound like to you?'

'A scam,' I said miserably.

'Too right. The first thing they'll want to know is, what's in it for you?'

'My fee,' I said. 'And it won't be much once I've paid the train fare out of what Tig gave me.'

'Who cares about your couple of quid fee from Tig? She's got no money – there's no point in you trying to get it from her. The Quayles will think you want money from *them* – because from the sound of it, they're pretty well set up. So, they'll be expecting you to ask them to pay you for acting as middleman. They won't believe you if you say you don't want anything. Look, who knows what they'll think? Maybe that you've got Tig locked in a cellar and don't mean to let her out until the Quayles have coughed up a really big amount. You'll turn up in this place, what's it called?'

'Dorridge.'

'Are you sure you've got that right? You'll turn up and find a police reception committee. At the very least, they'll call their solicitor. You know what I think you should do? You should tell Harford about it, ask his advice. At least, tell him what you're going to do so that you're covered if the Quayles turn nasty.'

'I can't!' I exclaimed in horror. 'Not Harford! He'd sneer. Besides, it's nothing to do with him. Nor have I got Tig's permission to bring the police into it – and I wouldn't get it. Tig would just disappear if I mentioned the cops.'

'How about Parry? He's a pain in the neck but he'd know all the ropes in a case like this. Don't the police deal with missing teenagers? Hey, it might even be illegal for you not to tell them about her.'

'It's not illegal to go missing if you're overage,' I pointed out. 'And if a person's over sixteen, the police won't do anything, either – not unless it's suspicious circumstances. She's got to be more'n sixteen. She was fifteen in Jubilee Street, and that was months ago. She's probably seventeen and anyway, she was only ever just a runaway. There's hundreds of them out there, up and down the country. The coppers don't want to know about another one.'

Ganesh tried another tack. 'They might not want her back. She's been a lot of trouble. They may think she's dishonoured them.'

'I don't think they're worried about honour, not from what Tig says. They're worried about respectability.'

'Well, same thing, isn't it?' he said. I began to feel this was one of the times when Gan and I found ourselves heading for a culture clash. It didn't happen often, but there was no way round it when it did.

'Look,' I said patiently, 'she hasn't run away from an arranged marriage. She just pushed off because of the pressure.'

'Don't think I don't know what that means,' said Gan testily. 'You want to know about family pressures? Try my lot. But have I pushed off to live rough on the street?'

This was getting me nowhere. I asked if I could use the phone. He told me to help myself and suggested I phoned from the flat upstairs. There was no one in the shop and he could manage. I think his head was hurting and he was fed up with talking about Tig. If I wanted more trouble, I was welcome to it. He was washing his hands of it.

I went up to the flat and sat in front of the phone for five minutes before I picked up enough courage to dial the number Tig had given me. It rang several times during which I went over what I'd rehearsed in my head – and decided none of it would do. I'd have to improvise.

It was still ringing. They were out. My heart lifted. I was about to replace the receiver when a woman's voice, breathless, asked, 'Hullo? Yes?'

'Oh, hullo,' I said stupidly. 'Is that Mrs Quayle?'

'Yes . . .' The voice was wary.

'My name's Fran Varady. I'm a friend of T— of Jane's.'

There was a silence. I could feel her gathering up her wits, steeling herself to deal with this. She asked in a careful way, 'Were you at school with Jane?'

I understood what she was getting at. If I was an old school pal who'd not been in touch for years, I mightn't know that Jane had left home. If that was the case, Mrs Quayle could invent some reason for Jane not being there and falsely promise to deliver a message.

'No,' I said. 'I'm phoning from London. I know Jane here.'

There was a gasp and a bump. After that came such a long silence I began to be afraid she'd fainted. I was anxiously repeating her name when she came back on the line.

'I'm sorry – it was such a shock. I – I had to sit down. You know Jane? Where— Why isn't she on the phone herself? Is she all right?' Panic began to enter her voice.

If I didn't watch out, I'd have a hysterical woman on the other end of the line. 'She's all right,' I said firmly. (I wasn't being untruthful. Tig's situation was grim. But she was in one piece and walking around, clean of drugs, and in street terms that was certainly all right.)

Her voice shaking, Mrs Quayle began to ask questions so fast, I couldn't have answered any of them if I'd wanted to. 'Where is Jane? What's her address? Why isn't she calling herself? Who are you? Where did you get my home number? Did—'

I managed to get a word in at last. 'Mrs Quayle, I'm sorry it's been such a shock, but if you'll let me, I'll try and explain. Tig – Jane would like to come home—'

'But of course she can come home! She always cou—'

I cleared my throat loudly and Mrs Quayle fell silent. 'She's too embarrassed to call you herself, so she asked me. Mrs Quayle, Jane's been living rough. Things haven't been easy for her. You ought to know that.'

'You said she was all right!' she retorted suspiciously.

'She is – but she can't – she doesn't want to go on living as she is now.'

Mrs Quayle was cudgelling her brain back into working order. 'Is my daughter in some kind of trouble?' Her voice was sharp.

'Not with the law, if that's what you mean,' I said. 'But things are difficult for her and she doesn't want to come to the phone and have to answer a lot of questions. Can't you understand that?'

'I don't know,' she said. 'I don't know who you are or even if you really know Jane.'

I had to play the one card Tig had given me. 'She asked me to wish you a happy birthday, by the way. She said it was today.'

Mrs Quayle moaned. It was a heart-breaking sound. I felt a louse. Ganesh had been right and I ought to have told Tig I couldn't do this.

'Mrs Quayle?' I asked. 'Would you like to talk this over with your husband? I can ring again.'

'Oh, no, please! Please, don't hang up!'

Now she was terrified she'd lose the one indirect contact Jane had made after so long. She truly didn't know what to do, poor woman.

'I will call back,' I promised.

'Can't I have your number? Can't I call you?' She was getting frantic. 'Look, you must tell Jane that of course she can come home. Daddy and I—'

'Jane thinks I ought to come and see you, Mrs Quayle. There's a lot I have to explain. She isn't the same girl who left you. She's changed. You've got to understand that. She can't just walk back in the way she walked out. I'm sorry if I sound brutal – but it's true. You'll have to be prepared to make, well, adjustments. It'll take time to pick up the pieces.'

She was quiet, thinking about it. Fretfully, she said, 'I wish Colin were here . . .' Then, making up her mind, 'When can you come?'

'Sunday, if it's all right with you? I can't come in the week, I've got a job.'

I should have said that earlier, mentioned that I was in employment, not skulking on street corners. It must have sounded reassuring.

'Oh, of course, we don't expect you to take time off from your job. Yes, come Sunday.' She sounded quite enthusiastic.

I told her I'd be there Sunday morning and to talk it through with her husband but not to get het up. She still wanted my phone number but I refused and I'd taken the precaution of withholding it from the system in case she dialled 1471 as soon as I put down the receiver.

'Well, you'll have to go now, won't you?' said Ganesh when I repeated the conversation to him.

After that, we didn't talk about it again. I could see he wasn't feeling well. I couldn't get him to go upstairs and rest, even though as the day wore on, he showed no willingness to do anything but sit in the storeroom, drinking coffee or dozing off with his head on the table. I managed on my own somehow, and at eight I closed up shop, checking the back premises were secure and the shop door bolted. I left the lights on low as added security. Then I confronted Ganesh in his storeroom retreat.

'What time is it?' he asked and looked bewildered when I told him.

'I've closed up. Can you manage to open that antique of a safe Hari's got upstairs for me to put the cash in?'

He stumbled upstairs to the flat and we managed to stow the cash away. I don't know what else Hari had in that safe; I could only see bundles of paper. But it seemed to me crazier than ever to put a dummy burglar alarm on the outside of the place if Hari had anything at all he wanted protecting.

'As soon as I've gone, will you go to bed?' I demanded.

He promised he would and followed me down the other flight of stairs from the flat which led to the separate street entrance beside the shop window.

'Promise, Ganesh?'

'Swear it, Fran.'

'I'll come early tomorrow, OK?'

I stood outside and listened to him lock and bolt this door, too. He hadn't completely lost his presence of mind. When he'd done that, he opened the letter box and addressed me through it.

'Fran, if by any chance when you get here in the morning the place is closed up because I've overslept or something – ring the bell on this door. It makes a helluva row.'

I set off home. Or at least, that was my intention. But I hadn't got a dozen steps from the shop when I heard my name hailed and recognised Harford's voice. I stopped and turned with a sigh.

'I thought you quit work at eight,' he said. 'I've been waiting.'

'Don't you lot ever quit work either? I had to close up, Ganesh isn't fit.' I glanced round. 'Waiting where? You can't park here.'

'I've been sitting in that grubby little coffee place over the road, by the window.'

'Police surveillance now!' I muttered.

'Look,' he said, 'I'm off duty, right? I need to talk to you. I thought we could go and have a drink.'

I squinted up at him in the poor lamplight. He still wore the suit, but had taken off his tie and unbuttoned the neck of his shirt. He looked and sounded genuine, wasn't sneering, and was even acting friendly. It had to be a trick.

I debated whether or not to go along with this. Nothing obliged me to go with him. On the other hand, if he'd been sitting over the road in Lennie's Drop-By Café (known jocularly among the locals as the Drop-Dead Café), he must want to talk to me about something that mattered.

'All right,' I conceded. 'There's a pub round the corner.'

'There's also a little Italian restaurant,' he said. 'It might be nicer. I checked it out earlier.'

I'd walked into that one. But it was getting late and I was hungry. We went to the Italian place.

It was nice, with green-checked tablecloths, a green-tiled wall behind the bar, real flowers in the vases and, inevitably, Christmas decorations.

'I eat Italian a lot,' he said. 'I hope you like it.'

'I eat anything,' I said ungraciously. Because I'd let him outmanoeuvre me didn't mean I had to go all sweet and girly. Anyway, it's not my style.

He leaned his elbows on the table, propping his chin in his hands, and stared at me thoughtfully. After a minute of this, I got fidgety.

'Something wrong?' I asked.

'No – nothing. Why did you cut your hair so short? I mean, it looks great – but it's a nice colour and it'd probably suit you longer.'

Heaven help us. Compliments from the Met. Was I, by any lunatic chance, being chatted up here? I opened my menu and took a quick look. Nothing was cheap but the *penne al tonno* was reasonable.

'I'll have that,' I said, pointing to it. 'And I pay my own way, right?'

'Fine. I'll buy us a bottle of wine. You did agree to a drink.'

When the wine had arrived and he'd poured us a glass each, I said, 'Look, Inspector—'

'My name's Jason.'

'Well, Jason, I'd like to know just what I'm doing here. I can't believe you're desperate for a date.'

He smiled. It transformed his face and if Daphne'd been there to see it, she'd have been bowled over. Not me, I'd like to make clear.

'Something tells me we've got off on the wrong foot, Fran. Obviously, we met in rather difficult circumstances – over a corpse.'

'Yes, what about the late Gray Coverdale?' I sipped the wine, which was rather nice. 'We're here to talk about him, I suppose? We don't have anything else in common.'

'Yes – and no. We might have more in common than you think. At least we could try and find out. I'd like to talk about you a bit. Or you can quiz me if you want. I'd like us to be friends. There's no point in glaring at each other like a couple of cats squaring up over territory. I thought we could bury the hatchet. It'd make life a lot easier.'

Friends, us? I spelled it out carefully. 'Just because this is a murder investigation and I found the body, doesn't mean that I've given up all right to a private life. Ask me about Coverdale and I'll tell you what I know – although you know it already. Anything else, *Jason*, is off limits. None of your business.'

'Why've you taken a dislike to me?' he asked, disconcerting me. 'Is it because you don't like coppers? A lot of people don't – or so I've been finding.' He frowned. 'I include respectable people. I never expected to be popular with villains, but I have been shocked, since I joined the force, by the general distrust shown by Joe Public. We're protecting them, for God's sake! We're not the enemy.'

'You should have thought about that before you joined the police,' I pointed out. 'If you wanted to be popular you should've formed a pop group. Why did you join the police, anyway? Couldn't you have got a job in the City or something like that? I should've thought that'd be more your mark.'

'Why?' He sounded offended. Then he hunched his shoulders. 'I could've gone for banking or something, I suppose. A lot of guys I know have done that. I just wanted something else, not just making money.' He fidgeted in an embarrassed way. 'I don't want to sound a pseud or big-headed, but I wanted to feel I was helping people, making a difference. I wanted to be able to think that what I was doing really mattered in the community. That somehow the world around would be a smidgen better for my efforts. I didn't just decide for all those high-minded reasons,' he added defensively.

'They sound all right to me,' I said.

He relaxed. 'The police force offers a good career structure for a graduate these days. It has to be more interesting than sitting at a desk. You meet a lot of unusual people . . .' Here he grinned at me and saluted me with his glass.

'What am I? A freak?' I snapped.

'Of course not. I think you're, well, bright, very attractive and probably fun if you'd get that chip off your shoulder. We could be friends, if you'd be prepared to give it a try.'

'Chip?' I goggled at him. 'Me? Chip?'

Fortunately the pasta arrived. We must have been equally hungry because conversation flagged while we concentrated on eating.

When we'd pushed our plates aside and Harford had refilled our wine glasses, he asked, 'How's Patel today, by the way?'

'A bit groggy. Could be worse.' I eyed him. 'Do you think the guy who attacked him will come back?'

'Not tonight. We've got a patrol car keeping an eye on the place, just in case. I'm more worried about you, Fran. He – the man who's looking for the film – may think you have it or can get hold of it.'

'Thanks, I worked that one out for myself. You're still not going to let the public know you've got it?'

He shook his head. 'Once he knows that, he'll vanish. As long as he thinks he has a chance of recovering it, he'll hang around and we'll get him. Don't worry.'

'Look,' I told him, 'I'm not thick. I do realise what you coppers are up to here. Ganesh and I are decoys, right? You're waiting for whoever-it-is behind this to get in touch with one of us – or failing that, Marco or Hitch. As I see it, the least you can do is offer us adequate protection.'

'We've got it all under control,' he assured me.

'Have you, heck. Why's Ganesh staggering round concussed if that's the case?'

'That was a slip-up. It won't happen again. We're keeping an eye on you, Fran.'

I supposed I had to take his word for it. I toyed with my glass. 'Why did the person who tracked Coverdale to my place kill the poor bloke? That was stupid if the tracker wanted the film back. He's not going to get it off a dead man, is he?'

'My guess is, he panicked. Or he threatened Coverdale with the knife but Coverdale took him on. There was a struggle and the stabbing was accidental.' He hesitated. 'I looked over your flat when I called round the other day and it's a pretty secure place. I don't think anyone could get through that little window on to the ditch and the lawn – but don't leave it open at night. I realise this time of the year you probably wouldn't. If it's got a weak point, it's not having burglar bars on the basement window. I saw you had safety locks on the window and a chain on the door and that's fine, but why don't you talk to your landlady about getting burglar bars sometime?'

I'd previously thought my flat secure, but this kind of talk was making me nervous.

'You sound pretty sure he'll come back.'

'His employer will insist. He's a worried man.'

'But I'm not to know who he is, this worried Mr Big?'

Harford looked serious and shook his head. 'No kidding, Fran. All discussion of those photos is embargoed.' Without warning, he made a jump of subject. 'You and Patel go back some way, or so I understood Wayne Parry to say.'

Wayne? Parry's name was Wayne? Had his mother liked cowboy films? And just how much gossiping was done about me down at the nick? 'Ganesh is my friend,' I said coldly.

'Just that, a friend?' His eyes met mine and there was no mistaking what he meant.

That made me angry. I leaned over the green-checked table. 'Listen, saying someone's a friend is saying a lot. I don't chuck the word "friend" about. A friend is someone who's there when you need him. You never have to explain yourself to a friend. You can have a stand-up row with a friend and when the dust settles, you agree to differ and you're still mates. I don't know what your background is, but I bet it's pretty comfortable. You've probably got a lot of people you call friends. But friends are thin on the ground when you're down and out. I wonder, if you ever find yourself really up against it, as I've been lots of times, whether your friends will still be there for you the way Ganesh has always been there when I've needed him.'

He was looking down at his clasped hands on the cloth as I spoke, avoiding my eye. As I fell silent, I realised that something had changed. The atmosphere had plummeted well down the scale and the chill factor had set in. He looked up and the good nature had gone from his face. He was back to the sneery cold look again. He signalled to the waiter.

'You'll want to get back home,' he said.

Now what had I said that had really upset him? Something had. I'd touched a nerve. I remembered what he'd said about the public not supporting the police and wondered if he found himself got at from all sides. I couldn't imagine he got on easily with the other CID people and as for the uniformed bluebottles, they probably wrote rude limericks about him on the bog wall. By my words, I'd made it clear I excluded him from my world, too. Well, if he was a misfit, it wasn't my problem. But to have accused me of having a chip on the shoulder was a bit rich.

'I pay my whack, like I said,' I told him, dragging my purse out from the neck of my sweater. I keep it on a leather string under my top clothing. I've always kept my money tucked well away. It's because of the sort of company I'd kept for too long and the crap places I'd lived – before I got the flat.

After the snug warmth of the restaurant, outside was really miserable. We stood on the pavement in the drizzling rain. I hunched down in my denim jacket, Harford stood with his hands in his pockets and a truculent expression on his face. 'Do you want me to walk you back?' he asked.

Put like that, how could a girl accept? 'I don't need an escort,' I told him sourly. 'Thanks for the wine.'

I don't know whether he watched me walk away. I didn't look back. *Brief Encounter* with a modern twist. You wouldn't catch me going for a drink with a bloke I didn't like again.

Chapter Ten

I didn't sleep at all well. My brain was too busy. It was only partly because of Harford's words about security at the flat. I'd checked everything and thought I was safe. Just to make sure of that little garden window, I'd blocked it by taking the medicine cabinet off the bathroom wall, and wedging it in the window space. It looked odd and was inconvenient, taking the light, but if anyone tried to get through the window, he'd dislodge it and it'd fall down with a heck of a noise.

As I lay there, drifting in and out of sleep, my mind ran on Coverdale, whom I'd hardly known, but who'd died just outside my door. Ganesh and I had rescued him from his pursuers once, but in the end it hadn't helped the wretched man. It did, however, leave me with a feeling of responsibility towards him – quite unnecessarily as I told myself, but hard to shift.

I speculated irritably about the perverseness of Fate. I remembered the story in which a merchant's told he's going to meet Death the next day, so he travels to Damascus to avoid it only to find Death has travelled there too. Coverdale had cheated Death at the shop, only to meet the Grim Reaper in my basement. I supposed there was a sort of sense in that. Coverdale had presumably poked his nose in where he shouldn't. He'd been an investigative reporter and that'd been his job. It had risks attached and they'd caught up with him. But me, why had I been dragged in?

In the end, I decided Ganesh was responsible. He'd allowed Coverdale to use the old washroom. He'd decided to get Hitch to rip out the fittings. So that settled that. It was Gan's fault.

I turned my thoughts to the fair-haired man in the photo and wondered where he was and what he was doing. His heavies were incompetent. They'd picked up Coverdale and lost him again the day he'd stumbled into the shop. Then one of them had contrived to kill the poor bloke before they'd found out what had happened to the—

I sat up in bed. 'Buck up your ideas, Fran!' I said aloud. Just because Harford thought Coverdale's death might have been unintended in a struggle, or because the killer had panicked, didn't mean that was how it had been. I was forgetting – and Harford was, too – that *Coverdale* hadn't known Gan and I had recovered the film any more than the villains did. Coverdale thought the film was still hidden in the washroom at the shop. He had come to the flat to ask me to retrieve it for him. When threatened by the knifeman, had he confessed this? If so, having told the knifeman what he wanted to know, Coverdale himself had then become expendable. In fact, he'd become too dangerous to leave alive. No accident, then. No panicking assailant. Coverdale had been murdered deliberately by a cold-blooded killer and any further knowledge he'd had about the fair-haired man in the pic had died with him.

It explained why the searcher had next tried the shop. It wasn't because he was blundering around, hoping to strike lucky, but because he'd been told, by the man who'd hidden it, that the film was there.

He must have had a terrific shock when he saw the

washroom with the partly installed new fittings. Coverdale hadn't known about that, either. Coverdale would've described the old washroom and the exact spot he'd stashed the packet with the film in it. The searcher had realised that someone else must have come across the envelope when the old fittings were torn out. But what he didn't know was what the finder had done with it. Had he or she simply chucked it in a waste-paper basket? Or kept it? The intruder had started up the back stair leading to the flat with the intention of searching there, but that's when he'd met Ganesh on the staircase. I wondered how long Gan had lain unconscious. Long enough for the intruder to complete his search? Hari's flat was a tip. Needles in haystacks would hardly have come into it. On the other hand, it was easier to search for something if you knew what it was, than if you didn't, if you see what I mean.

Having reached these various conclusions, it was difficult to get back to sleep at all. I looked at the clock and saw it was gone five. In an hour's time, Ganesh would be taking delivery of the morning papers – if he'd woken up. I got up, made some tea, showered, dressed, and set out for the shop.

It's surprising how many people are out and about just before six in the morning. The streets were quite busy, traffic already building up. People were bound for work, forming queues at the bus stops and hurrying into the entrance to the tube station.

Ganesh was at work already, taking in the stacks of newspapers, apparently much recovered, and surprised to see me.

'I told you I'd come early,' I said.

'You can give me a hand to put these out, then.'

I hate handling newsprint. You get filthy. I concentrated on the quality broadsheets, because that print is less likely to mess up your hands. As we worked, I told Ganesh about my encounter with Harford the previous evening, and also what I'd worked out about Coverdale's death. I didn't tell him how I'd concluded that our involvement was all his fault. I'd save that for later.

Ganesh agreed. 'What's more,' he said, 'I've been thinking over the business of that dummy alarm. That's typical of Hari and very bad thinking. Penny wise and pound foolish, that's the old fellow. I think I'll get a proper system installed before he gets back. It's for his own good and protection, not to say mine.'

It certainly made sense, but what with that and the new washroom, Hari's profits were in danger of disappearing fast. I felt a bit sorry for the poor old boy, holidaying out there in India, blissfully unaware what his nephew was up to.

When we'd finished the newspapers, I washed my hands in the nice new washbasin, and went down the road to the French bakery to buy us *pains au chocolat* for breakfast. I felt we needed a little treat and chocolate is supposed to cheer the spirit.

We needed cheering because the master craftsmen were back.

'Coppers not hanging around?' asked Hitch, putting his head round the doorjamb. He spoke in what passed, for him, as a whisper. I thought he'd have been good at stage asides, clearly audible to the audience.

Told they weren't expected, as far as we knew, he edged in and took a good look round the place to make sure, just in case Parry jumped out from behind the cold drinks cabinet. 'Got the back door opened up? Marco's bringing the tiles in. We can finish it all off by lunchtime. You all right today, sunshine? How's the old napper?'

Ganesh said he was fine, thanks, and glad they could finish

the job today. He went to open up the back door.

Left alone in the shop, I sold three newspapers, a tube of throat lozenges and a packet of disposable cigarette lighters, all to the same person, a brickie from a nearby construction site. If he cut back on the ciggies he mightn't have needed the throat sweets but I was more intrigued by what he was going to do with three papers. I asked.

'I buy 'em for me mates,' he explained hoarsely.

I didn't follow up the questioning although I was tempted. Two of the papers were downmarket tabloids but the third was the *Financial Times*.

After he left, trade, such as it was, fell off completely. From the rear of the premises came the muted roar of Hitch's normal speaking voice.

The doorbell tinged and I looked up.

'Hi,' said Tig, edging in nervously. Like Hitch earlier, she took a good look round. 'I thought I'd drop in and ask how you were getting on – you know, if you'd rung my parents.'

She looked worse than ever this morning. Her features had a nipped, chilled look and her lips had gained a blue tinge.

'You want a cup of coffee, Tig?' I offered. 'Things are quiet and the kettle boiled only a few minutes ago.'

She accepted, nursing the warm mug in her skeletal fingers and pressing it against her cheeks. She wore a dirty dark-coloured donkey jacket and a red scarf wound round her neck. Her hair was lank and straggly. I'd have to clean her up before I sent her home. Provided, of course, that I managed to bring off that little project successfully.

I explained about the phone call to her mother and that I hoped to go to Dorridge on Sunday.

'Not till then?' She sounded disappointed.

'Oy,' I protested. 'I'm doing my best. But I've got other

commitments, you know. Ganesh – the manager here – got bashed on the head the other night.'

Tig didn't ask how or why. Getting done over happened to everyone from time to time in her world. But she still looked restless and I guessed something had happened to worry her.

'Is it Jo Jo?' I asked, because that seemed the most likely explanation.

'He's getting really nosy,' Tig said. 'I'm afraid he'll get one of his moods when he thinks someone's plotting against him. He doesn't really trust anyone, not even me. He freaked out over that chocolate you gave me and if he knew about this, he'd go completely ape. I don't mean most of the time he isn't OK. But he can be scary.'

Scary, as in being a headcase. 'You've got to leave him, Tig,' I said firmly. 'Right away. I mean, as of now. Don't go back.'

'Where'm I going to go?' she asked. 'I gotta kip somewhere.'

That put me on the spot and I had to offer. 'You can come to my place until you go home. It'll be all right. I'm on my own there.'

And what if she didn't go home? Was I to be landed with her indefinitely? I didn't fancy the idea.

She wasn't exactly leaping at the offer, either. 'I dunno,' she said. 'What about my gear? Jo Jo's minding all our stuff.' Shrewd of him. Standing guard over Tig's few belongings might be enough to keep her by his side. If so, time to show him he was mistaken.

'Then ditch it. It's not worth the risk going back for it. You couldn't sneak it away without his noticing. Have you got anything you can't leave behind?'

She was nodding. 'Yes, sort of. There's – there's one thing

I've got to go back for.' She put down the empty mug. 'Tell me where your place is. I'll come over this evening, about nine. Jo Jo's got something on tonight, got to go and see a mate on business. I don't know what sort, he didn't say.'

Something connected with drugs, I shouldn't be surprised. Jo Jo didn't look the type to have scruples. I still didn't think it a good idea for her to return to him in the meantime but I could see she was adamant. I told her where I lived. As I finished speaking, there was the sound of Ganesh returning.

Tig said quickly, 'OK then, see you later, this evening sometime.' She was gone in a second.

I debated whether to tell Ganesh of this latest development and decided not to. He'd say I was getting in deeper and it was a really bad move. And what on earth was Tig carrying around with her that was so valuable she had to risk Jo Jo's violence to go back for it?

Ganesh said I could go at twelve if I liked. He was feeling better and Dilip had promised to come round for an hour around six when things tended to get busy.

I set off down the pavement and reached the chemist's shop where I'd taken the negatives to be developed. It occurred to me that my houseguest would be unlikely to bring a range of bathroom toiletries with her; from the look of her, soap might be a novelty these days. Poor Tig, once the dedicated tooth-brusher. Well, if she was going to stay with me, personal hygiene wouldn't be an optional extra. It'd be a basic necessity.

I pushed open the door of the shop. Things were quiet. One of the two regular assistants had gone to lunch and the other, Joleen, was leaning on the counter, reading *Black Beauty and Hair.* Her ambition was to be a beauty consultant with her own salon but selling cough mixtures and contraceptives in our local chemist's was as far as she'd got. I sympathised with her stalled ambitions, being in the same boat myself. I collected a bar of soap and a bottle of showergel from the open shelves and took them over to her.

'Hi, Fran,' she said. She held out her hands towards me, backs outward, so I could admire her purplish-red nails. 'What do you think?'

'Very nice,' I said.

'It's a new range. This shade's called Smouldering. Chip-proof. You ought to try it. I could do your nails for you. I'm a trained manicurist, you know.'

'Believe me,' I said, 'given my lifestyle, I wouldn't need chip-proof varnish, I'd need bomb-proof.' I put my purchases on the counter.

'Two ninety-five,' said Joleen, stabbing at the till with her vampire talons. I paid. She put the items in a plastic bag and propped herself on the counter again for a chat.

'Mike, he does the developing out back – ' she indicated the rear of the premises – 'he hoped those holiday snaps he did for you the other day were all right. He had a lot of trouble with them. It was some kind of foreign film, wasn't it?'

'Probably,' I said cautiously. 'They weren't mine. I got them done for a friend.'

'He had a coupla goes at them, as you'll have seen. The first lot came out really rubbish colours. The second lot were better, but he wasn't really satisfied. He said to tell you he couldn't do better – only it wasn't me gave them back to you, was it?'

'No, it was the other woman . . .' I said slowly, my brain grinding into gear. 'Joleen, what do you mean, as I'd have seen?'

She stared at me. 'He put both lots in the envelope, so you could see he really tried.'

'Hang on,' I said carefully. 'Are you telling me he took *two sets of prints from that film*?'

'Sure. He put them both in the envelope, like I said.'

'No,' I said, 'he didn't.'

'Oh.' Joleen thought about it and shrugged. 'He meant to. Must've changed his mind. Well, like I said, the first lot were no good anyway, so you wouldn't have wanted them.'

'But I would!' I said hastily. 'The friend – the person who asked me to get the film developed – he's lost the original negs now and can't get any more pics printed off. He'd like some copies to send to the other guys in the pictures. So, if the first prints are still out back somewhere, yes, I'd, I mean he'd, like them – even if the colour is duff.'

Joleen looked doubtful. 'They've probably been chucked out by now. I'll go and ask.'

She sashayed into the back room on her platform soles, her beaded braids swinging, and giving the impression she wasn't wearing an awful lot under that crisp white overall.

She came back a few minutes later carrying a metal waste-paper bin. 'Mike says, sorry, he meant to give them to you with the others. If they're still anywhere, they might be in this bin.'

The bell rang signalling a new customer. 'Here,' Joleen thrust the bin at me, 'take a look for yourself.'

She moved off to dispense corn plasters and E45 cream to an elderly woman.

I set down the bin and riffled through its contents eagerly (which distracted the elderly customer who gave me a funny look). Please, please . . . I was whispering to myself. Bingo! Right at the bottom, only one of the snaps – the other three must be lost for good. But one was better than none. I fished it out. The colours were bad, all right; no wonder Mike hadn't wanted to send these out. I'd have asked for my money back. The fair-haired man at the centre of the scene appeared to have had an orange rinse. But the images were clear enough.

'OK? Got them, then?' Joleen was back.

'Got one. Thanks, Joleen. I— My friend will be really chuffed.'

''Sall right,' she said cheerfully. 'Do you want a lipstick, free? I've got a box full of tester samples here, discontinued lines. Most of them have got quite a bit left.'

'Keep on smouldering, Joleen!' I called as I left the shop, and she let out a great shriek of a giggle. In the plastic bag I now carried the soap, the showergel, a half-used burnt sienna lipstick, which Joleen reckoned was my colour – and best of all, a luridly hued picture of Mr Big. It might prove dangerous property – but on the other hand, it might come in useful.

I got back to the flat mid-afternoon and sat on my sofa looking round the place, thinking my newly won privacy and independence were about to be invaded by Tig. I'd lived in squats and was used to sharing space and been grateful, often enough, when I'd first found myself on my own, to be offered shelter by anyone. I knew I couldn't have done anything else but invite Tig to stay, but it was harder to accept the reality than I'd imagined it would be. I'd got used to being on my own. This was my place. I lived here. I told myself not to be selfish but I'd got selfish. We all do the more we have. Anyone can be generous with nothing. Having Tig here to share would be good for me.

I did wonder if I ought to mention Tig to Daphne, because if she saw her going in and out, she might wonder. But I was perfectly entitled to have a friend to stay and anyway, I didn't think Daphne would mind. Charlie and Bertie, if they found out, would object strongly and it'd give them a weapon against me. I'd be accused of filling the flat with undesirables. But Tig wasn't going to stay long, or not if I had anything to do with it. It was, after all, up to me. I now had a perfect reason for fixing things up with the Quayles.

Tig didn't come until almost ten that evening. I was beginning to wonder if she'd managed to get away from Jo Jo or if he'd discovered her plan. When the bell rang, I called through the door, 'Who is it?' Because I now had a list of people I didn't want to see, including the Knowles twins, Inspector Harford, Wayne Parry and the killer of Gray Coverdale.

'Tig!' called back her voice and this was followed by a scrabbling sound and I heard her urge, 'Stop it.'

Had she brought someone with her? I opened the door cautiously.

'I'm here, then,' said Tig. She glanced down. 'I had to bring Bonnie. I hope you don't mind.'

I looked down. At Tig's feet sat a small brown and white rough-haired terrier, head on one side, ears pricked, gazing up at me expectantly.

'This is what you had to go back for,' I said. 'Bonnie.'

'That's right. OK if we come in?'

I let them both pass. Tig lugged in a bulging haversack which she dropped in the middle of the carpet. She looked round critically. 'Nice place, but why is the bathroom cabinet stuck up there where a window ought to be?'

'I'll tell you about that later,' I said.

Bonnie had started on her own tour of inspection, trotting round the furniture, sniffing out everything.

'She won't pee on the carpet, will she?' I asked nervously.

'Course she won't. She's really good. She belonged to the girl who died, the one I told you about. You remember I told you I got talking to that girl about her dog? Well, this is the dog and someone had to take her on. I had to bring her with me here. I couldn't leave her behind with Jo Jo, because he'd only sell her on to someone and I feel, you know, I've got to see she's all right.'

She felt about Bonnie the way I felt about Tig herself, so I understood. Bonnie came towards me and stood right in front of my boots, still looking up at me expectantly. She was mostly white, with a brown patch over the right eye and the ear above it. On that same right flank she had another large brown patch and a brown tip to her tail. On the left-hand side she was white all over – except for the tail tip. Looking at her from the right side or the left was like looking at two different dogs – on the one side a brown and white one and on the other, a white one.

'What about her food?' I asked.

''Sall right, I brought some.' Tig delved in the haversack and produced a tin of some dog food or other. 'She's no trouble, really.'

My attention had moved to the haversack. 'I see you've brought all your gear. Jo Jo will know straight away when he gets back that you've taken off.'

'Don't care. I've done it now. Can't go back.' She looked round. 'Where do I sleep?'

'On the sofa.' I indicated it. She was right. She couldn't go back and I couldn't tell her to leave. Like it or not, I was stuck with her.

There was something else I had to draw her attention to right away. 'That's the bathroom,' I said, pointing. 'You can have a shower. Why don't you take one now and I'll make us some sort of supper?'

'OK,' she said. 'It'll be nice to have the use of a proper bathroom again.'

Bonnie gave a short excited bark.

'Yes,' I told her, 'we can bath you, too.'

While Tig showered, I put bathing Bonnie into practice. I ran warm water into the kitchen sink, scooped her up in my arms and stood her in the pool. She didn't mind being picked up, but she was doubtful about being stood in the water. She sniffed at it, had a go at drinking it, and then looked at me reproachfully.

'Sorry, but it's for all our benefit,' I told her. I wet her all over and, careful to avoid her eyes, lathered her up with some washing-up liquid. She cringed miserably, her ears flattened and her tail drooped. By the time I'd finished rinsing her off, she looked like a drowned rat.

I'd found an old towel which I wrapped round her and lifted her to the floor. My intention was to dry her off, but she had other ideas about that, wriggled out of my grip and scuttled off. She then shook herself vigorously, waterdrops flying everywhere, showering the carpet and furniture.

'Oy,' I ordered. 'Stop that and come here—'

I set off in pursuit with the towel, but Bonnie was quicker than me, adept at squeezing through small spaces and, just when I thought I could grab her, putting on an extra spurt of speed and slithering through my grasp.

After five minutes of this, I was breathless. Bonnie – who'd regarded the chase as a great game – was wagging her tail and barking at me to keep going.

'Game's over,' I told her, collapsing on the sofa. Bonnie now came over to me and allowed me to pat her. The chase had pretty well dried her coat which was now quite silky, with a tendency in the longer hair to wave. Instead of smelling of grubby dog, she now smelled of lemon fragrance from the washing-up liquid.

'Hey,' said Tig, emerging from the bathroom, 'she looks pretty good.' Tig was looking an awful lot better, too, with her hair washed and a fresh look to her skin.

I hauled myself off to the kitchen to clean out the sink. I splashed a bit of bleach round to kill any germs or bugs which might have dropped off Bonnie. Then I turned my attention to supper. Having houseguests looked like turning out to be a lot of work.

I'm not a cook and when I opened my store cupboard, I realised I wasn't much of a housekeeper either. It held half-a-dozen eggs, the rest of the packet of pasta from last week, two tins of beans, a half-squeezed tube of tomato paste and some bread. I made us scrambled eggs and toast.

Tig ate it up appreciatively and while we dined in style, Bonnie gobbled up her dinner from a dented tin dogbowl Tig had brought with her. They were easy to please, I'll say that.

'How will your parents take to Bonnie?' I asked.

Tig looked over the rim of her coffee mug. 'Well, there might be a bit of a problem with that.'

My heart sank. 'Problem?'

'Yes, my mum's so houseproud, I told you. She doesn't like animals about the place. She says they shed hairs. So, um, I don't think I can take Bonnie to Dorridge. I thought, well, you might like her – or you could find a nice home for her. She deserves a nice home,' added Tig pathetically.

The pathos worked on old gents, not on me. 'Forget it,' I said robustly. 'I am not taking in Bonnie.'

There was a clatter from the kitchen and Bonnie appeared,

dragging along her empty tin dish. She dropped it in front of us and barked.

'There,' said Tig. 'She's telling you she wants a drink of water. She's ever so clever.'

I went to fill the dish. 'This is temporary,' I said to Bonnie as I set it down. 'You are just passing through, right?'

Bonnie gave an excited little yelp and fixed me with that expectant look. I was beginning to recognise it. It was the canine equivalent of Tig's Little Nell act. Resist me and have me on your conscience for ever, it said.

'Don't push your luck,' I told her.

We all three settled down cosily for the night, quite soon after supper. It had been a long day for all of us.

As I've mentioned before, my bedroom was the adaptation of a former Victorian coal-cellar under the pavement, and reached by a short passage from my basement living room, through the basement itself. The bedroom was, of course, windowless, although some light managed to get in through an opaque toughened glass panel in the ceiling, i.e., the pavement above, which replaced the former metal cover of the coal chute. I retired for the night in this tomblike little room, leaving Tig and Bonnie curled up together on my blue rep sofa in the living room.

Exhausted, I went out like a light. I was woken at some ungodly hour by a hand shaking my shoulder.

'Fran?' Tig's voice came as little more than a breath in the darkness. 'Wake up and don't make a noise.'

I was awake in an instant, every instinct straining. I couldn't see Tig but knew she was there by the bed. I also heard the sound of something struggling and realised she must be holding Bonnie in her arms.

'What is it?' I sat up and swung my legs to the ground. My

foot bumped against her leg and she moved back. The struggling sound was renewed together with a muffled whine.

Tig shushed the little dog and I guessed she had one hand clamped over Bonnie's muzzle to stop her barking.

'Someone's trying to get into the flat,' she whispered.

Chapter Eleven

Together we edged back into the living room where enough light seeped through the basement window from the streetlamps outside to reveal Tig's silhouette. In her arms Bonnie wriggled like a creature berserk, desperate to be allowed to do her job and see off any intruder.

He, the visitor, was at the basement window. The curtain was drawn and all we could see was his fuzzy outline and upraised arms as he worked his way round the frame. These were old houses and didn't, alas, have double-glazing, just old-fashioned single-paned windows in a wooden frame. He must have recced beforehand and had probably thought entry would be a doddle. Now he was probably realising that safety catches must be in place on the inside.

I felt slightly sick and was glad I'd wedged the medicine cabinet in the garden window. He'd have squeezed his way through there in a few seconds. The thing was, who was he?

'Do you think it's Jo Jo?' I whispered, not that I thought it really was. But there was an outside chance.

Tig dismissed it. 'No . . . he doesn't know I'm here. That guy at the window's not big enough for Jo Jo, anyway. Is it that bloke you were so scared of the other day?'

Tig hadn't been so wrapped up in her own problems that

she'd forgotten the fright she'd given me when she'd stopped me in the street.

'Sorry,' I murmured. 'Should have warned you this might—'

Tig hadn't got a free hand but used her elbow to jab me painfully in the ribs as a sign to keep quiet. We waited.

He'd moved away a little from the window but had now returned and began to do something down in the right-hand corner of the window pane. There was a faint squeaky scratchy noise.

Bonnie, frustrated to the point of madness, tried to tear her muzzle free of the restraining hand and renewed her efforts in Tig's arms, both of which were now tightly wrapped round the terrier's frantic body.

Whoever he was, he was a pro and had come prepared. He was cutting a hole in the glass. Tig leaned towards me and put her mouth to my ear.

'When he gets his hand through, you pull back the curtain and I let Bonnie go, right?'

I nodded, though she probably couldn't see it. There was a pause in activity at the window pane and then a soft tap. The small circle of glass fell inward but was prevented from falling to the ground and shattering noisily by the sticky tape he'd fixed to it to prevent this. He knew his stuff. We watched, horrified yet fascinated, even Bonnie stopped wriggling. Through the thin curtain, we saw a hand emerge through the hole into our space, and fingers feel about for the safety catch. It was like one of those old horror movies, you know, *The Mummy's Hand*, but I was beyond being merely scared, I was almost paralysed with fear.

He's not in yet, I reassured myself. And there are two of us, three with Bonnie.

'Now!' breathed Tig.

I leaped forward and yanked back the curtain. Bonnie, released, exploded out of Tig's embrace, flew at the hole in the window pane and sank her teeth into the searching hand. There was a scream of surprise and pain from outside. I dashed to the wall and switched on the light.

He was pressed against the window, his face contorted in pain and rage, but I recognised him as the little fellow who'd come to the shop. He was mouthing oaths in some foreign language, possibly Spanish or Portuguese. I'm not well up in either of those, but I knew it wasn't Italian. I could see his small white teeth and his eyes were like a wild animal's. I thought, this is the man who killed Gray Coverdale, and if he gets in here, he'll kill us for sure for doing this to him.

He was trying to get his hand back through the hole, but Bonnie, true to her terrier instincts, didn't let go but hung on grimly. Blood was dripping down the windowsill. Suddenly he pushed his hand forward, instead of trying to tug it back towards him, then jerked it viciously back again. It must have hurt him, but it hurt Bonnie too as her nose crashed into the cut edge of the glass. She yelped and fractionally loosened her grip.

Tig and I both yelled at her to let go. We didn't want her injured. Further confused, she dropped to the ground. The man pulled his free hand back through the hole a split second before Bonnie recovered enough to grab it again. Gripping injured fingers to his chest, he bolted out of the basement. We could hear the soft thud of his feet running away along the pavement.

Tig was kneeling on the floor trying to examine Bonnie's nose. Bonnie, cheated of her victim, was yelping and squealing, in no mood to stand still for a medical. She got loose and hurled herself at the front door, barking furiously.

We dragged her away and calmed her down. The side of her muzzle was scratched but she was otherwise unharmed. The blood on the windowsill was the intruder's. Serve him right.

'I'm really sorry, Tig,' I said. 'I should have explained things to you before you came here.'

'What's going on, then?' asked Tig. She disappeared into the kitchenette and could be heard switching on the kettle. We'd both come down in the world but we'd both been brought up on traditional lines and knew the golden rule: whatever the emergency, get the tea brewing.

Bonnie ran back and forth beneath the window sniffing at the carpet and from time to time, putting her paws on the sill and sniffing along there. She was reliving her victory over the would-be intruder in her mind. Probably, like many humans, she was garnishing it with a few extra heroics, although to my mind, she'd been quite heroic enough.

'The other evening,' I explained to Tig when we'd got our mugs of tea and settled down on the sofa on top of Tig's sleeping bag, 'a man was murdered out there, in my basement.'

Tig sipped at her tea and eyed me through a fringe of hair. There was a new air of friendliness about her. She'd woken up next to a body: I'd come home and found one on my doorstep. We had something in common.

'Why?' she asked.

'He'd come to see me because he thought I might have something a lot of people seem to want – or that I knew where it was.'

'Have you got it?'

I shook my head.

'You oughta move out of this end of town for a bit,' said Tig, after thinking this over.

'OK, I'm going to Dorridge on Sunday, remember? The thing is, you'll be here and he might come back.'

'I've got Bonnie and anyway, he won't try anything like that again now he knows the dog's here. She kicks up a real racket.'

Yes, she did. I wondered whether Daphne had heard anything. Her bedroom was on the first floor, which put her two floors above us here. It overlooked the garden and it was possible she'd slept through the whole thing undisturbed. I hoped so. I was less sure about the neighbours and their Watch Scheme which, after Coverdale's murder, must have gone into top gear.

'Tig,' I said. 'I'm going to have to report this to the police.'

She sat up, alarmed. 'I'm not staying here if the pigs are going to be crawling round the place!'

Bonnie got excited again at the tone of her voice and began rushing round the room, yelping.

'Calm down!' I begged them both. 'Look, you don't have to be involved. In the morning, first thing, we'll go upstairs and explain things to Daphne, my landlady. She'll have to know. I suppose the damaged pane can be fixed on her buildings insurance. I'll ring the police from her place. They *have* to know, Tig – Daphne will want to tell them – and anyway, the – this thing everyone wants, the police have – the police are interested. I'll ask Daphne if you can sit up there in her kitchen while whoever the police send does his stuff down here. You won't have to see them, the coppers. They won't see you. Not that it matters if they do see you does it? You're not wanted for anything?'

She shook her head. 'I just don't like the pigs.' She fidgeted about, undecided. 'Your landlady won't like me. Respectable old girls don't.'

'Daphne isn't like the others,' I assured her, and hoped I was right.

As I spoke, we heard the sound of a car turning into the street. I jumped up and switched out the light. Tig grabbed Bonnie again. Bonnie, hoping for a replay, took a dim view of this and whined pitiably.

I stood by the damaged window and peered up. I could just make out the top of the car as it cruised past.

'Neighbourhood Watch must've phoned through to the cop shop,' I said. 'It's the law, taking a look.'

'Shit,' muttered Tig.

We waited and after a while, we heard a regular plod's footstep approaching. From time to time it stopped and then moved on. He was checking out the basements. He reached mine and leaned over the iron railing. The beam of a torch flashed across the window. I heard him swear and call out to his partner.'Sorry,' I said to Tig. 'He's spotted it. You hide in the bedroom, take your stuff with you, and leave Bonnie out here.'

The officer was descending my stairwell, flashing the torch around. He shone it on the broken window again and turned aside to ring my doorbell. Tig had scuttled into the bedroom and there was no way I could ignore the summons. Bonnie was barking her head off.

I picked her up, switched on the light, and opened up. 'Good evening, officer,' I said, although it was the middle of the night.

'Evening, miss . . .' He looked rather startled. Perhaps it was the Snoopy nightshirt which had shrunk in numerous washes and was now little more than a long tee shirt. He dragged his eyes away and peered past me. 'We received a call a little while back from one of your Neighbourhood Watch members, old gent living opposite. You seem to have had some damage to a window pane. You know about that?'

I had to let him in. 'Someone tried to break in. My dog saw him off.'

Bonnie, in my arms, was behaving very badly. She clearly didn't like the police, either. Someone had taught her they were the enemy. She was growling ferociously, lips rolled back to bare her teeth, and the hair bristled along her spine. The encounter with the would-be intruder had given her a taste for blood.

'Yes,' said the copper, eyeing her nervously, 'she looks a real little scrapper. Did you call us?'

'I haven't got a phone. I was going to call in the morning.'

Pounding feet announced his partner. The first one turned to him. 'This is the place, all right. Dog drove chummy off.' He turned back to me. 'You on your own here?' He was eyeing the nightshirt again.

I said I was and they expressed some concern. I pointed out I had Bonnie, who, faced with *two* coppers, was doing her nut, longing to be allowed to get at 'em. I gripped her muzzle as Tig had done earlier. She spluttered, enraged.

'I've had a good look up and down the road, but he's gone,' said the newly arrived copper.

'We'll try and block up that gap for you,' the other said, 'and send someone round in the morning. You'll have to make a proper report then. OK?'

I promised them I'd be waiting. They were really rather nice, better than average anyway. It must have been the Snoopy nightshirt. They taped cardboard over the holed place and advised me to leave a light on.

'I'd offer you a cup of tea,' I said. 'But I'd have to put the dog down.'

They took the point.

When they'd driven off, I released Bonnie who, having had the last word in a defiant barking session, sat by the front door hopefully, waiting for the next arrivals. I opened the bedroom door and called to Tig that she could come out.

Tig sidled out, her white face defiant, as though she anticipated what I was going to say.

'You see,' I said. 'It was all right.'

'I don't like the pigs,' she said obstinately.

Daphne didn't let me down. Although she was clearly upset at the attempted break-in, she greeted Tig kindly and said how nice it was to meet one of Fran's friends. I saw Tig calm down under this civilised reception, but she remained wary and sat huddled in the corner of Daphne's kitchen, while we rang the police to see when they'd be coming round, and waited for them to turn up.

In the meantime, Daphne provided toast and coffee and made a great fuss of Bonnie.

'What a brave little dog and so lucky your friend had brought her along.'

Bonnie accepted all this praise as no more than her due, her stumpy tail thumping the ground.

Tig continued to sit awkwardly in the corner of Daphne's kitchen, her eyes studying every detail of the fixtures and fittings. I wondered what she was thinking.

'I'll get the glazier in today straight away,' said Daphne. 'And perhaps I'd better get a burglar-proof grille put in down there.'

'Inspector Harford's all for those,' I told her. 'But I don't fancy being locked in a cage, Daphne.'

'It's only at night or if you're away,' she pointed out. 'You can pull them back and forth, or so I understand. I didn't mean the fixed sort.' A thought seemed to strike her and she frowned worriedly. 'I suppose I can keep this from Bertie and Charlie.'

Oh blimey, the dreaded duo. I'd forgotten them. They'd love this.

'Who're they?' asked Tig, breaking her silence.

Daphne explained they were her nephews. 'And always so worried about my security, as they call it. Inclined to fuss, really, but it's all very well meant. Perhaps I can get the glazier to come quickly and get it all fixed up before they find out.'

There was the sound of a car drawing up outside and a door slammed.

'That'll be the police,' I said. 'You stay here, Tig.'

Parry was just climbing the steps to Daphne's front door as she opened it. He said, 'Morning, ma'am,' to her and, glimpsing me in the hall behind her, added less graciously, 'What's going on, then?'

We took him down to the basement and explained. He examined the window and sighed. 'I'll get the fingerprint boys over *again*. You say you can describe this bloke, Fran?'

I gave him a pretty good description: small, dark curly hair, Mediterranean appearance and foreign accent, injured hand. 'So you ought to be able to pick him up.'

'You may not have noticed it,' said Parry sarcastically, 'but the streets of London are littered with blokes speaking with foreign accents.'

'Tourists, I suppose,' said Daphne.

Parry gave her a jaundiced look. 'Yes, ma'am, and every petty crook and thug who likes to pop across the Channel. We make it easy for 'em these days.' I put Parry in the Eurosceptic camp. But then, I imagined Parry was sceptical about everything.

'When will these fingerprint experts come?' asked Daphne. 'I want to ring the glazier.'

'When they've got a minute,' muttered Parry to me. 'Seeing as they've got other things to do besides spend half their lives at this place or round at your mate Patel's.' He turned back to Daphne. 'I'll just take a statement from Miss Varady, and I'll be off.'

Daphne took the hint and left us. When we were alone, Parry took out a notebook and biro. 'I can't leave you for five minutes, can I?' he grumbled. 'I come in this morning and what do I find? Overnight you've had a break-in. First Patel, now you.'

'That's right,' I said. 'And the man who tried to break in here last night was the same man who came to the shop fishing for information about Coverdale.'

Parry, poised with pen above notebook, gave me a sharp look. 'You're on the level with this, Fran? You'd better be.'

I could have thumped him. There's just no getting through to Parry. 'I am sure!' I said tightly. 'So we know what he was after, don't we? Why don't you just release the information that you've got the flippin' negatives?'

'Been decided higher up,' he said. 'It's embargoed and it stays that way. We've all got to lump it. Right, let's have the rest of your statement, then.'

When I'd given it, he asked, 'Where's the dog?'

'Upstairs with Daphne.'

Parry wasn't stupid, despite his manner and general appearance. 'Since when have you had a pet pooch, then?'

'I'm looking after her for a friend.'

'Friend wasn't with you, then, last night?'

'Your boys were here,' I said. 'They talked to me. They saw the situation. You've got my statement. Now, if you don't mind, I've got to go to work.'

* * *

I went to work. I didn't tell Ganesh about my overnight visitor. He had enough worries. Instead, I excused my lateness by telling him I'd overslept. At least Hitch and Marco had finished the new washroom and, I had to admit, it did look good.

'See,' said Ganesh. 'The old chap won't be cross, not when he sees it.'

Looking at the shiny new tiles, the extractor fan which worked and sanitary fittings which didn't assault the would-be user, I had to admit Hari ought to be pleased. I still thought he'd make a fuss about the cost. Ganesh said that had been very reasonable. He'd haggled a bit and Hitch had brought it down. I privately thought that if Hitch had reduced the quoted price, it was because he'd increased it in the first place to allow for this. Still, it did seem mean to quibble. Hitch and Marco had done a good job and deserved to be fairly paid.

I did wonder, when I got home at lunchtime, whether I'd find Tig still there. I was relieved to hear Bonnie bark as I clattered down the basement steps. I noticed that the glazier had been and I had a new window pane. The putty was still soft.

'I've been out,' said Tig. 'You know, to walk Bonnie and get out of the way of the guys who came to fix the window. I brought us in some lunch and more dog food for Bonnie.'

'Watch out for Jo Jo,' I warned her. 'He might come back to this patch to look for you, seeing as you were working the area earlier.'

She'd brought in fish and chips. She heated them up in the oven and served them up to me on a tray. She obviously wanted to work her passage. I appreciated that. Tig had been no trouble in the old days, back in the Jubilee Street squat, because she'd always done her fair share. Reminded of her then, and seeing her miserable state now, I felt sad and worried. What would her parents think when they saw her? How could I prepare them?

We were washing up when the doorbell rang. Tig, who'd been chatting in quite a friendly way, was immediately back on the defensive, hissing, 'Who's that?'

'Hang on,' I said. 'I'll go and see.'

I peered out the nice new window and was rewarded with the sight of Jason Harford, who'd left the door and was prodding at the new putty in a critical way. Behind me, I heard the bathroom door click. Tig had taken refuge, dragging Bonnie in there with her.

I kicked Tig's rucksack behind the sofa out of sight and threw her sleeping bag after it. The coast clear, I let him in.

'You all right, Fran?' he asked, looking and sounding genuinely concerned. If we'd parted coolly on the last occasion, he appeared to have forgotten.

'As you see me,' I said. Behind the bathroom door, Bonnie was barking at the sound of a strange voice. 'I've shut the dog in there,' I explained, 'because she's been a bit overexcited since last night. She thinks she's got to see off any stranger.'

'Lucky you had her here,' he said. 'Parry said you're looking after her for a friend.'

'That's right.' He was standing in the middle of the room, fidgeting about, looking round him. He had his sharp suit on today and still didn't look your average CID man. I wondered again to what extent, if any, he fitted into the police scene. 'I made a statement,' I said, prompting him to explain his visit.

'Yes, I know, I read it. We've put out a description of the man you recognised. But he'll have gone to ground. I was going to suggest you came over to the station and took a look at the mug shots. He might have a record.'

'I can't come now,' I said. 'Maybe tomorrow.'

'I thought I could give you a lift over there now—' he began.

'I told you, tomorrow! I've had enough of coppers for one day, right?' I was beginning to sound like Tig.

I saw his features stiffen. The man was really sensitive about being disliked for what he did.

'Nothing personal,' I said wearily. 'But I'm sick to death of this whole business.'

He nodded. 'I understand that. Tomorrow, then.' He hesitated. 'Oh, by the way, you might like to know you weren't the only one to be burgled last night.'

If this was an attempt to console, it was cack-handed. I realised there must have been numerous break-ins of one sort and another in the Greater London area during the previous twenty-four hours.

'Don't get me wrong,' he went on hastily, noting my expression. 'What I meant was, a Mrs Joanna Stevens who lives in Putney came home last night to find someone had been in her house. Local police notified us because Mrs Stevens is Graeme Coverdale's sister.'

Light dawned. 'Oh,' I said.

'Coverdale used her house as a base in this country.' Harford's interest in property led him to reflect. 'That's a nice area. All those houses in Shaker Lane where she lives are big detached places. Four beds, quiet street, front shielded by laurel hedges, trees in the back garden.' He pulled himself together. 'Mind you, a burglar's dream. She's a widow with just one married daughter, so she was happy to give Coverdale a home. He wasn't there all the time, always coming and going, according to her. But one bedroom was kept as his and he left all his spare clothes, books, personal documents, that sort of thing there. Yesterday evening she went out as she always does to a church women's group. A friend called by to pick her up and off they went. When they got back, she invited the friend in for coffee. As soon as she got through the door, she says, she knew someone had been there.'

'There was a hole in a window?' I said.

He shook his head. 'No, different *modus operandi*, suggesting a different man. The same, perhaps, who broke into the shop. Nothing appeared to have been taken, just like the shop. There was little sign of disturbance, again just like the shop. But Mrs Stevens is a house-proud lady living alone and it didn't take much to attract her notice. A crooked mirror over the mantelpiece. Ornaments not facing straight forward. Coats on the hanger in the hall bunched together. When she went into the downstairs cloakroom she found the toilet seat had been left up. So she knew, she said, a man had been there – and he'd used the loo. She was more annoyed about that than anything else, I think.' Harford grinned. 'Anyway, we'd already been there and searched Coverdale's room ourselves with her permission, so backed by her friend, she rang her local station. They took a bit of convincing, as nothing was missing, but she urged them to get in touch with us. We didn't take any convincing.'

It wasn't good news. The unknown man behind this needed those negs desperately. He, or his employees, would be back. But I said, 'Thanks for telling me, anyway.'

'Look, Fran . . .' He'd flushed pink. 'I was going to come round and see you anyway, because the other evening at the restaurant . . . it didn't go the way I'd wanted it to. I mean, I wanted us to be friends, but we parted, well, a bit coolly. It was my fault.'

I hadn't expected an apology and it took me aback. I told

him it wasn't anybody's fault. No one struck up pally relationships over a corpse.

'I really hope this will all be settled soon,' he said. 'Perhaps we can be friends then?'

His persistence niggled me. He couldn't be that naïve. 'Look,' I told him, 'you lot have pegged Gan and me out to dry. You won't release news of those negatives and as long as *they* – whoever they are, and you won't even tell me that – think Gan or I have them, we're both of looking over our shoulders and waiting for more break-ins. It's time you spoke up.'

He looked unhappy, rubbing at his shock of hair. 'It's not my decision, Fran. Left to me, I'd do it, take the heat off you and Patel. There is a good reason for it, trust me.'

'It'd better be good,' I said sourly.

He hung around a few minutes more, perhaps hoping I was going to offer him coffee. I wasn't going to do that. I was afraid, apart from the fact that Tig and Bonnie couldn't stay in the bathroom indefinitely, that he'd wander into the kitchenette and see two plates, mugs, etc. He took the hint eventually and left, looking down in the mouth.

I tapped on the bathroom door and told Tig she could come out.

Bonnie rushed out and scrabbled at the front door. Tig emerged looking more frail and yet more determined than ever. She avoided my gaze and went past me in silence.

'OK, you can stop sulking,' I said crossly. 'I didn't know he was going to come.'

She'd found her gear behind the sofa and still neither speaking nor looking at me, began to stow it away in the rucksack. Bonnie ran over to her and put her front paws on the sofa, head tilted, her bright worried brown eyes asking to know what this meant. Tig's hand dropped absently to the little dog's head and then she carried on rolling up the sleeping bag.

My heart sank and I asked her what she was doing, knowing the answer.

She looked up, two red spots staining the white skin on her cheekbones. 'I'm getting out. I'll come back after Monday to see how you've got on with my people – but I'm not staying here. The place is crawling with bloody pigs. One lot here in the middle of the night, two lots here today. Every time anyone comes to your door, it's a copper, either in uniform or plainclothes. I might just as well have taken Bonnie and myself down to the nick and asked them to give me a bed in a cell for a few days. I'd see fewer of 'em down there than I've seen here.'

'It's not my fault,' I began, 'I don't want them here, either.'

'Then why're you so bloody thick with them?' she retorted.

I drew a deep breath. If she left, I wouldn't see her again. Jo Jo might find her, or she might go back to him, but she wouldn't come back here. Any trip I made to Dorridge would be for nothing. Pleading with her would do no good. I had to meet the problem head on. After all, it was her problem, not mine.

'Go on, then,' I said as brutally as I could. 'Run. That's what you do best, isn't it, Tig? Run?'

She looked up at me in surprise. Bonnie pricked her ears and looked puzzled and alarmed at my change of manner.

As they both stared at me, I went on, 'You didn't get on with your family, so you ran away from them. Where did it get you? Nowhere. You took up with Jo Jo and that didn't work out, so you ran away again – here. Now you're going to run yet again. Where to this time? You can't keep running, Tig, you've got to stand and face your problems. You've got nowhere else to go now. You've got to get a grip.'

Her lips moved stiffly as if she forced them to form sounds. 'I told you – I just don't like pigs.'

'So, how are you going to get on when you go home, back to your parents' place? People there, Tig, won't run at the sight of a copper even if they've done nothing. People there won't hide every time a stranger comes to the door. People there won't assume everyone's an enemy, or just won't like them – as you said Daphne wouldn't like you. Why shouldn't she?'

She stared at me for a brief moment, her face working soundlessly, her eyes blazing with unexpressed emotion. I braced myself for an earful of abuse, but I was caught out when, without further warning, Tig launched herself at me.

'Bitch!' she yelled. She wrapped both arms round me, pinning my arms to my side. The combination of the impact and being unable to balance myself left me helpless. I stumbled back, slipped and crashed to the floor. Tig threw herself on top of me, pummelling me with both fists and all the time, sobbing, 'Bitch – bitch – bitch!'

Bonnie darted around us hysterically as we struggled, not knowing whose side to take, and nipping indiscriminately at any bit of body within her reach. I managed to thrust Tig off me and roll aside. She scrambled to her feet and aimed a kick at me, but that was her undoing, because I caught her foot and twisted it. She yelped and crashed down to the floor where she scrabbled to a sitting position, her back against the sofa, and glared at me, her eyes bright with tears.

'All right,' I panted, taking advantage of the standoff to regain my feet. 'What's all this about?'

'You—' she gasped. 'You should bloody know—'

I interrupted her. 'Yes, I know. I understand why and how you've got like this, Tig, not trusting anyone, not even me. I know why you're scared of the police—'

She shook her head. 'You don't – you don't know . . . You know sod all.'

'All right, I don't know it all!' I was hanging on to my own temper here, more angry with myself than with her, because I didn't know what to do or say. 'Don't you see, Tig?' I pleaded. 'If you're to go home and get back into a different sort of life, which is what you say you want, then you've got to get over all these hang-ups. I'm sorry about the place crawling with coppers today, but it's not my fault, is it? It's because that guy tried to break in. I don't like them round here any more than you do, but I don't freak out. I deal with it and get rid of them.'

'You're you and not me,' she muttered.

'I'm not saying it's going to be easy,' I told her. 'But if you can't hack staying a week in my flat, how do you think you're going to cope with being home again with your family and dealing with them?'

I thought she might have another go at me, but instead she got up, smoothed back her hair, and with her back to me, resumed her packing.

I thought, I've blown it. She's taking off and that's that. I won't see her again. But after a few moments during which she struggled inefficiently with the rucksack, she chucked the whole lot to the floor and sat down on the sofa, head hanging, her wispy fair hair veiling her face.

'OK, now, Tig?' I asked tentatively.

'I've been thinking about it, too, Fran, you know,' she mumbled. 'I'm not the same person I was when I left home. How can I go back? They won't understand, my parents. They'll expect me to walk in just the same little girl who walked out. That's how they think of me, their little girl. I don't think I can cope with it and I don't think they can.

Perhaps we'd better scrap the whole thing.'

I hunkered down in front of her and took hold of her hands. They were icy to the touch. Bonnie jumped up on the sofa beside her and pushed her muzzle into Tig's side, wanting to add her own comfort.

'We made up our minds to do this, Tig, you and I. You asked me to go to Dorridge and I said I would. Neither of us is going to welsh, right? It's a pact. I'm going there on Sunday, and you're going to wait here until I come back. No one's saying this'll be easy, but it's like you said. It's your one chance. Don't muff it. Don't just duck out and run.'

She looked at me miserably through the curtain of hair. 'All right. I'll stay. But you'll have to tell them the truth, Fran. You'll have to tell them everything.'

'Sure,' I said encouragingly. It was all right promising. How I was going to manage that interview, I hadn't the slightest idea. In the meantime, however, I had other fish to fry.

'Come on,' I said. 'We're going out.'

'Where?' She was immediately suspicious again.

'Putney. We're going to do a bit of investigating. I want to know what's going on and there's only one way I'm going to find out and that's by doing it myself. Just wait here a tick while I nip up and ask Daphne to let me take a look at her A–Z.'

'You leave me out of this, whatever it is!' Tig burst out. 'You start going out there and pestering this woman he was talking about, the one who had a break-in, and you'll have all the coppers you want round here. But you won't have me! I don't know what you're into, but you're not involving me, right?'

'Take it easy. I won't involve you. I'll have to go and see this Mrs Joanna Stevens on my own. She'd be worried if two of us turned up. All I want is for you to come out to Putney with me, and hang around while I call on her. I'm not leaving you here on your own, Tig. You'll start brooding about going home and get into a state – and before you accuse *me* of not trusting *you*, let me tell you, that's not it. I just think you're better not left alone this afternoon. We'll leave Bonnie in charge of the flat.'

Chapter Twelve

We got out to Putney and found Shaker Lane all right. That was no problem. But I did have two other problems to deal with, before I ever got near Mrs Stevens. One was that the early dusk meant light was already fading by the time we got there. That worried me. I didn't want to knock on Mrs Stevens' door in the dark. She might be even more unwilling to let me in than I anticipated she'd be anyway. The other problem was Tig, who grumbled and threatened to desert all the way there. I wouldn't have brought her along if I could have safely left her back at the flat in the mood she was in. However, when we actually reached Shaker Lane, she bucked up a bit and started to get interested.

'This is it, then?' She looked up and down the road. The word 'lane' was a misnomer. Probably there had been a lane there once, donkey's years ago, but any trace of a rural path had disappeared. The road was as Harford had described it: prosperous. The houses pretty well all answered the description of Mrs Stevens' he'd given me. I wondered which was hers. 'What are you going to do now?' Tig asked.

Good question. 'Come on, Tig,' I said. 'Back to that little shopping precinct.'

The precinct in question wasn't much more than a row of shops and a paved area with a couple of wooden seats around a depressed-looking tree. It lay off the bottom end of Shaker Lane and we'd walked through it on our way there. I'd noticed, as we did, that it contained a florist's.

'They cost a lot of money,' said Tig, as we stood outside the shop, surveying the bunches of blooms in buckets. 'You could go inside and distract the assistant and I'll nick a bunch, if that's what you want.'

'It's not what I want!' I said firmly. 'I thought you wanted to stay out of trouble, Tig? You've got a funny way of going about it. We'll both go in.'

'I want some flowers to take to a lady who's bereaved,' I told the assistant. 'Only I haven't got much dosh. What can you let me have?'

The girl cast an eye over me and nothing she saw disproved my claim to be broke. 'Someone round here, is it?' she asked.

'A Mrs Stevens. She lives in Shaker Lane.'

'Oh, right!' She brightened. 'Several people have been in buying flowers for her. Her brother, wasn't it? He got knifed. Horrible, only it didn't happen around here, thank goodness.' She stared at us with increased curiosity.

'That's right,' I said, not parting with any more info, something which clearly disappointed her. 'So, what have you got?'

'Well, we've sold quite a lot, like I said, on account of her,' said the girl. 'And it's getting late in the day. You can have any of that lot, half price.'

I said fair enough, and parted with the cash for two bunches of freesias and some ferny stuff. They smelled nice and when I put them all together, they looked a lot.

'You don't know what number her house is, do you?' I asked. 'I had it written down but I left the bit of paper at home.'

'Hang on,' she said, going to the counter and opening a ledger. 'It'll be in the order book. She came in asking about wreaths. Yes, here it is, number fifteen.'

'See?' I said to Tig, as we left the shop. 'All you've got to do is haggle a bit. You don't have to nick 'em. And I found out the number of the house as well. That's being a detective.'

'They've got loads of them,' said Tig. 'They wouldn't have missed them. You could've gone in asking about the house number while I pinched some.'

It occurred to me that, if and when Tig got home to Dorridge, rehabilitating her was going to be a job and a half. Thankfully, it wouldn't be mine.

'You stay here,' I said. 'Sit on one of those benches. I won't be long.' If Mrs Stevens wasn't at home, or if she shut the door in my face, I'd be very quick.

It was darker by the time I got back to number fifteen, but someone had switched on a light downstairs, so I was in luck there. I rang the doorbell.

After a few minutes, it opened on the chain. I could just make out a woman's face, pressed against the crack. 'Yes?' she asked cautiously.

'Mrs Stevens? I've brought some flowers.'

'Oh, wait a tick.' She pushed the door to. I heard her unhook the safety chain. It reopened and I could see her properly in the hall light.

I judged her quite a bit older than her brother, a stocky woman of middle height with greying hair cut short and glasses. She reached out a hand for the flowers. 'Is there a card?' she asked.

'I'm not delivering them from a florist's,' I explained, hanging on to the bunch. 'They're from me personally. My name's Fran Varady. I – I knew your brother slightly.'

'Oh?' She hesitated, looking me up and down. 'Well, you'd better come in, then.'

That got me over the doorstep. I handed over my flowers in the hall. She thanked me and murmured something about just putting them in the sink for a moment. Then she disappeared into, presumably, the kitchen. I looked around. It was all very neat and tidy. The cloakroom, in which the incriminating loo seat was to be found, was off to my left. To my right I could see, through an open door, a comfortable sitting room.

Mrs Stevens returned and ushered me in. We took facing armchairs and studied one another. She was wearing a dark green dress with a cowl collar which did nothing for her, but was presumably a sign of mourning. She wasn't in any way remarkable – a middle-aged woman like thousands of others – and that a close relative should have been knifed in my basement seemed incongruous. I wasn't quite sure how I was going to break that bit of news to her, about it being my basement, or even if I should.

She spoke first. 'Are you a journalist?' When I denied this, she went on, 'Because my brother, being freelance, knew a lot of press people. I thought you might be one of them, a reporter or something.'

I supposed I did look disreputable enough to represent one of the more downmarket tabloids. 'I'm not sure,' I said, 'whether to call him Graeme or Gray.'

'His name was really Graeme, of course, but he's – he was always called Gray, right from childhood.' She faltered slightly.

Feeling bad, I told her sincerely that I was very sorry for her loss.

'I'm sure he always took unnecessary risks,' she said. 'He was always the same, even as a boy. There was a twelve-year age gap between us so I was the older sister who had to keep an eye on him. He arrived rather late in my parents' marriage and they found him a handful. He was always better with me.

Giving him a home here seemed natural. Although he was hardly ever here.' She paused. 'May I ask how you know Gray, if you're not a journalist?'

'He came into the shop where I work a little while ago. He sent a note saying he wanted to see me again – but –' I searched desperately for the words, but she made the connection.

'Are you the girl he was trying to see, when he – when he was killed?' She leaned forward.

I admitted it and decided to throw myself on her mercy. 'Look, Mrs Stevens, I'm really sorry to bother you. I don't know why such a dreadful thing happened to Gray. I don't know what sort of thing he'd got into, but whatever it was, I think it may affect me. In fact, I'm sure of it. I know your house was broken into last night. Someone tried to get into my flat last night, too, only I had a dog in the place and the intruder was scared off.'

'Oh, my dear!' she said, then, 'Would you like a cup of tea?'

I thought of Tig hanging about in the cold down at the shopping precinct. But the offer of tea meant Mrs Stevens was prepared to talk. I accepted.

'I'm afraid,' she said, when she'd brought the teatray, 'I really know nothing either. Gray didn't confide in me. I told the police all this because they were asking, too. He used to go on trips a lot, but often didn't say where he'd been. Sometimes he'd let me know when he was coming home and sometimes he'd just turn up. He was like that. I realise – I realise that this time he must have been doing something dangerous.' She paused and looked down at the cup and saucer she held on her lap. 'The police asked if anything had been taken from his room, but I had to tell them, I'd no idea. I didn't know what Gray kept up there. When I first called the police –

the local police – they didn't want to believe I'd had a break-in. They said the place was all too tidy and nothing was missing. I told them, tidy maybe, but not tidy enough! Then there was the downstairs toilet. He'd used it, I know, because he left the seat up. Do you know,' she was getting heated at the memory, 'the young policeman who came actually laughed when I told him that!'

'I believe it,' I said.

'I told him, I didn't think it was funny. Someone had definitely been in my house! Anyway, I could sense it, if you know what I mean. I just felt someone had been in while I'd been out. I still don't think they'd have taken me seriously if I hadn't told them about Gray's death. Then they got on to the other police – the ones investigating Gray's murder. They came out here and they were very sympathetic.'

'When did Gray come home this time? Had he been away long?' I asked.

'He'd been away about a month. Quite early on, he sent me a postcard from Switzerland, from Zürich. After that I didn't hear a thing until he turned up in his usual way, just a week before he died. I had a phone call from the station half an hour before he arrived to let me know he was on his way. I just had time to go up and make up his bed. He was very suntanned. I asked if he'd been skiing or something like that in Switzerland. He said, "I'll tell you—"' She broke off and fumbled for a handkerchief. 'He said, "I'll tell you all about it one day, Jo!" and that was all he said.'

I waited while she dabbed at her eyes and nose. 'I hate doing this,' I told her, 'but can I just ask, did he seem different in any way when he came home this time?'

She considered this as she tucked away the handkerchief. 'I must say, he did seem pleased with himself. But one morning he smartened himself up – because to be frank, he was a very untidy dresser – and said he was going to have lunch with a contact, he called it. When he came back,' she paled at the memory, 'he had a dreadful black eye! I asked what on earth had happened. He said, he'd tripped getting out of a car and hit his head on the kerb. I didn't know whether to believe him or not.'

I reflected that Gray Coverdale had been a practised liar. He knew to put an element of fact in his story, in this case, his abrupt exit from the Mercedes. Even a smidgen of truth adds confidence to the liar's voice, and it's always difficult to disprove a story that's partly true. I wondered what sort of journalism he'd gone in for. The sort that tracked down MPs in secret lovenests and interviewed the partners of men who'd been convicted of lurid crimes, I suspected. It all made sense. I was willing to bet he'd been following up some kind of dodgy story – only this time his luck had run out.

'I'd better go,' I said. 'A friend's waiting for me. I'm truly sorry about your brother. I expect the police will get it sorted soon.' I didn't believe any such thing, but you've got to say it. 'Would you mind,' I went on, 'not mentioning my visit to you to the police? They're sort of fussy.'

'Oh, that's all right,' she said. 'I won't say a word. They did tell me not to talk to journalists, but then, you're not a journalist, are you?' She gave a rueful smile. 'I'm used to not talking about Gray's business, partly because I knew so little about it, and partly because he wouldn't have liked it. Poor Gray. My father wanted him to be an accountant, you know? It would've been a lot safer.'

I made my way back to the shopping precinct, wondering whether Tig would still be there. It was quite dark now and had got a lot colder. Some of the shops, including the florist's, had closed up for the day, but a supermarket was still open and brightly lit. No one was sitting on the benches. I wondered whether she'd gone off to find a coffee or perhaps gone into the supermarket to buy a can of Coke or something. At least, I hoped she'd buy it and not try and slip it in her jacket, but by now, I realised I couldn't rely on her. As I approached the store entrance, I heard a familiar voice.

'Got any change?'

My heart sank. There she was, hanging by the exit, wearing that tragic look and waylaying shoppers. I grabbed her and hauled her away.

'What do you think you're doing?'

'Hullo, Fran,' she said. 'You were a long time and I got bored. I thought I could get back the money you spent on those flowers, but they're a stingy lot round here. I only made just over a quid. We could try somewhere else.'

'We're going home,' I said. 'Before you get us both arrested!'

The two days left before my trip to Dorridge passed off uneventfully, to my great relief. I worked extra hours at the shop because we were really busy now, Christmas being so close. We did a brisk sale in festive cards, decorations and wrapping paper, boxes of chocolates, all the things people pour out money on, grumbling all the while about how expensive a time of year it is. Tig behaved herself (or as far as I knew she did). She walked Bonnie by the canal and didn't encounter Jo Jo. With luck, he'd found himself another girlfriend by now. He hadn't looked to me the sort who'd pine.

I did go over to the nick to look at their book of criminal mugshots. At first they left me alone to study it but after a while Parry came in and asked if I wanted a cup of tea. I said yes, please. He brought it in a polystyrene cup and hung around for a few minutes until I told him he was distracting me. After that I had more time alone until Harford turned up.

'How's it going, Fran?' He took a seat beside me.

Normally I'd have given him the same treatment I'd given Parry, but by now, I was getting bored with looking at one broken nose, cauliflower ear and schizophrenic stare after another, so I took a break and said I was sorry, but really, so far I hadn't seen anyone remotely like the man who'd tried to break into my flat.

'Keep trying,' he encouraged. He moved his chair a little closer, his knee not touching mine, but not that far away either. Hmm, I thought. Now what?

He'd begun to turn the pages. 'Was he anything at all like this one, or this? You know, a year or two can make a difference and some of these mugshots are quite old.' He leaned towards me. He smelled quite nice, of expensive aftershave, unlike Parry who always seemed to niff of sweat, high-tar cigarettes and cough lozenges. He was also starting to confuse me. One minute I was getting the big freeze, the next he was trying to be friends. Well, I was prepared to be friends. I'm prepared to be anyone's friend. But, don't get me wrong on this, I'm not desperate for a shoulder to lean my head on and I like to know where I am with people. If Harford would stick to being snooty, it would be easier. At the moment, it was like the 'nice cop, nasty cop' scenario, all rolled into one man. I wondered if he'd quite got the hang of it.

I told him I really was trying, and we persevered onward through the book. Parry reappeared in the doorway midway and, seeing us with our heads cosily together, gave us a funny look.

'Yes, sergeant?' asked Harford crisply, looking up.

'Just come to see how she's getting on, sir,' said Parry, his look now indicating that he thought Harford was getting on all right, even if the identification exercise wasn't. 'OK, Fran?'

'All right, thank you!' Harford answered for me. Parry gave me a reproachful glance and left.

I did wonder vaguely whether Harford's hand might eventually stray to my knee, but he had more style than Parry – or Parry's interruption had put him off. We reached the end of the book without a word or move which could have offended a Victorian dowager.

'No,' I said. 'Not even allowing for old pics, blurred pics or plastic surgery. He's not there.'

Somehow, I wasn't surprised, and I could see that neither was Harford, who closed the book, looking resigned.

'If he's foreign,' he said, 'he might have arrived in this country only weeks ago. In fact, he probably has.'

I asked him why he was so sure of this. He replied evasively, because the man hadn't had time to get into trouble yet officially.

'No form,' as he put it, sounding a little self-conscious as he used this well-worn scrap of police jargon.

'Well, I've done my bit as good citizen,' I said, standing up.

'I'll run you home,' he offered. I nearly accepted, but then I remembered Tig back at the flat. If I turned up yet again with a plod in tow, she'd freak out. 'Thanks,' I said. 'I'll walk. I've got a spot of shopping to do.'

I did fancy he looked a little disappointed. But perhaps I was only flattering myself.

So Sunday dawned and Tig and I went over to Marylebone for me to catch the Dorridge train. It was early morning and none too busy at the weekend. Being at Marylebone awakened memories in me, however, and I found myself looking around the place, my eyes searching for ghosts.

'Who're you looking for?' asked Tig, ever suspicious.

'Someone who won't be here. I met an old wino here once, Albie Smith, he was called. I was just thinking about him.'

Tig wasn't interested in my past life. She pointed up at the smart computerised arrivals and departures screen, new since my last visit, and drew my attention to the platform number which had appeared alongside my train time.

'It's in, you'd better go on.'

I don't know why she was in such a rush. At that time of the morning and on a Sunday at that, it wasn't going to be full.

'Don't make a fool of me, Tig,' I said, before it drew out. 'Be here when I get back.'

'Promise,' said Tig. Bonnie, attached to a length of string and sitting on the platform at Tig's feet, gave a short bark of support. The train drew out and she waved at me. I had to trust her.

I sat back and reflected that even if I was successful in fixing up Tig's return, she'd declared herself unable to take the dog with her. I was going to be left with Bonnie on my hands. Still, getting Tig *off* my hands would be a start.

It was a long journey, much of it through nice countryside, but my head was filled with the forthcoming meeting with the Quayles. If Ganesh was right, I'd be met by a reception committee, probably including their solicitor and a magistrate or two who just happened to be their good friends. According to Ganesh, I oughtn't to be surprised to find a tactical response unit in body armour.

Tig had given me precise instructions on how to find the house. She hadn't described the place itself, but I'd guessed it would be a lot like Shaker Lane back in Putney, and it was. The house was thirties-built with bay windows and, even in winter, the front garden looked neat and cared for. Every other house in the street looked the same. Some had cars in the drive and all of them were polished and new. I felt out of place and apprehensive. There hadn't been that much money left over from Tig's savings once I'd bought the train ticket, and my fee was negligible. I was earning it several times over.

I approached the glass porch and rang the bell. The front door on the further side was opened almost at once. She must have seen me hovering outside as I sized up the place. We stared at each other through the porch door, then she came towards me and opened it up.

'Miss Varady?' she asked.

Her voice trembled. She was a small, slightly built woman and I could see Tig in her. Mrs Quayle must have been in her forties but had hung on to her figure. Her hair was done by a hairdresser, the grey rinsed away, and her very fine skin, starting to become lined as such skins do, was carefully made up.

I acknowledged my identity and said I was glad she'd agreed to see me. I wondered where Colin Quayle was.

She ushered me inside. The hall gleamed with new paint, new-looking carpets and shiny furniture redolent of the sort of perfumed wax you spray from a can. It made Mrs Stevens' place look scruffy. I had the feeling I ought not to come into contact with any of it, but shimmer across space a few inches above the ground in a sort of levitation experience.

As it was, I clumped my Doc Martens way into a painfully tidy drawing room (there was no other term for it) and sat down in a velvet upholstered armchair with snowy white, starched, crocheted protectors to save the soiling touch of the human hand. I could certainly see why Bonnie wouldn't be welcome in here.

'Coffee?' asked Mrs Quayle, still nervous. She stood in front of me, eyeing me in much the way the coppers had eyed Bonnie, as if I'd bite given half a chance.

'That would be nice,' I said, because I felt that was the answer she wanted. Still no Mr Quayle. I asked, 'Isn't your husband going to be here?'

'He's gone to church,' she said. 'He's a sidesman today. He'll be here shortly.'

She scurried out to make the coffee. I leaned back uneasily in my chair and studied the room further. There were china figurines of Edwardian belles on the mantelshelf and a photograph of a little girl in a ballet tutu.

I thought of Tig as I'd last seen her on the platform at Marylebone, in worn jeans, Doc Martens like mine, a grubby donkey jacket and holding on to a piece of string with a scruffy terrier attached.

Mrs Quayle was coming back. I got up to help her with the tray and she mumbled thanks. The coffee was in a cafetière, the cups were bone china, the spoons were proper coffee spoons with enamelled plaques at the end of the handles depicting flowers. There was a plate of homemade shortbread biscuits.

'Do you take sugar, Miss Varady?' She was observing the niceties in a desperate way, clinging to form as a drowning man might cling to a wooden spar.

I told her I didn't and asked her to call me Fran.

'I'm Sheila . . .' she said, handing me a cup of coffee. It slopped in the saucer. I felt sorry for her and wished I could put her at her ease. She was wearing a three-piece woollen outfit in a respectable, muddy brown: long skirt, sweater and long sleeveless jacket. It looked expensive. Her fingernails were painted a brownish-orange to team with it and matched her lipstick exactly. My feeling of pity for her increased. When Tig had walked out, this poor woman had been left with nothing to do but polish the furniture, visit the hairdresser and shop for painfully smart but respectable outfits. But how would she cope with Tig's return?

'Is Jane— You've seen Jane recently?' she asked now, leaning forward slightly, her eyes pleading.

I told her I'd seen Jane that morning and she'd been fine.

'I still don't know why she couldn't come herself,' Sheila Quayle said fretfully, and I recognised the tone of voice of the woman on the phone. She felt all this was unfair. She'd lavished care and attention on her family, her home, and in keeping herself looking nice. Her reward was this: desertion by her only child and a temporary desertion by her husband who, just when she needed him, was away doing his own thing. He'd left her here, facing a total stranger and one of an unknown species at that, begging for details.

She then floored me with a question I hadn't anticipated. 'There isn't a baby, is there?' There was a world of dread in her voice.

I gawped at her. 'No,' I said foolishly.

She flushed, her tissue-fine skin turning a dull rose-red. 'Only, these days— I mean there are so many single mothers and I thought, perhaps the reason Jane didn't come home – or even, the reason she'd left . . .'

I sighed. Since Tig had left, her mother had sat here asking herself, why? To her way of thinking, this perfect home couldn't be at fault. That must be nonsense. Her daughter had been working hard at school, so that couldn't be it, either. Sheila Quayle had come up with the only other thing she could think of. Explaining was going to be much more difficult than

I'd imagined in my wildest moments.

'There's no baby,' I said, underlining the fact.

She looked relieved but then that fretful expression came back. 'Then I really can't see why—'

We were interrupted by the sound of a car turning into the drive.

'Colin!' exclaimed Mrs Quayle as beleaguered drivers of wagon trains cried out 'The cavalry!' She jumped up and darted out into the hall to brief him as we heard his key turning in the lock.

She'd shut the drawing-room door behind her, but I could hear the slam of the front door and the muffled conversation which followed. The drawing-room door reopened.

He was a big, red-faced man in a houndstooth-checked suit worn over a mustard-coloured felt waistcoat. His shoes were highly polished brogues. The initial effect was that of a country squire rather than a businessman. At second glance, it was less convincing, all too new and too well pressed. It was a good suit, but I guessed off the peg. The shoes were top of the range, but likewise off the shelf, and the flashy gold wristwatch jarred. Such country gents as I'd come across – like old Alastair Monkton – wore suits of incredible age but beautiful cut and made-to-measure shoes cracking up with wear. When they wanted to know the time, they consulted ancient half-hunters which had belonged to their grandfathers.

I wondered about Colin's origins and guessed they'd been pretty ordinary until money had enabled him to move, as he'd probably term it, 'up' in the world. Perhaps the outfit was a sort of passport. Not all self-made men wore their success easily.

He didn't offer to shake hands but stood before me, towering over me, while he scrutinised me in a way no gentleman would do, as Grandma Varady would've said.

'You're the girl who phoned, then?' he challenged. 'The Londoner.'

I resisted the temptation to exclaim, in stage Cockney, 'Cor, swelp me, guv! Sit down and rest your plates of meat. Have a cuppa Rosie Lee.'

Sheila said nervously, 'Her name is Fran.'

'Oh, is it?' he retorted disagreeably. He lowered himself into the opposite chair and glanced at the coffee tray.

'I'll get you a cup!' his wife said at once, and darted off into the kitchen again. It was a telling moment – at least, it told me a lot.

He placed his hands on the chair-arms and I wondered if the crocheted covers were because this was his habit. His hands, I noticed, were large and coarse for all they were carefully kept. I decided the country suit had been chosen because it flattered his general build and style. I wondered, my fancy wandering as it's apt to do, how he looked when he and his wife went to a formal do and he was required to get togged up in a tuxedo. Like one of the door bouncers, probably. I liked the image and allowed myself a smile.

He interpreted it badly.

'While my wife's out of the room,' he said bluntly, 'I'll ask you a straight question, to which I want a straight answer. What's your part in all this? Also, if you think I'm paying you any money, you can forget that idea right now. So you needn't sit there smirking and looking pleased with yourself! You'll find me a hard man to fool and I'm impervious to sweet talk.'

Yes, he was a nasty bit of work and Ganesh had been right. He was the sort who put a price on everything and assumed everyone else did the same. He'd calculate success by financial reward. This house and its contents were proof, as was his well-dressed wife and – until a couple of years ago – his pretty daughter whom he'd sent to private school and ballet lessons. These things, which people could see and admire, these things only mattered.

I realised, with a stab of shock, how angry Tig's defection must have made him. His bubble of success had been punctured, his wealth rejected. His daughter had chosen God knew what sort of street life in preference to this. Could he ever really forgive that? I wondered.

'I don't want your money,' I said sharply to him. 'Jane asked me to come on her behalf. I'm doing it as a favour to her.'

His mind ran on the same lines as his wife's. 'She doesn't need anyone to speak for her. She could pick up the phone. She knows where we are. I'm not convinced you're on the level. I'm not even sure my daughter sent you. Why the dickens should she? She only had to pick up the phone,' he repeated doggedly.

Sheila was back, carrying a cup and fresh coffee in a little individual cafetière. She set them down with a clatter on the tray and took a seat nearby, smoothing her skirt over her knees. The action drew the eye to her manicured hands. Even diamond rings and nail varnish don't entirely distract from a looseness of skin on the knuckles and brown liver spots. I wondered briefly if it were possible she was older than her husband and all this care with make-up and appearance was to keep at bay the inevitable, the day when he'd look at her and decide she was no longer trophy wife enough. Time to trade her in as he'd do with his car. She was fixing anxious eyes on me. But though she didn't look at him, it was to her husband she spoke.

'Fran assures us there's no baby.' There was relief but also a hint of triumph in her voice, as if they'd argued this point over and over, she denying the possibility, he insisting. She wasn't daring to say, 'I told you so', but she couldn't quite keep it hidden.

'There'd bloody better not be,' he said. But he, too, looked relieved. 'Right, speak up. Where's my daughter? Supposing that you know and aren't just stringing us along. You'll be sorry if you are. I promise you that.'

'In London, staying at my place at the moment.' I ignored the threat though the impulse to get up and march out was strong. But if I did, Tig would be lost, and he'd be convinced he was right, I was conning them and he'd frightened me away.

'And what sort of place might that be?' His manner and voice were both insulting.

'I've got a basement flat in a perfectly respectable street, as it happens,' I replied, goaded into letting my anger show.

'And how do you pay for that? Got a job? Or just a welfare scrounger like the others?'

I was pleased to be able to say yes, I had a job. I worked in a newsagent's. I knew I had to get a grip on this conversation or I'd find myself sitting here being bullied by Colin until I was thrown out by him.

'Well,' I said briskly, putting my cup back on the tray, 'you'll be pleased to know T— Jane is fine. She has lost a lot of weight—'

Sheila let out a gasp and put orange fingernails to her lips. Her husband gave her an irritated glance.

'Has she been ill?' he asked me.

'No – but she's been living rough.'

Sheila moaned. Colin Quayle gave her another cross glare. 'Stop whimpering, Sheila, for God's sake. If you've got something to say, say it.'

He didn't give her any chance, however. Turning to me, he

went on, 'By living rough, do you mean under arches, in doorways?'

'Recently, yes. Not all the time. She's had different places to live. At one time she shared a squat with me and some others.'

'I thought you said you had a flat!' he snapped at me.

'Before I had the flat, I lived in several different places. Look,' I was getting seriously annoyed with him, 'do you want me to tell you about Jane or not?'

'Don't take that tone—' he began but, to my surprise, was interrupted by his wife.

'Let her speak, Colin. If you keep interrupting her, we shan't learn anything.'

He looked startled but fell silent. I took up my tale.

'Jane would like to come back home, but you'd need to be prepared – if she does come – for a lot of changes in her. She's had some bad experiences. She's had a rough time. She doesn't trust people any more. She's afraid of the police.' His eyes bulged and his mouth opened, but before Colin could speak, I hurried on, '*Not* because she's any reason to be, but because of the sort of life she's been living. The police have harried her and other homeless people like her. She's – she's been attacked during her time on the street. She's been hurt. Besides, she's had to do things on the fringes of the law . . .'

They were both staring at me in frozen horror. I knew I couldn't tell them that at one time Tig had been on the game, much less about the gang-rape.

I said, 'Like beg.'

'Beg!' Sheila screamed.

'Beg?' Colin took up the cry. Perhaps they'd have taken the idea of rape with less horror. His voice rose. 'My daughter? Begging on the street? For pity's sake – why didn't she just pick up the phone and ask us to come and get her? Or to send some bloody money? God, if it were only the money—'

'She – she was scared to,' I said, and thought I understood well why.

'My daughter begging . . .' He pulled out a handkerchief and mopped his face. 'Bloody hell. If people get to hear about this . . .'

Oh yes, that's what worried him. Prosperous, successful Colin Quayle the church sidesman – whose daughter stood on London streets with her hand held out to passers-by, asking if they had any change.

I said loudly, 'So you see, if she comes home, there will have to be a lot of give and take. You'll have to make allowances for her experiences, for the change in her. She's got to learn to live this sort of life again.' I indicated the room around us, but my heart was sinking as I spoke. Could Tig do that? Readjust to this? Especially with a blockhead like Colin around, a man as sensitive as Attila the Hun. 'It's going to be hard for all three of you,' I went on. I pointed at the picture of the child in the tutu. 'You've got to forget that.'

Sheila whispered brokenly, 'She was a lovely little dancer. She won prizes. You don't know what it's been like, Fran, since she's gone. I've hardly slept. I lie awake all night thinking of her. I think of her all day long. Every time the phone rings, or there's someone at the door, I've thought, perhaps it's Jane. I wait for the post . . .' She seemed to remember her husband. 'Colin has, too, haven't you?' she asked him.

Colin didn't answer that directly. He was afraid of showing even that allowable human weakness, I judged. I felt sorry for the man, really. He was in a sort of prison he'd made for himself, keeping up a set of unreasonable standards. The trouble was, he'd tried to impose those standards on Tig.

Now he asked grimly, 'Who attacked her?'

'Who knows?' I replied. 'That's how it is on the streets.'

'Is she on drugs?' he asked next. He was tactless but not stupid. He knew there was a lot I wasn't saying.

'She was.' I tried not to look at Sheila, who was swaying in her chair. 'But she's clean now. That took some doing. She's got courage.' I leaned forward. 'All she needs is some support and help. She can do it, she can get back into regular life. It won't be easy, but she can do it if you'll help. She does – will need – a lot of help. She hides behind the furniture when strangers come to the door. She thinks everyone is out to get her.'

They looked at one another and then both sat in silence.

'Dr Wilson could help,' Sheila said to her husband at last. 'He's known Jane since she was little. Perhaps a – some visits to a therapist.'

'I don't need some trick-cyclist telling me my daughter's crackers!' Colin growled. For him, having to turn to a psychiatrist would be another admission of failure. Frankly, I thought he was the one who needed the shrink.

'It might be a good idea to ask your doctor for advice,' I said. 'Anyway, T— Jane needs to go on some sort of proper diet to build her up again and, in my opinion, she won't last much longer if she doesn't.' It was make or break time. 'So,' I said, 'what do I tell her? Can she come home or not?'

Colin began, 'We need a bit of time—'

Sheila, again surprising me, broke in. 'Of course Jane can come home. This is her home. It's always been her home. She's our only child, Fran. Without her, what do we have? Nothing.'

Colin blanched. It was as if she'd hit him. He struggled for his former bullish self-composure. 'Yes, better tell her to come.

If she's ill, of course, she must.' He made another effort. 'I can drive down and collect her.'

'I'll put her on the train,' I said. 'You can pick her up at the station.'

There was a release of tension in the atmosphere now the decision was taken.

Sheila stood up, picked up the tray of used cups and asked, 'Would you like to stay to lunch?'

I ignored the glare of baffled fury Colin directed at his wife. I had no wish to stay here longer than I had to, anyway.

'Thanks, but no. I've got to get back. It's a long journey.' I got to my feet.

'I'll see you out, just let me pop this into the kitchen.' She trotted out.

Colin grunted but that was his only attempt at further communication. He had nothing more to say to me and stayed where he was as Sheila saw me to the front door. On the step, she touched my arm and said, 'Thank you.'

'It's OK,' I said. 'I'd like to think Jane was getting her life back together again.'

'Oh, yes,' she whispered, 'to think Jane will be home again. It's the best Christmas present I could've imagined. I've prayed for it. I honestly thought God wasn't listening, but He was.'

There were tears in her eyes. 'You will be prepared for changes?' I repeated anxiously. I really wondered how they'd cope.

But Sheila, I'd already decided, had hidden depths. 'We'll manage,' she said firmly. 'Jane and I always had a good relationship before.'

It didn't seem to occur to her that if it had been as good as all that, Jane would have been able to talk through her problems at home.

She had put her hand in the pocket of the woollen jacket and produced a small package wrapped in a paper napkin. She put it in my hand. 'Shortbread, for the journey.' She gave an apologetic smile. 'I'm sorry you're not able to stay for lunch. Have you got enough money to buy something?'

'I'm fine,' I assured her, 'but thanks for the biscuits.' There was nothing else to say but to wish her good luck, and put distance between myself and that house as fast as I could.

I felt really relieved as the train drew out, as if I'd put down a heavy weight I'd been toting along ever since Tig had turned up at the door with Bonnie. I'd done what I'd said I'd do and got away relatively lightly. My part was over.

A metallic rattle announced there was a trolley service on this line. The guy came along, hauling his load as I'd been hauling my symbolic one. He stopped and asked, without much show of interest, if I wanted any refreshments. I bought a coffee (black, white or cappuccino?) off him and unwrapped my shortbread biscuits. But somehow, although I was hungry, I couldn't eat more than one of them. I wrapped the others up again and put them away to give to Tig later.

Supposing Tig was still there when I got back. I'd raised Sheila's hopes and I couldn't bear to think of them being dashed. No, I would *not* worry about that. It wasn't my concern. I'd done my bit. You don't have to save the world, Fran!

A previous traveller on this train, who'd sat on the opposite seat to mine, had left bits of his Sunday newspaper behind, including the magazine supplement. To take my mind off Tig and her family, I reached for it, and sipping my coffee, opened it up.

'BRITAIN'S MOST WANTED MEN!' screamed the heading to the story which made centre pages. A row of smudged mugshots or heads taken from paparazzi snaps formed a border to the article which was, it seemed, about criminals who'd eluded the law successfully – the Mr Big figures of the underworld, who lived it up with flash cars and flashy girlfriends while the foot soldiers, who took the risks, did the time. I ran my eye down the rogues' gallery with only minor interest.

Then I saw it – saw him. His hair was darker in this pic but a bottle of bleach had since taken care of that. There he was and not a shadow of a doubt of it. Not sitting in a jazzy shirt in the sunshine as he'd been when the snaps Coverdale had acquired were taken. No, here he was leaving what looked like a nightclub, caught in the glare of the flashlight as he made for his limo. His name, I learned at last, was Jerry Grice.

Chapter Thirteen

At least, the article informed me, as I scanned it eagerly, that was one of two or three names he'd operated under. A warrant had been issued for his arrest in connection with a raid on a City bank vault which had netted an undisclosed sum in gold ingots and other valuables in safety deposit boxes. No one could ever be sure just how much the raiders had got away with, because many of the deposit box owners had been strangely coy about the contents, but the gold alone had made it a major robbery. Of the gang, most had been picked up and several gaoled. Grice alone remained at large and, more importantly, he knew where the loot was. Virtually none of that had been recovered.

Ironically, Grice was described as being not a violent man, but a planner, an ideas merchant. The journalist was being deliberately naïve, I thought. If you're in charge, you don't need to be violent yourself. You've got underlings to do that sort of thing for you, the actual orders issued by middle-ranking thugs in your employ. That way, Grice and others like him kept their hands clean. They were the clever clogs who got clean away with the dosh, while other mugs got banged up, and snoopers like Coverdale got dead.

I sat back, the cooling coffee in my grip, the magazine lying open on my lap. Coverdale had set his sights on tracking Grice down and thanks to Mrs Stevens, I knew he'd started in Zürich, home of the numbered bank account. Shrewdly, he'd tracked the money, because that would lead him to the man. It'd led him to a tropical location where he'd not only found Grice, but managed to get the photos as evidence. Then Coverdale's plans had gone disastrously wrong. What, I wondered, had Coverdale meant to do with the information? He hadn't handed it over to the cops. Had he envisaged some mega-deal with telly or a top magazine or newspaper, his name blazoned over everything? I didn't know, probably never would know, what Coverdale had wanted to do. He didn't get to do it, that's all I knew. Except that now I knew too what the police were playing at.

Grice's minions had failed to recover the negatives. Not knowing they were in police hands, he must be growing increasingly frustrated and angry – and very worried. Sooner or later, by police reckoning, he'd come back to take care of it himself. That's what they were waiting for so patiently; that was why they wouldn't reveal to the public that they held the negatives. They were forcing Grice's hand, confident that he'd show.

It wouldn't be difficult for him, after all. With that amount of money to play with, he could buy himself a false passport in any nationality he chose. He could hire a private plane to fly him in and out to a deserted air-strip or field. Heck, if SOE could fly agents in and out of Occupied Europe during the last war, then a seriously big-time crook like Grice could buy himself an away-day any time he chose. He'd probably done it a dozen times before, cocking a snook at detectives and half-a-dozen other concerned agencies.

So what made it so different, from the cops' point of view, this time? Why were they so sure this was their great chance to get him? Partly, I told myself, because this time they knew roughly when to expect him and a network of underworld informers must have been put on alert. But mostly, because this time they knew whom Grice would contact. He'd contact me.

By now, we'd rocked gently into the tunnel immediately before Marylebone Station. I was startled into awareness. The journey had passed with me deep in thought. I rolled up the magazine carefully and set out for home. To tell Ganesh or not, that was the question. On the whole, my instinct was not. On the other hand, there was nothing like a little insurance. If only one person knows (viz., Coverdale) he can be taken out. The more people who know, the more difficult it gets.

It was growing dark by the time I reached the house. The window of my basement flat was in darkness but a light was flashing around in the basement itself and indignant voices floated upwards on the cold air. I could also hear muffled, furious barking.

'She must be there, Charles. I'm sure of it. At least, the damn dog is. Ring again.'

I leaned over the railing. Bertie and Charlie had obviously heard about the break-in and come down in force to remonstrate with me. One of them was holding a torch to the window and trying to see in. The other was by the door, trying, for some reason, to see through the letter box. I toyed with the idea of calling the police or running across to the Neighbourhood Watch fanatic opposite to report prowlers. It was a nice idea, but I didn't need more hassle with the duo than I already had.

'What on earth are you doing?' I asked in a dignified way.

There was no way either of them could look anything but caught red-handed. The one by the door jumped up as if on a spring and the one by the window swung the torch round and shone it up into my face.

I shielded my eyes with my hand and snapped, 'Put that out!'

Rather to my surprise, he did. While I still had the advantage of surprise, I added, 'And come up here if you want to talk to me. I'm not coming down there.'

They huffed a bit, but climbed up the stairwell and arrived on the pavement. By the light of the streetlamp, I could see the one with the torch was Bertie. He was trying to shove it away in a battered briefcase he carried as if it'd suddenly become red-hot.

'We wish to speak to you,' said Charlie, getting his presence of mind back first.

'Go on, then,' I said. 'But don't waste my time.'

'Look here!' he began. 'You shouldn't take that tone with us, really you shouldn't! It's most unwise. We have genuine cause for grievance, as you very well know. Our aunt continues to be put in danger by your presence and we have come to insist—'

His voice was rising in indignation and Bertie, who'd been glancing uneasily at Daphne's windows, cleared his throat and took charge.

'Quite, Charles, quite. But not, um, here in the street perhaps? My dear,' he turned a sickly smile on me, 'can't we go down to the flat and discuss all this in civilised fashion, eh?'

'No,' I said. 'The flat is my home and I don't choose to allow either of you into it. Nor do I want you prowling in the basement. You've upset my dog.'

'We don't see anything in your lease which allows you to keep animals!' squawked Charlie.

'There's nothing in it says I can't. Anyway, Daphne knows Bonnie is there and she doesn't mind.'

Bertie, growing even jumpier, suggested we might, then, perhaps repair to a hostelry, as he put it.

'I'm not going into any pub with a couple of old goats like you two,' I said. 'I've got my reputation to think of.'

'That's slander!' gasped Bertie.

'No, it isn't. You ask your brother. He's got difficulty keeping his hands to himself and for all I know, you're the same. You're two and I'm one. I wouldn't feel safe. We talk here or, if you don't hurry up, we don't talk at all.'

Bertie had been distracted enough to turn to his brother. 'Charles? What's she talking about?'

'No idea,' bawled Charlie, oblivious to how many people might hear him. 'She's *non compos mentis*, if you ask me. Clearly not of sound mind.'

'You . . .' Bertie lowered his voice, shuffled a few steps away and drew his brother aside. 'You haven't . . .?' he whispered hoarsely.

'Of course I bloody haven't!' snarled Charlie.

'Not for want of trying,' I called.

They turned an angry but united front to me. 'It seems very strange to us,' said Bertie, appointing himself spokesman, 'that Aunt Daphne, after living safely and undisturbed in this house for forty years, should suddenly find the police virtually camped on her doorstep. First a murder, then an attempted break-in – what next, I wonder? There was also, we understand, a previous unpleasant affair which necessitated numerous calls at the house by the constabulary. You can hardly blame us for our concern. We do not, and cannot, consider you a suitable tenant in the light of all this. We have the safety of an elderly, frail lady to consider.'

'It's for Daphne to decide,' I retorted. 'And anyway, she hasn't been bothered, or not much, by the police. I have and I can cope.'

'Don't doubt it,' muttered Charlie. 'Practice makes perfect, they say.'

Bertie sidled up to me like an evil old owl. 'Tell me, my dear, what was the intruder after?'

'How should I know?' I snapped.

'But we think you do, eh? Yes, we think you do. Consider it. He didn't attempt to break into our aunt's house. He chose your flat – yet a look through the window, or a few minutes reconnoitring beforehand, would've told him you were unlikely to prove a rewarding target.'

'It's a basement,' I pointed out. 'They're always likely targets. No one could see him trying to get in.'

'The police,' Bertie insisted, 'seem to have made several visits and do not, in my experience, usually spend so much time on a failed burglary. One visit to take a statement and perhaps some fingerprints, would normally be enough.'

'So, what was he after?' growled Charlie, thrusting his unattractive mug into mine.

'Dunno,' I said. 'A rapist, perhaps?' I met his piggy little eyes accusingly.

Charlie stepped back. 'Come along, Bertram,' he said. 'We're wasting our time.' He turned back to me with a final shot. 'You've had your chance to discuss this, as my brother said, in a civilised manner. Very well. So be it. We shall have to see what may be done under the law.'

They marched off up the street, side by side, rigid with outraged dignity.

I wasn't too worried, because unless Daphne chose to evict me, there was little they could do. But they had a point. I couldn't go on causing this kind of disturbance. The entire neighbourhood would be signing a petition to get me out before long.

I let myself into the flat and switched on the light. Bonnie, who'd been lurking behind the door, began to jump up and down, whining an excited welcome. I picked her up, tucked her under my arm, and called out for Tig.

There was an upheaval behind the sofa and Tig crawled out on her hands and knees, her face concealed by a curtain of tangled hair. She got to her feet.

'I've been stuck behind there ages!' She glowered at me. 'They were at the door and looking through the flamin' window before I had a chance to hide in the bedroom or bathroom. All I could do was duck down behind there. They wouldn't go away. They kept ringing the ruddy bell and shouting through the letter box. You get a lot of visitors, don't you? And they don't mind insisting on coming in.'

'You could,' I said, irritated and tired after a long and difficult day, 'simply have answered the door and told them I wasn't here.'

'Answer? Not likely. They looked a real pair of weirdos.' She swept back a mess of hair from her eyes. 'So, how'd you get on, then?'

'OK,' I said. 'I'll tell you all about it later. I'm going to have a cup of tea first. I need it.'

When I emerged from the kitchenette, minutes later, with two mugs of tea, Tig was sitting on the sofa, reading my magazine. She tossed it aside and took one of the mugs.

'You saw them?' She sounded eager but nervous.

'I saw them.' I fished out the packet of shortbread. 'Here, your mum gave me this to eat on the train.'

Tig took the folded napkin and unwrapped the shortbread. She sat looking at it. 'You shouldn't have brought it,' she said in a muffled voice. 'Were they all right? Not ill or anything?'

'In blooming health, but been worried about you. They thought you might've been pregnant when you left.'

Tig burst out laughing. 'I bet that was Dad's explanation! I can imagine him shouting at Mum that it was a woman's business and she ought to have noticed and Mum denying the whole thing.'

'You weren't, were you?' It occurred to me that perhaps the Quayles' suspicions might not have been unfounded.

'No, of course I wasn't. When would I get a chance to get knocked up? I never went anywhere, never dated a boy. Dad thought they were all rapists – well, perhaps he wasn't far wrong at that.' Bitterness touched her voice.

'I thought your mum quite nice. A bit nervy.' I wanted to take her mind off her terrible experience.

'And my dad?'

'Wasn't so keen on him.' I couldn't politely say more but I didn't need to. Tig had given me a look of perfect comprehension but made no other comment.

'You can go home any time,' I said.

'You told them about the time I was on drugs?'

'I did. Not about your being on the game, though. They could only take so much and frankly, I don't think they need to know that.'

Tig fed a piece of shortbread to Bonnie, held out one to me which I took, and ate one herself. 'You think I'm doing the right thing, Fran? I know you said so before, but you hadn't met them then. It's one reason I wanted you to meet them. Do you still think I'd be doing the right thing in going back?'

'I still think you'll be doing the right thing, but I understand it won't be easy. You'll have to give each other time.'

Tig wiped the shortbread crumbs from her shirt. 'Did they say anything in particular? You know, did they make any conditions?'

I realised that the Quayles hadn't stipulated any rules beforehand. Perhaps they hadn't thought of it or perhaps they weren't quite so narrow-minded as I'd imagined. 'They mentioned a Dr Wilson.'

'That old boy? He's still practising? He must be eighty.'

'I warned them you'd lost weight – and I told them you'd been attacked while sleeping rough. That's all I said, no details.'

Tig looked away from me and muttered, 'Yes, sure.' After a moment, she said, 'I'll go tomorrow, then.'

I was startled enough to show it and she gave a wry smile. 'Strike while the iron's hot, that's what they say, don't they? I don't want to give myself too much time to think about it. I'll talk myself out of it if I do. It's all right if I leave Bonnie here, then?'

'Look,' I said, 'we'll have to phone them first so your dad can pick you up at the station.'

She was shaking her head. 'No. I don't want any contact with them beforehand. We'll start quarrelling on the phone and everything will just, you know, get screwed up. I'll just go. It'll be all right. If no one's in, I'll sit on the doorstep till they get back. Give the neighbours something to talk about.'

I imagined the neighbours would have plenty to talk about all right.

'Don't mess up that magazine,' I said. 'I haven't read it yet.'

I ran up to the shop first thing the next morning and explained to Ganesh that I had to go with Tig to the train. 'Not just to see her off, but to make sure she's really gone. I'll come back later.'

So Tig, Bonnie and I found ourselves at Marylebone again, only this time, our roles were reversed. Tig got on the train and I stood on the platform with Bonnie on her string. Bonnie lay down and put her nose on her paws. Her eyes looked up, rolling from side to side, and her expression said, 'Oh, are we doing this again? Is it going to be regular?' I thought that both she and I hoped not.

Tig had been in a funny mood since getting up. She hadn't said much although from time to time she'd looked as though she was about to speak, but then thought better of it. I couldn't blame her for being unsettled. I could only guess at how she must be feeling. The Quayles would probably be horrified when they saw her but even after only a few days with me, she was looking a lot better and taking more trouble with her appearance. She'd combed back her hair and secured it with one of those big spring grips. It suited her. I wondered if my hair would ever grow that long and how many months it would take, starting as it did from near zero.

She was standing in the open doors of the Chiltern Lines Turbo, studying me carefully in the way she had. I'd got used to it, mostly, but it was still unsettling.

'Something you've forgotten?' I asked.

Indecision flickered across her face before she seemed to take a deep breath and to have made up her mind to say something. 'Fran—' she began. Someone pushed past her and she moved aside, back into the carriage. When she reappeared something, some resolve, had gone out of her. 'I was just going to say, thanks.'

'No problem,' I said. But it occurred to me that wasn't what she'd been about to say and I wondered, if the other passenger hadn't intervened, if she'd have spoken out loud at last what had been on her mind since breakfast.

'You didn't get much of a fee,' she went on. 'When I get some more money, I'll send you some.'

'No, you won't,' I told her. 'We're quits. You've given me Bonnie.'

There was a whistle down the platform, a warning buzz from inside the train and with a pneumatic hiss, the doors slammed together. Tig, on the inside, waved at me as it drew out. I waved back.

'Just you and me then, Bonnie,' I said to the terrier. She jumped up and wagged her stumpy tail. 'You know, we're going to have to get you a proper lead,' I went on. 'This piece of string doesn't do anything for either of us.'

I rattled homeward on the bus with Bonnie sitting on my knees, attracting much admiration and petting, and looking as if butter wouldn't melt in her mouth. In the small hours of the morning, I'd thought out what I was going to do next. Not having the encounter with the Quayles looming over me had freed up my mind considerably.

I went to the flat first, collected the magazine, and the photo Joleen had unearthed for me, and made my way to the shop.

Hitch was there, leaning on the counter. 'Hullo, darling,' he greeted me. 'What's this then?' He meant Bonnie. He stooped to scratch her ears. 'This is a Jack Russell, this is.'

'It's a dog,' said Ganesh disagreeably. 'And they're not allowed in the shop. I've got a sign outside that says so.'

He was right. A yucky thing it was too, a picture of some soulful animals and the legend 'Please Leave Us Outside'.

'If I let you bring that one in,' Ganesh went on, 'I'll have to let everyone bring their dogs in. Loads of people round here have got dogs and some of them are big.'

Ganesh, you'll have gathered, isn't a dog-lover. Shop hygiene rules aside, he just doesn't like them and they don't like him. I leave it to you to work out which dislike sparked the other. All I know is, perfectly placid dogs, which had been rolling at the feet of little children moments before, would turn into snapping, snarling throwbacks to the wolf as Ganesh approached. Even Bonnie, catching the tone of his voice, made a soft growling noise in her throat.

By way of distraction, I asked after Marco. Hitch informed us he'd gone to the continent for a few days' holiday. I asked where.

'Amsterdam,' said Hitch. That made sense. Though his being away in the clouds half the time would've dulled my pleasure in Marco's company, I was still sorry we hadn't made it even to first base. I had fancied him.

'Catch rats, them little dogs,' said Hitch cheerfully, bringing things down to earth. 'Bloody good rat-catchers. Couple of people down our street, when we was kids, kept terriers like that. We used to pull up the manhole covers and drop the tykes down the sewers. They had a great time down there chasing rats. Then we had to squeeze down after 'em to get 'em back. Catching them was a job and a half down there. It was dark and stinking, all you could do to breathe. Had to watch where you put your feet, too. Do you know, a lot of them sewers are Victorian? Lovely bit of brickwork, wonderful workmanship, real skill.' He shook his head sadly. 'Kids don't have fun like that no more. It's all telly and computers stuffing their heads with rubbish. They learn nothing. They don't take no healthy exercise.'

I explained that Bonnie wasn't used to being left alone and

for today at least, I'd had to bring her. I took her into the storeroom and tied her up. She didn't seem to mind that and settled down happily on some flattened cardboard, with a clean plastic container of water, home from home.

When I went back Hitch and Ganesh were wrangling over payment of the bill for the new washroom. Ganesh wanted to write a cheque: Hitch wanted cash.

'It's easier, is cash,' wheedled Hitch. 'I can just stuff it in me back pocket. Cheques I've got to put through the books. I'll have to charge you VAT.'

'Don't tell me,' said Ganesh, 'that your turnover requires you to register for VAT. Not unless you've been putting in new washrooms from here to Battersea. I've got to put it through our books to show Hari what I've spent.'

In the end, Hitch took the cheque, though he clearly didn't have any confidence in such a method of payment. He trailed away looking as if Ganesh had given him a wad of Monopoly money.

'I told you to watch out if you were going to deal with him,' I reminded Ganesh.

Ganesh replied loftily that he could take care of business matters, thank you. He wasn't without experience.

It was time to dent his smugness. I unrolled the magazine and opened it out flat on the counter.

'What is it?' Ganesh peered at it suspiciously. 'Do we sell that one? It looks like one of those Sunday supplements to me.'

'It is. Just look at the photos, will you? Any of them mean anything to you?'

Ganesh scanned the pages, hesitated at Grice's picture, then moved on. After a few moments he sighed. 'I know what you want me to say, Fran. You want me to tell you that this one –'

he tapped Grice's pic – 'is a bit like the chap in those photos Coverdale left in the old washroom. I agree, there is a faint resemblance, but that's all there is. Don't start leaping to conclusions. You know what you are.'

I ignored that. I took out the print from the chemist's and put it beside the one in the magazine. 'Look again. Imagine him with bleached hair and perhaps four or five years older.'

Ganesh gasped and jabbed a finger at the print. 'Where did you get that?'

'It was in the darkroom waste bin, down at Joleen's place. Never mind how I got it. Look again and be honest.'

'It looks like him,' agreed Ganesh sulkily. 'But I'd better be wrong and so had you. From what it says here, he's bad news.'

'Coverdale's body in my basement's already told me that,' I retorted.

Ganesh closed the magazine and leaned his palms on the counter. 'So what are you going to do? Move house?'

'How can I? Talk sense. What I'm not going to do is spend my time jumping out of my skin every time someone walks up behind me, stay frightened to go down alleys, and sleeping with the light on. This has got to be settled. I'm going to take this down to the copshop and see what Harford and the others have to say.'

'You're mad,' said Ganesh simply. As I walked out, he added on a panicky note, 'Hey, don't leave me here with that dog!'

'You've got to get over this phobia of yours,' I called back. 'I won't be long.'

'Hullo,' said the desk officer when I walked into the station. 'You again?'

Honestly, there are professional safe-crackers, muggers,

even streetwalkers, who see less of the inside of the nick than I do, though I only get as far as the front desk, and occasionally an interview room. I've not yet been tossed in the cells. Give it time.

I told him I wanted to see Inspector Harford or, failing that, Sergeant Parry.

'Can't be done,' he said. 'They're in a meeting. Know it for a fact. Saw 'em all going up there ten minutes or so back and they gave out they wasn't to be disturbed.'

'What, all of them?' If they were, it had to be something important and I'd got a funny feeling crawling up my spine.

'You tell them,' I said, 'that Fran Varady is out here and I know who the man in the photos is.'

'What man in what photos?' he asked, being a simple bluebottle who didn't get taken into the confidence of CID.

'Tell 'em!' I instructed him. I sat down on an uncomfortable bench by the wall and picked up an ancient copy of *Police Review* lying there. It was that or a dog-eared copy of the *Sun*. From the corner of my eye, I saw him lift up a phone.

When he put it down, he called across, 'The inspector will be down in a minute or two.'

'Fine,' I said, calm and collected. The biggest mistake I could make now would be to storm in there ranting and demanding protection. I was a member of the public and I didn't have to do anything or go along with anything they'd dreamed up, if I didn't want to.

There was a clatter of feet on stairs nearby. Harford rounded the corner, face flushed and, contrary to his usual crisp business appearance, a little dishevelled. He jumped down the last three steps and marched over to me.

'What's all this?' he asked disagreeably. So we were back in that mode again, were we?

'Jerry Grice,' I said.

His face turned white. He glanced over his shoulder towards the desk and the officer manning it who was stirring his coffee.

'Don't say names like that out loud!' Harford hissed, stooping over me. He straightened up and recovered some of his aplomb. 'I think, in the circumstances, you'd better come upstairs and join us. We're just discussing that matter and we meant to call you in, anyway.'

'Oh, were you?' I asked sarcastically.

He retorted in like tone. 'Yes. So you've saved us the bother, haven't you?'

Chapter Fourteen

It was a meeting all right. The tribal chiefs had gathered for a powwow and the air was suitably thick with smoke. There must have been a dozen or so people in the room, perched on table corners, or leaning against walls, amid a litter of polystyrene cups, sweet wrappers and overflowing ashtrays. Most were men, two or three women and at least one who'd have doubled for either. I recognised Parry amongst them, and a couple of the others whom I'd seen before, but not a thin-faced man with grey hair and a grey complexion to match. He was the only one seated at a desk and everyone else hovered around him.

'This is Fran Varady, sir,' said Harford to him. To me, he whispered, 'Superintendent Foxley.'

His manner indicated I was being accorded an audience equal to that with a Chinese emperor. I wondered if I was expected to fall down and bang my head on the floor in obeisance, or merely retreat from his presence backwards. Well, I wasn't one of those struggling up the police promotion ladder. I was a free spirit and felt this was the moment to underline it. Apart from which, I'd choke if I had to stay in this foul atmosphere longer than a few minutes more.

'Do you think,' I said to Foxley, 'we could have a window open?'

There were looks of shock and bewilderment on all faces. They were quite unaware of the fug.

'Open it,' said Foxley without looking round. Some minion obeyed, creating a gap finger-thick, through which some of the haze began to seep.

'Sit down, Miss Varady, won't you?' Foxley offered and, again, an underling pushed a chair forward. 'Your arrival is perhaps timely. Can we offer you some coffee?'

I'd drunk their coffee on previous occasions and declined politely. I could see Parry in the background. When I'd walked in, his ginger eyebrows had shot up to meet his hairline. They hadn't far to travel. Now he was engaging in an elaborate pantomime, asking what on earth I was doing there.

'What's the matter, Sergeant?' asked Harford tersely, catching a particularly extreme example of Parry's mugging.

Parry mumbled some reply and buried his face in a cup.

'We've been having a case conference, as you can see,' Foxley went on to me. He didn't show surprise at my refusing the coffee. He probably understood and sympathised. 'We are not yet in a position to make an arrest with regard to the murder in your basement, but we're closing in.'

Closing in? Coppers said things like that in the old black-and-white movies I watched late at night. After someone says it, old-style black police cars race through deserted streets, sounding sirens fit to bust and alerting every villain for miles around that they're on their way. I had hoped police methods had advanced since then. Possibly the methods had – lots of technical wizardry and forensic leads – but not the approach.

Harford, standing behind and to one side of my chair, cleared his throat and said, 'Miss Varady believes she's made a discovery, sir.' He sounded nervous.

'Miss Varady knows she has,' I corrected him. I pulled out

my magazine and opened it. They all leaned forward, peering at the page of mugshots. I tapped the relevant one. 'Jerry Grice,' I said. 'That's the guy in the snapshots, isn't it? Give or take a bottle of bleach.'

Someone at the back of the room said, 'Shit.' Another said wearily, 'Bloody press.'

Parry turned purple and his eyes bulged at me.

'I told you not to muck about—' he began.

Foxley glanced over his shoulder and Parry fell silent. 'Yes, Miss Varady, that's right,' the superintendent said evenly. 'And you understand I'm sure, why we don't want to advertise the fact that he's the man we're after.'

'I understand,' I said. 'But I don't like being pegged out as decoy.'

He raised sparse eyebrows. 'Did we do that? I wouldn't say so. We have been keeping a friendly protective eye on you, I admit that.'

'Rubbish!' I retorted robustly.

Since Foxley was clearly the big cheese round here, my attitude was causing ripples of emotion round the room. I detected, on different faces, disapproval, anticipation and even glee. Parry looked about to faint.

'Someone tried to break into my flat the other night and if I hadn't had a dog on the premises, he'd have got in.' I did my best to sound like an outraged citizen. The very least they owed me was an apology.

The superintendent merely looked irritated. 'An oversight.'

I dismissed this with, I hoped, visible scorn. 'You bet it was an oversight. So, from now on, you include me beforehand when you want to use me. Otherwise,' I added on a brainwave, 'I'll take my case to the Police Complaints Committee.'

Parry turned aside towards the window to hide his reaction

to this. His shoulders were twitching. I didn't know whether from laughter or despair.

Foxley didn't snarl 'Feel free!' though it obviously hovered on his lips. Instead he gave a strained grimace and advised me that we hadn't got to that stage yet, surely?

I wasn't going to push the point, to tell the truth. But it did no harm to let them know I was seriously displeased.

Foxley had got the message. He leaned his elbows on his desk and placed the tips of his fingers together. 'I sincerely hope that you won't let a misunderstanding damage what I hope could be a profitable collaboration. The fact is, Miss Varady –' this was accompanied by his bleak smile. He was doing his best to be charming, but he wasn't cut out for it. I awarded him a point for trying – 'the fact of the matter is, we need your help. Now, of course, you don't have to say yes. You don't have to do anything unless you decide to help. It's your decision and no pressure will be put on you. But I'd be grateful if you'd just let me explain.'

Had Ganesh been there, he'd have told me to say no, and get out of there as fast as I could. But I reckoned it would do no harm to listen. A bit of police goodwill wouldn't come amiss. 'Go on, then,' I said.

Foxley launched into a seamless narrative which led me to believe he'd done this sort of thing before. I wondered briefly what had happened to others, such as myself, who'd been talked into helping in just such circumstances.

'Your magazine article will have told you why we're after Grice. He's been giving us the runaround but the net is closing.' (Did he, too, watch old films?) 'We believe that Grice will shortly be arriving in this country. There is an underworld rumour to that effect. We have it from a normally reliable source.'

I wondered about the 'source'. Say what you like, the professional grass earns his money. He probably wouldn't be in the business if the police didn't have some hold over him, but all the same, it's a risky enough trade to undertake in whatever circumstances. Rumbled and he's done for. His body is washed up and deposited on a Thames mudflat. The river police go out and scoop it up and add it to the statistics. If anyone enquires, and it's unlikely anyone will, a dozen people will testify to how depressed the late unlamented was, and how he'd spoken frequently of ending it all.

'Grice needs to recover that strip of negatives and any prints made from it, Miss Varady,' Foxley said. 'His hired help has bungled the job. He can't afford another body in a basement. Above all, you see, he seeks to avoid publicity. Pictures in magazines, murder reports on the evening news, police enquiries such as the one set in motion by Coverdale's death, all these things are anathema to Grice. Successful big-time crooks, you have to understand, view themselves as successful businessmen. It irks them that they make the money but can't spend it except in the society of underworld characters. They want out of that world. They're social climbers. They long to be on the Town Hall invitation list. They hanker to join the world of Rotary dinners and mornings on the golf course. In a word, they want to be legit. A respectable businessman is probably how Grice is passing himself off somewhere and the worst thing that can happen to him is that his new friends learn the truth, depend on it. It makes him vulnerable now in a way he wasn't when he was just a villain. He's displaying an Achilles' heel, you might say.' Foxley paused and then asked me, 'You know what that is?'

Prat, I thought. 'Yes, I do know,' I said aloud, crossly. 'I went to a good school, you know. Achilles' mother dunked him in the river Styx to make him invulnerable but forgot about the heel she held him by.'

'That a fact?' asked Parry, looking interested. 'I didn't know that. You'd think the poor little bugger would've drowned.'

Foxley gave him a dirty look and me an only slightly less dirty one. 'Your education wasn't wasted then, I see.'

He scored a hit, if only he knew it, but I wasn't going to let him see it.

Foxley regained his position effortlessly. 'To return to Grice. He'll try negotiation. To put it bluntly, he believes you have the film Coverdale hid – or you are in a position to obtain it. We are confident he'll offer to buy it off you.'

Oh, they were, were they? 'What if I tell the truth and say you lot have what he wants?' I asked.

His smile grew wider but no pleasanter. 'In Grice's world, people don't speak the truth. Why should he believe you? We haven't released any statement about the photographs. They are worth money. You could take them to a newspaper. They'd pay you well. Probably that was what Coverdale intended to do. Why should you not do the same? Grice will make you a pre-emptive bid, that's all.'

'An offer I can't refuse,' I said caustically.

'That's right.' His mouth stretched in a genuine grin. 'Got it in one.'

I thought it over, but not for long. 'What do you want me to do?'

There was a palpable relaxation of tension all round. This was what they'd all been in a huddle discussing before I arrived. How to get me to co-operate in this. Well, here I was, putting my head on the block. I had about as much choice as one of Henry the Eighth's wives. Grice was on his way and I was his target anyway. Either I worked with the police or it didn't bear thinking about.

'Good!' Foxley sat back in his chair. 'I'm glad we've got all that sorted.'

'What sorted?' I protested. 'What am I supposed to do?'

They'd been discussing that one, too. I got an encouraging nod.

'It's highly unlikely that Grice himself will approach you in the first place. An underling will do that. He'll tell you the deal. You agree, saying you don't have the negatives to hand, but you can get hold of them. You have one condition only, you'll only hand the negatives over to Grice himself. His representative will argue. But you stand firm. You say you don't trust intermediaries in view of what's happened before. They know they've screwed up and they'll take the point. So you say you want to be sure the deal's gone down as planned and the only way you can do that is for Grice to be there. It's likely Grice himself feels the same way. He'll want to be sure, too. The only way he can be is by collecting the negatives from you himself. Say you'll meet Grice wherever he wants, provided it's a public place in broad daylight. You'll bring the negatives. He brings the money. Straight swap. You then let us know where the exchange is to take place and we'll pick him up.'

Just like that. I must have looked unconvinced.

'He needs those pictures badly, Fran,' Harford said, beside me.

I fully realised that. Something on those pics not only betrayed Grice's location, it betrayed his current game. A project he'd planned carefully and executed beautifully had been thrown into jeopardy by Gray Coverdale, the man who took risks. Even Coverdale's death hadn't made Grice secure.

Only getting his hands on the film could do that.

Foxley was speaking. 'Oh, another thing. You make your own way to the meeting place. On no account get into a car. Just make it clear to them that you're broke, you have no interest in Grice's business, and your entire aim is to make a little cash. They'll believe that.'

I had an idea this last remark was probably insulting but I let it pass.

'How much money do I ask for?'

'They'll make an offer. I doubt it'll be extravagant. You can look a little disappointed if you like, but accept it. If you try to haggle, things might get nasty. It'll be enough to tempt someone in your circumstances, don't worry, but they won't make the mistake of dangling huge sums before your eyes. They'll calculate you're not a person used to dealing in large amounts of money and too many noughts could turn your head. You might decide that anything worth that much could find a higher bidder, and attempt a double-cross. Oh, and Miss Varady – ' he wasn't smiling now and his eyes reminded me of a dead fish – 'you wouldn't try that, would you? A double-cross, I mean. I wouldn't take it kindly. You'd find trying to be clever at our expense wouldn't pay you, Miss Varady.'

'Do me a favour,' I said wearily. 'All I want is for this business to be over and done with. One small point you seem to have overlooked . . .'

'Yes?' The sparse eyebrows shot up in genuine surprise. Parry, in the background, looked affronted.

'I don't *have* the negatives,' I said. 'You do. If I do go to meet Grice, he won't hand over an envelope of dosh without checking first that I've given him the kosher goods.'

There was a pause. 'When the deal's set up, we'll let you have the negatives.'

They would have as many prints as they needed, anyway. But then Grice might be concerned about prints, too. I pointed this out, though not mentioning the extra print I'd got from Joleen's waste bin.

'A fair point.' Foxley nodded. 'We'll put a set of prints in with the negatives. You swear to them that's all there are.' He gave his thin smile. 'I hear you're an actress, Miss Varady. I'm sure you can make it convincing.'

If only some casting agent somewhere had the same confidence in me.

Foxley's parting instructions were not to discuss this with anyone, understand? Anyone at all.

Parry made a move to escort me out, but Harford was ahead of him. He led me downstairs, through reception and out on to the station steps, where beneath the overhead lamp he made a very neat speech.

'I want you to know, Fran, that I admire your courage. It's really brave of you to agree to this and we're very grateful.'

That was easy on the ear, but I'd expected something of the sort. Now, however, Harford unbent sufficiently to add, 'The super's an old miseryguts but he's really chuffed that you're playing along with us in this. I don't want you to worry. Everything will be all right, I promise. I'm making it my personal responsibility to see nothing goes wrong. Whatever else happens, I'll be looking out for you.'

It was nice to think I had someone to look after me but since their priority would be to nab Grice, I couldn't help but be less than completely convinced all eyes would be anywhere but on the main prize.

He noticed the indecision on my face. 'What's worrying you?' he asked anxiously.

'Nothing,' I told him. 'I was just waiting for the spotlight to shine on us and the unseen choir to strike up.'

Concern faded in his face and the touchy look came back. He straightened up, stiff and wooden as a toy soldier.

'Relax!' I told him. 'It was a joke. I watch too many old films in the early hours of the morning.'

He looked faintly embarrassed and managed a smile. 'You see,' he said, taking my hand and squeezing it. 'You can even joke about it. That's what I mean, Fran. You've got guts.'

Another explanation would be that I was missing a few marbles but I just gave a noble smile back because it's not often someone tells me I'm a heroine, and it was nice to bask in approval for once.

Harford still had hold of my hand and I found I didn't mind too much. If he'd just get the chips off both shoulders, we might even get along quite well.

'We'll have the place completely covered,' he was saying. 'As soon as Grice has taken the envelope, we'll move in on him.'

'Look,' I said, 'he's going to be suspicious, you know. He hasn't stayed out of gaol this long by making silly mistakes.'

Harford leaned towards me earnestly. 'Let me tell you something, Fran. Sooner or later, they all make mistakes. They get to think they're invincible, you know? They're too used to calling the shots and getting away with anything. They really get to believe they can't be caught.'

'Grice thinks he can get caught,' I said. 'That's why he wants those photos back. The person who thought he could get away with it was Coverdale. Instead he got himself into something nasty and it caught up with him in my basement!'

Harford's hand, holding mine, gave a convulsive twitch before he let my fingers drop. 'Don't forget, tell us the moment he makes contact.' He turned on his heel and ran back up the steps into the station. A couple of uniformed men coming out gave me a curious look.

I went back to the shop to collect Bonnie. Both she and Ganesh welcomed me with flattering enthusiasm.

'Well, how did you two get on together?' I asked heartily. 'Friends?'

'I needed to go in the storeroom,' Ganesh said with emotion. 'And every time that animal growled at me. I had to keep feeding it crisps. It was the only way I could get past.'

Bonnie, sitting on her cardboard bed, thumped her tail. She looked pleased with herself.

'So?' Ganesh prompted. 'How did you get on with your police mates, then?'

'We're not mates. I told them it was Grice in the pics. They admitted it was. They told me not to discuss it with anyone.'

'Well,' said Ganesh. 'Now I hope you're satisfied and you'll leave it alone.'

I was glad I hadn't told him any more about the setup I'd agreed to back there at the nick. Gan wouldn't think me a heroine. He'd say I was nuts and make no bones about it.

A customer came in and he left me to go and deal with him. I untied Bonnie, called out goodbye, and set off slowly homewards, Bonnie pattering beside me.

Light was fading already. If I was to meet Grice in daylight, it would have to be quite early in the day to make sure of not being caught by gathering evening shades. I wandered down my street, lost in this and other depressing thoughts, and was almost at the house before my eye was taken by a glitter on the pavement ahead, just outside Daphne's front door. I approached wonderingly and gazed down at a silver patch of water which ran across the pavement slabs, over the kerb, into the gutter, and down that to the nearest drain. The silver patch had its origins in a tiny spring which had forced its way up between slabs. Around it were some painted marks which hadn't been there earlier. Bonnie sniffed around and tried to drink the spring. It bubbled up her nose and she jumped back and barked at it. Daphne's door opened and light beamed on me.

'Oh, Fran,' my landlady called. 'I've been watching out for you. The water board has been to inspect it and they're coming first thing in the morning to mend it. Unfortunately, they've got another emergency on and couldn't deal with it straight away.'

'But it's coming up through the pavement,' I pointed out.

Daphne came down the steps to view it. 'So it is. That's new. It wasn't doing that earlier when the water-board men came. There was just a lot of water seeping out. I have been worried. You know, there was a big puddle out here which never seemed to dry up? I assumed it was the aftermath of the rain, but it did seem odd.'

I told her I'd noticed it, too. We told each other we should have got in touch with the water board earlier.

'But they are coming in the morning,' Daphne comforted us. 'If it gets worse before bedtime or if they're late in the morning, I'll be on the phone straight away.'

She returned indoors. I dragged the fascinated Bonnie away from the spring, picked her up and carried her down the basement steps. As I felt for my key, she wriggled and growled.

'It's only water,' I told her. 'We'll go out and look at it later, see if it's worse, OK?'

I pushed the door open. Bonnie's growls intensified. In my arms, her body was stiff. The ridge of hair had risen along her back, the whites of her eyes showed and her ears were flattened.

A nasty sick feeling gripped the pit of my stomach. I peered into the darkness of the flat. There was complete silence but an odd feel to the place, something I could only sense. Bonnie sensed it too and to her it meant another presence. I stretched out my hand for the light and flipped it on. I could see into my living room and it was empty. Nothing looked as if it had been disturbed. Leaving the door open, I edged in. I put Bonnie on the floor and remaining by the exit, ready to run, watched to see what she'd do.

She ran round the place, nose to carpet and fetched up by the curtain and plastic strips which covered the entrance to the kitchenette. Here she stopped, pricked her ears and began to bark in short repetitive bursts.

That was enough for me. No way was I going in there unaccompanied. If I had to go back to the shop and wait for Ganesh to finish there and come back with me later that evening, so be it. But I couldn't leave Bonnie here with whatever danger threatened. I called to her but she wouldn't come. She remained in front of the curtain, barking, alternately rushing forward a little, then scuttling back as if caution tempered her combativeness.

I edged in a little further. 'Bonnie – come here, come on.' I crouched and whistled to her, but she was deaf to my urging.

The curtain shimmered, rustled and parted, and a man stepped out into the room. In my guts I felt sicker than ever, even though the dog's behaviour had told me he must be there. Bonnie hurled herself forward but the next moment yelped shrilly as she was propelled across the floor by a well-aimed kick.

'Hey!' I darted forward, heedless of the fact that I was distancing myself from the open front door and my escape route. 'Don't hurt my dog! She's only small.'

'Shut the door,' he said. His voice was low, cold, expressionless. 'Pick the dog up and shut it in another room. If you don't, I'll kill it.'

He meant it. I closed the front door behind me. I was shut in now with him, at his mercy. Bonnie wasn't easy to catch. She skittered round my outstretched hands, her eyes fixed on the intruder, still barking. At last I managed to grab her and shut her in the bathroom. In there, she began to scrabble at the door and keep up a noisy protest.

My visitor had remained by the kitchenette, his hands folded in the stance of the professional bodyguard. He was a big fellow in a dark suit, balding but with his remaining fairish hair tied back in a ponytail. His skull appeared to be perfectly round like a football. He wasn't so young – I supposed him in his forties – but as solid as a brick barn. I hadn't seen a Mercedes car on my way home – but no doubt that was parked nearby, possibly in the next street.

'Switch the light out,' he ordered in the same expressionless tone he'd used throughout our short conversation. For all that, it was an educated voice. 'And sit down there – on that sofa. We're going to have a talk.'

Chapter Fifteen

Once I'd switched out the light, the basement room was plunged into gloom, made worse by the fact that the medicine cabinet still blocked the small garden window. Ridiculously, I found time for a spasm of embarrassment. He had probably seen and guessed the reason for that pathetic attempt at barricading myself in. Totally futile, as it turned out. This fellow hadn't needed to break in by burglars' methods as had his Spanish-speaking colleague. This was the man who'd got into the shop, and, on the night the Spaniard (as I thought of him) had been trying to get in here, had effortlessly entered Mrs Stevens' Putney home. There he'd drawn a blank. Here the Spaniard had also been unsuccessful, thanks to Bonnie. He hadn't even got in. Ponytail had been forced to come here and try himself. I fancied a hierarchy was emerging. This sinister intruder, with whom I shared the darkness, was Grice's lieutenant, entrusted with his messages and orders. The other guy was a regular foot soldier. That Grice had sent his right-hand man suggested Foxley had been correct. Grice was taking personal control, albeit at one remove. Foxley would be pleased about that. I wasn't so sure.

I glanced towards the window. Up there, out in the street, it was still comparatively light, that steel-grey moment before dusk falls. Down here, I could barely see my visitor.

He had moved, taken a chair over by the television, which put him between me and the only exit. As my eyes adjusted to the poor light, I could make him out better but he was still little more than a silhouette.

I couldn't see his face and was glad of it. His voice was frightening enough.

Though Foxley had warned me that someone would contact me soon, I hadn't – and Foxley hadn't – bargained for it being as soon as this. As a result I was unprepared. In stage terms, I hadn't had time to learn my lines or rehearse. The interview would have to be conducted off the cuff. It would have to be a *tour de force* of improvisation. If I got it wrong, if he guessed I'd been primed by the cops or that I was uttering the smallest lie, he'd kill me. I found I was holding my breath and forced myself to breathe as naturally as I could in the circumstances, but my chest was rigid and it felt as natural as being in an iron lung must be. Even Bonnie had fallen silent. From the bathroom came only an occasional whimper and desultory scrabble at the door. She, too, was listening.

'Do you know why I'm here?'

I started. I hadn't expected a question. It was a clever one, straight to the point. It allowed for no evasion. If I lied, he'd know straight away.

'I can guess, I think,' I said. My voice sounded as if it were being forced out of a bag, like piped icing. 'Is it to do with the roll of film?'

'Yes.' I'd given the right answer. There was a touch of approval in his voice. I'd be a fool to bank on it. 'Do you have it?'

'Not here,' I croaked.

'I know you don't have it here,' he replied, now sounding reproachful.

Of course he knew. He'd used his time to search the place, just as he'd searched the house in Putney. It didn't look upside down because only careless, amateur searchers (or those bent on vandalism) leave a place looking as if it's been done over. The professional has been through your gear and you never know it. Mrs Stevens had guessed only because she was super-tidy and he'd made the error of leaving the loo seat up.

At the thought of him, searching methodically through my gear, the sick feeling returned. He'd been through everything, my clothes, including my underwear. My bed, looking under the mattress and inside the pillowslip and duvet cover. In the bathroom, unscrewing my tube of toothpaste and tin of talc. In the kitchen, shaking out the contents of the coffee jar, the packet of tea. Everything had been touched by him and soiled by him though he'd left no sign, not even a fingerprint, that was for sure.

'You've searched,' I said dully. 'Did you search the flat above the shop, too? After you knocked out my friend?'

'The Indian guy? He didn't have it.'

Yes, he'd calmly stepped over Ganesh's prostrate body and gone through Hari's flat. That must have taken a bit of time. There are a pile of papers to do with the business up there. At any moment, Ganesh could've regained consciousness but, thank God, he hadn't.

'How did it come into your possession? Did Coverdale give it to you?' Ponytail asked next.

'No, he didn't. He hid it in the old washroom at the shop the morning he stumbled in. The morning you— He was being chased. The washroom's been renovated since. That's when it came to light. It was in an old envelope, tucked behind some pipes.'

He thought that over and must have accepted it. His voice

went back to being expressionless. 'The person I'm representing would like the film. Can you get it?'

'Yes.' That was true. Foxley had promised that.

'He is a fair man and will pay you for your trouble. A thousand pounds. That's a lot of money. I'm sure you can use it.'

Yes, I could. But I'd rather earn it a different way. Come to that, the police would take it off me in due course, even if all went according to plan. They'd say it was evidence. I wondered if I could argue the case for being allowed to keep it. Then I thought wryly, why worry about that, Fran? A chance would be a fine thing.

'A thousand?' I said wistfully. It wasn't difficult to get the tone right. It came naturally.

'That's right. You agree?'

I hesitated. I wasn't acting. It was real. I was about to take the plunge. 'Yes, all right. I know you've been looking for the film but – but what about the bloke you— who was found dead outside my door here? I don't want to end up the same way. Don't take this wrong, but how do I know I can trust you? Look, I want to trade, but I'm not going to agree to hand over the film to you in some place, say like this flat here, where it's just you and me, like this. I'm not trying to be difficult. I'm trying to look after myself.'

I felt his anger though he hadn't moved. I hurried on. 'I'm not trying to shake more money out of you. You can have the film for a grand. That's fine by me. But I want to hand it over to – to the person you're representing, himself. That way, I'll know he's got it and that nothing's gone wrong. See, you say you represent him, but maybe you don't. Maybe you represent someone else. I don't know, do I? I give the film to your boss or no one, right?'

'You are not in a position to make conditions,' he said tersely.

But actually, I thought he was bluffing there. I was. I had the negs – or knew where they were. I was prepared to play along and return them for a grand in cash. They didn't want more trouble either, according to what Foxley had said. I hoped he was right. 'Look,' I said, 'just explain that to your principal, will you? You're right, I could use the money. I don't want the film. It's no use to me.'

He was hesitating. 'My principal may wish for some evidence that you do actually have access to it.' Sarcasm entered his voice. 'Since we don't know we can trust you, either.'

Tricky. I could hardly send him down the nick to ask. But if Grice himself were to come, he'd have to be persuaded. I gambled. 'I did get it developed,' I admitted.

At my words, he moved. He was across the room and towering over me in a split second. Bonnie, in the bathroom, began a determined attempt to scrape her way through the door, whining hysterically. He snatched me up off the sofa in a single move, holding my arms in a painful grip. I hung between his hands like a rag doll, helpless and wondering if I hadn't made the worst mistake of my life. But he had to know. If I handed the goods over, they'd know at once they hadn't got a film but a set of developed negatives. Explaining that if they were unprepared would be well-nigh impossible. They'd be sure it was a double-cross.

'Hold on!' I gasped. 'I'm not making trouble! When I got it printed up I didn't know, did I, that it'd be of interest to you? I thought it might tell me whose it was, but it didn't. I didn't – don't – know the people in the snaps. I only ever wanted to give the stupid thing back to its owner and if you want it, you can have it!'

He dropped me. I fell back on the sofa in a heap like the victim of a session on the rack. I was sure my shoulders were both dislocated. He still loomed over me.

'Where are the prints?' His voice was low and harsh.

'With the negs. Except one I've got here in my pocket. I meant to – to put it in a safe place with the others, in case the owner came asking, you know. Somehow it got left out. Look, it's only a holiday snap, what's the fuss?'

I was doing my best to sound thick, but I wasn't sure he'd bought the explanation. He held out his hand silently.

I fumbled in my pocket and gave him Joleen's print. He took it to the window and held it so the street lighting fell on it. I heard him give a little grunt. He put it in his inside pocket and turned back.

'How many of these prints do you say you have?'

'Four. Most of the film was unused, I swear. There were only four pics on it. You've got one print there, the three others are with the negatives, but not here. Look, I nearly threw them away! They're not interesting or anything.' I crossed my fingers beneath the cushion.

'The prints must be returned with the negatives, including any blanks that you may still hold. If we were to find you had held any back, we would be seriously displeased.' The threat in his voice when he said that would've chilled anyone's blood. It froze mine.

'Look,' I said pleadingly, and that wasn't acting, either, 'I really do want to give you the lot, get rid of it all, get the money, and then hear nothing more about it. I swear, I never wanted to get involved in any of this in the first place.'

That all rang beautifully true because it was. He was convinced at last. 'Very well. I'll tell the person I represent what you've said. I'll be in touch with you again. You'll speak to no one meantime.'

He stepped towards the front door, it swung open and he was gone, just a shadow on the basement steps. Despite being a large man, he moved almost silently, like a panther.

I got up by dint of pushing myself off the sofa with my hands. My legs were like jelly. I stumbled towards the bathroom and opened the door. Bonnie rushed out but I had no time for her. I staggered to the washbasin and threw up violently.

When I'd retched myself just about inside out, I went back to my living room and tried to think straight. I ought to let the cops know that someone had been in touch, but I was afraid to leave the flat. They knew I had no telephone here and they might be watching to see if I went to phone anywhere else – or went to see anyone else. I couldn't involve Daphne, and a public telephone box would be a dead giveaway. I'd have to wait until Ponytail got in touch again with details of the exchange arrangements.

Going to bed that night took some effort of will. To begin with, there was the picture in my head of Ponytail searching through the bedding. It wouldn't go away although I stripped pillowcase, sheet and duvet cover and put them to wash. Even if I'd been able to push away that image, the pain in both upper arms reminded me of my visitor. I showered, hoping that would make me feel better, and eventually crawled into bed around midnight. Bonnie hopped up on the duvet and settled down by my feet. I had discovered that Bonnie liked sleeping with people. I suppose it was because her original owner had been living rough.

In my bedroom under the pavement, sometimes I could hear feet walking overhead. Mostly it was a silent little cubbyhole, at times uncomfortably tomblike. Although there was a ventilation grille in the door to prevent my suffocating, I always propped the door open. I just didn't like being shut in there.

Perhaps Bonnie and I were both exhausted by the day's turn of events. At any rate, we both fell asleep.

I was awoken by a whining in my ear and opened my eyes to realise Bonnie was on the pillow, standing over me. She licked my face.

I sat up, startled and confused, wondering if this was a dream or, if not, what on earth was happening. Above my head, feet stamped back and forth. There was the noise of a powerful motor, something like a pump. Lights flashed across the overhead glass circle like the strobe lights in a disco. Voices were shouting and behind it all was an eerie trickling noise like running water.

Before I had time to work it out, someone began to thump furiously on the front door. The bell jangled. Bonnie jumped off the bed and landed with a curious splashing sound. I swung my feet out and yelled, 'Ugh!'

I had put them down, not on the carpet, but in a couple of inches of icy water.

The hammering on the door increased. As I ran out into the living room, splashing through more water, I heard a man shout, 'We'll have to break the window.'

'No!' I shouted back. 'I'm awake! Wait!'

I unlocked the front door and pulled it open. It flew inwards, propelled by a build-up of water on the further side. I lost my footing and fell back, landing on my backside in an icy cold wet mess.

A torch flashed over me and a large figure in yellow oilskins hauled me to my feet.

'Burst watermain, miss!' he bellowed. 'Emergency

evacuation. Get some clothes on, grab any valuables and get out of here – right away! Don't switch on any electricity.'

I splashed back to my bedroom, ankle-deep now in the flood. Luckily my jeans and sweater were on a chair, high and dry, but my boots, which I'd left on the floor, were filled with water. I grabbed my only valuable, Grandma Varady's gold locket, together with my purse and the envelope which held my birth certificate and the only photos of my family I had left, and stuffed them into my jacket. Then I waded out into the living room.

They'd set up emergency lighting outside and it beamed down into the room. In it, I could see a lake all around me, with furniture sticking up like islands. But all I could see of Bonnie in the rising water level was her head, with wavelets lapping at it. Her eyes looked up at me in bewilderment, asking whether she was supposed to swim for it now. I snatched her up and, with soaked dog under one arm and waterlogged boots in my other hand, sploshed my way back to the front door. As I did, Bonnie's tin dish floated past. I scooped that up, too.

The fireman had come back. He was waiting by the door and seized my arm. I was propelled through the mini swimming-pool which my basement had become, up the steps to street level, and found myself in the full glare of the temporary lights.

It was all go up there. There was a fire engine and another vehicle. A huge hose snaked across the pavement. People were working feverishly everywhere I could see. The tiny spring we'd inspected earlier had burst its corsets, flooding first the pavement and then, as drains proved unequal to the task, pouring down basement steps to gather at the bottom in lakes which had forced their way under my front door and those of my immediate basement neighbours.

Daphne's door opened and she scurried down the steps. She wore her usual jogging pants and sweater but in addition gumboots, a raincoat and a sou'wester. She was better equipped than I was. In her arms she held a large tin box.

'Oh, Fran dear!' she wailed. 'They say we've got to go to the church hall. I don't know why we can't stay in my place – that's not threatened.'

'The electrics, ma'am!' called the nearest yellow oilskin.

I realised that there were several police cars parked nearby. An officer appeared to escort us to one of them and we sped away through the night.

A group of us, about fifteen souls in all, inhabitants of the affected properties, huddled round a pair of portable Calor Gas stoves in St Agatha's hall. Bonnie, having shaken herself fairly dry, had taken the best place in front of one fire and curled up.

We basement dwellers had rescued a peculiar mix of valuables. One man had brought out an oil-painting. There was a crop of video recorders and home computer terminals, two guitars, a porcelain rococo clock and a cat, yowling miserably in a travelling cage. Bonnie had shown brief curiosity in that, but as it was safely locked away and couldn't be chased, lost interest. Otherwise, we looked typical refugees. We'd been handed blankets and mugs of tea by two stalwart ladies who'd appeared from somewhere. They were in the best of spirits. One said she was the vicar's wife. The other one informed us she was Brown Owl. They were obviously friends and lived for this kind of occasion.

At first, we, being British, affected an equal jollity, showing the spirit of the Blitz and so on, though we stopped short of the Vera Lynn songs. But it didn't last. Before long, we put our heads together and began to grumble about the water board, the incompetence of the council, the level of council tax, and those of us from basement properties, about where on earth we were supposed to go to, when the water was pumped out.

Clearly, none of the basements would be habitable. Carpets and furniture would be ruined. Electrical wiring would have to be checked. Insurance companies would have to be contacted. It would take weeks for the last dampness to evaporate, encroaching mould would need to be cleaned away, and then the business of redecoration would start.

A computer buff was sure he'd lost all his work. His floppy disks had got wet and, ohmigod, he didn't dare imagine what had happened to his hard-drive. Someone else had only just finished painting and decorating.

'And a week before Christmas!' groaned yet another.

A young woman burst into tears and declared she'd lost all the Christmas presents for sure. They'd been piled up in a corner. Everyone else turned to comforting her.

I brooded alone. I hadn't lost any Christmas presents because to date, I hadn't bought any and no one had sent me any, either. But it did seem likely I'd lost all my few possessions and worse, was left with nowhere to go. I had no family and no money for hotels.

Daphne, divining what was in my mind, tapped my arm and whispered, 'Don't worry, Fran. We'll be able to go back to my house once they've checked the wiring is safe. With the steps, the water couldn't rise to the level of my door.'

I hoped that was true.

'You can stay with me until the basement is fit to live in again,' she went on.

I thanked her, but said that wasn't on. 'It could be months,' I pointed out. 'I couldn't doss at your place for so long. It wouldn't be fair. There's Bonnie. Anyway, what about your nephews?'

'Oh, blow my nephews!' said Daphne.

But I couldn't stay with her for that length of time. Apart from all the other considerations, the flood had thrown a major spanner in Foxley's plans. When Ponytail came back, if he did, he'd find the flat empty and locked up.

'I'll go down the housing department in the morning,' I said, 'and ask for emergency accommodation. They can't refuse me, surely.'

They mightn't refuse, but they'd stick me in some God-awful hole of a place for sure. And what about Bonnie? Few places accepted animals.

'I might ask you to look after Bonnie for a bit, if you would,' I ventured.

'You listen to me, Fran!' said Daphne firmly. 'We're only days away from Christmas and I won't hear of your turning to the council at a time like this. I have a four-bedroomed house and I insist you stay with me – at least until New Year. Then we'll talk it over. In any case, I'll look after the little dog. She's no problem.'

Bonnie, in front of the gas stove, twitched her ears.

'We won't be able to use the tap water,' said a man gloomily. 'It'll be contaminated. They'll bring one of those water tankers round and we'll have to fill plastic containers.'

'I drink a lot of bottled water, anyway,' Daphne said. 'At least I've got a supply of that in.'

'Shops round here will soon run out of that,' said Jeremiah.

It was four in the morning. I pulled my blanket round my ears and wondered how my boots were drying. One of the stalwart ladies had stood them upside down on newspaper to drain, near to the fire. My co-refugees kept giving them mistrustful looks.

'The freezers will have shorted out!' screeched the young woman who'd lost her Christmas gifts. 'The turkey will be ruined!'

They all began again to talk about insurance. I didn't have that, either. That was to say, I supposed Daphne's house insurance took account of the building, but my personal possessions, well, that was another matter. Not that what I had was worth insuring. But that meant that, by Sod's law, I had neither the goods nor a cheque on its way in the post. The less you have, the more you have to lose at a time like this. I tried that line of argument out on the computer buff, but he didn't take the point at all. 'A year's work!' he moaned repeatedly.

I left him alone with his misery.

Daphne and I had steeled ourselves to finding a mess, when we returned home just before ten, but neither of us had anticipated the level of destruction in the basement flat. The water, before they'd pumped it out, had reached a level of some forty centimetres. A tidemark round the walls confirmed it. The old rep sofa had soaked it up like a sponge and would have to be thrown out. The telly would probably never work again. It hadn't worked well before. The pine coffee table might be salvaged. The carpet was ruined. Both bathroom and kitchen tiles had lifted. Worst of all, sewage had contaminated the water and the place stank. Bonnie picked her way fastidiously across the wreckage and returned with the bloated body of a dead mouse which she deposited at our feet.

'Come on!' said Daphne briskly. 'We'll move everything we can upstairs.'

It took us the rest of the morning, carrying the heavier items between us, up my steps, Daphne's steps and down her hall to the utility room at the back where we stacked them up. Some things we couldn't move, like the bed and the cooker, so they had to be left. The water tanker had turned up and so I also hauled plastic jerry cans back to the house to stock up. My arms, thanks to Ponytail's embrace, had ached before. Now the muscles shrieked protest at every movement. So busy were we, it wasn't until Daphne spoke of making something for lunch that I realised I'd quite forgotten about Ganesh and that I was supposed to have been at the shop. I went round to explain.

'I heard about it,' he said. 'It was on local radio, breakfast-time, with the traffic news. Motorists to avoid your street. I wondered if you'd been affected and when you didn't come in, I realised you must be. I'm really sorry. I was going to pop round later to see you.'

'You bet I'm affected,' I said. 'Flooded out and homeless again.'

He frowned. 'You can stay here until Hari gets back.'

'No, I can't. One of your family might turn up and find me and there'd be hell to pay. Daphne will give me a bed, at least until after Christmas.'

The bell jangled and Hitch came into the shop. He looked cheerful. 'Hullo, darling!' he hailed me. 'I hoped I'd find you here. I've been down your street and I saw your place was one of the ones flooded out. Here, you take my card and give it to the old girl who owns the house.' He thrust one of his business cards at me. 'You tell her, when she's getting quotes for the insurance, to come to me. I can give her a very good price for fixing that flat up.' He lowered his voice. 'And if you was to fancy lilac paint for the walls, I've got a job lot of that.'

I took the card without comment.

'Gan,' I asked, 'I need to use the phone up in the flat, OK?'

I left him with Hitch and ran upstairs. My luck continued out. I couldn't contact Foxley, Harford or even Parry at the nick. They passed me to someone I'd never heard of, called Murphy, and I had to tell him that Grice had been in contact.

'Himself or one of his boys?' asked Murphy, not sounding particularly interested.

I explained and he said, 'Fine, I'll tell the super. Let us know when he gets back to you.'

Then he hung up on me. I glared at the phone. For two pins, I'd have rung again and called the whole thing off. Then I remembered I couldn't.

Hitch had left when I returned to the shop. I told Ganesh I hoped to be into work the next day as normal, but he said if I needed to mop out the flat, he could manage. We left it at that.

I dropped Hitch's card in the waste bin on my way out.

I arrived back at the house in time to meet Daphne, who was just taking Bonnie out for a walk. An old leather dress belt in sky blue was looped round Bonnie's collar as a lead. 'Better than a bit of string, anyway,' said Daphne, setting off down the street.

I let myself in, went out into the kitchen and was just about to make coffee, when the doorbell rang. I froze. Had Ponytail tracked me down already? I crept into the front room and peered out the window. I was afforded the fat rear view of one of the Knowles brothers. I had just decided to let him stew out there, when he turned and saw me.

'Open the door!' he shouted. It was Charlie.

I opened up and he stormed in, passing me rudely and marching through to the back sitting room.

'Where is my aunt?' he demanded.

'Tied to the nearest railway line,' I said wearily. 'She's gone out.'

He huffed a bit, then made up his mind. 'Then we have time for a little talk.'

'I've nothing,' I said, 'to say to you.'

'Dare say not! Useless trying to justify yourself!' He was marching up and down Daphne's sitting room now, preparing to hold forth at length. 'But I've got a few things to say to you.'

'You're not going to blame me for the flood, are you?' I asked cheerfully, not because that was how I felt, but because I wanted to annoy him.

'This is not an occasion for levity,' he retorted. He had fetched up before the fireplace and stood there on his stubby legs, with his hands behind his back and his brogued feet planted apart.

'You're telling me,' I returned. 'That was my home.'

'No,' he said. 'It was, is still, part of Aunt Daphne's home. You were merely the tenant. Where is the other girl? The one with the dog? You had no right to sublet.'

'She was a friend staying a day or two and she left before all this happened.'

Charlie made his way to an armchair where he plumped himself down, his hands on his knees. 'And when will you be leaving?'

I took the opposite chair and braced myself for the outburst which must follow my reply. 'After Christmas. Daphne has asked me to stay here until then.'

I had been expecting Charles to rage, but instead he looked triumphant. He leaned forward and hissed, 'Staying here, indeed? I knew it! You just listen to me, young woman! I saw this coming, you know. So did my brother. We knew you were trying to work your way into our aunt's confidence. You think you've managed pretty well, eh? Well, it hasn't gone unremarked. We know what's what.' Here Charlie tapped the side of his pudgy nose. 'Don't count your chickens, that's all I have to say to you. We'll have you out of here before you can say knife!' He slapped his knees and sat back, looking pleased with himself.

I hit back by leaning forward myself and hissing back, 'Yes, and I know what's what, too! You're trying to gyp Daphne out of this house. You may be interested to know that I've already mentioned my concerns to a police officer I happen to know.'

Charlie collapsed in his seat as if I'd reached across and felled him with an uppercut. His eyes bulged, his face turned purple and I began to be seriously alarmed. Just when I was thinking that, revolting though the idea was, I might have to go over there and loosen his tie and unbutton his shirt collar (actions which he'd no doubt misconstrue), he found his voice, pitched low and full of real hate. The words hung in the air between us, each issuing distinct on a puff of breath.

'You-go-too-far!'

'Just remember,' I said, 'I'm on to your little game.' And I imitated his earlier gesture, tapping my nose.

Charles rose to his feet, straightened his jacket and tugged at his cuffs. 'You will be very sorry for all this. I shall come back later when I hope to find my aunt at home and have some private conversation with her. Don't make yourself too comfortable and don't trouble to see me out. I can find my way.'

I let him go. After a moment or two, it did occur to me that it was taking him a long time to walk down the hall, but just as I was about to go and investigate, the front door slammed. I went to look out the window and saw him marching away along the pavement. If I hadn't been so preoccupied with other matters, I'd have worried about him more.

Chapter Sixteen

The following couple of days passed uneventfully. Normally, that would be a plus. In this case, it meant that Ponytail hadn't contacted me with the reply to my offer to meet Grice. Uncertainty heightened my nervous state to the point where I jumped out of my skin at every ring of the doorbell or phone, every time a customer walked into the shop, every time a car slowed by me as I walked along the pavement. I took to hugging the buildings, so that it would be more difficult for someone to bundle me into a vehicle. I scurried home to Daphne's at the end of the day and, apart from walking Bonnie round the block at top speed last thing at night, didn't put my nose out of the door till morning.

A person can only go on like that for so long without it becoming noticeable.

'Are you all right, Fran?' asked Daphne. 'I know you're upset about the flat, but even so, you don't seem your usual bright self.'

'Winter blues,' I told her.

Ganesh, too, had noticed my jumpiness. 'What's going on?' he asked.

'Nothing,' I told him, but he didn't believe it.

'All I can say is, I hope you haven't done something stupid,

Fran. This hasn't got anything to do with that whizz-kid inspector, has it?'

'You know what I think of Harford,' I told him.

He snorted. 'I know what you thought of him when you first met him. It strikes me you might be changing your mind about him.'

I told him that was rubbish.

All the same, I felt a pang of disappointment when, Daphne having told me at breakfast-time the following morning the police were on the phone for me, I picked up the receiver to hear Parry's unmistakable tones. I did think Harford might have rung himself.

'Hi, Wayne!' I greeted him, just to let him know that his secret was out.

He answered grumpily, asking if I had anything further to report.

Whispering furtively into the receiver, I told him no more contact had been made and I was still awaiting confirmation of arrangements. I felt perfectly ridiculous saying things like this, as if I'd escaped from a spy thriller.

'You let us know what they are, straight away!' he ordered.

I needed to explain the call to Daphne. I put my head round her door and said, 'They haven't got any lead on my break-in yet. They don't suppose they will.' I didn't like telling her fibs.

'It all seems rather less important now than the flood,' said Daphne. 'But it was nice of them to ring and let you know their progress, or lack of it.'

She didn't know the half of it, that was the trouble. I wrestled with my conscience for the rest of the day. What would happen if Ponytail turned up on my landlady's doorstep? Poor Daphne would be totally unprepared. But ignorance was probably better in her case. Safer, certainly. I just hoped he'd contact me some other way.

That night, as we sat in her kitchen over a bottle of wine, I ventured, 'Have you had any callers today?'

She sighed. 'Only the boys. I wasn't going to tell you because I know you don't get along with them. I must confess,' went on Daphne, lowering her tone as one about to confide a startling secret, 'I am beginning to find them rather tiresome myself. I always found them unnecessarily fussy. But I believed – still believe – their hearts are in the right place. And they are, you see, my only family left.'

Who needs families? I thought, not for the first time, although mine hadn't been like that and I still missed Dad and Grandma. It was getting late. I said good night and went up to bed.

Bonnie bounced ahead of me. I had put an old blanket over the end of the bed to save the counterpane from dog hairs. An attempt to get Bonnie to sleep in a basket which Daphne had unearthed from somewhere, had proved doomed. Bonnie remained firmly convinced that we all slept together in a heap.

It must have been around three in the morning when she woke me, licking at my face and whining as she'd done on the night of the flood.

I sat up, bewildered for the moment, and thinking myself back in the flat. It was pitch dark in the bedroom. Daphne believed in thick lined curtains for winter. Bonnie slid off the bed, landed with a muffled bump on the carpet, and ran to the door where she whined again.

I thought, damn it, she wants to go out. She'd never done this to me before. Her late evening walk usually enabled her to last out till morning. I got out of bed, pulled on the old dressing gown my landlady had lent me, opened the door and made for the stairs.

I didn't want to disturb Daphne and hesitated to put on the light. Out here on the landing, streetlighting shone through an uncurtained window. I scooped up Bonnie and began to make my way downstairs with her tucked under my arm, the other hand clinging to the banister in case I lost my footing. Halfway down she began to struggle.

'Stop that!' I ordered her quietly. But she whined and then growled.

At the same moment, I heard a slight noise from the hall below. Immediately I clamped my hand over her muzzle and froze where I was on the stair. Oh my God, I thought. It's Ponytail! He's let himself in just as he did at the flat.

I didn't want to face the man but even less did I want Daphne to come face to face with him. I made my way down the remaining stairs as quickly as I could, Bonnie squirming beneath my arm.

The intruder had moved from the hall and was in the drawing room at the front of the house. More streetlight falling through the transom above the front door let me glimpse the erratic beam of a torch which was being flashed around in there. By now, I'd got a grip of my nerves and my brain was functioning better, too. If it was Ponytail, surely he didn't intend to search this large house, belonging to someone who had no connection with Coverdale, on the off chance I'd hidden the negatives here? I had told him I was prepared to hand them over. All he had to do was tell me where and when. Wasn't it more likely that, whoever was in that room, he was no more than a common thief?

I crept up to the door and cautiously stretched my hand through the gap, feeling for the light switch. He was on the further side of the room now. He stumbled over a piece of furniture and I heard a muffled 'Blast!' That wasn't Ponytail.

I switched on the light and dropped Bonnie to the floor.

Then everything happened at once. Bonnie rushed across the floor, barking. The burglar let out a high-pitched shriek, stumbled back and fell over, bringing down a little table over which he'd been bending. It was one on which Daphne kept a display of small silver antique items – spoons, salt dishes, pillboxes, that sort of thing. All these items spilled from the table as it crashed to the carpet, and rolled away in all directions. The burglar had become tangled up in the table legs and flailed about on the floor like an upturned tortoise. If you've never kept a tortoise, I can tell you that, once turned upside down, they can't get the right way up again, and lie there with all four legs working uselessly. Our intruder was, I was now able to see, somewhat tortoise-like in shape; round of body and short of leg. He was wearing dark pants and sweater and a ski-mask over his head. This round woollen head, with just two eyes showing, enhanced the tortoise impression.

Bonnie wriggled through the obstacle and grabbed the burglar's trouser cuff in her strong little jaws. She began to worry it, growling ferociously. I could see she was having the time of her life.

'Let go, you wretched brute!' came in a howl from the ski-mask. He struck out at Bonnie with his torch.

'Don't you hit my dog!' I shouted. I darted across and snatched the torch from him as he waved it wildly in the air. He was trying to kick out his snared leg and shake Bonnie off. No chance.

'Fran! What's going on?'

Daphne had appeared in the doorway holding a walking stick in businesslike fashion.

'Call the police, Daphne!' I gasped. 'Before he shakes Bonnie off!'

'No!' yelled the ski-mask frantically. 'Don't, I can explain!'

There was something familiar about that voice. Daphne and I must have recognised it at the same time. She put down the walking stick and I pulled Bonnie away.

Released, the intruder sat up and began to disentangle himself from the table legs. I reached over and pulled off the ski-mask.

'Bertie!' exclaimed Daphne. 'What on earth do you think you're doing?'

'If you weren't so obstinate, Aunt Daphne,' said Bertie a little later, 'Charles and I wouldn't have to resort to desperate measures.'

We had righted the table, picked up the silver objects and retired to Daphne's kitchen, the centre of operations in this house. Bertie sat on a wooden chair, his ski-mask lying on the table. His exertions, and being imprisoned in a woollen hood, had left his face very red and sweaty and his thinning hair ruffled. He was clearly conscious of the ridiculous figure he cut in his black polo-neck sweater and new-looking black jeans. Had he gone out and bought these items of clothing specially for tonight's expedition? No doubt he'd decided that was what house-breakers wore. Also on the table lay a dark blue canvas shopping bag.

'I don't know what you're talking about,' said Daphne. 'And how did you get in, Bertram?'

He looked sullen, crossed and uncrossed his short legs, and confessed, 'Charles took the spare key from the hook in the kitchen when he called round the other day. You weren't here.' His small angry eyes fixed on me. 'She was!' He pointed a stubby finger.

'I thought he took his time letting himself out,' I said. 'I should have escorted him to the door. Why did he send you? Why didn't he come back himself instead of sending you in, all togged up like The Shadow?'

'I don't owe you any explanations,' snarled Bertie.

'You owe me several!' Daphne told him. 'I hardly know where to start. Why did Charles take the key? Why have you embarked on this ridiculous escapade? If I, and not Fran, had heard you and come downstairs, I'd have been frightened out of my skin!'

'But I didn't mean you to hear me!' protested Bertie. 'For crying out loud, I didn't know she'd brought a blasted dog with her. It wasn't here when Charles came the other day. We thought that other girl, the one staying with her – ' the finger jabbed at me again – 'we thought she'd taken the dog away with her.' Bertie smoothed his hands over his ruffled hair and attempted some of his former confidence. 'If we'd known about the dog, we should have thought of something else.'

'I think,' said Daphne, 'that you've both taken leave of your senses.'

'I can explain, Auntie,' said Bertie. 'If you'll let me. But I don't choose to do it in front of that girl.'

'I hardly think,' said his aunt icily, 'you are in a position to make conditions. You've given Fran a terrible shock. You owe her an explanation as much as you owe me one.'

'Well, all right.' He folded his short arms awkwardly over the polo sweater. 'Charles and I have repeatedly told you that we think this house quite unsuitable for a lady of your mature years, living alone. Not only is there the responsibility, there is the security aspect. The recent and regrettable flood has, we hope, brought home to you the extent of the responsibility a house of this size carries with it. We wanted to underline the security aspect, or lack of it. She – ' finger jab – 'suffered a break-in, or an attempted one, at the basement flat. It gave us the idea to stage one here, in the house proper. All we thought we'd do was break in, just the one of us. We cut cards to decide who. My intention was simply to remove some small items. Then, in the morning, Charles and I would have called round openly, returned the articles missing, and pointed out to you how easily an intruder could get in.'

'An intruder wouldn't normally have a key,' I said.

'Bloody hell,' said Bertie. 'Neither my brother nor I are professional house-breakers. How on earth should we know how to get in without a key?'

'And what,' asked Daphne, 'if before you had called round, I had called the police?'

'Ah,' said Bertie, looking smug. 'Thought of that. We knew you didn't use this room much, never went in it from one end of the week to the other, unless we came. We knew about the collection on the table. I was just going to take one or two things. It was highly unlikely, even if you'd glanced in, that you'd have noticed.'

I'd been listening to all this with growing scepticism. 'Or,' I said now, 'Daphne might have been tempted to think I'd pocketed them – or I'd let in some accomplice to make off with the lot and anything else he could find. I can't see why you needed to bring that shopping bag if all you were going to remove was a couple of teaspoons.'

'Yes,' said Daphne grimly. 'You're sure this wasn't some ridiculous plan to get rid of poor Fran?'

'Look at the company she keeps!' squawked Bertie. 'When Charles called round the other day, he found her here alone. She could have gone through the place and taken every pocketable valuable you have, Auntie! We really think you're out of your mind to have invited her to stay here! I'm surprised the police haven't warned you. Or have they? For goodness' sake, surely you can see we've acted in your interest, Auntie?'

'This is enough!' Daphne ordered. 'I won't listen to another word of this rigmarole. Where is your brother?'

'He was waiting round the corner in the car,' said Bertie miserably. 'But he's probably pushed off home by now.'

'Hardly very loyal of him,' said Daphne. 'But I suppose I shouldn't expect Charles, or you either come to that, to be anything but cowards.'

Bertie opened his mouth to bluster but thought better of it.

'You had better go,' said his aunt. 'Kindly do not call round in the morning, or telephone, or even write. It will be a very long time before I want to see or hear anything of either of you again.'

Bertie got to his feet, picked up his ski-mask and shopping bag, and hovered uncertainly.

'Well?' Daphne asked.

'Look here,' he said. 'If Charles has left me here in the lurch – I mean, I've got no transport.'

'Walk!' Daphne and I said together.

Bonnie barked in support.

When Bertie had taken himself off, Daphne fetched the bottle of wine we'd started that evening and poured out a couple of glasses.

'I really can't believe it,' she said, taking a swig. 'The worst of it is, one doesn't know whether to laugh, cry or just scream in frustration. Whatever did he think he looked like? That silly sweater and the ski-mask! Oh, my God!' Here Daphne let out a great hoot of laughter.

I was rather taken with the image of them cutting cards to see who would take the risk. I was sorry it hadn't been Charlie

I'd trapped in the drawing room. That would've been sweet revenge for having been cornered in my basement bedroom by him.

Daphne sighed. 'I blame their upbringing. Their mother, Muriel, was a very odd woman. She dabbled in the occult.'

'Cripes,' I said, impressed.

Daphne waved her wine glass dismissively. 'She never took up anything properly. I always say, if you're going to do anything, do it thoroughly. Muriel fiddled round the edges, as it were, with things. Spiritualism, what she liked to call "white magic", oriental philosophies, whatever took her fancy of the moment. She was very beautiful, you know. That often means trouble. People forgive things of a beautiful person they wouldn't forgive in someone as plain as a pikestaff. She had a dreamy, slightly loopy way with her, which passed for charm. A lot of men fall for that kind of thing. My brother, Arnold, did. But then, he hadn't a jot of imagination himself. Believe me, Fran, I've met so many beautiful women who've been unstable. Arnold should've taken a grip on things, but he never did, of course. Putty in her hands.' Daphne snorted. 'You see, you can't blame the boys for turning out as they have. The atmosphere in that household was always unreal. I never had any looks and really, I thank God for it. I feel I've been spared so many complications.'

We'd finished the bottle. I added it to the pile of empties which had been growing in the corner since I'd arrived.

'I'll take these to the bottle-bank in the morning,' I said.

Daphne gazed at them as if she'd only just seen them. 'Goodness, I know the boys have been calling round rather more frequently than usual, but I never encourage them to linger. I mean, a glass or two is all I offer them. You and I, we couldn't have polished off all that lot, could we?'

I thought we probably could've. It was now almost five in the morning. It hardly seemed worthwhile going back to bed for me. Daphne went off but I stayed downstairs and fed myself and Bonnie on Weetabix. At six, I showered, dressed and walked round to the shop.

'Early bird!' observed Ganesh, staggering indoors with a load of newspapers which had been delivered to the pavement outside.

'Not much choice.' I told him about the events of the night.

'I warned you,' he said, 'those two wouldn't rest until they got you off the premises.'

'Daphne says their mother was a white witch, no kidding, Gan.'

He looked worried. 'You oughtn't to meddle with that sort of thing, Fran. You never know.'

'I might even take it up,' I returned. 'Nothing else seems to work for me.'

'Don't even joke about it!' he urged. He cleared his throat, preparing, I realised, to make a speech.

'You'll have to move out of there right after Christmas now,' he said, 'even if the council won't give you temporary accommodation. If you won't come here, you can sleep in Hari's lock-up, I suppose, until he gets back. But you can't stay with Daphne. Weird as the Knowles brothers are, and dodgy with it, they're Daphne's nephews and it's not for you to come between her and her family.'

'Even if they're trying to cheat her?'

'It's a family matter, Fran!' he said obstinately. 'She's not a fool. She knows what they're like. It's up to her whether she puts up with them or not.'

I supposed he was right. Daphne had to make her own

decision. Like Tig, she had to accept her family or reject them. Once she made up her mind, she had to live with the decision, same as anyone else.

Ponytail rang the shop at a little after eleven that morning. What with one thing and another, plus being tired after a disturbed night and the shop being busy, I'd even managed to forget about the wretched bloke for an hour or two.

When the phone rang, I answered, luckily. I afterwards wondered, if Gan had answered, whether Ponytail would just have hung up and tried again later.

'Miss Varady?' He didn't offer to identify himself but I recognised his voice at once. Even down the phone line, it gave me the shivers.

I croaked, 'Yes?'

'Tomorrow, twelve noon. At the statue of Nelson Mandela outside the Festival Hall cafeteria.'

He hung up.

'Who was that?' asked Ganesh.

'Nothing – someone wanting the chemist's. Gan, is it OK if I go upstairs and make a call from there?'

He said, 'Sure,' but gave me an old-fashioned look. He knew something was going on and I was keeping secrets. But one of Gan's many good points is that he doesn't badger me. If I don't choose to tell him, he lets it go. He knows it's one of the unspoken rules of our friendship.

I rang the police station and, thank goodness, got hold of Jason Harford. 'I need the negatives and snaps,' I said. 'Like as of now.' I repeated the message Ponytail had given me.

'I know the place,' Harford said. 'It's always pretty busy. Damn. There's umpteen ways in and out and it'll be difficult to stake it out. It's right by the Hungerford footbridge and look how many people go back and forth over that. We can't close it off. It'd be obvious and cause chaos.'

'He chose it for a reason, I suppose,' I said sourly. 'How you go about it is up to you. Just give me the negs. I give them to Grice and he gives me the money. That's all I'm contracted to do. Whatever else you're planning, make sure I'm clear, out of the way, before you do it. Grice has a very unpleasant minder.'

'Don't count on the money,' he said. 'What time are you leaving the shop today?'

I told him, probably at one. 'But don't come here, for God's sake. He might be watching.'

'Relax,' he urged. 'We've got it under control.'

All right for him to talk.

I walked out of the shop just before one feeling as if I were walking across red-hot coals. No cars lurked on the double yellow lines. The usual cross section of humanity surged past. A ragged, lunatic-looking old fellow, grasping a wad of badly printed leaflets, was trying to stop passers-by and press one of his scraps of paper on them.

'Bargain sale,' he urged in a piping voice. 'All quality goods. Fire-damaged stock.'

Most people hurried past. A few took a leaflet, perhaps to placate him, and dropped it to the pavement almost at once, turning the immediate surrounds into a litter-bug's dreamscape. A crisp wind blowing straight down the street picked them up and tossed them around, before bowling them off in all directions. They fluttered out into the road and were flattened by double-deckers. They fetched up in shop doorways. One had even been carried by an updraught clear up into the sky like a tiny kite.

'Here you are, dear!' He lurched at me, greasy old raincoat

flapping. His feet were wrapped round with plastic bags. Of a pair of trainers, all he had left were the soles, tied on to the wadded bags by string. His hair was long and unkempt. He might have been anything from just an old alkie to a lost soul condemned to care in the community. No wonder people scurried past.

I felt sorry for the poor old devil. He was probably being paid a pittance to stand out here for a couple of hours, kept going by the hope of getting enough out of it for a couple of cans of lager. I didn't want a bargain video recorder, 'fire damaged' being an euphemism, I suspected, for 'hot', but I hesitated.

He moved in front of me so I couldn't walk on. I cursed myself for the momentary weakness which had let him latch on to me. I knew from experience that people like him were often difficult to shake loose again.

'Go on, love,' he persisted, pushing his face into mine. Close to, he wasn't nearly so old nor so decrepit. His eyes met mine and sparkled with something which might have been intelligence or just malice. He pushed a couple of leaflets into my hand. 'Buy yourself something nice. Dead cheap!'

I said, 'Yeah, why not?' and thrust the leaflets into my pocket.

I didn't take them out again until I was safe indoors. I wasn't surprised to find I had not two leaflets, but one leaflet and a brown paper envelope.

I opened the envelope and shook out on to Daphne's kitchen table a strip of negs and four prints I recognised as old friends.

The police had kept their side of the deal. Now I had to keep mine.

Chapter Seventeen

Ganesh and I went out together to eat that evening. Given my guilty conscience, I wouldn't have chosen to go out with Gan that night of all nights. But he called round to the house just after eight to ask if I'd eaten and if not, whether I wanted to go out.

'We might have better luck this time,' he said. 'And not find a body lying around in your basement.'

I nearly told him he shouldn't count on that and the body might be mine – but he wouldn't have thought it funny and neither, come to that, did I.

'Is this another staff Christmas dinner?' I asked. No harm.

'No, it isn't,' he retorted. 'We can't take two staff outings! You'll have to pay your own way. Or I'll pay, if you like,' he added generously.

As it happened, Daphne had gone to see a friend and I was on my own and hadn't got round to making a sandwich – my idea of cooking dinner. So we went, having established that I'd pay my own whack. It was one thing to let the business pay, quite another to let Ganesh shell out. I don't mean because he's broke, but that's not the way our friendship works. He has lent me money in the past when I've been completely cleaned out or needed it urgently, but I've always paid him back. 'Neither a borrower nor a lender be,' as Mrs Worran used to say.

She was our neighbour when Dad and Grandma were alive. She belonged to some exclusive sect, so exclusive that if they were the only ones saved, Heaven must be a pretty empty place, just a few Mrs Worrans rattling around up there. She had a stock of such slogans, one for every occasion. They were uniformly negative. She also had a stock of badly printed tracts which she would post secretively through our door late at night, as if we didn't know they came from her. Once, at the age of ten, when I unfortunately fell off my bike into her privet hedge making a large hole, she shot out and told me that the way I was going, when the sheep were divided from the goats, I'd be in the wrong half of the draw for sure. When I was expelled from school, she was in her element. Even after Grandma died shortly after Dad, and I was left quite alone, Mrs Worran informed me by way of encouragement that she was sure I'd manage all right. 'The devil knows his own,' she said, which at the time I found rather obscure and never have quite worked out.

We left Bonnie shut in the kitchen. She took a dim view of this. We could hear her howling as we closed the front door. She probably added tonight's desertion to the list of things she had against Ganesh.

We ended up in a local burger bar where we both ordered the vegeburger. Ganesh is the vegetarian, not me, but somehow I'd gone off the idea of meat. It made me think of dead things. The vegeburger seemed to consist mainly of beans. On top of everything else, when I went to meet Grice the next day, I'd have wind. Not but what the very thought of going to meet Grice was enough to give anyone wind.

It gave me a chance to explain to Ganesh, however, that I

couldn't come to work the following morning. 'I'm sorry to let you down,' I said. 'But something's come up. It's just one of those things. Perhaps you can get Dilip to come in for a couple of hours.'

'You know,' said Ganesh, 'I don't interfere and I'm not about to start. But I want you to know that *I* know you're up to something and I just want you to be careful.'

'I'll be careful,' I promised. You bet I would.

'And you tell Harford,' he went on grimly, 'that if anything goes wrong with whatever it is, I'll be round to see him.'

'You've got a thing about Harford,' I said.

'I haven't. You have.'

'Rubbish!' I snapped through a mouthful of beans. 'You said the same thing about Parry. Really, Gan, you're turning into a real old matchmaker.' (I knew that would annoy him. That's why I said it.)

'I didn't say you were keen on Parry,' argued Ganesh. 'I said he was keen on you. And he is. So I was right. But you're not likely to fall for him, are you? Let's face it; he's gross. Harford's got education and prospects and is a good-looking bloke. Of course you're interested. But if it's led you into making silly decisions, it's not a good thing. That's all.'

I told him it was a good thing he'd finished his burger or I'd have shoved it down his throat.

The next morning turned out clear and bright, one of those winter days when the weather seems to have got it wrong, and spring is trying to get in early. The pale sunshine, the pleasant breeze, and the cheerful look on the faces of passers-by, all combined to mock me and the way I felt, which was like a woman on her way to the block. '*Tis a far, far better thing* — No, it wasn't. It was about the stupidest thing.

I began my long walk across the Hungerford Bridge shortly before twelve. Down below me on the Embankment I could see Cleopatra's Needle looking lonely and out of place, just like me up here really. The narrow walkway on the bridge was busy with people going in both directions. They slowed as they passed an old boy who was flying a kite from this vantage point. He was good at it. The kite, which was made of some silvery material, was way up high out over the water and he controlled it very niftily with what looked to me like a converted fishing reel. It shimmered around up there, dipping and diving, catching the eye of nearly everyone. Many stopped to take a second look, unsure whether it was a bird, a helicopter or – there's always one hopeful – a UFO. Then they saw the old man and knew it was a kite. I envied the kiteman his peace of mind as I walked on.

The river sparkled to my left and the view, if I'd been in the mood to admire it, was suffused with that pearly light which hangs over the Thames on days like this. The great dome of St Paul's, where the river sweeps round to the right, hung suspended above the buildings around it. Sometimes when I've seen it, I've really wished I could paint. I don't mean I aspire to being a Canaletto, just I'd like to be one of those hobby painters who can knock out a reasonable watercolour to hang on the wall and show off to their mates. But whenever I've tried, the result has looked like one of those expressive but out-of-sync efforts you see pinned up in infant schools. Even when I was in infant school, I couldn't get it right. I always got more paint on myself than the paper and in the end, they took the poster paints away and gave me crayons. I didn't like the crayons. They were too much like hard work.

To my right, the trains rumbled and clanked in and out of

Charing Cross Station, along the parallel rail bridge. I wished I was on one of the outward bound ones, going anywhere.

Ahead of me lay the South Bank complex, with its galleries, theatres and concert halls, its presence heralded by the line of fluttering blue and white flags along the riverside. I wondered briefly if I was ever going to make a career in the performing arts, or whether I'd no more hope of that than I had of painting in oils or flying a kite. I really did think I had more talent at acting than the other two. Everyone has a talent to do something, Grandma Varady used to say. It's finding it. (You see, Mrs Worran wasn't the only one with slogans. The difference was, Grandma's were intended to encourage you.) Finding this talent and making it work for you are two different things, however, as I've since discovered. Grandma's talent, she reckoned, was in making a very good strudel. She tried to teach me how to do it and, guess what, I couldn't do that, either. Flour and butter everywhere, stewed apple stuck to the pan, the air pungent with burned sugar. Result: a stick of pastry you could've knocked a hockey ball around with.

I wondered at greater length if I was even going to make the return journey back across the bridge this afternoon. In my pocket, the envelope with the negs was burning a hole. The Hungerford Bridge that morning seemed more like that bridge in Berlin where they used to exchange spies. I imagined finding a couple of heavies with long overcoats and trilby hats waiting for me on the other end. Come to think of it, that wasn't such a wild piece of imagination. God alone knew what I was going to find. Hopefully a well-organised snatch brigade from the Met. The problem was that in my experience, the police never seemed that well organised, more a case of trusting in the endearing British habit of muddling through. Grice, on the other hand, I was sure was organised to the nth degree. I began nervously to study the expanse of concrete promenades on the further side and the festival pier extending a long finger over the choppy khaki water. Was one of the strolling figures Grice?

In the angle where the walkway comes to an end and the flight of steps down to the bank starts, a young bloke was sitting on a grubby blanket, asking passers-by for change. No one gave him any. Even the tourists could tell he was fake. Probably they thought he was a professional beggar. I knew he was a cop who'd ousted the regular pitch-holder for the day. Cripes, I thought, is this amateur the best Foxley could come up with? I just hoped Grice wouldn't walk across this way and see him. Talk about dead giveaways. I don't know what betrays undercover coppers – the way they stand on their big flat feet or their haircuts perhaps? This one just didn't look hungry enough. But mostly, I think, I rumbled him because he hadn't got the voice right. Beggars repeat the same question of passers-by like a mantra, with dulled hope, resignation and not quite buried resentment. This guy sounded altogether too chirpy, as if he was selling flags for charity.

'You're rotten,' I muttered to him, as I passed.

'Sod off,' he managed to mutter back before I was out of earshot.

It was oddly comforting to know that, despite my present co-operation, nothing had really changed in my relationship with the rozzers.

I clattered down the steps. No going back now. There were always people around this large pedestrianised area, even in winter, especially on a fine day like today. I walked down the side of the Festival Hall to the cafeteria. Through its glass walls, I could see a few people having coffee. A young couple right by the door leaned across the table, gazing into one another's eyes. There was a whole world around me, living normal, peaceful lives. What had I done to be excluded from it?

Curiosity killed the cat, Fran, I told myself. You had to go and get that film printed up. You couldn't just have chucked it in the bin, could you?

The concreted area between the cafeteria and the rail bridge saw only a few visitors. I made my way to the larger-than-lifesize bronze head of Mandela on its plinth. No one stood by it and I felt a spurt of ridiculous optimism. Perhaps Grice wasn't going to show. Then I looked beyond it, up the short flight of steps to the higher level of walkway.

A burly figure stood up there, a man, with his back to me. He was leaning over the parapet and holding up a camera as if he were taking photographs of Waterloo Station's wonderful Victory Arch. The trouble was that from there he couldn't see it, only the topmost line of stonework, a couple of flags, and the legend 'Waterloo Station'. The rest was obscured by the grimy yellow brickwork of the rail bridge reaching down into Concert Hall Approach. Thoughts floated through my head in a discouragingly logical progression.

a) He was no photographer.

b) He was no tourist.

c) He might be an anorak obsessed with Victorian railway arches.

d) He was far more likely to be Grice.

As I neared, he turned and, pointing the camera down towards me, began taking snaps in my direction. He was prosperous in appearance, wearing a belted pale grey waterproof jacket and one of those little green felt Tyrolean hats. The angle he'd chosen allowed him to frame me in the viewfinder as I walked towards him. I heard the faint click as he pressed the button. He'd got a record of me, should he need it again. Nice thought.

He moved again, slipping rather incongruous shades on his nose, walking towards me, descending the flight of steps and pausing at the Mandela bronze. Slowly and deliberately he turned his body sideways on to me, apparently intent on getting a shot of Mandela from the best angle.

I had no doubt now this was Grice, who'd sussed out the area and taken up his position before I arrived. My heart sank to my boots. What did I do now? Walk up to him? It wouldn't do to look too familiar. I couldn't hail him by his name because I wasn't supposed to know it. In the end, I stopped by the plinth and stuck my hands in my pockets, as if I was waiting for someone.

Then someone else did turn up. Ponytail. My heart plummeted. I should have expected that he'd be on hand. Grice would hardly have come without his minder. He'd been close by near the top of the spiral stair which led down to Concert Hall Approach and, my eye distracted by the snapping camera, I hadn't seen him at first.

I was suddenly struck by an idea which I at first rejected and then decided wasn't so fantastic after all. Down that spiral stair, across the York Road, through the subway and Grice would be at Waterloo Station and the Eurostar Terminal. A few minutes' walk only. Was that what Grice had done? Come in on Eurostar, specifically to make this exchange? Having made it, he could just retrace his steps and get on the next fast service to the continent. It was so easy. I wondered if the cops had thought of it.

Ponytail moved to Grice's side and murmured something in his ear. Grice let the camera fall to hang from the strap round his neck. I swallowed with difficulty; my throat had clammed up. Where was Harford and his team? So far, all I'd seen was one phoney beggar back there on the bridge, nowhere near enough to be any use. He was presumably backup in case Grice took flight that way. I glanced round nervously, hoping Grice didn't think I was looking for help, just being prudent. The couple in the cafeteria had left their table and were coming out through the exit, hand in hand and still lovey-dovey. Grice was coming my way.

'Miss Varady?'

His voice was surprisingly pleasant. I'd been expecting a thug like Ponytail. But of course, Grice wasn't like that. Foxley had told me Grice was probably living a blameless life somewhere, masquerading as a respectable businessman, pillar of the community.

'You have something for me, I think,' he went on courteously.

I couldn't see his eyes through the shades. What I could see of his hair beneath the ridiculous hat looked reddish. He'd been at the bottle of colour again. He probably had one to match every photo in his selection of passports.

I fumbled for the envelope in my pocket and dragged it out. 'What about my money?' I forced myself to ask.

Grice glanced at Ponytail, who brought another envelope from his pocket. Grice held out his hand.

'I'd like to check the contents first, if I may?'

'Feel free,' I mumbled hoarsely, handing it over.

He opened it, riffled through its contents, held up the strip of negatives to the light, then looked at me. 'This is the lot? You're sure of that, are you?' His voice was no longer quite so pleasant.

'Yes,' I whispered, because it was a lie. I had removed the duplicate of the print I'd given Ponytail, otherwise there would have been one extra to the four I'd claimed existed.

Some tremor in my voice must have betrayed me. Between the brim of his hat and his shades, his broad forehead puckered into a frown. I felt his suspicion radiate in my direction. Fear made me speak up.

'Look,' I said, 'I don't know who you are and I don't care. They're just some blooming holiday snaps. He said you'd give me a grand.' I tried to sound both bolshie and dim. It must have worked.

The frown smoothed out. A slight smile touched his face. He turned to Ponytail. 'Give her—'

'Oy! You! I bloody know you! Where's my woman?'

Grice swore. Ponytail swung round, his hand moving inside his jacket. I goggled and nearly passed out.

At the top of the spiral stair, just climbed up from the street below, was a tall bearded figure in a plaid jacket and woolly hat. Jo Jo.

I had forgotten, in admiring the lay-out of this place as I walked over the bridge, just how close it also lay to the network of underpasses which offered shelter of a kind to the homeless. This was where Tig and Jo Jo had been reduced to sleeping, before desperation had sent Tig to me and consequently, back to the Midlands and the claustrophobic high-tension comforts of the Quayle household.

Jo Jo lurched forward, brandishing a clenched fist. 'I saw you talking with Tig! Where's she gone? What've you—'

Belatedly he realised he'd walked in on something he'd rather not be anywhere near. He broke off and turned to run back down the spiral stair. But a bunch of other guys were running up it, blocking it. Others had appeared round the side of the cafeteria from the direction of the river. The male half of the young lovers stopped cuddling his girl and shouted, 'Police! Stay where you are!'

Not bloody likely, as someone else said. I ran.

Jo Jo, unable to scuttle back down the stair to Concert Hall Approach, wheeled round and raced after me. We reached the corner of the cafeteria building neck and neck and made the turn right in unison. But Jo Jo wasn't interested in me any longer, only in escape. Jointly we negotiated the trestle tables set out for snackers, like a pair of runners in an obstacle race. After that, Jo Jo easily outstripped me. I could see him legging it ahead in great strides past the Queen Elizabeth Hall and Purcell Room. He reached the flight of steps leading down to the lower level and suddenly veered right between the blocks of concrete architecture towards the Museum of the Moving Image, making for the steps which led up on to Waterloo Bridge. From there, by turning right on the bridge and keeping going straight ahead, he'd be safe in the warren beneath the Bull Ring in no time. There were probably half-a-dozen blokes looking just like him in that general area.

I clattered down the steps and plunged on past the National Film Theatre. Beneath Waterloo Bridge, open-air second-hand bookstalls had been set up today. Long trestle tables barred my path. There were a lot of people there, sorting through the volumes. I dodged around them and thought I was clear when a dotty old girl with her nose in a book she'd just bought, stepped straight in front of me. I leaped to one side, slipped and crashed to the pavement.

The woman with the book yelled and dropped it. A couple of men by the bookstall left what they were doing and came running. I saw they were headed for me and didn't look friendly. They probably thought I was a fleeing mugger and had made a grab for the woman's bag, slung over her shoulder. I was about to be the subject of a citizen's arrest. A crowd began to form round me. I'd be lucky not to be duffed up as well.

I scrambled to my feet but before I could get away, a pair of hands grasped my shoulder. 'Leggo! I haven't done anything!' I squawked and hacked backwards at my captor's shins.

'It's me, Fran, it's me!' shouted Jason Harford's voice in my ear.

I froze and then, as his grip relaxed, turned. 'It's me,' he repeated breathlessly.

I was pretty out of breath too. I'd a stitch in my side and my chest ached as I dragged air in and out.

'Police!' Harford called to the two men. 'Under control. No problem.' People began to drift away, already deciding that whatever it was, they wanted no part of it. The mention of the word 'police' has that effect. Even the pair of gung-ho types keen to nab me seconds before, were deciding that, after all, they didn't want to be witnesses to whatever it might be.

'Grice . . .' I gasped, pointing a trembling finger over Harford's shoulder back the way we'd come.

'We've got him.'

'His minder, big guy with a pony—'

'We've got him too, don't worry. The only guy we haven't got is that loony in the woolly hat who came barging in. Who was *he*?' Harford asked indignantly.

'Nobody important. Just someone who thinks I did him a bad turn. Did you get Grice's camera?'

'His camera?' Harford scowled at me, not understanding.

'He took a picture of me. For God's sake, get the film out and destroy it! I've had enough trouble from bits of film left lying around!'

'Will do.' He grinned. 'Well done, Fran. Foxley will be pleased.'

I told him, rather impolitely, I didn't care whether Foxley was pleased or not. Never, but never again, would I agree to help out the cops. It was not my style. It was against all my principles.

'Do your own dirty work,' I said in one of my more printable phrases.

'You were always safe,' he said reproachfully. 'I said I'd look after you, Fran.' He put his hands on my shoulders again, but gently this time. 'And I will, you'll see.'

I am not good at handling this sort of occasion. I said, 'Oh, right . . .' and felt a fool. Fortunately, just then Parry turned up.

'Excuse me, sir!' he hailed Harford sarcastically. 'Can you come back to the control van? Mr Foxley would like a word.'

'I'll see you later,' Harford said hastily. He gave my shoulders a last squeeze and hurried away.

'Want a lift home, Fran?' asked Parry, when he'd gone.

I told him no thanks. I just wanted to get away from it all and be alone, like Greta Garbo.

'Going out with him, then, later, are you?' He jerked his head back to indicate the direction Jason Harford had gone in.

'Maybe,' I said.

'Watch yourself,' said Parry. 'He's got every WPC on the Force in a tizz. Still, he's a bright boy. He's going far, as they say.'

The depressed look which had accompanied these words was wiped from Parry's face as he added, 'You didn't half get a move on when you went belting like the clappers out of it back there. I thought you were going to break some record. They need you in the Olympics, they do.'

'Oh, go and arrest someone,' I said wearily.

* * *

He'd persisted in offering the ride home, 'in an unmarked car', until I eventually got through to him that he was wasting his time.

Instead I sat by the river for a while until my heartbeat had got back to normal and my legs were functioning again. Then I walked back, over Waterloo Bridge this time, cut through Villiers Street to The Strand and down into Charing Cross tube station. There was a lot I didn't understand, but it no longer mattered. I'd never even got my fingers on the envelope with the thousand in cash in it. That did rankle and I brooded darkly about it all the way home.

Bonnie was pleased to see me, jumping up and squeaking. I was pleased to see her, to be back in one piece, to have it all behind me. A distant rattle of typewriter keys pinpointed Daphne's location. The great masterpiece was being worked on again. Perhaps one day I'd get to read a bit of it.

'Only me, Daphne!' I called. A faint cry replied. The keys rattled on.

I went upstairs, stripped off and soaked in the bath. Feeling a lot better when I got out, I did my best to dress smartly (for me) though the best I could do was a repeat of the clothes I'd worn the night Coverdale had died. Hardly a good omen. To compensate, I applied the stub of lipstick Joleen had given me. Jason Harford had said he'd be round later.

I went down to the kitchen and was making a cup of tea when the phone rang. 'I'll get it!' I called out and went into the hall.

'Fran?' asked a female voice when I picked it up. 'It's Tig.'

I was surprised, though I'd wondered if she'd get in touch and let me know how things were going. I decided I wouldn't tell her I'd seen Jo Jo. It might lead to complicated explanations and anyway, she didn't need to know it. I told her Bonnie was fine, and asked her how things were.

'Mum's gone shopping,' she said. 'I had to wait till she'd gone out to call you. She gets suspicious if I use the phone.'

That didn't sound too good. 'How's your dad taking it?' I asked.

'Dad? He's gone.'

That threw me. 'Gone where?'

'Gone. Shoved off. He couldn't hack it, my being back and being "no longer his little girl" was his way of putting it. He's sleeping over at his office on a put-u-up.'

That was a turn up for the books. I hadn't anticipated that. Poor Sheila. She'd got her daughter back and lost her husband. 'Perhaps,' I said, 'he'll come back when he's got it sorted in his head. I expect your mum is upset about it, his taking off like that.'

'Not really,' said Tig. 'She just says we don't need him because we've got each other back again now. It's awful, Fran. She follows me round the house. She doesn't want me to go out. If I do, she wants to come with me. If she goes out, she wants me to go with her. I had a real barney with her earlier, because I wouldn't go to the supermarket. She's driving me nuts. I can't stand it. I'm going to have to leave again, Fran.'

'Give it time!' I urged. 'You've only just got there. You can't push off just before Christmas. It'd break your mum's heart. She'll calm down. Your dad will come back. He's bound to turn up for Christmas dinner. It's all been a shock for them. The strain's bound to show a bit.'

'Yeah,' said Tig. 'It's doing my head in for sure. But that's not what I'm phoning about. Look, Fran, I owe you. I know that. Even if it doesn't work out here, it's not your fault. You really tried. You did everything you said you'd do. If I screw up now, it's my problem. The thing is, there's something I wanted to tell you before, you know, before I left London, but I was scared to. I didn't want trouble. I still don't. But now I'm up here, away from it, it's not so bad and anyway, like I said, I owe you.'

'It's something I'm not going to want to hear, isn't it?' I said. The last fading beam of daylight moved away from the transom above the front door as I spoke.

'Yeah,' she said. 'You won't want to hear it, I reckon. But I couldn't be easy in my mind with you not knowing.'

So she told me, as I stood there in the darkening hallway, with Bonnie sitting at my feet and Daphne tapping away at her old upright in the background.

Chapter Eighteen

Jason Harford arrived just before seven. He'd changed out of the suit and was back in chinos with a casual shirt and leather jacket. He stood on Daphne's doorstep in the lamplight, with his hands in his pockets, smiling at me.

'You look nice,' he said. It must have been Joleen's lipstick.

I told him he looked pretty good himself, which was true.

'So, can I come in?'

'Sure.' I stood aside to let him pass. He hesitated in the doorway and leaned forward as if he was going to kiss me, but I slipped past him to close the door.

'No landlady?' he asked glancing around.

'Gone to see a friend, be back later.'

He wandered down the hall, studying the pictures and knick-knacks. 'It's been a great day,' he said over his shoulder. 'You've no idea how much Foxley's wanted to nail Grice. Grice is denying ordering anyone to kill Coverdale, of course. He says his "former associate", as he puts it, panicked and stuck the poor guy. After that, says Grice, he gave the killer his marching orders and doesn't know, surprise, surprise, where to find him now. Still, we've got Grice himself and he'll be angling soon to cut a deal. It's looking good. The super's as pleased as punch. I told you he's normally a sour old git. Right now, he's dancing on the ceiling.'

'Got it sewn up, then,' I said. 'Congrats.' I hadn't meant to sound frosty, but I did.

'Don't get me wrong. I don't mean anyone's going to make any deals with Grice,' he went on hastily, 'but it's been made clear it's in his interest to co-operate. He knows he's going to gaol, but he doesn't want to stay there any longer than he has to. The other guy, the one with the ponytail, has a record of violent offences and my guess is, he'll talk if Grice doesn't. There's a way to go yet but we'll get there.'

'No honour among thieves,' I said.

'Lord, no!' Harford looked quite shocked. 'Every villain I've ever come across would double-cross his own grandma.' He tapped the Victorian barometer, something Daphne had told me you shouldn't do. It upset it. 'You should listen to them volunteer to squeal when the heat's turned up.' He pointed to the barometer. 'Just like this. Guaranteed to be affected by current conditions.'

I wondered just how many villains he had met. His meteoric rise through the ranks to date, which niggled Parry so much, didn't seem to me the best way to build up a close acquaintance with the criminal world. In textbooks, maybe. In the flesh, less so.

Now, Parry, who had met hundreds of crooks in his day, would probably have said many villains were good family men, crime being their gainful employment, as they'd see it, and their families being chips off the old block. We're talking the professionals, of course, and not the bash-old-ladies brigade whom most of the regular type would abhor.

'That sort,' Parry had told me once, 'and the pervs who meddle with little kids or murder 'em you wouldn't believe how difficult it is to protect 'em from the other prisoners, once they get inside.'

It also crossed my mind, as I listened to my companion's optimistic forecast, that Parry would also have shown less confidence in the judicial system's ability to put Grice away. Perhaps Harford was showing a little lack of experience there, too.

If so, it wasn't the moment to suggest it to him. He'd abandoned the barometer. 'Time to go out and celebrate. I thought we might try the Italian place again. The food's good and this time, we might manage to talk.' He grinned.

'We need to talk,' I said. 'But perhaps we ought to do it here before we go out.'

He raised his eyebrows.

'You said,' I reminded him, 'that you'd explain to me why Grice was so anxious to get the negs back.'

'Oh, that, sure. I owe you the full story. You're right. We don't want to be talking shop over the spaghetti.'

'That's right,' I said. 'Come in the kitchen.'

At some point during the day Daphne had cracked open another bottle. It stood on the shelf with the cork sticking out at an angle. It was a Chilean Cabernet Sauvignon. I was going to have to keep my eye on Daphne. Among the bottles I'd taken to the bottle bank earlier, had been wines from France, Germany, Australia, Bulgaria and California. Daphne was making a boozer's world tour. I poured Jason a glass and half a glass for me and we settled down, either side of the big pine table. He picked up his glass and held it up in salute. I gestured towards mine but didn't pick it up.

'This is a nice kitchen,' Harford said approvingly. 'Mind you, this is a bloody good house. I thought so when I first came here – and met you. I'm not surprised the two old boys are after it. Any more trouble with them, by the way?'

'I think,' I said, 'they've been dealt with for the time being.'

'That's all right, then. I told you not to worry.' He leaned on the table. 'I remember that evening very clearly, when I first came here. I've thought about it a lot.'

'You looked at me,' I said, 'as if I'd been scraped up out of a blocked drain.'

'I was scared of you,' he said. 'You looked so tough and assured. It wasn't long, of course, before I rumbled your true nature.' He raised his glass again.

'My true nature,' I told him, 'is to be awkward, obstinate and bloody-minded. Nor am I about to forget that I was treated by your lot in all this as though I were expendable.'

'Hey!' he protested. 'That's not true! I admit we weren't as efficient as we might have been, all the time, but no one wanted *you* harmed. You know *I* didn't, don't you?'

'I don't suppose any of you wanted me harmed,' I said. 'Because without me, you wouldn't have got your hands on Grice.'

He pushed the glass aside. 'We're grateful, all right? But we were reasonably confident that, sooner or later, we'd find Grice.'

No, you weren't, I thought, but he could safely claim so now.

'It might have been a *lot* later, mind you,' he was saying, 'and we were bracing ourselves for that. But, you know, in the end a man like that has to break cover. Damn it, Fran, what's the use of the money if he can't spend it and live life to the full?'

'They never found Lord Lucan,' I pointed out. 'And when it came to tracking down Grice, poor Coverdale did an awful lot better than you. He did find the man.'

'And once he'd done it, he should have come straight to us!' Harford was getting nettled at all this criticism. 'If he had, he'd be alive today. And look here, Fran, we're saddled with always having to go through official channels. Coverdale got his information by God knows what means not open to us!'

I decided I'd made my point and could let it go. 'So where was Grice all the time? Where were the snaps taken?' I asked.

Harford's irritation was replaced by a smug grin. 'Cuba!' he said and laughed at my expression. 'On the level. I can see you think it'd be the last place on earth, but you've got to update your ideas. The leisure industry shifts huge sums of money around the world. In and out of different currencies, developing one playground for the rich after another. Grice may have first thought of Florida as a place to invest his money, but the Americans are canny. They don't like unknowns who turn up with huge sums to invest and no track record. They suspect organised crime and would've rumbled Grice straight away.

'So Grice looked around and saw Cuba. They desperately need hard currency. Cuba's broke but ambitious, keen to develop its tourist industry. The country's so run down it's having to start from scratch but it's making up for lost time. It's already getting to be the in place to holiday. The jet set are going out there for sun and sea. Everywhere else is getting overrun with plebs and package tours. If you've got a lot of money and you want to spend some of it in Cuba, they'll be delighted to see you and prepared to make sure you have the holiday of a lifetime. So when Grice turned up under a different identity, and proposed a joint venture in the tourist market for which he'd put up the bulk of the finance, they didn't ask too many questions of him. He was what they'd been waiting for. Officially, capitalism is still out of favour. But Grice knew how to present his package. He claimed to be a wealthy

European socialist. There are several French and Italian communist millionaires. The Cubans bought that, or pretended to. He was wined and dined, lodged in a government guest house – which was where Coverdale ran him to earth and, at a guess, bribed a servant to take those snaps.'

'And was about to tell the world where Grice was doing business.' I frowned. 'It was risky for Coverdale, but I'd have thought Cuba a high-risk investment for Grice.'

Harford spread his hands. 'Hey, before the revolution, fortunes were made in Havana out of hotels, casinos, nightclubs . . . Some pretty shady operators ran much of it then. Grice meant to run it this time round. The Cubans probably hoped his involvement meant otherwise; they want tourists but not the bad old days back again. Grice played that up. He presented himself as a financier with sound principles. Not just a money man and definitely not the Mob – which is what the Cubans would have been most worried about. No, he was a regular Mr Clean.'

I thought about this. 'So you've got Grice,' I said. 'And you think you know where he's stashed the money. But that's not the same thing as getting it back, is it?'

'Give us time,' said Harford with confidence.

I thought privately that the only one getting time would be Grice. But they couldn't lock him up for ever, even if they did manage to pin responsibility for Coverdale's murder on him. Good lawyers (which Grice must have) would make sure they had trouble doing that. No lawyer, and I doubted any accountant, could get that money back. Grice wasn't an old man. I judged him forty-two or -three at the most. He could sit it out. Besides I still wouldn't have put money on his definitely going to gaol. Maybe the authorities would get lucky. Maybe Grice would.

I had other things on my mind. So did Harford, who was in buoyant mood. 'Are you ready to go out and eat yet?'

'Not just yet.' I leaned my elbows on the table. 'Parry says you're destined for fast-track promotion. I suppose you're already on your way.'

He looked surprised. 'Why bring that up now?'

'Perhaps you should have thought about a different career,' I said.

He frowned, puzzled and a little angry. 'What are you on about, Fran? You're not one of these people with a down on the police, are you? The last thing I'd have thought you was bigoted! I suppose you've not always seen eye to eye with authority. I can understand that, but hell, that's not my fault. I know we met over a professional matter, but from now on, couldn't you try and see me as a normal person?'

'I'll always have difficulty,' I said. 'My problem is this. I'll always have in my mind that girl you and your two mates kidnapped over by King's Cross, took to the house belonging to one of you, held there for at least two hours and raped.'

I didn't think a room could go as quiet as that kitchen. The only noise was the faintest zizz from the fridge. All colour had gone from Harford's face, draining out as I watched.

He said, 'What the hell is this? What bloody stupid sort of joke is that?'

'No joke, Jason,' I told him. 'It was never a joke. You put her through a nightmare. She'll never forget it. She was abused, she was hurt, she was terrified. She thought you were going to kill her. The one who drove her back to King's Cross – I know it wasn't you – he threatened to take her down the river and hold her head under.'

'Who told you all this – this nonsense?' he whispered.

'I have a lot of friends out there on the streets, Jas,' I said.

'You forgot that.'

He ran his tongue over his lower lip. The expression in his eyes, watching me, was both hard and unpredictable. I felt a stab of fear, the faintest echo of what Tig must have felt.

'Then one of your *friends* lied to you,' he said.

'I don't think so.'

'Where is this girl?' He leaned forward so suddenly I couldn't help but recoil. 'You put her in front of me and have her repeat her story! She bloody won't, you know!'

'Of course she won't, Jason, you know that. You've always known that. You won't find her now. She's out of your reach.'

'I bloody well will find her! What's her name?' The fury spewed out of him now. He crashed his fist on the table. Bonnie, who'd been listening uneasily, jumped up and barked. Harford looked down at her. 'There was another girl here for a while, wasn't there? You kept her hidden away but the workmen who came to fix the window saw her and the scene of crime boys glimpsed her too. They said she was acting oddly. She had that dog. She left it here with you.'

'You see,' I said. 'None of you ever even asked her name. She wasn't human, she was just a thing, picked up off the street like garbage. Something to be used and chucked back in the gutter.' All the scorn I felt for him must have filled my voice. 'Only,' I said, '*she* wasn't the garbage. The three of you were that.'

He'd gone quiet again, leaning back in his chair. His features were frozen, his body tense, only his fingers drummed nervously on the table top.

'Why'd you go along with it, Jason?' I asked. 'Did you want to prove you were still one of the lads, despite being a copper? Was that it? Or was it a night out with old mates from university days – the ones who'd got City jobs – and it turned into something you hadn't anticipated and hadn't got the guts to stop?'

'You've got it all wrong!' He was shaking his head in disbelief, not at the outrageousness of my tale, but that this could be happening to him. 'I'm not proud of it. But it wasn't the way she told you. She was just a little tart and she was paid . . .'

'She was a barely sixteen-year-old kid down on her luck and desperate for money. She was paid a miserable eighty quid for two hours of horror. Twenty-five quid each, Jason. A quickie in a street doorway would've cost you that. A real professional prostitute would've cost you more.'

He stood up abruptly, the chair legs screeching on the tiled floor as he pushed it back. 'I take it dinner's off, then?' he asked coldly.

'You bet,' I said.

He put both palms on the table and leaned over me, his face dark now and threatening. His eyes held a mix of hatred, fear and desperation. I held my breath and hoped I hadn't judged it wrong.

'I swear, if you ever breathe a word of this—' he began.

'Calm down, Jason,' I told him as evenly as I could. 'No one would believe me. Just as you, all three of you, always knew no one would believe the girl if she was brave enough or daft enough to talk. You're safe. At first it really sickened me to think you'd got away with it so completely. But then I remembered what you've forgotten, Jas. You forget that besides yourself, your victim and now me, two other people know what happened that night. That makes five, and that's too many to keep a secret for ever.'

I saw alarm and then suspicion in his eyes. 'Who else? I don't believe you.'

'The other two guys involved with you. They know.'

He was staring at me, surprised, puzzled, not getting the message. I explained it to him.

'You think you can rely on them because you were all in it together. Wrong, Jas. You're a copper, remember? You're a copper destined for high things! Real senior rank. And one day in the future, just when you think it's all going swimmingly for you, one of those mates of yours is going to come to you and ask a favour. He'll tell you he's in a mess and you, his friend, can help him out. It might be any kind of jam. Fraud? An unreported fatal traffic accident? Perhaps he'll have picked up another girl for the same kind of games, only this time things may have gone really wrong and she's dead. Whatever it is, he'll come to you for help in some form or other. Perhaps for inside information on just what the police know or don't, or to request a report to be misplaced, a connection deliberately not made, information not passed on or a junior copper persuaded to tear a page out of his notebook. He may ask, tip me off, Jas old pal, if the police get close, so I can hop the country. You're a mate, you won't refuse. You won't be able to refuse, will you? Because he'll have the dibs on you.'

He was shaking his head.

'I know what's in your mind,' I told him. 'You're thinking, he won't be able to shop me because he'll be shopping himself. But when it happens, he'll already be in trouble and a little more old scandal won't make it that much worse for him. But you, you'll have everything to lose. So when I said you were safe just now, I meant, for the moment. After all, you were telling me that there was no honour among thieves. I'd be willing to bet there's none among rapists. Like you said, when the heat's turned up, every man's for himself, right?'

He looked like a man in the middle of a bad dream hoping

he'd wake up and afraid he never would. He walked slowly to the door and as he got there, I called, 'Inspector?'

He turned unwillingly. 'Yes?' His voice and face were stony. But I wasn't afraid of him any more. The fight was kicked out of him for the time being. He'd bounce back, outwardly anyway. But from now on, if I'd done any justice by Tig, he'd never go near any of his old mates again. He'd be alone, living with that niggling fear at the back of his mind, every achievement soured. Or I certainly hoped so.

'I've been homeless,' I said. 'And after Christmas I'll be homeless again. My old grandma used to say there were all kinds of people in every walk of life, and that's true. Good and bad everywhere. But I reckon there are fewer rats out on the street than there are living in comfortable houses.'

He was silent, then he said, 'It's a pity, Fran. I really liked you.'

He went out and I heard the front door close. I went and checked he'd really gone. I knew I had pushed him close. But I'd been taking a calculated gamble. I reckoned that at heart he was a coward. Only a coward would have stood aside and let all that happen to Tig – even worse, joined in. He'd chucked out the window everything he'd claim to stand for as a police officer. All that talk, I thought, remembering our conversation in the Italian restaurant. All that blather about making the community a better place and helping people. He'd sounded as if he'd meant it and I'd been taken in. Perhaps he had meant it. Perhaps he really thought the lapse, as he probably viewed it, with Tig hadn't mattered because she was nothing, just a street-dweller with a drugs habit she was financing by turning tricks.

Faced with the truth about himself and what he'd done, he'd folded. I had to admit there'd been a moment back there when he might've grabbed for my throat, but his brain had clicked in. I'd counted on his being bright enough not to do anything so dumb. Policework had taught him how murderers are caught. Parry, for one, knew he'd come here tonight. I'd probably mentioned it to Daphne before she went out. His fingerprints were all over the kitchen and he couldn't have been sure to clean them all off. Even so, I'd probably come as near to the edge that day as I'd ever want to be – twice.

'Cats have nine lives,' I said to myself as I poured my undrunk glass of wine down the sink. I hadn't touched it while he had been here. I'm fussy whom I drink with. I think I've told you that before. 'How many do you think you've got left, Fran?'

I hadn't wanted to believe Tig at first, although somehow, as soon as she began to speak, I'd had a premonition of just what she was going to say.

'I didn't know one of them was a copper,' her voice, echoing down the line from Dorridge, had said. 'Not until he came to your flat that afternoon. I caught a glimpse of him as he passed the window on the way to your door. I hid in the bathroom, you remember, but I took a peek through the door, just to make sure. It was him, all right.'

'You are positive about this, aren't you, Tig?' I'd asked.

'What?' asked Tig. 'Do you think I'm ever likely to forget their faces, any of them? I didn't tell you straight off, Fran, and I'm sorry. But I didn't know how thick you were with him. You seemed to be getting on really well with all the rozzers. I didn't know how far I could trust you. I didn't want you fingering me to him.'

'You think I'd have done that?' I'd been incredulous.

'I didn't know you wouldn't. Look, Fran, don't be angry. I

was scared. That's why I went for you. I was in enough trouble. I didn't want more. If he'd found out I'd told you about it, he'd have started looking for me, to shut me up. Maybe even to shut you up, too. Knowing some things is dangerous. Out there on the streets, I've seen all sorts of things – some really bad. But I've never talked about any of them, not once, not even to another street-dweller. You don't, do you? You see nothing. You hear nothing. That way you stay out of trouble and that's all I wanted to do. But after I got back here, I started thinking about it. You might really be starting to like him. He's a good-looking guy. He was being nice as pie to you. You had to know what he was really like. I wouldn't want anything bad to happen to you.'

Bad things had happened to me all my life, one way and another, but Tig had done her best to spare me one thing. I said, 'Yeah, I understand, Tig. Thanks.'

I fancied I heard her sigh in relief. There was a faint noise in the background and the echo of a woman's voice, querulous.

'Oh bugger it,' said Tig hastily. 'Here's Mum back from the supermarket and wanting to know who I'm talking to. I'll have to ring off.'

I could hear Sheila's voice now, shrill and frightened.

'All right, Mum!' Tig said crossly. 'It's only Fran. You remember her, she came here. I'm just calling her to let her know I'm OK.' Her voice came more clearly as she put the receiver back near her mouth. 'I've got to go. But I've got to ask, Fran, were you beginning to like him?'

'Not really,' I said. It was a lie. 'Cheers, Tig. Take care.' I hung up.

I'd sat for a long time in Daphne's rocking chair, following that call, with Bonnie curled up in my lap. At first I'd been so angry my stomach had churned. I'd wanted revenge for Tig, for myself. I'd wanted to race round to the police station and face Jason myself. Face them all, tell them all – Parry, Foxley, the lot. I could imagine their faces, horrified, disgusted but not at what he'd done. No, at my effrontery in suggesting such a thing of one of their brightest hopes. No one to back me. No proof. No Tig.

I could hear, in my head, Foxley's dry pinched tones, saying, 'There is no record of any complaint being made at the time. You are unable to produce the young woman who is making these claims. How do you know she isn't lying? How do you know, supposing that some incident of some kind took place, that her story isn't gross exaggeration? Do you expect me to accept an identification made through a crack in a door? The unsubstantiated word of a street-dweller? An amateur prostitute and drug addict?'

Then anger had died back and I'd gone through it carefully, testing to see if there was something I could do. Eventually it occurred to me that the one thing in my power was to let him know it wasn't a secret, what he'd done that night. Others knew and he'd never be safe. He wasn't only evil; he was stupid. I'd been wrong about thinking him bright. Mrs Worran would have called him a 'whited sepulchre' and she'd have been right. Game and match to you, Mrs Worran.

Chapter Nineteen

It was Christmas Eve. Throughout the country little kids were looking forward to Santa coming down the chimney or squeezing through the radiator somehow. I'm glad I'm not a mum trying to explain that one. As for me, I opened the door and found I'd got Sergeant Parry standing on the doorstep.

'Happy Christmas,' he said, leering.

If recent events hadn't already made it difficult to get any seasonal feeling going, the sight of Parry's straggling moustache and beady eyes would've nipped in the bud any enthusiasm I had worked up. He was wearing the oldest and dingiest green jacket I'd ever set eyes on. It was the sort which is meant to be waxed but all the wax had gone and the side pockets had bulged and sagged. He probably wore it when he wanted to blend with the crowd but something about it, something about all of Parry, screamed 'Copper!' Under it I could see he was wearing a peculiar hand-knitted pullover in cable stitch. It had to have been a present from some elderly female relative. Even a first glance at the front of it showing between the open sides of the waxed jacket revealed several pattern mistakes, cable twists going the wrong way and lots of bits of purl where it should've been plain, and the other way round. Whoever had knitted it, she'd either had poor eyesight or one eye on the television. But who am I to criticise? The only thing I've ever knitted was a Dr Who scarf, and that was when I was about twelve. It took me a year and was out of fashion by the time I'd finished it.

I wasn't feeling kindly about policemen anyway. The showdown with Harford might've been the main reason, but I had others. I'd had time to review my recent co-operation and to decide that whatever might happen to me in the future, nothing would persuade me to stick out my neck like that again. I'd had little choice because Ponytail had been coming for me anyway, but you know what I mean. On reflection, I should've told Ponytail the police had taken the negatives and let him get on with it. That walk over Hungerford Bridge was burned into my memory. As for Jason Harford, I'd nearly made the worst mistake of my life there. It just goes to show you should trust your instincts. I hadn't taken a shine to him when I'd first met him and I should've stayed that way. Still, everyone can be a fool sometimes and I'm no exception. There's no shame in doing something daft provided you don't repeat it and I certainly meant never to repeat it.

'Whaddya want?' I asked sourly.

'Come to see you're all right,' he told me with oily insincerity.

I spelled it out. 'I don't want to see or talk to any coppers. I've had it up to here –' I indicated my throat – 'with rozzers and their dodgy ways. If Foxley wants me to do anything else, you go tell him from me to take a running jump.'

'Oy,' said Parry, looking hurt. 'I've always been straight with you.'

If he had, it was only because subtlety wasn't his strong point. Over his shoulder, I could see the old fellow from the house opposite standing on the pavement, doing a bit of neighbourhood watching. The number of times Parry had been round here lately, he must know it was an officer of the law on the doorstep. For this reason only, I decided to let Parry in.

'Ah, Sergeant!' called Daphne, passing through the hall. 'Season's greetings to you!'

'And to you, ma'am,' he said. He made what was probably meant to be a bow, leaning forward without bending, and inclining slightly to one side like the Tower of Pisa.

'You are always sickeningly polite to her,' I told him. 'Not that I'm objecting, but you never give me that sort of treatment. Aren't I a citizen? A member of the public?'

'Miss Knowles is a lady,' he said, affronted.

'Oh, thanks. What do you want?' I asked again more firmly.

Parry's blotchy skin turned even more unattractive with a dull flush. 'As it happens, I brought you a Christmas present.' He put his hand in one of the bulging pockets and brought out a small package. It was wrapped in red paper with green reindeer on it, all stuck down with Sellotape.

'What is it?' I asked suspiciously. Parry pretending to be Santa was just not on.

'Go on, then, open it,' he said, looking all pleased with himself.

I did and found a rather squashed box of Maltesers. He hadn't broken open his piggy bank, that was for sure. Even though I like chocs, I was anything but delighted because the last thing I wanted to do was accept presents from Parry. I had a horrible feeling it might be leading up to a request for a date. It gave 'not if he was the last man on earth' a whole new meaning. On the other hand, it was Christmas and I didn't want to seem churlish. Goodwill to all men, and all that.

'Thanks,' I said hollowly. 'It's a nice thought. I appreciate it. But if I accept it, it's only because I'm taking it as thanks for risking my neck recently to help you nab Grice. And remember to tell Foxley,' I added, 'what I said just now. He needn't bother to ask me to save police bacon again. Not a chance. The more I think about it, the more I'm sure I was bonkers even to consider it.'

'Oh, we can do a bit better than chocs for that,' said Parry. He lowered his voice confidentially. 'I do believe, no letting on I've told you, now! I do believe Mr Foxley is going to ask if you can be given a reward from public funds. Probably about fifty quid. How about that, eh?'

'Fifty quid?' I squeaked. 'Fifty— If Jo Jo hadn't turned up when he did, I'd have got my hands on a grand from Grice!'

'But you'd have had to give that back,' he pointed out.

I knew it. I put the chocolates down on the hall table. 'Well, I hope you have a very nice Christmas and I'll wish you a Happy New Year as well, while I'm about it – because I don't suppose I'll be seeing you for quite a while.'

'Don't count on it,' he said. 'But I get the message. Still, while I'm here, I'd better give you the news. Which do you want first? The good or the bad?'

So he hadn't just come to bring me his box of chocs. 'Tell me the bad,' I invited. 'Why not? It's Christmas Eve. Finish it off for me completely.'

'Don't be like that,' he said. 'It's just I thought you ought to know your pal Inspector Harford has asked for a transfer. If you don't know it already, that is.'

'He's not my friend,' I told him. 'And I didn't know it. It makes no difference to me.' I tried not to sound too relieved.

Parry twitched his ginger eyebrows but also looked, I fancied, relieved. It occurred to me the chocs had been intended to soften the blow of what he'd feared would be devastating news for me. Was there a sensitive streak well hidden in the man, after all? On the other hand, he might just be fishing for information.

'There's me,' he said, confirming this last suspicion, 'thinking you were getting along pretty well with Wonderboy. You couldn't hazard a guess as to why he's suddenly decided to love us and leave us, could you?'

'Not a clue.' But I wasn't surprised. Harford had decided not to stay around here where there was a chance he might walk into me again. He was going to cut and run. He was going to find out, eventually, that he couldn't keep running. No one can, whatever the reason. Even his victim, Tig, had found that out. I'd been a bit hard on her, but it'd been for her own good because she deserved a helping hand. As for Harford, I felt nothing but scorn for him.

'I thought he might've confided in you.' Parry gave his rictus grin. 'Must have been something *I* said, then. Tell you the truth, Fran, I'm glad you're not upset or anything. It's a bit sudden, his deciding to move on. I fancy Mr Foxley's not too pleased. Caused a bit of gossip in the canteen.'

'What doesn't? seems to me,' I retorted. 'What's the good news?'

Parry's manner changed and became more official. 'It's good in the sense it clears up a problem for us – for you, too, maybe. It's not so good for the bloke concerned. I'm talking about Coverdale's killer.'

'You've got him?' I couldn't believe it.

'In a manner of speaking,' Parry replied cautiously. 'We've got him down the morgue, so I suppose you could say we have him. He's a stiff.'

I sat down on a nearby chair. Parry grinned down at me evilly. 'Got his name, too. Miguel Herrera, Spanish national, wanted by the French police. Description answering the one you gave us of the herbert who tried to break in here. Half-healed bites on the fingers of his right hand, probably made by a small dog of the terrier type. You haven't got to worry about him any more, Fran.'

'What happened to him?' I asked.

Parry shrugged. 'He got into an argument in a pub night before last. When he left at the end of the evening, the other bloke in the spat was waiting outside for him with a crowd of his mates. Kicked his head in and ran off.'

'So, how'd you tie him in with Coverdale?'

'When we tried to ID him, his fingerprints matched some we lifted at the scene of the murder and sent to Interpol. Knife found lying near Herrera's body showed the same fingerprints on the hilt and the blade's the same size and shape as the fatal wound in Coverdale. This Herrera johnny must've pulled it to defend himself outside the pub, but didn't get the chance to use it.' He beamed at me until he remembered that a serious crime had occurred. 'Course,' he added quickly, 'we're looking for his attackers.'

'You won't find them,' I said.

'Nah – no witnesses, never is, a barney like that. Still, saved us a job, didn't they? We mightn't have picked him up otherwise and the taxpayer won't have to keep him as a guest of Her Majesty. French can cross him off their list, too. You won't have to look out for him again. We can close a murder file. Suits everyone, really. It'd have been nice to be able to link it to Grice, but you can't have everything, can you? Not in this line of business, anyway. Thankful for small mercies, that's what, if you're a police officer. We can't prove Herrera was on Grice's payroll. It might've been a revenge attack. Still, don't,' finished Parry a trifle obscurely, 'look a gift horse in the mouth.'

I'd better take back what I wrote above. Parry isn't sensitive. I'd no sympathy for Herrera, but the passing of a human being ought to be met without hand-rubbing glee. I suppose to Parry it was just another statistic. As for me, I have to say it was a relief to know Herrera wasn't out there, nursing his bitten hand and plotting a nasty revenge attack of his own.

But Parry had missed my meaning when I'd said they wouldn't catch Herrera's killers. I didn't bother to explain it. The police might choose to believe that Herrera had died as a result of a random violent attack – and his attackers had thoughtfully left his knife by his side on the pavement. It just confirmed my previous notion that Grice was a very well-organised man. Herrera had been a weak link. Picked up by the police, he'd have told them everything he knew about Grice and whether or not he'd been told to eliminate Gray Coverdale. Now he wouldn't have the opportunity. I shivered.

'I hope,' said Parry, 'that after all this, you're going to make a New Year resolution, Fran, to keep out of trouble.'

'With a little help from my friends,' I told him.

'Well, I'll be off then,' he said. 'Give us a kiss for Christmas.'

He should be so lucky. I pushed him out of the door and slammed it behind him.

I went round to the shop to tell Ganesh Parry's news about Herrera. He was just closing up. We finished off and went up the back stairs to the flat.

'Don't know what Hari wants done about the unsold Christmas cards,' he said. 'Whether I'm supposed to flog them off half-price or put them away till next year. We'll leave the decorations up until after New Year.'

'You're supposed to leave them until Twelfth Night,' I told

him. We counted up on our fingers to work out exactly what calendar date they would bring us to.

'Nice to think we've got a couple of days off,' said Ganesh. 'I'll have to pop down to High Wycombe and see Mum and Dad at some point, but we could go somewhere.'

'Like where? Everywhere's closed.' I had an idea. 'We could go and see a pantomime.'

A bell rang loudly, making us jump. 'Street door,' said Ganesh. 'Hang on.' He went to lean out of the window to see who it was. 'Usha,' he told me over his shoulder. 'I'll just chuck her down the key.'

He dropped it down to his sister and went to open the door on to the staircase which led up from the street. We heard the outer door slam and footsteps running up the stair. Usha burst in.

She was dressed in a new-looking scarlet wool coat, black ski-pants and nifty little boots. Obviously, being married to an accountant pays off. She was also clearly in a bit of a state and hadn't just come round to wish us a happy holiday.

Hands on hips and long black hair flying, she demanded, 'What's been going on here?' As an afterthought, she added, 'Hi, Fran. Happy Christmas.'

It was such an open question that we both stayed silent, wondering quite what or how much to tell her.

'How do you mean?' Ganesh asked cautiously.

She advanced on him, jabbing a finger at each word. 'Don't try wriggling out of it. We know! What's more, Dad's writing to Uncle Hari tonight!'

'If you mean the washroom—' Ganesh began, drawing himself up to begin his defence.

'Of course I mean the washroom! What have you been doing to it? How much has it cost? Hari didn't say anything about getting decorators in before he left. Did you get more than one estimate?'

'No, I didn't,' said Ganesh, rallying before the onslaught. 'Because I got a very good deal from Hitch. And before you go on, tell me how you all know about it.'

'Dilip saw them working here. He told his mum. She told—' Usha gave a hiss of exasperation. 'It got passed down the line. You know how it does. Dad says you must have gone barmy.'

Trying to help, though it wasn't my spat, I offered, 'It looks really good, Usha. Have you seen it?'

'No, I haven't, but I'm going to. I've got to go back and tell Dad exactly what you've done so's he can put it in his letter.'

We trailed downstairs to the new washroom. 'You wait till you see it,' said Ganesh belligerently. 'The old one was a health hazard. See!' He threw open the door.

Usha stared round it. 'Sure, it looks good. But how much did it cost?' She swung round, eyes bright with suspicion. 'And where's the old loo?'

'Hitch took all the old junk away. Did a complete job,' said Gan proudly.

Watching Usha's face, I somehow knew this wasn't the right answer.

'Took it away?' She flung both hands out dramatically to indicate the new loo, resplendent where the old one had been. 'Took away that lovely Victorian loo? He didn't, I suppose, pay you for it? You didn't knock the value of it off the bill?'

'What value?' asked Ganesh. 'It was nearly a hundred years old.'

'Too right it was!' yelled Usha, erupting in fury. 'People seek out those Victorian patterned lavatories! Collectors of Victoriana and old domestic equipment. They're what's called highly desirable. That one of Hari's was in perfect condition, glaze hadn't crazed, no chips, nothing! It was manufactured by Doulton. At auction those things fetch between five and six hundred quid!'

There was the sort of silence in which you're supposed to hear pins dropping. Ganesh was shaking his head slowly, a dazed expression on his face.

'Now,' Usha went on with the calm which makes you want to run for cover, 'I don't know what you paid Hitch for fixing up the washroom, but he must have nearly doubled it by getting the old blue and white loo, which you described as junk, thrown in. And please, don't tell me he didn't know what it was worth. Hitch knows what everything's worth. He's a fixer, a middleman. And the worst of it all,' Usha was working up the Richter scale again, 'Jay and I were going to approach Hari about selling it to us, you know, family price.'

There was a silence. 'Well,' Ganesh said at last, very faintly, 'who'd believe it?'

'I would,' I told him. 'I warned you Hitch was always on the fiddle. Honestly, Ganesh, all those magazine supplements you've been reading, didn't any of them have articles about antiques?'

Or, come to that, hadn't any of the holiday supplements featured Cuba? Even I'd been able to see the location of the photos hadn't been the Canary Islands. What's the point of being able to list the world's most eligible bachelors, in order, if you don't know anything really useful? But it wasn't the moment to get at Gan about that. He was looking utterly miserable.

'They didn't have any articles about old loos,' he was saying. 'Only silver and china and stuff.'

It was time for me to make a discreet departure. 'When you

see your mum and dad, Usha,' I said, 'give them my good wishes.'

'Happy Christmas, Fran, dear.'

It was Christmas Day, breakfast-time. Daphne and I exchanged kisses and good wishes and produced our presents.

It was difficult to know what to buy Daphne but, inspired by the mistake over the loo, I'd ended up with the latest edition of one of those antique guides. She was interested in that sort of thing and went round the salerooms. I'd checked in it before I wrapped it up and Usha was right about that Victorian loo. Ganesh had said he was going to ask Hitch to pay for it, but we both knew he hadn't a hope. Hitch would swear he didn't know it had any value and that he'd dumped it. But Hitch knows the value of everything. Usha was also right in saying he was a middleman. He'd probably already got a buyer in mind when he'd first agreed to do the work in the old washroom.

I presented Daphne with the book. Bonnie sat by with tinsel entwined in her collar and waited hopefully, sensing goodies were being handed out. I gave her a chocolate-flavoured rubber bone. She carried it off and began to chew it happily.

Daphne handed me two small packages. I opened the one labelled 'Bonnie' first. It was a smart new lead. 'Thanks very much, Daphne,' I said. Then I opened the second, smaller, packet marked 'Fran' and said, 'Oh, Daph . . .'

'I want you to have them,' Daphne said firmly. 'Before you say anything.'

'But they belonged to your mother.' I put the amethyst earrings, lying on cottonwool in a neat little box, on the table. 'I can't accept those, Daphne.'

'Whyever not? Who else should I give them to? I've got no young female relatives. Neither Charles nor Betram is married so it'd be no good giving any of my jewellery to either of them. They couldn't wear them.'

I wasn't sure of that but tactfully kept quiet.

'I've got a sort of cousin, way up in Shropshire, who's got a daughter, and my pearls and a hideous tiara thing which no woman in her right mind would wear these days, are left to her. But I want you to have the earrings. I thought they'd match that purple skirt of yours,' my landlady concluded.

'Thank you, Daphne,' I said humbly. 'I'll treasure them, promise.'

'I am so sorry,' she said, 'that you'll be alone for Christmas lunch. I really don't want to go over to my nephews', but they have been apologising nonstop and really, I know I've got to make it up with them eventually, so it might as well be on Christmas Day. Bertie is a very good cook, you know.'

I didn't doubt it. 'I'll be fine,' I said. 'I've got Bonnie.'

'I had thought you might be spending the day with Mr Patel.'

'He's had to go to High Wycombe,' I said. 'He's got a family dispute to patch up as well.'

'Well, that's what Christmas is for,' said Daphne, adding on a note of doubt, 'I suppose.' She cheered up. 'I'll be back this evening. We can have a glass of wine then. Tomorrow I'll poach us that nice piece of salmon in the fridge. Oh, there are plenty of things in the freezer, meantime. There's an individual portion of chicken *à la provençale.* Why don't you pop that in the microwave?'

'This is it, Bonnie,' I said to her, when Daphne had left. 'This is independence. Christmas Day, just you and me, with a frozen chicken portion between us.' I brandished the foil container at her. Bonnie's ears drooped. 'All right,' I said, 'you can have a tin of dog's chicken dinner. It'll probably have more chicken in it than whatever's in here. We'll eat Wayne Parry's Maltesers for pud.' The thought didn't cheer. Activity was called for. 'Want to go out for a walk?' I asked Bonnie, producing the new lead.

We set off up the road. There was a Christmas Day sort of feeling in the air, people wearing silly smiles and greeting complete strangers. Cars passed filled with people and presents, all off to lunch with family or friends. Kids cycled along the pavements on new bikes. I'd thought going out in the fresh air might have cheered me up, but it made me feel worse, isolated. All I had to look forward to was a new year which would start off with dossing in Hari's lock-up with my belongings in a couple of plastic sacks. I understood why Daphne was making it up with the gruesome twosome. In the end, they were her family, just as Ganesh had said.

When I reached the shops, things began to look up. To my surprise, I saw coming towards me Marco, blond hair flowing. He was snazzily turned out in a blue jacket in some shiny material and clean jeans without paint splashes. My heart rose.

'Hello, Fran,' Marco said. 'Happy Christmas.'

'Same to you,' I returned happily. 'I thought you were in Amsterdam.'

'Got back last night. I'm just going down The Rose for a drink,' he said. 'It's open till lunchtime. Crowd of us meeting up there. Want to come?'

What do you know, Fran? I told myself in delight. There is a Father Christmas, after all. I asked about Bonnie.

'Don't worry about her,' he said. 'They don't mind dogs in The Rose. The landlord's got a pit bull. It's out back,' he added, by way of encouragement. 'And it's tattooed and lost its knackers and everything, all legal. The police come round and insisted. Don't seem right, somehow.'

We made our way to The Rose. It's an old pub and hasn't changed its style much in fifty years. Downmarket is where The Rose feels it should be and downmarket it resolutely stays. It was packed to the door, the air filled with nicotine and boozy Christmas cheer. I picked Bonnie up because it seemed likely she'd be trodden on, and followed Marco to a corner table surrounded by people.

'This is Fran,' he announced, propelling me forward. A chorus of voices greeted me and wished me a happy Christmas. 'This is Mike,' Marco began to make a round of the table for my benefit, 'this is Polly and this . . .' It went on until we reached a red-haired girl in an advanced state of pregnancy who was prudently on the orange juice.

'And this is Bridget,' said Marco happily. 'Meet the wife, Fran.'

You know, that Scottish poet had it right. The best laid plans of mice and men are apt to go pear-shaped. And there's not a lot any of us can do about it.

Watching Out

Ann Granger

Fran Varady fell into private detective work by chance. Now she's got a 'real' job at a trendy pizzeria, she's back on track with her acting ambitions, and she's even found a nice flat to rent. But things aren't as straightforward as they seem.

The job, for a start: there's something sinister about the way the pizzeria is run. And the play rehearsals are riddled with problems. On top of all this, Fran has rashly undertaken to help a young boy, illegally in the country, find an elusive people-trafficker called Max.

When the trail Fran is following is tragically interrupted by a horrifying death, she finds herself up against dangerous men and a ruthless organisation. Fran's in big trouble this time . . .

Praise for Ann Granger:

'A good feel for understated humour, a nice ear for dialogue' *The Times*

'Ann Granger's skill with character together with her sprightly writing make the most of the story . . . she is on to another winner' *Birmingham Post*

'A delight. Darkly humorous but humane . . . fluent, supple and a pleasure to read' *Ham and High*

0 7472 6802 9

headline

A Restless Evil

Ann Granger

It sends a shiver down Detective Superintendent Alan Markby's spine when he hears that a rambler has stumbled on human bones in Stovey Woods in the heart of the Cotswolds. Twenty-two years ago, he had a rare failure in the hunt for a brutal serial rapist preying on local women. After the fifth rape, the attacker went to ground, never to be heard of again. Now, with a new investigation prompted by the grisly remains, the trail could be warm once more. But almost at once Markby is confronted with another body and a thoroughly up-to-date murder. Could the two be connected? It seems that some of the village residents would be just as happy to let sleeping dogs lie and secrets – both old and new – stay hidden . . .

The critics love Ann Granger's mystery novels:

'Characterisation, as ever with Granger, is sharp and astringent' *The Times*

'You'll soon be addicted' *Woman & Home*

'Ann Granger has brought the traditional English village crime story up to date, in setting, sophistication and every other aspect of fiction writing . . . sheer, unadulterated bliss' *Birmingham Post*

'A good feel for understated humour, a nice ear for dialogue' *The Times*

0 7472 6804 5

headline

Risking it All

Ann Granger

When Fran Varady, aspiring actress and part-time sleuth, is approached by Private Investigator Clarence Duke, she mistrusts him on instinct. But she can't ignore what he has to tell her. Her mother, Eva, who walked out on Fran when she was only seven years old, has hired Clarence to find her daughter. And for good reason. Eva is dying.

Within days, Fran is reunited with the mother she hasn't seen for fifteen years, and is soon to lose again. But the biggest bombshell of all is still to come. Eva has another child – a daughter she gave up soon after her birth – and she wants Fran to find her.

Matters aren't helped by the fact that slippery Clarence Duke seems intent on discovering what she's up to. But it's when he's found dead in his car outside Fran's home that the trouble really begins . . .

Praise for Ann Granger:

'Ann Granger's skill with character together with her sprightly writing make the most of the story . . . she is on to another winner' *Birmingham Post*

'A good feel for understated humour, a nice ear for dialogue' *The Times*

'A delight. Darkly humorous but humane . . . fluent, supple and a pleasure to read' *Ham and High*

0 7472 6801 0

headline

madaboutbooks.com